From the reviews of *The Accursed*:

'Joyce Carol Oates has written what may be the world's first postmodern
Gothic novel: E. L. Doctorow's *Ragtime* set in Dracula's castle. It's dense,
challenging, problematic, horrifying, funny, prolix and full of crazy
people. You should read it. I wish I could tell you more ... feverishly
entertaining'   STEPHEN KING, *New York Times Book Review*

'Enthralling ... In Oates's practised hands, the story of the moral hysteria
afflicting a repressed community is effectively told ... A commentary on
the art of Gothic fiction, and a marvellously sustained piece of Gothic
writing itself'   STEPHEN ABELL, *Daily Telegraph*

'Expertly crafted ... Part of what's enjoyable and impressive about *The
Accursed* is the chance it offers to watch Joyce Carol Oates recycle and
reinvent the conventions of genre fiction to achieve something more substantial and ambitious than the chills we expect from the horror novel'
          FRANCINE PROSE, *New York Review of Books*

'A belated candidate for the Great Oates Novel ... *The Accursed* is a big, mad, colourful romp, respectful of the literary traditions in which it participates, leavened with a piquant humour. It may not be the definitive work to crown the singularly fascinating Oates oeuvre but, for the uninitiated, it is a great place to begin' DAVID EVANS, *Financial Times*

'Oates's "vampire" novel succeeds superbly as a political statement ... But its bold and authentic portrayals of real-life figures also anchor it in the realist tradition Oates has claimed for her own for so long. With a pinch of humour, and a sense of fun that some of us never quite expected'

LESLEY MCDOWELL, *Scotsman*

'Spectacular – a coalescence of history, horror and social satire that whirls around for almost 700 mesmerizing pages ... The delights of this macabre novel gather thick as ghouls at midnight in the cemetery. I've never been so aware of Oates's weird comedy'

RON CHARLES, *Washington Post*

'Much of *The Accursed* is slyly hilarious ... There is a barely suppressed, almost mesmeric urgency in many of her sentences ... A weird and wonderful book: one senses that Oates had great fun writing it'

ELIZABETH WASSELL, *Irish Times*

The Accursed

JOYCE CAROL OATES

FOURTH ESTATE • London

Fourth Estate
An imprint of HarperCollins*Publishers*
77–85 Fulham Palace Road
Hammersmith, London W6 8JB

This Fourth Estate paperback edition published 2013

1

First published in Great Britain by Fourth Estate in 2013

Joyce Carol Oates asserts the moral right to
be identified as the author of this work

A catalogue record for this book is
available from the British Library

ISBN 978-0-00-749422-4

Designed by Suet Yee Chong

Printed and bound in Great Britain by
Clays Ltd, St Ives plc

MIX
Paper from
responsible sources
FSC™ C007454
www.fsc.org

FSC™ is a non-profit international organisation established to promote
the responsible management of the world's forests. Products carrying the
FSC label are independently certified to assure consumers that they come
from forests that are managed to meet the social, economic and
ecological needs of present and future generations,
and other controlled sources.

Find out more about HarperCollins and the environment at
www.harpercollins.co.uk/green

From an obscure little village we have
become the capital of America.

—ASHBEL GREEN, SPEAKING OF PRINCETON,
NEW JERSEY, 1783

All diseases of Christians are to be ascribed
to demons.

—ST. AUGUSTINE

CONTENTS

Part Four

THE CURSE EXORCISED

The Accursed

AUTHOR'S NOTE

An event enters "history" when it is recorded. But there may be multiple, and competing, histories; as there are multiple, and competing, eyewitness accounts.

In this chronicle of the mysterious, seemingly linked events occurring in, and in the vicinity of, Princeton, New Jersey, in the approximate years 1900–1910, "histories" have been condensed to a single "history" as a decade in time has been condensed, for purposes of aesthetic unity, to a period of approximately fourteen months in 1905–1906.

I know that a historian should be "objective"—but I am so passionately involved in this chronicle, and so eager to expose to a new century of readers some of the revelations regarding a tragic sequence of events occurring in the early years of the twentieth century in central New Jersey, it is very difficult for me to retain a calm, let alone a scholarly, tone. I have long been dismayed by the shoddy histories that have been written about this era in Princeton—for instance, Q. T. Hollinger's *The Unsolved Enigma of the Crosswicks Curse: A Fresh Inquiry* (1949), a compendium of truths, half-truths, and outright falsehoods published by a local amateur historian in an effort to correct the most obvious errors of previous historians (Tite, Birdseye, Worthing, and Croft-Crooke) and the one-time best seller *The Vampire Murders of Old Princeton* (1938) by an "anonymous" author (believed to be a resident of the West End of Princeton), a notorious exploitive effort that dwells upon the superficial "sensational" aspects of the Curse, at the expense of the more subtle and less evident—i.e., the psychological, moral, and spiritual.

I am embarrassed to state here, so bluntly, at the very start of my chronicle, my particular qualifications for taking on this challenging project. So I will mention only that, like several key individuals in this chronicle, I am a graduate of Princeton University (Class of 1927). I have long been a native Princetonian, born in February 1906, and baptized in the First Presbyterian Church of Princeton; I am descended from two of the oldest Princeton families, the Strachans and the van Dycks; my family residence was that austere old French Normandy stone mansion at 87 Hodge Road, now owned by strangers with a name ending in *-stein* who, it is said, have barbarously "gutted" the interior of the house and "renovated" it in a "more modern" style. (I apologize for this intercalation! It is not so much an emotional as it is an aesthetic and moral outburst I promise will not happen again.) Thus, though a very young child in the aftermath of the "accursed" era, I passed my adolescence in Princeton at a time when the tragic mysteries were often talked-of, in wonderment and dread; and when the forced resignation of Woodrow Wilson from the presidency of Princeton University, in 1910, was still a matter of both regret and malicious mirth in the community.

Through these connections, and others, I have been privy to many materials unavailable to other historians, like the shocking, secret coded journal of the invalid Mrs. Adelaide McLean Burr, and the intimate (and also rather shocking) personal letters of Woodrow Wilson to his beloved wife Ellen, as well as the hallucinatory ravings of the "accursed" grandchildren of Winslow Slade. (Todd Slade was an older classmate of mine at the Princeton Academy, whom I knew only at a distance.) Also, I have had access to many other personal documents—letters, diaries, journals—never available to outsiders. In addition, I have had the privilege of consulting the Manuscripts and Special Collections of Firestone Library at Princeton University. (Though I can't boast of having waded through the legendary *five tons* of research materials like Woodrow Wilson's early biographer Ray

Stannard Baker, I am sure that I've closely perused at least a full *ton*.) I hope it doesn't sound boastful to claim that of all persons living—now—no one is possessed of as much information as I am concerning the private, as well as the public, nature of the Curse.

The reader, most likely a child of this century, is to be cautioned against judging too harshly these persons of a bygone era. It is naïve to imagine that, in their place, we might have better resisted the incursions of the Curse; or might have better withstood the temptation to despair. It is not difficult for us, living seven decades after the Curse, or, as it was sometimes called, the Horror, had run its course, to recognize a pattern as it emerged; but imagine the confusion, alarm, and panic suffered by the innocent, during those fourteen months of ever-increasing and totally mysterious disaster! No more than the first victims of a terrible plague can know what fate is befalling them, its depth and breadth and *impersonality*, could the majority of the victims of the Curse comprehend their situation—to see that, beneath the numerous evils unleashed upon them in these ironically idyllic settings, a single Evil lay.

For, consider: might mere pawns in a game of chess conceive of the fact that they are playing-pieces, and not in control of their fate; what would give them the power to lift themselves above the playing board, to a height at which the design of the game becomes clear? I'm afraid that this is not very likely, for them as for us: we cannot know if we act or are acted upon; whether we are playing pieces in the game, or are the very game ourselves.

M. W. van Dyck II
Eaglestone Manor
Princeton, New Jersey
24 June 1984

PROLOGUE

*I*t is an afternoon in autumn, near dusk. The western sky is a spider's web of translucent gold. I am being brought by carriage—two horses—muted thunder of their hooves—along narrow country roads between hilly fields touched with the sun's slanted rays, to the village of Princeton, New Jersey. The urgent pace of the horses has a dreamlike air, like the rocking motion of the carriage; and whoever is driving the horses his face I cannot see, only his back—stiff, straight, in a tight-fitting dark coat.

Quickening of a heartbeat that must be my own yet seems to emanate from without, like a great vibration of the very earth. There is a sense of exhilaration that seems to spring, not from within me, but from the countryside. How hopeful I am! How excited! With what childlike affection, shading into wonderment, I greet this familiar yet near-forgotten landscape! Cornfields, wheat fields, pastures in which dairy cows graze like motionless figures in a landscape by Corot . . . the calls of red-winged blackbirds and starlings . . . the shallow though swift-flowing Stony Brook Creek and the narrow wood-plank bridge over which the horses' hooves and the carriage wheels thump . . . a smell of rich, moist earth, harvest . . . I see that I am being propelled along the Great Road, I am nearing home, I am nearing the mysterious origin of my birth. This journey I undertake with such anticipation is not one of geographical space but one of Time—for it is the year 1905 that is my destination.

1905!—the very year of the Curse.

Now, almost too soon, I am approaching the outskirts of Princeton. It is a small country town of only a few thousand inhabitants, its population swollen by university students during the school term. Spires of churches appear in the near distance—for there are numerous churches in Princeton. Modest farmhouses have given way to more substantial homes. As the Great Road advances, very substantial homes.

How strange, I am thinking—there are no human figures. No other carriages, or motorcars. A stable, a lengthy expanse of a wrought iron fence along Elm Road, behind which Crosswicks Manse is hidden by tall splendid elms, oaks, and evergreens; here is a pasture bordering the redbrick Princeton Theological Seminary where more trees grow, quite gigantic trees they seem, whose gnarled roots are exposed. Now, on Nassau Street, I am passing the wrought iron gate that leads into the university—to fabled Nassau Hall, where once the Continental Congress met, in 1783. Yet, there are no figures on the Princeton campus—all is empty, deserted. Badly I would like to be taken along Bayard Lane to Hodge Road—to my family home; how my heart yearns, to turn up the drive, and to be brought to the very door at the side of the house, through which I might enter with a wild elated shout—I am here! I am home! But the driver does not seem to hear me. Or perhaps I am too shy to call to him, to countermand the directions he has been given. We are passing a church with a glaring white facade, and a high gleaming cross that flashes light in the sun; the carriage swerves, as if one of the horses had caught a pebble in his hoof; I am staring at the churchyard, for now we are on Witherspoon Street, very nearly in the Negro quarter, and the thought comes to me sharp as a knife-blade entering my flesh, Why, they are all dead, now—that is why no one is here. Except me.

PART I

Demon Bridegroom

ASH WEDNESDAY EVE, 1905

1.

Fellow historians will be shocked, dismayed, and perhaps incredulous—I am daring to suggest that the Curse did not first manifest itself on June 4, 1905, which was the disastrous morning of Annabel Slade's wedding, and generally acknowledged to be the initial public manifestation of the Curse, but rather earlier, in the late winter of the year, on the eve of Ash Wednesday in early March.

This was the evening of Woodrow Wilson's (clandestine) visit to his longtime mentor Winslow Slade, but also the evening of the day when Woodrow Wilson experienced a considerable shock to his sense of family, indeed racial *identity*.

Innocently it began: at Nassau Hall, in the president's office, with a visit from a young seminarian named Yaeger Washington Ruggles who had also been employed as Latin preceptor at the university, to assist in the instruction of undergraduates. (Intent upon reforming the quality of education at Princeton, with its reputation as a Southern-biased, largely Presbyterian boys' school set beside which its rival Harvard University was a paradigm of academic excellence, Woodrow Wilson had initiated a new pedagogy in which bright young men were hired to assist older professors in their lecture courses; Yaeger Ruggles was one of these young preceptors, popular in the better homes of Princeton as at the university, as eligible bachelors are likely to be in a university town.) Yaeger Ruggles was a slender, slight, soft-spoken fellow Virginian, a distant cousin of Wilson's who had introduced himself to the university president after he'd enrolled in his first year at the Princeton Theological Seminary; Wilson had personally hired him to be a preceptor, impressed with his courtesy, bearing, and intelligence. At their first meeting, Yaeger Ruggles had brought with him a letter from an elderly aunt, living in Roanoke, herself a cousin of Wilson's father's aunt. This web of intricate connections was very Southern; despite the fact that Woodrow Wilson's branch of the family was clearly more affluent, and more socially prominent than Yaeger Ruggles's family, who dwelt largely in the mountainous area west of Roanoke, Woodrow Wilson had made an effort to befriend the young man, inviting him to the larger receptions and soirees at his home, and introducing him to the sons and daughters of his well-to-do Princeton associates and neighbors. Though older than Ruggles by more than twenty years, Woodrow Wilson saw in his young kinsman something of himself, at an earlier age when he'd been a law student in Virginia with an abiding interest in theology. (Woodrow Wilson was the son of a preeminent Presbyterian minister who'd been a chaplain for the Confederate Army; his maternal grandfather was a Presbyterian minister in Rome, Georgia, also a staunch religious and political conservative.) At the time of Yaeger Ruggles's visit to President Wilson, in his office in Nassau Hall, the two had been acquainted for more than two years. Woodrow Wilson had not seen so much of his young relative as he'd wished, for his Princeton social life had to be spent in cultivating the rich and influential. "A private college requires donors. Tuition alone is inadequate"—so Woodrow Wilson said often, in speeches as in private conversations. He did regret not seeing more of Yaeger, for he had but three daughters and no son; and now, with his wife's chronic ill health, that had become a sort of malaise of the spirit, as well as her advancing age, it was not likely that Woodrow would ever have a son. Yaeger's warm dark intelligent eyes invariably moved Woodrow to an indefinable emotion, with the intensity of memory. His hair was very dark, as Woodrow's had once been, but thick and springy, where Woodrow's was rather thin, combed flat against his head. And there was something thrilling about the young man's softly modulated baritone voice also, that seemed to remind Wilson of a beloved voice or voices of his childhood in Virginia and Georgia. It had been a wild impulse of Woodrow's—(since childhood in his rigid Presbyterian household, Woodrow had been prone to near-irresistible urges and impulses of every kind, to which he'd rarely given in)—to begin singing in Yaeger's presence, that the younger man might join him; for Woodrow had loved his college glee clubs, and liked to think that he had a passably fair tenor voice, if untrained and, in recent years, unused.

But it would be a Protestant hymn Woodrow would sing with Yaeger, something melancholy, mournful, yearning, and deliciously submissive— *Rock of Ages, cleft for me! Let me hide myself in Thee! Let the water and the blood, that thy wounded side did flow . . .*

Woodrow had not yet heard Yaeger speak in public, but he'd predicted, in Princeton circles, and to the very dean of the seminary himself, that his young "Virginian cousin" would one day be an excellent minister—at which time, Woodrow wryly thought, Yaeger too would understand the value of cultivating the wealthy at the expense of one's own predilections.

But this afternoon, Yaeger Washington Ruggles was not so composed as he usually was. He appeared to be short of breath, as if he'd bounded up the stone steps of Nassau Hall; he did not smile so readily and so *sympathetically* as he usually did. Nor was his hurried handshake so firm, or so warm. Woodrow saw with a pang of displeasure—(for it pained him, to feel even an inward rebuke of anyone whom he liked)—that the seminarian's shirt collar was open at his throat, as if, in an effort to breathe, he'd unconsciously tugged at it; he had not shaved fastidiously and his skin, ordinarily of a more healthy tone than Woodrow's own, seemed darkened as by a shadow.

"Woodrow! I must speak with you."

"But of course, Yaeger—we *are* speaking."

Woodrow half-rose from his chair, behind his massive desk; then remained seated, in his rather formal posture. The office of the president was booklined, floor to ceiling; windows opened out onto the cultivated green of Nassau Hall's large and picturesque front lawn, that swept to Nassau Street and the wrought iron gates of the university; and, to the rear, another grassy knoll, that led to Clio and Whig Halls, stately Greek temples of startling if somewhat incongruous Attic beauty amid the darker, Gothic university architecture. Behind Woodrow on the wall was a bewigged portrait of Aaron Burr, Sr., Princeton University's first president to take office in Nassau Hall.

"Yaeger, what is it? You seem troubled."

"You have heard, Woodrow? The terrible thing that happened yesterday in Camden?"

"Why, I think that I—I have not 'heard' . . . What is it?"

Woodrow smiled, puzzled. His polished eyeglasses winked.

In fact, Woodrow had been hearing, or half-hearing, of something very ugly through the day, at the Nassau Club where he had had lunch with several trustees and near the front steps of Nassau Hall where he'd overheard several preceptors talking together in lowered voices. (It was a disadvantage of the presidency, as it had not been when Woodrow was a popular professor at the university, that, sighting him, the younger faculty in particular seemed to freeze, and to smile at him with expressions of forced courtesy and affability.) And it seemed to him too, that morning at breakfast, in his home at Prospect, that their Negro servant Clytie had been unusually silent, and had barely responded when Woodrow greeted her with his customary warm bright smile—"Good morning, Clytie! What have you prepared for us today?" (For Clytie, though born in Newark, New Jersey, had Southern forebears and could prepare breakfasts of the sort Woodrow had had as a boy in Augusta, Georgia, and elsewhere in the South; she was wonderfully talented, and often prepared a surprise treat for the Wilson family—butternut corn bread, sausage gravy and biscuits, blueberry pancakes with maple syrup, creamy cheese grits and ham-scrambled eggs of which Woodrow, with his sensitive stomach, could eat only a sampling, but which was very pleasing to him as a way of beginning what would likely be one of his complicated, exhausting, and even hazardous days in Nassau Hall.)

Though Woodrow invited Yaeger Ruggles to sit down, the young seminarian seemed scarcely to hear and remained standing; in fact, nervously pacing about in a way that grated on his elder kinsman's nerves, as Yaeger spoke in a rambling and incoherent manner of—(the term was so vulgar, Woodrow held himself stiff as if in opposition to the very sound)—an incident that had occurred the previous night in Camden, New Jersey—*lynching.*

And another ugly term which made Woodrow very uneasy, as parents and his Virginian and Georgian relatives were not unsympathetic to the Protestant organization's goals if not its specific methods—*Ku Klux Klan.*

"There were two victims, Woodrow! Ordinarily, there is just one—a helpless man—a helpless black man—but last night, in Camden, in that hellish place, which is a center of 'white supremacy'—there was a male victim, and a *female*. A nineteen-year-old boy and his twenty-three-year-old sister, who was *pregnant*. You won't find their names in the newspapers— the Trenton paper hasn't reported the lynching at all, and the Newark paper placed a brief article on an inside page. The Klan led a mob of people—not just men but women, and young children—who were looking for a young black man who'd allegedly insulted a white man on the street—whoever the young black man was, no one was sure—but they came across another young man named Pryde who was returning home from work, attacked him and beat him and dragged him to be hanged, and his sister tried to stop them, tried to attack some of them and was arrested by the sheriff of Camden County and handcuffed, then turned over to the mob. By this time—"

"Yaeger, please! Don't talk so loudly, my office staff will hear. And please—if you can—stop your nervous *pacing*."

Woodrow removed a handkerchief from his pocket, and dabbed at his warm forehead. How faint-headed he was feeling! This ugly story was not something Woodrow had expected to hear, amid a succession of afternoon appointments in the president's office in Nassau Hall.

And Woodrow was seriously concerned that his office staff, his secretary Matilde and her assistants, might overhear the seminarian's raised voice and something of his words, which could not fail to appall them.

Yaeger protested, "But, Woodrow—the Klan murdered two innocent people last night, hardly more than fifty miles from Princeton—from this very office! That they are 'Negroes' does not make their suffering and their deaths any less horrible. Our students are talking of it—some of them, Southerners, are joking of it—your faculty colleagues are talking of it— every Negro in Princeton knows of it, or something of it—the most hideous part being, after the Klan leaders hanged the young man, and doused his body with gasoline and lighted it, his sister was brought to the same site, to be murdered beside him. And the sheriff of Camden County did nothing to prevent the murders and made no attempt to arrest or even question anyone afterward. There were said to have been more than seven hundred people gathered at the outskirts of Camden, to witness the lynchings. Some were said to have crossed the bridge from Philadelphia—the lynching must have been planned beforehand. The bodies burned for some time—some of the mob was taking pictures. What a nightmare! In our Christian nation, forty years after the Civil War! It makes me ill—sick to death . . . These lynchings are common in the South, and the murderers never brought to justice, and now they have increased in New Jersey, there was a lynching in Zarephath only a year ago—where the 'white supremacists' have their own church—the Pillar of Fire—and in the Pine Barrens, and in Cape May . . ."

"These are terrible events, Yaeger, but—why are you telling me about them, at such a time? I am upset too, of course—as a Christian, I cannot countenance murder—or any sort of mob violence—we must have a 'rule of law'—not passion—but—if law enforcement officers refuse to arrest the guilty, and local sentiment makes a criminal indictment and a trial unlikely—what are we, here in Princeton, to do? There are barbarous places in this country, as in the world—at times, a spirit of infamy—evil . . ."

Woodrow was speaking rapidly. By now he was on his feet, agitated. It was not good for him, his physician had warned him, to become excited, upset, or even emotional—since childhood, Woodrow had been an over-sensitive child, and had suffered ill health well into his teens; he could not bear it, if anyone spoke loudly or emotionally in his presence, his heart beat rapidly and erratically bearing an insufficient amount of blood to his brain, that began to "faint"—and so now Woodrow found himself leaning forward, resting the palms of his hands on his desk blotter, his eyesight blotched and a ringing in his ears; his physician had warned him, too, of high blood pressure, which was shared by many in his father's family, that might lead to a stroke; even as his inconsiderate young kinsman dared to interrupt him with more of the lurid story, more ugly and unfairly accusatory words—"You, Woodrow, with the authority of your office, can speak out against these atrocities. You might join with other Princeton leaders— Winslow Slade, for instance—you are a good friend of Reverend Slade's, he would listen to you—and others in Princeton, among your influential friends. The horror of lynching is that *no one stops it;* among influential Christians like yourself, *no one speaks against it.*"

Woodrow objected, this was not true: "Many have spoken against—that terrible mob violence—'lynchings.' I have spoken against—'l-lynchings.' I hope that my example as a Christian has been— is—a model of—Christian belief—'Love thy neighbor as thyself'—it is the lynchpin of our religion . . ." (Damn!—he had not meant to say *lynchpin:* a kind of demon had tripped his tongue, as Yaeger stared at him blankly.) "You should know, Yaeger—of course you know—it has been my effort here, at Princeton, to reform the university—to transform the undergraduate curriculum, for instance—and to instill more *democracy* wherever I can. The eating clubs, the entrenched 'aristocracy'—I have been battling them, you must know, since I took office. And this enemy of mine—Dean West! *He* is a nemesis I must defeat, or render less powerful—before I can take on the responsibility of—of—" Woodrow stammered, not knowing what he meant to say. It was often that his thoughts flew ahead of his words, when he was in an emotional mood; which was why, as he'd been warned, and had warned himself, he must not be *carried away* by any rush of emotion. "—of confronting the Klan, and their myriad supporters in the state, who are not so many as in the South and yet—and yet—they are many . . ."

"'Supporters' in the state? Do you mean, 'law-abiding Christian hypocrites'? The hell with them! *You* must speak out."

"I—I must—'speak'—? But—the issue is not so—simple . . ."

It had been a shock to Woodrow, though not exactly a surprise, that, of the twenty-five trustees of Princeton University, who had hired him out of the ranks of the faculty, and whose bidding he was expected to exercise, to a degree, were not, on the whole, as one soon gathered, unsympathetic to the *white supremacist* doctrine, though surely appalled, as any civilized person would be, by the Klan's strategies of terror. *Keeping the Negroes in their place* was the purpose of the Klan's vigilante activities, and not violence for its own sake—as the Klan's supporters argued.

Keeping the purity of the white race from mongrelization—this was a yet more basic tenet, with which very few Caucasians were likely to disagree.

But Woodrow could not hope to reason with Yaeger Ruggles, in the seminarian's excitable mood.

Nor could Woodrow pursue this conversation at the present time, for he had a pressing appointment within a few minutes, with one of his (sadly few) *confidants* among the Princeton faculty; more urgently, he was feeling unmistakably nauseated, a warning signal of more extreme nausea to come if he didn't soon take a teaspoonful of the "calming" medicine prescribed to him by Dr. Hatch, kept in a drawer in the president's desk.

"Well, Yaeger. It is a terrible, terrible thing—as you have reported to me—a 'lynching'—alleged . . . We may expect this in south Jersey but not in Camden, so near Philadelphia! But I'm afraid I can't speak with you much longer, as I have an appointment at . . . Yaeger, what on earth is wrong?"

Woodrow was shocked to see that his young kinsman, who had always regarded Woodrow Wilson with the utmost respect and admiration, was now glaring at him, as a sulky and self-righteous adolescent might glare at a parent.

The carelessly shaven jaws were trembling with disdain, or frank dislike. The nostrils were widened, very dark. And the eyes were not so attractive now but somewhat protuberant, like the eyes of a wild beast about to leap.

Yaeger's voice was not so gently modulated now but frankly insolent: "What is wrong with—who, Woodrow? Me? Or you?"

Woodrow protested angrily, "Yaeger, that's enough. You may be a distant relation of mine, through my father's family, but that—that does not—give you the right to be disrespectful to me, and to speak in a loud voice to upset my staff. This 'ugly episode'—as you have reported it to me—is a good example of why we must not allow our emotions to govern us. We must have a—a civilization of *law*—and not—not—anarchy."

Stubbornly Yaeger persisted: "Will you talk to Winslow Slade, at least? If he could preach from his pulpit, this Sunday—that would be a good, brave thing for Princeton; and maybe it would get into the newspapers. And if the president of Princeton, Woodrow Wilson, could give a public comment also—"

"Yaeger, I've told you! I can't discuss this now. I have an appointment at three-fifteen, and I—I am not feeling altogether well, as a consequence of our exchange."

"Well, I'm sorry for that. Very sorry to hear that."

(Was Yaeger speaking sarcastically? Woodrow could not bring himself to believe so.)

Woodrow wanted to protest: he was a friend to the Negro race, surely!

He was a *Democrat*. In every public utterance, he spoke of *equality*.

Though he did not believe in women's suffrage—certainly. Very few persons of his close acquaintance, including his dear wife, Ellen, believed in so radical and *unnatural* a notion.

Woodrow would have liked to explain to Yaeger how systematically and explicitly he was fair-minded toward Negroes. Over the protests of certain of the trustees and faculty, he saw to it that Booker T. Washington was not only invited to his Princeton inauguration, as a sensible, educated Negro promoting a "gradualism" of racial reform, unlike the radical W. E. B. DuBois, but that the Negro educator was asked to give one of the speeches at the ceremony, alongside several of the most distinguished white persons of the day.

Also, Booker T. Washington had been made welcome at a commencement luncheon at Prospect, where he'd been seated among the other guests in a most relaxed manner; though an invitation to a lavish dinner at the Nassau Club, given the night before, had not been extended to him, since the Nassau Club did not admit Negroes onto its premises (except as servants). *That,* President Wilson had been powerless to modify, since the Nassau Club was a private club.

In addition, Professor van Dyck of the Philosophy Department often told the tale of how one Reverend Robeson, of the Witherspoon Street Presbyterian Church, had aspired to a meeting with the president of Princeton University, to suggest that his son Paul, allegedly an "outstanding" student and athlete, be admitted to the university; scarcely knowing, from the courtesy with which Woodrow Wilson greeted this remarkable request, how audacious it was; and how gentlemanly Wilson's reply— "Reverend, I am sure that your son is indeed 'outstanding.' But it is not quite the right time in history for a Negro lad to enroll at Princeton—that time, I am afraid, will not be for a while." So long as Negroes—*darkies*, as they were more fondly called, in Woodrow's childhood—knew their place, and were not derelict as servants and workers, Dr. Wilson had very little prejudice against them, in most respects.

"Yes," Yaeger said, with a turn of the knife-blade, not unlike the cruelty of an adolescent boy with regard to his father, "it would be tragic if you were not feeling 'altogether well'—as a consequence of my unwelcome appeal."

In a part of Woodrow's mind, or of his heart, which was hardly so calloused as Yaeger Ruggles seemed to be implying, Woodrow was deeply wounded, that the young man he so cared for seemed now scarcely to care for *him*. Stiffly he said:

"There is some mystery here, Yaeger, I think—as to why you are so very—so very *concerned* . . ."

" 'Mystery'? D'you think so, Woodrow?" Yaeger spoke with an insolent smile; all this while he had been smiling at his elder kinsman, a mirthless grin, like the grimace of a gargoyle. He too was agitated, and even trembling, but he could not resist a parting riposte as he prepared to leave the president's office, "You have never looked at me closely enough, 'Cousin Woodrow.' If you had, or if you were capable of such insight, you would know exactly why I, and others like me in this accursed United States of America, are so very *concerned*."

As Yaeger turned away contemptuously yet Woodrow saw, suddenly—saw the young man's facial features, his lips, nose, the texture and tone of his skin, even the just-perceptible "kinkiness" of his hair—saw, and, in a rush of sickening horror, understood.

PRESIDENT WILSON! OH—President Wilson!

Are you all right? Did you injure yourself? Let us help you to your feet—back to your desk . . .

Shall we summon Dr. Hatch? Shall we summon—Mrs. Wilson?

***

NEITHER DR. HATCH nor Mrs. Wilson was summoned. For Woodrow was quite recovered, within minutes.

Yet, he had had enough of Nassau Hall, for the day.

Though unsteady on his feet, and ashen-faced, yet President Wilson insisted upon walking unassisted to the president's mansion, Prospect, located at the heart of the university campus: an austere example of Italianate architecture built by the architect John Notman, that was the president's *home*.

Something of a fishbowl, Woodrow thought the house. And Ellen and their daughters were made to feel self-conscious there—for prankish undergraduates could circle the house at will, in the dark, peeking into windows beneath blinds.

Still, Prospect was a very attractive and imposing residence. And Woodrow was unfailingly grateful that he lived in it; and not, as fate might have devised, another man.

Fortunately, Ellen was out. The girls were still at school. Clytie and Lucinda were in the cellar doing laundry—the smells of wet things, a deeper and harsher smell as of detergent and even lye soap provoked in Woodrow one of his *memory pangs* of childhood, that increased his sense of excited unease and dread.

It was a household of *females*. So often, he could not *breathe*.

Yet this afternoon he was allowed unimpeded to ascend to the dim-lit atmosphere of the master bedroom where, in the privacy of his step-in closet, he was free to select a pill, a second pill, and a third pill from his armamentarium of pills, medicines, and "tonics"—that rivaled his mother's armamentarium of old.

Woodrow's dear mother! How he missed her, in his weak moods especially.

She could guide him. *She* could instruct him in what course to take, in this matter of his nemesis Dean West.

As to the matter of the ugly Klan lynching—Mrs. Wilson would not have spoken of so obscene an event, if she had even heard of it.

For there are some things too ugly for women to know of. Genteel Christian women, at least.

A man's responsibility is to shield them. No good can come of them knowing all that we must know.

Woodrow's Southern relatives would have pointed out that mob violence against Negroes was a consequence of the abolition of slavery— blame, if there be blame, must be laid where it is due, with the abolitionists and war-mongers among the Republicans.

The defeat of the Confederacy was the defeat of—a way of civilization that was superior to its conqueror's.

Hideous, what Yaeger Ruggles had revealed to him!—he who had liked the young man so much, and had, precipitously perhaps, appointed him a Latin preceptor.

That appointment, Dr. Wilson would have to rethink.

And perhaps too, he must have a private conversation with Reverend Shackleton, head of the Princeton Theological Seminary.

Unfair! And very crude! The charges Yaeger Ruggles had brought against him.

In such times of distress it was Woodrow's usual routine to soak a compress in cold water, lie on his bed and position the compress over his aching eyes. Soon then he felt a shuddering voluptuous surrender to—he knew not what.

The Bog Kingdom. Bidding him enter! Ah, enter!

There, all wishes are fulfilled. The more forbidden, the more delicious.

He had not had the energy to undress. Only his black-polished shoes had been removed. Carefully placed side by side on the carpet.

So unmoving Woodrow was in sleep, he hardly risked rumpling his white cotton shirt, his vest and neatly pressed trousers. So still did he sleep, at such times, he did not risk sweating and dampening his clothing.

Yet, his thoughts raged like hornets.

Never can I tell Ellen. The poor woman would be distraught, appalled—the deceptive young "cousin" has come into our house, at my invitation; he has sat at my dining room table, as my guest; he has exchanged conversations with my dear daughters . . .

Now the full horror of the revelation washed over Woodrow—the danger in which he'd put, in all ignorance, his Margaret, his Jessie, and his Eleanor.

2.

It was a secret late-night meeting on the very eve of Ash Wednesday, recorded in no document except, in code, in the diary of Woodrow Wilson for March 1905.*

It was, one might say, a *clandestine* meeting. For so Woodrow Wilson, troubled in spirit, considered it.

I will implore him. I will humble myself, and beg for help.

I am not proud—no longer!

This meeting, more than the earlier meeting between Woodrow Wilson and his impetuous young kinsman Yaeger Ruggles, marks the first true emergence of the Curse; as an early, subtle and easily overlooked symptom marks the emergence to come of a deadly disease.

As, one might say, the early symptoms of Woodrow Wilson's breakdown, stroke and collapse of May 1906 were prefigured here, in the events of this day, unsuspected by Woodrow Wilson, his family and his most trusted friends.

For that evening, after dinner, feeling more robust, though his brain was assailed by a thousand worries, Woodrow decided to walk a windy mile to Crosswicks Manse on Elm Road, the family estate of the Slades. It had been his request to see Reverend Winslow Slade in private, and in

---

* Which diary, included in the Firestone Library Special Collections, was provided for my perusal by the kindly curator who had no idea, for how could he have known?—that I alone, of the numerous researchers who have contemplated *five tons* of Wilsonia, managed to crack the ingenious code.

secrecy, at 10 P.M. precisely; Woodrow, who had a boyish predilection for such schemes, as a way of avoiding the unwanted attention of others, was to enter the dignified old stone house by a side door that led into Reverend Slade's library, and bypass the large rooms at the front of the house. For this was not a *social meeting*—there was no need to involve any of the household staff or any of Dr. Slade's family.

The last thing Woodrow Wilson wanted was to be *talked-of*; to be the object of *speculation, crude gossip*.

His dignity was such, yes and his pride: he could not bear his name, his reputation, his motives so besmirched.

For it was beginning to be generally known in Princeton, in this fourth and most tumultuous year of his presidency of the university, that Woodrow Wilson was encountering a cunning, ruthless, and unified opposition led by the politically astute Dean Andrew Fleming West, whose administrative position at the university preceded Woodrow's inauguration as president; and who was reputed to be deeply aggrieved that the presidency, more or less promised to him by the board of trustees, had unaccountably been offered to his younger rival Woodrow Wilson, who had not the grace to decline in his favor.

All this rankled, and was making Woodrow's life miserable; his primary organ of discomfort was his stomach, and intestines; yet nearly so vulnerable, his poor aching brain that buzzed through day and night like a hive of maddened hornets. Yet, as a responsible administrator, and an astute politician, he was able to disguise his condition much of the time, even in the very company of West, who confronted Woodrow too with mock courtesy, like an unctuous hypocrite in a Molière comedy whose glances into the audience draw an unjust sympathy, to the detriment of the idealistic hero.

Like a large ungainly burden, a steamer trunk perhaps, stuffed with unwanted and outgrown clothing, shoes and the miscellany of an utterly ordinary and unexamined life, Woodrow Wilson sought to carry the weight of such anxiety to his mentor, and unburden himself of it, at his astonished elder's feet.

It would not be the first time that "Tommy" Wilson had come to appeal to "Win" Slade, surreptitiously; but it would be the final time.*

"Woodrow, hello! Come inside, please."

A gust of wind, tinged with irony, accompanied Woodrow into the elder man's library.

Reverend Slade grasped the younger man's hand, that was rather chill, and limp; a shudder seemed to run from the one to the other, leaving the elder man slightly shaken.

"I gather that there is something troubling you, Woodrow? I hope—it isn't—anything involving your family?"

Between the two, there had sometimes been talk, anxious on Woodrow's side and consoling and comforting on Winslow's, about Woodrow's "marital relations"—(which is not to say "sexual relations"—the men would never have discussed so painfully private a matter)—and Woodrow's disappointment at being the father of *only girls*.

Woodrow, breathless from the wind-buffeted walk along Elm Road, where streetlights were few, and very little starlight assisted his way, and but a gauze-masked moon, stared at his friend for a moment without comprehending his question. *Family?* Was Winslow Slade alluding to Woodrow's distant "cousin"—Yaeger Washington Ruggles?

Then, Woodrow realized that of course Winslow was referring to his wife, Ellen, and their daughters. *Family.*

_____

* In order to give shape to my massive chronicle, that has been assembled from countless sources, I intend to "leap ahead" in time whenever it seems helpful. Also, I should note here that Thomas Woodrow Wilson, born 1856, soon saw the advantage, as an ambitious young man, of a more distinctive-sounding name: *Woodrow* Wilson. It was a proud if somewhat fantastical claim of Woodrow's that his lineage extended back to one "Patrik Wodro" who had crossed the English Channel with William the Conqueror; and that no one of significance had yet asserted himself in American politics who was not of Scots-English origin—a somewhat contradictory claim, it would seem.

"No, Winslow. All is well there." (Was this so? The answer came quickly, automatically; for it was so often asked.) "It's another matter I've come to discuss with you. Except—I am very ashamed."

" 'Ashamed'? Why?"

"But I must unburden my heart to you, Winslow. For I have no one else."

"Please, Woodrow! Take a seat. Beside the fire, for you do look chilled. And would you like something to drink?—to warm you?"

No, no! Woodrow rarely drank.

Out of personal disdain, or, if he gave thought to it, out of revulsion for the excess of drinking he'd had occasion to observe in certain households in the South.

Woodrow shivered, sinking into a chair by the fireplace that faced his gracious host. Out of nervousness he removed his eyeglasses to polish them vigorously, a habit that annoyed others, though Winslow Slade took little notice.

"It is so peaceful *here*. Thank you, Dr. Slade, for taking time to speak with me!"

"Of course, Woodrow. You know that I am here, at any time, as your friend and 'spiritual counselor'—if you wish."

In his heightened state of nerves Woodrow glanced about the library, which was familiar to him, yet never failed to rouse him to awe. Indeed, Winslow Slade's library was one of the marvels of the wealthy West End of Princeton, for the part-retired Presbyterian minister was the owner of a (just slightly damaged and incomplete) copy of the legendary Gutenberg Bible of 1445, which was positioned on a stand close by Winslow's carved mahogany desk; on another pedestal was an early, 1895 edition of the *Oxford English Dictionary*. And there were first editions of works by Goethe, Kant, Hegel, Fichte, Schelling, Schleiermacher, Ritschl, James Hutchinson Stirling and Thomas Carlyle among others. In his youth Dr. Slade had been something of a classics scholar, and so there were volumes by Plato, Aristotle, Epicurus, Aeschylus, Sophocles, Euripides and others in Greek, as well as Latin texts—Virgil, Caesar, Cicero, Seneca, Livy, Cato, and (surprisingly, considering the unmitigated pagan nature of their verse) Ovid, Catullus, and Petronius. And there were the English classics of course—the leather-bound works of Chaucer, Shakespeare, Milton, Dryden, Pope, Swift, Samuel Johnson through the Romantics—Wordsworth and Coleridge, Byron, Shelley, Keats and, allegedly Dr. Slade's favorite, the fated John Clare. The library was designed by the celebrated architect John McComb, Jr., famous for having designed Alexander Hamilton's Grange: among its features were an ornate coffered ceiling, paneled walls of fifteenth-century tooled leather (reputedly taken from the home of Titian), and portraits of such distinguished Slade ancestors as General Elias Slade, the Reverend Azariah Slade, and the Reverend Jonathan Edwards (related by marriage to the original Slade family)—each rendered powerfully by John Singleton Copley. Portraits, daguerreotypes, and shadow drawings of Dr. Slade's sons Augustus and Copplestone, and his grandchildren Josiah, Annabel, Todd, and little Oriana, also hung on the wall, just behind Dr. Slade's desk; and should be mentioned here since all but the child Oriana will figure prominently in this chronicle.

(Is this unobtrusively done? I am a historian, and not a literary stylist; so must "intercalate" such details very consciously, that the reader will take note of them; yet not so obtrusively, that the sensitive reader is offended by over-explicitness.)

In this gracious room, commanding a position of prominence, was a fireplace of stately proportions in whose marble mantel was carved, in Gothic letters, HIC HABITAT FELICITAS—which caught Woodrow's eye, as always it did when he visited Winslow Slade. With a morose smile Woodrow leaned over to run his fingertips over the chiseled inscription, saying, "*Here*, Dr. Slade, I have no doubt that happiness abides; but at my home, and in the president's office in Nassau Hall—not likely."

During the conversation to follow, the fire in the fireplace blazed and waned; and blazed again, and again waned; until, without either man noticing, the logs collapsed in a crumbling of smoldering coals, like distant, dying suns, into darkness and oblivion which not even a belated poker-stirring, by the younger man, could revive.

AT THIS TIME, before the terrible incursions of the Curse would prematurely age him, Winslow Slade, partly retired from his longtime pastorship at the First Presbyterian Church of Princeton, was a vigorous gentleman of seventy-four, who looked at least a decade younger; as his visitor, not yet fifty, yet looked, with such strain in his face, and his eyes shadowed in the firelight, at least a decade older than his age.

Since the death of his second wife Tabitha some years before, Dr. Slade had remained a widower, and took what melancholy joy he could largely from his several grandchildren.

Though fallen now into quasi-oblivion, known only to historians of the era, Winslow Slade was, in the early years of the twentieth century, one of New Jersey's most prominent citizens, who had served as a distinguished president of Princeton University, three decades before, in the troubled aftermath of the Civil War and into the early years of Reconstruction, when the academic state of the school was threatened, and Dr. Slade had brought some measure of academic excellence and discipline into the school; and, in the late 1880s, when Dr. Slade had served a term as governor of New Jersey, in a particularly tumultuous and partisan era in which a gentleman of Dr. Slade's qualities, by nature congenial, inclined rather more to compromise than to fight, and in every way a Christian, found "politics" far too stressful to wish to run for a second term. In Princeton, a far more civilized community than the state capitol in Trenton, Winslow Slade was generally revered as a much-beloved pastor of the Presbyterian church and community leader; and how much more so, than Woodrow Wilson could ever hope to be!

Not that the younger man was jealous of the elder: he was not. But, quite consciously, he *wished to learn* from the elder.

Though very likely Winslow Slade knew a good deal of the animosity blooming between the university president and his most powerful dean, being the beneficiary of his wife's network of local news, yet Winslow tactfully asked his young friend if it was a faculty matter, that was troubling him?—or, an undergraduate issue?

Woodrow's reply was reluctantly uttered: "No, Dr. Slade. I think that I have won the boys over, after some initial coolness—they like me now. This generation is more concerned with making their own worldly way than I would wish, but we understand each other." Half-consciously Woodrow rose to his feet, to pick up, from Winslow Slade's desk, a brass letter-opener, and to turn it in his fingers. A thin smile distended his lips. "The mischief of boys I would welcome, Dr. Slade, at this point—if it could spare me this other."

" 'This other'—?"

For an unsettling moment Woodrow lost the thread of his concentration: he was hearing a muted yet vehement voice daring to accuse him. *The horror of lynching is, no one speaks against it.* Behind the silvery glint of his glasses his eyes filled with tears of vexation. The little brass letter-opener slipped from his fingers to fall onto Winslow Slade's desk. He said, "I'm speaking of—of certain underhanded challenges to my authority—as president of our university. You know, Dr. Slade, I take my responsibility to be—well, God-ordained; certainly I would not have had this exceptional honor bestowed upon me, if God *had not wished it*. And so, I am baffled by the calculated insults, malicious backbiting, and plotting among my administrative colleagues—and their secret liaisons with the trustees. Surely by now you've heard how my enemies conspire against me in skirmishes that have not the dignity of *battle,* still less of declared *war.*"

There followed an embarrassed silence. The elder man, regarding his friend with grave sympathy, could not think how to reply. It was kept fairly secret among Woodrow Wilson's family and intimates that he had already suffered several mysterious collapses in his lifetime, the earliest as a young adolescent; Woodrow had even had a "mild" stroke at the premature age of thirty-nine. (At the time, Woodrow had been teaching jurisprudence at Princeton, preparing his lectures with great urgency and intensity, and working on the multivolume *A History of the American People* that would one day solidify his reputation.) Now, a decade later, Woodrow's nerves were so keenly strung, he seemed at times to resemble a puppet jerked about by cruel, whimsical fingers. Yet, like any sensitive, proud man, he shrank from being comforted.

With a wry smile Woodrow confessed to his friend that, as pressure on him lately increased, he suffered from such darting pains in his head and abdomen as he lay sleepless through much of the night, he half wondered if his enemies—("Led by that careerist whose name I do not care to speak")—were devouring his very soul, as a sinister species of giant water spider sucks the life out of its helpless frog prey.

Winslow responded with a wincing smile, "Woodrow, my dear friend, I wish I could banish from your vocabulary such words as *battle, war, enemy*—even, perhaps, *soul*. For your nature is to take a little too seriously matters that are only local and transient, and you see *conspiracy* where there may be little more than a healthy difference of opinion."

Woodrow stared at his elder friend with a look of hurt and alarm.

" 'Healthy difference of opinion'—? I don't understand, Winslow. This is life or death—my life or death, as president of the university."

"When the issue is whether to build the new Graduate College at the heart of the campus or, as Dean West prefers, at the edge? *That* is a matter of your life or death?"

"Yes! Yes, it is. And the eating clubs as well—my enemies are massing against me, to defeat my plan of colleges within the university, of a democratic nature. You know, I believe that the highest executive office must centralize power—whether the chief executive is the President of the United States, or of a distinguished university. And right here at home, I am met with *mutiny*."

"Woodrow, really! 'Mutiny.' " Winslow Slade smiled.

"*Mutiny*, yes," Woodrow repeated grimly, "and I have no doubt that they are meeting in secret at this very minute, somewhere close by."

For Woodrow had learned, from a remark of Mrs. Wilson's when she'd returned from a luncheon at the Princeton Women's Club two days before, that Andrew Fleming West was to be a houseguest at a dinner party at the home of the Burrs, of FitzRandolph Place, to which the Wilsons had conspicuously not been invited.

Winslow Slade murmured that none of this boded well for the university, if it was true; still less for Woodrow and his family.

"Dr. Slade, it *is* true," Woodrow said irritably, "the prediction around town that I will be 'outflanked' by Easter, cornered like a rat and made to resign the presidency! Please don't deny it, sir, in the interests of kindness or charity, for I know very well that Princeton whispers of nothing else— even the washerwomen, and the Negro servants, and every sort of local riffraff, gloat over my distress."

At this, Winslow Slade leaned over to touch the younger man's tensed arm. "Tommy—d'you mind if I call you 'Tommy'?—I hope you remember the advice I gave you, when you accepted the trustees' offer of the presidency: 'A wise administrator never admits to having enemies, and a yet wiser administrator never has enemies.'"

"A banal platitude, sir, if I may say so," Woodrow said, with increasing vexation, "—that might have been put to the 'enemies' of Napoleon, as his armies swept over them and devastated them utterly. It is easy for you to think in such a way—*you* who have never known an enemy in your life, and have been blessed by God in all your efforts."

"I had political enemies enough, when I was governor of the state," Winslow said. "I think you are forgetting the vicissitudes of real life, in your airy allegorical dramas."

Woodrow, pacing in front of the fireplace, spoke now rapidly, and heedlessly—saying that Ellen and his daughters were "sick with worry" over his health; his doctor, Melrick Hatch, had warned him that the palliative medications he'd been taking for years to steady his nerves might soon have a "reverse" effect. (One of Woodrow's medications was the morphine-laced Mrs. Wycroff's Soothing Syrup; another, McCormick's

Glyco-Heroin Throat Lozenges; yet another, Boehringer & Soehne's Antiseptique, with its high quotient of opium. Woodrow was also somewhat addicted to such home remedies as syrupy calomel, bismuth, and Oil of Olmay; cascara sagrada and Tidwell's Purge.) Again, Woodrow picked up the brass letter-opener, to turn it restlessly in his fingers— "The dean, it's said, boasts that he intends to drive me into an 'early grave' and take my place as president. And a majority of the trustees align themselves with *him*."

"Woodrow, please! This isn't worthy of you. I think that you and Dean West must meet face to face, and stop this absurd plotting. I would guess that Andrew goes about Princeton complaining of *you*, and declaring that *you* should drive *him* to an early grave, if you had your way."

Woodrow stiffened at this remark. For indeed, it had frequently come to him, even when he knelt in prayer at Sunday church services, feeling himself an empty vessel to be filled with the grace of God, that, if *something would happen* to his enemy Andrew Fleming West: how easy then, his life would become!

"All opposition to my ideas would evaporate at once, like harmless smoke. *All opposition*."

"Woodrow, what do you mean? What have you said?"

Had Woodrow spoken aloud? He was sure he had not.

Winslow Slade said, quietly, yet with feeling, "Sometimes I think you scarcely know me, Tommy. Or, indeed—anyone. You so surround yourself with fantasies of your own creation! For instance, you claim that I seem not to have known an enemy in my career, and that God has 'blessed' my efforts; but you must know, this was hardly the case. There was a very vocal opposition at the university, when I pushed forward my 'reform' of the curriculum, and insisted upon higher admissions standards; very nearly, a revolt among the trustees. And then, when I was governor of this contentious, politician-ridden state, there were days when I felt like a battered war veteran, and only the solace of my religion, and my church, kept me from despair. Yet, I tried not to complain, even to my dear Oriana; I tried never to make careless public remarks, or denunciations. This is not in keeping with our dignity. Remember the doomed Socrates of *The Crito*—a public man in his seventies condemned to death by the state: it was Socrates' position that one abides by the laws of his time and place, and that death is preferable to banishment from society. So I've long kept my own counsel, and not even those closest to me have known of my secret struggles. So it is, dear Tommy, in the waning years of my life, I can't allow myself to be drawn into 'politics' yet again. I know that your office is a sacred trust in your eyes, very like that of the pulpit; you are your father's son, in many ways; and you have been driving yourself these past months with a superhuman energy. But it must be remembered, Woodrow, the university is not the church; and your inauguration, however splendid, should not be interpreted as an *ordination*." Winslow paused, to allow his words to sink in. It was a misunderstanding of the elder Slade, that he was without sarcasm or irony, as he was without guile; that, being by nature good-hearted and generous, he was one to suffer fools gladly. "So, my counsel to you is *compromise*, President Wilson—*compromise*."

Woodrow reacted like a child who has been slapped. Slowly, dazedly, he sank into his chair by the fireplace, facing his host. Waning firelight played on his tight, taut features; his stricken eyes were hidden behind the wink of his eyeglasses. In a hoarse voice he said: "*Compromise!*—what a thing to suggest! What—*weakness, cowardice!* Did our Savior *compromise*? Did He *make a deal* with his enemies? My father instructed me, either one is right, and compelled to act upon it; or one is in error, and should surrender the chalice to another man. Jesus declared, 'I bring not peace but a sword.' Does not our Lord declare everywhere in His holy writ, that one must be either for Him or against Him? I have reason to believe that all evil begins in compromise, Dr. Slade. Our great President Lincoln did not compromise with the slavers, as our Puritan ancestors did not compromise with the native Indians whom they discovered in the New World, pagan creatures who were not to be trusted—'drasty Sauvages' they were called. You might not know, Winslow, but our Wilson family motto—from the time of the Campbells of Argyll until now—*God save us from compromise.*"

When Winslow didn't reply, only just shook his head, with an inscrutable expression, Woodrow said, a little sharply: "Ours is a proud heritage! And it would go hard against my father, as against my own conscience, if I weakened in this struggle."

Winslow said, gently, "But after all, Tommy, you *are not* your father, however much you love and honor his memory. And you must bear in mind that he is no longer living; he has been dead this past year, and more."

At these words the younger man stared into a corner of the room as if he had been taken by surprise: *was his father dead?*

And something else, someone else, another tormenting voice, had been beating at his thoughts, like buffeting waves—*You can speak out against these atrocities. Christians like yourself.*

Clumsily Woodrow removed his eyeglasses. His vision had never been strong; as a child, letters and numerals had "danced" in his head, making it very difficult for him to read and do arithmetic; yet, he had persevered, and had made of himself an outstanding student, as he was, in his youth, invariably the outstanding member of any class, any school, any group in which he found himself. *Destined for greatness. But you must practice humility, not pride.*

Woodrow wiped at his eyes with his shirt cuff, in manner and in expression very like a child. It seemed to be so, he did not recall that Joseph Ruggles Wilson, his father, had passed away; into the mysterious other world, into which his mother had passed away when Woodrow had been thirty-two, and his first daughter Margaret had been recently born. "You are right, Winslow—of course. Father has been dead more than two years. He has been gathered into the 'Great Dark'—abiding now with his Creator, as we are told. Do you think that it is a realm of being contiguous with our own, if inaccessible? Or—*is it accessible?* I am intrigued by these 'spiritualists'—I've been reading of their exploits, in London and Boston . . . Often I think, though Father is said to be deceased, is he entirely departed? *Requiescat in pace*. But—is he in peace? Are any of the dead departed—or in peace? Or do we only wish them so, that we can imagine ourselves free of their dominion?"

To which query Winslow Slade, staring into the now-waning fire, as shadows rippled across his face, seemed to have no ready reply.

REQUIESCAT IN PACE is the simple legend chiseled beneath the name WINSLOW ELIAS SLADE and the dates 14 DECEMBER 1831–1 JUNE 1906 on the Slade family mausoleum in the older part of the Princeton Cemetery, near the very heart of Princeton. It was said that the distressed gentleman, shortly before his death, left instructions with his family that he wished the somber inscription *Pain Was My Portion* would be engraved on his tomb; but that his son Augustus forbade it.

"We have had enough of *pain*, we Slades," Augustus allegedly declared, "and now we are prepared for *peace*."

This was at a time when the Crosswicks Curse, or, as it is sometimes called, the Crosswicks Horror, had at last lifted from Princeton, and peace of a kind had been restored.

I realize, the reader may be wondering: how could Reverend Winslow Slade, so beloved and revered a Princeton citizen, the only man from whom Woodrow Wilson sought advice and solace, have come to so despairing an end? *How is this possible?*

All I have are the myriad facts I have been able to unearth and assemble, that point to a plausible explanation: the reader will have to draw his or her own conclusions, perhaps.

At the time of our present narrative in March 1905, when Woodrow Wilson sought him out surreptitiously, Winslow Slade retained much of his commanding presence—that blend of authority, manly dignity, compassion, and Christian forbearance noted by his many admirers. No doubt these qualities were inherited with his blood: for Winslow's ancestry may be traced on his father's side to those religiously persecuted and religiously driven Puritans who sought freedom from the tyranny of the Church of England in the late 1600s; and on his mother's side, to Scots-English immigrants in the early 1700s to the Massachusetts Bay Colony, who soon acquired a measure of affluence through trade with England. Within two generations, a number of Slades had migrated from New England to the Philadelphia / Trenton area, as, in religious terms, they had migrated from the rigidity of belief of old-style Puritanism to the somewhat more liberal Presbyterianism of the day, tinged with Calvinist determinism as it was; these were compassionate Christians who sided with those who opposed the execution of Quakers as heretics, a Puritan obsession. Sometime later, in the Battle of Princeton of 1777, General Elias Slade famously distinguished himself, alongside his compatriot Lieutenant Colonel Aaron Burr, Jr. (Elias Slade, only thirty-two at the time of his death, had boldly surrendered his powerful positions in both the Royal Governor's Council and the Supreme Court of the Crown Colony in order to support George Washington in the revolutionary movement—a rebellion by no means so clear-cut in the 1770s nor so seemingly inevitable as it appears to us today in our history textbooks. And what an irony it is that Aaron Burr, Jr., a hero in some quarters in his own time, has been relegated to a disreputable position scarcely more elevated than that of his former compatriot Benedict Arnold!)

It was a general characteristic of the Philadelphia / Trenton branch of the Slade family, judging by their portraits, that the men possessed unusually intense eyes, though deep-set in their sculpted-looking faces; the Slade nose tended to be long, narrow, Roman and somewhat pinched at the tip. In his youth and well into old age, Winslow Slade was considered a handsome man: above average in height, with a head of prematurely silver hair, and straight dark brows, and a studied and somber manner enlivened by a ready and sympathetic smile—in the eyes of some detractors, a *too-ready* and *too-sympathetic* smile.

For it was Winslow Slade's eccentric notion, he would try to embody Christian behavior in his daily—hourly!—life. In this, he often tried the patience of those close to him, still more, those who were associated with him professionally.

"It's my considered belief that the present age will compose, through Winslow Slade, its *spiritual autobiography*"—so the famed Reverend Henry Ward Beecher declared on the occasion of Winslow Slade's inauguration as president of Princeton University in 1877.

As a popular Presbyterian minister, who had studied at Union Theological Seminary in New York City, Winslow Slade had long perfected the art of pleasing—indeed, mesmerizing large audiences.

Though, in contrast to such preachers as Reverend Beecher, Winslow Slade never stooped to rhetorical tricks or empty oratorical flourishes. His Biblical texts were usually familiar ones, though not simple; he chose not to astonish, or perplex, or amuse, or, like some men of the cloth, including his formidable relative Jonathan Edwards, to terrify his congregation. His quiet message of the uniqueness of the Christian faith—as it is a "necessary outgrowth and advancement of the Jewish faith"—is that the Christian must think of himself as choosing Jesus Christ over Satan *at every moment;* an inheritance from his Puritan ancestors, but rendered in such a way as not to alarm or affright his sensitive followers.

It is no surprise that Reverend Slade's grandchildren, when very young, imagined that he was God Himself—delivering his sermons in the chaste white interior of the First Presbyterian Church on Nassau Street. These were Josiah, Annabel, and Todd; and, in time, little Oriana; when these children shut their eyes in prayer, it was Grandfather Winslow's face they saw, and Grandfather Slade to whom they appealed.

As *The Accursed* is a chronicle of, mostly, the Slade grandchildren, it seems fitting for the historian to note that Winslow Slade loved these children fiercely, rather more, it seems, than he had loved his own children, who had been born when Winslow was deeply engaged in his career, and not so deeply engaged with family life, like many another successful public man. While recovering from a bout of influenza in his early sixties, watching Josiah and Annabel frolic together for hours in the garden at Crosswicks Manse, he had declared to his doctor that it was these children, and no other remedy, that had brought him back to health.

"The innocence of such children doesn't answer our deepest questions about this vale of tears to which we are condemned, but it helps to dispel them. *That* is the secret of family life."

"AND HOW IS your daughter Jessie?"

"Jessie? Why—Jessie is well, I think."

Woodrow's eighteen-year-old daughter, the prettiest of the Wilson daughters, was to be a bridesmaid in the wedding of Winslow Slade's granddaughter Annabel and a young U.S. Army lieutenant named Dabney Bayard, of the Hodge Road Bayards.

Winslow had thought to divert his young friend from the thoughts that so agitated him, that seemed, to Winslow, but trivial and transient; but this new subject, unexpectedly, caused Woodrow to fret and frown; and to say, in a very careful voice, "It is always a—a surprise—to me—that my girls are growing into—women. For it seems only yesterday, they were the most delightful little girls."

Woodrow spoke gravely, with a just perceptible *frisson* of dread.

For the intimate lives of *females* was a painful subject for a man of his sensitivity to consider, even at a little distance.

Winslow smiled, however, with grandfatherly affection. For it was the more remarkable to him, his "fairy child" Annabel was now nineteen years old, and about to take her place in society as Mrs. Dabney Bayard.

"Ah, Lieutenant Bayard!—I think I've glimpsed the young man once or twice," Woodrow said, without the slightest edge of reproach in that, perhaps, his wife and he had been excluded from recent social occasions at Crosswicks Manse, "and he seems to me an upstanding Christian youth, and a patriot as well: the grandson, isn't he, of John Wilmington Bayard?—hearty Presbyterian stock, and most reliable."

"We shall see. I mean—yes of course. You are quite right."

More than once, Winslow Slade had caught an unwanted glimpse of his dear granddaughter walking in the garden behind the Manse, with Lieutenant Bayard; a handsome boy, but impetuous, whose hands too frequently made their way onto Annabel's petite body, at her waist, or lower, at her slender hips . . . It was not a vision the seventy-four-year-old wished to summon, at this awkward time.

Woodrow said, yet still gravely, "Our Margaret, you know, was born in Georgia—not in the North. My dear Ellen took it into her head, near the very end of her pregnancy, that she could not bear for our firstborn to be delivered north of the Mason-Dixon line, and so I—I humored her of course . . . And I think that, in a way, it has made a difference—Margaret is our most gracious daughter, not nearly so—emphatic—*headstrong*—as the younger girls, born here in the North."

Winslow Slade, whose ancestors did not hail from the American South, but rather from the Puritan north of New England, tactfully made no reply to this peculiar remark, in its way both apologetic and boastful.

"Would you like a cigar, Tommy? I know that you don't 'smoke'—at home, certainly. But I have here some very fine Cuban cigars, given to me by a friend."

"Thank you, Winslow—but no! I think that I have told you, how my dear mother cured me forever of a wish to smoke?"

Winslow Slade inclined his head politely, that Woodrow might again tell this favorite story. For Woodrow was quite practiced at the recitation of certain family tales, as if they were old tales of Aesop.

"I was seven years old when Mother called me, to enlist her in killing the aphids on her roses. It might have been that I had been watching my father and other male relatives smoking cigars, and may have appeared admiring; Mother was quick to take note of such details, and I have inherited her skill. 'Tommy, come here: I will light one of Father's cigars, and you will blow smoke on the nasty aphids.' And so—that is exactly what I did, or tried to do." Woodrow was laughing, a wheezing sort of laugh, without evident mirth; tears shone in his eyes, of a frantic merriment. "Ah, I was so ill! Violently ill to my stomach, not only repelled by the horrific tobacco smoke, but vomiting for much of a day. And yet, Mother's wisdom was such: I have never smoked since, nor have I had the slightest inclination. Observing the trustees lighting up their ill-smelling cigars, when we are meant to have a serious meeting, leaves me quite disgusted, though I would never betray my feelings of course."

"A most thoughtful mother!" Winslow returned the cigars to their brass humidor.

In a corner of Dr. Slade's library an eighteenth-century German grandfather's clock chimed a quiet but unmistakable quarter-hour: Winslow Slade was hoping that his young friend would depart soon, for Woodrow was clearly in one of his "nerve" states, and the effect upon Winslow himself was beginning to be felt; of all psychic conditions, anxiety verging upon paranoia/hysteria is perhaps the most contagious, even among men. Yet, Woodrow could not resist reverting to his subject, in an indirect way, to lament that the United States was burdened with "an insufferable buffoon" in the White House: "A self-appointed bully who fancies himself a savior, mucking about now shockingly in Panama, and swaying the jingoists to his side. The presidency of the United States is not an office to be besmirched but to be elevated—it is a sacred trust, for our nation is exceptional in the history of the world. And I, here at home, in 'idyllic' Princeton, must contend with Teddy Roosevelt's twin, as it were—who pretends only to have the interest of the university at heart, while wresting my power from me."

Winslow sighed, and could not think how to reply. He seemed to know beforehand what his young friend had come to ask of him; and did not want to encourage him; yet, inevitably, Woodrow made his plea, with the blinking simplicity of a small child, his moist eyes gleaming behind his polished eyeglasses: "Dr. Slade, if *you* might indicate your support of me, or rather, your preference: Woodrow Wilson or Andrew West . . . It would be such a relief to me, as to my family."

Pained, Winslow explained that he thought it a wiser course, for one like himself in retirement from all politics, to remain neutral.

"I am sure that, in the end, wise heads and wisdom will prevail. You will have a vote of the trustees, and that will decide it—soon, I would think?"

"Winslow, that is—that is not—this is not quite the answer I had hoped for, in coming here . . ."

Winslow persisted: "I prescribe for you, my dear friend, the simplest and most fundamental of all Christian remedies—prayer. By which I mean, Woodrow, a deep examination of your soul, your motives, and your ideals. *Prayer.*"

The younger man blinked at Winslow, as a tic in his left cheek seemed to mock his enfeebled smile. "Yes, you are right—of course. You are invariably right, Dr. Slade. But, I'm afraid, you are uninformed—for I have already spent countless hours on my knees, in prayer, since this hellish situation first manifested itself, months ago. Of course, it has been a gathering storm. I have enlisted prayer from the start, yet the results have been disappointing: for West continues his sorties against me, even laughing behind my back, and *God has not seen fit to intervene.*"

So astounded was Winslow Slade by these words, he could think of no adequate reply; and silence uneasily fell between them, as smoldering logs in the fireplace shifted, and darkened; and Woodrow reached out, in a nervous sort of curiosity, to take up a small jade snuffbox on a table, to examine closely. It was an engaging object, though hardly beautiful, covered in a patina of decades, its lid engraved with a miniature yet meticulously wrought serpent that, coiled, looked as if it were about to leap out at the observer. Strikingly, the cobra's eyes were two inset rubies of the size of pumpkin seeds.

Fascinating to Woodrow, in his somewhat dazed state, how these rubies glittered, with the fantastical potency of an actual serpent's eyes . . .

Now daringly Woodrow said, as he had been preparing to say, perhaps, this past half hour: "*He* seeks power in a very different way, you know."

"*He?*"

"West."

"Ah yes—West is still our subject?"

"It is not mere rumor, Dr. Slade, it has been whispered everywhere in town, and Ellen was reluctant to upset me by repeating it—but Andrew West has consorted with clairvoyants and mesmerists; in a pretense of 'scientific inquiry,' like his Harvard psychologist-friend William James, he has delved into what we must call occult practices—that fly in the face of Christian teaching."

" 'Occult practices'—? Andrew West?"

Winslow Slade laughed, for Andrew West had the solid, burly build of a wrestler; certainly an intelligent man, with degrees from Cambridge (England) as well as Harvard, yet not in any way a sensitive or inwardly-brooding person, of the kind who might take the occult seriously.

"Yes, Dr. Slade, though you may smile at the prospect—'occult practices.' By which he hopes to influence 'powers'—thereby, to influence the more impressionable minds in our community, and among the trustees. I told you, it is a battle—in an undeclared war."

"You are saying that our colleague and neighbor Andrew West, dean of the graduate school, is an—occultist?"

"Well, I am saying that it is said—it is said by many—that West dabbles in the occult, in a pretense of scientific inquiry; one of his allies is Abraham Sparhawk, in philosophy; but a newfangled sort of philosophy in which *up* is proved to be *down,* and time and history not *fixed points* as we know them to be, but something called—I think the term is—*'relative.'* What they are cooking up together, to defeat me, I have no way of knowing in any detail." Woodrow continued to examine the little jade snuffbox, as if the cobra's glittering eyes had transfixed him. "And d'you know, as a result of his campaigning, Mr. Cleveland scarcely returns my greeting at the Nassau Club—he has become a favored crony of West's, this past winter."*

Winslow said, a little sharply, "It must be the lateness of the hour, Tommy—you are saying things that will have to be consciously 'forgotten' by us both, in the light of day. Frankly, I don't believe for an instant that Andrew West, or anyone else at the university, is 'delving' into occult practices; and I ask you to reconsider what you have said."

So speaking, Winslow lay his hands upon the younger man's hands, that were visibly trembling; meaning to extract from his fingers, before he dropped it, or crumbled it, the little jade snuffbox, which Woodrow continued half-consciously to grip.

Yet, Woodrow would not surrender his position: for, despite his appearance of neurasthenic intensity, and the watery weakness of his blinking eyes, the man was yet endowed with a most powerful, indeed near-unshakable *will*. Vehemently he said, "Dr. Slade, you of all people should know that some loosening of the tongue is prudent, when Evil appears in our midst. I am not saying—I am not accusing—West of summoning the Devil, but of consorting with those who might, or do. Just last night, in my library, Professor Pearce van Dyck spoke at length with me, defining the principles of 'mesmerism' and 'animal magnetism'

---

* Grover Cleveland, twenty-second President of the United States, had retired to Westland Mansion in Princeton after leaving office in 1897; a considerable presence in Princeton, both by repuation and by girth, Cleveland lived scarcely a half-block from Crosswicks Manse, on Hodge Road; he too was a trustee of the university and, as Woodrow Wilson feared, a supporter rather of Dean West than of Woodrow Wilson. It was invariably a social coup to include Grover and Frances Cleveland in any gathering, despite Grover's uncouth manners and buffoonish laughter, and the disappointment of his second term in office; worse yet, as many knew, Grover Cleveland had, as sheriff of Erie County in upstate New York in his early career in politics, personally executed, by hanging, at least two condemned men, rather than pay a hangman ten dollars.

as best he could; for Pearce is, as you know, as much of a rationalist as any Christian might be, and professes an abhorrence of 'occult practices' as much as I—including even Spiritualism, which the ladies so extol. According to Pearce, those European scientists and physicians who have advanced such bizarre notions, like Mesmer and Charcot, that make a mockery of Christian free will, are best ranked with alchemists, sorcerers, and witches; and are held in very low esteem by true men of science. Yet, the theory that a 'magnetic fluid' might pervade the Universe, including the human body, and that this fluid might somehow be controlled, if one only knew how—this theory is not without plausibility, I think. It is like holding the key to certain chemical processes—like knowing the recipe for gunpowder! And while the ostensible aim of mesmerism is the improvement of mental health, any fool can see that the reverse can be true as well: there being a *diabolical* side to man, more prevalent, in some quarters, than the *angelic*."

This outburst of speech left Woodrow breathless. His stiff-laundered white cotton collar, that had been spotless that morning when he had arrived in his office in Nassau Hall, was visibly wilted; a faint glisten of perspiration shone on his furrowed brow.

Winslow said, in an even voice, like one who feigns a tactful kind of deafness, "Well! Let me pour you some brandy, Woodrow, to soothe your nerves, and then I will ask Henry to drive you home. I think you're not quite yourself—and Ellen must be awaiting you."

Hotly Woodrow said: "Thank you, Dr. Slade, but I do not drink brandy—as you must know. And I am not in any womanish state of 'nerves.' My dear wife has not the slightest idea where I am—she has retired to bed by ten P.M. and would assume that I am working in my study as usual. I find it upsetting—and baffling—that you, Winslow Slade, with your thorough grounding in Calvinist theology, and the practical experience of being a Presbyterian minister, should take so lightly the possibility of 'diabolism' in our midst . . . I wonder whether West himself hasn't sought you out, in this very room, to poison you against me, who has long been your devoted friend—and to *influence* your thoughts!"

Woodrow spoke with such adolescent sarcasm, his friend was taken aback.

It was then, the little accident occurred.

Though the men certainly could not have been described as *struggling together*, in any sense of the phrase, it somehow happened that, as Winslow Slade sought to take hold of Woodrow Wilson's (flailing) arm, to calm him, the younger man shrank from him as if in fright; causing the jade snuffbox to slip from his fingers onto a tabletop, and a cloud of aged snuff was released, of such surprising potency both men began to sneeze; very much as if a malevolent spirit had escaped from the little box.

Unexpectedly then, both Woodrow Wilson and Winslow Slade suffered fits of helpless sneezing, until they could scarcely breathe, and their eyes brimmed with tears, and their hearts pounded with a lurid beat as if eager to burst.

And the austere old grandfather clock against a farther wall softly chimed the surprising hour of *one*—unheard.

POSTSCRIPT:
"ASH WEDNESDAY EVE, 1905"

It is not generally acknowledged to the reader that much is *left out* of any complex account. A reader must be trusting, and assume that what has been included is all that is necessary; what has been *left out* is extraneous.

But I am troubled, in assembling the previous chapter—for so much has been *left out* that might have been of interest, and might even be essential to a reader's fullest understanding.

Therefore, I suggest: the reader who wants to know a little more of my chronicle should read this postscript, as well as the others to follow. (I am sure that there will be other postscripts to follow!) Readers who are satisfied that they know enough of Dr. Wilson and Dr. Slade should simply proceed to "Narcissus"—a total change of scene, I promise!

Here is a miscellany of details regarding Woodrow Wilson that could not find their way into the narrative.

—WOODROW'S "WIND-BUFFETED" walk to Crosswicks Manse was in fact an ordeal for the troubled man, who had not fully recovered from what he would recall as the *unprovoked attack* of his (alleged) kinsman from the hills of rural, western Virginia.

For, in leaving Prospect House, without telling his wife or daughters, all of whom (he assumed) were in bed, Woodrow Wilson was obliged to walk alone across the darkened Princeton University campus, and to pass close by undergraduate residences; though friendly to students by day, smiling his wide grimace of a presidential smile at virtually everyone he encountered, which never failed to enlist boys' startled smiles and greetings, Woodrow quite dreaded being sighted at such a time; for a nocturnal journey, by foot, on the part of the president of the university, would seem suspicious—would it not?

So, Woodrow walked quickly, and furtively; more than once he ducked into a doorway, or around a corner, to avoid being seen by late-carousing undergraduates, returning from the Alchemist & Barrister pub on Witherspoon, or the rowdy taproom of the Nassau Inn.

The darkened tunnel of evergreens and rhododendron leading from Prospect to the inner campus was fraught with a kind of childish dread, which Woodrow recognized as unwarranted; but the deep, somehow *writhing* shadows behind the most Gothic of buildings, Pyne, gave him pause; nor did his fluttering heartbeat subside, at the rear of Alexander Hall with its fantastical towers, turrets, arches, walkways, and ornamental windows on all floors that, though darkened, seemed to wink with an extra-terrestrial light. (Did a voice faintly cry out from one of these high windows? Did a spectral face appear fleetingly? The hurrying man could not take time to pause, and did not dare to glance back.)

It was a sore point among the Princeton University administrators, that a high percentage of their undergraduate population were inveterate *carousers* for whom "clubs" were of more significance than academic studies, and persons of questionable repute of more significance than their revered professors. Indeed, an alarming number of *carousers* kept mistresses in rented rooms on Witherspoon, Bank, and Chambers streets, an old and seeming inextricable tradition at the university, despite its Presbyterian affiliation; as, at one time, Southern boys from slaveholding families were allowed to keep their personal slaves in the residence halls. (It had come to be a tradition among these boys, at least among the more affluent, that they would "free" their slaves upon graduation: with the result that many ex-slaves lived in the ramshackle neighborhood of lower Witherspoon, and swelled the local workforce with capable workers willing to work at very reasonable wages. Dr. Wilson's house servants Clytie and Lucinda were descendants of freed slaves.)

Woodrow felt some relief when he left the university campus, and made his way southward along Nassau Street, quite deserted at this hour of the night; and past Bank, and Chambers; taking note of the forlorn cries of nighthawks, that made his skin shiver; and of the gauzy-masked moon overhead, like a face glimpsed out of the past. At the shadowy junction of Nassau and Stockton there came noisily a handsome ebony brougham drawn by a matched team of horses, that swung smartly past Woodrow to continue along Bayard Lane.

Woodrow recognized the carriage as belonging to ex-President Grover Cleveland. Quickly he calculated that the Clevelands had been dining at the palatial home of the Morgans on Hibben Road; they were returning to Westland, their own palatial home on Hodge Road, absurdly named for Andrew Fleming West, who was an intimate friend of Grover Cleveland. (Who can comprehend such perversities? Woodrow would not even try.)

"O God! If I am seen! They will *know*."

Fortunately, Frances Cleveland was so absorbed with her fretting, elderly and obese husband, who was suffering a bout of dyspepsia following a lavish four-hour dinner, that the usually sharp-eyed woman failed to notice Woodrow Wilson's shadowy figure on the sidewalk; if she had recognized him, Mrs. Cleveland would have guessed at once that he was on a mission to Crosswicks Manse, and the tale would have spread through the village of Princeton by teatime of the following day.

Note. As a disinterested and fair-minded historian it isn't my place to delve into old local feuds and squabbles; to stir up old misunderstandings, slanders, and hatreds, dating back to the turn of the century; to evoke once again a time in our peaceful community in which everyone, not excepting schoolchildren, felt obliged to take sides in the dispute between Woodrow Wilson and Andrew Fleming West; and a good portion of the congregation of the First Presbyterian Church chose not to speak to the remainder.

I hope I won't compromise my objectivity as an historian, as to whether Woodrow Wilson ought to have been obeyed, as he wished, in every particular concerning major issues at the university; or whether his opponent, the strong-willed dean of the graduate school, ought to have had his way. (My van Dyck relatives were said to favor Woodrow; my Strachan relatives, Andrew West.) In any case the reader should know that Woodrow Wilson's campaign for complete control over the university, as it parallels his campaign for complete control over the issue of whether the United States would go to war with Germany in 1917, when he was President, is a subordinate issue here, set beside the domestic tragedies to befall the leading Princeton families.

—CROSSWICKS MANSE, the home of the Slades, has not been properly described; only just the interior of Winslow Slade's library.

As male readers have a predilection for military history, so female readers have a predilection for learning about houses, furnishings, and ornamentation. Yet I hope that both sexes are intrigued, to some degree, by the Slades' residence on Elm Road, as fine a house as one could discover in the Princeton vicinity, including even the Henry Morgan estate on Hibben Road and the Carlyle estate on the Great Road.

There was no more splendid example in all of New Jersey of the architectural style of early Georgian, in combination with the newer Palladian, the novelty being that the Manse was built along these lines reflecting classical Renaissance architecture at a time when, in England, the influence was yet very rare. The history of the Manse is most impressive, dating back to the early 1700s when one Bertram Slade of Margate, Massachusetts, purchased a large tract of land from William Penn in a region known as the "wilds of West New Jersey"; and encompassing that time when one of the great battles of the American Revolution was fought in Princeton, in 1777—indeed, scarcely one mile from the Manse itself in open parkland now designated Battle Park.

What must it have been for our young people, Josiah and Annabel Slade, and how subtly and magically did it shape their lives, to have spent their childhood at Crosswicks Manse!—in that house of countless rooms, spacious courtyards, and splendid vistas opening onto terraces, and gardens, and mirror-like ponds. (As a boy, Josiah tried to count the rooms of Crosswicks Manse, but ended with a different number each time—twenty-six, twenty-nine, thirty-one; nor did Annabel, the more patient and exacting of the two, fare much better. "It is like a dream, living here," Annabel said, "except the dream isn't my own but another's.")

It was in the Manse, for instance, that the fate of the young Republic was determined: for such illustrious men as George Washington, Alexander Hamilton, General Nathanael Greene, Baron Steuben, "Light Horse Harry" Lee, Benedict Arnold, the Chevalier de la Luzerne, Don Juan de Mirailles, and many another figure of history, frequently met. If I had more space I would like nothing better than to dramatize the "unspeakable insult" endured by the Slade family when, in 1777, the British General Cornwallis seized the great house for his private headquarters and proved so little the gentleman that, when at last driven away by patriotic Continentals, he encouraged his soldiers to loot, desecrate, and burn the magnificent house. Ah, if he had only lived *then!*—so Josiah thought, as a boy. He would have sought out the cowardly general himself and demanded satisfaction—that is, insisted upon a duel—for the personal nature of the outrage.

Yes, it is so—Josiah, born in 1881, in the waning years of the nineteenth century, naively yearned for a lost world in which, he believed, his courage and manhood might have been better tested, than at the present time; Josiah's most impassioned readings were of Sir Walter Scott's *Waverly Novels*, Tennyson's *Idylls of the King*, any and all treatments of *King Arthur and the Knights of the Round Table*, and such homegrown American romances as Washington Irving's *Sketch Book* and James Fenimore Cooper's *Leatherstocking Tales*, his favorite being *The Last of the Mohicans* which he had virtually memorized by the age of twelve; more recently, he had fallen under the spell of Jack London's *Tales of the Klondike* and *The Call of the Wild*, and Owen Wister's *The Virginian*.

"To be born 'too late'—is it possible? Or am I born at just the right time, unknowingly?"

Yet, God must have smiled upon the Slades of 1777: for damage to the beautiful house was minimal, in the end. Fires started by Cornwallis's men soon smoldered out, in a cloudburst of autumnal rain as if indeed, as the Continental army was given to believe, *God was on the rebels' side*.

The Slades took particular pride in the fact that when the Continental Congress met in Princeton, in 1782, under the presidency of Elias Boudinot, it was at Crosswicks Manse that quite a few of the representatives stayed, and all of the representatives dined, before their formal congress in Nassau Hall. So the prized local legend, that Crosswicks Manse was the first "White House" of the Republic.

It cannot be denied that the vision of the luminous Manse, even by partial moonlight, had the force of intimidating Woodrow Wilson, as he made his way up the graveled drive, beneath overarching white oaks; as he approached the side door, to Winslow Slade's office, the troubled man swallowed hard, and shaped his lips in an inaudible prayer—*Have mercy on me, O God: I am Your humble servant seeking only how best to serve You.*

—TO THE RESPECTFUL titles in Winslow Slade's library on the eve of Ash Wednesday, 1905, there should be added others, not alphabetized, but stacked on tables, that failed to capture Woodrow Wilson's full attention: the unscholarly but much-perused *Phrenological Studies* of Dr. Phineas

Lutz; *Beyond the Gates of Consciousness* of Stanislav Zahn; *Heaven and Hell* of Emanuel Swedenborg; and that rare and arresting treatise in quarto Gothic, the manual of a "forgotten church"—the *Vigiliae mortuorum secundum chorum ecclesiae maguntinae*; still more, volumes in French, by the controversial Jean-Martin Charcot, and a recent copy of *The Journal of the American Society for Psychical Research* of Cambridge, Mass., in which an essay by a founding member of the Society, Professor William James of Harvard, appeared under the title "Is There a 'Natural' Barrier to Consciousness?"

Yes, the reader is correct in wondering why, when Charcot and James were mentioned by Woodrow Wilson, Winslow Slade remained silent and did not suggest in any way that he was familiar with the work of either man.

—WINSLOW SLADE'S PREOCCUPATION on the night in question.

It was Dr. Slade's custom to dine with his family before eight o'clock, then to retire to the bachelor solitude of his library, which few in the family ever visited; nor did Dr. Slade encourage visits from the children who, when young, would have poked and pried amid his special collections, like the (allegedly) Malaysian jade snuffbox, that had been a gift to Winslow Slade by a woman friend, a world-traveler of decades ago, and, of course, the invaluable Gutenberg Bible, one of but forty-eight copies remaining in all of the world, of that first monumental printing. (That Dr. Slade's copy of the Gutenberg Bible was not complete scarcely diminished its worth, for very few of the original copies remained undamaged by the incursions of centuries.)

Often, Winslow absorbed himself in fireside reading, of newer books (like those listed above); more recently, in the late winter of 1905, he had taken up the task of revising his sermons for a collection which a Philadelphia publisher of theological texts had pressed him into completing. ("Why would anyone want to read my old sermons?" Winslow asked wryly; and the publisher rejoined, "The mere name 'Winslow Slade' will assure quite a sale in New Jersey and the Mid-Atlantic states generally.") When this task proved too boring, Winslow turned with more enthusiasm to his translations of one or another book of the Apocrypha, upon which he'd been laboring for years, with the assistance of a Hebrew scholar at the seminary; his particular interest was "The Epistle of Jeremy" and the Books of Esdra and Tobit, and, in the New Testament, those curious gospels attributed to Thomas, Matthias, and Judas.

"Of all Biblical figures, surely Judas is the most misunderstood, as he is the most condemned!"—so Winslow believed.

For it had always seemed evident to him, Jesus adored his faithless Judas above the other disciples.

As Winslow was frequently plagued by insomnia, but resisted taking the myriad "home remedies" favored in great doses by his young friend Woodrow Wilson, out of a fear of clouding his thoughts, so he reserved for the early hours of the morning his transactions with his journal: not a single volume but more than a dozen eight-by-twelve "scribblers."

The reader will naturally think that I have had recourse to Dr. Slade's journals—would that were so! It is a tragic fact, all volumes of the journal were destroyed, with most of Winslow Slade's personal papers, in a bizarre act of self-mortification that seemed to have occurred in late May 1906, shortly before Dr. Slade's death.

—WOODROW WILSON'S MYRIAD physical ailments.

Why people are, or were, so intensely interested in Woodrow Wilson's panorama of ailments, as in the ailments of U.S. Presidents generally, I am not so certain. It is not to be attributed to mere morbidity, I am sure— perhaps rather more a wish to peer into the private lives of exalted others, to compare with our more meager estates.

In addition to what I have already mentioned, and to reiterate— among Woodrow's medical complaints were gastric crises, raging headaches, neuritis, nervous hyperesthesia, arrhythmic heartbeat, "night sweats" and "night-mares," and the like. In some quarters, as early as Woodrow's first years as president of Princeton University, the question was raised, if the man was "entirely" sane, given his intense preoccupations and obsessions with enemies real and imagined; and his frantic need *never to compromise*.

It had been a passionate belief of the Campbells of Argyll, that battle was preferable to peace, if that peace was determined by *compromise*.

There was not a conspiracy exactly, but certainly an understanding, among Woodrow's intimates, that talk of the man's ailments should be curtailed. With much justification, Woodrow felt that if it became generally known that his health was erratic, confidence in his leadership might be undermined.

In fact it was impressive how Dr. Wilson soared above such shackles of the spirit, frequently climbing out of his sickbed to attend to university affairs, or to travel by rail to Philadelphia, Baltimore, Washington, Richmond, even so far as Chicago and St. Louis, to give a speech. "The flesh may be weak," Woodrow quipped, "but the spirit *is* willing." As a precocious young boy Woodrow had sent away for a mail-order chart depicting the postures and declamatory gestures of classical oratory, in order to learn the art of public speaking; as a result, he had unwittingly become imprinted with a set of mechanical gestures, and in times of stress and fatigue he was likely to lapse into them, as his students had soon discovered, in his lecture courses at Bryn Mawr, Wesleyan, and Princeton. (In those days, students suggested discontent and boredom by *shuffling their feet*. How Woodrow had come to dread, and to abhor, that *shuffling* sound, as of brooms being swept along floors, maddeningly; and when students were reprimanded by university proctors at Princeton for *shuffling their feet* during chapel sermons, Woodrow was not at all sympathetic, and refused to mitigate expulsions from the university.)

Yet, audiences felt positive about him: for he was so very *earnest*, and so *idealistic*. He had hoped to be loved by multitudes, he said, but, failing love, to evoke admiration, awe, and even fear in audiences was not such a bad thing.

Sow yourself in every field of the world's influence; knead yourself into its every possible loaf of soul-nourishing bread. Be vitalizing wheat, indeed—hide not your talents. So Woodrow's father Joseph Ruggles Wilson had warmly advised him.

—THE KU KLUX KLAN lynching in Camden, New Jersey, on March 7, 1905: had Woodrow Wilson entirely forgotten about this, and his impetuous kinsman's request, when he visited Winslow Slade; or had Woodrow Wilson, in the heat of his greater concern, simply brushed all thought of the terrible incident from his mind?

And did Winslow Slade know of the incident?

Could Winslow Slade *not have known of it?*

NARCISSUS

E xcuse me—hello?"

On a sun-warmed morning in early spring she saw him, at a little distance: a man of indeterminate age, his face turned from her, who seemed at first to be one of her grandfather's gardener's assistants, as he was gripping in his gloved hand a small hand-sickle, cruelly hooked and gleaming in the sun; and, at his feet, stricken flowers, presumably past their prime, and a heaping of last-year's grasses, that had been cut down.

Annabel had never seen this man before, she was sure. Though often there came to Crosswicks Manse, to visit with Grandfather Slade, individuals not known to her, of significance.

She supposed that the stranger, not in gardening attire but in formal, just slightly old-fashioned clothes, like clothes Winslow Slade had worn decades ago, was one of her grandfather's visitors: possibly a Presbyterian minister, or seminarian, who'd wandered out of Dr. Slade's shadowed library to breathe in the freshness of the April morning; and, out of restlessness perhaps, had decided to try his hand here, with the sharp little sickle.

"Hello! Are you a friend of Grandfather's?"

There was laughter in Annabel's voice, as there was so often a light sort of laughter, or joyousness, in her face.

The reader must not think that nineteen-year-old Annabel Slade was accustomed to addressing strange men, even in her grandfather's garden; she was not a bold girl, still less a brash girl; but some sort of childish elation had come over her, on this perfect April morning, with her diamond engagement ring—(square-cut, fourteen carats, surrounded by miniature rubies, an heirloom of the Bayard family)—sparkling on the third finger of her slender left hand, in the sun. When Woodrow Wilson had spoken critically of "headstrong" young women born in the North, lacking the natural graciousness of his daughter Margaret, as of his wife, Ellen, both Southern-born, he would certainly not have included Annabel Slade in this category!

Strange it seemed to Annabel, yet not alarming, that the mysterious visitor didn't seem to hear her, or to acknowledge her—"Hel-*lo?*"—as with childlike persistence she called out to him again, though shyly too, smiling as her mother might smile, or her grandmother Slade, in the feminine role of welcoming a guest to the house.

On this April morning several weeks after Woodrow Wilson's visit to Crosswicks Manse, Winslow Slade's beloved granddaughter Annabel was picking flowers for the dining room of Crosswicks Manse. In her hands was a small gathering of jonquils, Grecian windflowers, daffodils and narcissi—how fragrant, narcissi!—almost, Annabel felt light-headed. It seemed probable to her, this stranger would be dining with them at lunch, which gave to her task an added urgency.

She recalled now, she'd heard it mentioned at breakfast, that an emissary from the highest echelon of the Presbyterian Church was coming to visit with Winslow Slade that day, and to enlist his support in the awkward matter of a "heresy trial" within the ranks of the Church.

(Poor Grandfather! Annabel knew that he wanted very badly to be totally retired from his former life, yet fervently his "former life" pursued him!)

Annabel knew little of such matters but understood that, through his many years of service in the Church, Reverend Winslow Slade had participated from time to time in such closed trials; for heresy was a terrible thing, and must be combated at the source, though such disagreeable matters upset him deeply. Josiah had told her that in such actions, their grandfather was not to be distinguished from any responsible Protestant clergyman of his day, charged with the mission that the "special character" of Anglo-Saxon Christianity be protected from "anarchist" assaults arising both within, and without, the Church.

"Of course," Annabel had said to her brother, in an undertone, so that no adult could hear, "these are not *real trials*—no one is imprisoned, or sentenced to death, I hope!"

"Not in our time," Josiah said. "Fortunately."

Annabel knew that, fierce as Protestants might be in their zealous protection of their Church, they were not nearly so fierce, or so blood-thirsty, as their Roman Catholic predecessors had been in the time, for instance, of the Inquisition; or the Thirty Years' War, or the Crusades.

So, judging the attractive stranger by his outward attire, and a certain air of good breeding in his manner, the innocently naïve Annabel Slade was led to believe that Axson Mayte was a gentleman of her own social station: a friend of her grandfather's, in short.

A profound misreading, as the historical record will show.

VERY ODD, HOWEVER, Annabel was beginning to feel, how the stranger continued to hold the hand-sickle, at his side; now he'd turned to her, seeing her, yet without an air of surprise, as if he'd known she was there, observing him; he smiled, in a rapt sort of silence, as no gentleman would ever do, in fact; as if he and Annabel Slade had met by chance in a public place, or in some dimension in which the sexes might "meet" impersonally, like animals, with no names, no families—no identities. In that instant, Annabel felt both chilled and flushed with warmth; and somewhat faint; and had to resist the impulse to hide her (burning) face in the little bouquet of flowers she had picked, that the bold stranger would not stare so directly upon her with his penetrating gaze.

A tawny-golden gaze it was, like a certain kind of beveled glass.

Disturbing it was to her, that they had not been introduced, he had not said a word to her, yet the stranger smiled more insidiously at her, with thin, yet strangely sensual lips!

I will ignore him. I will walk away, as if I were alone. We will be introduced at lunch, maybe—and if not, that can't be helped.

Yet Annabel failed to leave the garden, as she might have done, but only moved to another corner, where she reasoned she wouldn't be so clearly observed by the strange bold visitor. Here was a lavish bed of wind-rippled daffodils that made her smile; for words of a favorite, memorized poem ran through her thoughts: " 'And then my heart with pleasure fills, and dances with the daffodils.' "

In times of unease, excitement or dread, what comfort in *rhyme*!

As poets of old well knew, and poets of our vulgar and atonal contemporary life seem to have forgotten.

Unfortunately for Annabel, her brother Josiah wasn't at home this morning, nor did anyone from the Manse appear to be taking notice.

Annabel could not resist glancing back at the stranger with the hand-sickle. What a shock, he was still observing her.

He is rude. I don't like him. Dabney would not like him!

If he is one of Grandfather's associates, he must be older than he looks. His clothing is—old. Or, it may be—he is one of Father's younger business associates—"brokers."

For his part, the stranger was drifting in Annabel's direction, yet not very deliberately. As if, in some way, he were *being drawn* to her, by some (unconscious) motion or motive of Annabel herself.

Why else, that smile? A smile of—was it *recognition*?

Not wanting to betray her unease, and resisting the impulse to flee, Annabel continued picking flowers, though not liking it, how the narcissi broke between her fingers, and wetted them with a syrupy sort of liquid, she had to refrain from wiping on her skirt. And when she straightened, feeling just slightly light-headed, as if she were very hungry, she saw to her surprise that the stranger had somehow advanced close to her; he could not have been more than twelve feet away where, a moment before, Annabel would have sworn he was on the farther side of the garden.

Why, he has moved in silence, seemingly without effort.

Now, Annabel dared look at the visitor more openly: as she had surmised, he was in his early thirties perhaps; he was of more than medium height, as tall as her brother; slender in the shoulders, with a noble, well-shaped head, and very dark, silken, tight-curled hair. His skin may have been just slightly coarse, of a curious darkish-olive hue, that yet contained a sort of pallor, as if, beneath his robust masculine exterior, he was not entirely healthy. His eyes were large, and both slumberous and piercing; possessed of a fiery topaz glow that was not obscured, but the more enhanced, by the deep-shadowed sockets that enclosed them. The forehead was prominent, the eyebrows thick, of that hue of blackness of the raven's wing; the teeth small, and pearly, and almost overly white, of a uniform regularity—except for one incisor, which jutted a half-inch below its fellows, to give an impression somewhat carnivorous.

Though the stranger's attire was in very good taste—a silk-and-woolen dark-blue suit, in a light texture; with wide-padded shoulders and a tight-waisted coat; white dress shirt, with silver cuff links, striped necktie, polished shoes—yet Annabel had begun to think the mysterious stranger was somehow foreign, exotic. *A Persian prince perhaps, exiled in America; or, one of the Hebrew race—for is there not something most noble and melancholy about him? And his eyes—why, those are basilisk-eyes!* *

---

* As Annabel Slade's surprising words are sure to puzzle the reader, as, initially, they puzzled me, I am obliged to note that, so far as I have been able to learn, the young woman had not ever personally gazed upon "foreign" or "exotic" individuals, whether female or male; but she had avidly read many books, of a more fancifully romantic cast than those read by her brother Josiah, namely novels by the Brontë sisters, of which her longtime favorite was *Wuthering Heights* as well as verse by Byron and Shelley; she had been told of a fabled colony of Russian and Polish Jews—the Alliance Israélite Universelle—which had settled in Woodbine, New Jersey, some years ago. (This settlement, too, had been threatened by zealots costumed in white sheets, to disguise their identities: very likely, these anonymous

Descriptions of female beauty are tedious, and often unconvincing. Is a young woman really so *beautiful* as her admirers claim? Would Annabel Slade with her conventionally pretty, pleasing features—her shyly downcast eyes of blue, or deep violet; her perfectly shaped lips, untouched by cosmetics; her nose, the Roman nose of the Slades, but snubbed—have been so celebrated a Princeton beauty, were she the daughter and granddaughter of more ordinary Princetonians? What is the distinction, in fact, between *beauty* and *prettiness*—the one rare and austere, the other commonplace? It is frankly beyond my writerly powers to suggest the delicate and unstudied *charm* of Annabel Slade, unless by summoning the image of the narcissus—the most exquisite of spring flowers with its fragile, fluted petals and its miniature center, all but invisible at a glance, and its just-slightly-astringent perfume, in which resides the quicksilver essence of spring: fresh, unsullied, virgin.

For if beauty is not *virgin*, it is *despoiled*. In the Princeton of 1905, such

---

individuals were neighbors of the colony, as well as local law enforcement officers. A cross was burned, as a warning; when the warning was not obeyed, the main house of the Alliance Israélite Universelle was set on fire the following night, and its inhabitants routed into the wintry dark with what fates awaiting them, I do not know—the incident, or incidents, was not recorded in any detail in newspapers of the era.)

As for the basilisk reference—how perverse that a young, virginal girl from a highly sheltered background should seize upon so unlikely, and so ugly, an image; for the lizard of the genus *Basiliscus* resides in the more tropical zones of the Americas, and not in central New Jersey. Yet, the other day, while examining a carton of aged and mildewed books in my study, I came upon *The Castle of Kashmir*—a child's book published by Lippincott Publishers, 1884, that had once belonged to Annabel Slade and her brother Josiah; the title page being inscribed with both their names. (It was a wild stroke of good luck, that, at an estate sale in Hopewell, I was able to buy this carton of books, among other prized items, for a mere eight dollars!) On the cover of this much-worn little picture book there is a (faded, but still stirring) illustration of a young knight on his steed, doing battle with a legendary species of basilisk, or dragon, possessed of cruel talons and teeth, and fiery breath, and eyes of glaring topaz: the very stare of Axson Mayte; as Axson Mayte is the very image, in corporeal form, of the demonic—wholly unguessed-at, at this time, by poor Annabel.

a sentiment was hallowed as a love and fear of the Protestant Almighty.

The previous year, Annabel had "come out" at a number of balls and parties in Manhattan, Philadelphia, and Princeton; it was said of her, as perhaps it is said of many debutantes, that she was the most "beautiful" of the crop, along with being, to speak bluntly, one of the wealthiest. (The Slade wealth was in railroads, real estate, manufacturing, and banking; for some decades in the late 1700s and early 1800s, until high-minded Slades insisted upon divestiture, there was considerable revenue generated by the slave trade. Even divided among a number of heirs, it remained one of the great fortunes of the nineteenth century, having virtually doubled its worth in the era known as the Gilded Age. But Annabel, like her brother Josiah, gave little thought to the Slade fortune, not even to their probable inheritances which they took for granted as they took for granted the very air they breathed, which was not the coarse and smoke-sullied air of Trenton, New Brunswick, or Newark.)

So famously sweet-tempered was Annabel, she could not bear to hear ill of anyone, and often became downcast when an unkind or a thoughtless word was uttered in her presence; profanities, still more obscenities, of the sort undergraduate carousers scrawled on walls in white chalk, for all to see in the bright daylight, truly shocked her, as if she were personally attacked. (Though, fortunately, Annabel had but the vaguest notion of what these crude words and expressions actually meant.)

As the naïve young woman had but a vague notion of what it might mean to exchange such glances, and be the recipient of such smiles, with a man she had not glimpsed before this hour.

In addition, Annabel was devoutly religious. She could not have clearly stated what set her Presbyterian faith apart from other Protestant faiths, or, except in the most obvious terms, how it was to be distinguished from Roman Catholicism, an old and much-feared enemy; though she had long outgrown the childish notion that Winslow Slade *was* God, she cherished in her heart the fervent belief that her grandfather was one of the chosen few in his generation; certainly, Grandfather had been the instrument by which countless individuals, many of them grave sinners, had been brought to Jesus Christ and to salvation. Unlike the more strident "outspoken" female—including Annabel's friend Wilhelmina Burr—Annabel would never have wished to discuss with the "free thinkers" among her Princeton circle such fashionable issues as whether the Bible is literally, or figuratively, true; or whether it is revelation, or history. Those yet more disturbing new theories springing from Darwinists, Marxists, Bolsheviks, Anarchists, and other atheist-ideologies, were utterly perplexing to Annabel, who could not imagine why anyone wished to argue for such beliefs, that so lacked kindness and comfort. In her family it was considered unseemly for women to concern themselves with such matters—a very harsh judgment: "unladylike." In the words of the poet—

Be good, sweet maid, and let who will be clever!

—embroidered on one of Annabel's hand-stitched pillows; a sentiment that has not lessened, in my opinion, with the passage of years.

Annabel had been an excellent scholar at the Princeton Academy for Girls, as at the two-year collegiate Kingston Academy for Women, in nearby Kingston, New Jersey; her strongest subjects were poetry, art, and calligraphy; in her fantasies of an independent career, she had liked to imagine herself as an *artiste* of some sort, designing children's book covers for instance, or creating original art for children; or, more ambitiously, illustrating her own verse in small, exquisitely designed books like those by Elizabeth Oakes Smith, Mary Anne Sadlier, and the wonderfully mysterious and cryptic Emily Dickinson, who had died in 1886, the year of Annabel's birth—(Annabel's favorite of these poets, though she understood that Dickinson's verse was considered "rough" and lacking "feminine sentiment" by the literary establishment). She had not liked math, science, history—"So hobbled by *facts*! And *facts* are the least revealing, of any aspect of our lives."

Yet, Annabel had received reasonably high grades in these disliked subjects, for, lacking in aptitude as she was, she was yet more capable than the majority of her girl-classmates.

On this weekday morning in April, Annabel was not showily dressed; though she wore beneath her clothes, on her already slender body, a straight-front corset tightened to make her small waist appear smaller still, so that she could scarcely breathe; this cruel restraining undergarment being mandated for her, since the age of fourteen when it was perceived by her uneasy elders that she was becoming *womanly* in the bosom and hips.

Though it was not a rainy day, Annabel was wearing a "habit-back," or "rainy-day" skirt of pale blue flannel-and-cotton; a skirt fashionable at the time, that dropped to shoe-top length, ideal for rainy days but proper enough for casual wear at home. Her silken white blouse sported stylish puff sleeves, with tight cuffs, and as many as twenty-five mother-of-pearl buttons at the front; her little bolero jacket was pale yellow quilted cotton; her straw hat, prudently worn in the sun, was trimmed with a green satin ribbon tied beneath the chin. Since Annabel would be seeing her fiancé Dabney Bayard later in the day, with the assistance of one of the younger Negro maids she had fashioned her silken hair into a sleek pompadour and numerous small curls. Annabel's hair was a fair brown, that might appear blond, or even silvery, in certain lights; it was held in place by ornamental amber combs that had once belonged to her grandmother Oriana, a woman departed this life long before Annabel had been born.

As her fair complexion was too delicate to brave even the rays of an April sun, Annabel kept the rim of her straw hat strategically lowered over her eyes; yet it must be presumed that Axson Mayte, staring so frankly at her, as at an exotic animal-specimen on display, could see how arrestingly *pretty* she was, and how fragile, like the very narcissi she held in her hands.

Suddenly there issued out of the wind-rippled flowers at Annabel's feet a faint hissing whisper—*Annabel, Annabel!* In her confusion, Annabel thought *It is Grandmother Oriana. She is worried about her amber combs, she regrets leaving them for me.*

(This was a curious thought, since Annabel had not known her grandmother, who'd died many years before her birth; nor had she known her grandfather's second wife, Tabitha.)

Yet, a moment later Annabel had forgotten the whisper. So distracted was she by the stranger in her grandfather's garden, she couldn't seem to concentrate. That she had not turned away from the man with the hand-sickle, and walked quickly up to the house, as she had every opportunity to do, seemed to encourage him for, smiling still, the tip of his pink tongue darting at his lips, he stepped forward again in a single gliding stride, now less than five feet from her.

Now, surely, he would speak to her?—but he did not.

Annabel lifted her bouquet of flowers and in a kind of child-miming gesture indicated that the visitor should note her task, and its urgency, and not detain her any longer; aloud she murmured, for the visitor to hear, or not—"I have tarried too long, already." For overhead the sunny sky was becoming riddled with rain clouds; a giant thumb and finger pinched shut the sun. Yet for some reason, as if she were paralyzed, Annabel didn't turn away; and again the hissing *Annabel, Annabel!* seemed to rise from the wind-buffeted petals of the flowers at her feet.

Then—in the literal blink of an eye!—there stood the gentleman be-fore her, now just twelve inches from her; for now he did seem like one of Winslow Slade's emissary-gentlemen, on a churchly mission that would be kept secret from the rest of the family, who were but lay-Presbyterians in the faith. Out of giddy nervousness Annabel may have murmured "H-Hello" or "G-Good morning"—which had the immediate effect of unlocking the gen-tleman's silence at last. For now he bowed a second time, with an eager sort of stiffness, and announced that his name was "Axson Mayte, of Charles-ton, South Carolina"—"an associate of Winslow Slade's"—"overcome with rapture, *chère mademoiselle,* at the prospect of making *your* acquaintance."

At this, Annabel stammered her name, for she could not think of a polite way of avoiding it: "I am—Dr. Slade's granddaughter—Annabel Slade . . ."

The visitor seized Annabel's small hand, and bent as if to bestow a kiss upon it, in the German manner—hardly more than a sociable gesture, with no actual touching of the lips to the back of the hand, yet Annabel felt the imprint of a considerable, impassioned kiss; she was certain, she'd felt the imprint of the snaggle-tooth incisor against her sensitive skin. And she'd smelled the stranger's breath—harsh and dry as ashes.

In that instant, the very marrow of her bones seemed to shiver, and the satin tie beneath her chin felt dangerously tight, like the long straight-front corset, too tightly laced that morning by Harriet, the frowning Negro girl who seemed both fond of her young white-skinned charge, and resentful of her. Half-fainting Annabel yet clearly thought—*Must I pay now for my vanity! O God have mercy.*

If Axson Mayte of Charleston, South Carolina, had taken note of Annabel's shudder of distress, he gave no sign; for he was a smooth-mannered gentleman, with his sharp deep-set eyes and sidelong glances, that might have been as ironic as they were yearning. He proceeded to cut for Annabel, with his borrowed hand-sickle—(the blade of which was wickedly sharp, Annabel saw with a shiver)—a dozen or more fresh flowers: daffodils, miniature iris, star-of-Bethlehems, narcissi—which he then made a gallant ceremony of presenting to her, with another grave bow.

"Oh! Thank you, sir."

Annabel felt that she had no choice but to accept these flowers, though juices from their cut stems dripped, and darkened her rainy-day skirt in tiny splotches; she had no choice but to thank Mr. Mayte, for he *was* very kind; and as gallant, she was sure, as any Princeton gentleman.

More gallant than her fiancé, certainly! For Dabney could be curt and ill-tempered, when he and Annabel were alone, with no elders to observe him; Dabney could confound Annabel with paradoxes she wasn't sure were serious, or mocking: "Do you *think*? Your face is so like a doll's—a painted ceramic doll."

Annabel saw with relief that Axson Mayte had set aside the wickedly sharp hand-sickle, letting it fall carelessly on the path.

The gardener would discover it there, or—possibly—Annabel's

mother, Henrietta, who "gardened" in pleasant weather, in beds kept weeded and lushly fertilized by the grounds staff.

In a confused sort of happiness Annabel was smiling. Or—perhaps it was sheer nerves, unease. So many spring flowers, some were falling from her hands. Impulsively she selected a long-stemmed narcissus to offer Axson Mayte, for his buttonhole.

"Compliments of Crosswicks Manse!"

Mayte seemed genuinely surprised by this gesture; warmly and effusively he thanked her. "From the depths of my soul, *chère mademoiselle*, I thank you—you are too kind—you cannot know, in fact, how kind you are—a rare quality in 'ladies' of your station, in my experience."

Though Mayte's words were flattering, or were meant to be, the man next behaved in an odd, crude manner: he shortened the narcissus stem by clamping his strong teeth upon it near the flower and biting down hard, that it might fit with ease in his buttonhole—where in fact it looked very striking.

"Will you, mademoiselle—?"

Looming over Annabel, from his height of at least six feet, Axson Mayte extended his arm for Annabel to take, hesitantly, that he might escort her back up to the Manse where now, on the rear terrace, Winslow Slade himself was waving and calling urgently to them.

THE SPECTRAL DAUGHTER

Now, we arrive at the first *public* manifestation of the Curse, on Sunday morning 20 April 1905—except that no previous history credits this episode, nor did any of the principals know, or could have guessed, what the vision of the Spectral Daughter portended.

That is, what the vision portended for those like the Slades, and Lieutenant Dabney Bayard, who might have supposed themselves mere bystanders, astonished and pitying witnesses to a mental collapse of ex-President Grover Cleveland.

This chapter, intended to be brief, is pivotal in my chronicle, and difficult to execute, I think—for, prior to this, my dramatized scenes were between but two persons; now, I am attempting a larger *dramatis personae*, and must try to hint to the reader, without being over-explicit, some of the subtleties of emotion that existed among the young people Josiah, Annabel, and Annabel's fiancé, Dabney Bayard.

(Yet, some readers will complain: the chronicle is *too subtle*. Even as others will complain, *it is not subtle enough*.)

***

ON THIS MORNING, following Sunday church services in Princeton, a party of approximately two dozen persons traveled to the "old Craven estate" on Rosedale Road, which had recently been purchased by the Slades, as its grounds of several acres abutted the three-hundred-acre property of Crosswicks Manse, that stretched back from Elm Road; the revelation being, that the elder Slades were making the Craven estate a wedding gift to the young couple, for them to take occupancy there following their honeymoon in Italy.

Of course, I have seen photographs of the "old Craven estate" which was razed years later, to make way for a larger and grander country estate at the height of the economic boom of the 1920s; at this time, among the Slades and their party, the house was considered a "honeymoon cottage" though it contained as many as twenty rooms, with twelve high, narrow front windows bracketed by black shutters; its steep roof was made of gleaming Holland tile. So large a house, with an impressive exterior of Boonton limestone—(incidentally, from the Slades' quarry at Boonton)—would not seem, to most readers, unfamiliar with the vagaries of the rich, appropriately designated a *cottage*.

Later, the house was to acquire an ironic, or perhaps a purely ignorant misnomer—"the old Bayard estate"—though neither Lieutenant Bayard nor his bride Annabel was ever to live in it, nor even spend a single night beneath its roof; at the time of this narrative, in 1905, the house was still named for its original owner, the Revolutionary hero Major Dunglass Craven, who, as George Washington's most intimate aide, uncovered the scheme of the spy André, and brought about his execution.

It was a gay and splendidly dressed party, driving out in several surreys trimmed in pink dogwood from Princeton for brunch at the house, which was to be presented by Crosswicks kitchen staff on-site, as china, cutlery, tables and chairs and linens, and a vast quantity of food and drink, had to be brought from Crosswicks, to the (vacated) house. So far as I have been able to determine, from various diaries and letters, the party consisted of Grover and Frances Cleveland, Pearce and Johanna van Dyck, Edgerstoune and Amanda FitzRandolph, Ezra and Cecelia Bayard (Dabney's uncle and aunt), Dr. Aaron Burr III and his wife Jennifer, and her daughter Wilhelmina (who was to be Annabel's maid of honor at the wedding), the Reverend Nathaniel FitzRandolph (since Winslow Slade's retirement, the full-time pastor of the First Presbyterian Church of Princeton) and Mrs. FitzRandolph and the Reverend Thaddeus Shackleton, head of the Princeton Theological Seminary, as well as a number of the Slades—Winslow and his son and daughter-in-law Augustus and Henrietta, and Copplestone and Lenora Slade, Annabel's uncle and aunt, and their young son Todd, as well as Annabel and Dabney, and Annabel's brother Josiah.

"Grandfather! You are so kind! You make us happy as children—we scarcely know what to say . . ."

So Annabel exclaimed, seeing the house with its somewhat austere and even forbidding limestone exterior, and the great weight of the Holland tiles, that looked like an avalanche about to flow; yet the greening grasses and overarching elms and oaks, just beginning to come into leaf, gave the scene a picturesque air, like a fairy-tale dwelling; Lieutenant Bayard stammered his gratitude as well, having lost some of his usual composure at the sight of the property, soon to be deeded to *him*.

It would be disclosed afterward that negotiations to acquire the house had been discussed with Dabney's father and his uncle and aunt, before the Slades had moved forward with the purchase. But Dabney himself had not guessed—the plot was kept secret from him, as from Annabel.

(Though very likely, as a shrewd young military officer who had graduated with honors in his class at West Point, Dabney had surmised that the wealthy Slades would give their dear Annabel and her bridegroom a gift commensurate with their love, and their wealth.)

Still, confronted with the "Craven estate" on this sun-lit morning in April, in the midst of a gathering of jovial well-wishers, Dabney seemed quite surprised, and somewhat tongue-tied. A fierce blush rose into his face and in his eyes too sprang some sort of moisture which surreptitiously he brushed away with his fingertips.

The atmosphere of this outing was light, admiring, and festive, for the spring day was perfection, and the stone house with its handblown leaded-glass windows, and its Tiffany-stained glass framing the front door, struck all as ideal for the "honeymoon couple." Hearing the words *honeymoon couple* caused Annabel to blush, and Dabney to smile awkwardly; though Annabel couldn't fail to have noticed a certain reserve in her brother Josiah, and a matching discomfort in Dabney when, a few minutes later, by chance the three young people found themselves together in a downstairs room, while the rest of the party ascended to the second floor, to admire the several bed-rooms and the splendid vistas framed by each window. (Most of the rooms were empty of course, but Annabel's mother, Henrietta, had been out to the house numerous times with a retinue of servants on a confidential errand of "decorating" the house in a temporary sort of way. The real effort of decorat-ing, and of furnishing, would fall to the young married couple.)

"How exquisite!—how *very* lovely! I quite envy the young couple"—Mrs. Cleveland's forceful soprano voice carried down the staircase—"the house is a *tablet rosea*—they will make of it their own. Unlike the house I stepped into, as a young bride . . ."

(Mrs. Cleveland was coyly referring, as often she did, to the White House: she had married the much older President Cleveland in the East Wing of that house, as a girl scarcely out of school.)

And there came Grover Cleveland's booming voice, in a playful sort of rejoinder—"Dear Frances! You have overcome your initial disadvantage, that is certain. Many times!"

Out of a stubborn sort of diffidence, perhaps, the three young people had stayed behind. Dabney Bayard, erect and handsome in his dress uni-form, made a game effort to engage Josiah Slade in a quasi-masculine conversation on one or another topic: the fortunes of the New York High-landers against their rivals the Cincinnati Reds, and the caliber of both teams set beside the Boston Americans; horses, most hopefully—for Dabney was something of a horseman; and the latest antics of the President—Teddy Roosevelt proudly photographed with a spread of animal-corpses at his feet—wild sheep, bison, deer and pumas on a lavish hunting expedition in the West; Teddy threatening to intervene in Venezuela, that was defaulting on its debts ("It will show the Dagos that they will have to behave decently"*); Teddy in virtually every edition of every daily newspaper, grinning out and eyeglasses winking as he trumpeted the virtues of the imperialist Roosevelt Corollary to the Monroe Doctrine.

Lieutenant Bayard was particularly interested in discussing the "outlaw mining strikes" in eastern Pennsylvania, lately the focus of much newspaper coverage. How "itching" Dabney was, to be involved in some sort of U.S. Army intervention! (That morning, Reverend FitzRandolph at the pulpit had alluded to the "anarchist and atheistical outrages" perpetrated by the United Mine Workers of America against the mine owners and, by extension, against the "law-abiding citizenry" of the American people as a whole.) Yet, though the Slades of Crosswicks had investments in the Pennsylvania mines, as in New Jersey and Pennsylvania textile mills, and Josiah might be expected to concur with Dabney's sentiments, Josiah only shrugged indifferently, and held himself aloof; and Annabel stood blushing at her fiancé's side, not knowing whether to be distressed by her brother's rudeness, or vexed.

(Josiah had no way of knowing that Annabel had, that morning, happened to overhear a brief exchange between him and their mother, Henrietta; and that Annabel was wounded, to hear of Josiah's studied indifference regarding the day's outing. If he joined the party, Josiah said, it was only to please *her*, and the other, elder Slades; for he doubted that his sister, so distracted by wedding plans, would notice if he accompanied them, or not.)

---

* This quote from Teddy Roosevelt's letter to his Secretary of State John Hay was not, to be precisely accurate, a matter of public record in April 1905 and would not become known to historians until years after his death in 1919.

What was wrong, Annabel wondered; why could not the three of them be easy in one another's company? Before Josiah had realized that Dabney Bayard was "interested in" Annabel, he'd seemed to like the robust young man well enough; the two had attended the Princeton-Yale homecoming football game, the previous fall, with a rowdy contingent of other young Princeton males. But Josiah had soon surmised Dabney's reasons for visiting Crosswicks, and had begun to withdraw from him, though he was too polite, or, in a way too shy, to speak of any reservations he had for Dabney to Annabel.

Annabel wished that her friend Wilhelmina had stayed downstairs with them, at this crucial time. But Wilhelmina—"Willy"—had been the first one to dash upstairs, on an impromptu tour of the house.

Frequently, since early April, Annabel was finding herself lapsing into silence when she and her fiancé were alone together: for their romantic acquaintanceship had been fashioned amid parties and social gatherings, and the tricky matter of "intimate conversation" seemed to baffle them both. Of what did one speak, if no one else overheard? And too, Annabel was beginning to sense that for all his Virginian predecessors, Dabney was not always so well mannered and patient; she had reason to believe that he had a considerable temper, for she'd overheard him speak sharply to servants, waiters, and the like; he had never spoken harshly to her of course, but, at times, his remarks were tinged with a light sort of irony, putting her in mind of the young, greenish thorns on her mother's prize rosebushes, that looked harmless yet could inflict some small damage if one were not careful.

As to Lieutenant Bayard's temper, Annabel thought: *He is only expressing his nature. He is a man, and he is a soldier.*

For all of Dabney's pose of confidence, however, he was often unsettled by Josiah Slade, who was, at twenty-four, two years younger than he; but of the two, the more seemingly self-reliant, whose habits of silence made Dabney uneasy, and prone to talk all the more, sometimes boastfully; though he was not, he believed, a boastful person—the most impressive army officers, it was well known, were those who remained reticent, while others told of their exploits.

It was an awkwardness between them, that Josiah Slade had attended West Point after his graduation from Princeton—but only for four months. Abruptly, he had renounced his appointment, quit, and spent several months traveling in the West, before returning home. (When asked why he'd dropped out of West Point, about which he'd been so enthusiastic before enrolling, Josiah had said, with a shrug, that he'd had more than enough of "marching in uniform" for one lifetime.) During the months he'd traveled in Wyoming, Utah, Idaho, and northern California, no one in the family had known very clearly what Josiah was doing though, like a loving son, he wrote home each week, if briefly, to assure his family that he was alive and well.

And so, confronted with his fiancée's brother, Dabney Bayard was often at a loss for words. How unnerving it was, and how maddening!— for young Bayard, with close-clipped chestnut hair in undulant waves, and long eyelashes, and a quick forthcoming smile, was accustomed to the admiration of women, and of his elders; and yearned only for the admiration, or, at least, the acceptance, of young men of his own age and background, like Josiah Slade.

"Is there some reason you don't like Dabney?"—so Annabel had asked her brother, shyly; but Josiah had said, with as much sincerity as he could muster, "No! Not at all. What matters, Annabel, is that *you* like *him*."

This was an oblique answer, which Annabel did not know how to decode. But she noted the bland *like* and not the more forceful *love* out of her brother's mouth.

And what of Josiah Slade? His character is so complex, and contradictory, and problematic, and, it may as well be said, so "fated," I don't feel qualified to analyze it here, as I would not feel qualified to analyze the character of Shakespeare's Hamlet, of whom Josiah sometimes reminds me. A young man of deep-smoldering passion overcome by too-cerebral meditations; a young man of an "elevated" family, not at ease in society; a young man set upon a course of destiny—with no knowledge of what his destiny must be.

Since Augustus Slade had accepted the suit of Dabney Bayard for Annabel's hand, effectively cutting off, at the knees, a small battalion of suitors about to declare themselves, Josiah had behaved strangely—capriciously. Yet, when Annabel approached him with her tentative query, he seemed stiff with her, and evasive: "You must follow your heart, Annabel. And Father has said 'yes'—it can only be up to you, to persevere in the engagement."

Persevere in the engagement! Annabel laughed, somewhat hurt; as if marrying Dabney Bayard were some sort of military campaign.

Though Josiah was five years older than Annabel, and had not always had much time for his sister while they were growing up, he had always been fond of her, and protective; if by nature blunt-mannered, and inclined to impatience; yet it had always seemed to Annabel, that Josiah loved her dearly. (As he loved, or tried to love, their ever-restless and intrusive young cousin Todd, now eleven years old.) But when Annabel tried to take Josiah's hands in hers—(ah! how large they were, how strong and big-boned)—he drew away with a frown; and when she begged him to have no secrets from her, as when they were children, he said, with a vexed sort of smile, "But Annabel, you must realize—we are children no longer."

WHILE THE SLADES' numerous guests made their festive way from room to room upstairs, Annabel, Josiah, and Dabney Bayard continued to stand rather awkwardly before an empty fireplace, in one of the first-floor drawing rooms; no recent ashes littered this empty space, but rather some very fine bones, that had dried to splinters. Out of desperation Dabney said, "Your grandfather Winslow is the most remarkable man—it's true, as everyone says. And he has been so *generous* . . ." Annabel agreed; but Josiah only grunted in reply, as if the inane remark did not warrant a serious response.

Surreptitiously Annabel poked her brother in the ribs. She cast a sidelong glance at him, as if to implore *Please don't be rude. Don't ruin this happy day.*

Six weeks before her wedding, Annabel Slade had never looked more beautiful, with her skin slightly heated, and her violet-blue eyes moist, and her lower lip trembling with emotion. For this Sunday brunch at the "old Craven house"—soon to be the "honeymoon cottage" of the young people—she was wearing a new dress of cream-colored crepe de chine in the "Fluffy Ruffles" fashion of the day; her lavishly feathered "picture" hat, of a hue matching her dress, was perched atop the mass of her honey-brown pompadour, with a bandeau secured beneath the crown for more height. In her shimmering cascade of ruffles, that trembled with her every intake of breath, Annabel struck the eye as the very emblem of feminine loveliness—of feminine *mystery.* For why was it, so adored a young lady, so clearly blessed a young lady, stood between her fiancé and her brother, her gaze downcast, and her forehead lined with worry?

It would have taken a more perceptive observer even than Josiah, to note that Annabel was distracted, and her thoughts elsewhere; it may have been, the warning hiss *Annabel! Annabel!* could just faintly be heard, from the winter-ravaged, as yet untended, flower beds at the rear of the house.

And it may have been, Annabel's thoughts were moving surreptitiously to the memory of a hand-sickle wickedly glinting in the sun—fresh-cut wildflowers and grasses fallen into a heap, soon to rot—the memory of a bold grasp of her hand, and a yet bolder kiss on the back of her hand—*chère mademoiselle! How kind you are! A rare quality in ladies of your station . . .*

Annabel had many times examined the back of her hand, looking for the imprint of the stranger's sharp incisor. But the skin was smooth, quite thin and creamy-pale, with only a fine filigree of bones beneath, and a translucent web of bluish veins.

As Annabel was glancing, another time, at her hand, there came from the second floor sudden cries, and shouts; female screams; and, following almost immediately, a sound of struggle, or scuffling—as of persons grappling about on the floor directly overhead.

Josiah ran unhesitatingly upstairs, bounding the steps two and three at a time; Annabel and Dabney came following after, though not running. In her fear, Annabel had grasped Dabney's arm; and Dabney leaned to her, as if to protect her.

"Oh, what is it? Is someone hurt? It sounds like President Cleveland—is that his voice?" Annabel cried.

Upstairs, Josiah discovered, in a bedroom of the Craven house, one of the most astonishing sights of his young life: Grover Cleveland, our former President, a rotund gentleman of nearly seventy years, and three hundred pounds, badly flushed in his face, and loudly wheezing, had fallen to the plank floor in a convulsive thrashing, being held in place, clumsily, by several persons including Josiah's father, Augustus, and the distraught Mrs. Cleveland. The corpulent old gentleman, yet panting, and wheezing, so that one feared he was on the brink of an apoplectic seizure, would not cease his struggling, and cried in a grieving voice:

"Let me up—please let me up—O stand back, if you have any heart! *Here's Pappa! Here's Pappa,* I say! My dear daughter, do not abandon us again!"

In the doorway Josiah stood transfixed. What was this? Had the world suddenly gone mad? It was like a scene out of a film—*The Great Train Robbery* which everyone had seen, two years before—calamitous excitement, jerky and uncoordinated movements, a rapid, headlong pace, sensational music to rouse the blood—yet, though you stared at the moving images, you could not make immediate sense of them; you could not *slow* them, to comprehend.

Grover Cleveland, it seemed, had fallen to the floor, or had possibly been pushed to the floor, to save him from falling out a window that opened out onto a section of tile roof; it seemed that Josiah's father was wrestling Cleveland down, and Mrs. Cleveland herself—ripely Junoesque, darkly handsome, and, ordinarily, complacent and composed in her every gesture—was trying to pin her husband to the floor by the rough application of a silken knee, to his immense midriff; which effort had bared the woman's shapely leg, in a sheer white stocking, that drew Josiah's astonished attention, like nothing he had ever seen in actual life, nor had even imagined.

IT IS TRUE: my fellow historians have bungled this episode, having not a clue of what had happened in the old Craven house on Rosedale Road, at midday of 20 April 1905; their collective failure is to be attributed to the zeal of Frances Cleveland in suppressing the lurid facts, that she might protect her elderly husband from censure and ridicule; for the former First Lady was most sensitive to cruel remarks made behind her husband's (massive) back, correctly assuming that such derision reflected upon her, as well. After Cleveland left the presidency, under a considerable cloud, in 1897, and sought to retire to the "sleepy village" of Princeton, New Jersey, it fell to his young wife to shield him from over-excitement, as from over-eating and –drinking, for it was said that Grover could "no more stop himself from gluttony, than a gold fish in a bowl, that eats all that is given to him, until his stomach bursts." Despite her youth, Mrs. Cleveland soon cultivated an arch and imperial style in society, as in public; so it was, knowing her and her husband both *sought-after,* and *shamelessly talked-of,* Mrs. Cleveland was not one to suffer fools gladly. Not just Woodrow Wilson, as we have seen, but many a Princeton citizen, of a higher social rank than he, came to fear the woman's flashing eye, sarcastic tongue, and her power to enhance, or damage, one's social ranking, depending upon her whim.*

---

* The Clevelands remain a fascinating couple, seven decades later. Grover Cleveland, twenty-eight years older than his wife, was reputed to have first glimpsed her as an infant; after the death of her father, who was one of Cleveland's oldest friends, Cleveland became the guardian of the eleven-year-old girl to whom, hardly a decade later, when she was an undergraduate at Wells College for Women, he proposed. At twenty-one, Frances was the youngest First Lady in history, as she remains the youngest to this day. The Clevelands had five children, of whom the

Despite the confusion of this incident at the old Craven house, I have managed to piece together, like a skilled, if somewhat eccentric, maker of quilts, a more or less coherent narrative, as follows.

After ascending to the second floor of the house, which was an exertion for one of his girth, Grover Cleveland idled at the rear of the excited little group making their way through the rooms, hoping to catch his breath; while others were elsewhere, marveling at one or another charming feature of the house, Cleveland wandered into an empty room, as it happened, a children's nursery; he chanced to pass one of the tall windows in this room, that was part-shuttered, and overlooked a steep corner of the roof; there, he saw, or seemed to see, a terrifying sight, there at the very edge of the roof; imagining it at first to be a large, ungainly bird, a great blue heron perhaps, for such prehistoric-looking waterbirds were not uncommon in rural Princeton, the affrighted man literally rubbed his eyes to see a child, a young girl, perched at the edge of the roof; playfully, or prankishly?—the girl was tearing into pieces a handful of calla lilies, letting their torn petals fall to the ground below; her wavy dark hair tumbled loose down her back; her gown long, and white, and curiously soiled; her bare feet ghastly pale—all of her skin ghastly pale, with the unmistakable pallor of the grave. Oblivious to the astonished observer, the child managed to get to her feet, at the edge of the roof, laughing, and tossing the remainder of the calla lilies into the air, as if she were about to step off into space; and how should Cleveland save her?

He shouted—"No! No! Stop! You must not!"

---

firstborn, Ruth, died of a childhood illness in 1904, at the age of thirteen. Growing up in Princeton, I saw Mrs. Cleveland often—that is, as a widow—for her corpulent husband did not long survive the vicissitudes of the Crosswicks Curse, though an innocent victim of the scourge, it seems. My mother was a friendly acquaintance of Mrs. Cleveland both before and following her second marriage, at the age of forty-nine, to an archaeology professor at Princeton University; I wish I could claim to having spoken with her but I have only blurred memories of this striking dark-haired and dark-complected woman, rumored (by female detractors in Princeton) to have been a distant relative of an Indian chief in the Choctaw Nation of Oklahoma!

Cleveland was at the window, grunting to raise it, and to push open the shutters, shouting wildly—with the result that, to his further astonishment, and horror, he saw the girl turn to him to reveal herself as *his own beloved daughter Ruth*—who had died but the previous year, of diphtheria, at the Clevelands' summer home at Buzzards Bay, Massachusetts.

Ah, what was this? How could it be? Cleveland's beloved Ruth, of whom he so often dreamt, and for whom he continued to grieve in the privacy of his thoughts—why had she appeared to him here? And what must be done?

It is a fact, though Grover Cleveland suffered from a battery of ailments, beyond even those of Woodrow Wilson, yet he had never suffered from any mental illness, or hallucinations.

Priding himself on being the most commonsensical of men, with scarcely a thought of an "after-life" or a "realm of spirits," yet Cleveland did not hesitate for a moment, convinced that his daughter had returned to him, in this mysterious way; attired in the very raiments of the grave, and peeking over her shoulder at him, with that look of coquettish mischief that, in life, Ruth had often looked at her dear Pappa, to tease, and to make him laugh.

It is no wonder that Cleveland forgot that Ruth was dead, and had been buried; in a frenzy he shoved the window as high as it would go, leaning out, reaching his arms to her, begging her to come to him. Giving no thought for his own safety and trying, despite the handicaps of age and girth, to force himself through the open window, he cried, "Ruth! Dear Ruth! It *is* you! Do not step off—your Pappa begs you, darling—here!— here's Pappa! Come to Pappa! O my poor darling! My little one! My angel! Do not step off! *Come to Pappa's arms, O do—*"

The phantom at the edge of the roof could not be seen by the others, evidently; yet, as they rushed into the room, the situation was instinctively grasped—at least, that Grover Cleveland was suffering a violent hallucination, and was trying to force himself out a narrow window, to his probable death on the ground below, if he was not restrained.

So it was, the struggle ensued, which Josiah a moment later witnessed: the elderly rotund gentleman being wrestled to the floor by several persons including his wife, who threw aside her silken parasol, and hiked up her heavy skirts and petticoats, enjoining Cleveland, in a ringing voice, to cease his struggles at once: "Why, what is this! What can you mean! Dear husband, what can you mean!"

"Frances, it's Ruth—our daughter, Ruth! Look! She is beckoning to me—to us! Let me go, please—"

"Ruth? What do you mean? Where?"—now Mrs. Cleveland was on the verge of hysteria, crouching at the opened window; but she seemed not to see any apparition on the roof, unless, by this time, the apparition had vanished.

Soon then, held down against the hardwood floor, the raving man lapsed into a merciful faint; his plump, roughened face covered in sickly perspiration, and his breath stertorous and terrible to hear. His tight-starched collar was torn open by his rescuers, and his vest, and shirtfront; his face was sprinkled with water, and wiped with a cold compress. One of the surrey drivers was sent to fetch Cleveland's physician Dr. Boudinot, who resided at Lilac Lane, that intersected with Hodge, and was not far from Rosedale; by the time the doctor arrived, the immediate danger to Cleveland's life appeared to be past, though such a seizure did not bode well for the future, and Mrs. Cleveland tearfully begged the party that they should not spread the unhappy news.

Of all of the party, only three others seemed to have "seen" or "sensed" the apparition, so far as I can determine.

Eleven-year-old Todd Slade, Annabel's and Josiah's cousin, the son of Copplestone and Lenora Slade, had not actually witnessed Mr. Cleveland's collapse, nor had he been allowed to enter the nursery afterward;

yet, the excitable child would wake from nightmares for several nights in succession afterward, claiming that a *girl-ghost* was chasing him.

Then there was the adamant testimony of Amanda FitzRandolph who insisted afterward that she had glimpsed a "shimmering efflorescence" of some sort on the roof, exactly where Cleveland had been pointing; but she could not have identified it as poor Ruth Cleveland for "wraiths so resemble one another, returning from the Other Side."

Less clearly, there appeared to have been a distinctive emotional reaction from Winslow Slade, who had entered the nursery after the others, when the stricken Mr. Cleveland had lost consciousness, yet who seemed to grasp the situation immediately: what it was outside the window that had "beckoned" to Mr. Cleveland, with so catastrophic a result.

For, in the confusion of the moment, when help was being summoned, and Mrs. Cleveland was weeping loudly in distress, Winslow had tried to comfort her by saying it would be all right now, as "the spirit of your little daughter appears to have left us."

Though asked afterward by Josiah and Annabel if he'd seen the apparition, Winslow Slade said, curtly: "No. There are no 'spirits' in Christendom."

While in the company of the distressed others, Annabel had said very little; but when at last they were alone together, in the evening, at Crosswicks Manse, Annabel confided in Josiah: "Ruth, you say? He saw his daughter Ruth outside the window? Oh the poor child—you know, Josiah, I had rarely seen her, in life—but lately in dreams, since her death, Ruth has beckoned to me, too—I am so frightened *why*."

ANGEL TRUMPET; OR,
"MR. MAYTE OF VIRGINIA"

It was just two days later, on the Princeton University campus, that Josiah Slade had an adventure of sorts of a significance he couldn't have guessed at the time; though he felt its disagreeable nature and was chilled to the soul, as if sensing some of what lay ahead.

His mission was to visit Professor Pearce van Dyck, a former philosophy teacher of his, whose office was on the second floor of the new Gothic building called Pyne, eventually to be known as East Pyne; and whose advice, or informed counsel, Josiah very much desired. Josiah recalled his undergraduate days at Princeton when he had flailed about in his studies, never quite knowing what he wanted to do: study ancient languages, including Hebrew and Aramaic, that he might read the Holy Scripture for himself, to satisfy the many questions raised by the King James translation, which his grandfather Slade had not been able to answer for him; or was he inclined to science—botany, biology, geology; or was he inclined to history—the blood-steeped soil of Europe, or the more virginal, though scarcely less bloodied, soil of the New World? As he had grown restless after a few weeks at West Point, so Josiah had been restless as an undergraduate, taking time off from his studies to "travel"—to "prowl about," at times not unlike a common vagabond, under the spell of Jack London's Klondike tales or, less desperately, the Mark Twain of *Life on the Mississippi.* (In some way not entirely explained, Josiah had earned a fair amount of money in the West; though the sum was being rapidly depleted, he did not yet have to depend upon his family to support him.)

At Princeton, Josiah had been conscripted to play on the football team, and on the hockey and softball teams; he'd spent a few back-aching weeks on the crew team, practice-rowing in the chill dawn through spectral mists rising from Lake Carnegie with the consoling thought that such a cooperative sport was a rebuke to the exhibitionist athlete he so disliked, and recognized in himself. And Josiah had ignored a bid from the most exclusive eating—(and drinking)—club on Prospect Avenue, Ivy, without offering any explanation to his surprised, disappointed and disapproving club-brothers, other than a shrug of the shoulders: "One evening is fairly much all evenings, at Ivy; having sampled three and a half weeks of such evenings, I am satisfied that I have sampled them all."

There was a spirit of forced camaraderie among the Princeton boys—or as they wished to think of themselves, *young men.* As if nothing mattered so much as one another: to be respected, to be liked, to be admired, to be "popular." Grades scarcely mattered—if you studied, you were mocked as a *poler.* A gentleman had no need of a grade beyond "C"—for a gentleman was not going to make his living by his wits, surely. And so you joined a club, or two clubs; or three. You went out for sports as others did, in an affable herd. But, as at West Point he would soon learn that marching *in uniform* was deeply boring, so too Josiah had learned at Princeton that any effort that reached no higher than the height of his classmates had not the power to engage him for very long.

To please his father, he'd persevered at Princeton until after several years he was granted a B.A. degree. The sheepskin diploma he hid away at once, and may have lost.

Such independence filled him with a reckless sort of elation—but then, he felt such a reaction of melancholy, he could not bear to be alone.

And so he sought out his most sympathetic instructor, Pearce van Dyck, who had always welcomed him into his commodious office with its floor-to-ceiling bookshelves, leather chairs and sofa, and a view, through leaded-glass windows, of the university "chapel"—large and impressive as any church.

Josiah thought *Professor van Dyck will speak frankly. Of all persons I know.*

So it happened, Josiah knocked on the opened door of van Dyck's office, and was invited inside; Pyne Hall was agreeably bustling, and popu-lated by undergraduates hurrying to lectures, or departing lectures in thun-derous herds on the stairs, and no one took notice of Josiah in his worn tweed "blazer" and gabardine trousers, who might have been one of them, except for his furrowed brow and a more mature intensity in his eyes. "Jo-siah, hello! This is a very pleasant surprise."

Between the philosophy professor and the young man there had long existed a relaxed and companionable relationship, for their families were acquainted, and van Dyck had known Josiah since earliest childhood. In his classes, Josiah was enough of a good student to merit high grades; at times, even a brilliant and capricious student, but not one subject to troubling moods, or at least not in van Dyck's company. The professor, a specialist in Kantian idealism, was middle-aged at this time, taciturn by nature, scholarly and earnest rather than "popular" with his students; Jo-siah did not feel nearly so comfortable with his own father, as he did with Pearce van Dyck.

The great value of philosophy is, one cuts through subterfuge at once; one "goes for the jugular." And so Josiah said, with no preamble, before he'd even taken a seat in van Dyck's office, "Professor, what do you make of this?"—holding out for van Dyck to see, in both his hands, a gath-ering of broken and bruised lily petals, and a few stems and leaves, badly desiccated and pungent-smelling.

Van Dyck stared at the lily-remnants, that seemed, in the unsparing sunshine that slanted through a tall window, to be rather a simulacrum of lilies than the actual flowers.

"I think these are 'calla lilies'—it's hard to tell, they are so rotted. Where did you get them?"

"I found them."

" 'Found them'—? Where?"

"Beneath my feet, where I happened to be walking. I looked down—and there they were."

Josiah did not explain that he'd stepped on the calla lily petals when he'd left the Craven house, after the Sunday visit. Glancing down, and he'd seen the desiccated petals, and felt a shiver of recognition.

The dead girl left these behind. The dead child is making a claim on us.

Josiah's motive for coming to Professor van Dyck was more than merely personal: for van Dyck was known, in addition to his scholarly pursuits, for his extensive amateur's knowledge of botany and horticulture; the van Dyck garden, behind the family's house at 87 Hodge Road, was one of the glories of Princeton's West End.

"I don't recall where I found these, Professor van Dyck. But I wondered what you thought of them. How you would identify them."

Josiah spoke slowly, like one who is weighing his words with care.

Van Dyck had spread the bruised petals, the broken stems and leaves, out on his desk. He peered at them, frowning. "The blooms seem aged—very old. Not an ordinary sort of decomposition but something else . . ." He lowered his head to smell, and recoiled at once with a look of consternation. "Why, the odor is *vile*."

"A sort of chemical odor, I thought. Not organic."

"Why, look! They are visibly *decomposing* . . ."

Josiah and Pearce van Dyck observed the desiccated lilies crumbling to pieces, and then to dust. A few dried wisps of leaf remained, a single calyx, a near-nauseating odor of rot.

"It must be the reaction of the strong sunlight on the lilies. Some sort of accelerated chemical process . . ."

Van Dyck's effort to explain the eerie phenomenon seemed to Josiah the very essence of the philosophical temperament: to wrench some sort of sense out of senselessness; to determine logic where there is none. Like the rhyming of poetry, such an effort gives an illusion of comfort.

"Yes. A 'chemical process.' I think that must be so."

"But where did you say you found these? 'Underfoot'?"

"It was at the Craven house, Professor. On Sunday."

As Pearce van Dyck and his wife had been at the house also, it was natural for Josiah to explain; but, a moment later, he regretted having said these words, that had the effect of intriguing van Dyck, and whetting his curiosity.

"But—no one had 'funeral' lilies there, I'm certain? And these are so *aged* . . ."

"I was just wondering—what you might think. Since you are a horticulturalist."

Josiah, restless, was on his feet. In his face was an expression of excitement and fatigue—as if he had not slept well the previous night, but had been "tossing and turning" in the grip of Paradox.

A predatory bird with a great sharp beak and vicious talons—Paradox. To be in its grip is to suffer, yet so exquisitely, one might mistake the experience for a kind of ecstasy.

Josiah shook his head, to rid it of such cobwebs of thought. Ah, he was not himself this morning! He had not been "himself"—to a degree—since the episode at the old Craven house, when Grover Cleveland had collapsed; and Annabel had confided in him that the Clevelands' dead child had come to her in dreams, and had beckoned to *her*.

"Josiah, why don't you sit down, please? You are in no hurry to leave, I assume?"

Josiah, who hadn't been aware that he was on his feet, and pacing about the office, could not think how to reply. *Was* he in a hurry? But to arrive—*where*?

"There's a sort of beating pulse in my head, Professor. If I become very still, it is more noticeable, and distracting."

Van Dyck squinted at him. He had been stooped over his desk, examining the crumbled remains of the calla lilies, and now looked up at Josiah, concerned.

"I hope it wasn't the smell of these flowers that has made you ill, Josiah. It's fading now, but it doesn't seem a *natural* smell . . ."

"Well, Professor! Thank you! You have been very helpful and now—now—I'll say good-bye."

"My dear Josiah," van Dyck protested, "you aren't leaving so soon, are you? Why don't you sit down—we can talk about that extraordinary episode on Sunday—poor Grover Cleveland, quite raving, and out of his mind . . . There had been an old story of the Craven house being haunted by the deceitful André, bent on revenging himself on Major Craven. Yet, it seemed, Mr. Cleveland hadn't seen the ghost of the executed spy but that of his poor daughter Ruth—what do you make of that?"

"There are no 'spirits' in Christendom. That's what I make of it."

Not quite rudely, Josiah walked away with an airy wave of his hand; and Pearce van Dyck was left behind, baffled that his young friend should be in so curious a mental state, over a handful of desiccated funeral flowers.

Carelessly then Pearce brushed away most of the flower-debris, not noticing that some curled little petals, and fragments of a stem, remained in an opened copy of Spinoza's *Ethics,* at the very beginning of *Part IV, Of Human Bondage, or, of the Strength of the Emotions.*

CROSSING THE UNIVERSITY campus, at a rapid clip, his broad shoulders hunched in his tweed coat and his head slightly bowed, Josiah was intercepted near the steps of Chancellor Green by the president of the university, Woodrow Wilson, who called out familiarly to him, and who smiled with warmth as if Josiah were one of his family. With a sinking heart Josiah thought *Waylaid! Damn.*

Of course Josiah did not continue on his way, as he'd have liked; instead, he paused to speak with Woodrow Wilson, or rather, to allow Woodrow Wilson to speak with him.

Wilson was in the company of a stranger, to whom he introduced Josiah: a singularly ugly man Josiah thought him, with a flaccid skin, fish-belly-white, and close-set eyes of some intense though unnatural-seeming color like bronze; and a reptilian manner about the lips, his tongue quick-darting and moist, as he smiled an unctuous smile that Josiah found particularly offensive. Yet it was not possible to escape, for Woodrow Wilson insisted upon introducing the stranger to Josiah, and Josiah to the stranger, as if the exchange gave him inordinate pride.

So it happened, Josiah Slade found himself forced to shake hands with "Axson Mayte," here identified as a lawyer from Carnahan, Virginia, with an association with the Presbyterian Church, whose services, Wilson told Josiah, he hoped to engage in his altercation with the university's board of trustees. Josiah, who'd heard only the rudiments of gossip concerning Wilson's feud with Andrew West, the dean of the Graduate School, and considered the issue entirely trivial, smiled courteously and murmured a friendly/perfunctory response, eager to be on his way; but Dr. Wilson adroitly detained him, by laying a paternal hand on his arm, and inquiring after his family—the health of his parents, and his sister and young cousin, and his grandfather Winslow.

How predictable, these social exchanges! How numbingly repetitive! And yet, how to escape them?—Josiah had a vision of himself breaking free, and running out to Nassau Street.

That is madness. From madness, no turning back.

Dr. Wilson was clearly eager to talk; there would be no easy escape. Despite the presence of the stranger from Virginia, whose gaze was fixed upon Josiah with a discomforting intensity, Wilson began to ask particularly after Annabel, for he knew that Josiah and his sister were unusually close; he said he'd heard a "most distressing, and curious" report the previous day regarding the health of Mr. Cleveland, and wondered if Josiah knew anything about the incident.

Discreetly, Josiah said he did not. No.

Discreetly, Josiah would have excused himself and slipped away, except that Woodrow Wilson detained him with a hand lightly on his arm; all the while smiling at the young man, with the familial warmth of Pearce van Dyck, yet with something more intense and more compelling beneath, a subtle sort of coercion. The conversation flailed about like a small bird in a large cage, as Wilson tried also to draw in "Mr. Mayte."

(How loathsome this "Mayte" struck Josiah!—his loathsomeness had little to do with mere physical ugliness, for such did not usually offend Josiah, but with the man's fawning, craven, yet presuming manner, and the euphonious nature of his voice; even the inappropriate sportiness of his clothes—for, though he was Woodrow Wilson's age or more, with a squat, stocky build, he wore a costume suitable for a Princeton undergraduate: a brick-colored blazer with wide-padded shoulders, and a white shirt and narrow dark tie; peg-top trousers, and circular-toed shoes, and a cap resembling a baseball cap set rakishly on his head. It would not have surprised Josiah to see "Mayte" with an eating-club insignia in his lapel, so absurdly did he try to emulate an undergraduate. When Axson Mayte smiled it was to reveal yellowed teeth of which one, an incisor, hooked a good half-inch below its fellows.

Yet, to Josiah's shrewd eye, the most repellent touch was the delicate white narcissus worn in Mayte's lapel, that had begun to turn brown, and to wither.

Though Annabel was admiring of the Wilson daughters Margaret, Jessie, and Eleanor, and always spoke in the most exalted terms of President Wilson, Josiah had never felt comfortable in the man's presence, for he thought him pompous, and grasping, and ambitious, and far too interested in the Slade family. (Wilson would run for a major political office one day, Josiah believed. And he would want Winslow Slade's public blessing, as well as some private cash.)

It did not help Josiah's uneasy feeling about Woodrow Wilson that, some years ago, when he'd been a young boy of about ten, and already a very good softball player, he'd overheard Wilson say to his father, Augustus, that he greatly envied him his *manly* son; for, as fortune would have it, he had *only girls;* and the venerable Wilson name was in danger of being lost. ("Yes, your Josiah is the child I would have wanted, if God had seen fit.")

Now, in Axson Mayte's presence, Woodrow Wilson brought up the subject of Annabel's wedding; he could not resist saying how pleased he was, that Jessie would be a bridesmaid; and all of Princeton was anticipating the happy event. Hearing this, Axson Mayte brightened, and said in a buttery Southern drawl to Josiah, "Why, I had not realized that you are Annabel Slade's brother!—let me shake your hand again."

This was so ridiculous a request, Josiah would have drawn away in irritation; but Axson Mayte quickly reached out to shake Josiah's hand a second time. Josiah felt a current of cold run up his arm.

Fortunately, the bell of Old North began to sound. Within seconds undergraduate men swarmed along the path, many of them wearing oddly shaped hats, the arcane insignia of one or another club; there were sophomores "hazing" hapless-looking freshmen; in the roadway, bicyclists sped past. Josiah was able to make his excuses though Woodrow Wilson called after him, almost wistfully—"Please say hello to your grandfather for me, will you? And—of course—your mother . . ."

Hurrying toward Nassau Street, where a stream of horse-drawn carriages and motor vehicles passed, Josiah couldn't resist glancing back over his shoulder to see the tall thin ministerial figure of Woodrow Wilson beside the squat figure of Axson Mayte—both men gazing after him and engaged in conversation, Josiah hated to think, about *him.*

Annabel Slade's brother!—so that contemptible creature had called Josiah. What right had he to make so casual a reference to Annabel, as if he knew her?

Did he know her? But—how?

So shaken was Josiah by this unpleasant meeting, that grated against his sensitive nerves like a fingernail against a chalkboard, he began to feel faint; it was a sensation he'd had in the Craven house, as he'd stared at the fallen and terrified Grover Cleveland, and felt the hairs at the back of his neck stir in a kind of animal sympathy with the old man, that such horrors were imminent in his life, too.

Suddenly, Josiah Slade doubted his strength to walk back to the Manse; and felt obliged to catch the Johnson trolley off Witherspoon, amid a gaggle of chattering women and schoolchildren; and, at the rear, dark-skinned workmen and laborers, some of whom were carrying lunch pails, who glanced up at him with veiled eyes, and faces emptied of expression.

"Hello! Room for one more?"—so Josiah took his seat among the men, at the very rear of the trolley; hoping to relax among them, as he could not relax elsewhere; and trying to take no note that, with his arrival in their midst, the men had abruptly ceased talking.

AUTHOR'S NOTE:
PRINCETON SNOBBERY

In our egalitarian American society, it is considered a kind of evil to *feel superior* to other Americans; though the lower strata of all human societies yearn to *feel superior* to other, yet lower, strata, still it is sacrosanct to pretend that this is not so; that *snobbery*, in all its forms, is aberrant as well as evil.

This may be a convenient time for me to provide to the reader some information concerning the subtle yet crucial differentiations in social rank between those persons in our chronicle who belong to the old "county" families, of long-established lineage and wealth, and those of a more recent sort who have but lately, that's to say within the past century, migrated to the area.

The original category is *pilgrims*, *settlers*, or *colonists*; the second, much vaster, is *immigrants*.

On one hand we have the old Jersey families of the stature of the Slades, initially inhabitants of the Massachusetts Bay Colony who had moved to the Crown Colony of New Jersey at a time when "Princeton" did not exist, being but one of three small villages—"King's Town," "Queen's Town," and "Prince's Town"—on the old pike road between New York and

Philadelphia. Along with the Slades, if not rivaling them in reputation and wealth, are the Morgans, the FitzRandolphs, the Bayards, the van Dycks, the Pynes (of the magnificent mansion Drumthwacket, in more recent years the residence of the governor of New Jersey), the several families of Burrs (descended from Reverend Aaron Burr, Sr.)—and others, falling beyond the periphery of this history. That these noble old families predated Princeton University by decades should be kept in mind, for, in its earlier guise as the College of New Jersey, the institution was first founded in Elizabeth, New Jersey, and later moved, in 1748, by the Reverend Aaron Burr, Sr., to Newark; then, a decade later, the college was moved by President Samuel Davies to its present location in the village of Princeton, on Route 27, or Nassau Street as it is called, near the intersection with state highway 206. From this modest beginning, with its close ties to the Presbyterian Church, the university has grown, and grown—and has now overgrown itself, one might say, in a crowded and cramped campus in which "green" is scarcely glimpsed and unsightly high-rise structures fly in the face of the elegant Collegiate Gothic architecture of the earlier era. In the West End of Princeton, to this day, descendants of the old families yet reside, some very nearly anonymously; for time has passed them by, as the admission of women, "blacks," and a quota-less quantity of Jews to the great university would indicate, a trickle of anarchy at first in that low decade, the 1970s, and now a flood.

Thus, one can see a clear division between the old "settler" families and the swarm of "new persons" who had moved into the area merely to be employed by the university, at decidedly modest salaries.

(It was held against Woodrow Wilson, by individuals like Adelaide McLean Burr, that, being too poorly paid to afford a motorcar, the president of the university was obliged to bicycle much of the time; this is a cruel sort of snobbery, indeed. Yet we must laugh with Adelaide, for she is very witty!) Naturally there was some overlapping as in the case of my father Pearce van Dyck, the son of one of the most distinguished "county" families, who was also a scholar and philosopher of national reputation, with degrees from Cambridge (U.K.) as well as Princeton. To reason more finely, Ellen Wilson was related, on her paternal grandmother's side, to the Randolphs of Virginia, by way of which she might have claimed a familial connection with the wealthy FitzRandolphs of Princeton, except, we have to assume, Mrs. Wilson lacked the courage to do so, and risk being *snubbed*.

As to Josiah and Annabel, the principal characters of *The Accursed*—though they are wholly sympathetic, and indeed very good-hearted individuals, it is inescapable that they, too, are *snobs*—all unconsciously and helplessly, as they are *Slades*.

THE UNSPEAKABLE I

(Excerpted from the secret journal of Mrs. Adelaide McLean Burr,
April–May 1905)

This invaluable journal, transcribed in a secret code which no other historian has "cracked" until now, was originally discovered amid a miscellany of papers, household accounts, and other memorabilia, at Maidstone House, long after Mrs. Burr's premature death. At the time, inscribed in an eccentric and near-unreadable code, in a spidery hand, in lavender ink, in the Crimson Calfskin Book, the journal was not recognized for its worth.

The present narrator is hesitant to put himself forward as the sole living person capable of reading Mrs. Burr's journal with full comprehension, yet I think that false modesty is remiss; and rival historians of the period are hereby warned against infringing upon my labors, which are fully protected by copyright.

(I hope it will not seem over-protective of my rights, but I have decided not to reveal to the reader the way in which, after months of frustration, I managed to "crack" Adelaide's code, which would seem, to the untrained eye, the most egregious gibberish, festooned with eccentric Theosophical symbols and doodles.)

The reader should be informed that Adelaide McLean Burr was stricken with a mysterious "malaise" shortly after her wedding, in September 1891, to Horace Hu-

diger Burr, Jr., which manifested itself in a variety of physical and mental complaints, including partial paralysis, extreme fatigue, and breathlessness; among the female invalids of Princeton at this time, Mrs. Burr was quite the most prominent, and often sent "bulletins" to friends whom she could not see socially. It was not uncommon that the invalid would ask to be carried downstairs, to greet distinguished visitors at Maidstone House, for instance Mr. and Mrs. Grover Cleveland, when they were new to town, or to visit with a select sisterhood of Princeton ladies at teatime primarily; though it was believed that she had not left the confines of the Maidstone property since returning from her Bermuda honeymoon in October 1891.

Another detail that the reader should know: Maidstone House, the ancestral home of the Pembroke Burrs, who had, like the Slades, originally settled in the Massachusetts Bay Colony, but moved to the Crown Colony of New Jersey in the 1700s, is one of the more striking of the stately homes in the West End of Princeton. It is located at 164 Hodge Road, having been built in 1803 in a quaint (and somewhat forbidding) style of "bastardized" Romanesque and Gothic, in somber-hued granite tending toward the luminous, depending upon the strength of the light. With more than twenty-five rooms in the house proper, and a dozen more in the old carriage house and in the slaves' quarters to the rear, Maidstone exerts a curious spell upon the observer: suggesting, in its somewhat blunt, foursquare architecture, and its towering chimneys and exceptionally tall, narrow, and "brooding" windows, frequently kept shuttered, an unusual blend of the funereal and the sublime.

As the reader knows, my childhood was passed at 87 Hodge Road, which is but a half-block from Maidstone House. It was a childish fancy, though taken very seriously by our impressionable servants, and other household workers and tradesmen who came often to the house, that Maidstone House was "haunted"—well before Adelaide Burr's horrific death.

_____ . *UNSPEAKABLE!*—the incident of which all Princeton whispers this morning.

But how shall a *lady* inquire of it?

I know not for certain when it took place—(two nights ago?)—& whether the woman to whom it happened—(an outrage, was it?—so delicious!)—was the sort to embark out alone, at dusk; whether she was a resident of Princeton proper, or dwelt in some pokey little village nearby.

How unjust, to be denied this crucial information!—but if the crime against the lady be UNSPEAKABLE how then can it be spoken of, to a lady? Horace will tell me nothing. Horace is grim and close-mouthed like all of his kin. Horace murmurs only, in response to my teasing inquiries, "Nothing is wrong, dear Adelaide, that would concern you"—and so the matter rests; for Horace would shield his Puss from all wickedness, as he has—beloved husband!—for the fourteen years of our union.

_____ . (My handsome curly-mustach'd husband could never guess, in his innocence, how wicked his Puss is, in her heart; how bold & daring & untrammeled her thoughts!)

_____ . An afternoon of tea & tarts & luscious mocha trifles. Yet how dull, when Puss craved only to hear news of the UNSPEAKABLE in our midst, of which ladies are not supposed to know; & the chatter was all of prune-face Dr. Wilson & glad-hander Andrew West quarreling in their silly Teacup. I know, I am considered "rude"—at the very least, "irreverent"—scarcely disguising a yawn at the L E N T I S S I M O of Mrs. FitzRandolph's gossip; & Cousin Wilhelmina, that overgrown child, shot me a glance of mischievous sympathy while her mother droned on & on accounting of who is for Dr. Lantern-Jaw Wilson & who for Dean Sixty-Two-Around-the-Vest West among the board of trustees; for it suddenly seems, the entire town is divided. Trustees & alumni of the university & powerful widows & of course the Clevelands with their considerable *weight* (Grover is chair of the board, & it is said strongly favors West), etcetera! Puss consoled herself by eating a half-dozen of the mocha trifles, with dollops of extra cream—which had the effect of making me quite ill that evening, as I should have known. But ah!—what measures Puss will take, out of exquisite B O R E D O M.

_____ . It is teasingly unclear: the UNSPEAKABLE seems to have involved one of our most distinguished West End households!

So cruel & frustrating, no more details are yet reveal'd.

_____ . & another UNSPEAKABLE incident has been hinted-at: this, involving ex-President Cleveland who somehow came to be, so very mysteriously, at the old Craven house on Rosedale Road, in a company of individuals including many of the Winslow Slade family—thus, our leading citizens; a gathering that must have had something to do with the upcoming Slade-Bayard nuptials. But Horace quite disappointed, he seems sincerely to know nothing of this incident which took place only last Sunday.

_____ . Dr. Boudinot comes to visit. In the wake of the mocha trifles such gastric distress, & 18 hrs. malaise, Death is preferable.

Doctor must be fetched by motorcar. Yet another medication is prescribed for Puss. She has not had a clear head in 14 yrs.

This new medication in the form of chalky pills is fetched from the Princeton pharmacy by Abraham: the most coal-black of boys, new on our staff, related to our cook & housekeeper Minnie. At least, I think they are related. I think these are their ridiculous names.

_____ . On Mother Burr's silken chaise longue Puss lies innocent & breathless shivering in her Vale-of-Kashmir shawl & thinking secret thoughts to annihilate all of Princeton! Would Satan come to Maidstone House, if summoned? What are the "black rituals" required, to summon such a fellow? Would punishments—i.e., small humiliations—wreaked upon Puss's Princeton enemies be a sufficient reason, for Puss to "sell" her soul?

_____ . Cousin Wilhelmina! How I wish that she would confide in me, as to an older cousin; speak to me of the (anguished?) secrets of her life; for I believe that "Willy" is grievously in love with Josiah Slade, as other girls & women in Princeton are said to be.

Has Josiah Slade cast the girl a second glance? Except she is the friend of his sister Annabel? One doubts it!

But Willy is so impetuously young, she & the exquisite Annabel who are such fast friends, since they were schoolgirls; I do envy them!

I fear that, in their eyes, I am old—older than they; no matter that Puss's face is unlined & eyes brightly dark & quick; & skin always a little fevered, & breath quickened; & my smile that of a slyboots little girl all dimples—the smile that pierces Horace's heart, as he says. And my hair remains fine & light as smoke lifting about my head—though thinner than when I was a girl—a very pretty light brown threaded with red hairs—& if there be uglier gray hairs of a coarse texture, my maid Hannah has become skilled at henna rinse; & dear Horace, like all husbands, is none the wiser.

Do you still love your poor little Puss—so I asked Horace yesterday at dusk, shivering against his vest—or would you wish for a stronger wife, a huskier Juno of a wife like Frances Cleveland? To which wistful query Horace replied with but a kiss on my warm brow.

_____ . In secret Puss devours The Secret Doctrine of Madame Helena Blavatsky. Tho' the prose is obscure & difficult of access as a thorn-chok'd garden. & much is forgotten, in the course of a single page.

Yet: Puss so longs for comrades in Theosophy! Individuals courageous enough to brave such truths of the Occult Science (as it is called: for it is a Science). But—we are all Presbyterians & Episcopalians here; the most radical among us, Unitarians!

The Theosophical Society of America has its headquarters in Manhattan, at Gramercy Park. Meetings are held there to which only invitees are allowed. My heart gives a leap, I am so hopeful—for I believe only the Theosophists can comprehend my desire, for a world of the spirit to which only the very special have access, through superiority of Intellect & Striving.

Yet a little child shall lead ye—is not a teaching of the Theosophists!

(If only Puss were not a pathetic invalid, & might journey by motorcar!— yet Horace would disapprove.)

(All of the Burrs & the McLeans would disapprove for they are but narrow-minded provincials, at whom Madame Blavatsky would laugh in scorn.)

Madame Blavatsky has said THERE IS NO RELIGION HIGHER THAN TRUTH.

Madame Blavatsky has promised WE SHALL PASS TO OUR ETHERIC BODIES WHEN THE THIRD EYE IS OPENED GRANTING SPIRITUAL SIGHT.

Madame Blavatsky has promised A GUARDIAN DEVI (ANGEL) WATCHES OVER US IF WE ASCEND TO A HIGHER PLANE.

To which Puss adds a fervent AMEN.

_____ . More of Cousin Willy. I think there is some fever'd secret in *her*.

I am not able to judge if Wilhelmina at age twenty is handsome as some say or as others say too blunt-jawed, her face "hearty" & high-colored in a way not befitting a lady. I <u>wish</u> we might be friends. But she is young, & keeps her distance; less frequently comes to tea at Maidstone with her mother & aunt; or, if she is here, casts a dreamy eye on us all, as if her thoughts were elsewhere; is drawn into talk of the upcoming wedding of course, for she is Annabel's maid of honor, indeed a singular honor here in Princeton; for the Slade-Bayard nuptials will be the great social event of the season.

Yet, Wilhelmina has hopes to enroll in the New York School of Art, to study with the renowned painter Robert Henri. No sooner speaking of this wish than her mother interrupts to chide her, the daily commuting trip would be exhausting, by rail; & Wilhelmina's father would never consent to her living in the city; so, the notion is absurd.

So, the blushing girl is silenced & blinks tears (of rage?) from her stark brown eyes. Dear Willy is brash & forthright & I find that I cannot dislike her, as a girl who might have been my closest friend, at the Girls' Academy; when I was the happiest of girls, I believe; & somewhat the most mischievous. Willy wore a most striking costume—a white pique skirt, smartly starched; a white cotton blouse, with puff sleeves & tight cuffs; a dark-striped jacket to accentuate the length of her torso & the narrowness of her hips; a hat of just under-size, a black straw Merry Widow without adornment; shoes black & plain & styled for walking, from our Bank Street cobbler. (For Willy claims to "walk, walk & walk" each day—along the canal, & the wild banks of Lake Carnegie; most shockingly, <u>alone</u>.) On her jacket lapel, a charming ladies' pin-on watch, its sly little face upside down; at which, I saw, my dear cousin covertly glanced often as her elders prattled on, & on. Dear Willy, I cannot blame you!

_____ . (Such rumors fly about Princeton, in the wake of the Wilson-West discord! The most exciting being, Andrew West is accused in some quarters of <u>dabbling in the black arts</u>. Horace has said that there is some truth to the charge, for there is known to be a cadre of research scientists at the university who venture into areas of experimentation involving the human brain through dissection (ugh!) & the like; kept secret from the university administration & the majority of the faculty, these scientists, under the guise of Natural Biology, pursue their illicit research in the bowels of Guyot Hall.)

_____ . Horace refuses to even hint at what the UNSPEAKABLE is, in our midst—"Nothing to concern you, dear Adelaide." Yet I know, it is something shocking & horrific; as bad as <u>dissection</u>. My lady-visitors know less than I do, it seems, & are so very disappointing, they make me want to <u>spit</u>. "Was it a robbery, a beating, a <u>murder</u>?"—so I persisted in inquiring of Horace, "—please tell me <u>was it a murder</u>?" (For I could not give utterance to the UNSPEAKABLE, that horrific insult that might be inflicted upon a woman or a girl, by a man; & the disgust & dismay of it ever afterward casting a shadow upon the poor victim's life, of which she could no more speak than if her tongue had been cut out like poor Philomela.) But Horace says grimly it is nothing to concern his dear Puss.

_____ . Horace's nephew Dabney Bayard drops by for tea, with several Bayard relatives of such antiquity, I could have sworn they had <u>passed away</u> years ago; Lieutenant Bayard as he is now called, in his handsome officer's uniform; all mustach'd smiles & Virginia charm & a curious persistence (did the young man believe that sharp-eyed Puss did not <u>see</u>?) in staring after young Hannah as she passed the tea things, for the girl is ever-more <u>buxom</u>, I am afraid, & otherwise shapely as a grown woman; with a mocha-taffy-colored skin, thick lips & nose; very quiet, deferential & obedient; not "bright"—one can see, in the sometimes lack of focus of her eyes. Yet in every way young & innocent, I am sure; for Minnie would see to this. And when Hannah was absent from the room, Lieutenant Dabney quickly became restless; chattered vaguely of the nuptials in June & the honeymoon trip—(Venice, Florence, Rome—ah, those fabled cities, poor Puss yearns to see!)—& the Craven house on Rosedale Road which will be deeded to the young couple—(though it is said to be haunted: has Lieutenant Bayard no fear of ghosts?)—casting me a blank embarrassed stare when I inquired, as if I had only just thought of it, what on earth had happened at the Craven house the other day?—of which no one will speak? After a startled silence Dabney drew breath and said, "Aunt Adelaide, I don't think I know what you mean. I pay very little attention to gossip."

Why, this was a rebuke! Such rage coursed along my veins, I could wish that I had recourse to the Prince of Darkness & his quick ways of revenge; if only Andrew West were a close friend of Horace's, & a confidant of poor Puss!

As well as rebuke, something in Lieutenant Bayard's gaze frightened me. For the Lieutenant, too, seemed frightened—for just a moment. & when he left escorting his doddering elders I felt very faint, & Henriette Slade, who had lingered behind in sympathy with me, ministered a dollop of snuff—Ladies' Snuff, it is called—much milder than Gentlemen's—& badly needed—out of her little crystal snuff bottle, carried concealed in her sleeve & wrapt in a lace handkerchief; a delicious fit of sneezes to clear the head, I might have wept with relief.

_____ . Horace kisses my brow & says that I am feverish. He says that Dr. Boudinot must be obeyed—no undue excitement in Puss's life! Warns me against the swirl of local gossip, which resembles a windstorm of dirt, sand, chaff, bits of manure—it is <u>very dangerous</u> to breathe! When I inquired after Lieutenant Bayard, that there has been said something to the effect that, at West Point, the young man was chastised for a violation of— is it the honor code, so-called?—yet not expelled, for his family influence— Horace at once pressed his forefinger to his lips frowning—<u>No, Adelaide! This is nothing of which I have ever heard & it must go no farther.</u>

_____ . Later assuring me, I am well protected in this house; all of the inhabitants of Hodge Road & vicinity are well protected; it is not after all Camden, New Jersey!—which drew from me a quick response, <u>Why do you speak of Camden?</u>—& Horace seemed confused for just a moment, as if he had misspoke. As if to weary my curiosity then, he went on to speak at length of Mr. Harrison our investment attorney, & matters of Wall Street, & Mr. Depew, & Mr. Hill—& Mr. Roosevelt—(which livened me just a bit for the exploits of "Teddy" are always amusing in the papers). Yet, talk of the unions & strikes continues to weary—no more do I care for such sordid matters as Madame Blavatsky herself might have cared for them—recoiling from talk of rabble-rousers who have begun to plague society with demand for HIGHER

WAGES & their crude threat of STRIKES. Horace grows livid, says they are but criminals; Pinkerton's must be hired, if the U.S. Army will not help our cause; the anarchists must be kept down, that Justice be served. Such craven greed, to wish only HIGHER WAGES, as if there is not a HIGHER CONSCIOUSNESS to which we must all strive.

Did the rabble & their leaders not ever learn—man must not live by bread alone?

_____ . B O R E D O M through the week; & on Monday, an ambitious tea, & Puss was feeling strong & gay, & most of the ladies looking very well.

Frances Cleveland came, a very pleasant surprise; at her dashing best, all plumes & jewels & high-colored complexion—(for it is whispered, the ex–First Lady has a touch of Indian blood, which throws Grover into a fit of fury if the gutter press pursue it); & Cousin Mandy in good spirits, despite her health; & the angelic Annabel Slade, our reigning Princeton debutante & bride-to-be; & her tedious mother Henrietta who is so damned good; & handsome Johanna van Dyck, tho' dressed just a bit shabbily it seemed to me; & old Mrs. Washington Burr, Horace's mother whom I did not recall having invited; & little Ellen Wilson in an unfortunate outfit, not at all flattering to her plain horsey features & stolid figure. (I am most angered, "Willy" sent regrets! Her excuse was so feeble, I did not even listen to it uttered by her silly aunt.)

Poor Ellen Wilson, invited to Maidstone House out of a sense of obligation & courtesy; & because her husband is president of the university, & cannot be avoided. A naïve woman, allowing herself to be drawn out by us in the matter of Dean West & the Graduate College, stammering that the dean & his supporters would "be very regretful if Woodrow's wrath is finally aroused, & his health threatened"—& we ladies sat startled into silence. Is the woman vulgar, or merely gauche?—is this how the company at Prospect common talks? Cousin Mandy discreetly changed the conversation by inquiring of Lenora Slade her recipe for the coconut meringues she had brought us, which were delicious. Thus, some embarrassment was curtailed, & Mrs. Wilson spared further folly.

From thence, discussion of the upcoming wedding: Annabel's gown which will be a "vision," Mrs. Slade promises, in the new <u>Directoire</u> style, & her maid of honor & bridesmaids so very thrilled; & the many distinguished guests journeying to Crosswicks Manse, from various parts of the country including Washington, D.C.; & the honeymoon trip, to Venice, Florence & Rome; & Josiah's plan to study German idealist philosophy at Heidelberg, or, it may be, to join a Polar expedition to the Klondike!— & all matter of chattering, pleasing at the time if forgettable a half-hour later. <u>Ladies!</u>—so I wanted to cry, rising from my chaise longue like a Valkyrie—<u>ladies! Does not one of you know that an UNSPEAKABLE crime has been perpetrated here in Princeton, that it involves a female & is very serious & mysterious, & no notice has appeared in the local papers, & the men conspire to know nothing, that they might shield us from evil?</u> But of course Puss said nothing, except to ask if Hannah might serve more tea.

_____ . Here is a surprise. Amid gales of laughter Frances Cleveland confides in me, the latest development of the Wilson/West feud: each gentleman is courting the 99-yr-old dowager Mrs. Horatio Pyne, of Baltimore; her late husband Horatio Pyne, Class of '22, having earmarked some 6 or 7 million dollars for Princeton. The nut to crack, as Frances says with a flash of her fine white teeth, is whether the money goes to the university with no specific instruction, or will it go to the canny Dean West, that he might exercise its use and build his Graduate School empire upon a high hill, some distance from campus? (For so it appears, Dean West wishes to establish a counter-campus of his own, to rival that of the president of the university who would preside over undergraduates, from Nassau Hall.) Mrs. Cleveland reports charges to me of "occultism" & "mesmerism" leveled against West by the Wilsons; while the tub-size dean remarks that he has experienced of late "uncanny vibrations of harm & ill-will" emanating from the president's house at Prospect; which foolishness caused the ex–First Lady & me to fall into fits of laughter. Frances is very handsome; very full-bodied; beside her, Puss feels scarcely <u>female</u>.

A striking woman who has been young in the eyes of her countrymen for so long, having married at 21 in the White House, Frances Cleveland is at last beginning to show the ravages of time; as a consequence, no doubt, of the bereavement of last year; the sudden death of her daughter Ruth; &

the daily & nightly task of <u>wife-ing</u>, as she calls it, the bejowled old 300-lb. Grover.

Ah, what it must be, Puss wonders suddenly, fearful—to be <u>truly a wife</u>?

_____ . One of my weak-minded days when I dare not venture downstairs. Scarcely the energy to change from bedclothes to <u>negligee</u>.

& have Hannah brush out my hair, & arrange my shawls. Already by 11 A.M. quite exhausted.

Recalling the old, ghastly days as a girl when I was obliged to be <u>corseted-up</u>, that I might gasp for breath, & stagger in mere walking. Those days long past, for Puss does not venture out, & is thus spared the whalebone torture all others of my sex must endure, save the tribe of invalids.

& this evening Horace knocked softly at my door, as he had heard from Hannah & others that Puss was feeling poorly. & brought me a small vase of bluets & wild columbine & a bowl of blueberries purchased from the Stockton farmers' market. & so we had a light tea together. & so it seems we have never been happier despite the Tragedy of 14 yrs before. As the windows darkened with rain Horace tried to cheer me singing snatches of nonsense tunes & lullabies & one of the sweet songs of our courtship days:

> *Ah! May the red rose live always*
> *To smile upon earth & sky!*
> *Why should the beautiful ever weep?*
> *Why should the beautiful ever die?*

_____ . Poor Puss naively wished a friendship with Mrs. Cleveland & now regrets her folly for it is in very questionable taste, such sudden revelations & unwanted confidences!—I am sick & headachey all this morning, & have swallowed too many of Dr. Boudinot's chalky white pills, recalling yesterday's exchange. For the ex–First Lady wrenched our conversation onto the topic of her (exceedingly boring) husband Grover, & asked of me if I had heard of a "collapse" at the Craven House, while they were visiting there two weeks ago this past Sunday; & what had Horace reported to me, & what was being said in town? "Adelaide, I must know what is being said of us. I cannot abide people whispering behind my back." For the first time I saw a shadowy down on her upper lip. Yet she is no less handsome to me. I assured her that nothing was being said & that no one in Princeton was more respected than Mr. Cleveland & she. This she seemed to wish to believe; & plunged on further, inquiring about what had been reported to me of the "ghostly visitation" & most curious of all, if I had, in my boudoir, at any time recently during the day or the night, imagined that I had seen the deceased Ruth?

(How desperate the poor woman, & how unsightly in her distress! If this be a grieving mother, I thank God that I had not ever given birth to any child, & never shall.)

Stammering I assured the distraught woman that I had not; nor had I dreamt of the child. All that I have heard, Mrs. Cleveland, is that your daughter was a most beautiful angelic child. Beyond that, I know nothing.

At this moment my little French clock prettily chimed the hour. I hoped Mrs. Cleveland might rise, & shake out her skirts, & leave; for her carriage awaited at the curb. (Had Puss the energy to walk, so short & idyllic a walk as that between Maidstone House & Westland, scarcely a quarter-mile, would be a great reward for the airlessness of this life; but such, unfortunately, is not for poor Puss.) Yet, Mrs. Cleveland did not leave. Instead, in a lowered voice she pursued the dread subject—explaining that since the morning of April 20, when Ruth (it seemed) appeared to her father, several persons had told Frances that they had seen, or dreamt of, her poor daughter: among them the Wilsons' youngest daughter, Eleanor, who had claimed to see Ruth's face pressed against her window pane on the second floor of Prospect House, in the middle of the night; her eyes "huge as a owl's" & her lips parted as if she sought to draw breath yet could not. The poor dead child had craved admittance to the Wilson daughter's room but Eleanor Wilson was too affrighted to act in any sensible way, & hid beneath her covers. "Of course it is only a dream," Frances Cleveland said bitterly, "yet it is very rude & vulgar of the Wilson's girl, to make such a claim for our Ruth; who never, in life, was a friend of hers; as Grover & I are not 'friends' of the Wilsons— hardly! Yet"—and here Mrs. Cleveland's tone softened—"Annabel Slade has reported a similar experience, in a lovely handwritten note to me, which I received just yesterday; & Lenora Slade's son Todd, that queer child, claims to being chased from room to room in his sleep by a girl with 'large staring eyes'—it must be our Ruth! I had thought, dear Adelaide, I know it may be foolish & hopeless, yet I thought to beg you, for all of Princeton marvels at your sensitivity: if Ruth comes to you, you will not deny her—but bid her, if you will, to come to me, her grieving mother, who loves her with all her heart, & has not forgotten her."

& so on, & so forth: some very awkward minutes passed before I roused my courage, & explained that I am a Christian woman, & did not believe in such phenomena as "spirits."

_____ . (I know, Madame Blavatsky would be distressed with me, to recoil in so conventional a way from one who had enlisted my solicitude; yet, it seemed to me then, I could not have the dead Cleveland child haunting my sleep, that was troubled enough most nights, & left me wrack'd with exhaustion in the morning. In life, I did not know Ruth Cleveland; scarcely do I know the Clevelands, & Horace did not at all approve of Mr. Cleveland's second-term presidency, which was something of a disaster & a scandal.)

(Unless: could the dead child be a _devi_?)

_____ . Feeling out of sorts & mean. Scolded Hannah, & made the girl cry. I fear that I have lost Frances Cleveland's friendship; & so rarely see dear Willy; & care for no one. (As for cousin Wilhelmina—I let drop in a greedy gossip's ear this afternoon that my young cousin is helplessly in love with Josiah Slade, while Josiah feels only "brotherly" toward her; this, Wilhelmina's secret, which sharp-eyed Puss has found out.)

_____ . (Another Princeton rumor, told to me by Caroline Fitz-Randolph, with a plea for secrecy: it seems that, his first year as a cadet at West Point, Lieutenant Bayard was chastised for violating one or another principle of the honor code; whether "cheating" in the usual manner, or in another, more ambiguous manner; or "plagiarizing" written material; or "intimidating"—"threatening"—another cadet: such details are not known. When reported by me to Horace the response was scarcely friendly: Do not speak of it, Adelaide. The young man was not expelled, & will soon marry into the Slade family.)

_____ . Confided in Caroline all that Mrs. C. had told me & begged me not to repeat; thus we shivered, & gripped each other's chill hands, & giggled in fright, over the "phenomena" of ghosts, spirits & apparitions that surround us. Throughout the visit Caroline was behaving strangely I thought—as if, when I was not observing, she were rocking an invisible baby in her arms—a most distracting sight; for almost, I could see the infant in its swaddling clothes, its eyes queerly pale & lacking in focus & lips wetly slack; a pathetic little creature, perhaps lacking a soul. & in this way I came to understand that Caroline had "had" such a baby, sometime in her life; & had "lost" it; & was now childless as Puss, but not nearly so content as Puss in this condition.

Though laughing with me, too—for Caroline is no fervent admirer of our ex–First Lady—then breaking off & clasped her (invisible) baby to her bosom saying chidingly Adelaide! It is wicked for us to mock, we must pray to God for forgiveness.

_____ . Horace who reads most voraciously in scientific journals as in the Atlantic & Harper's has said, the invisible spirit world is akin to the pathogene-world as hypostatized by Joseph Lister some decades ago, to account for disease. As you would not voluntarily venture into the pathogene-world for fear of great harm, so you would not voluntarily venture into the spirit-world.

_____ . Lower Witherspoon Street it is being said—a wild uninhabited area said to be a marsh—a most snaky, evil place—where the body was discovered. A young girl—it is said—& how horrific the words, that leave me faint—Where the body was discovered. This was several nights ago, it is being revealed at last. & all of Princeton whispers of nothing else save of course we ladies of the West End, & in particular we invalid Ladies above all, who are spared.

_____ . News has come to me, through Mandy & Caroline, of a "most ambitious if indiscriminate" tea at Pembroke House where Mrs. Strachan evidently spoke of the "new man" in Princeton—one Axson Mayte— whom it seems that everyone has met, for President Wilson has been introducing him to favored members of the faculty. Mrs. Strachan praised the man as "impressive, with a strong intellect"—especially for the law; Mrs. van Dyck thinks the man "cold & studied & not altogether a gentleman"; though my aunt Jennifer was adamant in declaring him a most judicious young man, in his verdict on the duel of Alexander Hamilton & Aaron Burr, Jr.—a legitimate duel in all ways, fought on New Jersey soil. (Our poor ancestor Aaron, Jr., whom the world condemns as having shot down "in cold blood" the revered Founding Father & Federalist Hamilton, Washington's Secretary of the Treasury! Yet it was Hamilton who had hoped to "rig" the dueling pistols, thus to allow him to shoot Aaron, Jr., through the heart; as fortune would have it, Hamilton fired quickly, & first; yet not accurately; so that, taking his time, the grievously insulted Aaron, Jr., could return his shot accurately. For which, why is Aaron, Jr., to be blamed? Had Hamilton shot <u>him</u>, would the world mourn? We Burrs have suffered enough calumny I think! It is time to defend our good name.) Praise to the stranger Axson Mayte who spoke quite reasonably along these lines, without the slightest knowledge, it is believed, that there were descendants of Aaron Burr in the company. I dearly regret I have not met this man, said to be a "most distinguished lawyer" from south of the Mason-Dixon Line.

_____ . Sickly & faint-headed & suffering from palpitations. Dr. Boudinot has prescribed another medication, that leaves my mouth quite dry & my heartbeat quickened. Read Mrs. Corelli's <u>The Sorrows of Satan</u> & felt quite strange afterward—as if the fever'd voice of the author were murmuring in my ears; grew quite restless with Mrs. Wharton's <u>The Decoration of Houses</u>; could not make sense of a single paragraph of <u>The Secret Doctrine</u>. VERY NAUGHTY PUSS slipped into Horace's library to take up the receiver of the "telephone"—our very new Bell 'phone—dialed the number of the Princeton police department & asked in a hoarse whisper if they had apprehended the "murderer in our midst" but quickly then slipped the heavy receiver into the cradle panting & gasping for air—my poor heart hammering. (For by this time I am reasonably certain, there was a murder, & doubtless worse perpetrated upon the body; & the body found in the marsh of lower Witherspoon, unless the wilds of Kingston by the canal & Millstone River; & the victim was <u>female</u>—but am not certain as to her age or other details of her life; having been still as a churchmouse overhearing the Negro servants chattering, as they will when they do not believe <u>we</u> are around. <u>Horace must not know.</u>

To cheer me, Horace read from <u>The Gentleman from Indiana</u>. He & Booth Tarkington having been in the same eating club at Princeton & the Glee Club & Triangle Club. I lay back laughing in the chaise longue, till suddenly I began to feel faint; then, suddenly vexed; I know not why, swept from the table all my medications, & a pitcher of water Hannah had only just brought me; half an accident, & half not. Horace was astonished as I wept, & wept; & Horace comforted me; though I thought him somewhat stiff & startled; & an air of weariness in his limbs, as he carried me to my bedchamber. When I inquired of him about Axson Mayte whom he had met that day at lunch at the Nassau Club, he spoke curtly: saying only that Mayte was not, in his eyes, a gentleman. And there was <u>something in his complexion & the shape of his nose, that was not quite right</u>. But when I begged him to explain, he would not. "You are in a state of nerves, Adelaide. I will give you your nighttime medication, it is time for bed." Gravely my husband spoke, & I knew not to confound him. For it is wisest not to confound them, at such times. Yet how unfair, when all of Princeton is buzzing with excitement, & every sort of news & gossip, at only 9 P.M. poor Puss's eyelids are drooping & soon—all spark of what Madame Blavatsky calls the divine spark of being is <u>extinguish'd</u>.

_____ . Disguising my handwriting to emulate that of Frances Cleveland, & using a dark-purple ink for which the lady is known, I wrote to PRESIDENT & MRS. WILSON, PROSPECT HOUSE, PRINCETON: <u>Dear President & Mrs Wilson you are very foolish people to believe that any in the community might favor you over the virile Andrew West. & you are not of good breeding tho' you persist in putting on "airs." & your daughters homely & "horse-faced" like their father & of most dowdy figure like their mother & in addition "buck-toothed." Sincerely, A Friend.</u>

This missive, in a plain envelope, stamped, I entrusted to Hannah, to run out & post in a box on Nassau Street, while on errands in town.

_____ . Horace in the city, visiting our broker at Wall Street; for there is some complications in his will, or in our joint will; of which I never think, for Dr. Boudinot has told me not to worry, in the slightest—"You will outlive us all, Mrs. Burr!" & by stealth & shy questioning like that of a maiden lady of ample years I put questions to Minnie, & to Abraham; as to Hannah, & one or two others; for it is known when a Negro lies to a white person, you can see deceit in their eyes for they are childlike & without guile, in their hearts. In so querying, I think that I have learned that the murdered girl was but eleven years old; father not known & mother a slattern who works at the Bank Street dairy. So there it is, after all my speculation! Poor child! Poor innocence!—for I am sure the child must have been innocent, being so young. Yet she was of a rough background & (it was hinted) of "mixed" blood. Such things will happen to such people, God have mercy on their souls.

_____ . "Mrs. Burr, please do not ask, no more, Mrs. Burr, please"—so Minnie begged, just this morning; when I summoned her to my bedchamber, to speak frankly to me as to the circumstances of the murder; & whether the child was "tampered with unnaturally." For this is crucial to know, for the well-being of all in the community. Tho' it is too beastly, & will only make me ill to learn. "All right then, Minnie, don't tell me," I said, wounded; adding, "But if some grievous harm befalls me, it will be on your head." Minnie began to quiver, & to shake; she is not so strong a woman as you would think, though the daughter of slaves out of Norfolk, & thus strong & reliable stock; yet, it is said she has not been well, with some sort of female illness of which it is best not to speak. Enough to know, I suppose, that there is monstrousness in our midst, in Princeton Borough.

_____ . A wild windy night & we two are cozy by the fire in the master bedroom, that Abraham has stoked & teased into a blaze. & Horace is less irritable, since his meeting with our broker; our wills have been drawn up, & I have signed, without taxing my eyes, as Horace advised, in attempting to read the arcane legal-babble. & the unease with the unions has subsided, I think. At least, Horace is not raging over it now. Innocently I inquired of Horace, has any progress been made in solving the murder?—& he seemed quite startled, that I knew it was murder; & did not consent to this knowledge, but spoke vaguely that he knew of no serious crime in the Borough, in recent years. Then taking up Mr. Tarkington's novel, & beginning to read; & I lay my hand on his wrist & begged of him, not to <u>condescend</u> to me; for I wanted to know the Truth, & would know the Truth, as all Theosophists must. & Horace said to me, with a laugh, that the only upset in Princeton of which he has heard, at the Nassau Club, was of some undergraduate pranksters again hammering down a section of Dr. Wilson's wrought iron fence, he had had built to surround Prospect House; for the boys <u>do</u> take offense, that the president & his family of females should seek privacy for themselves, in the very midst of the campus. ("Dr. Wilson is one of those persons," Horace has gravely stated, "who may one day succeed in impressing the world, but who can't be taken seriously in Princeton, New Jersey.") Later I fell into a headachey sulk, & scarcely consented to take my medicine from Horace's hand, & dear Horace sought to comfort me, & perhaps wished to cuddle; so I allowed him to lie on top of the quilt & to press his weight gently against me, but very gently—for Horace has grown stout these past few years. & some other exertions may have transpired on Horace's part, of which I took no heed; for already Puss's eyelids were drooping. "Do you regret it"—so I asked in a whisper, & the dear gentleman kissed my closed eyes—"do you regret your invalid wife, that never yet <u>has been</u> a wife, nor ever <u>shall be</u>" & he denied all emphatically, as he always does; & hummed a gentle little tune; & his curly mustache tickled, & I thought of the ravaged child in the marsh, & felt an exquisite pain in the very core of my being, & in the next instant—was gone . . .

_____ . Here is a surprise: there was no child of eleven murdered in Princeton, nor of any age. There were <u>two persons</u> said to be murdered— "executed"—for misbehavior & insult to their superiors—not in Princeton but in Camden, New Jersey. These persons, of whom I have been reading in the <u>Philadelphia Inquirer</u>, discovered by chance in Horace's study, were called <u>Jester & Desdra Pryde of Camden</u>. All that was done to them, or why, was not explained in the paper, in a brief article on page eight; but the sheriff of Camden County stated that, of 500 persons observing the executions, "not a single eyewitness" has stepped forward. It is an ugly story but too distant from Princeton for pity, I am afraid. & you would know from the intent of the article, that the <u>Prydes</u> were Negroes, & not white; & that they were punished for misbehaving of some sort, that might have been avoided by more discreet judgment on their part.

_____ . & so, there is no UNSPEAKABLE crime in Princeton after all, but, as Horace warned, a swirl of mere gossip. I am not sure if I am relieved, or disappointed. Poor Puss, misled!

I have put away Horace's newspaper where he will not know that it has been touched; & next is nap, & teatime in the late afternoon & ah!— B O R E D O M in gusts like airborne ether.

THE BURNING GIRL

One afternoon in late May, Annabel Slade, Wilhelmina Burr, and Annabel's cousin Todd were walking along the bank of Stony Brook Creek, at the edge of Crosswicks Forest; the young women were intensely engaged in conversation as the boy—(at this time eleven years old but looking and behaving like a younger child)—frolicked about, and shouted commandments to the Slades' dog Thor, who was accompanying the small party in their ramble.

"Thor, here! Thor, *obey*."

The boy's voice was sharp, provoking the dog to bark. The dog was a mature German shepherd with a gunmetal gray, whorled coat.

"Thor, *run*! Go!"

How noisy the boy was! And the handsome dog, that did not ordinarily bark, was barking now, excitedly.

Out of the May sunshine and into the splotched light of the forest the boy and the dog ran. The young women could hear their crashing into the underbrush, like a deliberate thrashing of sticks.

Annabel called: "Todd? Please! Wait for us."

Yet deeper into the forest the child ran, driving the dog before him.

Unless the dog was on the trail of some creature, and leading the boy forward in an ecstasy of blood-excitement.

"Todd! You promised . . ."

Vainly—laughingly—Annabel called after her headstrong cousin.

But Annabel was not truly complaining of Todd, her little cousin whom she loved dearly. His unfailing energy was a marvel to her, who was herself capable of walking for miles, in her good hiking shoes, in Crosswicks Forest and along the creek bank; nearly as far as the Craven house, and back again, on Rosedale Road. And Wilhelmina was an even more experienced hiker.

On this May afternoon the young women were very sensibly dressed for out-of-doors: Annabel in a blue-striped shirtwaist, with a high collar and a tight-clasped belt; Wilhelmina, or "Willy," in stylish Turkish trousers and a belted blouse. Annabel had tucked a water iris into the silken coil of hair gathered at the nape of her neck: a flower of extreme delicacy that mimicked the violet-blue of her eyes. Her straw sailor hat gave her a pleasing and piquant childlike air and, once out of the sight of the Manse, she had, in imitation of her bolder companion, lifted her chiffon veil off her face, for she found it confining, and disagreeably warm. "Mother worries about my 'fragile, English' complexion," Annabel said, "but I can't think that the sun will make an aged crone of me in a single hour."

"Not a single hour, but an accumulation of hours. *That* is the danger our elders perceive."

But Willy spoke lightly, dismissively. Annabel's schoolgirl friend had long cast off a daughterly reverence for her mother's cautious admonitions, and had a way of speaking so impetuously, Annabel had to laugh.

"Well. We must take the risk, then. After all, the century is very young—it will go on for a long time."

In Princeton circles, it was acknowledged that Annabel Slade and "Willy" Burr were close as sisters, though very different. While Annabel possessed the sylphid grace of a fairy-tale princess, unstudied and seemingly spontaneous, yet with a dreamy air, Willy presented a dramatic contrast: brash, brusque, heavy-jawed, with eyes that engaged too directly, and too often ironically. Willy's considerable charm was at first obscured, to the superficial eye, by a certain *stolidity* in her figure, as in her character. She was a brunette, with a somewhat dark, and very healthy, complexion, while Annabel was ivory-pale, with very fair hair, and very blond eyelashes and brows; Willy was more forceful, as Annabel seemed to glide; yet both young women were likely to be gay-hearted in each other's company, and to whisper together, and laugh a good deal. ("If only Dabney could make me laugh, as Willy does!"—Annabel said sighing.) Young men complained of Wilhelmina Burr that she was given to unpredictable—"unprovoked"—moods; she could not be relied upon, to turn up when she'd promised; if engaged in croquet, lawn tennis, or court tennis, she could not be relied upon to *graciously lose* to her male opponents, but seemed rather too intent upon winning; and, having won, was likely to express some satisfaction. Nor did Willy take care with her hair, or her clothes and grooming, as other young Princeton ladies did, conscientiously; Willy's "Turkish trousers" would have been appropriate for a girl-cyclist, or even a girl hockey player; the plain straw hat on her head looked as if it had been hurriedly clamped in place, with no effort at charm. Willy had cast her gloves away, or had lost them; and carried over her shoulder, like a vagabond in an illustration, a canvas bag into which her sketch pad, pastel chalks, and other art supplies had been thrust. Her high-necked blouse was white cotton, with limp throat-ruffles, and cuffs just perceptively soiled.

Poor Wilhelmina, who struck the eye as distinctly disadvantaged, beside her beautiful friend!—for Mrs. Burr was always nagging at her, and complaining, and worrying that no one would ever wish to marry her, except for her family's position and wealth. (Willy had "come out" in New York a year before Annabel but had, as yet, received only a scattering of unacceptable marriage offers, from either young men of no fortune, or young men of no family: which only amused the young woman, who commented that she looked forward greatly to declining an "irresistible" offer, like a governess in a romance novel, for the splash it would make in Princeton circles; but was being prevented by Fate.) So little did Willy care for feminine adornment, or for her own feelings, she did not take offense when Todd Slade, earlier in their walk, had presented his cousin with the exquisite water iris but gave to her a sprig of white baneberry, with the remark: "*You* shall have this, 'Willy'—for it is said to be poison; and Todd senses, how you dislike him." Indeed, so far from being offended by the boy's curious, stiffly uttered words, Willy laughingly accepted the sprig from him, and tucked it into the chignon at the nape of her neck.

IT IS TIME to acknowledge that Mrs. Adelaide Burr, "poor Puss," had not been entirely misinformed, regarding an UNSPEAKABLE crime in the Princeton vicinity; and this not the ugly episode in Camden, New Jersey, but the disappearance of a young girl of thirteen, sometime during the night of April 30, out of her parents' home on the Princeton Pike, about midway between Princeton and Trenton; after a search, the body of *Priscilla Mae Spags* was found floating in the Delaware-Raritan Canal, not far from the family home; though details concerning the nature of the crime were unclear, either because law enforcement officers did not wish to release them, or knew very little. Nor was there any mention of the sordid crime in the weekly Princeton paper. Trenton authorities had acted with commendable swiftness in apprehending and interrogating, in Trenton, a male of "unfixed" address, an immigrant from eastern Europe who handily provided them with a signed confession—signed, that is, with crudely executed initials, for the wretch seemed not to know how to read or write English, or speak English very coherently, nor seemed even confident of his birth date!

So it was, or seemed, that the danger of further unspeakable outrages may have abated in the area; certainly, there should not have been any danger in the forested property belonging to the Slades, that stretched for several miles along Rosedale Road. (Crosswicks Forest, as it was locally known, and the adjoining countryside, were posted against all trespassers, of course; any hunter or poacher among the locals would have been very brash indeed, to set foot on the Slade property, and to risk the hot temper of the Slade gamekeeper, a close acquaintance of the county sheriff.)

The young women strolled briskly, yet with their arms linked, as was their custom; trying not to be nettled by the commotion of Annabel's young cousin and Thor rushing ahead into the woods; calling out to him, not chidingly, for like a part-bridled young horse the boy balked at being scolded even by Annabel whom he adored, but sweetly—"Todd! Please try to stay in sight, will you? Don't make us fret over you"—even as the boy shouted back to them, out of the forest underbrush, of the "devils" he and Thor were scaring up—"witches"—"trolls"—the famed "Jersey Devil" itself;* then, with diabolic slyness, doubling back and rushing at them from

---

* The Jersey Devil is a legendary creature whose natural habitat is the Pine Barrens of South Jersey, reputedly a seven-foot predator bird/reptile with a long neck and a long, very sharp beak and sharp talons. Historically, the Jersey Devil is said to be the thirteenth child of a witch named Mother Leeds, or, in some documents, Mother Spags, living in the Pine Barrens at the time of the Revolutionary War. (Yes, it is a coincidence, this repetition of the name "Spags"—the sort of awkwardness historians encounter more often than the layman would suspect. But there is no "meaning" to most coincidences, as I am sure there is no meaning here.) The Jersey Devil has been sighted hundreds of times in the twentieth century alone, and has been the object of many amateur searches; the Devil leaves behind enormous bird-feet prints in snow and mud, and mounds of scat so vile-smelling, dogs have been known to vomit, even to convulse and die, that have come imprudently too near. In 1909, the Jersey Devil was sighted in numerous areas in New Jersey and Pennsylvania, near the New Jersey border; most frequently in Camden, where, according to newspaper reports, the Devil "attacked" a group of worshippers at the First Methodist Church of Camden; and later, in another part of Camden, a social club. (By which is meant a gentlemen's private club? Or, perhaps, "social club" was a journalist's euphemism, indicating a tavern or saloon.) Camden police officers allegedly fired upon the Devil at this second sighting but the Devil escaped by taking flight over the Delaware River, resulting in such panic in South Jersey, schools and government offices were officially shut down for several days, until it appeared that the Jersey Devil had returned to the desolate swamp of the Pine Barrens. At

behind, with Thor noisily barking at his heels, meaning to frighten them; and indeed, to a degree frightening them. In a high-pitched singsong voice Todd demanded of the tensely smiling young women: "The Jersey Devil asks: What is round, and flat, and blank, and *tells no lies?*"

" 'Round, and flat, and blank, and *tells no lies . . .'* "

Unlike her brother Josiah who was skilled at riddles, as at charades, and other parlor games, Annabel was at a loss at such times; and sought to deflect the boy's intensity by brushing his damp hair from his fevered forehead, and picking burrs from his clothing, and declaring that his riddle was "too difficult" for her—which caused the boy to react in frustration, to gnash his teeth, leap into the air and clap his hands loudly; Annabel was accustomed to such childish tantrums, and only tried to laugh, while Willy shrank away, that the antic boy might not stumble into her. (It was true, as Todd sensed, that Willy did not quite share in Annabel's indulgent affection for him.) And now Todd confronted Wilhelmina: "What is round, and flat, and blank, and, for you especially, *tells no lies?*"

Willy tried to smile, as one tries to smile at the over-bright, unsettling children of relatives or friends; she offered the boy a fig bar which he accepted from her, and devoured within seconds; then rudely declared that, though she was "Willy" she had not the "wit" to solve a riddle. In childish contempt Todd said: "It is a mirror, Miss Burr. A mirror, and you know it. You big Burr: mirror. The reverse side of a mirror, its back. Like *your* back, telling no lies, as a face does. Now, give me another fig bar! Thor and I are hungry."

Annabel protested: "Todd! You must not be rude."

Todd said, "*You* must not be rude, the two of you, to pretend not to know my riddle."

---

the time of this writing, in 1984, the Jersey Devil endures still in legend, but has not been sighted, except by unreliable children and adolescents, in some time. For a detailed history, see *The Jersey Devil* by James F. McCloy and Ray Miller, Jr. (Middle Atlantic Press, 1976).

So mercurial were Todd's moods, however, he soon quieted after de-vouring the second fig bar, which he broke in half to share with the eager German shepherd; and insisted that Annabel and Willy stop where they were, for it was time for a story—had not Annabel promised Todd a story, if he was good on their walk; and he was sure that he had been good, for he and Thor might have been *so much less good*.

The young women had not intended to sit down just at this time, or in this place; but Todd found for them some exposed, gnarled tree roots, that formed a kind of seat; so they sat down, beside the quietly flowing Stony Brook Creek, and Annabel took out of her straw bag a children's book, to read to Todd that tale of Hans Christian Andersen's which was Todd's favorite, "The Ugly Duckling"; and taking care not to intrude, Willy sketched her friend in pastels; for she very much wanted an intimate por-trait of Annabel as she was before her wedding, to keep as a memento; as Willy felt, for some reason, that she would lose her closest friend once the young woman became Mrs. Dabney Bayard and lived in the old Craven house.

(Yes, it is strange that Todd, at eleven years of age, would request being read to, as if he were a very young child; but Todd did not easily "read," claiming that letters and numerals were "scrambled" in his eyes, when he tried to make sense of them.)

At the end of the story Todd clapped his hands and declared that when *he* became a swan, he wouldn't be so kind to the ducklings who had mocked him—"For Todd has a very good memory for wrongs, and will not forget or forgive his enemies." Which provoked Annabel to say, in repri-mand: "But once you are a swan, Todd you *will* be a swan, and have a swan's code of conduct—that is, you will be manly and noble."

"But will Todd be *Todd*, then?"—the child's query was couched with some anxiety.

"Why yes! Of course."

Resting in the grass, the boy considered this statement of his cousin's, with an air of mock gravity; but responded then in typical Todd-fashion by rolling onto his back, kicking frantically, and protesting in a high-pitched whine as if he were being tickled, or attacked, by an invisible adversary.

(POOR TODD SLADE!—the reader may be curious about him, particularly in the light of developments to follow; for surely of the "accursed," Todd was primary.)

Through Todd's first two years he had seemed to be displaying superior traits—(walking, talking, even "reasoning" to a degree)—of a precocious sort, but then, for no reason anyone could know, he had seemed to "regress"—as if wishing to remain an infant a little longer, and a particularly difficult infant displaying flashes of brightness, even brilliance, amid much else that was infantile. In stature Todd wasn't below the average for a child of his age, being in fact somewhat tall; but his frame was peculiarly under-developed, and his head over-large, and his feet so poorly coordinated that he was always stumbling, or falling down, to the dismay of his parents and the derision of other boys. Yet more puzzling, Todd often reached for things that were *not there*—but rather a few inches to one side. The more futile his behavior, the more frustrated and impatient he was.

Todd particularly upset his father Copplestone, a man of shrewd business acumen, and financial success in trade; who prided himself on his speaking and writing abilities, as he had been head of the Princeton Debate Club, and a popular "man on campus" during his undergraduate years; and who could not bear it, that his only son "refused" (as Copplestone put it) to learn to read, and write; and was so stubborn as to hold a book several inches to one side of his head, or even upside-down. This "prank" as Copplestone judged it was especially infuriating, and had to be met with discipline—"Why, the child is either a devil, or harbors one," Copplestone would declare to Todd's weeping mother, after one of their father-son contests, which, in the matter of sheer lung volume, and franticness of behavior, Todd triumphed, sending Copplestone charging out of the room.

(Yet it was said, perhaps irresponsibly, that, in private, Copplestone applied "discipline" to his unruly son: whether by hand, or switch or belt, is not known. Certainly, Winslow Slade was not known to have disciplined his sons Copplestone and Augustus, nor even to have raised his voice to them when they were young.)

Yet Todd would not learn his ABC's, still less arithmetic, despite the efforts of his father and of numerous tutors; with the result that, by his twelfth year, his family had given up forcing him, and had become reconciled to the boy's stubbornness, obstinacy, or whatever it might be called. (Later, when Todd was older, after the trauma of the Curse had run its course, it would seem that he could "read" and even "write" after a fashion; even, it was claimed, that Todd was "above average" in many respects; for Todd was enrolled in the Princeton Academy, when I entered first grade there in 1911, and must have been taking regular courses.) Though prone to temper tantrums, Todd could also behave very sweetly; he had long been taken up by his cousin Annabel as a favorite; and even, from time to time, by Josiah, who lacked his sister's patience for their young cousin. (Josiah was most frustrated that, in board games like checkers and chess, Todd often won; not because Todd was a superior player but because Todd so shamelessly and skillfully cheated, with a touch so light he was rarely caught. "He will make a brilliant politician at Tammany Hall, where money evaporates in plain air," Josiah said, "if, unlike some at Tammany Hall, he can stay out of jail long enough.")

Wilhelmina instructed herself that Todd Slade was only a child—*only* a boy of eleven; yet she feared something precocious and penetrant in his gaze, and halfway wondered if the child might be possessed of clairvoyant powers. For one Sunday at Crosswicks, a few months before this time, Todd made his way through a gathering of adults most deliberately to Wilhelmina, to shake her hand gravely and offer his condolences in a low, insinuating voice; saying that, as Josiah was absent from the party, Miss Burr was condemned to a "mere mastication of tasteless food" and the "auscultation of tuneless music"—a statement so preposterous out of the mouth of a child, Willy could scarcely believe what she'd heard. Then, when the impish lad repeated his words, eyeing her with a semblance of genuine sympathy, she flushed crimson, and found it difficult to breathe, to realize that Todd Slade knew—(could it be general knowledge through Princeton?)—the secret of her love for Josiah Slade.

But I have not told anyone! Not even Annabel.

Following this, Wilhelmina felt very cautious about Todd Slade, yet grateful to him, he had not divulged her secret to any other person, so far as she knew.

So it was, Todd still wished to be *read to,* and not *to read;* and Annabel liked to indulge him, for it made him happy, as if he were a child of but three or four, to be so easily made happy. After "The Ugly Duckling" Todd requested "The Hill of the Elves," an old nursery favorite, and after that "The Snow Queen"—which Annabel hesitated to read, for reasons of her own. Yet Todd so persisted, kicking his heels against the ground, and rolling his eyes back into his head, that she had no choice but to give in; but her voice seemed thinner, and her manner less animated, and after a few minutes Todd grew bored, and hummed, and sighed, and began to yank out clumps of grass to toss at Thor, and excite him. When Annabel read of the little boy's sleigh ride with the Snow Queen, and of how they "flew" over woods and lakes, over sea and land, while beneath them the cold wind howled, and the wolves cried, and the deathly snow glittered, Todd nervously yawned, as if *he* were indifferent to such terrors; and at last knocked the storybook out of his cousin's hands!—then, before the startled Annabel could protest, he leapt to his feet and ran in the direction of the forest, driving the excited dog before him, both child and dog barking with a crazed sort of elation.

Wilhelmina said, "Annabel, you've spoiled your cousin. He will only get worse, if you persevere."

"But—what would I do? What would any of us do? Todd is—as Todd *is.*"

"Are you so sure? That is a way of giving up on him, you know—for he can never become an adult, nor even a young person in high school or college, if he is so indulged."

Surprisingly, Annabel didn't deny this; but, her sweet face unpleasantly flushed, and her eyes shimmering with tears, she did no more than shut the storybook, and let it fall.

"Yes, you're right, Willy. This is my reward."

When, afterward, Willy examined her sketch of Annabel she discovered that her friend's likeness was so shadowed with worry, and melancholy, and some queer insinuation of the cynical—(in a curve of Annabel's lips)—she didn't want to show it to her, and thought it most prudent to fold the sketch quickly, and hide it in her bag. Seeing this, Annabel asked, with a hurt little laugh, if the drawing was so *very* hideous; and Willy said, "Yes, it is, a bit—but the failure is the artist's, and not the model's. I will try again, soon—another time."

The young women resumed their stroll, following Todd into the forest; though, a mood of gravity having overtaken them, they were not now inclined to walk arm in arm.

After several strained minutes Willy said, in a voice low and chastened with emotion, "Annabel, I hope you won't 'drift away' from me— and from other friends, who love you—after you and Dabney are married. Sometimes I fear you are already 'drifting away'—for, unless I've been imagining it, you've been a little distant, and distracted, lately, at least in my company . . ."

Quickly Annabel protested: "Willy, that is untrue! You are my anchor—you and Josiah. I will never 'drift away' from either of you—I swear not to lose either of you."

Willy smiled, hearing her name so coupled with Josiah Slade's name; and remarked only that it struck her ear as odd, that Annabel should swear she *would not lose* her brother, or her oldest friend—"Which makes me think that you are somewhat troubled, Annabel?—and hesitant to speak?"

Again quickly Annabel protested, with a little laugh: "Willy, *no*. You are beginning to tease and torment me, now. Maybe we should change the subject?"

"Of course. Consider the subject changed."

"In my heart, Willy, in my soul—*I am not troubled in the slightest. I am— very happy...*"

But Annabel's voice so suggested otherwise, Willy turned to her, slipping an arm around her waist: "Dear Annabel, what is it? Please tell me."

"I've told you—there is nothing to tell."

"Where I love, you know I don't judge. Is it something between you and Dabney? Has it to do with—your parents? Are there no words, dear Annabel, to express what you are feeling?"

"No words," Annabel said softly, with a sigh, "—no words."

The young women were following Todd and Thor into the forest, at a little distance. By degrees their conversation was shifting into a tone compatible with sun-dappled shade, or shadow, as they left the open sky behind. Willy said that she was feeling just a little hurt, that Annabel wasn't more confiding in her; after all, she had confided in Annabel many times, since they'd become "fast friends" in fifth grade at the Princeton Academy for Girls. "To whom would you speak, Annabel, if not to me, your closest friend?"

Annabel laughed. Without mirth, and with an air of vexation.

"Why, maybe with your aunt Adelaide, of whom such things are said, of an 'accident' on her honeymoon."

"My aunt Adelaide? But why?"

"Because—such things are said of her. And of the 'accident' on her honeymoon."

"Why do you speak of it?—no one knows what happened. At least, I don't. Within our family, such things are not spoken of."

"What I don't understand, Willy, is: was there an accident in travel, or at an inn where the honeymoon couple was staying? And the 'accident' has been irrevocable?"

"An 'accident,' it has always been said, of an 'unspecified sort.' I believe it happened in Bermuda, or on the cruise ship bound for Bermuda."

"And so, your aunt Adelaide is both a 'married woman'—and yet, in many respects, a mere 'girl'—not so much older than we are, in essence. And her figure is unaltered, for she has not borne children. And she and her husband are so very close, it's said—they remain a romantic couple."

"Yes, so it's said. I find it difficult to talk to Horace, however—as he, with me."

"So that one doesn't know if Adelaide Burr has suffered a kind of tragedy," Annabel said, musing, "or a kind of blessing."

All this while, Annabel was turning the diamond heirloom engagement ring on her finger, where it fitted her loosely.

For several minutes the young women walked together, in a brooding silence; though ahead, Todd was shouting to Thor, and Thor was barking; and there came wafting out of the interior of the forest a subtle brackish odor, where the land sank into a sort of bog.

"Todd? Where have you got to?"—so Annabel called, without much expectation that her young cousin would answer her.

More quickly the young women walked now. There was a sort of path into the woods, which gradually broadened, to spread out in all directions, soft, yielding, and springy beneath their feet. Willy exclaimed how delightful it was, to walk here—"It feels as if I am floating, weightless."

Annabel laughed, startled. "Yes—'weightless.'"

But something was catching at the hem of Annabel's shirtwaist, and at the petticoats beneath. To her dismay she saw that the hem of her pretty blue-striped dress was both torn and soiled; the undersides of her frilly white petticoats were quite filthy. With a little sob she brushed at the dirt, then let her skirt fall back into place and said, as if the thought had only just struck her, "Please don't think that I am crazy, Willy—and please don't repeat this—but I've often wondered why it is that sisters and brothers can't continue to live together, after they are grown; not eccentric old bachelors and old maids, but—perfectly normal people!

Why is it, the world so insists upon *marriage*? Since I was a girl of twelve, I swear my mother has thought of little else, for me; every female relative in the family has been *plotting*. When I'd hoped to be a children's book writer, or illustrator, or artist—that was all they said to me: maybe, after you are married, and have your own children, you can take up a 'hobby' like that. But no boy or young man who wants to be a writer or an artist—or a musician, or a scientist—is told that he should take it up as a *hobby*, why is that?"

"For the same reason that we are not 'allowed' to vote. We are but second-class citizens, though residents of the same United States of America as our brothers."

"Father has explained, female suffrage is 'redundant'—a woman will vote as her husband votes, or, out of willfulness, she will vote against his vote, thus canceling it. In either event, the female vote is wasted."

"Hardly! We will want to try it, first."

"But why is it, sisters and brothers are not encouraged to live together? Entire families might live together, as they used to do, in the past? I will feel so—alone—strangely alone—with just Dabney; as he will feel alone with me, I think. And, as you know, there is no one quite like Josiah, for getting along with people—at least, with me. We have no need even to talk, much of the time; we are quite happy being quiet together. Whereas, with Dabney, there is a need to be always talking—nervously . . . Which leads me to wonder," Annabel said, in a rapid low voice, "why it must be, we marry strangers, and dwell apart from our loved ones. D'you know, my cousin Eleanora, who lives in Wilmington, was married a few years ago, and nearly died giving birth to a husky big boy, for she'd had rheumatic fever as a child, and her heart had been strained; and it's said, she and her husband live together now *as sister and brother*, and no one feels obliged to criticize them. Yet it seems, if an actual sister and brother, related by blood, were to establish an independent household, society would look upon them with much disapproval, and disdain. How unjust, Willy, and how illogical!—do you agree?"

Willy murmured a feeble assent. (For she did not like the drift of this conversation, or its one-sided vehemence.) Adding, with girlish wistfulness: "Only think, we three might all live together, in such a household, if we'd lived in a happier time—for instance, at Fruitlands, or Oneida, or in the Shaker community. Why can't 'sister and brother' be expanded to include 'sisters and brothers' in the plural?—there being no harm, surely, in that."

So, Willy had spoken: brashly, recklessly, and irrevocably!

Feeling the need now to press her hands against her warm cheeks, to cool and soothe; for she had grown unpleasantly warm, in the sun-splotched shade of the forest, with its damp, springy forest-bed; her hair felt disagreeably damp, coarse as a horse's hair, at the nape of her neck. And why had she thought her "Turkish trousers" so chic, that were now stippled with burdocks, and muddied at the hem?

The young women paused, and Annabel plucked at the burdocks on her friend's clothing, as on her own. Gnats, mosquitoes, and tiny stinging blackflies had begun to swarm, in the forest interior. Fretfully Annabel said: "Yes, Willy—you are right. Yet, it is too late—for me. I have fallen in love and am damned—I belong now to another, in body as well as spirit—and neither Josiah, nor the dashing Lieutenant, can save me: not even *you*, dear Wilhelmina."

IT WAS AT this moment that the young women made their discovery, that Todd and Thor were nowhere in sight; though the boy's shouts and laughter, and the dog's wild barking, seemed to be echoing from all directions of the forest.

Annabel led the way deeper into the forest, calling her cousin's name; then, faltering, she surrendered the lead to Willy, who led them in another direction, calling out: "Todd! You are very bad! Why are you hiding from us? Come out at once!"

After some stressful minutes, as the young women made their way ever more deeply into a soft, sinking, bog-like part of the forest, into which Stony Brook Creek evidently emptied, at last they sighted Todd at the same moment, in a sort of clearing, in which gigantic logs lay in a jumbled profusion; the logs being ossified, it seemed, and formidable as fallen monuments. The sunshine that fell slantwise into this open space, having taken on the peculiar quality of the great forest, did not seem, somehow, a natural sunshine, or the light of the sun itself, but rather a queer, silvery, lunar effulgence, unsettling yet not entirely disagreeable.

There Todd stood, his head lowered, and his wild dark hair rising in tufts above his pallid face; but though both Annabel and Willy called to him, he seemed not to hear; nor did Thor leap up from the lichen-bed in which he lay, to approach them with his tail wagging, in his usual manner.

The young women then noticed that Todd was not alone in this strange space: but there stood before him, engaging him in earnest conversation, a young girl unknown to either Annabel or Willy, of slender proportions, indeed wraith-like, with long and unruly dark hair, and a round, dusky-skinned, sharp-boned face; and dark eyes that seemed to blaze with passion. The girl was very coarsely dressed in what appeared to be work-clothes, that had been badly soiled, torn, or even burnt. The fingers of her right hand appeared to be misshapen, or mangled. Most remarkably, small flames lightly pulsed about the girl: now lifting from her untidy hair, now from her tensed shoulders, now from her outstretched hand!—for the girl was reaching out to Todd, as if to grasp his hand.

More remarkably still, around the girl's neck was a coarse rope, fashioned into a noose; the length of the rope about twelve feet, and its end blackened as from a fire.

And ah!—how the girl's topaz eyes blazed, with vehemence!

Was the hellish vision a trick of the sunlight? Did Annabel's and Wilhelmina's widened eyes deceive them? The flames pulsed about the girl, and rippled, and subsided; and flared up again, lewdly vibrating, tinged with blue like a gas-jet, at their core; so subtle, in hellish beauty, they might have been optical illusions, or mirages, caused by some fluke of the fading light.

"Todd! Come here . . ."

In a faltering voice Annabel called to him, but Todd gave no sign of hearing.

For it seemed that Todd had fallen under the spell of the demon girl, and could not rouse himself to flee from her, as if not comprehending what the pulsing blue flames might mean, or the coarse rope around her neck; or the danger to him, as she came very close to touching him, caressing him, with her burning fingers, and he did not shrink away.

"Todd! It's Annabel—Annabel and Wilhelmina—come to take you home. *Todd!*"

Yet, was the burning girl not most mesmerizing?—though dusky-skinned, with a flat, slightly thick nose, and thick lips, and unruly and unwashed-looking hair tumbling down her back; and those uncanny luminous eyes; and the noose around her neck, that must have been uncomfortable, for it seemed tight enough to constrict breathing . . . It might have been that Todd believed the girl to be his own age, yet a closer look suggested that she was considerably older, at least the age of Annabel or Wilhelmina, a young woman and not a girl.

And there was the German shepherd Thor so strangely stretched on the lichen-bed a few yards from the feet of the burning girl, muzzle extended, ears pricked into little triangles, eyes adoringly fixed upon the girl—why was Thor not barking but only just panting, audibly, as if he had run a great distance to throw himself down, as if in worship?

When Annabel and Willy, clutching hands, ran forward, with little shrieks of concern, the burning girl turned to them, with an expression of rage, dismay, and anguish; now, a paroxysm of flames whipped over her figure, to obliterate her entirely; and, in the blink of an eye, as if she had never been, the *burning girl* vanished.

"Todd! Thank God, you are unharmed!"—so Annabel cried, rushing to Todd, to embrace him; and quite shocked, when Todd wrenched himself from her, and fixed upon her a look of angry contempt.

"Here is Cousin Annabel," Todd began to chant, in the singsong that so maddened his father, "who has come too soon; here is Miss Willy, who has come unbidden; here is Todd, who had at last found a friend in the forest, but who has lost his friend—poor silly Todd, left all alone."

Most alarmingly, the German shepherd, who had known Annabel since he was a puppy, and had known Wilhelmina Burr nearly that long, had leapt to his feet and was growling deep in his throat, ears laid back and hackles raised, and formidable teeth exposed as if—(could this be possible?)—*he failed to recognize the distraught young fair-haired woman and her dark-haired friend.*

AUTHOR'S NOTE:
THE HISTORIAN'S CONFESSION

Though it is the rare historian who will speak candidly of such matters, all of us who are engaged in the rendering of the past—by way of the amassing, selection, and distillation of a multitude of pertinent facts—are commonly beset by two dilemmas: the phenomenon of *simultaneity of event*, and the phenomenon of the *authenticity of evidence*.

In assembling my materials for *The Accursed: A History of the Tragic Events of 1905–1906, Princeton, New Jersey,* which has been an effort of decades, if not my entire life, I have been forced to eliminate a great deal, that the reader will not be distracted by an excess of information; yet it would be disingenuous of me to pretend that, as my narrative moves forward in the mimesis of a "fable," with its focus upon certain key individuals, the others are arrested in a kind of frieze, and refrain from thinking, feeling, speaking, and acting—indeed, in participating in History. While I write about Annabel Slade, Wilhelmina Burr, and Todd, in Crosswicks Forest, it is certainly the case that Woodrow Wilson, Winslow Slade, Adelaide Burr, Josiah Slade, the Clevelands, Lieutenant Bayard, and all the rest continue their lives uninterrupted, with no awareness that the "focus" has shifted elsewhere; as they have not the slightest awareness that they are participants in a chronicle of a time long past as an historian labors to illuminate the pathos of their situation. But, as I am confined to a linear chronology, and to the exigencies of print, how otherwise can I proceed? And even should I wish to include in this chronicle everything that transpired in Princeton, at this time, how could such a Herculean undertaking be accomplished?

So, though I am tempted to examine certain scenes of unusual interest, which would surely throw some light upon the chronicle, I can't, but must pass quickly by, with regret: for here is the partly clad Woodrow Wilson lying sick upon his bed, upstairs at Prospect; writhing in gastric agony, after a grand luncheon at the Nassau Club in honor of President Teddy Roosevelt; an event that exasperated, frustrated, and finally maddened the sensitive president of the university, who could not bear to hear such fulsome boasting, and such lurid accounts of animal-slaughter in the West; as the distraught Ellen Wilson hovers over him, administering what medicines the suffering man will take, and praying that her husband will not die!—all this, nearly on the eve of the Slade-Bayard nuptials of 4 June, in which their dear daughter Jessie will play so prominent a role. Mutters Mr. Wilson through tight-clenched teeth: "He is crass. He is vulgar. He is a buffoon—a bully. He does not respect me. He condescends to *me*—in Princeton of all places! *It is insupportable*." (Thus the president of Princeton University, on his ill treatment by the President of the United States.) As elsewhere, a sorry scene unfolds:

"Mr. Ruggles, I am sorry. The contract was for one year, as you know. It will not be renewed."

"But—why not?"

Somberly the chair of Classics shakes his head.

Why? Why not? Questions impossible to be answered, it seems.

"But—I'd thought—I mean, I was led to believe . . ."

The young man appears to be genuinely shocked. He has had a lively and productive teaching experience, he believes, as a preceptor in Latin; indeed, Yaeger Ruggles has devoted much of his time to act as a kind of personal tutor for a number of his undergraduate students, grievously deficient in Latin.

"The boys have all learned a great deal. Several have told me, particularly . . ."

"Mr. Ruggles, thank you."

" . . . even their parents have expressed gratitude, and have sought me out . . ."

"Unfortunately the contract will not be renewed, as I have tried to explain—we're so very sorry."

"But—who is 'we'?"

Somberly still the white-haired chair of Classics shakes his head, with a look of muted pain. As if to inform the astonished and deeply wounded young man *Do not ask. You will not be told. You are being expelled from our great university and there is no re-entry.*

"Sir, how can you treat me so unjustly?—so unreasonably? On what grounds are you firing me?"

"Mr. Ruggles, you are not being 'fired.' Your contract is not being renewed, that is a very different matter. There have been anonymous reports, you see."

" 'Anonymous reports'—but—"

"Mr. Ruggles, please close the door on your way out, I beg you."

Shortly thereafter, in another scene of ignominy, Yaeger Ruggles is summoned to the austere book-lined office of the head of the Princeton Theological Seminary, Reverend Thaddeus Shackleton, who informs him, in much the same somber and implacable tone as the chair of Classics, that it is believed to be "for the best of all concerned" if Mr. Ruggles departs the seminary at the conclusion of the spring term, which is the following Monday.

"But, Reverend Shackleton—why?" Yaeger Ruggles demands. "What is the reason? How have I failed? You must point out to me the ways in which I have failed."

Ruggles's first year at the seminary had gone "exceptionally well"—his instructor in Ancient Languages of the Bible had been ful-some in his praise for the young scholar, and his instructor in Minis-terial Duties had predicted that he would make a "very attentive and responsible" minister one day soon. In his second year, academic reports had continued strong until March, when there was reported to be a "de-cided falling-off" of his work at the seminary, including even a number of unexplained absences.

"The seminary is confronted with many more applicants than there are openings in our school. We have a waiting list of more than one dozen—who are quite as 'deserving.' And so, unfortunately, Mr. Ruggles . . ."

"But, I don't understand . . ."

"It is not given to us, Mr. Ruggles, to 'understand.' We must have faith, and we must prevail."

In a haze of incomprehension the young man staggers away. So wounded, an observer from a short distance away might have discerned a limp in his walk.

He would not have betrayed me—would he? My cousin Woodrow . . .

At Nassau Hall, Yaeger is curtly informed that President Wilson is not in his office. And that his appointment schedule is so filled for the remainder of the week, it will not be possible to see him.

Yaeger protests: "But—I am a cousin of Mr. Wilson's, from Virginia. He knows me. He would want to speak with me."

His name is taken, by the president's secretary.

"Please tell Mr. Wilson—there has been some terrible misunder-standing. He will know what I mean, I hope. Tell him—Yaeger will not give up!"

A mile away, at Maidstone House, Mrs. Adelaide Burr has fallen asleep reading *The Secret Doctrine*, and wakes from a light and unsatisfying nap to see, or to imagine that she sees, a face pressed against her bedroom window: a dark-skinned child-wraith, bold, impetuous, with features dis-tended by rage, or by hunger; a stranger to Mrs. Burr, for she bears no relationship to anyone Mrs. Burr has ever seen. Yet, before Mrs. Burr can draw breath to scream, the creature vanishes, with the unspoken hint, that she will return soon.

And here in the nursery at Mora House, at 44 Mercer Street, a half-mile from Maidstone, Mrs. Burr's young cousin Amanda FitzRandolph is interrupted in the midst of nursing her infant son Terence, disturbed by a footfall, or a sigh, or a shadow, or—could it be?—the diaphanous figure of a man gliding by a mirror on the wall. Turning, and hugging her baby to her bosom, Mandy sees nothing, and hears nothing; knows herself alone with Terence, except for servants in another part of the house; yet is so beset by a fit of trembling, she must lay her baby back in his cradle, to prevent dropping him, or hurting him—for there is a moment of confusion when it seems to Mandy that her baby is no longer Terence but another, stranger's baby—his nose broader than Terence's dear little nose, his lips fleshier, his thin dark baby-hair coarser, and the very tincture of his baby-skin cloudier. A fit of vertigo overcomes her. A thought assails her *Edgerstoune would not do such a thing to me.* Beside the rarely used fireplace in the bedroom there is a wicked-looking poker, Mandy's fingers yearn to wield, but she resists, she will resist, stooping to soothe the fretting infant, whispering, "Why it is nothing, Baby must *sleep*."

Close by, in a distinguished old Colonial house at 99 Campbelton Circle, Miss Wilhelmina Burr stares at herself in a full-length bedroom mirror, as a French seamstress kneels at her hem to make adjustments in the pale pink satin dress she will be wearing in Annabel's wedding; her critical eye absorbing little of the appealing vision in the glass but fastening, with a cruel sort of intensity, upon *defects*—in face, figure, person. Wilhelmina is not in a "Willy" mood today—her "Willy"-self is dependent upon others, like Annabel, and Josiah; alone, she is but Wilhelmina, the daughter of parents who cannot seem to look at her except with disappointment, for she is not a beauty; and she is not the sort of charmingly submissive, sweetly acquiescent young woman whom lack of beauty might reasonably yield. Nor does Wilhelmina take note of her dress, its long graceful skirt edged in a double row of ruffles that rise to the front, to mesh with a set of delicate pleats, all of which is flattering to her somewhat angular figure. To the contrary, the subdued young woman, forced now to draw breath to accommodate the gown's narrow waist, feels suddenly that she might burst—must burst: feels that she is in danger of weeping, or laughing, or crying in despair, or whispering words of profanity. (This, sometimes in her sleep, Wilhelmina finds herself doing, such foul words! such unexpected words!—that, in daylight, Wilhelmina scarcely knows.) For the imminent wedding of her closest friend throws into humiliating relief her own loneliness. *Josiah does not love me, and will never love me.*

At most, Josiah is "fond" of Wilhelmina, whom he calls "Willy" with the casualness of a cousin, or a brother; he is admiring of her intelligence, and her skill at croquet; yet, he has not truly looked at her in years, she is sure. In their last conversation, Josiah had spoken eagerly of his new, numerous plans—(to study philosophy in Germany, to travel back west or rather north, to the Arctic; to join the Young American Socialists League, in New York City)—not one of which will involve Wilhelmina Burr.

As Wilhelmina had been a very good schoolgirl and had memorized many passages from Shakespeare, she has absorbed enough of the great poet's keen insight into human nature to know that while intense hatred might reverse itself, and erupt as "love," mere fondness can never. And Willy can never be a sister to Josiah as Annabel is—there is no competing, in Josiah's affections, with Annabel.

Not hearing a query put to her by the seamstress Wilhelmina continues to stare at herself in the mirror, as if astonished by her own singular ugliness; perhaps it would be better, kinder, for her to fade away, like Ophelia; to remove herself from the Hamlet of her obsession, who has no obsession for *her*. Thinking, with a vindictiveness that is not characteristic of her good, generous nature, how she would like nothing so much as to possess, for even a brief period, that mysterious power over the male species that young women like Annabel Slade wield, in their very innocence and beauty; for what, in her unhappiness, does Wilhelmina care for her supposed intellectual and artistic talents, if no one loves her; if Josiah Slade does not love her. Her heart beats rapidly with the mean wish that Josiah might be wracked with bitter jealousy over *her*, for her appeal to a rival-gentleman. *Then he would suffer as I have suffered. We would be well matched for life.*

Somewhere near this hour, in the vast lecture hall in McCosh, on the Princeton University campus, Professor Pearce van Dyck is interrupted in the midst of a lecture on Kantian ethics, to turn aside from the lectern and cough into a handkerchief; Professor van Dyck has been suffering from a mysterious allergy, or infection of a lung, for several weeks, intermittently; the malady does not appreciably worsen, yet it does not go away; as some fifty undergraduate men stare at him in a fascinated sort of pity, Professor van Dyck coughs, coughs, coughs; tears shimmer in his eyes, behind his wire-rimmed glasses, and threaten to spill onto his cheeks as in desperation he tries to clear his throat; tries to wrangle, out of the depths of his lungs, or his sinuses, whatever viscous substance it is, that threatens to choke him; until at last the young preceptor, who sits in the front row, rises to his feet, to approach him in trepidation—"Professor van Dyck? May I help you?"

As, on Nassau Street, at Witherspoon, Dean Andrew West encounters the dark-brow'd and richly dressed Mrs. Grover Cleveland, shopping in town with one of her daughters, and accompanied by a Negro maid; and engages in several minutes' amiable conversation with the lady during the course of which a subtle sort of flirtation ensues; or, rather, the semblance of a flirtation; for neither Andrew West nor Frances Cleveland feel any genuine attraction for the other, except a "social" attraction; Andrew West learns that Mr. Cleveland's health has been "fully restored"— Grover has so recuperated from his nervous prostration of several weeks before, he is now able to take his customary breakfast, which Mrs. Cleveland delights in reciting, for such is proof of her husband's well-being: beefsteak, Virginia ham, pork chops, whiting, and fried smelt; even, occasionally, corned beef and cabbage, while he perused his usual fare of several newspapers—"For Grover is very *O current*, you know; it is his very life's-blood." All this while, Andrew West listens with an air of extreme interest, for it is the man's dean-temperament, to make the most of any opportunity. So it is, Mrs. Cleveland says, turning the ivory handle of her sunshade, "that the rumors that have been circulating in Princeton, about Grover, are entirely unfounded; and I hope, Mr. West, you will do your part in combating them."

According to the diary kept by Henrietta Slade, Winslow's daughter-in-law, Dr. Slade is, at this hour, sequestered away in his favorite corner of the *jardin anglais* at the Manse, immersed in one of his scholarly pursuits; whether work on Biblical translations, or labor at assembling his old sermons, or scribbling entries in his journal—(this journal to be, unhappily, destroyed in the spring of 1906)—she does not know; but Henrietta does note a "troubling change" in her father-in-law, who had always been of an even, placid disposition, as well-disposed to his family as to his public, rarely irritable or even fatigued or distracted; but lately, Winslow has been "not himself"—quite irritable, fatigued, distracted; and less inclined to spend time with his family, or with friends in the habit of dropping by to visit him in his library, than he had been. *Perhaps he is anxious about the wedding, for so many people have been invited. Perhaps he is worrying about the weather, for an outdoor fete is planned here at the Manse.* And Henrietta, mother of the bride-to-be, drifts onto pages of fretting about the wedding, of very little interest to History.

And Josiah Slade makes the impulsive decision to join several friends bear hunting in the Poconos, though it is but a few days before his sister's wedding, in which he is to play a prominent role. "But what if—something happens to you?" Annabel asks, pleading; and Josiah says laughingly, "Nothing will happen to *me*, I promise," and Annabel says, "You will return, won't you? The night before? No later? Josiah? "—almost begging her brother, *You will return, you won't leave me alone to this—will you?*

And handsome Lieutenant Dabney Bayard, being fitted in an

Egyptian cotton shirt, and slim-tapered trousers, chances to note, out of boredom, a small black insect on the neck of the Italian tailor kneeling before him; idly he reaches down to pinch the thing in his fingers, and give it a sharp dig with his nails, with the result that the tailor screams in surprise and pain, and lurches away from Dabney—for the black speck isn't an insect but a mole or tiny wart, deeply rooted in the man's flesh.

THE SPECTRAL WIFE

On the humid morning of June 4, 1905, which was the very morning of the Slade-Bayard nuptials, young Upton Sinclair, who lived with his wife and infant son in a ramshackle farmhouse on the Rosedale Road not so very far from the old Craven estate, had walked several miles into town, badly needing to stretch his legs after a long stint of writing; and, knowing nothing of the wedding, and nothing of the principals except, dimly, the name *Slade*, with which the young Socialist naturally associated the extremities of capitalist exploitation of the masses, he chanced to see, on Nassau Street, a stream of stately motor vehicles and horse-drawn carriages, as in some sort of royal procession—"Not a funeral, for there seems to be no hearse. A wedding?"

For some minutes, Upton Sinclair stood on the sidewalk gazing at the conspicuous opulence on display: for the motor vehicles arriving at the First Presbyterian Church of Princeton were exclusively luxury touring cars, of such manufacturers as Pierce-Arrow, Lambert, Halladay, Buick, Cadillac, and Oldsmobile; the fittings were all of brass, very smartly gleaming, as the windshields were of gleaming glass. And the horse-drawn carriages, which were fewer each year, being inexorably displaced by motorcars, here exuded an air of the timeless and romantic, very smart too. Upton, who owned neither a motorcar nor a horse, looked on with an abashed smile, for in his subdued state of mind the young Socialist wasn't roused to indignation, but rather to a kind of envy—not of the opulence, but of the evidence here of families, and couples. Here was the ruling class of the province, Upton supposed; yet, when you considered them, they were a tribe comprised essentially of families; and at the heart of each, a couple.

It was a *bourgeois* social institution: the family, and at its heart the couple. Yet, Upton considered it with much wistfulness.

His own marriage, his own dear wife Meta—ah! how troubled, and how precarious, lately; Upton had walked into town, rather than borrow a horse and buggy from his neighboring landlord-farmer, to escape the confines of his writing-cabin and the confines of his brain, lately obsessed with his marital dilemma to the detriment of his creative energies.

For Upton dearly loved his wife: yet, he knew that such love is hobbling, and enervating; and not worthy of the Socialist ideal. And he knew that such love can be precarious, based upon a bedrock of sheer emotion, and not the intellectual rigor of Marx, Engels, and other Revolutionary thinkers.

In the open air, that was just slightly over-warm, and distinctly humid, Upton brooded upon his wife: her unhappiness, her desperation, her mysterious *change of personality*, in the past several weeks. How was he, in his mid-twenties, untutored in the skills of marriage and parenthood, to contend with such an alteration? Just the previous night after a botched dinner she had prepared in the ill-equipped farmhouse kitchen Meta had been weeping angrily, and then weeping hopelessly; declaring that she "could not go on, but prayed for the strength to be delivered from her misery"; to the horror of her husband, Meta had dared to press the barrel of a revolver against her forehead, and could not be persuaded to surrender the weapon to Upton for at least ten agonized minutes.

At this time, their infant son was sleeping in his cradle in the next room.

So, the immediate crisis had passed. But Upton was left stunned, demoralized and confused; as dazed as if he'd been struck a blow to the head with that very revolver, that his wife had brought with her when they'd married. (That is, Meta had brought the weapon with her in secret, that had belonged to her father, an ex–army officer whom Upton had not yet met.)

Yet, Upton was resolved to go about his domestic duties, and fulfill his Saturday's shopping and errands in town, as if nothing were wrong; for his wife's moods were so mercurial, it might well be that, when he spoke with her again, later that day, nothing really was wrong, and Meta would have forgotten her distress of the previous night.

Still, she had come to dislike the "idyllic surroundings" in which the young couple was living, in the countryside near Princeton; and each meal prepared in the bleak kitchen with its wood-burning stove and hand-pump sink, was a plunge into the unknown, as each effort of nursing a colicky baby was fraught with the possibility of disaster.

"I think that I am not a good mother," Meta had begun to lament, "as I am not a good revolutionary. If this were the French Revolution, I should be guillotined." Her humor was senseless, to Upton. Her laughter was harsh, and upsetting—not the sweet throaty laughter of the young woman with whom Upton Sinclair had fallen in love, only two years before.

The future, which had seemed so promising to Upton, was now uncertain; like the progress of Socialism in the capitalist societies of Europe and America, precarious and somewhat haphazard, unpredictable as a vast game of chance. It was evident that reform was needed on every side, from the shame of child-labor in factories throughout the entire country, to the debased and dehumanizing conditions of the Southern Negroes, whose lives were hardly improved from the slavery of their grandparents. Yet, how should he and his fellow Socialists confront such a massive entity? *Had he the requisite courage?*

Brooding upon these matters, Upton lost track of time; it was like him, to lapse into a sort of waking fugue, from which the baby's crying or his wife's sharp voice would wake him, scarcely knowing where he was. On the Nassau sidewalk, he was being jostled by pedestrians, who stood about gazing and gaping at the now shut front doors of the First Presbyterian Church across the street, where the private wedding ceremony must have been in progress. The stately procession of motor vehicles and carriages had ended; the select wedding party was all inside the church, it seemed.

"I hope they will be happier than Meta and I have been. I *hope* it isn't the institution of marriage that is the dilemma, but only just our passing—transient—moods . . ."

There was a murmur in the crowd, as, across the street, the wide white doors of the church were flung open; and a young woman in a wedding gown and a man in formal attire quickly descended the stone steps—could this be the bride and groom, so soon? The young woman wore a wedding gown of dazzling silken-white beauty, with a long train that trailed against the grimy pavement; the gentleman, a formal coat and tails, and white gloves, and a high top hat that gave him a grotesque sort of height, like one on stilts. Despite the elegance of their clothing, this newlywed couple moved with an air of clumsy haste, even of urgency, as if in flight; climbing into a brougham that awaited them at the curb, a carriage of another era, drawn by four horses—four! (And each of these horses a splendid specimen, Upton saw—purely black, with high heads, braided manes and tails, and not the smallest patch of white at their forelegs or ankles to distract the admiring eye.) Such was the young Socialist's somber mood, he failed to respond in his customary way to this display of capitalist greed, but sadly wondered how so lovely a young woman, probably not twenty years old, should have been aligned with a gentleman so singularly repulsive!—the bridegroom being at least three times her age, squat-bodied, flaccid-faced, with a face like a toad's.

Upton, who kept a journal hidden away beneath the floorboards of his writing-cabin, rehearsed what he would write there, when he returned home; for very few minutes of the young writer's life were "lost"—that is, would fail to be converted into useful prose, for future reference, if not for publication.

> *Revolutionary theory isn't required to reason that such a marriage is a forced one. The bride has been SOLD—like chattel. Shame to her family, and to all her tribe! For all her youth and angelic beauty, she shall soon regret her life.*

ONCE IN MOTION, afoot, Upton soon lost himself in the very mundane nature of his errands, making his way along crowded Nassau Street, along Chambers, and Bank, and Witherspoon; frequently consulting his notes for the morning: flour, sugar, cornmeal, eggs, soap, bread, tea, barbershop, library—this last underscored several times, for Upton was immersed in a Civil War novel of "Socialist ideology," and had come to reside near Princeton University primarily to use the university's special historical archives. (Does it strike the reader as ironic, that Upton Sinclair of all persons should wish to peruse the library holdings of Princeton University, while inwardly denouncing the institution as a bastion of Caucasian privilege; still more, that such covert behavior contradicted the secret principle of Socialism: NO COMPROMISE WITH THE ENEMY.)

How Upton Sinclair, author of the youthfully ambitious *King Midas* and the misguided creator of the hoax-experiment *The Journal of Arthur Stirling,* came to live near Princeton, New Jersey, is a complex tale on the surface; yet, beneath, fairly simple—being penniless, after the failure of his first two books, he had entered into a financial arrangement with the wealthy Socialist George D. Herron, in which he and his family would be supported at thirty dollars a month, in surroundings very different from their pestilent garret room in New York City, while Upton labored at a Civil War trilogy destined to convert the masses to Socialism. The first novel, *Manassas,* was completed; the second, *Gettysburg,* was well under way; with

Appomattox yet to come: the very pinnacle, Upton believed, of Socialist vision. Neither Upton Sinclair nor his sponsor Mr. Herron could doubt that the trilogy would have a vast popular appeal, if the masses were made aware of it, and urged to read it; for had not Jack London a remarkable success, with similar "popular"—"adventure"—materials. Though there was always frustration in trying to convert the downtrodden, who clutched to their hearts the delusions of the ruling class as if such delusions could be their own.

The dilemma is, in the United States, each penniless citizen believes that, with luck, he might become a millionaire; and so doesn't want to put restraints on "robber barons"—he might become one, one day!—so Upton mused, and would inscribe in his journal that night.

On such matters Upton had often lectured Meta, in the early months of their marriage. Particularly, Upton was given to quoting Nietzsche's Zarathustra—*Only where the State ends, there begins the human being who is not superfluous.*

Though Upton knew himself ideologically estranged from Princeton, indeed an enemy alien in its midst, nonetheless he and Meta had several times strolled, on twilit evenings, along leafy Prospect Street, in order to overhear undergraduates singing in their palatial eating clubs— "Why, the boys sound like angels! How is it possible?" Meta exclaimed; or in the yet more sumptuous West End of the village, where great old houses from Revolutionary times were to be seen: Maidstone, Mora, Pembroke, Arnheim, Wheatsheaf, Westland (said to be the home of ex-President Grover Cleveland, on Hodge Road) and, not least Crosswicks Manse, dimly visible from Elm Road. Taking care not to be swayed by the architecture of these grand houses, or the society to which it belonged; for all wealth sprang from the labor of others, wage-slaves to the machine. This would come about, Upton said, when the "historic phase of classes" had completed itself. So, while Meta listened, Upton lectured her on the threefold dialectic of Marx and Engels, the St. Simonean concept of class struggle, and the Smith-Ricardo labor theory of value; and those eminent predecessors frequently cited by Marx and Engels: Fourier, Owen, Feuerbach, Hegel. It couldn't have been an accident, Upton said excitedly, that both Marx and Darwin published revolutionary books in the single year 1859; nor an accident in his own life, during a period of despondency when he was working his way through the City College of New York, a copy of Nietzsche's visionary *Thus Spake Zarathustra* fell by chance into his hands—"In an hour, my life was changed." For it seemed clear to him, as to an increasing number of contemporaries, that the future would see Zarathustra as the true savior of mankind— "The Jesus Christ of bourgeois Christianity being discredited."

Closing his eyes, so moved, Upton recited for Meta several exhilarating passages of *Zarathustra,* that couldn't fail to sway anyone of sensibility; ending with the thrilling words—" 'A free life is still free for great souls. Verily, whoever possesses little is possessed that much less: praised by a little poverty!' "

To which Meta said, "Then we are much praised, I guess! For we are more than a little poor."

WHY HIS YOUNG WIFE wept so much, and allowed herself to sink into sickly depressive states, Upton didn't know, for his temperament was entirely different: he liked to think of himself as a *go-getter.* So he felt constrained to lightly chide her, for her immersion in *the self-serving throes of private life* while the Revolution was in the making, and needed all their energies. Wasn't there the prospect of the Good Time Coming, when the working class would go to the voting polls, and overthrow the existing bourgeois government, and seize the means of production, and precipitate the *classless* and *stateless* society which Marx had predicted? "No matter how poor we are, or how much we are made to suffer, so long as we know the future, Meta, that is enough."

"But we don't 'suffer' nearly as much as most people," Meta said, hesitantly, "like Negroes, and the poorest immigrants. And we can *read*—there is always the prospect of escape, through books."

"Books are not a means of 'escape,' Meta! Books are a means of knowledge, and of learning how to cope with the future."

Upton had spoken curtly, for, though he often lectured Meta on the particular injustices endured by Negroes and by poor immigrants, he did not like her to seem to contradict him when he was in his idealist mood.

He'd been surprised and gratified—very surprised, and very gratified—by the unexpected response his novelistic exposé of the Chicago stockyards, *The Jungle*, was receiving in its serialized form in the Socialist publication *Appeal to Reason;* the editor himself had expressed amazement at the newspaper's mounting sales, and predicted more remarkable things for the future. (Upton hadn't wanted to over-excite Meta and raise false hopes, but several New York publishers, including the capitalist bastions Macmillan and Doubleday, had expressed interest in publishing the novel in book form; and it had begun to seem not merely a fantasy, that Upton might soon have the means to pursue cherished goals: producing a play, founding a magazine, organizing a Socialist society in Brooklyn.)

It was true that the "idyllic romance" of the New Jersey countryside had turned somewhat sour, for life in the ramshackle old farmhouse was arduous, though conditions had been much worse when the young couple and newborn son had to spend their first Princeton winter in a tar-paper-insulated cabin heated by a single wood-burning stove and all were freezing, and sickly much of the time. (If it had not been for the charity of the landlord-farmer and his wife, little David might have died of the croup; but on the coldest, most bitter nights, the young Sinclair family was invited to sleep in the farmer's house, where it was reasonably heated, if not precisely "warm.") Now, though they were living in a farmhouse of their own, it was a very primitive dwelling, with a roof that leaked, and rotted floorboards, and mice that scrambled about inside the walls; and it was so, Upton's nerves were unusually sensitive to the baby's near-ceaseless whimpering and crying, that distracted him from his concentration. And so, in warmer weather, Upton returned to the tar paper cabin, to work in solitude, on the ambitious *Gettysburg*. (So devoted was Upton Sinclair to his work, he'd resolved never to spend less than twelve hours a day at his desk, with the unfortunate but necessary consequence that Meta was obliged to milk the cow, that had come with the farmhouse; and deal with a flock of mangy chickens, that yielded very few eggs; and attempt to protect the meager fruits of a small orchard and garden from armies of worms, insects, and slugs that infested them in overlapping shifts. Upton sympathized with Meta's frustration, as with her exhaustion; but he did not condone her frequently voiced despair—if they were to one day help found a Socialist colony it would be in a rural environment, and so the present farm work was excellent training.

Upton was made to feel guilty, thus to feel resentful, when Meta complained of being "lonely"—and "bored"; for hadn't she Upton, and little David, and the farmer's wife to speak with; and any number of Socialist comrades with whom she might correspond, as Upton did, daily. But, Meta pleaded, she yearned for a change of scene, even for the small novelty of riding in the "moth-ridden" surrey into town; yet strangely, Meta often became over-excited when dressing "for town," as Upton was clumsily hitching up the mare, and declared that she couldn't come with him after all—her breath was too short, or her heart racing, or a "trouble in her womb" had flared up. (At this time, Meta suffered from a malady of the female reproductive organs, a result of the fourteen-hour labor she had endured in the poorly staffed maternity ward at Bellevue, for which she'd been advised, by a Socialist comrade-doctor, to take Lydia Pinkham's Compound, and avoid red meats. And not to become pregnant again until she was in stronger health.)

Yet, there was the hope of Revolution to come—soon. The probable date was now set for 1910, by Socialist theoreticians whom Upton Sinclair most respected.

FREQUENTLY IN THE months following Upton's adventures in the Chicago stockyards and slaughterhouses, the young writer succumbed to vivid recollections of those days, that had passed with the swiftness of fever-dreams; going about his errands on the morning of June 4, 1905, he was struck anew by the folly of the *bourgeoisie* surrounding him, on Princeton's streets and sidewalks, how these well-to-do individuals resembled beasts doomed for slaughter, all unknowing of their fate. Five years until the Revolution! It would not be *heads rolling* but *fortunes gone up in smoke, tribal delusions exploded.*

Yet, Upton felt a sharp disparity between these individuals and himself: for he wore workingman's clothing, trousers of some plain inexpensive fabric, a faded shirt; a frayed straw hat on his head, pillaged from the farmer's barn. And the citizens of Princeton were so well dressed! Only a very few, who must have been common laborers, and most of these dark-skinned, wore clothes like his; house servants of the well-to-do were better dressed, in their fresh-laundered uniforms. He had spent two months in Packingtown, in Chicago, living among the slaughterhouse workers, and badly missed it now. *In such places the hellishness of the class struggle is evident to the naked eye while here in gilded Princeton you must delve beneath surfaces, to see with an "uncanny" eye.*

These entries Upton would make in his journal, faithfully each night. One day, the multi-volume *Journals of Upton Sinclair* would be read by the masses, he hoped.

Making his way along the Saturday crowds of shoppers on Nassau Street, trying to keep his thoughts vibrant and optimistic, nonetheless Upton found himself thinking obsessively of the scene of the previous night: Meta sitting at the rickety kitchen table, revolver in hand, the long barrel of the weapon pointed at her head—indeed, pressed against the pallid skin at her temple. How vulnerable the poor young woman had looked, at such a moment! It was more telling than nakedness; Upton had wanted to turn his eyes away. He would never forgive Meta's crude soldier-father for giving his daughter such a weapon, or allowing her to take it from his household, for what purpose Upton couldn't guess. (He didn't want to think that Meta's father believed that Meta would need protection from *him*.) Her thin cheeks had been streaked with tears; her hand visibly shaking; in a flat hopeless voice she spoke of the contempt she felt for herself, as a "bad mother," for her failure in being able to pull the trigger.

A terrible sight, Upton would never forget. And would find very hard to forgive.

"She is the mother of my son. The poor boy must never know."

Distracted, Upton found himself gazing at his lanky reflection in a shop window: a kind of scarecrow, with a battered-looking straw hat. To care little for appearances is very different from being made to realize how eccentric one looks, in the public eye. Like a vagabond he was carrying a few items, his recent purchases, in a contraption that consisted of two wheels, with a vertical carrying-case and handle-bar. He saw that he was standing at the window of Joseph Sweet's Confectionery on Palmer Square, facing an opulent display of peppermint sticks, *petits fours*, caramels, bonbons, and glistening candies; most elaborately, chocolates fashioned into ingenious shapes (baby chicks, soldiers, bears, even miniature musical instruments and dirigibles)—another display of what Thorstein Veblen called *conspicuous consumption*. To one who, like Upton, avoided all rich foods, as well as meat, such a display was fairly sickening to behold. Ah, he wanted to step inside the shop, to protest! To point out to the proprietor, the clerks, the smiling customers, what a waste such luxuries represented, what vanity, when in nearby Trenton and New Brunswick, not to mention the wretched sweatshops along the Delaware River, children as young as five or six labored for fourteen-hour days, for mere pennies. Did the citizens of Princeton not know—did they not *care*?

Upton had not read firsthand accounts, but he had heard of a particularly sordid incident that had taken place in Camden several weeks before: a public lynching, of a young black man and his sister, executed by white-clad hooded figures of the dread Ku Klux Klan and observed by as many as five hundred persons crowded into a field. Sequestered in the Princeton vicinity as he was, Upton had no way of learning more about the incident, except through letters sent to him by New York comrades, that dealt primarily with other matters. It was significant to Upton, *no one in the Princeton area with whom he had spoken knew anything about this outrage*. Yet, just the other day, the President of the United States, Teddy Roosevelt, had visited Princeton, as the houseguest of wealthy political patrons. He regretted that he hadn't found out more about Roosevelt's visit, and picketed outside the residence in which the President had stayed. One day, he would be a martyr to the Revolution—arrested, beaten by police, charged with trumped-up acts of creating a public disturbance, public lewdness, treason. *The true Revolutionary does not wait to be called, but seeks his destiny himself. His faith is his courage.*

It was at that moment, as Upton turned, that he happened to see, in one of those accidental moments that can alter a life, his wife Meta across the square—somehow, Meta had come into town after all, leaving the baby behind? with the farmer's wife?—was this possible?—though in the next instant, as the young woman moved on, in the company of another person, Upton halfway doubted it could be she. This young woman, though resembling Meta in startling respects, including even her wavy honey-colored hair, and a pert little straw hat identical to Meta's, was wearing a long flounced skirt in a floral design, which Upton might have recalled from the days of their courtship; but which he had not seen on his wife in some time. At the farm, Meta wore shapeless clothing, sometimes a man's clothing—for appearances did not matter, obviously, in their new bohemian life. His eyes had to be playing tricks on him, Upton thought. And when he squinted across the busy square, a moment later, the honey-haired woman had vanished.

Even so, Upton felt faint with emotion. If Meta had made her way into town without him, it was an act of virtual infidelity—deceit. And to leave little David behind! He wondered how it had happened that his marriage, entered into with such romantic sentiment and Socialist idealism, had turned sour; had become a *trap;* for him no less than for his wife. Yet it was a trap whose bars were human beings, a woman and an infant son whom he loved more than his own being. *Unthinkable that we can part. Yet, how can we continue to live together? And if—if we suffer another "error"—and bring another innocent child into the world* . . .

So Upton brooded, crossing busy Nassau Street onto the university campus, and so to Chancellor Green Library; into the dignified, high-domed reference room, where, as in the past, Upton felt a thrill of joy—for the hopeful young author had no doubt that books might change the world; his model was Charles Dickens, as well as America's great author Harriet Beecher Stowe whose *Uncle Tom's Cabin* was popularly credited with having precipitated the Civil War!* And so why should it not be Upton Sinclair who should take his place among the great authors of Western civilization? Frankly, Upton had grown secretly bored with the fustian melodrama of his Civil War trilogy, though George Herron purported to find the first novel "thrilling"; but, as he was contracted to finish it, he would; for Upton Sinclair was a man of integrity, even, at times, as his wife charged, a foolish sort of integrity. What he most yearned to do was begin another novel like *The Jungle*—an "incendiary bomb of a novel" as it had already been called by his Socialist comrades—that would advance the cause of social reform in the world. The entire United States—if not the entire world—would be forced to take note of him: for his targets were the Beef Trust, and the Railroad Trust, and the Oil Trust, and the shameful "profits" (as a Socialist wit called the evangelical "prophets") of bourgeois religion; Upton

---

* It is a popular misconception, that President Abraham Lincoln said, upon being introduced to (the very petite, and very unprepossessing) Mrs. Stowe, "Here is the little lady who started the great war!" Thus the reader is made to think that a single individual, in this case a female novelist, might help direct the course of history for the better. Thus the reader is made to smile, as one might smile seeing an affable dog staggering upright on his hind legs. The historian is one who must expose and correct such misconceptions, in the service of authenticity.

was taking on also the hypocrisy of American "public education" and the sham of journalism itself, in particular the "yellow" gutter press of Hearst. Though he was only midway in *Gettysburg*, with the great bulk of *Appomattox* yet ahead, Upton had already begun to plan two new novel projects, satirical attacks upon the arts in a bourgeois culture, to be titled *Mammonart* and *Money Writes*. For it was certainly true, as the prophet Zarathustra preached, *Rather be angry than be put to shame. And if you are cursed, I do not like it that you want to bless. Rather join a little in the cursing.*

By nature, Upton was a gentle person, and had never "cursed" in his life. But, he was determined to learn.

ANOTHER TIME, crossing Washington Road after having spent several fruitful hours in Chancellor Green Library, amid toiling and serious-seeming undergraduate boys, Upton saw, or seemed to see, his wife Meta on the farther sidewalk; this time, she was wearing a cream-colored frock Upton didn't recognize, and she was in the company of a tall gentleman in a linen suit, a total stranger to Upton. Yet, the young woman was certainly Meta: the chestnut-red curls escaping from beneath her wide-brimmed straw hat, the pert uplifted profile and the "Scots" coloring to her cheeks, that had been pale these past several months. And, for a scant moment, it seemed that she had glimpsed *him*.

Unless Upton was light-headed from having eaten very little that day. And quite the fool, to imagine that his adoring young wife was deceiving him with a stranger.

Yet he stared after the couple, making their way in the opposite direction; the young woman carrying a yellow sun-parasol, and her arm casually linked through the arm of the tall gentleman; and after a long moment roused himself, to stagger in the direction of Witherspoon Street, his last stop before returning home.

Though it went against Upton's principles to dine out, since restaurant food was shockingly expensive, and not likely so nutritious as meals prepared at home, Upton thought it might be a good idea to fortify himself at the Knight's Court Tavern on Witherspoon Street; otherwise he might be susceptible to light-headedness and hunger pangs. Entering the unpleasantly smoky interior of the tavern he tried not to notice the undergraduates at most of the tables, for he was obliged to dislike them, even to detest them, as scions of the wealthy who attended college as if it were a country club and theirs by hereditary privilege. (While Upton had toiled away at part-time jobs to put himself through the City College of New York amid an eager, at times frantic swarm of immigrants and immigrants' children of whom many were exceptionally intelligent, and unabashedly ambitious and opportunistic. But they were the sons and daughters of the proletariat, generally, and so he did not resent them.) Upton had heard surprising things about Woodrow Wilson's hope to reform Princeton University, particularly to raise academic standards, which were far below those of Harvard and Yale at this time, let alone the fabled English universities upon which the American Ivy League universities were modeled.

As an undergraduate, with no family income to support him, Upton had lived in unspeakably impoverished conditions. Yet he did not regret his experience, for it was at that time he had converted to Socialism, and felt a powerful kinship with all workingmen, the victims of the capitalist juggernaut. By contrast, these Princeton students, many of them sporting the cocked hats of their clubs, were deprived, in a sense, of this kind of knowledge, and had no comprehension that the bourgeois way of life was in fast decline; that they and their families were doomed to early extinction; that the Apocalypse close at hand would usher in a new era. Ah, the New Jerusalem to come!—when all men and women of all races and colors should know themselves *kin,* and never again *enemies.*

It was not yet known how the Revolution would develop. But Upton supposed that the arguments of the philosophical anarchists were most convincing: society would fragmentize into independent, self-governing communities of mutually congenial individuals, requiring no police, no army, no guardians of morality, and no government. The old Deity being dead and dethroned, Humankind would come at last into power. And the Proletarian, transformed, would teach its former class enemies the virtues of self-restraint, charity, communal sharing, and contempt for greed.

In the bustling tavern, Upton ordered cheese, dark bread, and a glass of milk from the bemused waitress and sat lost in such thoughts, that had the effect of consoling him. Then, as the young male voices on all sides were so loud, gay, and fired with the myriad enthusiasms of youth, he couldn't help eavesdropping; hearing excited news of a recent crewing victory over Brown; crude and jocose commentary on President Wilson and his "family of females"; and rumors that a "coal-black nigger" had been detained, as the possible murderer of the young Spags girl; except that a prior detainee, an immigrant from eastern Europe, had signed a confession to Trenton police, this newer detainee was believed to be the actual murderer, and not the other. (Discussing the Spags murder, of which Upton had heard only rumors, the young Princeton undergraduates were indignant and incensed; several of them infuriated that a "coal-black nigger" should defile a white girl, and yet voices were raised in his defense . . .)

At this news Upton frowned, and lowered his milk glass to the table. The abduction and murder of a young girl in the Trenton-Princeton area had greatly frightened Meta, and had originally inspired her to take the Smith & Wesson revolver out of its hiding place in a closet, and see that it was properly loaded. But now it seemed that the murderer might not be apprehended after all: very likely, considering the integrity of the local police, an innocent man, or men, had been detained and questioned and made to "confess." Mixed with the smells of beer, ground beef, and corned-beef hash, which boys at a nearby table were consuming, and the pervasive odor of smoke, the atmosphere of the tavern grew increasingly oppressive; Upton felt a wave of revulsion for the meat-eaters, who had not the slightest awareness of what they were eating: neither its true nature, that of suffering terrified animals, and the debased nature caused by the meat-packing industry. He passed a trembling hand over his eyes and for a moment seemed to smell again the raw, rancid, sickening and yet strangely sensual odor of the stockyard-slaughterhouses in which he'd lived for two months. The odor of blood, guts, animal excrement, raw flesh, and animal terror . . . The very air alive and shuddering with the stench of living creatures turned into mere flesh; screams of animal panic, and horror; the eyes of sentient creatures bulging in terror of death, tongues protruding . . . *The hog squeal of the universe* Upton Sinclair had called it, in his novel; shrieks mounting to the very Heavens, that paid not the slightest heed to their sufferings. And if humankind were aware of this suffering, there was an easy way to assuage guilt—*They are only animals*.

As it had been argued by Southern Christians, that black slaves did not feel pain, like the white race.

Feeling ill, Upton pushed aside his part-eaten meal and staggered from the tavern. He wondered if he'd hidden the revolver carefully enough in the hay barn, that Meta could not find it; then, unaware of any contradiction in his thoughts, whether it had been wise to hide the little box of bullets beneath the crude floor of his cabin, where dampness might corrode them.

BY THIS TIME most of Princeton was buzzing with the scandalous news of the abduction of Winslow Slade's granddaughter Annabel, just seconds after her wedding; unless the young bride had fled of her own volition, in a kind of illicit elopement, following her wedding vows to Lieutenant Dabney Bayard. But Upton Sinclair was unaware of such scandal as he made his way, somewhat dazed, to Stockton Street, and so to Hodge Road; pulling his two-wheeled contraption behind him, filled with the day's purchases. He recalled how he and dear Meta had played duets together, early in their courtship: he on the violin, Meta on the piano. Their best pieces were compositions by the young Mozart, that lifted their hearts. He recalled how eagerly Meta had read the lengthy manuscript of his verse narrative on the subject of the Haymarket Massacre of 1886; how Meta had declared the work a masterpiece, and how he'd kissed her—impulsively, daringly. Meta believed that Upton Sinclair would be one of the most brilliant writers and thinkers of his generation of Americans. How innocently happy they'd been, then!

And now they were trapped together—not as lovers any longer (for that relationship had proved deadly following the unanticipated pregnancy, that must not be repeated) but as brother and sister, emotionally estranged. Lately, mere glances and tender words on Upton's part were repelled by Meta, who feared unwanted consequences. Can it be, Upton wondered, that he was no longer *loved*?

Suddenly it seemed urgent to him to return home. As he hurried along the roughly paved sidewalk of Hodge Road in the direction of Rosedale Road and the open countryside he was seized by the conviction that he must get back to the farm, to his wife and infant son—"Before it's too late."

THE DEMON BRIDEGROOM

*A*nnabel! Annabel!

A nnabel! Annabel! Midway in the wedding ceremony. A low hissing sound issuing from all the corners of the austere old Colonial church.

The sound was inaudible to most of the guests but distinctly heard by Annabel Slade standing tremulously beside her husband-to-be Lieutenant Dabney Bayard at the altar of the First Presbyterian Church of Princeton.

Annabel? Come.

Though hardly more than a whisper yet the summons exuded the authority of a shouted commandment. As Reverend Nathaniel FitzRandolph enunciated the sacred wedding vows *Annabel Slade do you take this man* the hissing sound grew louder and more persistent and the distracted bride was observed to be glancing sidelong, away from Lieutenant Bayard who knelt beside her, and toward the very rear of the church. Her expression, it would later be claimed by witnesses, was one of apprehension, and guilt.

Annabel! I tell you, come.

A sepulchral tone, grave, lofty and yet intimate. As if the humid air of late spring were taking elemental form.

Annabel: come with me.

Now the bride found it impossible to maintain her composure but with each hissed ejaculation of her name glanced over her shoulder—now to the right, now to the left—her skin ashen, and her lips visibly trembling.

So much has been written on the subject, and so high did local feeling run for decades following, the historian must proceed cautiously in presenting an "objective" picture of the scene. For, in what appears to have been a denial of their senses, a majority of the spectators—(those who might describe themselves as close friends of the Slade family, for instance)—would afterward insist that the young Annabel had been "abducted" from the altar, in the very wake of her marriage to Lieutenant Bayard; for no one could have believed that the bride would have been capable of an action so mad, and so criminal, as *walking away of her own volition.*

The reader must imagine for himself the interior of the First Presbyterian Church of Princeton on that Saturday morning in early June 1905. A church interior of white, bedecked with sumptuous white flowers—lilies, roses, carnations; the walls otherwise unadorned, with a beautiful Protestant simplicity; narrow windows in stone walls, whose wavy glass emits a wavy sort of sunshine. Presiding at the altar is Reverend Nathaniel FitzRandolph, Winslow Slade's able successor; middle-aged, gentlemanly, with an earnest bald head and a frowning sort of smile, conscious of the solemnity of the occasion; above, at the rear of the church, rich resonant organ-notes intoning Bach. The bride in dazzling white has been delivered to the altar, and to the bridegroom, by her beaming father, Augustus Slade, seated now in the front pew of the crowded church; Lieutenant Bayard has come to stand, and then to kneel, beside his bride, in his U.S. Army dress uniform; women's eyes are fixed upon the bride, and her bridal gown of creamy-white satin, with its stylish "monobosom," high collar, yoke of ribbon inserts, feather stitching, and nine-inch-deep waist shirrings; the long skirt deceptively plain, with but a few horizontal tucks ending in a lacy train; the sleeves double-puffed at the upper arm, then slim to the wrist, in ribbon and feather stitching about which Mrs. Grover Cleveland would lament in her diary *she could not ever again wear so slim a fashion.*

To the surprise of all who knew her, Mrs. Horace Burr, that is, Adelaide Burr, has risen from her invalid's bed to attend the ceremony, supported on one side by her devoted husband Horace and on the other by an older McLean brother; Adelaide who began to weep even as Annabel was led up the aisle by Augustus Slade, and all the more as Annabel and Lieutenant Bayard knelt at the altar, heads bowed, like beautiful children to be disciplined, and Reverend FitzRandolph began the solemn intonations of the Presbyterian wedding ritual. That evening, Adelaide would record in her journal, in a cascade of hieroglyphics, that the mere trim of satin lilies-of-the-valley on the bride's gown so moved her, she yearned to be a girl again, a silly little unsuspecting goose, another time joined in holy matrimony with dear Horace, if she could be outfitted thus! Adelaide, as well as other female observers, take particular note of the bride's floating veil which had been handed down through the Slade family, dating back to England in the late 1600s, before the early, adventurous crossings to the New World.

The reader should probably know, however, that the fashionable "narrow silhouette" of the bride, which renders the young woman's waist exquisitely small at about eighteen inches, is the result of artful corseting; the monobosom of 1905 is cleverly built up so that, of necessity, and to continue the harmonious line, the entire body of the female is forward-tilting. Like the waist, the hips are remarkably slim—a controversial innovation, as fuller hips in the female are preferred by the more conservative of fashion-makers, as by, in general, the male sex.

The reader should imagine the Slade family in the front pews of the church—the dignified old gentleman Winslow— his sons Augustus and Copplestone and their wives; Annabel's brother Josiah, prominent among the groom's party, not fashionably but handsomely dressed for the occasion in a dark suit, with a dark necktie; for, fortunately, Josiah had returned from hunting in the Poconos with his friends, just the previous night. And there is Annabel's cousin Todd forced to wear a "little gentleman's suit"—(chocolate-brown linen, hand-stitched white satin vest, white gloves, gleaming black patent-leather shoes)—seated beside Josiah, itchy and restless and with a threat of his eyes rolling back in his head like those of a captive wild pony.

Here too is Miss Wilhelmina Burr in the front pew, the much-envied maid of honor; clearly nervous in her snug-fitting flounced pink gown, and not smiling calmly as she would wish; and the six beautiful bridesmaids in their matching dresses, like upright breathing pink-satin flowers; there is little Oriana, Todd's sister, the flower girl—an angelic little blond child with very bright eyes and a shy smile. Of the groom's men only Josiah Slade figures in this narrative, so I think I will not elaborate upon these others— handsome young men, friends and comrades of Lieutenant Bayard, whose names are lost to posterity even as they find themselves eyewitnesses at close range of the extraordinary events of that day, when the Curse first manifests itself to the public in the most dramatic of ways.

ANNABEL: NOW.

According to Adelaide Burr, seated in the second row, directly behind the Slades, it was Todd Slade who first exhibited an awareness of the low hissing sound in the church, judging from the boy's restlessness, and agitation; another was Woodrow Wilson, possibly, with his acute hearing and the extreme sensitivity of all his senses, who glanced about frowning, and squinting; then, with disapproval. One by one, numerous persons heard the hissing, or imagined that they heard; though what it was they were "hearing," no one could have said; nor could they have sworn that the sound was audible, and not rather an uncanny vibration of the air, as if a high-pitched whistle were being blown, undetectable to the human ear.

Yet Dabney Bayard, kneeling at the altar, seemed to hear nothing, and to be aware of nothing except the minister's gravely intoning voice— *Dabney Bayard do you take Annabel to be your lawful wedded wife*—and his own solemn reply *I do*. The muscles of Lieutenant Bayard's jaws clenched as if in a sudden spasm of nerves and he turned to his beautiful bride only to see, with some shock, that the demure Annabel was scarcely aware of him, or of Reverend FitzRandolph; her blue-violet widened eyes sought someone or something in the church, not visible, though perhaps at the very rear of the austere old Colonial building.

Annabel: come.

Yet, the ritual proceeded: Reverend FitzRandolph made his final pronouncement, in the name of the Lord: *I now pronounce you man and wife.* And yet, even now, when the bride and groom should be embracing, and kissing, the low hissing grew louder, like rising waves, and Annabel shuddered, and drew away from Lieutenant Bayard in a fainting gesture, as if she failed to recognize him.

By this time the whispering had increased in volume. Each individual who heard it was perplexed, and some frightened; stricken with a numb sort of panic; not knowing if he or she heard truly, or had lapsed into a temporary sort of faintness, or madness, in this humid public place that had seemed now to have turned hostile.

For such is the Devil's power to tease us, and terrify us, as to whether we are in his spell, or merely caught up in childish fantasies.

AS THIS INFAMOUS EPISODE in Princeton history moves to its inevitable conclusion, I will acknowledge that I am relying almost exclusively upon my predecessor Q. T. Hollinger, as well as a miscellany of letters, journals, and diaries written by local observers. For otherwise, the episode is totally beyond my comprehension. Yet it is clear that the bold summons—*Annabel! Come to me*—is from Annabel's seducer Axson Mayte, who stands at the rear of the church, in the opened doorway, not taking a step inside.

Not daring to take a step inside, commentators will note. For the sanctified church is a holy place, into which the Devil, or any of his demons, cannot enter.

Yet, though Axson Mayte cannot enter the church, he has the power to draw Annabel Slade, now Mrs. Annabel Bayard, from her husband's side, as forcibly as if he has stridden into the church and along the crimson carpet to seize the trembling young woman by the nape of her neck, and lead her away with him.

Annabel: it is time. You will come with me at once.

And so, the bride turns from her bridegroom, blindly; drops her floral bouquet onto the carpet; glancing to neither side, but with her gaze fixed to the commanding figure in the doorway, hurries up the aisle, with the wounded grace of an injured bird, her lips parted in breathless subjection, and in the most subtle, and most sensual, of female smiles.

"Annabel, my love! Have you been not naughty?"—so Axson Mayte declares in a low, mocking voice; and, while the wedding guests turn to stare in gawking horror, the toad-like creature grips the bride roughly in his arms and presses upon her lips a kiss of the most carnal heat, and manly authority.

PART II

The Curse Incarnate

FOR HYSTERICAL MAIDENS
I WOULD PRESCRIBE MARRIAGE,
FOR THEY ARE CURED BY PREGNANCY.

—*Hippocrates*

THE DUEL

I pray for you, Josiah, as I have prayed for your sister—that you will not succumb to barbarism."

In a voice scarcely raised above a whisper Winslow Slade spoke to his distraught grandson in the hours following the hideous public shame of the "abduction" from the First Presbyterian Church of Princeton, in full view of more than two hundred invited guests.

As if, and not for the first time, the distinguished older man seemed to have the power to read another's mind.

"If our enemies be evil, beware that they draw us into evil with them."

So saying, Winslow Slade reached for his grandson's hand; but Josiah was no boy, and his hands not a boy's hands, to be placated in this wise Christian way, even by a beloved grandfather.

HE WOULD DO IT, he vowed.

For hadn't he the example of his (male) ancestors?—some of them very young men indeed, younger than he, who had been willing to surrender their lives in battle; others, their manhood challenged by an adversary's careless insult, immediately responding with the challenge of a duel. There was thirty-two-year-old General Elias Slade who had signed the Declaration of Independence, and who had fought bravely during the Battle of Princeton, said to have been bayoneted seven times, by a cowardly cadre of British soldiers, and brought to die at the old Clark farm on the Princeton–New York Pike. There was Major Vreeland Slade, another of Washington's aides, who had distinguished himself at the first Battle of Springfield; and Colonel Henry Lewis Slade, who had defied the demagogue Andrew Jackson; and Bingham Slade, who had died in a duel fought with a law school classmate at the University of Virginia as a consequence of their disagreement over a popular Democratic scheme of the 1850s, to annex Cuba and Central America for slavery! (For such were the dreams of our American democracy, in the middle years of the nineteenth century.) And there was Abraham Lewis Slade who had fought a duel, at the age of sixty-seven, to repair the honor of his very young third wife—an incident celebrated in the gutter press that had occurred in 1889 in Manhattan's Central Park and was, as Josiah had gathered since boyhood, a source of both family embarrassment and family pride.

For Abraham Lewis Slade had, according to legend, calmly returned his adversary's (missed) shot with a perfectly aimed shot of his own—that had penetrated the other's forehead in a "ghastly, gaping" hole between the man's astonished eyes.

Arrested by police officers on the spot, with a charge of murder, Abraham Lewis Slade did not spend more than an hour in police custody, being at once freed, and all charges against him dropped, by an act of the New York mayor, a political friend and confidant of certain wealthy friends of Abraham Slade, all members of the prestigious Century Club.

So far as Josiah's Strachan relatives were concerned—(Josiah's mother was a descendant of the Strachan family, originally of Bride's Head, Rhode Island)—Josiah knew of fewer heroes, and fewer heroic deaths; yet from earliest boyhood he'd been intrigued by tales of Walton Strachan, from whom his mother was directly descended, who had at the age of eleven proved himself so capable a spy for General Edward Braddock, in western Pennsylvania, in a campaign against the French, that he was decorated by the general himself, in full view of hundreds of assembled troops. Only a few years later, Walton had distinguished himself as an officer in the Colonial army, in the Battle of the Monongahela River, in 1755; two decades later, Walton Strachan had died in a duel in Philadelphia, over a freed slave woman who had seemingly come under Strachan's protection.

"Am I so courageous? Even with Mayte mocking me at every turn?"

By which Josiah meant, the memory of Axson Mayte taking hold of his sister Annabel in the doorway of the church, in full view of the assembled guests; the hellish image of Axson Mayte multiplied in Josiah's imagination like a mirror-image multiplied to infinity.

Like any young man bent upon an honor revenge, Josiah feared that another man would exact justice before he could; in this case, Lieutenant Dabney Bayard, who had gone into hiding, it was said, soon after the incident in the church, when his newly wed bride had been stolen from him and cast him into the intolerable role of *cuckold*. For it might be presumed that the wrath of a betrayed husband and lover was more potent than the wrath of a brother.

(According to Bayard relatives, it was believed that the betrayed husband was on the track of Annabel and her "abductor"; now that a week had passed, and now twelve days, it became known to the Bayards that their disgraced Dabney had been involved in "drunken altercations" in public houses in Trenton, Washington Crossing, and New Hope, across the state border in Pennsylvania; that it was being whispered, in West End Princeton circles, that Lieutenant Bayard was "going to the dogs" and that, in a fit of temper, fueled by shame, the distraught young man had "severed all communications" with the Slade family, who should have been his allies.)

Josiah, who had not been a friend of Dabney Bayard, and would not have wished to be an ally, except under duress, was relieved by this; for he intended to find his sister by himself, and to exact a just sort of revenge upon Axson Mayte, no matter the consequences to himself. He had read, as a student at the Princeton Academy for Boys, translations of both Homer's *Iliad* and *Odyssey*; he had read those romantic-action novels listed previously in this chronicle, in which the exploits of courageous men and boys were honored, by Sir Walter Scott, James Fenimore Cooper, Jack London, Owen Wister; stubbornly he had wished to interpret, in Mark Twain's *Huckleberry Finn*, those passages in which the Hatfields and the McCoys make war upon one another, and barbarously kill one another, as exalted by Twain, and not instead deplored. As Josiah traveled from one Jersey town to another, in pursuit of the missing couple, he found himself in the wake of the enraged husband Dabney Bayard, who preceded him, at times, by merely hours; and wondered that, if Dabney were in one of his drunken tempers, and spoiling for revenge, declaring his intentions to any and all who would listen in public houses, Dabney might be reported as saying things insulting to Josiah's sister's honor, necessitating that Josiah must fight *him*. To Winslow Slade he felt obliged to speak in this way, as he could not have spoken to his own parents: "If the 'wronged husband' insults the 'unfaithful wife,' if he so much as hints at his displeasure with Annabel, you know, Grandfather, what I must do. I will have no *choice*."

And Winslow Slade said quietly: "No, Josiah. You will have a choice, as we all do. Even as she did—our lost Annabel."

IT SOON BECAME EVIDENT to Josiah, with the intolerable passage of days, and finally weeks, that there were unique problems involving the search for Annabel and the demonic Axson Mayte: for not only had the illicit couple disappeared from the church on Nassau Street, in a dignified old brougham pulled by four matched horses, "as if into thin air along the Old King's Highway" (now Route 27), but, in the aftermath of the scandal, very few persons could account for Axson Mayte during the weeks of his residence in Princeton.

It was true, Mayte had been entertained at several of the most distinguished old Princeton houses, and had been a visitor at Crosswicks Manse; he had been a guest for several days at Prospect, the president's house at Princeton University; everyone in the West End seemed to have met him, and to have shaken his hand which was recalled by some as "strong, vigorous, hot" and others as "limp, chill as a dead fish, boneless." Yet, Josiah had great difficulty piecing together information about the man. His grandfather Winslow had not been very helpful, saying only that Axson Mayte, a Virginian associated with the Presbyterian Church, had virtually invited himself, to speak with Winslow in his library—"On a theological matter, of no interest to the lay person"; the meeting had been brief, not two hours; but Axson Mayte had not left town, turning up elsewhere, at others' homes, and at Prospect, to shake the hand of Woodrow Wilson. Why had he come to Princeton in the first place; where, indeed, had he come from—(by this time the Presbyterian-Virginia background had been proven false); was he a man of the law, as Woodrow Wilson believed, an "ethicist" and an "educator"; was he a wealthy man, as others believed, or was he a gambler and card shark, as others claimed; how had he become associated with Winslow Slade's sheltered granddaughter Annabel; and, most mysteriously, *what precisely did Axson Mayte look like?*

No two persons seemed to agree. Josiah himself remembered with a vivid sort of revulsion—the squat man's toad-features, and ditch-water eyes; a sly, sensual, insinuating smile, of wormy lips. Yet others whose opinion Josiah valued, like Horace Burr, insisted that Axson Mayte looked "altogether ordinary: neither tall nor short, thin or stout, attractive or ugly"; several of the women, including Johanna van Dyck and Florence Chambers, claimed to have found Mayte "handsome, in an arrogant-Southerner way" but "soft-spoken, courteous." No one could agree: did Mayte have "coarse, dark hair"—or "fair, thinning hair"; or was he in fact bald? Professor Pearce van Dyck, still ailing with a mysterious infection of the lungs, could speak in only a hoarse voice, insisting that Axson Mayte was "a kind of golem"—(a golem being a creature out of Hebrew tradition, a humanoid creature fashioned of clay and lacking a soul). Of West End Princeton residents not one would confess to having brought together Axson Mayte and Annabel Slade: indeed, no one could recall having glimpsed the two together at the same gathering, beneath the same roof.

The barkeep at the Sign of the Hudibras on Fort Street, Trenton, recalled a "friendly Southern gentleman" while the hotel manager at the Nassau Inn exploded in an angry tirade against the uncouth guest who'd left evidence of his "bestiality and animalism" in his suite, for which he had neglected to pay; the hackney driver who'd taken Mr. Mayte's luggage from the shuttle train claimed that he had never in his life carried such heavy suitcases—"Filled with rocks, like the graveyard, they were." This same gentleman complained to Josiah that after having driven Mr. Mayte to the Nassau Inn, and helped him settle into his suite, the several dollars Mayte had given him had somehow "vanished" out of his pocket within the hour.

At the Coachman's Inn in Brunswick, Mayte had been "brooding and secretive"; at the Nassau Inn, he had been "wonderfully animated," and had shown respectful curiosity about the Inn and its history; he'd spoken with a "cultivated" Southern accent, or with a "clipped, British accent"; or in the flatter tones of Maryland, or South Jersey. He was above average in height, slender, and handsome; then again squat, and lumpish, and ill-featured, with slack sneering lips and "pink, pig-eyes." Public house waitresses spoke guardedly of him to Josiah; other women, having learned of Mayte's "abduction" of the Slade daughter, were anxious for Josiah and his family to know that they had been deceived in believing that Mayte was a gentleman, a "close, personal" friend of the former Reverend Winslow Slade.

As Josiah made inquiries after Mayte, his own initial impression was in danger of fading; eventually, Axson Mayte would lose all distinctive features, only the *demonic* remaining, like dark-tinctured skin and topaz eyes.

In desperation Josiah went to the Mercer County sheriff's headquarters on Route 206 to inquire whether "Axson Mayte" had been questioned in the matter of the Spags murder and was informed that since the attack upon the child was clearly the work of a deranged beast, the sheriff's deputies would hardly have questioned a gentleman about it.

Josiah asked how was Axson Mayte a *gentleman;* and the reply was, when Mayte's name was first mentioned to sheriff's deputies, Mayte had been a houseguest at Prospect, on the Princeton University campus—"A personal friend of the president of the university there, that could have nothing to do with the Spags family on the Princeton Pike."

Hotly Josiah said, "Then you are fools. You are collaborators with the Devil. I will make my own way."

AND NOW AT LAST. The hour of reckoning has come.

The setting: the Raven Rock Inn of Raven Rock, Pennsylvania, on the Delaware River north of New Hope; the time, a midsummer night near one o'clock in the morning, six weeks and two days following Annabel Slade's disappearance.

Or, as poor Annabel was likely to be identified in the press, *Mrs. Annabel Bayard.*

The other day was Josiah's twenty-fifth birthday. By his own firm wish, the Slades did not insist upon celebrating it, at this somber time.

Nor would a birthday of Josiah's be truly celebrated, without the presence of his sister Annabel.

And so Josiah, in the bloom of indignant and heedless youth, has driven in his brass-trimmed Winton motorcar into the Delaware Valley, through the sleepy villages of Hopewell and Lambertville, and so to New Hope; then north along the curving River Road, to the scenic crossroads

Raven Rock, eleven miles away. Josiah has come to Raven Rock alone, on his mission of vengeance: to bring his (dishonored) sister back to her family, and to fight to the death, if necessary, with her seducer.

To this end he has brought with him in a kidskin case, lined in crimson velvet, two fine-wrought dueling pistols with carved mahogany grips, prize specimens from the workshop of Trinity Morris, Jr., the revered gunsmith of Philadelphia of the mid-1800s.

Josiah recalls his grandfather's plea: *That you will not succumb to barbarism.*

Being a young man confirmed in the Presbyterian faith, in the very bedrock of Protestant Christian faith, Josiah understands that his behavior is reckless, and dangerous; it is surely not *Christian*. Yet, his Slade and Strachan ancestors would cheer for him, if they knew. For nothing is more precious than the honor of a family, even Christian redemption.

"If I am doomed to Hell for my behavior, then I must accept it. And if there is no Hell, except what men have fashioned for one another, then I will be spared. I will be *redeemed*."

His dishonored sister, poor Annabel, he would forgive—of course. Vaguely Josiah thought that she might simply return to Crosswicks Manse, to live in seclusion for a while; at some point, perhaps she would travel with Josiah to Italy, and live in Rome, or Florence or Venice, for a while; eventually, with the passage of time, Josiah and Annabel might share a household together, as Josiah set about his life's-work of—well, he wasn't yet sure: Philosophy? Journalism? Medical school? Law? Exploration of the West, or the Arctic, in the mode of the great Lewis and Clark? Political reform? Socialism?

Josiah is well aware that dueling is illegal—it is a class-A felony—in the State of New Jersey. Already in the time of the infamous duel of Aaron Burr, Jr., and Alexander Hamilton, in 1804, dueling was a class-A felony in the State of New York, though somewhat less stringently outlawed in New Jersey, where the duel was set, in Weehawken. In Southern states, where laws are legislated with an eye toward preserving "tradition"—(statutory laws banning miscegenation, for instance, and "sodomy")—law enforcement officers are less likely to seize and arrest dueling gentlemen, as they are less likely to seize and arrest individuals who have participated in "lynchings" of Negroes, still less are juries likely to vote such individuals *guilty*.

Josiah knows that if he wounds or kills Axson Mayte, he will be arrested; and there is the possibility, for Josiah is not a fantasist about such matters, but a fatalist, that he himself may be wounded, or killed. Yet, the risk must be taken. For Annabel's sake, as for the sake of the Slade family.

Weeks of thwarted effort have led to this journey along the River Road, beside the broad, beautiful Delaware River; weeks of "tracking down" the illicit couple, through every sort of inquiry, and bribes, and some coercion; at last, by chance, Josiah had encountered a former "valet" of Axson Mayte, living in Camden, in a rooming house. Against all his Slade principles Josiah found himself begging, threatening, and cajoling the man, at last pressing fifty dollars into his (unwashed) hand, in return for being presented, to his surprise, a half-dozen "aliases" of Mayte's, commonly used in New Jersey/Pennsylvania.

For it seems, "Axson Mayte" is not the seducer's name; and what the name is, Josiah has no idea.

"The Devil has no name, and no face."

At the Raven Rock Inn, Josiah learns that "D'Apthorp, Mr. & Mrs. François" are registered there, as the ex-"valet" had speculated. For "François D'Apthorp" is one of Mayte's aliases. ("If you look hard enough you will find him—you will always find him." So the ex-valet said with a wink at Josiah, that quite chilled Josiah.) But having learned this fact, from having pressed a ten-dollar bill into the palm of the desk clerk, Josiah feels demoralized suddenly, and exhausted; where a fierce coursing of blood had fueled him on the drive from Princeton to Raven Rock, now he feels uncertain; he wanders into the public room of the old inn, and sits at a solitary table, resting his head for some minutes on his crossed arms; then, chides himself—for what would "crafty Odysseus" do at such a juncture? What would a hero of Jack London do, in close proximity to an individual who had dishonored the hero's name? To restore his strength Josiah orders a tankard of dark bitter ale, which he drinks quickly, scarcely tasting; and so within a half hour he will make his way upstairs to knock on the door of the "honeymoon suite" overlooking the river, taken by "François D'Apthorp" and his alleged wife; and only God knows what will happen then.

He can't refuse a duel, Josiah thinks, *but if he does—what shall I do? Attack him, beat him? Kill him outright? And what of Annabel? Must she be a witness?* He did not want to consider whose "side" Annabel might be on, in such a struggle.

For Josiah had clearly seen, Annabel had gone of her own free will to join Axson Mayte in the doorway of the church. She had been deathly pale, blinking and staring as if under a hypnotist's spell; but no one had forced her to leave the side of her new husband Dabney Bayard, and to move beyond the protection of her aggrieved family.

Still, Josiah would not judge Annabel. There was no need even to consider "forgiving" her—Josiah did not judge his beloved sister at all.

"It's as if she is ill. She must be saved from her illness!"

In the shadowy quiet of the Inn's public house, at a plank-board table, Josiah surreptitiously opens the kidskin case on his knees, to examine yet again the large, ungainly-looking dueling pistols. He finds the sight of them, and their chill oily scent, and their weight in his hand, not consoling as he had anticipated, but alarming. Josiah has been a hunter of pheasants, geese, deer, bears; he has handled rifles and shotguns, and knows to respect firearms. But he has had virtually no experience with a *hand-gun*. Though fantasies of duels had drifted through his boyish dreams for years, he had not ever exactly anticipated a duel in its particulars. The heavy steel pistols, the finely carved wood, the silver trim so exquisitely wrought—in one, a *fleur-de-lis* pattern, and in the other an equally delicate *serpentine* pattern. Another time he hears the hissing summons—*Annabel! Annabel!*—hears again his grandfather's warning words, and feels again his grandfather's fingers groping against his, weaker fingers than his own, easily eluded.

"Grandfather, thank you. I know you mean well—I know that you are *right*. But I have no choice. I must avenge our family honor, for no one else will."

Yet, if Josiah should actually kill a man! How Grandfather Slade would grieve for him, and his beloved parents!

Fleetingly, Josiah thinks of Wilhelmina Burr. She, too, would grieve for him . . . But there is nothing to be done, Josiah is the descendant of heroic men and must avenge the family's honor.

"HELLO? PLEASE OPEN this door."

Boldly Josiah has knocked at the door of room 22, the "honeymoon suite" at the Raven Rock Inn. Leaning his ear to the door, to hear inside an exchange of muffled voices.

His voice is more forceful than he would expect: "I am Josiah Slade. Please open this door."

There is another exchange of voices inside the room and then with startling swiftness the door is flung open.

"Yes? Hello? Who are you?"

In the doorway stands a man of youthful and vigorous middle age, whom Josiah is certain he has never seen before; a curious combination of gentleman and ruffian, with ruddy face and rude staring eyes. The man's white linen shirt is partway unbuttoned, exposing a brawny chest covered in metallic hairs. Of a height near-identical with Josiah's, the gentleman-ruffian shows no apprehension at seeing him, only rather a kind of bemusement.

"Excuse me, *monsieur*—I am asking *who are you*?"

Behind the staring man, at the rear of a fussily furnished room, is a woman with loosed pale-blond hair, a face both beautiful and hardened; the woman is wearing a peacock-blue kimono, carelessly tied at her waist so that it falls partway open at the throat, like her companion's linen shirt. In her fingers is a small gold cigarette case, from out of which she draws a long white cigarette with mannered slowness.

"I—I am Josiah Slade—I'm looking for—my sister Annabel . . ."

Josiah hears his awkward stammering voice. Josiah feels a blush rise into his face. In both hands he is gripping the kidskin case containing the dueling pistols, that feels to him conspicuous and foolish; by the way the gentleman-ruffian eyes the case, and contemplates Josiah's abashed expression, it seems to Josiah that he must understand what is contained in the kidskin case, and why Josiah has knocked so brashly on the door.

" 'Josiah Slade'—'Annabel'—what have they to do with *us*? You must have the wrong room, Mr. Slade. We are François and Camille D'Apthorp, and we are no one you know."

Josiah sees the pale-blond woman in the kimono cast a sidelong glance at him, of contempt, as she lights a cigarette and exhales a small venomous-seeming cloud of smoke. The woman is not young, perhaps as old as forty, and seems to Josiah both utterly strange, and yet familiar. *She knows me. But she will not acknowledge me.*

Confused, Josiah draws back from the doorway, that the woman might not see him so clearly, and deduce from the kidskin case in his shaky hands what his reason is for knocking at their door. In a stammering voice he apologizes, explaining that he is looking for another couple; the gentleman-ruffian smiles at him, with a sly, insinuating smile, and surprises Josiah by not shutting the door in his face but opening it wider.

"*Monsieur*, will you join us for a glass of Champagne? We are returned to this charming inn to celebrate our twentieth wedding anniversary, and would be so pleased if you would help us celebrate."

Almost, the gentleman-ruffian is winking at Josiah.

"Thank you but I—I think—I hadn't better . . ."

"But why not, *monsieur*? Whoever you are seeking, will surely be there a little later this evening, eh? In the meantime—a glass of Champagne?"

At the rear of the room the pale-blond woman, her untidy hair spilling down her back, lifts her hands as if to warn Josiah away, even as the gentleman-ruffian glances back at her, with a severe frown.

"Camille begs me, to insist that you join us. Since you have knocked at our door, which can be no accident, yes? You will?"

"N-No. No thank you. Good night!"

Blindly Josiah turns away, his heart beating hard. Gripping the kidskin case he walks swiftly along the corridor with its soft worn carpet, its just slightly tarnished-looking wallpapered walls, electric lights in the shapes of candles every six feet or so, to light his way back to the staircase.

In the doorway of the honeymoon suite the gentleman-ruffian calls after Josiah, with a mocking laugh: *"Bonsoir, monsieur! Chaque chose en son temps, peut-être."*

POSTSCRIPT:
THE HISTORIAN'S DILEMMA

Numerous times I have reread the previous scene, bringing Josiah Slade to the door of room 22 of the Raven Rock Inn; numerous times I have brooded upon the meaning of the enigmatic exchange between Josiah Slade and "François D'Apthorp"—and the significance of the "warning" gesture of the blond woman in the kimono—but to no avail. Whatever meaning the scene might have, it does not yield its meaning to me.

The reader will smile to learn, I have been so baffled by the scene, I've visited the Raven Rock Inn and investigated that very same honeymoon suite, that has not been altered much in the intervening decades, but with no illumination.

Perhaps it is the historian's dilemma: we can record, we can assemble facts meticulously and faithfully, but only to a degree can we interpret. And we cannot *create*.

THE UNSPEAKABLE II

I n Nassau Hall behind closed doors they met.

No secretary would take notes.

"Matilde, you may leave us."

"Sir? 'Leave you—'?"

President Wilson reiterated his command, in a voice that threatened to quaver. His face was very pale, his skin taut and drawn. At the corners of his thin lips, a faint chalky substance had dried. Those who passed close to the agitated man, which is to say within three feet, would note that his breath smelled of camphor and ashes.

"Matilde, I have instructed you. *Shut the door as you depart.*"

For the meeting was hastily called. And in secrecy.

For the meeting was *without a stated agenda.*

In the president's outer office, around a spare wooden table that looked as if it had survived from Colonial times, indeed from the very firestorm of the Battle of Princeton of 1777, the men gathered, perplexed and apprehensive. Several deans, several departmental chairs, the university attorney, the master of the residence in question and the master's young assistant Thomas Tremain (Princeton '95) who was also a preceptor in Romance Studies and who had never before this fraught hour stepped foot in historic Nassau Hall.

Gravely President Wilson chaired the meeting. Beside him, just slightly behind him, the chair in which the president's secretary Matilde usually sat, to record the minutes of the meeting, was stunningly empty.

Awkwardly the men sat. Awkwardly glancing at one another, and at the somber drawn face of the president, who seemed to be waiting for another individual to enter the room; or, it may have been, was simply sitting in his usual stiff public posture, lost in thought, frowning, polishing his eyeglasses vigorously with a fresh-laundered handkerchief as he summoned from the depths of his soul the appropriate words with which to open this exceptional, because *unrecordable*, meeting.

After some minutes, when the silence grew oppressive, as if oxygen were slowly being sucked from the room, President Wilson cleared his throat, positioned his *pince-nez* at the bridge of his nose, and began, with the air of a man teetering at the edge of an abyss.

"You are wondering why you have been summoned so quickly. And why you have been cautioned to tell no one—I repeat: no one—of the meeting. And why there is no stated agenda for the meeting."

Here, Wilson paused. A sudden ghastly smile stretched his thin lips.

"You are wondering, gentlemen—yes, you have reason to wonder. As, in your place, I would have reason to wonder. But—I am pained to inform you—the situation is so grave, and so—lewd—it is literally *unspeakable*."

Unspeakable! The individuals gathered about the table in the president's outer office stared at Wilson, and at one another, in bewilderment; yet almost at once, bewilderment melted into a kind of shared horror, and profound embarrassment.

"Mr. Eddington, whom some of you know is the master of West College, has come to me with a very upsetting report; as, just yesterday, his assistant Mr. Tremain came to him, with a very upsetting report."

At this, Wilson passed his fingertips over his eyes, as if for a fleeting moment he felt faint.

Eddington and Tremain sat rigid as statuary, as the others gloomily regarded them; of these, most were sitting with their arms folded tightly across their chests, like a kind of armor.

(It should be noted here that, unknown to Woodrow Wilson, rumors had been racing like wildfire through the university community, that he'd had a "nervous collapse" of some kind recently; this collapse believed to be related to the mysterious/scandalous incident involving the granddaughter of Winslow Slade who'd been allegedly "abducted" from her wedding ceremony in the Presbyterian church, in which Wilson's daughter Jessie had been a bridesmaid. Since very few individuals associated with the university had been invited to the wedding, much was speculated, but little was known.)

"Mr. Eddington, would you like to speak?"

But Mr. Eddington, looking miserable, could only mutely shake his head. Wilson regarded him sympathetically, with an expression of some relief.

"Mr. Tremain, then?"

But Thomas Tremain, a bony-faced boy of twenty-nine, in an ill-fitting suit of the kind worn by undertakers' assistants, could only shudder, and swallow audibly, and shake his head *no*.

"It seems, there were—there are—boys—that is to say, undergraduate men—involved—as well as, I am very sorry to say—several preceptors." Wilson paused, to allow the weight of such a revelation to be absorbed: *preceptors*!

"But the facts, as reported to me, or rather as presented to me, not in words precisely because, as I have said, the situation is *unspeakable*, are clear enough: grounds for immediate expulsion, and all records expunged, regarding the undergraduates; and immediate termination of contracts, regarding the preceptors. So that, so far as the world will know, *not one of these unspeakable persons ever stepped foot on our campus, still less was expelled from it.*"

This statement was uttered with steely control. Yet you could see, if you were seated close by President Wilson, that the man's grainy eyelids trembled, and the chalky dryness in the corners of his mouth gleamed like arsenic.

"Gentlemen, we will have to—proceed. Are we in agreement? We will want to end this meeting as quickly as possible, I think."

"Sir? May I—"

"Yes? Yes? What is it, Dean Fullerton?"

The dean of the faculty was sitting with his arms tight-slung across his chest, and seemed to be having difficulty breathing. For one who looked ill, he spoke bravely, almost recklessly—"Granted the situation is *unspeakable,* and we would not wish to *speak of it,* yet, still, under civil law, the accused would be allowed to defend themselves, you know—before they are punished. Mr. Eddington, how many boys are involved?"

Miserable Mr. Eddington squirmed in his chair. Wordless, he lifted his hands—two hands—wriggling his fingers as if to count: exactly ten?

No, twelve. *Thirteen.*

Thirteen!

"That is—well, that is . . . shocking. That is . . . not what we would wish." The dean of the faculty, who had spoken so bravely a moment before, now seemed to have lost his way; his eyes were blinking rapidly, downcast.

"None of this is 'what we would wish,'" President Wilson said cuttingly. "We are agreed, what is *unspeakable* cannot be articulated, yet, it must be acted upon—swiftly. 'Justice delayed is justice denied.'"

"The boys—that is, the young men—will be expelled? So quickly?"

"In fact, they are expelled. They have been asked to vacate their rooms this very morning."

"So *quickly?*"

"Sir, you need not repeat yourself: we have heard you, the first time. 'Justice delayed is justice denied' and so the boys involved in the *unspeakable* have been asked to leave, and may in fact have left already; or are awaiting their parents' arrival, to help them vacate their rooms and depart. As for the preceptors, who have crassly violated the university's trust in them, as young gentlemen of intellectual and moral distinction, they are—gone."

"Gone?"

"Is this an echo chamber? Is this mockery? When I say that these sub-human creatures are *gone*, I mean precisely that they are *gone*. And where they have *gone* is not Princeton's concern."

"Sir, on this matter of—'defense'—"

"What is *unspeakable* is also *indefensible*. I think we are in agreement?"

"But, President Wilson, sir, it might be that the charges are—inaccurate? Or exaggerated? *Fabricated?* Until we organize an investigation, and allow the accused to speak in their own defense, we can't be certain that—that—'justice' will be done."

These bold words fell into an abyss of silence. Such was the stillness in the president's office, over which portraits of several of President Wilson's distinguished predecessors—(Reverend Jonathan Edwards, John Witherspoon, James McCosh)—brooded, each man became acutely aware of his own breathing, heartbeat, and digestive processes; Thomas Tremain, in a state of sheer nerves, swallowed hard with a gulping sound, and a spasm of his Adam's apple. You could see that the stricken young man, himself guiltless of the *unspeakable,* had yet been tarnished by his proximity to it; and his contract with the university, very likely, would be allowed to dissolve, somewhere beyond the current term.

With a barely restrained air of sarcasm President Wilson continued: "And how do you propose to allow these *unspeakable* individuals to—*speak*? It is just not possible, in decent company, and in civilized quarters."

"But—granted it is *unspeakable,* yet, still, there must be a way . . . It seems unfair simply to . . . *expunge* these persons, who were a part of our university family until just yesterday."

"Yes. That is the horror of it—'part of our university family until just yesterday.'"

A shudder seemed to pass around the spare Colonial table, touching each man in turn. And Thomas Tremain most conspicuously, who had to jam his knuckles against his mouth, to keep from coughing louder.

Yet still, the faltering objection was voiced: "If you have already 'expelled' and 'expunged' these individuals, President Wilson, why are we meeting? It would seem to be *ex post facto*."

"We are meeting, sir, because I have called a meeting of the chief university administrators. Because I am asking you to ratify an *ex post facto* action of the executive, as it were."

"Yes, but, sir—"

"May I revive your memories—for perhaps some of you have forgotten—my much-reprinted speech *Princeton in the Nation's Service* concluded with the words 'As we at Princeton are in the nation's service we are obliged to be not merely *good*, but *great*.'"

President Wilson glanced about the table, eyeglasses glittering.

Like abashed children the men seated at the table made no more objection.

"Then, I think this meeting—which never occurred, and will never be spoken of—is adjourned."

With visible relief the men departed. Wordless.

THE CRUEL HUSBAND

(From the secret journal of Mrs. Adelaide McLean Burr;
June–October 1905)

_____. Cruel! Very cruel. My hand trembles so that I can scarcely hold this pen.

Though six hours have passed since the ignominy; the bafflement; the inexplicable *hurt*.

For it seems to have come about, as in a malevolent tale of the Brothers Grimm, that my beloved Horace has <u>turned</u>—he is <u>not himself</u>—on the very eve of our fifteenth wedding anniversary; while my love for him remains as unsullied as when I was a bride.

_____. I shall not weep another tear, for I have none. He loves me no longer—& I must die.

_____. "One day, Adelaide, you will see, they <u>turn</u>," my own dear mother whispered in my ear, when I was a girl. "Husbands <u>turn</u> because it is their nature: they cannot help themselves, & we cannot help them. & then there is little solace but the grave."

_____ . Handsome stout-bodied curly-mustach'd husband Horace who has always adored & prized & pampered his dear little Puss; & laughed at her little breathless ways; & made light of her terrors; after 15 years of Christian matrimony of uncomplaining devotion, why, he has revealed another side to himself—a lewd & unlook'd-to aspect of the masculine soul.

_____ . "Horace," I inquired of him, in a voice so faint it could hardly be heard over the sound of the man's hoarse breathing, "why are you but partly clad? Why have you burst into my room in the night, & so afflicted me with the sight of you, my poor heart is near to bursting? And—can it be, you smell of <u>spirits</u>? Horace, please—come no closer! Or I shall ring for a servant!"

_____ . Or was it but a nightmare; the work of Dream-Hawks that swoop & stab & claw . . . This morning finds me disheveled & fainting, too weak to tolerate my new medicine, coaxed upon me by Hannah, who is very worried on my account; & midmorning Mrs. Joris our housekeeper ventured to see me, greatly troubled—for all the staff whispers of Mrs. Burr's crisis of health.

_____ . (It has been thus, this crude behavior, laced with <u>spirits</u>, following Horace's business visits to Manhattan, when he stays overnight at the Madison Club; for it is whispered by Mrs. Cleveland, women of a <u>loose reputation</u> are readily available there, to the most distinguished & dignified of gentlemen. & if the man does not succumb, yet, in his inflamed imagination, he has been tempted; & cannot control himself when he returns to his own household. & in my naiveté I said to Frances—"Ah, but not Horace! Not ever my dear Horace.")

_____ . (It is not a secret, the coarse-mannered ruffian Grover Cleveland had "relations" with women before his marriage to Frances; & God knows, very likely afterward. For there is a beast in men, if once released cannot then be confined. & all the world knows, Mr. Cleveland sired a bastard child upon one of these wretched females, yet, our civilization being depraved as it has become, this fact was not held against the man, & did not prevent his being elected President of the United States—not once, but twice!)

_____ . So lonely & nervous & why does my heart pound so. I am a high-strung young lady, Dr. Boudinot declared, when I became mistress of Maidstone, "to be compared with a musical instrument of such subtlety & artistry as the Stradivarius violin"—for which little Puss was praised & admired, for as a girl of seventeen I had but an eighteen-inch waist <u>without corsetry</u>; & a complexion of such translucence, it was marveled that I resembled a <u>porcelain doll</u>. In those happier years it seemed Horace—& many others—prized me for all that I was high-strung & "sensitive" & prone to fainting spells & required petting & comforting & the gentlest of caresses.

_____ . (What is happening in this house? In which I am "mistress"—yet captive? Horace is so often away, at his office on Bank Street, or in NYC; here, I am aware of the servants whispering & plotting behind our backs; there is evidence that they are stealing from us, that Horace discounts. Hannah is stiff in my presence & when reprimanded for a blunder, grows resentful; & Minnie has become close-mouthed; the boy Abraham, having grown inches within mere months, from gorging himself in the kitchen, I am sure, is stiff-faced in my presence & rudely mumbles <u>Mz Ad'laide</u> as if the taste of my name in his mouth was most bitter. Just now ringing & ringing the bell, & no one comes to my aid & if I had fallen into a faint, or worse . . . & so I think <u>Why, they could rise up against me, in this very house! Like slave massacres of old, and terrible things perpetrated upon helpless white women, of which no one will then speak for such are UNSPEAKABLE</u>.)

_____ . Thus the accursed summer passes. Days & nights in hellish succession & poor Puss lies prostrate beneath the attacks of the Dream-Hawks—great carrion birds with wing-spans of ten feet & eyes of blazing coals & cruel talons to rake against my soft cheek & tangle in my hair. & the wisdom of Madame Blavatsky lies fallow in me now, I am not strong-minded enough to comprehend her; the most insipid Sunday school catechism is quite enough, for poor Puss's strained mental state.

& nothing is further known of the unhappy Annabel Slade, now Mrs.

Annabel Bayard; though it is believed that her brother Josiah has vowed to revenge himself upon her abductor, & reclaim her. Poor dear Annabel!—a mere
child, not so canny as Puss; for Puss alone feels deep sorrow for her, & not a
<u>frisson</u> of satisfaction, that the high & mighty Slades are in this vulnerable
way laid low. For Annabel is lost to all society now, & all decent company; as
she is lost to her beloved family. & my unhappy nephew Dabney Bayard has
fallen into drunkenness & it is believed lewdness, of which his female relatives
are not supposed to know. & Horace says, It is not our concern, Adelaide:
do not think of it. & yet, which woman in Princeton, horrified by the public
abduction of Annabel Slade, does not think of <u>it</u>.

_____ . To my horror & disgust I am ever more often visited by
Horace, staggering in the dark, & smelling of bourbon; this partly-clad, disheveled stranger who mumbles, begs, threatens me, that I must "embrace"
him—"as a wife should." & in my bed he grovels, & grunts, & squeals, &
groans; & collapses, like a sack of flour, weighing so heavily upon me, I am
in danger of suffocation. & the shame is such, I must change my own bed
linens in the morning, for fear that the servants will know, & pity me; or
worse yet, laugh at me—mistress of Maidstone, no more respected than a
harlot! & yet stranger visions come to me, in my troubled sleep, the frolick-
ing ghost-shape of Ruth Cleveland who is far more familiar to me now in
death than ever she had been in life; & little Oriana Slade, who was flower
girl at Annabel's wedding, now Ruth Cleveland's nocturnal companion, it
seems. & most upsetting, the transmogrified shape of cousin Wilhelmina
who smiles at me & lisps <u>Dear Cousin Addie!</u> as she has never done in
life; & contorts her young body in a most sinuous way as, by daylight, that
high-minded & chaste young woman would never do, I am certain. & most
hideous, the naked form of the house-boy Abraham, who is no more than
thirteen years old, I am sure, yet, in such visions, a muscled & "developed"
youth, & his skin as dark as the ebony inlaid in my bedroom bureau, & his
white-rimmed lascivious eyes . . .

_____ . (Yet I have learned of bold women of our time who have
themselves <u>turned</u> from the merely female, & acquiescent: the poet & suffragette Charlotte Perkins Gilman & the Jewish anarchist Emma Goldman of

whom it is said she conspired to assassinate President McKinley! Would that poor Puss had such boldness, & such opportunity; would that poor Puss were not a pathetic <u>invalid</u> which is the most extreme state of that more general malady <u>femaleness</u>.)

_____ . I shall not forgive any of them. My heart, that is frail, yet pounds hardily, & with pride. I am <u>sickened</u> by Horace in his transmogrified state, when he is cruel & swinish & "not himself"—afterward kneeling in the corridor outside my door & begging me through the keyhole, <u>O my darling forgive</u> me—for he knew not what he did, what pleas he has made to me, having over-indulged at sherry & bitters & smoked oysters at his accursed <u>gentlemen's club</u> in the city.

_____ . Thank God for my female friends!—as Mother had warned, in the end you will have only women to rely upon, & to love you. For here is Johanna van Dyck bringing me the sweetest honeycomb, from her groundskeeper's bee hives; & she & Mandy concerned that I am looking "very pale, & sickly"; & reading to me from Mr. Ade's amusing <u>The College Widow</u>, & Mrs. Corelli's <u>The Wicked Suitor</u>; & frothy glamour pieces out of <u>The Smart Set</u>. (When these & other ladies come to visit, sly Puss hides her Theosophical & anarchist texts, & Charlotte Gilman's <u>In This Our World & The Yellow Wallpaper & Other Stories</u>; it is enough, that I betray to them that I am reading Mrs. Wharton's <u>The House of Mirth</u> which is faulted, in the very best families of New York & Newport, as a crude & unfair satire of their society, with a heroine who behaves in a most unladylike fashion.) & there is the solace of Gossip, that rages unabated through the summer & into autumn, that the Slade family is <u>accursed</u>, in the way of the Hebrew God testing Job; & that the feud between prune-face Woodrow Wilson & Dean Sixty-Two-Around-the-Vest Andrew West grows more heated each week. Tongues wag freely in town, some merrily & some in distress; for it is said, not one, not two, not three, but <u>all four of the Wilson females</u> are suffering Woodrow's chagrin; & poor Jessie, hardly eighteen years old, has badly suffered the loss of her friend Annabel Slade, to whom she looked as an ideal friend, & a model of behavior. Elsewhere, in Wilmington, the elderly Mrs. Pyne clings fast to her millions of dollars as she clings to her crabbed life, & plays Wilson & West against each other: whether she will leave her husband's fortune to Princeton University under the direction of Wilson or of West: quite the trick, my girl, to make these pompous "academicians" dance to your tune! A fresh development, however: yet a second elderly millionaire is drawn into the squabble, one Isaac Wyman of Boston, Mass., Princeton Class of '86, who is said to be leaning "just slightly Westward" with his bequeath of four million dollars. Horace shakes his head over these developments, for he is sympathetic with President Wilson, who is so very earnest a man; yet, Horace is sympathetic with Andrew West too, for Andrew preceded Wilson by many years at the university, and is seen to have been slighted by the board of trustees, in not having been offered the presidency. Wilson's latest humiliation is that the site he has proposed for the new graduate school, in defiance of the dean's proposal, has turned out to be unfit for reasons of sanitation; evidently, the acreage had been at one time a sewer field. (& yet it did shock me, that there was anything like a sewer field in Princeton Borough! I am sure, I have never heard of it until now.)

_____ . Next day, perusing The House of Mirth, I find that the novel is ugly & grating, as it had been suggested; disagreeable for its cruelty toward that very set to which Edith Newbold Jones was born, if I am not mistaken. Hurriedly skimming the pages, I find that it is even worse, that the arriviste Jew Mr. Rosedale should prove in the end gentlemanly—as if in rebuke to the Christians. I shall toss the novel into the trash where it belongs for Mrs. Wharton is indeed a traitor to her class, like her dear friend the buffoon "Teddy" as well.

_____ . Thrilling, to learn that as a young woman, Emma Goldman conspired with an anarchist comrade to murder Henry Clay Frick of Carnegie Steel; for Andrew Carnegie is not a favorite in this household, nor a friend of the Burrs. So much is confused & complicated in the world, it is very exciting to think of murder, as a solution. For, how the men in Princeton worry & fret! Poor Augustus Slade, since his daughter's shameful "abduction," is said to be miserable with ulcers & arthritis; my Burr relatives are distressed with the financial scene, on Wall Street; & of course the van Dycks, & the Strachans, & the Bayards, & Horace. For the world threatens to turn upside down, & Roosevelt for the mere purpose of publicity hammers away at what it pleases the bully to call TRUSTS; & his conspiracy with the outlaw Mitchell, "president" of the miners, is scarcely to be believed. Like his friend Mrs. Wharton, Roosevelt is a class traitor, yet strutting & preening before us—a friend to the Socialist Labor Party (as the anarchists call themselves) & sympathetic doubtless with the riots & arsonists of Paterson. Ah, I hate them all: I am tired of hearing of them: riffraff, rubble, the unwashed & the unlettered & the poor. Mr. Armour, Horace's friend, is sorely abused by a series of attacks in a Socialist newspaper; all about town it is whispered, his meat-packing companies in Chicago have been "exposed" by a young muckraker named Sinclair, who has published a series called <u>The Jungle</u>—Dr. Boudinot shudders to speak of it saying that Adelaide must never so much as glance at this infamy, she would be violently sick to her stomach, & could never again eat meat, nor suffer it to be eaten in her presence. If Mrs. Armour comes to tea this week, I will offer her my sympathy, for if Horace were "exposed" in the public press, how should his Puss respond! We must take solace from the wisdom of the ages as Reverend Beecher has preached <u>God intended the great to be great, and the little to be little; and the workingman who cannot live on one dollar a day, and bread and water, is not fit to live</u>.

This, a Christian preacher of great renown & reputation.

_____ . Late September & yet humid & oppressive as midsummer. & the Slade girl has not yet been found; & poor Dabney has resigned his commission, out of shame. & it is said, divorce proceedings have been initiated, not by Dabney but by the Bayards; for the two families, that had once been friends, are now irrevocably split. & Puss is often vexed & peevish & has little patience for fools. Reverend FitzRandolph came for tea & I quite shocked the man saying I wished to drop two of my charity cases—Sarah Crum, of Kingston, who has presented the world with yet another unwanted Crum—this, the seventh, I believe—& <u>truly enough</u>. & the Windvogel family as well, scarcely less fecund, though the father is said to be crippled, & the mother diabetic; they have moved out to Valley Road, & can no longer be considered in our parish. Reverend FitzRandolph, who will never recover from the shock & shame of having "wed" Annabel Slade & Dabney Bayard, & being in a sense responsible for some part of the scandal, purses his lips at me & worries that it will be difficult to explain to the Windvogel father, badly injured in a furnace mishap in the cellar of Nassau Hall, & without insurance, that the Burrs' charity must cease, as his father has moved a few miles from their original home, since they are not able to afford Princeton Borough taxes & expenses. Whereupon Puss's temper & wit flared up & I said, "Why, dear Reverend, shall our charity—by which I mean yours, and not just ours—so inflate itself to encompass the entire globe?" & the good reverend gaped at me, quite unable to reply.

So much for the Crums & the Windvogels. I have been sick of their mewling & begging for years. It is a good thing, I am sure that Emma Goldman would concur, to XXXX these creatures from my charity list & XXXX them from my conscience.

Ah, I am weakened by my Neftel treatment[*]—& Dr. Boudinot by my bedside overseeing the treatment, murmuring to me, as if it were a well-known & controversial fact, that the tragedy of the Slades would never have occurred, if he had been allowed to perform his "delicate surgery" on Annabel, at the age of seven, as he had recommended to the Slades; for as a young child, the little girl was deemed to be "over-sensitive" & of an "inflamed imagination"; but the family unwisely declined, with the explanation that such young children must be allowed to develop as they will, naturally; without medical or even adult interference. The Neftel procedure is one that Dr. Boudinot & other physicians are often called upon to perform as, in pre-pubescent females, it is adamant that they be spared the indecencies of certain types of physiological sensation; & spared all risk of succumbing to madness by way of the habit of

---

[*] The popular Neftel treatment for nervous invalids involved a complex electrical mechanism by which "galvanic currents" were applied to the spinal column of the invalid, resulting in therapeutic shocks, spasms, or actual convulsions; the theory behind the radical treatment being that both the "nervous" and the "muscular" systems of the body operated on the basis of transmitted electrical messages which must, in afflicted persons, be radically redirected. Often it happened that the invalid exhibited some progress as a result of the therapy; then again, she frequently relapsed, & grew sicker, & more "high-strung" with the passage of time, lapsing finally into paralysis. Adelaide McLean Burr, the reader will be relieved to hear, is to be spared this tragic fate.

unspeakable practices. Thus Dr. Boudinot prattles, & sighs; in the service of the many invalids of Princeton, the doctor has grown white-haired, & elderly; bestowing a kindly paternal tapping on my wrist & commending my parents for having acted prudently in my case. (Yet I remember little. Or nothing. A chloroformed handkerchief, perhaps; a stinging & burning sensation afterward, when required to "make water"—(as Nanny called it); ah, is it not distasteful, ugly—& too trifling to be recalled.)

Autumn, & yet warm. Strange solar winds blow through Princeton & vicinity, it is said. Horace, of late restless nearly all the time, & thinner-cheeked than he was even a few months ago, has installed an <u>electric fan</u> in our household, from Dr. Schulyer Skaats Wheeler's famed laboratory of invention in Ampere, New Jersey; a curious yet wonderfully effective contraption. (& how did Horace learn of it?—by way of my cousin Wilhelmina, it seems; for the two quite by chance sat together on the train to New York, Willy paging through the <u>Post</u> & commenting on the diverse advertisements therein, of which one was for Dr. Wheeler's novelty invention.) & so here it is, in Puss's boudoir, where it is much appreciated. Idly I switch the noisy motor on & off & on & off amusing myself with the fresh little breeze it generates against my heated cheeks & unloos'd tresses. "You are so good to your Puss, dear Horace," I whisper; & Horace says, "Dear Puss, it is the least that a husband might do."

_____ . <u>Inspired by E. Goldman I am in a nervous ecstasy thinking how all of them might be dispatched including the crude sweating Husband, their food laced with arsenic; for arsenic is a white powder, I believe, & might be dissolved in milk, or stirred in mashed potatoes; & spooned into suety grits, which the servants particularly favor. & who would suspect? For the poor invalid Mrs. Burr is scarcely able to lift herself from her divan, on most days; let alone make her way into the rear of the house, where she has not ventured for years. & she is not likely to even know of arsenic, let alone how to employ it.</u>

_____ . (For so it was argued of Lizzie Borden of Fall River, Mass., no "lady" could take an ax & murder her parents; & so the jurors agreed, idiot sheep as they are. & under the law, Lizzie Borden is as innocent as you or I; the more so, as guilt was never proved against her, & guilt might yet be proved against you or I.)

_____ . Boudinot & his son Boudinot, Jr., & a new specialist Dr. Danke from Philadelphia shake their heads & mumble of <u>neurasthenia, rheumatic gout, nervous hyperesthesia, spinal neurosis, temporal lobe inflammation, & the newest & most virulent of plagues from the Orient: Laotian sleeping sickness which paralyzes the brain & spine</u>—& so they recommend a new therapy called Motorpathic Treatment. So, Puss is meant to comply; & not to shriek at the carrion birds, they have come to Maidstone because Mr. & Mrs. Burr are well-to-do Princetonians, & can pay for such quack remedies. So, my temper flared & I wept & thrashed my legs beneath the comforter & told them to leave, to leave at once, I will not succumb to more medical experimentation & more pain that quacks may enrich & amuse themselves. & Dr. Boudinot who has known me since my girlhood stared at me in astonishment, & alarm—"Why Adelaide, this is not like you," etc.—"Why then, Adelaide, we must appeal to Horace."

_____ . To defy them, & quite surprise Horace when he learns of it, I ventured out today to my first tea of the autumn; in fact, it is the first time I have left Maidstone since hideous 4 June when poor Annabel was abducted before our eyes by that beast. Would that the tea were more significant, but it was a welcome respite from my sickbed: our hostess was Mrs. Wilson at Prospect, that poor-man's "Tuscan mansion" on the university campus, about which the Wilsons make such a fuss, giving themselves airs & at the same time complaining that the boys look into their windows! (Who would care to look into *these windows*?) Henrietta Slade kindly stopped for me, to be driven with her in the Slades' new motorcar, a handsome Pierce-Arrow a-gleam with brass fittings; dear Henrietta is solicitous of my health, for the poor woman misses her daughter, of course; & of her daughter no one dares speak. At Prospect, there was the disappointment of so many faculty wives & wives of the Seminary instructors (who are all ordained ministers, I believe)—all very stiff & self-conscious & most of mediocre breeding & shockingly badly dressed in outdated "fashions" of the kind West End ladies have passed on to the poor years ago; Henrietta & I were very quiet, though Mrs. Cleveland condescended to speak with her usual warmth, with Mrs. Wilson, to humor the vain woman, who has announced her intention to establish a women's club—"The Present Day Club"—with a meeting-place on Stockton Street. (So, we were made to realize, this invitation to tea was but a ruse to involve West End ladies in this club—a mingling of West End Princeton & academic Princeton *that will never be*.) Departing, Mrs. Cleveland laughed slyly into my ear—as if we were making our escape but narrowly—& in the Pierce-Arrow, Henrietta said not a word but seemed to be weeping quietly into a lace handkerchief. The company of women—*the wrong sort of women*—is very shrill & weary-ing. And now, I am headachey & out of sorts & must pay for my dash for freedom, with some of the new medication, & a nap.

Item. Henrietta Slade, fortified by several strong cups of tea, shocked a circle of ladies with a tragic & repulsive episode of the other day, at Cross-wicks; the Slades' dog Thor, a handsome German shepherd, was attacked by an unidentified species of snake, black-scaled & very thick of body & unnaturally long: the creature having thrust its wicked head into the poor dog's mouth & forced itself down his throat for some fifteen inches of its hideous length! And this horror, at the edge of the beautiful rose garden at Crosswicks. At this, several of us, certainly including Puss, were feeling very faint; & disgusted; & Johanna turned quite white; & Mrs. Wilson ran to fetch ether-and-water, to revive us. We knew not which was more horrific & perplexing, the strangulation of a dog under such circumstances, or Hen-rietta Slade speaking in such a way—for the poor woman smiled inanely, as she recounted the horror, saying several times But as we Slades are accursed, anything may happen to us now. No one will mark it.

_____ . Accursed! The very word rippled through us, like an elec-tric current. For now the Slades' fate had been defined, it would soon seem to us, who would wish to imagine ourselves but observers, that this was our general fate, as inhabitants of Princeton.

_____ . "All is not well at Westland." This bleak declaration, from out of the beautifully shaped lips of Mrs. Grover Cleveland, came unexpectedly, the next day; & poor Puss quite amazed, to be told by the excitable Hannah that "Mrs. Cleveland" is downstairs & awaiting her, as if a visit had been planned beforehand, which assuredly it had not.

Imagine my surprise, that dark-eyed & olive-skinned Frances Cleveland falteringly confessed, over several cups of Earl Grey liberally sweetened by honey, that <u>all was not well</u> in the stately old Colonial on Hodge Road; for, since the episode at the Craven house, poor Grover could scarcely sleep of a night; cannot seem to find a position to accommodate his stomach, or his back-side, or his chest; thus, he wanders the house in his nightgown & nightcap; is discovered in prayer, or in tears, or rants pertaining to his lawyering days; refuting charges made against him by the Tammany Hall villains, or the Republicans in their cruel campaign that Cleveland had fathered a bastard child & was thus unfit to be President. & most grievous of all for the effect it had upon him, his tearful pleadings with McKinley on issues of the War, & the <u>Maine</u>, & whether Grover had profited from the assassination & rejoiced in it.[*] "He is closeted away with the old President for hours at a time," Mrs. Cleveland confided in me, "and, one wretched night last week—(indeed, the very worst night of our married life!)—Grover woke from sleep shouting in terror, believing that the assassin Leon Colzigna—Czolginga?—Czolgoz-something—was in the room with us, with a fire-arm. Grover had broken into a chill sweat and I could not calm him, nor even attempt to calm him, for he pushed away my arms and seemed not to recognize me. I did not see the anarchist assassin but Grover certainly seemed to see the man, except the creature was now partly decayed, it seemed; as, after his electrocution, quicklime and acid were heaped onto the body. 'He is here, Frances!—the anarchist!—they have come for me at last! My crimes were so petty—my faults, my flaws—yet,

---

[*] That is, with the spirit of McKinley. For William McKinley, twenty-fifth President of the United States, had died in Buffalo, New York, at the hand of the self-proclaimed anarchist and admirer of Emma Goldman, Leon Czolgosz, on September 6, 1901; though police tried assiduously to tie the anarchist female to the assassination, they could discover no evidence linking the two; nor did informers step forward, to involve Goldman, who, nonetheless, refused to denounce the assassin. At this time, Teddy Roosevelt was vice president and was quickly sworn into office. It is not recorded that any assassin had ever threatened Grover Cleveland, during or following his term as President.

they have come for me and will drag me to Hell.' " Mrs. Cleveland fell silent, as if exhausted by this account; and poor Puss scarcely knew what to say, for a fit of shivering and queasiness. & soon after, Mrs. Cleveland departed, with a squeeze of my chill little hand—"Pray, Adelaide, it will never happen to you, that your beloved husband _turns_."

Item. Having resigned his U.S. Army commission, my troubled nephew Dabney Bayard is said to be glimpsed often at the Belmont, Saratoga, & Pimlico racetracks; more grievously, he is said to be a patron of illicit & illegal gambling establishments in New York City.

(No doubt, Dabney frequents worse establishments, even the mention of which we ladies are spared.) Henrietta Slade speaks in a tremulous voice of this unhappy young man, whose marriage to her daughter was just recently annulled by a decision of the local court; for it seems, unjustly, Dabney has become an enemy of the Slades & refuses to communicate with them, etc. There is a prevailing rumor that Dabney & Josiah Slade will soon fight a duel; that each young man has chosen his dueling pistol; yet, Henrietta insists: "Josiah is a young man of Christian morals & fortitude who would never be party to an act of forbidden violence. He commiserates with Dabney as he would with a bereaved brother."

When Mrs. Slade absented herself from the drawing room at Wheatsheaf for a few minutes, we ladies spoke excitedly of her revelation; & compared notes, that, so strangely, there has been no news of Annabel from any quarter, as if the young woman and her abductor had indeed vanished into thin air. Josiah is often absent from Princeton, rumored to be ceaselessly searching for his sister in every part of Jersey—cities, towns, hamlets & wild forests and mountains to the Northwest, along the Delaware River. (For Jersey is a greatly varied state, its rural regions scarcely imagined by inhabitants of its cities, or visitors from New York City.) Johanna van Dyck confided in us that in meeting Josiah one didn't immediately grasp the nature & degree of his obsession; nor had his appearance altered greatly, except for the fact that he had lost weight—his handsome face just slightly gaunt, & his eyes unpleasantly glittering; it seems too that he has cultivated a rough sort of beard. When he returns to Crosswicks, he is said to be "very quiet"—"melancholy & resigned"—yet hides away in his grandfather's library perusing old maps, even, it's said, maps drawn up in Colonial times, of little accuracy now. "The most pathetic of all tales of Josiah," Johanna said, in a lowered voice, "was told to Pearce by several undergraduates who were camping last weekend near the Water Gap, and wakened from sleep before dawn by a 'bearded young hunter' tramping in the forest alone, armed with a deer rifle, and wearing a backpack, searching, as he said, for his <u>lost sister</u>. The campers roused themselves to give aid, for, being Princeton boys, they are naturally gracious and schooled in courtesy; but were taken aback to learn that the <u>lost sister</u> had been missing for ninety-seven days, and had been last seen on Nassau Street, Princeton. Have you ever heard a more piteous tale?"

_____ . & there is my young cousin Wilhelmina—"Willy"—who has quarreled with her parents, & has applied to the art school in New York City which they had forbidden, & <u>will</u> move out of her parents' house soon, she has vowed. Since the rude departure of Annabel, Wilhelmina has certainly not been herself; very rarely comes to see me, in fact has not come to Maidstone for months. & further trivial news, Ellen Wilson informs the party of ladies gravely in her soft-melting Southern accent that Dean West "persecutes" Woodrow in the most diabolical ways: if the two men happen to meet while playing golf at Springdale, for instance, West, who is the more skilled golfer, stands observing & sneering as Woodrow tries to play with equanimity, quite embarrassing himself & his golfing companions. Since there was no way to prevent it, Woodrow has allowed the opening of Merwick House, on Bayard Lane, as the temporary residence of the Graduate College, housing twenty young men and patterned in "slavish" imitation, as Woodrow has said, of Oxford & Cambridge. The students are forced to dress in formal academic attire, Mrs. Wilson said, solely that Dean West might sport his fulsome academic regalia—for the vain creature, as Woodrow calls him, boasts a crimson hood from Harvard; on Wednesday evenings guest speakers are invited to the college & evening clothes are worn beneath the gowns! As if this were not outrageous enough, Mrs. Wilson said, her Southern accent now flattening in vehemence, the young men escort West back to his private residence at the close of the lengthy evening, at which many courses of fish, fowl, Virginia ham, beaten biscuits, sherry, wines, & God knows what all else are consumed, costumed still in their voluptuous academic gowns & carrying large candles—"As if they are altar boys, and Andrew West their prelate!" Beyond this, Ellen Wilson told us there was a great deal of tobacco consumption at Merwick, & "orgies" of bridge-playing; & it may soon develop, <u>female visitors</u> allowed in the public rooms downstairs. "The dean has even resumed his frightful clarinet playing," Mrs. Wilson said, hotly, "with the sole purpose of tormenting Woodrow: for the abrasive sounds carry across campus to Woodrow's study in the tower at Prospect." At which Mrs. Cleveland said, sharply: "Andrew West is a very fine man, a gentleman; his experience with graduate education is much superior, I am told, to that of Mr. Wilson, as he has traveled widely in England & Europe; & it is said, Mr. Wilson, like any provincial Protestant minister, has scarcely traveled in the United States." & the reaction of Ellen Wilson was such, the poor woman opened her mouth to speak, & confronted with the Junoesque authority of the former First Lady, & a sense that her audience did not sympathize with her, could not think of a thing to say; & soon after, deeply blushing, murmuring one or another excuse, left the drawing room as if to consult with the kitchen staff; whereupon Mrs. Wilson's unfashionable clothes were exclaimed over, & her "uneven" features & ill-styled hair, as well as the singularly dowdy & second-rate furnishings of the president's house. "Yet, you know, they are perfectly suited for each other: Mr. & Mrs. Wilson"—so Frances Cleveland said, with schoolgirl insouciance; and all laughed.

Ah, it is so good to <u>laugh</u>!

_____ . And now, a new gentleman in Princeton.

<u>Count English von Gneist</u> is an abbreviation of the man's name, I am told; he is a guest at Drumthwacket, on Stockton Road, near the seminary; he is in fact a distinguished theologian, from Heidelberg, Germany, who presented himself to the Moses Taylor Pyne family with a letter of introduction, & quite impressed Mr. Pyne with his bearing and conversation. Evidently, the Count is a widower; his entire family was lost in a tragic accident on the Rhine River; but no one should speak of this loss, it is warned.

"Is the Count an attractive man?" I asked Johanna van Dyck, who had met him at Drumthwacket, & Johanna said, with a shivery sort of smile, "Ah, yes! Very." & Clarice Biddle volunteered that she had never seen so unusual an individual in her life, so "well-bred"—"noble of features & figure"—"quite the social catch of the season!" (Clarice Biddle! How has it happened, Clarice Biddle who lives with her dour judge-husband in a pokey little stone house on Hibben Road has been invited to Drumthwacket to meet the Count, & not Horace or me?) Unfortunately the Pynes are not so very social, Johanna & Clarice agree, & have done little to introduce Count von Gneist to their neighbors . . . At which moment the sonorous bell of Old North sounded & I know not why, a sensation of faintness swept over me; & I heard myself inquire in a most nonchalant way, "What is the Count's age, do you think?"—& Johanna said, "Fairly young: no more than forty" & Clarice Biddle said, "Or, if fifty, a very virile fifty."

_____ . Sluggish this morning after yesterday afternoon's excitement—can it be the virulent Laotian sleeping sickness—at last?

& Hannah calling "Mrs. Burr? Mrs. Burr" from a great distance; for it seemed I was in another land, in a castle overlooking the Rhine; in which I was not "Mrs. Burr" nor even "Adelaide"—or "Puss." The appellation the Count bestowed on me was crude & blunt & brooked no resistance: Woman he commanded in a heavily accented baritone come here.

_____ . Only Dr. Wheeler's ingenious mechanism soothes me, its blades turning & turning & stirring a voluptuous breeze against my fever'd face.

_____ . "How am I cruel, Adelaide," Horace demanded of me impatiently, "—no man possessed of his wits would wish to provoke such a response!" (For in settling the tray on my lap he deliberately pressed against my left bosom, that is uncorseted; I would swear to it.

(Cunningly with the edge of the tray & his thumb. Causing me to flinch & shriek & all went tumbling—teapot & hot water & cream & sugar & spoons & he did not apologize afterward.)

_____ . Bored & tearful. So very weak, my Bible slipped from my fingers & struck the floor with a thud. Though uncorseted on my divan it seems that an iron bar encircles my ribs & stomach & hips; I cannot breathe;

I shall faint. For Horace has ceased to love & respect me & naught but the grave awaits.

_____ . The new issue of <u>Vanity Fair</u> is the talk of Princeton as it features an article on John Singer Sargent; his portrait of Mandy—("Mrs. Edgerstoune FitzRandolph of Mora House, Princeton")—a splendid reproduction—I am wildly jealous!—no, I am truly pleased, for Mandy is my dear friend, & worthy of attention. (But why has she stayed away so long? It has been told to me, the Count has been a dinner guest at Mora House; & Horace & Adelaide not invited.) (Why does she not bring the Count to visit <u>us</u>? Does she expect me to <u>beg</u>?) Mandy is a handsome woman if not beautiful; what is called "strapping"—a sort of "Gibson Girl"—& not <u>petite</u> like me, if I may say so. Is it foolish of me to wish that my portrait might be painted by Sargent? Or is it—too late?

_____ . (Ah, how my heart leaps! But it is nothing—no one—the door blown gently ajar & then pausing—as if someone waited, breath inheld, in the hall. "Yes? Hello? Hannah?—Mrs. Joris?—Minnie? Is it you, Horace?" (But no, Horace has taken the train to Philadelphia, where he has a business meeting, he has said; & will not return until Friday.) It is no one; & Puss is being foolish again, to take such alarm over a trifle.)

_____ . <u>The true founder of Anarchy was Jesus Christ & the first Anarchist society the Apostles. For the weak will rise up against their oppressors, & the last shall be first, & the first last; the Proletariat shall prevail against its class enemies, & the Bourgeoisie & all Government wither away. Until such time, we teach the Propaganda of the Deed, & Individual Reappropriation.</u>

Reading thus in <u>Revolutionary Thoughts of Mikhail Bakunin</u> which I have sent for, in the mail; unknown to Horace, who would soundly disapprove, as to my simpering lady friends; & a thrill rushes through my body, at such stirring words!

By <u>Propaganda of the Deed</u> is meant destruction: anarchic bombings, assassinations. By <u>Individual Reappropriation</u> is meant bold & fearless acts of theft against the <u>bourgeoisie</u>.

Would that an anarchist revolutionary stormed Maidstone House, to <u>reappropriate</u> poor Puss! The first house I would lead him to would be Drumthwacket, if not Crosswicks: for each is far too "palatial" for good taste; each deserves fire-bombing & looting at the grubby hands of the Proletariat.

_____ . "There is at least one saint among us: Winslow Slade."

These surprising words Horace said to me this evening; for it turns out that my husband has <u>sought counsel</u> recently, on an issue not known to me. "Dearest Puss, I would not trouble you with the subject, for it is inconsequential"—so Horace says smilingly; leaning to kiss my brow, & I am amazed to sense the new calm that lifts from him, & the spiritual equanimity of old, absent these many weeks. My handsome gentleman-husband, returned to me: freshly barbered on Witherspoon St. with a faint but pleasing scent of lemon-pomade; his curly mustache flecked with gray, but distinguished; his strong teeth displayed in a smile so broad, his cheeks are creased; eyes brimming with love for his Puss, whom he has slighted of late. Ah, I <u>am</u> loved; I will not doubt Horace again.

(Though it is strange, & worrisome: Horace refuses to tell me what <u>counsel</u> he has sought from our former Reverend Slade* as if I am a silly little goose to be concerned with anything beyond the boudoir, or the drawing room. Is it a Wall Street matter? Is it our mutual investments? (For my inheritance & trust fund have been freely mingled with Horace's, in acknowledgment of his comprehension of such matters.) Tiresome Mr. Lodge who urges Horace to buy & sell & buy & sell again: Northern Securities Co.—Northern Pacific—Great Northern—Colorado Smelting & Mining—Panama Canal

---

* Though Winslow Slade destroyed the vast majority of his private papers in the unhappy spring of 1906, some partly charred pages of his Journal remain; and so we know that the subject of Horace Burr's several anguished conversations with him involved one of the knottiest moral problems in Christianity: whether the marital act is <u>innocent</u>, while the carnal desire is <u>evil</u>, as the Church Father Gregory taught in the sixth century; or whether, as the Thomists later calibrated, evil lies less in carnal indulgence than in the <u>ligamentum rationis</u> (the suspension of the rational being). But what did Winslow Slade advise Horace Burr; & why indeed did Horace feel the need to seek him out, after fifteen years of marriage?

Co. of America—Pennsylvania Railroad—Standard Oil—so very boring! I shall not even trouble to lift the receiver & overhear when Horace next confers with Mr. Lodge etc.

The world passes me by, it seems. For Dr. Boudinot has cautioned Horace—I am not to be over-stimulated & must keep to my couch; & must not "incite" my thoughts by a rough or promiscuous sort of reading. For this reason I have missed the performance of Count English von Gneist at the Pahaquarra Valley Hunt yesterday, about which everyone is marveling. For it seems that this well-born gentleman rides a superb stallion, starkly black, of the Arabian Thoroughbred breed; his posture is noble, but agile; his riding manners impeccable; when most swiftly galloping across a field, the Count & his steed seem scarcely to be hurrying. & his English-tailored riding costume, so gracefully fitting his figure, it is said to have put our local men to shame—so my eager informant Johanna van Dyck has told me.

"His face, Adelaide, is both bold & poetical: the forehead high, & the iron-gray hair retreating from it, yet giving the impression of unusual thickness," Johanna says in a slow voice, "which adds to the Count's look of nobility, yet melancholy. For he reminds me of no one so much as Lord Rochester, of Jane Eyre." The von Gneists are said to have descended from an ancient noble family in a region of central Europe called Wallachia, a former principality of Romania; the warrior blood of Magyars, Saxons, Lombards, Bulgars, and even the infidel Turk flows in their veins. Yet the von Gneists are sadly depleted in number, & their once-enormous fortune has been much reduced; Count von Gneist calls himself "The Sole Living Heir of Nothingness" & has spent his adult life in travel from one capital city to another. Though a graduate of the distinguished Munich Theological Seminary, the Count did not become a Protestant minister, but rather a writer of "theological texts"; in addition, he is poet, playwright, novelist and composer. And an exceptional horseman, and hunter. By nature prone to melancholy, the Count thinks of himself as "essentially without a home"— "an exile"—not unlike the legendary Flying Dutchman; except he is not an immortal, but decidedly mortal.

"And he is a widower, totally without a family."

Johanna's voice quavers imparting such news.

_____ . I think that I shall meet him at last: Count von Gneist.

For Amanda has invited Horace & me to dine at Mora next week; & I am optimistic that I shall prove strong enough to venture forth, if Horace will allow.

_____ . A strange incident, reported to me second-hand: in the train depot, Horace was snubbed by Mrs. Cleveland; that there could be no mistake on his part, Horace attempted courteously to address the woman, provoking her to turn her back on him, most rudely. Even her footman blushed for the woman's rudeness, Horace says.

I will not defend Mrs. Cleveland: I do not like her, & she is not my friend. Nor is the obese guzzler Grover Cleveland an individual to be admired.

Yet, Horace gazes oddly at me stroking his mustache—"The mysteries of the female sex! We men can never hope to fathom your depths, but only try not to drown in them."

_____ . A strange itching & burning sensation between my eyes— and I am wakened from sleep startled, like one who has eased out of her mortal body just slightly, in sleep; the etheric body comprises us, who are enlightened, it is said; & sometimes in sleep this body becomes dislodged from the moral body. (Mrs. Blavatsky teaches.) But oh!—this so queer sensation between my eyes, in my lower forehead—is it the third eye, of enlightenment? Opening, at last?

THE SEARCH CONT'D

It was months after the "abduction" that Josiah learned of at least one of the ways in which his sister and her seducer had cultivated their illicit relationship.

On a chilly October morning when Josiah was walking in the *jardin anglais* behind Crosswicks, tormented by thoughts of where he might search next for Annabel, for all his attempts to find her had come to naught, he was approached, hesitantly, by the head gardener—an older man who'd been in the employ of the Slades for decades, and had known each of the Slade grandchildren from infancy.

The gardener confessed to Josiah, in a voice of chagrin and regret, that he hoped *he* had not failed to prevent the tragedy of Josiah's sister's disappearance by remaining silent when he might have spoken out to Mr. Slade, or Annabel's parents, or Josiah himself.

For, it seemed, he had "many times" observed Miss Annabel leaving sealed letters in the rotted hollow of an enormous, ancient wych elm in the lower garden, through much of April and all of May; and though he kept watch a dozen times, in secrecy, he'd never so much as glimpsed the person who came for Annabel's letter, and left another in its place addressed, in a firm hand MISS ANNABEL SLADE. (All that he was certain of, the man said, with an attempt at wit, was that whoever took away Miss Annabel's letters was not Lieutenant Bayard.) Upon three distinct occasions, in that uncertain twilit hour before dawn, he had, from his greenhouse, happened to see a man and a woman gliding swiftly along the dewy grass in the direction of Crosswicks Forest—"With such little weight to their bodies, their feet seemed to leave no impression at all."

Josiah was so astonished by this revelation, he quite forgot to be angry at the gardener; nor would anger, so belatedly, have made much difference.

" 'A man and a woman'—but was the woman Annabel?"

Somberly the gardener shook his head: he did not know, the figures were too distant.

"How were they dressed?"

Again, the gardener didn't know. Though he believed their clothing wasn't new, or fashionable—"Like the clothes of some other time, when I'd been a boy, maybe."

Josiah said, frowning: "It seems strange, Hendrick, you wouldn't have recognized my sister, even at a distance."

Quickly the gardener agreed: yet, it was so, he couldn't have identified the man and the woman except to think, at the time, that they were not familiar to him, but strangers.

"But I did find cigarettes in the grass, that should not have been there. Some kind of foreign cigarette it looked like, not much smoked, only a little part burnt away."

"Cigarettes! But Annabel doesn't smoke, of course."

Still, the smoker was very likely the man. *Was* this Axson Mayte?

"And when did they stop appearing here? Was it after the wedding?"

Gravely the gardener nodded *yes*. He believed so.

He hoped, he said, that Josiah would forgive him. For he wished now, so very badly, he'd said something to someone, that the tragedy might have been prevented.

Josiah said there was nothing to forgive—of course he wasn't to blame.

"No more than any of us, Hendrick. For it seems we hardly knew my sister, though imagining that we did."

AND SO MAYBE this was her escape from us—from Crosswicks Manse, and the Slades. And maybe she does smoke, and did—and none of us knew.

AT ABOUT THIS TIME, Josiah received a curious note from Woodrow Wilson asking him, in the most humble terms, if he would be free to drop by Prospect sometime soon, to discuss a "private matter."

A time was arranged; yet, when Josiah arrived, and was let into the house by Mrs. Wilson herself, he was disappointed to learn that Woodrow was "feeling unwell" and could not see him after all.

Josiah expressed concern, and asked if Mr. Wilson was seriously ill; and Mrs. Wilson said, in an outburst of emotion, "Why yes of course he is *seriously ill*; he would not shirk his responsibilities otherwise."

Josiah apologized for the interruption, and was about to leave, when Mrs. Wilson said, in a softer voice, yet not without an air of reproach, "Woodrow has been in a perpetual state of nerves since—since that terrible day. He fears you all blame him, at the Manse; no matter that he scarcely knew this creature 'Mayte,' and certainly hadn't involved the university in any business dealings with him."

Josiah assured Mrs. Wilson that no one in his family blamed anyone for the episode, except Mayte himself; and that his conversation with Mr. Wilson would be along other lines. He added that he might want to speak with Jessie, too, since Jessie and Annabel had been close friends, and perhaps Annabel had confided in Jessie, or at least hinted of her situation . . .

At this Mrs. Wilson became visibly upset, and said it was not possible—as Jessie, too, had suffered a nervous collapse, and couldn't come downstairs; and, in any case, Josiah could be sure that she herself had closely questioned her daughter on the subject of the "abduction," and was satisfied that Jessie knew nothing, and was absolutely innocent.

As Annabel was innocent, once. As we wished to believe.

Josiah apologized again to the agitated woman, and went away; but was summoned back the next day by a telephone call from Woodrow Wilson himself, asking Josiah to meet him in the late afternoon, when he would be returned from Nassau Hall to Prospect; and would be working in his "tower"—which turned out to be hardly more than an attic room sparely fashioned into a study, with excellent views from several windows looking out onto the university campus through a thicket of evergreens and elms.

This was the "tower" of which Josiah had heard: the president's hideaway from his *all-female household* about which he sometimes joked rather awkwardly.

Josiah thought that Woodrow Wilson was looking rather more ashen-faced than usual, though Wilson was not a man to ever look "hale and hearty"—the very antithesis of his nemesis Andrew West, a burly Falstaff of a fellow with ruddy cheeks and an ebullient, infectious laugh. Out of politeness Josiah inquired after the older man's health, as he knew he was expected to do, and was presented with a grimly comical recitation of maladies, a number of which, Wilson said, he'd been enduring in stoic silence, not wanting to alarm those around him; or to "give hope to" those who stood apart from him.

Dyspepsia, and chronic nervous spasms in his upper torso, and an intermittent tremor of his hands, and occasional "occlusions" of vision—this particularly alarming to him, for he had numerous important speeches to write and articles to prepare. (Mr. Harvey, editor of *Harper's*, had requested an article from him, and he was anxious to oblige.) These ailments,

Wilson told Josiah, before even he thought to ask Josiah to be seated, were the result of intense pressure put upon him by the university "situation"—about which, he was sure, Josiah knew? "The latest outrage is, Dean West has gone to the board of trustees to inveigle their support of him, for the Graduate College—the man has been offered the presidency of the Massachusetts Institute of Technology, in Cambridge, Mass.—*at a salary rumored to be higher than that of the president of Princeton University*." Wilson paused, that Josiah might absorb this revelation.

"But the double-dealer won't leave Princeton, I know. There is some devilish business about this 'Institute of Technology'—the Harvard president Mr. Eliot is seeking to annex it to Harvard, as a 'science department.' How, then, is Dean West to be *president*? It's all very complicated—diabolical. Yet the trustees will believe him, especially Grover Cleveland who is the man's *crony*."

As Wilson ranted, and rambled, in a "stoic" voice, Josiah glanced about the room, which was both Spartan and cluttered; only just a desk, a table, and chairs, but the windowsills, as well as the table, were stacked with papers and documents; on a low sideboard close to the desk were a startling number of medications and syrups; Josiah noticed even a package of wide white gauze bandages, and a tin bottle with the Gothic legend *Hebes Liniment* on its side. Stained spoons, soiled handkerchiefs and tissues—from these, a stale, dimly cloacal odor emanated.

"Might I open a window? It's a little close in here . . ."

But no, Woodrow Wilson frowned at the suggestion: for he was fighting bronchitis, and could not risk further infecting his lungs.

Following his complaints of Dean West, Wilson complained of the difficulty he was having clearing away "dead wood" from the university, which he had inherited from the genial, ineffective president Francis Patton; yet more difficulty, in his campaign to abolish the eating clubs, that held a "veritable chokehold" on university undergraduate life, and had the power to intimidate the faculty and administration as well. And sports—"The sports teams dominate, crudely; and their coaches and trainers imagine themselves as deserving of their salaries as our faculty."

Josiah recalled how Annabel had often defended Woodrow Wilson, when others were criticizing the man as "cold"—"coldly ambitious"—a "self-righteous prig"—a "Byzantine logothete"; Annabel had protested, saying that her friend Jessie's father, as she knew him, loved to talk with children, and to amuse them with his comical dialect stories in a "darky" drawl. Particularly little girls, Annabel said, in recollection of several occasions in Jessie's company, when Mr. Wilson lowered himself into a squatting position, to speak more comfortably with them, and to make them laugh harder.

Several times Josiah tried to interrupt Wilson's monologue, which persisted in a dogged, quiet way, like a slow movement of molasses; he was eager to ask about Axson Mayte, but Wilson deflected him by suggesting to Josiah that he pursue a career in *law*, as he had, initially; for he'd intended to go into politics, with a law degree, and not to practice law. He then lectured his visitor on the fact that their Calvinist faith did not countenance withdrawal from the world for the world was, as the Bible makes clear, a battleground between the forces of Good and the forces of Evil—"The Devil likes nothing better than for the best of us to retire to private life, and let the world go hang!"

"The 'best of us'—but, sir, how are we to know?"

"How are we to *know*? Why—God allows us to know. There can be no mystery here."

Irritation flared in Wilson, as if a match were being struck. The grainy-lidded eyes grew sharper in contention, and the languid posture immediately straightened. Yet Josiah said, not quite insolently, but in the manner in which he might have tried to refute any of his older Slade relatives, "So far as I've learned from my studies, here at Princeton and after, all nations, tribes, clans, and sometimes even individuals, believe themselves to be 'God's chosen people' and their enemies the Devil's. In which case, Dr. Wilson, it requires quite an act of faith to imagine that

God is exclusively on our side, and has only our interests in mind, when there are so very many others—*millions*."

Wilson blinked slowly at Josiah through his bright-polished eyeglasses as if he'd never heard anything so extraordinary, and so disturbing, in his life. "Josiah, I wonder if I've heard you correctly? Such 'free-thinking'—'anarchic'—notions have no place at Princeton, and can't be blamed on your course of study, I'm sure. At the seminary, Reverend Shackleton has gone on record stating that 'no new ideas' of any sort will be entertained there, unlike that bastion of 'free thinkers' Union Theological Seminary; and my commitment to Princeton is, as I have said, 'reform' in the service of tradition. Ideas like yours make for lively debating subjects but, in actual life, are unacceptable, relativistic nonsense."

Josiah had all he could do to keep from rolling his eyes; or, in the undergraduate way of muted derision, shuffling his feet against the bare hardwood floor. Instead he said, with an air of placating an excited elder. "Well. I know enough, sir, to know that I'm very ignorant."

He didn't like the tremulous way in which Wilson was staring at him, or the twitching motions of Wilson's lips, that appeared caked at the corners with a powdery white substance.

He wondered why Wilson had invited him to visit. It could not have been to recite his usual grievances, surely?

He ventured to say: "Now, sir, on this matter of a former associate or acquaintance of yours, Axson Mayte—"

"No, no! That accursed individual is no 'associate' or 'acquaintance' of mine, I assure you!"

To this, Josiah could think of no reply. For certainly Woodrow Wilson had been seen in the company of Mayte frequently, for a fixed period of time; Josiah himself had seen them together.

"He was coarse and barbaric and no gentleman, like Jack London"—Wilson spoke now as if inspired, by an association of ideas—"who, the other day, dared to state in public that he would not deny that Socialism *is* a menace! 'Its purpose is to wipe out, root and branch, all capitalistic institutions of our present-day society'—so the ruffian boasts. The Revolution, as they call it, will have taken place by 1910. And what of the influx of multitudes of immigrants of the lowest classes from southern and eastern Europe?—for the sturdier stocks of the northern Europeans, the British and the Scots-Irish, are increasingly threatened; as, it is said, bad money drives out good."

Josiah sighed, and made no reply. In the near distance Old North was tolling the welcome hour of 6 P.M.

"When I was an undergraduate at Princeton, and something of a 'poler,' I was blackballed by Ivy," Wilson said, with an ironic twist of his lips; as if nothing could be more incredible, than this revelation. "I vowed then, to take my revenge where I could, and when. I have waited twenty years. The Campbells of Argyll know *patience*."

An objective observer could not have drawn any connection between this impulsive utterance of Wilson's and Wilson's repugnance for "anarchy"—but Josiah understood.

Josiah, who had disdained bicker at Princeton, as one of the more sought-after freshmen in his class, had received a bid from the exclusive eating club Ivy nonetheless, unofficially and indirectly—which he'd ignored, in his Slade arrogance. And so on campus during his undergraduate years he'd been the envy and the awe of all, even certain of his professors. To have ignored Ivy! He had made his friends elsewhere, a few. But friendship and popularity had not seemed to him the point of college, then or now.

Now the expression in Wilson's long-jawed face, of an old humility but partly mollified by the hope of vindication, made Josiah feel that, for a moment, he'd been cast back to his adolescent self on this very campus: essentially, a claustrophobic little world of privilege and anxiety in which one was made to *care too much about too little.*

"I'm sorry to hear that, sir. The eating clubs can be tyrannical, if they are not checked."

"*They will be checked*. I will fight the entrenched alumni and the G—damn'd board of trustees and accursed Dean West who supports them, *till the death*."

Woodrow Wilson was trembling now, through his long lean body.

It was very extreme of the ministerial Wilson to have said *G—damn'd*.

Josiah felt an impulse to comfort the older man, even to wipe at his damp mouth with a handkerchief. Yet he would never touch Woodrow Wilson—of course! He was remembering, in a European lecture in Mc-Cosh, years ago, one of his professors declaring that while madness in individuals is relatively rare, it is virtually a prerequisite for a certain sort of political leader: "He is not functionally mad, but mad in his intellect. He will know by instinct how to rally others to his madness, in the pretense that he is in their service and their lives depend upon him—Napoleon, for example."

Josiah thought *At least here in the U.S., in our democracy that can't happen*.

It was said about town that Woodrow Wilson had had "political ambitions" since boyhood. In a ribald moment Frances Cleveland had remarked at a dinner party that the "most potent male organ" in all of Princeton was the mouth of Woodrow Wilson.

Josiah smiled at the thought. But ceased smiling at once, as Woodrow Wilson was glaring at him.

"You are amused, I see! *You*, as I recall, were a member of Ivy."

"No. I was not."

"I had heard, you were. Or, you'd declined their bid."

"It was all long ago, Dr. Wilson. It's best to believe that the eating clubs will 'wither away' with the rise of democracy on campus—as the Socialists and Marxists predict, the state will 'wither away.'"

"No way of life so entrenched will ever 'wither away'—it must be helped, with dynamite, if need be. As well expect that Nigras and—and women—will be admitted to Princeton University, one day, as to fantasize the 'withering-away' of the eating clubs." Wilson laughed, at such a ridiculous notion.

"And does Dean West oppose you on that issue, too?"

Wilson saw no undue familiarity on Josiah's part, in asking this question; but rather responded with heat, as if Josiah were a confidant.

"Yes. Of course. West opposes me *on every possible issue,* as it is my soul he wants, in a nutshell, he has said."

" 'In a nutshell'—really?"

"He has said. It has been reported to me."

Now in a state of quivering nerves, Wilson lurched to his feet. Josiah took advantage of the moment and quickly stood as well, with the excuse that he had to leave, for he was expected at dinner at Wheatsheaf that evening. With a curious smile of elation, Wilson laid his arm on Josiah's shoulder, and escorted him down the narrow stairs to the first floor, and to the foyer. (Josiah wondered where in the house Mrs. Wilson and the daughters were. The "tower" was just enough detached from the main part of the household, so that Woodrow Wilson could slip up there, and even have visitors, without being detected.) Just as Josiah was about to leave, eager to step outside into the fresh air, Wilson said, bringing his mouth close to Josiah's ear, "You will wonder why I invited you? It is very hard to say this, Josiah, but—my dear daughter Jessie has been unwell, you know—after the—that terrible day—to which she'd so long looked forward, as a bridesmaid. Dr. Hatch has been administering to her, with some success. But I must tell you—Jessie is tormented by terrible dreams. The sleep-medicine Dr. Hatch prescribes seems almost to exacerbate them. Nights in succession she has dreamt of poor Ruth Cleveland—and the murdered Spags girl, whom none of us knew of course—these wraiths tease and torment her, scratching at her window and begging to be allowed inside; lately, the two have been joined by a third girl, a blond girl, which seems to Jessie to be your sister Annabel, as she was some years ago—young, innocent, terrified, begging to be let inside Jessie's room; but Jessie reports that she is too transfixed by horror, to move from her bed. Jessie says—*What if they are vampires?*"

Wilson's voice quavered. Josiah stepped away, as if he'd been stabbed to the heart.

Wanting to protest *My sister is not dead. My sister is not a vampire!*

Instead, Josiah could only thank Wilson, and hurriedly depart.

The bell of Old North was tolling an unknown hour.

OCTOBER 1905

Vampire! Josiah is incensed. He has never heard anything so ridiculous in his life.

For Josiah is purely a rationalist. Josiah's heroes are Aristotle, David Hume, John Stuart Mill. He is not widely read in philosophy and logic but feels a repugnance for all that is *murky, mystical.*

Yes, to a degree: Josiah is a Protestant Christian. But Josiah does not subject his faith to reason; his faith is bound up with family loyalty, which is not to be questioned.

"There is no 'supernatural' world—only just this, the 'natural' world. All the rest is nonsense."

"NONSENSE."

In her opulently furnished boudoir-library at Westland, Mrs. Grover Cleveland has distracted herself from her marital worries by typing, on her new frontstroke, Underwood typewriter, the concluding pages of an article on female suffrage that had been begun by her ailing husband at the invitation of *The Ladies' Home Journal;* but Frances Cleveland has revised the article in her own far more conversational voice so that it is a chatty effusion, and not a dreary sermon. Frances smiles to think it will make a considerable "splash" when it is published: " 'Sensible and responsible women *do not want to vote.* The relative positions to be assumed by Man and Woman, in the working-out of civilization, were assigned long ago—by a far higher intelligence than ours." Frances pauses before typing, with fierce strokes of the machine, the final riposte: "Female suffrage is, in a word, *nonsense*."

From an adjoining room, poor Grover is calling to her. Frances has the excuse that the typewriter-mechanism is very noisy, and she can't hear; in any case, a servant will come running, soon.

"It is what we pay them for, after all."

ITEM. COUNT ENGLISH von Gneist, of late the most sought-after dinner guest in Princeton, in a dark-hued evening suit with a ruffled white shirt and silver-embroidered vest, has escorted Mrs. Amanda FitzRandolph and her great-aunt Thomasina Bayberry to a lavish dinner at Drumthwacket—for Edgerstoune is away in San Francisco, on business. It is at this dinner that von Gneist exchanges significant glances with another guest, Miss Wilhelmina Burr, who feels a sensation of cold come over her even as, with girlish laughter, she responds to the remark of a dinner-table companion to her right. *Such a powerful personality!—and so handsome, though his cheeks are creased with melancholy. But what interest would the Count have in* me!

Since Annabel's departure, and Josiah's continued indifference to her, Wilhelmina has vowed not to withdraw from the world in heartbreak, or in invalidism; often she is seen in hiking shoes and tweeds striding along a bank of the Delaware-Raritan Canal, as it runs parallel to Lake Carnegie; often, she is seen striding along Nassau Street, in the direction of the public library; at least once a week, in the early morning, she is seen on the train platform at Princeton Junction gripping an artist's portfolio, on her way into the city and the New York School of Art where she receives instruction from the renowned Robert Henri himself—though forbidden by her anxious parents to *stay the night* in New York City, even at a relative's home.

Item. It is at Wheatsheaf, the home of his uncle Copplestone Slade and his aunt Lenora, that Josiah hears news to tear at his heart: that, according to his uncle, Annabel and "that man, Mayte" have been sighted at the Waldorf-Astoria in New York City and yet again at a private dinner party at the Frick mansion on upper Fifth Avenue. With a snort of disgust Copplestone hands Josiah a newspaper clipping from the *New York Herald,* a photograph of a couple in a smart Paige motorcar, the young blond woman wearing a veil about her head and shoulders and the gentleman in linen duster, dust-hood, and goggles; the caption beneath reading simply *The fashionable set tours abroad.*

This photograph, Copplestone said, was fresh evidence of the "infamy" their family would never outlive.

"But is this Annabel? The man is certainly not Mayte."

Josiah examined the photograph closely. Possibly, the young woman might have been his sister, or her twin; but the gentleman was certainly not Axson Mayte, for he was slender and darkly handsome, and Mayte was squat and ugly as a troll.

Copplestone raged: "And to think that I played cards with that scoundrel, in fact, lost money at cards to that scoundrel, at Andrew West's! And more than once."

"But—is this 'Mayte'? He doesn't resemble 'Mayte' at all."

"Though, Josiah, bear in mind—I didn't trust him from the first. His manners were those of a Rooshian Bolshevik, and his 'luck' with cards too good. He stank, too, of ambergris—like a silly female."

Stung by this remark, perhaps, though ordinarily Lenora remained silent when her husband gave himself up to one of his rants, Josiah's aunt said quietly: "Why, Copplestone, I remember you saying of Axson Mayte that he was a most lively fellow, 'a man among men,' and very clever in his mimicry of both Woodrow Wilson and Teddy Roosevelt."

Copplestone grunted, in a kind of grudging assent.   was cruelly funny. But I did not laugh."

Lenora said, bent over her embroidery as if it, and not the co   sation, drew her deepest concentration: "Why yes, Copplestone, I believ   you did laugh—quite cruelly, I thought at the time. For Woodrow Wilson would believe himself a friend of yours, as he is a friend of your father's."

"He *is not* a friend of my father's. He is a hanger-on, who wants my father's support—the support of all of the Slades."

Josiah sensed that there was tension in the air of the drawing room, between his uncle and his aunt; badly he wanted to question Copplestone about Axson Mayte, but this did not seem like an opportune time.

And how dank and chill Wheatsheaf felt that evening, like a mausoleum.

Wheatsheaf, inhabited now by strangers, is one of the oldest and most regal houses on Bayard Lane, having been originally built in 1769, with numerous additions to follow over the decades. It is in a palatial Georgian style with a "soft" redbrick facade, high roofs, a prominent portico, and narrow shutters framing its many windows, at the corner of Bayard and the road now known as Cleveland Lane. Through Josiah's childhood his uncle's house, a quarter mile from Crosswicks, had always seemed a more relaxed house than his own, or, at least, the household was given an air of gruff levity by Copplestone, who had no wish to compete with his older brother Augustus as a "serious" son of Winslow Slade. (Josiah's family had always lived with the elder Slades, as Crosswicks was an enormous house, and might easily have benefited another family.) Like his friend Andrew Fleming West, Copplestone was admired through the West End for his generosity, hospitality, and "masculine" sense of humor; though social acquaintances knew little of the strain of his relationship with his son, Todd, a subject which Copplestone was not likely to discuss with them, or indeed with anyone.

As he'd approached the house Josiah had heard a shout from a second-floor window and, glancing up, had seen his cousin Todd gesturg to him; during his conversation with Copplestone and Lenora, Josiah had heard similar outcries from the top of the staircase, but knew that, if he sought out his young cousin, Todd would hide from him—that was the boy's sort of humor, for which, at this time, Josiah hadn't much patience.

At this time Copplestone was forty-seven years old, having been born in 1858; yet, as the man was bald, and favored muttonchop whiskers, and was rotund as Dean West, he looked a decade older. Copplestone had always had an easy and relaxed attitude toward life, as an heir of the Slade fortune: why others taxed their brains with riddles about the nature of God, and the divinity of Christ, and whether God be *in* or *above* nature; why did the innocent suffer, and the evil reap harvest—Copplestone could not guess. "The distinction between 'eternity' and a tankard of ale is a simple one: I can close my fingers around the tankard, and drink, while with 'eternity'—I'd wait a very long time before my thirst was quenched, if I looked to sustenance from that."

Since Copplestone's income was assured, he'd frequently indulged himself in speculations of a reckless sort: several years ago, he'd gone in with Trillingham Bayard in backing a private militia, to be hired by companies who needed protection against picketing strikers and the like, as with the United Mine Workers of recent notoriety, and the much-publicized strife in the "Silk City," Paterson; he'd lost as much as $200,000 in backing Thomas Edison's revolutionary scheme of cement furniture which had, as Copplestone affably said, "sunk without a trace."

Copplestone had also invested in the Cape May–Atlantic City resort area and he was involved in the Cape May Challenge Cup Race, betting lavishly, but not always wisely. It was a measure of Copplestone's habit of favoring the underdog in such competitions, he'd financed a motorcar from the experimental workshop of Henry Ford, of Greenfield, Michigan, in a race on the Cape May sands, with the result that the Ford motorcar lost badly and the young inventor was so penniless he had to sell his racer in Cape May City, to a rival, in order to buy a railroad ticket back to Michigan! For Copplestone, in a swift change of mood, was so disgusted with the car's performance he refused to finance the inventor's return home. He'd had enough of "homegrown American" products—"Next time I'll back the Ace Frenchman, *Chevrolet*."

Josiah's ruddy-faced uncle was a very social person, unlike his older brother and his father Winslow; his presence at West End dinner tables assured a certain intensity of *bonhomie*. His skill at dialect stories was far in advance of Woodrow Wilson's, though the men both favored "darky" accents; Copplestone had cultivated, too, a set of jokes featuring "Rooshian Jews" and "immigrant Poles." Copplestone was a popular club-member in Manhattan, as well, though the effort of taking the train, or being driven by motorcar such a distance, was not appealing. In more than twenty years of marriage Copplestone had never been less than absolutely faithful to his wife, so far as anyone in Princeton knew.

Copplestone felt obliged to punish his rowdy son Todd from time to time, but he doted upon little Oriana, who was clearly his favorite. He'd always expressed a great affection for his niece Annabel, and he was fond of Josiah who, as he complained, ought to have been his son and not his nephew; for they would have gotten along well, and he should have minded it less, that Todd was an idiot.

(*Idiot?* Did Copplestone carelessly speak of his only son in this way? I'm afraid that, yes he did. And not always when Todd was safely out of earshot.)

Josiah's aunt Lenora, née Biddle, was Copplestone's age; not a beauty but a "handsome" woman, if somewhat fleshy; though small-proportioned when seated beside her portly husband. Her hair was of no memorable style and in any case usually covered by a morning-cap, or afternoon-cap, or bonnet, or hat; she rose early each morning, and always bathed twice— the first immersion was for soaping and washing; the second, for rinsing. She attended church services nearly as often as church services were available, and always read her Bible before bedtime; it did not greatly matter to Lenora which book of the Bible she read, only that she read a few pages, as intently of Hosea, or Nehemiah, or Zephaniah as of the Gospels or Genesis, for she would not remember what she'd read only a few minutes later, only that her mood was calmed, and prepared for bed. Each day also Lenora prayed that Todd would revert himself to normal boyish ways as, she seemed to recall, he'd behaved when he was younger; for, like her husband, Lenora found it difficult to believe that their son wasn't choosing to behave badly, and might have learned to read and write if he'd tried harder; but Lenora never scolded Todd, and was brought to tears when Copplestone decided it was "time for a whipping."

Of her many activities, Lenora was most proud of her prominent position in the New Jersey Society of the Colonial Dames of America, and her role in the Ladies' Altar Society of the First Presbyterian Church. But Lenora was most famous in the community for her excellent way with foods, particularly pastries: her specialties were cream-and-custard cakes and tarts of all varieties from quince to boysenberry. It was declared that a West End lady could scarcely sink into her sickbed before Lenora arrived with a prettily trimmed basket of dainties from her kitchen; she was most solicitous of the chronic invalids in town, visiting them weekly. "Ah, it is Lenora Slade again," Adelaide Burr would say with a little scream of a laugh, "so I know I am *sick;* and have little hope of recovery."

Yet there was in Lenora an inclination to be severely critical of behavior that deviated from her own, and, with her nephew Josiah present, Lenora couldn't resist bringing up the subject of Wilhelmina Burr whom, she said, she had never entirely trusted, for her "wanton" influence on Annabel, since the girls were classmates in elementary school. Wilhelmina was "outspoken"—"capricious"—"disrespectful of her elders"; she dressed scandalously, in "Turkish trousers" and "unskirted bloomers." Most alarming, Wilhelmina had quarreled with her parents about living in Manhattan, and she was attending art classes in which, it was said, nude persons *of both sexes* were known to pose; Lenora had heard too, from the Stocktons, that Wilhelmina now smoked cigarettes occasionally. It was common knowledge in Princeton, Lenora said primly, that this aggressive young lady had "set her cap" for a certain young man whose name she would not mention.

"Aunt Lenora, you're right—you should not mention it." Josiah was both bemused, and irritated; he felt a pang of guilt, for Wilhelmina whom he meant to contact, but seemed never to have time, or the opportunity.

"Well. Others do, you know. Quite frequently."

"I'm sure all that you've heard is just the usual gossip, invented to injure feelings rather than illuminate truth."

This was a prim statement of Josiah's own, in which he could hear a faint echo of his grandfather Winslow.

"Wilhelmina might have known, you know—about Annabel."

"What about Annabel?"

"She might have known, or suspected—something. She has behaved very strangely, very stiffly and guiltily, since—that day."

At this moment the tall doors leading to a rear, flagstone terrace of the drawing room were flung open, and Todd whom no one had known had crept outside, now came in, brashly; humming and singing to himself as if he were alone, and quite ignoring his cousin Josiah. Lenora tensed, as if awaiting a crash of her elegant tea-table; but seemed to take no notice as the glittery-eyed boy snatched at the remaining crustless sandwiches and little cakes. Todd then flung himself daringly into the divan beside his glowering father, and chewed noisily, all the while loudly humming "Zip Coon" and stroking an imaginary, immense belly, in mockery of Copplestone.

Neutral of expression, his posture now rigid, Copplestone stared fixedly before him, at Josiah, and gave no sign of his son's intrusive presence. When Josiah greeted Todd, Todd only just nodded, without a glance at his cousin, and continued eating.

He is accursed. But he has always been. Yet, he is my cousin, and I love him.

Badly Josiah wished he'd left Wheatsheaf a few minutes before, to have escaped Todd. Now, he feared a sudden outburst of his uncle's temper, and the possibility of Copplestone "disciplining" Todd.

Since the outing in Crosswicks Forest months before, Todd's skin had become noticeably darkened from the sun, for he spent a good deal of time outdoors and now looked, as his sister said, like a "Red Indian." He had always had a playful/feral manner but lately, he behaved as if his clothing, or perhaps his skin, chafed him. Clearly he'd been upset by Annabel's abrupt disappearance, as by his relatives' reaction to it; he was both noisier than usual, yet at times quieter—prattling to himself, then lapsing into stony muteness during which times, to his mother's distress and his father's rage, he appeared to be deaf as well as mute. (It was known to Josiah that his nephew hadn't uttered a coherent sentence since that Saturday morning in June, though his parents would not speak of it.) His appetite had grown so erratic, he ate only at wayward, unexpected times, preferring to feed himself in the kitchen, to the alarm of the cook. Though he'd been many times forbidden to leave Wheatsheaf unaccompanied, Todd often disappeared for baffling periods of time as if into "thin air"; then, he reappeared, with no explanation. More than once, his parents had been on the brink of alerting the Princeton police, for Todd could be found nowhere; nor did he seem to be at Crosswicks, or any other house in the neighborhood, when worried calls were made. The domestic staffs at Wheatsheaf, Crosswicks, and elsewhere whispered of Todd as a *demon*; and there were several older women servants who, when they encountered Todd, rapidly made motions in the air of an old German *Hexenbanner*.

Josiah's aunt Lenora was trying gamely to continue speaking with him, as if nothing were wrong, but Josiah was distracted by a new prank of Todd's—for Todd had produced an old cap of Josiah's which Josiah had not seen in years, and had set it atop his spiky hair at a rakish angle. When Todd stood, saluting Josiah in a mocking way, Josiah said sharply, "That's enough, Todd." He was as much a boy as to snatch the hat from his young cousin, at the risk of overexciting Todd, but Todd only just looked hurt, and reproachful; and now began to whistle "Zip Coon" in a particularly high-pitched tone, that at last provoked his father to rise from the divan, seize hold of his antic son, and begin cuffing and boxing him about the head, chuckling angrily: "Have I not told you and told you, Todd—*you must not upset your mother.*"

Josiah at once intervened, managing to separate father and son; but suffering one or two of Copplestone's blows to his own face; as Todd had already been injured, it seemed, for his nose was bleeding, and his wail was loud as an infant's. Muttering still, and loudly panting, Copplestone reached around Josiah to seize Todd again, and give him a final violent shake, before turning on his heel to storm out of the room.

During these upsetting seconds Lenora remained sitting very straight in her chair, presiding over her tiny gleaming kingdom of tea things, and gently chiding her son: "You see, Todd, you have aggravated your father again. God have mercy on us all, if his wrath does not abate."

COME TO TEA, Josiah! I have no news—but feel the need to speak to you of what has happened to alter all our lives.

Since June, Josiah had avoided Pembroke, which was Wilhelmina's family home, on Campbelton Circle, though the FitzRandolphs had several times invited him to dinner, and Wilhelmina to tea, or to simply "drop by." And it troubled Josiah, that Princeton gossip conspired to say that poor Wilhelmina was hopelessly in love with him. This Josiah neither believed nor wished to believe, for he was too gentlemanly to wish to hurt any-one; yet had too much pride, to consider "Willy" Burr a suitable mate for himself—for she and Annabel had been so close, for so long, he'd come to think of Willy as a *sister*.

Yet, she continued to invite Josiah, at some expense, he thought, to her own pride. And he felt sympathy for her, and a wish to make amends to her, and so accepted.

Pembroke, one of the smaller and less distinguished of the larger West End homes, was razed in the 1940s, to make way for newer houses; at this time, it was a striking specimen of the Tudor style, as it was generally copied in America, with an impressive front door boasting original brass rim locks, brought from London; a high-ceilinged foyer and spiral staircase leading to the upper floors; a rather dark interior, paneled in walnut; but, at the rear, a charming little garden or breakfast room to which Josiah was led by Wilhelmina herself, who'd answered the door when he rang the bell. In this room, which was filled with lushly flowering plants and small fruit-bearing trees, as well as Egyptian vases containing remarkably large and beautiful feathers, Willy appeared to have been reading, on a comfortable rattan couch, for there lay a slender, opened volume of poetry. Josiah asked what it was and Willy said, "I'm not sure, Josiah! I have been reading, and rereading, and I have vivid *sensations*—but scarcely know what to think." Josiah took up the small book: *Poems*. Its author he'd never heard of: Emily Dickinson.

"Josiah! Please take a seat. It has been *so long*."

Wilhelmina spoke gaily and with no trace of reproach, only her usual frank friendliness and dimpled smile.

Quite surprising Josiah by offering him a cigarette out of a Turkish morocco miniature case which he declined, with the excuse that he only smoked in the evenings, after dinner; and then, only cigars.

"Why then, I hope you will not mind if I smoke. For I find, it calms my nerves." Wilhelmina spoke with a slight betrayal of breathlessness, lighting a cigarette with a tiny gilt-trimmed match. Josiah had never seen any West End woman, of any age, smoke a cigarette before, and was quite fascinated by this new, unexpected behavior of his sister's friend.

"Tell me, Willy—did Annabel smoke?"

"Annabel! Of course not. You would have known it, if she had."

Willy was wearing casual clothes, in fact a pair of those Turkish trousers which Josiah's aunt deplored, that looked like pajamas; but over this she wore a middy-blouse and an attractive quilted duster, or housecoat. High on her bosom she'd pinned a lady's watch. Her day shoes were of dark leather, and her stockings of silk, Josiah saw when by chance he glanced at her ankles.

It was whispered of Wilhelmina Burr that she cared not for the fashionable extremes of corsetry, and so could boast nothing like a Gibson Girl figure; far from being wasp-waisted, like her more stylish contemporaries,

Willy struck the eye as solid, sturdy; a healthy girl, with no subterfuge. Yet, it seemed that Willy had spent more time than usual at her toilet that day, for her thick, often unruly dark hair was now smoothly drawn into a pompadour, and affixed with amber combs and pins. It was with a playful air of *dress-up*, rather than feminine affectation, that Willy had tucked a lacy perfumed handkerchief into the V of her middy-blouse, and insinuated a tiny pink tea rose into her hair.

"This smoking is new to you, Willy, isn't it? And who gave you that fancy cigarette case?"

Willy smiled evasively, tucking the case into a pocket of her Turkish trousers. "A friend."

"A new friend?"

"Yes. New. And no one you know."

By her expression, Josiah was prompted to suppose that the gift was from a male admirer. He felt just the slightest prick of jealousy.

Willy murmured: "A new presence in Princeton, a houseguest at Drumthwacket."

Yet stubbornly, Josiah would make no further inquiry.

Though Willy had hurried to open the front door herself, to prevent its being opened by one of the household staff, she had no choice but to allow the housekeeper to bring in tea, for that lady would have been scandalized if she had not, and might have informed Mrs. Burr. But Willy took a visible pleasure in presiding over the tea service, and pressing upon Josiah the usual sort of fare—cucumber and watercress sandwiches on crustless white bread, and buttered scones, and quince tarts topped with cream. It may have been the radiant heat of the old, silver teapot, or the fumes of steam that rose from Josiah's cup of Ceylon tea, or the sub-tropical atmosphere of the garden room itself, that caused Josiah to begin to feel warm, and yearning to tear open his stiff-starched shirt collar.

As if she had no pressing reason for having asked Josiah to visit her, Willy spoke in an animated voice of the new Broadway hit, Mr. Belasco's *The Girl of the Golden West* which she hadn't yet seen, but wanted very much to see. (Was Willy suggesting that she and Josiah go together?) And there were other, Princeton topics about which Willy spoke, in her open, frank, friendly way, until Josiah, beginning to become restless, intervened to ask if she had heard anything at all—anything—of Annabel; and Willy said, with a look of hurt, that of course she had not—"If I had, I would have told you all immediately. I would have *called*."

Josiah then asked if Willy could recall anything Annabel might have told her, however slight it might have seemed, about "Axson Mayte."

Willy said, not quite meeting Josiah's eye, "I think that's why I asked you to drop by, Josiah. I may have made a terrible mistake . . ."

"What sort of mistake?"

"Of the man himself, whose name I can't bring myself to say, Annabel never spoke, to me. Though I'd been hearing news of him, as a new presence in town, befriended by many of our friends and neighbors, and Dr. Wilson; and my mother had got it into her head, he and I must meet."

"Yes. I'd heard that."

"But Annabel wasn't present, at that awkward meeting—a dinner party here, and only ten at the table. In actual words, Annabel said very little about the great change that was coming into her life; but in actions, gestures, and sighs, and sudden outbursts of nervous laughter, she said a great deal. For it was evident to me, on several of our walks, and quiet times together, that Annabel was, if not unhappy, then clearly not *happy*, as she should have been. I'd thought she was feeling some anxiety about marriage to Dabney, whom she really didn't know very well, or maybe about marriage itself—Annabel was so very sheltered, as you must know. It's a curious thing, a man who marries must pretend that he has no 'experience'—a woman who marries in fact has no 'experience'—in our class, at least. And nothing must be *uttered aloud*."

Josiah said, slowly, "Annabel was sometimes *too happy*—at her engagement party, for instance. She seemed to have fallen in love with Dabney's uniform, or some idea of him, rather than *him*. Or maybe she'd fallen in love with our fantasy of what Annabel Slade should be, the most beautiful bride, the most obedient daughter."

Carefully Willy stubbed out her cigarette, which she'd scarcely smoked, into a little silver bowl.

"Josiah, I think that I let Annabel down. She seemed to want to talk about something, one day when we were walking in Crosswicks Forest, but I—I felt shy about pursuing it, or just too ignorant. Since then, I blame myself every hour."

Josiah waited, as Willy went on: "She hinted to me that she'd 'fallen in love and was damn'd'—'I belong now to another, in body as well as spirit, and no one can save me'—I tried to see how this was in reference to Dabney Bayard, even when I knew it could not be. It was very strange, Dabney seemed to have nothing to do with Annabel's agitation."

"And—what? You chose not to hear?"

"I chose not to *understand*."

"What exactly did Annabel say, can you remember?"

"She was speaking emotionally—not very coherently. She said 'neither Josiah, nor the dashing Lieutenant, can save me'—something like that. So I knew, I should have known, that Dabney wasn't the object of her concern."

"Poor Lieutenant Bayard! I could feel more sympathy for the man, if he hadn't made himself an enemy of the Slades." Josiah was on his feet, agitated. He'd set his cup of Ceylon tea down in haste. "If I could lay my hands on this 'Mayte,' I could revenge both Dabney and me. But—where have they fled!"

Hesitantly Willy said, "It might be that Annabel did fear Dabney—she feared you all. She didn't want to disappoint her family, or his family. She might have behaved out of desperation, simply to escape."

" 'Escape'—where?"

"She might not have known what would happen. If she became at all 'involved' with this man, in secrecy."

"And you never saw them together, or heard her speak of him?"

"I've told so many people, Josiah—no, and no! Of course not."

"Annabel was by nature a very shy girl. She knew nothing—I'm sure—of 'marital relations'—and I'm sure that my mother did not disabuse her ignorance."

Willy, staring into her teacup, could not reply. Josiah saw her face color with warmth. He said:

"There should be a kind of 'free love'—as the revolutionaries say—for those who are fearful of marriage. Or better yet, a way for a woman to live her life without either—'free love' or 'marriage'—but just as an individual, as a man might live, undefined by the opposite sex."

"Yes. That is so." Willy paused thoughtfully, biting her lower lip. "But Annabel was not ready for such a life, no more than I am, really. Though I'm closer to it than Annabel could have been. To live freely, as the suffragettes argue, a woman must be self-sufficient, financially. She must have decent *work*, and a decent *income*. Neither Annabel nor I have this—yet."

"Annabel was brought up to be *wed*. You, I think, are different—you are almost of a newer generation."

"How I wish that that were true! But I will try."

"People say you want to live in New York. You should, somehow. Princeton is not the place for you, right now."

"It is churchly humbug here, isn't it? And such good, kindly, Christian people, whom we love, and whom it would hurt to leave."

"Well, Annabel has left. By this time, I should think that she might have returned if she'd wanted to."

Willy said, in a lowered voice, "If Annabel has cast her life here aside, even if she has made a mistake, shouldn't she be allowed her freedom? Her freedom even to be made miserable?"

"I would kill the son of a bitch, if he made Annabel miserable. If I could find him, and get hold of him."

A roaring in Josiah's ears, and a hot flush in his face. It was made very obvious to him, he and Wilhelmina Slade were alone together, in this room; had they not the freedom to do what they wished, even to be made miserable? And what delight, in such freedom.

"I suppose we're all selfish, as I know I am, Josiah. I want Annabel back with us, where we know she's safe."

"How could we ever believe that, again—'safe'!"

"Or maybe the truth is, Annabel didn't 'choose'—she was the victim of a sort of spell, like hypnosis or mesmerism. That is what most people think, and what I would prefer to think."

"It's what I think—what I prefer to think. And if I can find the man, I will make him pay. For my sister's situation calls for rescue, and for revenge, even if she herself does not."

In such emotion, as if he had no idea what he did, Josiah seized Willy by the elbow, and lifted her to him and kissed her mouth, wetly. Then stepped back from her, the heartbeat in his chest so wild, he felt that he might faint; only fresh air could help.

Kissed by Josiah Slade, even in so distracted a way, Willy could not seem to respond; then, as Josiah left the room, she followed after him, daring to pluck at his arm. "Josiah!—my friend. Will I see you again?"

"Yes. Yes of course. You will see me again—many times. Good-bye!"

Josiah stammered, eager to escape. A few minutes later, striding along Campbelton Road in the direction of Elm Road, he could recall of the heated emotional exchange only the admonition *Shouldn't she be allowed her freedom? Her freedom even to be made miserable?*

"GOD'S CREATION AS VIEWED FROM THE EVOLUTIONARY HYPOTHESIS"

This is the intriguing title of Winslow Slade's sermon, delivered at the Germantown Unitarian Church just outside Philadelphia, on October 19, 1905; the last such public appearance the renowned former minister was to make in his lifetime.

Through the lengthy, humid summer, Winslow Slade had virtually hidden away in his library at Crosswicks, in a paralysis of grief and (it may have been) shame, following the loss, as he called it, of his beloved Annabel. Unlike Josiah, and most of the Slades, Winslow shrank from speaking of the situation; he showed so little animation at the prospect of locating Annabel, bringing her back, "revenging" her honor, you would almost think that he'd given her up—the "loss" was irrevocable, and out of human hands.

When his daughter-in-law Henrietta burst into tears in his presence, as several times the poor bereft mother did, Winslow allowed others to comfort her, and quietly excused himself, and left the room to return to the sanctuary of his library.

In the autumn, Winslow roused himself, to a degree, to accept an invitation from Colonel Harvey to write an essay for *Harper's* on the delicate subject of the "popular preaching" of the day, and its danger to the stability of a more mature faith; he accepted invitations to give guest sermons here and there in Jersey, and, most successfully, at the Germantown Unitarian Church in an affluent Philadelphia suburb, on "God's Creation as Viewed from the Evolutionary Hypothesis." So many admiring faces, so many heartfelt handshakes!—reminiscences of Dr. Slade's many years as a Presbyterian minister, and president of Princeton University, and governor of New Jersey—and much else, that Winslow Slade had nearly forgotten, as if it had been the effort of another man, a stranger to him. If there were murmurs behind his back of the *terrible scandal* in his family, these were tactfully hidden from him, and may have provoked a greater sympathy for him among his hosts. *What a good, saintly man! And what a cross to bear, in his twilight years.*

For weeks Winslow had worked on "God's Creation"—he'd never been a minister who avoided intellectual issues, or who glossed over scientific challenges to faith; for weeks, he'd consulted books and journals from his library, and newer material, from Chancellor Green Library, which he'd quite enjoyed visiting, in a pretense of being a young, curious scholar once again. He'd discussed his talk with his grandson Josiah who seemed to be, among Winslow's relatives, the only one familiar with what Christian theologians called the "evolutionary hypothesis," but their discussions proved contentious, and upsetting: Josiah claimed that the view of Darwin's theories which Winslow was presenting was "so simplistic as to be erroneous," and that Winslow's willingness even to consider the theory, advanced by numerous theologians, that the Devil had scattered false fossils to undermine faith in the Biblical creation, was "absurd." Most upsetting, Josiah suggested that his grandfather really didn't understand Darwin's basic concepts of survival of the fittest and survival by natural selection—"It is all random, Grandfather: there is no 'creation' at all."

"Josiah, of course there is a 'creation'! Look at the world—the world is *there*."

"But the world, all worlds, are 'accidents.' I think that is what Darwin meant."

"Darwin could not possibly mean that there is no *design*. Without design, there would be chaos."

"Well, I think the theory is: out of 'chaos' arises something that resembles 'design.' But it's all random."

Winslow, usually soft-spoken and courteous, even with very stupid people, was beginning to lose patience now with his arrogant grandson: "But Josiah, how is that possible?"

"Grandfather, how do I know? I'm not a biologist, a geologist, or a geneticist! I'm trying to be a rational person, amid a most irrational world."

"It is not 'rational' to think that our world, humanity itself, might have evolved out of—nothingness. It is only rational to conclude that if there is a creation, there is a Creator. If you discovered a complex Swiss watch cast away on a beach—"

Josiah interrupted: "But there is no 'creation,' Grandfather. You are trapped in your theistic vocabulary."

Now angrily, Winslow persisted: "—a Swiss watch cast away on a beach, and you would conclude that the watch 'evolved' by itself? That there was no watch-maker, and no creation?"

"It isn't the same thing, Grandfather. One is a biological phenomenon, and the other is an 'invention.' It's a foolish argument. Of course, there is an inventor, and there is a manufacturer, of a watch! A watch does not reproduce itself."

But Winslow seemed not to understand, doggedly returning to the thesis of his sermon: "The existence of so complex a mechanism proves a 'Creator'—so too, our complex species, and the vast world . . ."

"Grandfather, no: given the astonishing variety and processes of the world, and so much that goes horrifically wrong in the world, it is more rational to assume that there is no 'Creator'—it is all an accident, and we must try to understand it."

"Never! I can never believe that the world is an 'accident' and not a 'creation.' And the people to whom I will be speaking, who have faith in our teachings, will never believe, either."

Winslow spoke hotly, furiously. His usually affable eyes shone with rage. Josiah had never seen his grandfather in such a state and felt immediate regret, for what was the practical purpose of such a discussion? The older generation must believe what it must believe, Josiah thought. Younger generations will supplant their elders, and feel pity for their ignorance which they were proud to call "faith."*

With a mumbled apology Josiah excused himself, and slipped out of his grandfather's study.

They were never to discuss the subject again.

He is trapped, like a butterfly in a jar. So long as the oxygen remains in the jar, he can survive. But no longer.

AS IF TO REFUTE Josiah, and what Winslow Slade called, in his sermon, the *younger generation of quasi-rationalists,* the Germantown congregation was very receptive to his ideas, and to their expression in a form in which the youngest listener, as well as the least educated, might understand; the essence of the sermon was that "faith" and "science" inhabit totally different spheres, and do not overlap, even to share the same vocabulary. There was no applause in the beautiful old church, as there would have been in a lecture hall, but the Unitarian minister and his company were enormously pleased with the sermon; and numberless people came up to Winslow Slade afterward to shake his hand, with the praise that he had explained their own beliefs to them, in a way they could not themselves.

How very good it felt, or should have felt, to bask once again in such

---

* Is Josiah Slade prescient here, or naïve? So captivated by his precious *theory of evolution,* he imagines a similar sort of progression, of ever-more complex ideas, in the human sphere? For faith will never be supplanted by reason, not so long as *Homo sapiens* endures.

public adulation! And in the cause of defending the Christian faith, against atheism. But Winslow was feeling tired, and mildly anxious, as the elderly are likely to feel, when some distance from home; and so he excused himself before the elegant luncheon at a church member's house had ended, saying that he had to make a 2 P.M. train.

On the return to Princeton, Winslow could not keep his eyes from drooping; he could not concentrate on the book he'd hoped to read, the newly published *The Life of Reason* by George Santayana, of the Philosophy Department at Harvard. In a light doze in his private compartment on the train Winslow woke abruptly to stare out the window at a creature of some sort—a horse? a deer?—running and stumbling alongside the speeding vehicle—seeing then to his astonishment that the figure was human, and wraith-like. Why, it was Annabel!—his beloved granddaughter Annabel!—running barefoot in the rough terrain, thin bare arms pitifully extended to him; her long tresses blown wild, and her fair, childlike face wildly contorted. *Grandfather! Help me! Don't abandon me! Intercede with your God for me!*—even as the train seemed to be gathering speed, and pulling away; and Annabel was left behind, staggering desperately through the sere and tangled grasses beyond the railroad bed.

So noisy was the train's clattering, no one heard the elderly man's cries of horror, and for help. No one was to discover him collapsed on the floor of his compartment, half his face contorted in a look of terror, and his eyes rolled back inside his head, until a conductor slid open the door, at Princeton Junction.

THE PHANTOM LOVERS

*M*an's belly is the reason why man does not easily take himself for a god.

This curt aphorism of Nietzsche had a special meaning for Upton Sinclair this autumn: not because, like billions of impoverished beings throughout the world, he suffered from daily hunger; nor, certainly, because he over-indulged in rich foods. Upton's peculiar condition was a lack of appetite, or, even, at times, a revulsion for food; he was rarely "hungry" in the usual sense of the word and, after forcing himself to eat a meal, often writhed in silent agony as if the acids of his digestive system were in turmoil.

How mysterious his predicament was, and how unjust, that he of all persons should be so afflicted!—when he religiously adhered to the tenets of vegetarianism, avoiding not only meat and poultry but fish; and kept to a rigorous asceticism, working for as long as fifteen hours a day at his desk, and denying himself all but heated skim milk when he felt light-headed. It was Upton's theory that fasting would stimulate him to sustained feats of prose, as he believed it had others; hadn't Balzac labored at his desk for as long as thirty hours at a stretch?—and Upton Sinclair believed himself to be cleaner, healthier, and more ascetic in his habits than Balzac, and more selflessly dedicated to his ideal.

Meta worried that Upton was making himself "anemic"—and generally ill—but the young author replied that children as young as six toiled all night before burning furnaces in the Allegheny steel country; and his work, set beside theirs, was light indeed. "I don't want to spoil myself, and grow lazy," Upton said, "when the Revolution will need all the strength we can provide it."

"But you aren't 'lazy,' Upton—of course you are not. And you don't eat much, as it is, and are very thin."

"Not so thin as others are!" Upton retorted. (Though secretly he felt a little distress, that he could not seem to gain weight, but only to lose it; that, after eating the most mild of foods, like unsalted and unsweetened porridge, a single boiled egg, a bowl of warm milk in which bread had been soaked, he experienced a stoic and silent sort of pain in his stomach. And he felt most grievously sorry, that, as a consequence of the asceticism he imposed upon his little family, his son David had developed rickets, according to the diagnosis of a stern-faced Princeton doctor.)

Meta would never forgive him for that, he feared—the puny bone-development of little David.

Yet it was difficult for her to argue with Upton, who retreated as always to his Socialist beliefs. He was convinced that the ulcerous condition of his stomach and the over-sensitivity of his nerves were mere symptoms, the cause of which was finance capitalism: the "mighty fortress of Greed" which he and his Socialist comrades detected on all sides in the United States of the early 1900s.

"In so sick a society," Upton said to Meta, "how is it possible that anyone is healthy, at all?"

But this riposte was too precious to fling away without recording it, that night, in his journal.

> *In so sick a society as ours how is it possible that any citizen is healthy, at all?*

***

IN THE RELATIVELY less stressful era before Meta's "suicide attempt" the young couple often went strolling of an evening, with their infant son carried in a sort of Eskimo-backpack, strapped to Upton; as the countryside was less hospitable to strollers than the village of Princeton, its private lands being marked by NO TRESPASSING signs every one hundred yards or so, Upton and Meta walked in town, and on the Princeton University campus; so idyllic a setting, Upton observed, yet so much a bastion of privilege, it could make him physically ill if he allowed himself to dwell upon it. Hastily then, Meta directed him away, to Alexander Road; where, at the little stone train depot, Upton was inspired to speak of all that the "monopolistic" railroads had done to American citizens; and to tell her, and any others who chanced to overhear, on the railway platform, that the forcible Revolution must be made, if the peaceful transition failed. Gripping Meta's slender arm tightly he quoted one of his favorite passages from *Zarathustra:* " 'Behold, the pale criminal has nodded: out of his eyes speaks the great contempt. *My ego is something that shall be overcome: my ego is to me the great contempt of man*—that is what the pale criminal's eyes say.' "

Meta listened courteously, as Meta usually did; but Meta did not seem to comprehend.

"Nietzsche speaks in riddles, Meta. Yet, if you have the key, his words aren't riddles but crystal-clear. I am a pacifist, as you know—but—what prophecy! There will one day be gunfire, and bombs, and high-leaping flames, and cries in the streets, if the worshippers of Mammon don't heed our warnings."

"It will be the U.S. Army that fires upon the Revolutionaries, I'm afraid. Or Pinkerton's, as they've done at the strikes." —So Meta murmured, in an unassertive voice.

Taking little heed of his wife, except that he required her as an attentive listener, Upton led her from the platform onto the graveled railroad bed, as no train was imminent; and onto the dully gleaming rails and wooden ties. He spoke of the old fascination the railroad had exerted upon him since boyhood: the railway cars, the steam locomotives, the monsters of iron and steel and speed and romance—that same romance the contemptible J. P. Morgan and his Railroad Trust tried to exploit in the name of greed. Upton did love the railroad, he confessed, by which he meant the machinery itself, and the sheer wonder of it—the pride, the great noise, the happy sight of thick black smoke curving backward; the "melancholy music" of its calls in the night; the whistle, the clattering of wheels, the deafening roar, the marvelous O of the locomotive's boiler face.

"When Jack London and I meet, and we two must meet, I will ply him with questions about 'riding the rail,' as I know he has done such things. I will ask if he has ever witnessed a railroad accident—they are terrible to behold, it's said. It's all bound up," Upton said excitedly, "with the New Brotherhood of Man, as it is wrested from the Old Tyranny. For how could it be otherwise, in the dialectical history of the class struggle? Life is a simple and clearly defined *evolutionary process* in which the strong overcome the weak, and are in turn overcome by the yet stronger; and so entire species may pass away into extinction. The old way of belief—that God 'created' the heavens and the earth and all that dwell on the earth—has been thoroughly refuted by Darwin and Nietzsche and their followers; now, we look to Marx, and Kropotkin, and Bakunin as our visionaries—and Jack London."

Upton went on to speak of the role of "chance" in the dialectic process; the way in which, for instance, President McKinley was killed by the assassin Czolgosz, who'd functioned unwittingly as an agent of historical necessity, though the world dismissed him as a rabid anarchist-madman. And with McKinley's sudden death, the elevation of Roosevelt to the presidency. "By such 'chance' history is altered forever," Upton said, "and it can't be an accident that *The Jungle* is appearing now, during Roosevelt's administration. For there is much more likelihood that Roosevelt will take note of it, than McKinley."

Meta may have smiled to herself, at the possibility of her young, unprepossessing husband, invited to the White House to discuss his exposé of the Chicago stockyards.

"For isn't the artist by nature a revolutionary?"

Meta concurred, *yes.*

As there can be no social progress without genius, Upton continued, so there is no genius without social progress. "Thought is power, as Victor Hugo believed; and God creates art by way of man. So, God continues to add poets of genius to the world when the needs of progress require, and if the Revolution brings violence, even of a monstrous sort, why then the poet must be in the service of *monstrousness.*"

Meta murmured gently, "But do you believe in 'God,' Upton? I'd thought you had said we should not, any longer."

"Of course I don't believe in 'God' in the old, discredited way," Upton said, "but as 'God' in a kind of dialectical history. Though I am a pacifist, as I am a vegetarian and a teetotaler, yet it gives me a sort of thrill to consider what *monstrousness* the Revolution may bring forth. A new breed of humankind, perhaps; a new morality—'Beyond good and evil,' as Nietzsche has said."

"Like the French Revolution?" Meta shivered. "The guillotine—how horrible it seems to me. And so many revolutionaries were beheaded by it."

"*Not* like the French Revolution, Meta," Upton said, with exasperated patience. "This is an entirely new sort of Revolution, which our Socialist comrades have worked out. It will involve a 'crash' of the bourgeoisie—of capitalism. Think of a railroad accident—the wild exhilaration of such drama—for here we have the image of all that's most powerful brought to a sudden stop; the virile forward-motion arrested; the brute strength stymied; the billowing black smoke of the locomotive stilled; the complacent passengers in their private Pullman cars, with every sort of luxurious accouterment, thrown through the smashed windows, and broken in body and spirit, their blood draining into the common earth. What remorse then, when it's too late—what terror at the destruction of vanities! The mighty engine overturned, flames billowing forth, and oily black smoke—panicked cries and screams—mangled faces, bodies like those of wounded snakes, impaled frogs—godly steel corrugated as if it were cardboard. What power has the Railroad Trust *now?*"

Upton was speaking with such passion, Meta had to pluck at his wrist, to quiet him; for individuals on the platform were listening, very curiously. And Upton fell silent, abashed. For in the next seconds there came along the track the three-car shuttle called, by locals, the Dinky, making its way from Princeton Junction to the village of Princeton, its thin perky smoke puffing upward. Upton Sinclair hurriedly scrambled out of the railroad bed and up onto the platform, helping his wife beside him; he would have stayed to watch the half-dozen passengers climb onto the little train, with a kind of envy, had not Meta, hugging her cotton shawl close about her, murmured: "Upton, please—I want only to go home now."

THE FOLLOWING WEEK, Upton discovered his wife seated at their bare kitchen table, late at night; the barrel of the ugly revolver held against her forehead, and her finger pressed tremulously against the trigger. (Upton had never fired a gun, and had no idea how hard one must press the trigger; the prospect would have terrified him.) He'd wakened to find Meta slipped from their bed; he'd lighted a candle, to search for her; not wanting to call for her, for fear of waking little David, and provoking an onslaught of ear-splitting wails.

It was a hellish sight—seeing Meta in the kitchen, beside a sullenly burning kerosene lamp. Yet further distressing was the fact that, in surrendering the weapon to him, Meta wept bitter tears saying how she detested herself as a bad mother, and lacked courage to do what God had whispered to her, to do.

"God would not ask of you such a cruel thing," Upton protested, "even the Old Testament God of wrath."

For weeks afterward Upton was haunted by his wife's piteous words, and couldn't think how he deserved to hear them. Had he not been a devoted husband and father, despite their frugal circumstances?

Did his wife not realize that he loved her, despite his commitment to the Socialist cause? "Yet it seems, for a woman, this isn't enough."

In his journal noting, for posterity

The Revolutionary must not marry, no more than the martyr.

A POISON HAD SEEPED into their marriage, if not into their very souls, since their arrival in Princeton and the "rural experiment" on the old farm on Rosedale Road: but the young author could not determine what this poison was.

Could it be a poison of *place*? Or, less clearly, of *time*?

For this part of New Jersey was quite beautiful, and Princeton an idyllic town lacking the ugliness of most towns. Upton had remarked in letters to his Socialist comrades how there appeared to be, in public at least, no "poor" people; certainly, no beggars; even the Negro house servants and laborers were respectably dressed, and lived in a respectable residential neighborhood on lower Witherspoon Street one might mistake for a "white" neighborhood. Yet, there seemed to Upton a kind of free-floating *poison* . . . Where once his young wife had doted on him and his writing, detecting in even his dashed-off pieces for the New York papers evidence of genius, she now showed but a perfunctory interest, and seemed scarcely to care that *The Jungle* was selling out every issue of *Appeal to Reason* in which it appeared. ("Since you are only being paid the usual rate by the magazine, it hardly makes any difference if the issues are 'best sellers.' We're still poor"—so Meta pointed out with cruel accuracy and not at all the kind of sympathy a man might expect from a loyal wife.) It had been their custom for Upton to give his wife reading matter to study by kerosene lamp in the evening, so that they could discuss the pieces together; but by degrees Meta had lost interest, and even lost the material—which included Upton's own "The Scientific Basis of Utopia," which he planned to present at the first meeting of the Intercollegiate Socialist Society that summer.

A terrible thought came to Upton: could his wife be in love with another man?

Or, at least, seeing another man in secret?

So the unhappy husband tormented himself while hunched over his writing table in his sacred work-place in the little cabin behind the farmhouse.

This autumn, since the murder of the Spags girl not many miles away, and a rumor of other, "unspeakable" crimes in the vicinity, Meta had set out on solitary walks as if in defiance of circumstances; several times she declared she was "not fearful" as other women were; for it was crucial to her, to slip away from little David, when she could, to be alone with her thoughts and in no danger of being interrupted. At such times the frail young woman exhibited a remarkable, if not febrile energy, and could walk long distances— at least two miles into town, and back; or, in the woods and fields behind the farmhouse, an incalculable distance. She walked on Province Line Road and on Carter and Poe roads, in the area of Stony Brook Creek, as well as along Rosedale; by chance, Upton learned that she'd walked as far as Pretty Brook Road, that ran parallel with Rosedale, on the farther side of the creek. Sometimes, Meta dared to walk in Crosswicks Forest, though the land was prominently posted against "trespassers" of any sort; she returned with muddied shoes, as if she'd been tramping in a bog. And when she returned from an illicit walk, having failed to inform Upton that she was leaving the house, she was likely to be scant of breath, sunburnt, her clothing torn by brambles and her hair disheveled. "Meta, where have you been?" Upton would ask, disapproving; for after all, he'd had to interrupt his work, to take care of the baby. And Meta would say only vaguely that she'd been "on a walk—and lost track of time."

Upton had hidden the revolver. And the bullets, too. Yet, should Meta want to injure herself, how could he prevent her?—for all the sincerity of his love, and the passion of his moral beliefs, he knew himself helpless.

Sensuality often grows too fast for love to keep up with. Then love's root remains weak and is easily torn.

Upton had noted this remark of Friedrich Nietzsche in his journal. It was not clear that it applied to him and Meta but there was a disturbing wisdom here.

At first, as the Sinclairs had decided to live chastely, as "sister and brother," to prevent another pregnancy, Meta had appeared pallid, nervous, anxious and short-tempered; yet strangely, with the passing of time, she began to exude an air of well-being, and secrecy; even, Upton thought, sensuousness.

(Or did he imagine it?)

There were the lengthy, unexplained walks, for which Meta scarcely troubled to apologize; there were occasions when Meta slept luxuriantly well past dawn, as she had not slept in the past, with an air of utter abandon, oblivion; and a notable reluctance to wake up, and resume her housewife-duties even when little David screamed for his mother's attention.

She played with the baby less. If she and Upton chanced to touch, to bump into each other in the cramped space of a room, she froze at once; which Upton did not find at all flattering.

Naturally, the Sinclairs no longer shared a bed; Meta elected to sleep on a narrow cot in the front room, assuring Upton that she didn't mind in the slightest.

As autumn deepened into early winter, Upton became ever more conscious of his wife's undefined air of well-being; the play of a smile about her lips, instead of a frown, as she prepared meals, or cleaned the kitchen after meals; the way she gazed at her reflection, in the sole mirror in the house, attached to a bedroom bureau, with an expression of wistfulness, hope, and—(unless Upton was imagining this, too)—coquetry. He was not by nature a suspicious person, yet it seemed to him significant that Meta now spent five or more minutes brushing her hair and, with girlish expectancy, viewing herself from several angles in the mirror, and fashioning her hair into unusual styles, he could only conclude were copied from sleek magazines like *Vanity Fair*, which certainly didn't come into his household.

Once, Upton came into the farmhouse from his cabin unexpectedly, to discover Meta trying on one of her old bonnets which she'd "livened up" with a bit of satin ribbon; another time, while searching in a drawer, he discovered, hidden behind items of feminine apparel, an expensive-looking brooch he'd never seen before, of mother-of-pearl inlaid with small red stones. (Rubies?) Meta claimed that this was a gift from her grandmother but Upton was suspicious, for why hadn't he seen it before?

Evasively Meta said it was but a "trifle"—she'd never worn it in his presence.

One morning in late October when Upton was sitting at his writing table, in the little cabin overlooking a desiccated cornfield, he found himself so distracted by thoughts of Meta that he couldn't write; and sat for a long while with his head in his hands. He'd been writing a letter to a comrade in the city but the passage of wind through the dried cornstalks seemed like whispering to him, though no words could be discerned.

It was at this moment that Upton saw, some distance away, yet within the (evident) border of the cornfield, a horse and buggy moving at a leisurely pace, though no road or lane existed there, and no horse and buggy could cross a cornfield in so smooth-gliding a way . . . The buggy was attractive, though old-fashioned in style; yet, in this rural place, where no farmers owned motorcars, it did not appear so extraordinary as it would have appeared in Princeton.

This had to be an optical illusion, Upton thought. Or a moment of weakness, from overwork. Or maybe the horse and buggy were passing along a road, invisible from the cabin. He returned to the letter and forced himself to reread it: the general subject was the Intercollegiate Socialist Society, which had been organized early in the year with the purpose of counteracting the teachings of American professors in their ignorant and biased presentations of Marx, Engels, Kropotkin, Feuerbach, Bakunin, et al.; the specific subject, the hoped-for election of Jack London to its presidency. For Upton revered London; he considered London one of Socialism's proudest figures: handsome, bold, outspoken, provocative, and widely acknowledged as a genius for the "fireball" success of such best sellers as *The Call of the Wild* and *The Sea Wolf.* What excellent publicity the Society would reap if London were elected, and agreed to take office!—the fledgling organization would be flooded with applications for membership.

So Upton Sinclair was arguing that the Society must elect London, and not Eugene Debs; though Debs was a veteran of the Socialist struggle, the man had undeniable problems—(excessive drinking, marital complications, ill temper)—and could not hope to command such general attention from both Socialists and "unbelievers" as the dashing London.

Hadn't London already distinguished himself in several confrontations with the enemies of Socialism?—hadn't he addressed hostile gatherings, and launched an ambitious if ill-advised campaign for the mayoralty of Oakland, California? He was brash, but well spoken; "rough" yet "poetical"; a man among men but popular with women, including "ladies" of the upper classes. Inspired, Upton wrote: "He has been a salmon fisher, an 'oyster pirate,' a longshoreman, a sailor. He has tramped our great nation and knows it inside and out; he has lived in the horror of the Whitechapel slums, and searched for gold in the Klondike. He has been beaten by police, and jailed."

(Though Upton didn't think to mention it, London had dashed off a generous blurb for *The Jungle,* soon to appear in hardcover: "Here it is at last! The book we have been waiting for! The *Uncle Tom's Cabin* of wage slavery! Comrade Sinclair's *The Jungle*! And what *Uncle Tom's Cabin* did for black slaves, *The Jungle* will do for the white slaves of today . . . It will be read by every workingman. It will open countless ears that have been deaf to Socialism. It will plough the soil for the seed of our propaganda. It will make thousands of converts to our cause. *Comrades, it is up to you!*")

Upton took pains to defend Jack London against "vulgar and meretricious gossip" circulating at the present time about London and the "temptress" Charmian; for if London remained with his wife, or chose to leave her, how should that matter to Socialism? In any case, London had denied even knowing the exotic "Charmian" and that was enough for Upton Sinclair to endorse.

At this moment he glanced up to see, or to seem to see, the apparition of the horse-drawn buggy yet again—now making its way in his direction.

"Is it coming for *me*?"

The vehicle seemed to be solid enough, drawn by a bay horse with a splotched white star on its forehead; it was more commodious than the ordinary two-seater buggy, in fact a *landau*, gray or pearl in color; its black top was partly lowered and its fringed hammer-cloth distinctly white. A gentleman was driving it, flicking a whip light over the bay's withers, and a lady sat close beside him, her head inclined against his shoulder and a part-opened silk fan raised to shield her face from the sun.

In astonishment Upton stared. And in that instant he blinked, and rubbed his eyes, for the vision had abruptly vanished, and the cornfield was empty again.

"Am I losing my mind?—*me*? Who has always prided himself on his *rationality*?"

UPTON RETURNED TO his writing, as swiftly and powerfully as he could. Though it was difficult to keep his mind from wandering: for perhaps the *landau* had something to do with the *poison* in the Princeton atmosphere? A man had been arrested and, probably by now, condemned, in the matter of the Spags murder; but Upton had no faith in the local police, that they'd arrested the actual murderer. And there had been other acts of violence and vandalism in the county, it was rumored. And sporadic demonstrations of the white-hooded Ku Klux Klan, that sprang up overnight, in rural enclaves of New Jersey, like deadly nightshade.

It was sobering to recall, as Marx and Engels had taught, that the proletariat isn't invariably saintly but, as a consequence of brutalizing labor, often transformed into *brutes*. Drunkenness—prostitution—licentiousness of all sorts; robbery, manslaughter, murder, "lynchings"—all were inevitable consequences of the capitalist crime against human nature. Why should the proletariat not steal, or become brutalized, even against their brothers and sisters? Who has taught wage slaves to be *good*?

Once, on her way home from a long tramp across the Stony Brook Creek, Meta had accepted a ride from a neighboring farmer in his crude horse-drawn wagon; Upton had been distressed to see his wife in the company of so uncouth an individual. As a Socialist, he was bound to identify with all workingmen and all exploited persons; yet, as a well-bred young man of a good family, with a love of the arts, and a wish to believe in the natural goodness of humankind, he was frankly dismayed by the degenerate behavior of some persons in the area. Wife- and child-beating, venereal disease, drunkenness, outright madness and rampant cruelty were all to be found within a few miles of the Sinclairs' rented property. Most widespread was sheer stupidity, for Upton had discovered that few farmers knew how to farm intelligently, or seemed to care; their most lucrative undertakings were the illegal manufacture of "applejack" (sold, it was said, surreptitiously to the most exclusive eating clubs at Princeton University) and the shameless prostitution of their voters' rights as male citizens of the United States—such votes were sold, in Mercer County, for a meager two dollars! Nor could it fail to astonish the young Socialist who'd written so passionately of wage slavery in Chicago, with a special grievance against child labor, to discover, in his very backyard, so to speak, that the young children of neighboring farmers were expected to work for as many as sixteen hours a day on their family farms; the more cruelly in that their fathers' crops were haphazardly sowed, and each farm chore involved a waste of human energy and spirit. Most sickening, when the scanty crop was at last harvested and sown, the father was likely to "drink it up" as quickly as possible.

Upton had learned that the only efficient farmers in the Hopewell Valley seemed to be those who'd acquired, through superior intelligence, cunning, conniving, or outright cheating, farms of substantial size, above one hundred acres; which farms replicated, in a sense, factories, in the mass means of production and in the employment of "dirt-cheap" labor. These farmers, though genial enough in conversation, God-fearing Christians of Protestant stock, could not have prospered as they did without a *systematic and sustained exploitation* of others, including their own families. Rural America was no paradise, indeed; the farm no idyllic retreat, as some urban Socialists seemed to think.

Upton was particularly distressed that even poor farmers had so little sense of camaraderie with others like themselves, or worse off than themselves; he and Meta had both been shocked by jocular references to the terrible lynchings in Camden, some months before, made by neighbors—"If it takes that to teach 'em, it's their own fault."

And: "A Nigra has got to learn he ain't a white man and if it's a female Nigra, her too."

At the same time, Upton wished to believe that in the near future a special cadre of Socialists would establish a co-operative "home colony" in a secluded rural place like Mercer County. Was there a contradiction? What was one to believe? As Upton fiercely noted in his journal:

> We must, like the prophet Zarathustra, overcome our own weakness, that we may become Übermensch.

YET, A HALF hour later, Upton happened to look up from his writing table, to see an astonishing spectacle outside his window: in fact, an *obscene spectacle,* not thirty yards from the cabin, at the edge of the cornfield.

The gentleman and the lady from the *landau* had alighted from the vehicle and, imagining themselves alone and unobserved in this rural place, were now embracing most intimately, and passionately. Upton rubbed his eyes: was the woman Meta, his own wife?

"It can't be! No."

The man had a ruffian's swagger, a solid body and a ruddy complexion; for his excursion into the country he was wearing "sporting" clothes, and a yachting cap. Judging by the fashionable cut of his clothes, his class was that of the *capitalist exploiter;* and judging by the extreme ruddiness of his skin, he could be nothing other than a *carnivore.*

The stricken Upton Sinclair found it difficult to make out the woman's features, as in mock protestation of her companion's forwardness she squirmed, butted, punched (lightly, with playful fists), tried to kick, and wildly laughed, while her amorous suitor held her in a lewd embrace; the silk fan had been allowed to fall to the ground. The young woman was wearing an attractive striped silk dress in the fashionable "hobble" silhouette, now partly undone; her red-blond hair, fashionably coiled at the top of her head in a Gibson Girl style, had loosened in the amorous struggle. Upton had never seen the striped dress, he was sure, nor had he noticed his wife's hair so styled; yet there was no mistaking Meta's pert Scots profile, or the girlish ring of her laughter.

"Stop! You must stop! Meta!"

Upton threw down his writing things, and ran outside.

But now, another time: where had the lovers gone?

Nor were the pearl-colored *landau,* and the bay horse with the splotched white star, visible.

"Meta? Where are you? Where are you hiding? *Answer me.*"

Yet it seemed that the cornfield was empty, as before. Only the desiccated stalks moved, in a continuous teasing whisper. In a moment's madness, Upton ran to the barn, to locate the revolver on a high ledge, where he'd hidden it beneath a canvas; next, he returned to the cabin, where, beneath a loose floorboard, he'd hidden the bullets. With shaking hands he forced bullets into the revolver's chambers, he knew not whether in the correct direction, or not; for he had no clear idea how to load a gun. A great artery was beating in his head as he ran outside, waving the gun: "I've seen you! I know, now! I will murder you both!"

Though there was no one in sight, Upton lifted the gun, aimed it recklessly and pulled the trigger. A terrible, deafening *crack!* nearly split his eardrums.

Yet, the wildness was upon him: Upton pulled the trigger again, and again. Where the bullets flew, into the rippling cornstalks, he had no idea. But there were no outcries, there was no sign of anyone hiding—"Where are you! Devils! Adulterers! How dare you taunt me!"

To this there was no reply. Only the dry mock-whispering of the cornstalks; and, as he began at last to hear, the faint crying of an abandoned baby in the farmhouse.

FOR IN TRUTH there was no one in the field, nor had ever been, it seemed. After returning to his son, to strap him into the awkward backpack, which Upton had yet to adjust correctly, Upton hurried back to the field, to look more closely, making his way along rows of broken stalks.

In the field, he discovered skeletal remains of—something. Some small creatures, rabbits perhaps. Tufts of grayish fur, or feathers—the devoured prey of an owl?

At the farther edge of the field he discovered a sizable mound of horse manure, but couldn't decide to his satisfaction whether the excrement was fresh, or a day or two old.

"And no other damn'd clue!"

A few hours later, near dusk Meta returned.

In a drab cotton skirt of some faded floral design, that looked as if it had been fashioned out of a seed sack, her bonnet limply askew and her shoes covered in dust, a scattering of thistles on her clothing, Meta approached the house in no great haste, yet not in apparent dread; rather, like a young woman in a dream. Through the kitchen window Upton observed her, still in his astonished state, with a headache now, and a sickened sense of malaise through his body.

"Meta! Where in hell have you been?"

There was a familiarity to this question, that quickened the sense of malaise in Upton.

Meta protested: hadn't she told Upton that she was "going for a walk"?—she was sure that she had.

"I've only been gone for an hour, or a little more."

An hour! But Upton bit his tongue, not wanting to quarrel. He returned to the table where Meta would see, as she entered, yawning, removing her bonnet, that her disheveled hair would tumble about her shoulders, that he'd been cleaning the revolver: unskillfully oiling its parts, with greasy fingers.

Upton didn't doubt that his narrow, clean-shaven and fiercely indignant face was shrouded in a melancholy of its own, or that his deep-socketed eyes were moist. At his elbow the kerosene lamp gave off a feeble flickering glow.

Seeing the revolver, Meta stared for a moment; then asked, casually, or carelessly, why the gun was "allowed" back in the house, since Upton had forbade it?

"The murders in New Jersey are mostly unsolved. It shouldn't surprise us if there are more to come."

"Murders? Have there been more than one?"

"I think, yes. Many more."

Meta shivered, shaking her hair loose, and removing a fragment of cornsilk from it.

THE TURQUOISE-MARBLED BOOK

D isgust! And dismay.

That's what I feel, to be utterly frank, as I approach one of the most painful episodes of this history, the subject of the chapter that follows, titled "The Bog Kingdom."

This is Annabel Slade's "confession." It is a very disturbing and in some respects an obscene document, which I choose to present without censorship or distortion, as earlier historians have done; it has been taken nearly verbatim from a notebook identified (by me) as "The Turquoise-Marbled Book."

Historians must rely upon sources. Historians do not "invent" sources. Yet it is as much of an invention, that's to say a lie, to omit or distort sources, in the interests of protecting "innocent parties."

The fact is, my historian-rivals have dealt with Annabel Slade's confession in very unprofessional ways. They have been misleading, obfuscatory, and timid; they have not been honest, and they have not been professional. (Ironic that I, an "amateur" historian, should accuse these others of unprofessional behavior; but so it is.)

Granted, the subject matter is disconcerting, if not frankly repulsive. And its exact authenticity can't be guaranteed.

(But then, what of the past can be verified *exactly,* even if we were eyewitnesses?)

Yet there is no excuse for the historian Q. T. Hollinger to relegate the "unconfirmed tale of a 'bestial' birth" to a mere footnote in *The Unsolved Enigma of the Crosswicks Curse: A Fresh Inquiry* (1949), and to so vaguely paraphrase Annabel's story that one can't grasp the poetic flavor of its highly refined language. As for Hiram Tite in *The Unsolved Mystery of the "Crosswicks Horror"*—this sensationalist study isolates the final humiliation and (evident) death of Annabel Slade in a separate chapter, yet deals with it so ineptly in its particulars as to suggest to the skeptical reader that it is nothing more than rumor or gossip, or that category of twaddle dismissed as *old wives' tales. The Vampire Murders of Old Princeton,* by an "anonymous" author, is too contemptible to justify serious comment; yet little more can be said for Croft-Crooke, with his impressive academic credentials (Harvard B.A., Yale M.A., longtime headmaster of the Lawrenceville School), or Miss Helena Worthing, with hers (Barnard B.A., Columbia M.A.). What is most disturbing to me are several articles written, in obvious haste, for New Jersey newspapers, that confuse Annabel's tragic fate with the alleged fates of victims of the "Jersey Devil." (This quasi-mythical creature went on a rampage in January 1909, when reports of miscarriages, stillbirths, and other abnormalities among women were noted, including at least one of a *monstrous birth* to a young woman in the Pine Barrens—improbable and unverified incidents which fall entirely beyond the scope of my fact-based chronicle.)

My primary source of information for this section of the chronicle is a journal measuring eight inches by twelve with a turquoise-marbled cover in which Josiah Slade seems to have written sometime after the New Year of 1906, at the bedside of his sister Annabel; though not transcribed in code, like Adelaide Burr's journal, this account has been difficult to transcribe because it was clearly written in haste, and with emotional anguish, resulting in numerous disjunctions, confused figures of speech, abrupt breaks and elliptical statements. And the reader will note the abrupt ending—as, it is believed, Annabel Slade began labor, with a sequence of powerful contractions of the womb, that would continue for twenty excruciating hours.

On the flyleaf of the journal is the poignant inscription, in Josiah's hand: *God grant me the strength to be equal to all that my sister will reveal.*

SINCE THIS IS a chapter many readers will wish to skim, or to skip altogether, as it is concerned with the historian's trade, and of as much interest to admirers of screen actors as an account of the "backstage" of film production might be of interest to those admirers, I think it is judicious at this point to enumerate certain of my prized research materials, which are not to be found, nor even alluded to, in most of the libraries, special collections, historical archives, etc., that contain information pertinent to the subject. The Turquoise-Marbled Book is one of the most precious, obviously; and though in Josiah Slade's hand it is kept separate from the morass of letters, notes, newspaper items, and other memorabilia relevant to Josiah, to be found between the pages of the Beige Morocco Book—Josiah's diary for the years 1901–06. (Typical of a young male diarist, Josiah did not faithfully record each day of his life but rather went for long stretches without writing a word. And there are pages roughly torn out.) In addition, as the reader knows, I have relied heavily upon Mrs. Adelaide Burr's Crimson Calfskin Book—now so faded and shabby, it seems a melancholy document indeed, despite the vivid and "perky" writing of that inveterate invalid; and also Mrs. Johanna van Dyck's multi-volumed journal, known to historians as the Ivory Book, as it resides in the Princeton Special Collection, and has been consulted by numerous historians. (Unknown to these historians, Johanna van Dyck kept a second, secret diary, which I have called the Black-Dappled Book. It is a small-sized diary of about sixty written pages, much of the entries undated, and not very coherent; for it did happen, Johanna van Dyck gave (premature) birth to a baby boy in February 1906, at about the time that Annabel Slade gave birth; during which time her usually devoted husband Pearce suffered from a variant, it seems, of the Princeton *malaise,* with unfortunate consequences about which I do not wish to comment.) Most consistently rewarding has been Wilhelmina Burr's Brown-Dappled Book which is filled to bursting with notes, personal documents, news clippings, love letters (?) from unidentified individuals, photographs, and even tradesmen's receipts, as well as Wilhelmina's minutely observed diary-entries; yet more crowded and untidy, the Sandalwood Box, in which I store a miscellany of Woodrow Wilson material that has made its way into my private possession; and the Rose Brocade Box, in which materials pertaining to the Grover Clevelands are kept. I have also at hand the Orange-Marbled Book which was once the diary of Mrs. Henrietta Slade, but it is disappointing in its particulars, and of little use to the historian; and the Fleur-de-lis Book of Mrs. Amanda FitzRandolph, whose confused and hallucinatory accounts of her "possessed" infant son are both shocking and questionable, and of little practical use.

Most prized, and kept under lock and key here in my study, is the Ebony-Lacquered Box in which are stored all materials pertaining to Winslow Slade; though I am doubtful about this material also, and sometimes wake in the night wondering if I should destroy it at once. Priceless matter it is, to me, throwing light, and a great deal more, on these events of long ago; but the wisdom of introducing certain facts into my chronicle, that so refute the material of the Princeton Special Collection regarding Dr. Slade, that cannot be verified, and cannot fail to disturb, is an ethical issue not easily resolved.

For *The Accursed* is intended as a work of inquiring moral complexity, and not a "sensationalist" rehashing of an old, dread scandal far better left to molder in the grave!

AS FOR THE DOCUMENT known generally as "The Confession of Annabel Slade"—or, as I prefer, "The Bog Kingdom"—Josiah didn't date it exactly but since Annabel (evidently) returned to Crosswicks in the second week of December 1905, and since her confinement and its (unspeakable) aftermath took place within a fortnight, it is reasonable to presume that Josiah transcribed his sister's distraught tale sometime between December 12 and Christmas Day. It is possible that the entire confession was told during a single protracted period, for Annabel's voice seems to falter, and grow faint, and takes on a sporadic strength again, with the rhythms of a human soul baring itself utterly; no revisions were made afterward by Josiah or by Annabel, one can tell from the document.

So far as I've been able to discover, by collating diaries, no one except Annabel's mother, her grandfather Winslow and her brother Josiah, of course, was present in her bedchamber at this time. (Annabel's father, Augustus, it was said, could not bear to look upon his daughter's face; her cousin Todd, literally "under lock and key" at Wheatsheaf, clamored to see her, but was forbidden; and Wilhelmina, who also wanted to visit Annabel, and whom, possibly, Annabel would have liked to see, was forbidden as well, by a curt decree of Annabel's parents.)

There were visits by the astonished Dr. Boudinot, but either that gentleman was sworn to secrecy, which he did not violate; or, his accounts of the monstrous delivery have been lost.

THE BOG KINGDOM

F aster, yet ever faster, the horses galloped along the old King's Highway foaming at the mouth, and snorting—our carriage wildly rocking from side to side . . .

So faintly Annabel spoke, so uncertain and faltering her voice, it was very difficult for Josiah to hear, and to transcribe what she said.

Poor Annabel! Returned in disgrace, and in physical distress, to her girlhood room at Crosswicks Manse.

In a fever—delirium, her lower body grotesquely swollen in pregnancy.

Also with Annabel were her mother, Henrietta, in a state of great anxiety, and her grandfather Winslow Slade, only partly recovered from a stroke of several months before, that had paralyzed the left half of his face, and caused his left eye to squint, with but minimal sight in that eye. And the elderly man's speech had been slowed, as if each word came of its own, like a rock rolled with effort, and independent of words preceding and following. For it was as Winslow Slade had foreseen, through the window of the railway car: his granddaughter would return home not only alone, but afoot; in a condition exhausted and broken, beyond hysteria; on a particularly cold and snowy night in December—*cast off from her lover.*

This is a scene of flickering candlelight, and not electricity. (Though the Slades' house was fully electrified by 1905.) As Annabel's room had not been at all changed since her girlhood: very prettily decorated in a "feminine" Victorian style with rose-colored fleur-de-lis French wallpaper, a charming little chandelier of Irish crystal, white-lacquered furniture and a cherrywood writing desk overlooking a view of the rose garden, desiccated now in winter. There was a marble fireplace, of Sienna marble, rarely used; above it, a mirror that resembled a woodland pool, flickering with candle-flame amid shadows. At the several tall narrow windows were curtains of chintz-and-damask, in bright colors now muted and indistinct. Annabel's girlhood bed was a beautiful old eighteenth-century "sleigh" bed that had come down through the family, with a white silken canopy, and mostly white bed-linens and quilts; it was bizarre to see, in a girl's narrow, single bed, a young woman in the last stage of pregnancy, clutching a chaste-white comforter with desperate fingers.

Dr. Boudinot had been hurriedly summoned, and had been sent away again. For Annabel wished to speak openly to her brother, her mother, and her grandfather, and would have felt restrained by the presence of a stranger.

(In his place, the Slades' longtime housekeeper Cassandra, trained in midwifery, would help with the delivery. But Cassandra was downstairs at this time, waiting to be called.)

(Readers should be warned: the various first-person and "eyewitness" accounts of the delivery of Axson Mayte's hideous offspring that have been reported, in previous chronicles by Hollinger, Tite, Worthing, "Anonymous," et al., are utterly meretricious and inauthentic. Cassandra, who loved her employers' granddaughter dearly, did not ever reveal what she'd seen, or even that she'd assisted at the birth, though many individuals would question her, some of them quite persistently, for years. *All that is known of this episode is by way of Josiah's recording in the Turquoise-Marbled Book, which is in my keeping.*)

One more item should be noted, to "set" the scene: a pastel portrait (by Winslow Homer, a friendly acquaintance of the elder Slades) of little Annabel, at about the age of eleven, in a beribboned sailor cap and with a shyly sweet smile, hung on the wall near the canopied bed; this image of childhood innocence and trust, in painful contrast to the young woman in the canopied bed, her delicate features contorted in humiliation, and in pain.

. . . . *THE wind tearing at my hair and ripping my bridal veil from my head—causing my eyes to fill with tears—though not—(not yet!)–tears of regret and shame.* Do you love me above all men, dear Annabel *he whispered* and will you be my bride, and Queen of my Kingdom . . .

So strange it was, trees flew past us—meadows beside the King's Highway that should have been the freshest green were now starkly gray and drained of all color as in a solar eclipse. More strangely, we seemed to be passing Crosswicks Manse, my beloved home for all of my life, set back from the road beneath tall trees and yet to my dazed eye the house was leaden-dull lacking all color, and beauty; and the sky beyond no longer blue but of the transparency of washed glass. Hedgerows looming close to the road were startling in their uncanny chalkiness—*and the newly cultivated soil in farmers' fields was no longer a rich deep earthen color but reversed in tone, strangely pale as if a fine powdery snow had fallen upon it, on a fair June day!*

He had warned me—I must not look back. Must not glance back over my shoulder not once at all that I had left for his sake.

The wind, the wind! Whipping at my hair—and my lover's powerful arm clasped about me that I might bury my face in his neck— Do you pledge your troth to me and only me as your true husband?—*bringing his lips to my eyelids and a tightening of his arm that made me cry out, in sudden pain.*

My breath was drawn from me by the hot whipping wind that had acquired a brackish odor though we were traveling through a familiar landscape which I'd known since childhood—yet, what were these strange creatures at the roadside?— fluttering into the air, on dark leathery wings, as we approached?—they appeared to be birds, yet not birds of the kind one usually sees here but rather goatsuckers, or nighthawks, with great flat heads and long pointed wings and eyes mere slits glaring at us, like smoldering coals. Their cries were angry and impatient and close to human, seeming particularly to be addressed to Axson, as we passed; as if they knew him, and he them, in some unknown way.

My brave Annabel!—to have cast off your old life, for my sake!

The horses were galloping faster, and more fiercely—almost I could believe that flames snorted from their nostrils—their long manes blown in the wind and their tails uplifted—their eyes rolling—yet impatient Axson flicked his whip over their withers—as if he feared pursuit.

Soon we shall be safe in my kingdom, where no one can follow.

No one, dear Annabel, to wrench you from my arms.

Chalk-hued hedgerows, and great looming leafless trees, and desolate countryside in which creatures of an unknown species grazed—so eerie and glowering with light, yet a pallid light, my eyes ached and I could not look too closely at anything I saw; for all was faded like an engraving of many years past, or one of Grandfather's daguerreotypes of his youth. O wild frenzied ride! O drear changed world! But once we encountered another vehicle at the junction of a narrow road—a farmer's wagon drawn by a swaybacked horse—this vehicle though surely moving yet appeared frozen in motion and the grizzled farmer seated behind his horse in overalls and shabby straw hat gazed upon us with blank glassy eyes as if he saw us, yet did not see; the wagon moved, yet its crude wheels did not turn, nor did the horse trot forward. And I seemed to know, it was for Axson's sake: time might be stopt for us, that Axson might plunge forward with his bride.

We saw a forsaken cemetery that had been a Quaker graveyard, by an old ruin of a church; and all the grave markers, and the gutted church, were of the identical hue of lead. We saw a convict gang toiling by the roadside in shapeless prison clothes and leg-irons—not a one of these men was of Caucasian features but African in descent with flat blunt noses and fleshy lips and yet their skins were chalky-white!— astonishing to the eye, one would have thought that the world had turned inside-out and Heaven had drunkenly reversed itself with Hell.

Hours passed, or days—I was confused in Time, like one buffeted in a rough *surf—scarcely knowing where I was being taken in such haste; for love had entered me like chloroform, through the nostrils and mouth and causing a mist in the brain. The rough motion of the carriage was a comfort to me, as the carriage was a confinement; in my dazzling-white bridal gown that had become soiled, rumpled and torn. Never again would I be Annabel Slade, never again that ignorant child but a woman bound to her lover, forever more; it was a part of my enthrallment, I gave no thought to my lawful wedded husband Dabney Bayard, as one would not give thought to a dream that has been supplanted by a newer, more powerful and demanding dream. As the carriage lurched along a sandy rutted lane leading into the depths of the forest—which was meant to be the Pine Barrens—and yet our own forest, at Crosswicks.* You are all to me, dear Axson as a shadow absorbs a fainter shadow, or a single powerful stream absorbs countless small tributaries.

How strange, the great trees locked overhead to form a kind of arch—these leafless trees of a ghostly hue, and nothing of life visible in them; though these appeared to be the oaks, elms, beeches and chestnuts of Crosswicks Forest. Presently we passed through a clearing of some size, that was most painfully familiar; an uncanny space filled with sultry glaring light; my eyes leapt upward, to the limb of a great oak from which two bodies hung, by their necks; lifeless, hideously burnt, very still despite the whipping wind. My eyes were affrighted, I could not look but buried my face in my lover's hot neck and he laughed Dear Annabel, you are almost safe—do not be frightened—no one will ever hurt *you* as others are hurt—by your beauty you will be spared—I vow to you as your lover for eternity.

So the horses drew us onward into the Bog Kingdom, which I did not yet know was the Great Dark, or the Kingdom of the Accursed—the narrow roadway growing more narrow still, and subsiding to mud—the beautiful matched horses so cruelly used by this time by their impatient master, their bits were scummed over with froth and blood and their poor straining backs brightly gleaming in crosshatched stripes of blood. Of a sudden we were in the Bog and surrounded by enormous trees of some moss-bearded sort, also of the hue of ash; and marsh water lay in dark pools on all sides, rippling with unseen serpentine creatures beneath the sur-

face of the water; and the smell was brackish and sharp like an odor of drains, and rich with vegetative decay. Be patient, my love, my sweet, pure bride!—for we are almost there, where our bridal bed awaits in the most sumptuous bedchamber of my palace.

A heady paludal air so ripe, so rich—almost, I could not breathe. The beeches of Crosswicks Forest gave way to the moss-bearded trees, and to others which were unfamiliar to me, tall straight smooth-barked trees of a species I didn't recognize—unless they were mangroves, with snaky roots in dense clusters. Birds circled about us with angry cries—the nighthawks, with renewed ferocity; and other great predator-birds, flapping leathery wings like Lucifer making his way through the void, to the despair of humankind. I had begun to feel alarm now, the hairs at the nape of my neck stirring in animal panic, and my protector the more tightly squeezed me to his bosom. Be patient, my dear! We have some small distance before us yet, and cannot force these lazy brutes to trot faster!

Presently we came to an aged and rusted gateway of wrought iron, its arch crowned with gryphon-like figures, and spikes; that lent it both a kindly and a forbidding air. Yet the gate was opened wide, and no gatekeeper in evidence. Here my lover gripped my hands in his so hard, I feared he would break my fingers, and passionately whispered Do you hereby reject your family, and your lawful wedded husband; do you stand by your decision to cleave to your heart's true lover, forevermore?

And I could scarcely breathe to vow Yes! Yes.

IN THIS WAY I was brought to the Bog Kingdom in my ruined bridal gown; in my veil, and my Spanish lace, and my satin lilies-of-the-valley each exquisite as an actual miniature blossom. And in my pride and ignorance I was brought, in the very vanity of my innocence. Dear Annabel! Sweet Annabel! In my Kingdom at last.

In my intoxication of love that fed upon even as it shrank from the fire of my protector's gaze. In my blindness of wishing only to sink into another's being.

For Axson Mayte was the most handsome man I had ever seen, I was sure. Tall, and well-formed, and exquisitely well-mannered; gentle-voiced, and loving.

Thus in my blindness, and sinful, sickly nature.

Brought to the Bog Palace deeply hidden in that lightless swamp, that no one might find it; that no one from that other world might venture into it, to bring the deluded Annabel home.

Soon we alighted from the mud-splattered carriage, and the panting horses were led from us; it was a murmured aside of Axson's, they were to be put down—for he never used the same matched pair of horses twice, after such a journey.

Leading me then—somewhat roughly it seemed to me, by fingers shut about my wrist—into the central hall of the cavernous Palace, which astonished me, and silenced me, with the high gloomy granite arch of its vaulted ceiling, like an old, great cathedral, and the echoing emptiness all around, and the overwhelming odor of damp, earthen rot, and fetid decay.

And with no further words, my bridegroom led me up a great spiral staircase littered with the broken bones of delicate, small creatures, the which I could not help stepping on, in a frisson of horror; no further words, except Annabel: come! To our bridal bed.

IN THIS WAY, the Bog Palace.

In the very interior of the Bog Kingdom.

And I, Annabel—Queen!

Queen Annabel, of the Bog Kingdom.

And the cruel "Axson Mayte," beside her as King.

OF HOW MY bridegroom used me, it is very difficult to speak.

Even of the bridal bed, it is very difficult to speak.

The master bedchamber at the top of a flight of badly worn and mossy stone steps, overlaid with grime, and the hard-dried excrement and remains of vermin—

overlooking, from its single (barred) window, a marshy graveyard, the aged markers tilted and filthy from neglect, spiky grasses growing all around, and pools of brackish water interspersed among the graves. Here, creatures of a kind I have never glimpsed before freely disported themselves, like overgrown, rowdy children; such strange species, I shrank in terror from even gazing upon them for many days: great ungainly birds that were yet reptilian, with sharp talons; giant lizards with darting tongues, and topaz eyes; soft fleshy bulbous creatures like mollusks without shells, of the size of pigs, that drew sustenance from sucking from numerous mouth-tentacles at once. And how horrible!—the soil of the graveyard was torn and churned from the feeding of these creatures.

Who is buried in the graveyard, Axson?—*so I dared to ask my husband; who remarked casually, indifferently*—Why, your predecessors, dear Annabel. For I am a widower, many times over.

THE BOG PALACE, in which Annabel reigned as (mock) Queen—for a brief spell.

The Bog Palace, with its dank mossy chambers—some, rooms as large as private chapels; others so cramped and airless, and dark, they might have served as dungeons, or places of torture. Many corridors leading in many directions into the very depths of the Palace, and outward, through breaks in the crumbling stone wall, into the depths of the swamp; slope-ceilinged hallways that lurched to one side, then to the other; windowless, or with narrow (barred) windows that overlooked fetid courtyards heaped with broken masonry, and profuse with sickly-smelling swamp lilies. Many flights of steps there were, that led nowhere; or to heavy locked doors that gave every impression of having been locked for centuries.

The Bog Palace! But one day Axson took pity on me, or so I supposed, leading me into his library; which was far larger than my grandfather Winslow Slade's famed library—Anything you wish, you can read, my dear wife. With my blessing.

Yet a shock to me, and a torment, that on shelves reaching to the fifteen-foot ceiling there were leather-bound books that, when opened, revealed smudged print, as if there had been a flood in the Palace; worse yet, many books had utterly blank pages, which I examined with mounting dismay, and a sense of great desolation.

Why is this, Axson, I asked my bridegroom, what has happened to your books?—*and again Axson replied casually, with an indifferent shrug*—All pages, all books, are equally useless: what's the fuss?

THE BOG PALACE, staffed by "servants"—and these creatures that seemed but part-human!—repulsive, yet piteous. They were misshapen, female and male alike; of greatly varying ages, but mostly older; their skins were ghastly-pale, like the underbellies of frogs or snakes; their grieving eyes were dark-shadowed and hollow; their manner craven and abashed yet sly, even furtive. How hard they worked!—yet how fruitlessly. That is one of your predecessors, dear Annabel, if you are curious—*so Axson indicated a stoop-backed old crone wrapped in what appeared to be a winding-shroud though she was animatedly scrubbing steps, on her hands and knees; if this piteous creature heard Axson's off-handed remark, she did not give any sign; nor did I continue to stare at her, in a state of light-headedness. (How terrible it seemed, that the poor woman seemed to be laboring in vain, spilling dirty water onto dirty steps, scrubbing vigorously at them, yet with not the slightest change in the grime on the steps; and on the wetted steps, Axson indifferently strode, with not a glance downward.)*

At a distance, I was allowed to view Axson Mayte's sister Camille—a woman of a particularly hard-faced beauty, with very pale skin, pale-blond hair loosened down her back, and a pitiless gaze.

You must never approach Camille. You must never speak with Camille, unless she speaks with you first.

Axson spoke of his sister admiringly. On his face, that had become a splotched frog's face, with bulging eyes, and a slack spittle-damp mouth, was a look of commingled wonderment, apprehension, and sibling-dislike.

***

CHILDREN OF THE NIGHT *he named them. The ugly creatures sporting outside our bedchamber window, in the desolate graveyard. Though they were nearly as active during the day-hours: shrieking, squawking, squabbling among themselves, poking about in the moldering graves with manic greed, and in black infested pools of water.* Children of the Night *Axson Mayte* murmured which you would do well not to scorn, my proud Annabel, for you and they will become well acquainted soon, before many months have passed; and I, and my companions, weary of your creamy skin and insipid ways.

IT WAS NOT entirely true, that Axson's former brides were dead; but some varying number of them, as many as twenty, it sometimes seemed, were fully alive, kept captive in rooms in the Bog Palace, or allowed to emerge, to work as manual laborers, like the piteous crone in the winding-shroud. My harem is not so showy as the harem of an Arab prince *Axson Mayte* remarked for our females are not so well disciplined, and soon pine away, and die; or are helped to die; if they are not *loved*. In a true harem, it is not realistic to expect to be *loved*. Dear Annabel, be wise!

So broken in mortification, so weakened by cruel and crude usage, and repugnant food, I could not even pray to our merciful God (whom I had abandoned, in my vanity and stupidity) but lay senseless for days, for weeks, while Axson Mayte plied upon my limp and unresisting body such obscene acts, I am sickened and speechless to recall. That my body was limp and resisting sometimes pleased him, but at other times aroused him to fury. Soon, there will be no need to "play dead," dear Wife!

Soon, too, bored with the sameness of our marital bed, Axson Mate invited into it his lewd drinking companions.

UPON THE HOUR a great bell tolled. An undersea bell it sounded like, and we the inhabitants of an ancient sea.

And sometimes the tolling had a hollow ring, dull, ponderous, leaden, and muffled; as if the sound were coming from within, in the marrow of one's bones.

So Axson Mayte said, seeing my look of baffled horror Dear Annabel, it is but the music of Time you are hearing. Why take foolish alarm as if you were still a child at the Manse? You have left your paradise forever, you cannot return. Now, as each note sounds—each tolling of the bell— understand how quickly it passes; each note, imagining it is Eternity, while so very fleeting, one can scarcely grasp that it existed at all.

Upon the hour, and the half hour, and the quarter hour—tolling, tolling, to make a mockery of Time.

For in the Bog Kingdom, Time did not pass.

Or, as Axson Mayte gloatingly said, it passes so fleetingly, one cannot measure it, or experience it.

So, feverish Annabel lay in her filth-encrusted bridal gown, which had become a kind of nightgown, or housecoat; sometimes, she lay in a bed of mere rags on the stone floor of a nameless room; hearing, close by, the cries of luckless females and men, singled out, as Axson chanced to remark, as "medical" or "scientific" subjects; for certain of his drinking companions, it was revealed, were men of medicine, or science; though Annabel would know them but dimly, through a scrim of horror, repugnance, shrinking pain as Macalaster!—"Scottie"!—O'Diggan!— Pitcairn!—Pitt-Williams!—Skinner!—*jocularly introduced to Annabel, as Axson ushered them into the bedchamber.*

Later, there was water thrown on her: lukewarm, fetid water but welcomed, desperately. And there was food, of a kind—tossed into the room where she lay, or, as Axson and his friends looked on, to their vast amusement, dumped onto the filthy floor of the kitchen so that Annabel and the others were made to eat from the floor, like animals; and, like animals, greedy and grateful for what they were given.

Rancid food, garbage food, bones mostly picked clean of meat—these were tossed at the starving, no matter that flies and beetles had gotten into them. Where is your Slade pride now, my darling?—*so Axson mocked, and laughed.*

Why these disfiguring tears? Men despise tears—it is the very weakness of the female sex that most disgusts them. Did you not foreswear all you'd known, to cleave to me; did you not cast your lot with Axson Mayte, who flattered you; did you not repudiate your family, the infamous Slades, who made their fortune in the slave trade, decades ago, and have been most holy-and-righteous Christians, since? Did you not cast aside your baby-faced Lieutenant, that fatuous gentleman, yet to moisten his lips in blood? Did you not break your parents' hearts, and devastate your brother Josiah? Does not your foolish virgin-heart yet swoon in amorous abandon, in my presence?

Thus coldly and jeeringly Axson Mayte laughed. Changed utterly from the Southern gentleman I had known, in my grandfather's garden.

His close-set eyes of the color of mucus, in the flaccid-toad face.

His forehead low, and furrowed, and sickly-white; his thin lips glistening lewdly, in the way that Annabel saw, or imagined she'd seen, in the faces of certain gentlemen of Princeton, who could not have known that Annabel, or anyone, was observing them at such a time.

In the secrecy of her filthy bed begging God to forgive her. Begging God to show her the way out of the Bog Palace, and the Bog Kingdom, that was not the way of death.

So badly she missed her dear family—her mother, and her father; her grandfather; her beloved brother Josiah, whom she had wantonly injured, and now could not recall why.

For she was not yet desperate enough to comprehend how a Christian of purer heart and greater resolve than she might have preferred death, to the continued horrors of the Bog Kingdom; how a woman of purer heart than her own should have eagerly embraced the grave, and given herself to the loathsome scavengers of the cemetery, than willingly surrender to the bestial lusts of Axson Mayte and his companions.

FORGIVE ME, for this abject wish to live! To be returned to my beloved family, whose hearts I have wounded, and whose reputation I have defiled.

During this time and afterward, when I was yet more abused as a servant-girl and a cast-off wife, I found some small relief in moments of quiet; by summon-

ing the Manse, and my family, and girlhood friends like Wilhelmina; and many another kindly face of childhood, as if the years could run backward. Often I lay too exhausted and demoralized to move, even to be kicked into action by Axson Mayte, or one of his drinking companions; and so I was allowed to lie in filth for as many as two or three days, as the brutes ignored me in their excited interest in one of their experimental subjects—electric shocks, blood-transfusions and "organ transplants" with creatures of another species, and if the poor wretched died, dissections with surgical instruments. (For so I came to know, though I had not ever looked upon such horrors directly.) During such times my soul seemed to pass from my body to drift about the airless cell; my fingers resumed an old, playful life, at the pianoforte in the drawing room at Crosswicks where I'd played sonatas by Mozart, Schubert, Beethoven, and Chopin; or sang with my beloved family from sheet music at the piano, as I played, songs of Stephen Foster, Gilbert and Sullivan, and these words of Thomas Moore set to such exquisite music, that Josiah particularly loved—

> Oft, in the stilly night,
> Ere Slumber's chain has bound me,
> Fond Memory brings the light
> Of other days around me;
> The smiles, the tears,
> Of childhood's years,
> The words of love then spoken;
> The eyes that shone,
> Now dimmed and gone,
> The cheerful hearts, now broken!
> Thus, in the stilly night,
> Ere Slumber's chain hath bound me,
> Of other days around me.

In such desperate ways, by slow degrees, I gathered in myself the strength to endure. And held out before my tear-swollen eyes the hope that I would someday escape the Bog Kingdom and return to the Manse and to my beloved family I had so cruelly wounded.

THE FEMALE IS the most contemptible of creatures: deficient of wit, repulsive in her mammalian nature, lecherous, and "frigid"; scheming, and stupid; entirely devoid of the moral and rational motive that guides men. For a short while, some of these creatures possess *beauty*—but it no more endures than spring blossoms, and soon festers, and stinks, like these.

So Axson Mayte and his drinking companions spoke, not vehemently so much as affably, and bemusedly; some of them men of "science," and some of them it seemed men of "the cloth," and some "businessmen"—or so Annabel gathered. And there was Axson Mayte's declaration, to which the men drank toasts: Yet, we must allow uses for the female!—seeing that the world must be continuously repopulated, and we would not wish to spill our precious seed into the Bog.

AT THIS TIME it had become evident that I was with child. Which further provoked Axson Mayte to be repelled by me, and to consider if perhaps an "experiment" might be performed upon me, and the unborn child, by one or another of his companions.

Yet, Axson seemed to forget this; or to take pity on me; for as I was deemed of little use to the men as an amorous object, lacking in feminine beauty and desirability, my position in the Palace reverted to that of servant-girl; which allowed me to learn from other servants that Axson Mayte and his sister Camille and certain of the churlish houseguests had themselves been mere servants in the household, or farm-laborers; and had some time ago risen against the rightful King and Queen and all of the royal family, and the nobles of the kingdom, slaying most, in heartless fashion, and forcing the others into lifelong servitude.

One of the ravaged female servants, who had once been a young bride of Axson Mayte, told me You have come to the very edge of the world, in coming here. Poor child, how will you find your way back!—the distance is so far.

WHAT SORROW! WHAT ignominy!

And yet, what gratitude, simply to be alive.

For I could not bring myself to hate the baby in my womb—that so drained my energy, and roused me to the most terrifying hunger, that I might almost have eaten as the graveyard scavengers ate, in the fierce desperation to live.

Axson Mayte's sister Camille would appear, to the neutral observer, the more "noble" of the two; for so Camille Mayte comported herself, in a queenly fashion; yet she was of plebeian origin which she betrayed in small gestures, as in an unseemly scowl that contorted her sculpted-looking face; or a flashing stare of hauteur, yet of pity, directed toward such wretches as me. (It was Camille who at last, repelled by seeing me in my grossly altered state, banished me out of the central part of the Palace and commanded that I be put to work in the cellar, which other workers called the "tunnel," or the "pit," or "the hole of Hell.")

In this way it was revealed to me, piecemeal, the true nature of the Bog Palace, and of the Bog Kingdom: presided over by murderous former servants of an era long past, whose particular history seemed to be lost now; for no one remembered when the uprising had occurred, and the public executions of the royal family and their retainers; and the forced servitude of many in the kingdom of aristocratic and genteel blood. The majority of the younger servants were certain that the insurrection had not taken place during their lifetimes; yet there were some, a very few, who claimed that they'd seen massacres with their own eyes, and had narrowly escaped being killed. These events had taken place thirty, or only twenty, or only ten years before. The elderly servants disclaimed such tales, and were more convincing to my ear.

That they concurred in the general detestation and fear of the present regime was evident; and how pathetic it seemed to me, that a crowd of former menials should be raised in such a way, and now waited upon by their former masters and mistresses. And these menials of old were of coarse untutored stock hailing from the more desolate regions of Europe, as from the west of Ireland where the "black Irish" are said to abide with their peasant superstitions, their Gaelic, and their wild melancholy so provok'd by alcohol!

Yet we are all grateful, we escaped with our lives—*the more stoic of the servants would say*—if indeed this is life, in such a hell of servitude.

EVER MORE DESPERATELY I prayed for deliverance from this place, that my child would be born elsewhere; for though it kicked and cramped inside me, like a little fiend, I could not but love him; though it be Axson Mayte's son, as I feared it must be, I could not but love him—for such is a woman's nature.

Yet I lacked courage to try to escape, for I knew that Axson Mayte would punish me severely if he caught me; and my ever-swelling body was very awkward, since my limbs were somewhat thin, and lacking in muscle. In my weakness, I am ashamed to reveal, as in a fever-dream, I caught myself in the most absurd fantasies: that Axson was but testing me, as in the old medieval tale of Patient Griselde, we had had to read in English class at the Academy, in a translation from the Middle English. For could it be, Axson was hoping to determine if I loved him purely, or was so shallow as to foreswear my vow to him . . . At such times the hissing Dear Annabel! Fair Annabel! *seemed to rise to me, from a lost world; the which, in my feverish imaginings, I so craved to regain, I would have sold my soul, or bartered it wildly—another time! Yet this too was mere foolishness, and had no weight in the actual, exterior world.*

In that world, I was most piteous indeed; beginning to appear grossly pregnant, with every accompanying symptom of morning sickness, and a bloated belly, and swollen ankles; sinus infections and bronchitis swept through me, as did a ravaging stomach flu; merely to wait table to that crew of drunken ruffian louts was a torment, and exhausting; for quite "by accident" one or another of the men would jab an elbow against my belly, or ram into me with a bottle, or a chair; this provoked much laughter. Merely to witness the men devouring their food with bestial greed, not hesitating to devour raw beefsteak that leaked blood down their chins . . . (This "cannibal sandwich" was a favorite of the Palace, raw steak in a thick cut placed between two pieces of coarse bread.) As my condition grew more pronounced such displays of savage manners increased my bouts of nausea, and vomiting, so that I was disgusting to others, as to myself. Fair Annabel!—beauteous Annabel!—go away and hide yourself, you are VILE. *So mocking words echoed in my reeling brain.*

Exiled to the dank cellar, which was a vast cavernous space like a cave, amid garbage, raw sewage, rats and other vermin, I found myself a comrade of similar laborers; one of our tasks was to bail excessive sewage out of the cesspool, and carry it to a woodland ravine a quarter mile from the house; our task was the continuous filling of buckets, and the continuous emptying-out of buckets, hour after hour, day following day, amid the most nauseating of odors and sights; with provision for no more than a few minutes' respite for a frantic feeding, of poorly baked dough, and leftovers from the kitchen; and brief periods of scanty sleep, amid the very stench of the cellar in which we toiled. Sixteen hours of stoop labor daily—and then eighteen—twenty!—as autumn rains fell thunderously, and increased the water-level of the cesspool, and the Palace was threatened with flooding; entire days were spent in such labor, under threat of death from Axson Mayte, who could not abide "mutiny." Our miserable cellar-crew of which I was surely the weakest member were obliged to crawl where we could not walk upright, and where the jagged stone ceiling was low we had to squirm like snakes, on our bellies . . . At which times the thought came to me stern and judicious This is your Hole of Hell, to which you have brought yourself.

Yet it might be that this final mortification worked for good; for it came to me soon after that if it was so, I had brought myself to the Hole of Hell, and so could take myself away, if I had courage; all the while sprawled facedown, on my swollen belly, in a filthy composition of mud, slime, sewage, and offal, not excluding the bones of fellow menials of an age long ago. And a new thought came to me If I am freed from the Hole of Hell I will consecrate my life to freeing my fellow-sufferers and it was astonishing to me, this thought did not seem to be from God but from the depths of my own soul, and in my own voice.

ESCAPE FROM THE Bog Kingdom was only possible if my fellow-slaves did not report me, as evidently they did not; though pleading with me, it was "too dangerous" to chance, crawling through a sort of cave, or tunnel, to reach the outside of the Palace, by night; then making my way through the Bog Forest, by the most pallid moonlight. It was the purest chance, Axson Mayte had not the slightest awareness of me at this time, as I was banished from the better part of the Palace; it may even have been, Axson

Mayte had brought a new bride to the Bog Palace by this time, without my knowing. And so I set off, less in desperation than in resolution, on a cold night of intermittent rain and sleet; in which month this was, I had no idea; nor even which year; for in the Bog Kingdom, Time did not exist as we know it elsewhere. And so—somehow—I made my way back—beginning to recognize my surroundings after dawn of the next day—seeing with amazed eyes the hills outside Princeton, now a latticework of the brightest snow.

Hearing these terrible words from one so debased, you cannot help but feel repugnance, for the depth of sin, degradation, bestiality and even worse to which your Annabel has fallen. Yet it is my prayer that you will see it in your hearts to forgive me, and perhaps one day again to love me; and to allow me, and my baby soon to be born, a refuge at the Manse.

POSTSCRIPT:
ARCHAEOPTERYX

It might be of interest to the reader of scientific and naturalistic inclinations to learn that at least one of the strange species of scavenger which Annabel describes in the graveyard of the Bog Palace—the one that is part-bird and part-reptile—is evidently no mere phantom of her delirium but an actual creature to be found in certain isolated regions of the eastern United States.

Though few living persons have claimed to have actually seen these terrifying birds—(for "birds" they are classified, with the capacity for limited periods of flight)—it is evidently the case, according to a biologist at the university whom I have consulted, that they must be descendants of *Archaeopteryx*, an extinct "flying reptile" of the Jurassic period. Such creatures are to be found today primarily in the Florida Everglades (where they are companions of the Everglade kite), in the Ogeechee region of Georgia, in the Dismal Swamp of North Carolina, and, closer to home, in both the remote Pine Barrens of southeastern New Jersey (encompassing more than seventeen hundred square miles) and the smaller Great Bog, or Crosswicks Bog, several miles south and west of Princeton.

THE CURSE INCARNATE

How exhausted I am, and drained of emotion, following the account by Annabel Slade of her nightmare adventure in the Bog Kingdom! Though I have read it numerous times, each reading leaves me more upset, and with a fear that my objectivity as an historian might be jeopardized.

And a feeling of great sympathy for poor Josiah, who recorded this upsetting material verbatim, over a period of hours, often near-overcome by emotion as well, with such fury that his hand ached and his fingers could scarcely clutch at his pen.

If only it could be that this book of *The Accursed* might end with Annabel's return home, her family's forgiveness of her and great relief to have her back, and the birth of her child—*her* child, and not the Fiend's.

Yet, unfortunately, it was not that way. So far as I have been able to determine, Annabel died in, or shortly after, childbirth; near the end of her labor she lapsed into a coma, and did not awaken; with the effort of the skilled midwife Cassandra, the baby was "born"—but did not live for more than a few seconds.

Called to the Manse, Dr. Boudinot could do nothing for the young mother, who had ceased breathing, and whose skin had begun to chill; the distraught physician signed a death certificate declaring that Annabel had died of "complications" following childbirth. (Which certificate I have located, in the Princeton Borough Records; but I was not able to locate any birth or death certificate for the unnamed and unbaptized Slade infant, the great-grandson of Winslow Slade.)

Both Annabel and her infant son were interred in the Slade family mausoleum in Princeton Cemetery, in a private ceremony attended only by family and barred to all others, by a special decree of the Princeton police which the Slades had arranged.

So it was said, and so it was widely believed.

THE TURQUOISE-MARBLED BOOK contains nothing but Annabel's words, as I have said; so, for a comprehension of the confused events that follow, the historian is obliged to consult a miscellany of sources of which no single one, unfortunately, can be thoroughly trusted.

Though all concur that Annabel Slade passed away in her childhood bed, after an arduous delivery, and was entombed shortly thereafter, yet there is considerable disagreement about the infant: was it a monster, or a normal infant?

The Beige Morocco Book, Josiah's diary, contains no entries for this time, but several pages have been raggedly torn out.

Mrs. Johanna van Dyck's Ivory Book devotes a dozen pages to the subject; but, having had no firsthand experience of the events at Cross-wicks, and dependent solely upon gossip and rumor, her account is of limited value. It seems to have been Mrs. van Dyck's assumption, which was common in Princeton, that the baby was a "premature birth" precipitated by the mother's physical ordeal. *So the unhappy tale winds to its close* Mrs. van Dyck wrote. *God have mercy on these poor souls!*

Adelaide Burr in the Crimson Calfskin Book seems to have been in possession of more bits of information, presumably by way of gossiping friends and tattling servants, or of Dr. Boudinot's breach of confidence; for, though suffering from some undiagnosed fever, which Mrs. Burr feared might be *incipient Laotian sleeping sickness,* the invalid devotes some thirty close-written pages to what she calls THE TRAGEDY OF CROSSWICKS MANSE. So enthralled is Mrs. Burr by her salacious subject matter, there are passages in which she neglects to write in her usual crabbed hiero-glyphic but lapses into English as she speculates on the "nature of the mis-shapenness" of the infant, which she had heard from "reliable sources" was *black-skinned;* whether this "cruelty of nature" should be interpreted as a "just & necessary Act of God" for the sin of forbidden "race-mixing"; or whether such a phenomenon was a sort of natural "mutant"—like con-joined twins, or dwarfs. Adelaide's earliest entries deal with the "new & piteous fact that horrifies all of Princeton"—that poor Annabel Slade, re-turned to her family, has died in childbirth, having given birth to a *stillborn baby;* it is not until a day later, having been informed of a "fresh onslaught" of news, that the diarist adds that the baby's skin is *black;* not until several days later that she writes that the baby had indeed been a "freakish prod-igy of nature" born with two heads and foreshortened, flipper-like arms and certain of its vital organs, heart, liver, kidneys, carried on the outside of the body. "How merciful, there *is* God—to deny breath to such afflic-tion." (Adelaide then indulges herself in an unwholesome sort of specula-tion, questioning whether, if she and Horace had had a child, "it would have been in the shape of anything decently Human; or so mischievously deformed, as Horace sometimes appears to me in his disheveled state, I would have been locked away in a madhouse forever, like the legendary Mrs. Andrew West.") (For so cruel rumors circulated about Dean West's wife, who had passed away twenty years before.)

At Prospect, the Wilsons were naturally shocked and grieved over what Woodrow referred to as the "undeserved tragedy of the Slades"; for he had been very fond of Annabel, as of Josiah, and believed that the young woman's "fall from grace" was to be attributed to the growing immoral-ity of the secular world—indeed, in the very heart of Presbyterian ortho-doxy. Dwelling in what observers slightingly called "Dr. Wilson's petticoat haven," with a wife and daughters and a frequently visiting mother-in-law,

Woodrow was of two minds concerning Woman, and doubted that the "natural propensities" of the sex could include a moral and rational depth equivalent to Man's. So, the mysterious behavior of Annabel Slade seemed to him but a vindication of certain doubts, and a warning to all, that years of Christian upbringing cannot always overcome the biological fact of *ab initio* femaleness.

Jessie Wilson, Annabel's friend from school, was deeply shaken by news of her death; but did not want to talk about it, nor certainly about the rumor of a "misshapen black-skinned baby," except to say that, since Annabel's death, her nightmares seem to have lessened, for which she was grateful. "Instead of Annabel, I dream about—nothing! As if Annabel drew all with her of my emotions, and I am left behind."

Jessie's pink satin bridesmaid's dress would hang in her closet at Prospect for years, unworn a second time; for the young woman sincerely believed that there was a curse on the dress, that would afflict her should she ever dare to wear it.

In her Brown-Dappled Book, Wilhelmina Burr set down an emotional account of what she was able to learn of her dear friend's ordeal; initially, she records her dismay at being denied entry to the Manse, to visit Annabel; she records her concern, that Annabel might be very ill; then, a number of rumors: that Annabel had succumbed to madness, and tried to injure herself and her baby with an overdose of laudanum; that Annabel had not died in childbirth, but some days later, while nursing her misshapen baby; that the Fiend had come for his son, and taken away the infant, from all the Slades who dared not lift a finger to prevent him . . . Then, news came that Annabel had died: which Wilhelmina at first refused to believe.

Like other West End residents, Wilhelmina would be "baffled & incensed" by not being invited to Annabel's funeral, and lapsed into melancholy, that she would never see her friend again; but began to dream, that in fact Annabel *had not died;* and that she and Annabel would be reunited one day soon, *this side of the grave.*

Wilhelmina would hear of the burial in Princeton Cemetery that, as the mausoleum doors were slowly closed, Josiah broke into sobs and refused to be comforted by his mother, or anyone; and Todd woke from a transfixed state to rush at the mausoleum, clawing at the doors and wrestling with the attendants who were shutting them, crying angrily that his cousin Annabel *should not die, and would not die; because Todd would not allow it, and Todd would bring her back.*

Among Princetonians, by this time, every sort of crazed rumor was circulating, the most bizarre being relayed to Amanda FitzRandolph by a neighbor on Edgehill Road, that the infant born to Annabel Slade was no human creature at all, but a *black snake;* with a blunt bullet head, topaz eyes, and a length of at least two feet, thick, muscular, with "diamond" scales covered in its mother's blood. Amanda had felt faint with disgust, and disbelief; asking what had become of this hideous thing she was told that it had *escaped*.

For all who were in attendance at the delivery in Annabel's room, it was reported, had been stunned by horror and incredulity, and too frightened to take hold of the snake, or beat at it with any weapon. "So that the horrible thing slithered from the bed, made its way downstairs, and out of Crosswicks Manse. And it was the sight of the snake that so terrified Annabel, she sank into a coma, and never awakened."

Mrs. FitzRandolph cried: "Ridiculous! It is utterly absurd, such a rumor."

So her neighbor went away chastened; but would relay to others that, as she'd told of the hellish birth, Mandy FitzRandolph had not looked nearly so surprised as one might have expected.

PART III

"The Brain, within Its Groove . . ."

THE WRITER MUST APPEAL TO PHYSICIANS
& TO MEN CONVERSANT WITH THE LATENT
SPRINGS & OCCASIONAL PERVERSIONS, OF
THE HUMAN MIND.

—*Charles Brockden Brown, Advertisement for*
Wieland, *1798*

"VOICES"

Following his sister's death Josiah Slade was generally noted to be "gravely altered" and to "behave strangely"; yet observers, seeing only the outward man, had no idea how very much altered and how strange the young heir to Crosswicks Manse had become.

Where before Annabel's death Josiah had been frantic with activity in searching for her, and hoping to exact revenge upon Axson Mayte, now he became a virtual hermit sequestered away at Crosswicks, rarely consenting even to dine with his family. He had tried to locate the Bog Kingdom in which Annabel had been held captive, but without success; nor did maps of New Jersey, of early eras, suggest any such vast marshy area, apart from the Pine Barrens and the smaller marshland in Crosswicks Forest, covering only a few acres, which Josiah had explored numerous times, to no avail.

Many times, Josiah fantasized having murdered Axson Mayte when he'd been introduced to the man, by Woodrow Wilson, on the university campus; except of course, he would never have committed such a mad act.

"Our lives can only be interpreted in retrospect, yet must be lived from day to day, blindly. What folly, the human condition!"

Through the winter and spring of 1906 Josiah spent most of his time locked away at the Manse, brooding and berating himself for his failure;

for he did truly believe that he was to blame for his sister's death, as he had not prevented it. Through the long nights he read and reread such books as he considered crucial to his understanding of human nature, and possibly illuminating in suggesting a course of action for him to take: Robert Louis Stevenson's *Dr. Jekyll and Mr. Hyde,* Edgar Allan Poe's *Tales of the Grotesque and Arabesque,* Charles Brockden Brown's *Wieland;* the 1818 edition of Mary Shelley's *Frankenstein; or, The Modern Prometheus;* and not least, Milton's epic *Paradise Lost* and such tragedies of Shakespeare—*Macbeth, Othello, Lear, Hamlet*—that seemed to pertain particularly to his situation. So restless was Josiah, he could rarely sit still for more than a half hour, but had to pace about, or rush outside to walk hurriedly by moonlight; it was his habit to read several books at once; no sooner did he begin a book than he pushed it aside to take up another—now Theodore Dreiser's *Sister Carrie,* now Jack London's *The Call of the Wild;* now Plato, Thucydides, Goethe and Hegel, from his grandfather Winslow's library; now, the magnificent if rather shopworn Gutenberg Bible enshrined in the library, that could never be removed from it. (At such times, Winslow Slade sat silently nearby, observing his frowning grandson, but making little comment; for, like Josiah, Winslow seemed to have felt that he was in some way to blame for Annabel's death, in having failed to prevent it; and, since his stroke of some months before, the elderly man had lost much of the vigor and goodwill for which he'd been renowned and seemed rather more simply a melancholy individual whom life had left behind, marooned amid the debris of his old, former life and reputation.) "Do you have any question, Josiah?"

"Question? What question?"

"About what you're reading . . . You look as if you might have a question."

Winslow Slade spoke in a kindly and unassuming voice, having seen his grandson grimace, in perusing the Bible; for there is much in the Bible to provoke grimaces of incomprehension. But Josiah only just shrugged.

"I have plenty of questions, Grandfather. But not questions the Bible can answer."

But Josiah's concentration was poor, no matter the ferocity of his intention, for his thoughts assailed him increasingly, in the form of alien "voices."

You will, will you?—eh? Yes of course you will—you!

When the voices rose to a din, Josiah had to flee the house and wander into the forest, or tramp along back roads; his nerves were so tightly strung, he could not bear the company of other people; he had ceased seeing, or even speaking with, his male friends in Princeton, who had ceased trying to contact him after numerous rebuffs. He'd have liked to visit Pearce van Dyck in his office at the university but could not bring himself to step onto the college campus. The fatuous college boys roused him to impatience and contempt, and the intelligent, serious-minded college boys roused him to envy, and a yearning for his lost youth.

As much as possible Josiah avoided the busyness of Nassau Street. For he imagined, not unreasonably, that, as he made his way along the sidewalk heads turned in his wake; in pity, in sympathy, yet in cruel satisfaction as well.

Is that one of them?—the Slades?

Think they'd be ashamed to show their faces . . .

In Micawber Book Store, Josiah had formerly liked to browse in a pleasurable sort of trance, collecting an armload of books to purchase; now, he made a furtive course through the aisles, in search of a particular title that might strike his fancy and that he must own immediately, and read, as if his life depended upon it. So Josiah had, in recent weeks, impulsively purchased books as diverse as Mark Twain's *Pudd'nhead Wilson,* whose "calendar" of sharply observed little ironies struck his fancy, and Ulysses S. Grant's *Personal Memoirs,* that seemed to him a frank, fearless, yet melancholy document; and, belatedly, Harriet Beecher Stowe's *Uncle Tom's Cabin,* that roused Josiah to emotions of sympathy and indignation, and settled for him, for all time, that the responsibility of "white" Americans was to establish a society in which "Negro" Americans might be freely at home, as equals.

One slender book, Josiah had ordered, and picked up now, with much anticipation—*Poems* by Emily Dickinson. The little volume of mostly short poems had gone through several editions, Josiah saw, since its publication in 1890; the edition he held in his hand had been published in 1896. Yet, apart from Wilhelmina's remarks, Josiah had never heard anything about the poetess, and was doubtful of the worth of his purchase until, on his way back to Crosswicks, a distance of about a mile, he leafed through the pages, and was struck by a "voice" of uncommon timbre, far from any poetic voice he had yet encountered:

Tell all the Truth but tell it slant—
Success in Circuit lies
Too bright for our infirm Delight
The Truth's superb surprise
As Lightning to Children eased
With explanation kind
The Truth must dazzle gradually
Or every man be blind—

"If I am to be haunted by 'voices,' how wise it would be, to be haunted by this one!"

Yet, there were times when Josiah felt that he must escape from Crosswicks, and from Princeton; not by train (where he would have encountered fellow Princetonians) but by motorcar he traveled to New York City, to walk the streets, marveling at the throngs of people of whom many appeared to be immigrants, speaking languages utterly foreign to him. Though Josiah had relatives and family friends who lived in mansions on Park Avenue, and overlooking Central Park on Fifth Avenue, he made no effort to contact these individuals but far more preferred to walk aimlessly along the teeming streets of the Bowery, as it was called—long ago, a verdant Dutch farm; equally attractive were the congested streets of the West Side, the open "fresh produce" markets and meat-packing district near the Hudson River, the garment district, the "fresh flower" district, the blocks of brownstone tenements of the Lower East Side filled with life as a hive is filled with bees . . . Simply to cross a street wide as lower Fifth Avenue, Sixth or Seventh Avenues, or the aptly titled, so cunningly slanting Broadway, upon which traffic rushed in ill-defined lanes of two general directions—horse-drawn cargo-trucks, horse-drawn fire trucks, carriages and taxicabs; a frequent incursion of motor-vehicles compounding the confusion, in a constant blaring of horns—was a challenge that made Josiah's blood leap as at the prospect of battle. For the drivers of both cargo-trucks and fire trucks plunged forward into slower traffic, heedless of horns and the screams of pedestrians; the more whipping their frothing horses, as the congested way should have made them cautious. Josiah was several times almost struck by galloping horses, and by a brass-trimmed motorcar whose uniformed driver but glanced at him as it passed within inches as if the heir to the Slade fortune were of no more consequence than a luckless street cur; yet his most dangerous moment came when a careening fire truck pulled by four ill-matched horses veered out of the street, to avoid a head-on collision with a careening cargo-truck, and onto the crowded pedestrian walkway. Badly shaken Josiah shouted at the driver— "Damn you! Keep to the street!"—but within seconds the fire truck had plunged onward. Quickly one felt rage, but quickly rage subsided, for the fact of Manhattan street-life, Josiah saw, was its *drumming vividness*, and its *transience*.

Where rarely Josiah smiled in Princeton, frequently he found himself smiling in Manhattan, bemused by such impersonal activity, and such a spirit of brashness.

How vast the world was, and how mysterious! How small, how provincial, how *dreamlike* was Princeton, New Jersey; how sheltered from the rough vitality, vulgarity, and *foreignness* was the university, that seemed to float, like an enchanted island, somewhere just a little above the Earth. Especially, the bookstores of Manhattan were very different from Micawber Book Store, with its fastidiously shelved books and high-quality journals and magazines and, in special glass cases at the rear, first-edition and antiquarian books, that sold at high prices. In a large, bustling store on upper Broadway, that more resembled a small warehouse than a bookstore, Josiah acquired Lincoln Steffens's controversial *The Shame of the Cities*, which was not sold at Micawber, as well as several issues of a crudely printed Socialist magazine called *Appeal to Reason*, which he'd never before seen, whose title attracted him. "For that is our only hope—an 'appeal to reason.'" And afterward, sitting in Union Square, oblivious to the hubbub on all sides, Josiah began reading an excerpt of *The Jungle*, that dealt with the squalid conditions of the Chicago slaughterhouses and meat-packers, in a most personal, even intimate way, that quite captivated Josiah, even as it sickened him.

Indignantly he wondered—could such revelations be true? The wealthy and unscrupulous Chicago meat-packer "Durham" of the novel appeared to be a thinly disguised J. Ogden Armour.

Thinking, "But the Armours are our friends. They are my grandparents' and my parents' friends. Are the Armours themselves aware of *this*?"

Josiah could not believe that the well-bred Princeton family, whose sons he'd known at the Academy, had anything directly to do with the Chicago branch of the family, of which J. Ogden Armour was the head; though surely, they owned stock in the thriving company, as perhaps the Slades did as well . . . At the time of a massive strike in Chicago two years before, which had involved the hiring of thousands of Negro strike-breakers, to replace the striking union workers, Josiah had been traveling in the West and had rarely seen a newspaper, or cared about "news." Now, reading of these incidents in *Appeal to Reason*, he was ashamed of himself for being so ill-informed.

The Princeton Slades and the Princeton Armours were distinguished families of the West End, thus allies and friends *by tradition*. Annabel had been a classmate and friend of Eloise Armour, in a little circle that had included Wilhelmina Burr. And one of the Armour sons, Timothy, an upperclassman at Princeton University when Josiah had been a freshman, had been instrumental in acquiring for Josiah, who'd scorned it, the precious invitation to join Ivy. Josiah wanted to think that the Armours' reaction to *The Jungle* would be similar to his own.

Yet, reading further, in other issues of the Socialist magazine, Josiah was increasingly appalled, and sickened. That workers labored in such conditions, not unlike his dear sister Annabel's experience in the cellar of the Bog Palace, was outrageous; so poor, so trapped in the economic vise, even sickly men, and injured men, had no choice but to return to the conditions that were killing them: tuberculosis, rheumatism, "brown lung" and blood poisoning, and every kind of physical injury from accidents on the killing-floors that were slick with blood and offal. Most hideous were the fertilizer rooms and the "steamy tank" rooms where, Josiah read, workers sometimes slipped into vats of boiling water and were dissolved within seconds, to be sent out into the world as "Durham's Pure Leaf Lard"! (After reading the notorious chapter nine of Upton Sinclair's exposé, Josiah had had to close the magazine to recover.)

"Can it be, I've unwittingly eaten some part of a fellow human being? At Crosswicks, at our dining room table, my family and I have been *cannibals*?" The thought was so awful, Josiah could not bring himself to eat anything, even bread and cheese, for the remainder of that day.

VOICES! LIKE HOUNDS of hell, in hot pursuit.

Infrequently Josiah attended church services now. And, when he did, he resisted sitting in the Slades' pew at the front of the church, for he felt a revulsion for his Slade-self, seeing this individual through the eyes of others, as one of privilege and shame in about equal measure. And so, Josiah slunk into the First Presbyterian Church hoping to be undetected, by even his own family; he slipped into a pew at the rear of the church, and hid his face, in a paroxysm of remorse.

As much remorse for his having failed to murder Axson Mayte, as for his failure to have detected his sister's unhappiness as the fiancée of Lieutenant Bayard.

He had not ever been one to pray openly, in a church setting; nor had private prayer meant much to him, who could not perceive how, considering the millions of inhabitants of the world, the Creator could be aware of any of them, as individuals; still less could he understand why. He'd long abandoned the hope of acquiring his grandfather Winslow's combining of faith and intelligence, that had made Winslow Slade so revered a figure—among those of his kind.

Scarcely listening to Winslow's successor Reverend FitzRandolph, who derived the most familiar and the most trite conclusions from Holy Scripture, and addressed the congregation as if they were indeed *sheep*, Josiah lapsed into an open-eyed reverie; and became vulnerable to the flood of voices that rushed at him in the high-pitched mocking voices of cherubs to blend with his own prayer-voice: *Our Hellish Father who art in Hell damn'd be Thy name damn'd Thy* Kingdom *forever & ever AMEN.*

BLUESTOCKING TEMPTRESS

Josiah! I am your friend, please come to me when you can. Or when you wish. Please!"—so Wilhelmina murmurs to herself, testing the thrilling, unspeakable words while adjusting her new "slouch" hat in a mirror, or struggling to button the tight cuffs of her crisp white cotton middy-blouse, or preparing her cumbersome art-portfolio, to carry into the city for her lessons with Robert Henri.

Yearning, yet headstrong Miss Wilhelmina Burr!

In the spring of 1906 Wilhelmina has begun teaching as a part-time instructress in Art, Elocution, and Eurythmics at the Rocky Hill Seminary for Girls just outside Princeton, on the old King's Road to New Brunswick, to the distress of her family; for the Burrs think it déclassé, indeed embarrassing, that their debutante daughter should wish to "work" at all, let alone side by side with (spinster) females of middle-class families, and worse.

Yet more alarming to the Burrs, those alternative days when Wilhelmina takes the early train into the city, to indulge in her "fevered, if undirected" interest in art.

For Wilhelmina exults in her very stubbornness, that she might be self-supporting if necessary, and independent of all the Burrs.

"Otherwise, I shall have to marry. If I can't marry for love, I shall have to marry for money. *I will not.*"

In this way Willy believes herself content. Or believes she should be content. For in this new phase of her life it has happened that men have begun to take "interest" in her, as they had not earlier; except, none of these men are quite ideal. And none of them of course is Josiah Slade.

Indeed, the attention of these men has come to be worrisome to Wilhelmina, and not so pleasurable as one might expect.

Her encounter with Count English von Gneist, for instance—of which, resolutely, Wilhelmina does not wish to think.

"A misunderstanding. A misfortune. Never again!"

On her left wrist the incensed young woman carries still the mark of the Count's strong fingers—like an iron vise, they had seemed. And she carries still the memory of the man's broad grinning teeth. And the glowering topaz eyes. Never again!

Yet, as a sympathetic biographer, shall I suggest, this outspoken young woman is not so innocent as she imagines herself?

For it seems, a sly sort of female-demon peeps out through Willy's serious brown eyes, and distorts her smile with its own; a becoming blush comes into her cheeks, unbidden, in masculine company; even as she shrinks from the most innocent sort of coquetry, for fear of being misunderstood. Though Willy has brushed her springy hair back from her face and fashioned it into a schoolmarm's chignon, and Willy has scrubbed her face until it shines like soapstone, defiant in its plainness, yet, she has become a figure to "turn heads."

With particular care for her Kingston days as instructress at the girls' school, Willy dresses in white cotton blouses with high starched collars, tight sleeves, and full, rather than "hobbled," skirts; though she hates the sensation of being suffocated, Willy binds herself up each morning in a straight-front corset with long hips, to make of her soft, resilient flesh a kind of armor. (Inadvertently, Willy's tight-corseted figure attracts admiring glances, for she is made to appear, beneath even her fullest skirts, distinctly shapely.) Willy scorns excessive hairstyles, and wide-brimmed befeathered hats; wears no jewelry except for her pin-on watch and a miniature ivory brooch in the shape of a swan, a family heirloom recently given to her by her aunt Adelaide. (Though brought to her at Pembroke by her uncle Horace Burr.) And her stockings are thin black wool or cotton, and her day shoes of black leather with prim black buttons. Yet, still, there is something *covert* and *lascivious* in her step, in the inclination of her head, and most of all in the veiled sweep of her gaze. For why else do Princeton men, some of them proverbially *happily married men*, gaze at her as they do?

"It must be my fault. It is something new, but—what?"

Of a single week, from the stout, middle-aged Copplestone Slade, from taciturn Hamilton Hodge, from ministerial Dr. Woodrow Wilson of the university and Reverend Thaddeus Shackleton of the seminary, even from the gout-stricken Grover Cleveland, Willy receives unsolicited, unwelcome, and disagreeable attentions. Drivers have brought to her house sealed love-letters for her, and several prettily wrapped packages from the prestigious Hamilton Jeweler; so many packages from Edmund Sweet's—chocolates, bonbons, Black Forest tortes, even jelly beans. (Jelly beans! Willy is baffled, for who would eat such juvenile candies, that had not the slightest appeal to her since she'd turned sixteen.) Flowers are of course the most favored gift: these have included dozens of long-stemmed roses from the Bank Street florist, plus gardenias, lilies, daisies and lilacs, potted orchids. Even at the seminary where Wilhelmina is Miss Burr, with a reputation for making her girl-students work, and with no patience for girlish silliness, she is the recipient of illicit letters pressed into her hands by these very girls, which is embarrassing to her; she is stern about declining gifts, even those from a girl's grateful parents, given for "disinterested" reasons.

With a reluctant hand Willy opens one of the unsought *billets-doux* from a gentleman, sighing at the clichéd salutation—*My dear adored Miss Burr, Dear Beauteous Miss Burr;* impatiently she skims the protestation of love, couched in the language of subtle male reproach, and notes the signature, or, as often happens, the absence of a signature.

"It is a kind of sickness, a plague. But who is to blame?"

When these unwanted attentions first began, sometime in the early spring of 1906, as the scandal and tragedy of Annabel Slade began to wane, and sightings of Annabel's "bestial child" had all but ceased, Willy did feel, to her shame, a kind of girlish pleasure. These were not the sorts of attentions her mother had hoped for her, following her expensive coming-out in Manhattan, but they were authentic-seeming, and passionate. It is not surprising, nor should we judge Wilhelmina Burr harshly, that the young woman, only just twenty-one, would be flattered by such masculine interest; she may have interpreted the attentions from married men as but playful, and not serious. Perhaps such attentions are common in Princeton, and she has not known?

Regarding herself in the mirror, with an air of critical yet hopeful inquiry: "Can it be, 'Willy' is beautiful after all? And will *he* take notice—finally?"

For all such masculine interest is to Wilhelmina but a prelude to the interest of Josiah Slade, of whom she continues to think obsessively.

In her sweetest dreams, she feels Josiah's lips—warm, assertive, yet tender—pressing against her mouth; for the impulsive kiss in the garden room, now months ago, is as vivid to her as if it had happened just the previous day. Wakened from this sweet sleep, she could weep aloud—whether for joy, or sorrow, she cannot know.

For Willy has learned, from numerous sources, that Josiah is *in retreat* from life, since Annabel's death. Like a monk he seems to her, a penitent, and wholly admirable. She would never judge Josiah Slade harshly, as one who'd trifled with her feelings, as she would never have judged Annabel, her dearest friend.

Though Wilhelmina may have been flattered to receive cards and gifts, she knew that she must ignore the cards, and return the gifts when possible. (How is one to return flowers, though? Willy kept these, filling the garden room with such beauty and fragrances, visitors laughingly commented that one could *fall into a trance* in such surroundings.) It was also not possible to return gifts that were anonymously sent to her; or to reject the exquisite heirloom brooch that her aunt Adelaide had allegedly given her, by way of her uncle Horace.

(Willy thought it strange that there was no note from Adelaide accompanying the brooch. And that Horace thought it necessary to bring the brooch to her, in person, on a Sunday afternoon when no one else in the family was home, with the explanation that the antique brooch was too precious to trust to a delivery boy.) "But—how is Aunt Adelaide? Is she well, or—not so well?" Willy asked her stout mustached uncle, who told her, with a sorrowful smile, "Not so well, Willy, I'm afraid. Some days it seems almost poor Puss can't fully *wake herself up*.")

With the passing of weeks, however, Willy has begun to be vexed by such "attentions"—the more so, the majority of men who pursue her are older, and married, and in some inevitable way undesirable.

As disturbing as the men's behavior, the behavior of the women is yet more disturbing.

For instance, encountering the three Wilson daughters in Edmund Sweet's, Willy smiles her friendliest smile and invites the young women to sit at her table with her, and have some tea and cakes; but the eldest, Margaret, sharply shakes her head *no*, and Jessie and Eleanor nervously decline; for it seems, their father awaits their return from an errand at the pharmacy, and they have come only to purchase a few little cakes, to eat on their walk. Not long after this, Mrs. Johanna van Dyck, who has always been so sensible and friendly, turns away with a frown when she and Willy chance to meet at Micawber; and Mrs. Cleveland, buxom and glamorous in sable coat, hat, and muff, and high-buttoned kidskin boots, so cruelly "cuts" the smiling young Wilhelmina in Palmer Square, poor Willy feels faint with shock.

And, in days and weeks following, Willy is also snubbed by Mrs. Sparhawk, Mrs. Morgan, Mrs. Pyne, Mrs. Armour and her daughter Eloise; even Mandy FitzRandolph (about whom ominous whisperings have begun to accrue), who had always been her friend. Thinking *Oh Annabel, if you could help me! What have I done, what can I do to make amends?*

Most upsetting to Willy is the fact that Josiah Slade has not dropped by to see her, nor even contacted her, since the day of that sudden kiss. Several times she has imagined she'd seen him, in Princeton, but at a distance; she had not wanted to pursue him, so unmistakably, and risk another snub. And once, to her astonishment, she was sure she'd seen Josiah making his way along a crowded sidewalk at Fourteenth Street and Fifth Avenue, in the vicinity of the New York School of Art, which was her destination; again, Willy suppressed the impulse to run after Josiah, and to call to him—"For in Manhattan, perhaps Josiah doesn't want to be confused with *Josiah Slade of Princeton.*"

"YES! THIS BEGINS to be *vexing*."

With a sigh Willy unwraps a little present from LaVake Custom-Made Gifts, and stares inside the box at what appears to be a gold collar-necklace adorned at its center with a square-cut diamond. The unsigned card reads, bizarrely—

> To the Cruel & Beauteous Bluestocking Temptress
> From One Who Harbors no Ebullition Against Her
> For All She has Prick'd Him in Torment of Love.
> Your Faithfull Suitor

How beautiful, the gold necklace; yet how frightening, its resemblance to a dog collar.

And the hand? Though far looser and scrawling than normal, with a clumsy attempt at disguise, Willy is sure she recognizes it, with a sharp intake of breath, as that of her uncle Horace Burr, her father's younger brother, and husband of poor Puss.

THE GLASS OWL

Through Princeton it began to be remarked upon how, in a time of general sorrow and strife in the Slade households, the boy Todd, Copplestone and Lenora's "idiot" son, was undergoing an unexpected change; less in his appearance, for Todd was yet very young for his age, with a spindly nervous frame and darting eyes, than in his behavior.

So strangely, Todd seemed to have taught himself the rudiments of *reading and writing*, which tutors and governesses had despaired of teaching him for years.

Since his beloved cousin Annabel's death, Todd was less conspicuously vexing than he'd been to his family; he did not incur Copplestone's wrath quite so often, or provoke his mother to tears. Where previously the very sight of a book might throw him into a fit, unless it was a children's picture-book, now Todd was spending hours in the library at Wheatsheaf, which was not a room much frequented by either of his parents.

Of course, Todd's handwriting was primitive, set beside that of any twelve-year-old Princeton schoolboy; it fell between script and "printing," and was executed at great cost to the boy, who concentrated so fiercely, perspiration shone on his forehead, and his fingers sometimes gripped a pencil so tight that it snapped. One afternoon, while visiting Crosswicks Manse with his mother, Todd hid himself away in a corner of the drawing room and wrote out, in labored letters resembling Gothic—

Vammovv ivanmcct omnomomiia

—which no one could read; until, by chance, Woodrow Wilson dropped by to visit Dr. Slade, and was shown the curious printing, and, holding the sheet of paper at a slant, read straight out—

AMOR VINCIT OMNIA

—which thrilled Todd, very much.

How delighted everyone was!—Todd's first *writing*.

And how nice it was of Woodrow Wilson, president of Princeton University, to take the time to decipher the boy's writing and to very kindly speak to him of his own childhood, and the difficulties he'd had with reading and writing himself. "My family thought I was 'lazy' when in fact I could not 'make sense' of words as others did. I'm embarrassed to admit that I was at least your age, Todd, before I could read with any ease. I was always a poor student, and my undergraduate performance at Princeton was so undistinguished, I graduated *fiftieth* in my class, a fact I don't know whether to hide or reveal, so that other boys may take heart from my example." Seeing that Todd Slade was listening raptly to his words, and staring at him with his uncanny dark-liquid eyes, Dr. Wilson said: "I'll tell you a secret, Todd—what seems a curse may prove a blessing. For those of us who begin our lives with 'disabilities' quickly learn to work much harder than those who find their studies easy; and as the race proceeds, we commonly pull ahead." Dr. Wilson's sallow skin glowed with an inner fervor.

" 'Race'—like a horse-race? Are you a horse-race-rider, Mr. Wilson?"

"No, Todd! I meant metaphorically. 'The race is not to the swift'— it's an old saying."

"But—is it a horse-race? Or just on foot?"

"Neither, Todd. I'm sorry to confuse you."

"Why don't you know, Mr. Wilson, if it's a horse-race or a foot-race? Which did you do?"

"A foot-race, I suppose."

Pointedly, Todd looked at Dr. Wilson's feet, in narrow black shoes with neatly tied black laces.

"A race," Dr. Wilson said, with some feeling, "that never ceases, and with every sort of obstacle put in the runner's path to make his victory, when it comes, all the sweeter."

THAT NIGHT, Todd woke the household at Wheatsheaf, that had settled in to sleep, with excited shouts.

For it turned out, the restless boy had only pretended to go to bed; instead, he'd sat at his little desk with a single light burning, covering sheets of paper with hopeless scribblings, unintelligible even to him. When his mother hurried to him he told her that there was a "message" that was meant to come to him, through his fingertips, which he would record on paper; but the message was trapped inside him somewhere, and could not get free.

Todd knew not why, but he understood that it was urgent to warn Mrs. Cleveland across the lane, and the Strachans, and the van Dycks, and Annabel's friend Wilhelmina Burr, that something *very bad* would happen soon, he thought at the Rocky Hill school where Miss Burr taught.

Oriana, wakened, quavered at her brother's side; for it seemed that the little girl, too, had had a dream of something *very bad*.

"Todd! Oriana! *You* are bad children, to be up at this time of night!"—so Lenora cried, in fear and dismay.

Todd stood resolute; Oriana began to cry, so piteously that Lenora hugged the child, and assured her that all would be well.

Lenora hurried to wake her husband to tell him of this development, but Copplestone had little patience for her.

"Todd says we should warn these people. At least—we might warn Wilhelmina."

But irritable Copplestone thought not. "There are enough ridiculous rumors circulating about us, without inviting more. You will make fools of us. Go back to sleep."

In this way, no "warnings" were sent. It is a temptation for the historian to speculate what the effect of Todd's premonition would have been, in Wilhelmina's life, if the boy's father had not responded so dismissively.

All the following day, the children remained together, subdued and shivering. It was not like Todd to tolerate the presence of his much-younger sister, who was only nine; yet, this day, he seemed to take pity on her, for she was looking forlorn; and very shyly confessed to him, that Annabel had come to her, in her sleep—"She is very pretty, like before. She said to me, 'Oriana, there is a place for you here—you must come to me!' But when I tried to, I could not—there was something like a door in the way."

"Annabel is in Heaven, Oriana. You can't go *there*."

"Yes I can. Annabel says so."

"You *can't*."

"I *can*."

"I said, stupid—*you can't*."

At this, Oriana began to cry as if her heart had broken.

IF CROSSWICKS WAS, as Winslow Slade accepted, an *accursed* household, so Wheatsheaf, close by, appeared to be cursed by ill luck as well. It was an open secret in Copplestone's business life that over the past eighteen months he'd become ever more immersed in a scheme in which certain South American countries as well as Cuba, Haiti, and Puerto Rico, were to form a military and trade alliance under the auspices of an (unnamed) American company; the primary problem being, as Copplestone and his associates lamented, the "resistance of the little monkeys to being civilized."

Copplestone tried to appeal directly to Theodore Roosevelt, for (*sub rosa*) support; but Roosevelt was elsewhere engaged, in other political battles.

And too, though this was certainly not known by Lenora, rumor had it that Copplestone had been several times sighted in the Hopewell area, in his Winton motorcar, in the company of a wanly pretty young woman twenty or more years his junior, a stranger to the West End entirely, with a Scots flush to her cheeks and the pert manner of one who has risen above her station.

Accursed households, are they not!—so Josiah's jeering voices assailed him, often out of nowhere, as his thoughts were attuned to other subjects entirely—*that should be put to the torch, to purify Princeton.*

OBLIVIOUS OF HIS adult relatives' preoccupations, Todd continued with his "studies," more or less unaided; a young male tutor, hastily hired by Lenora, met with opposition in the boy, and quit after a few lessons. Though often alone, Todd did not appear lonely; he tramped about the Wheatsheaf estate in a heavy hooded jacket and boots, creating eerily lifelike snow-sculpted forms of human figures and animals, and "disappearing" as he'd often done, for hours at a time. When Lenora called for him, and sent a servant to find him, it was revealed that Todd's footprints in the snow ceased abruptly, as if the boy had taken flight, or been snatched up, from the ground, by a great-taloned bird. Later, it was discovered that Todd had managed to escape over the twelve-foot stone wall at Wheatsheaf and hike to the Princeton Cemetery a mile away, to visit his cousin's grave.

Have I noted the engraved letters beneath *Annabel Oriana Slade* (1886–1906)—PAIN WAS MY PORTION, JESUS MY SAVIOR.

And beneath this a single, brief line—BABY SLADE (1906).

Returned home, Todd was silent, brooding; then irritable, and restless; when Lenora tried to comfort him he exploded in startling bitterness against his cousin, saying that "Todd will not forgive Annabel for leaving him and going to that place on the hill with the doors locked against him. Todd wants dynamite, to burst it open!"

One day, in late winter, about eight weeks after Annabel's funeral, Todd discovered a glass owl beneath one of the tall fir trees behind Wheatsheaf. He'd been shoveling snow with a child's shovel, to fashion another of his lifelike figures, when the glass owl glittered at his feet, and he pried it free of snow and ice to examine it in the bright winter sun.

Here was an artifact of striking beauty and detail, the size of a barn owl, made of clouded milk-glass, with agate-eyes. Each feather was distinct, even the downy feathers in the creature's pricked-up ears. The sharp talons were particularly life-like.

"How did you know that Todd would find you, Owl? Can you see through the snow, Owl?"

This curiosity the child brought back to the house to show to the servants, in great excitement, as he believed it must be a "good luck sign"; but the housekeeper and the cook believed it must be an omen of *bad* luck—possibly because Todd Slade had found it.

"Better to take it away, Master Slade. Not keep it here."

Todd ignored the pleading servants, as he often ignored the pleas of adults. And the dark-skinned household staff was always so *worried*, that something terrible would happen because of Todd, or to Todd, and they would be blamed.

The child was convinced that the glass bird was somehow "real"—an actual, living bird that had frozen in the cold—for were the feathers not precisely defined, snowy-white edged with pale gray; and the eyes lifelike, starkly open and staring, a milky orange with black pupils that seemed, uncannily, to possess sight?

So, Todd busied himself with "bringing the owl back to life"; fussing and crooning over it in the warmth of the kitchen, and rubbing it vigorously with his hands; until, after an hour or more, the "glass" owl did in fact revive, and came suddenly to life, to the terror of the servants. For now, the owl was a sharp-taloned bird, with a sharp beak; its snowy feathers edged with gray were wet, and smelled. Except that Todd gripped it tightly, the owl would have flapped its wings and risen into the air.

"Get it away! Get it away!"—so the servants begged, as Todd laughed at their discomfort; boasting that he'd heard the owl's heartbeat as soon as he'd pried it out of the snow. Before anyone could stop him Todd ran back outside coatless and hatless to release the bird, which was now struggling in his hands, flinging it into the air crying, "Fly away! Fly away! Go to *her*, and bid her come back, Todd is waiting *for her*."

The servants talked of nothing else but Master Todd's "devil-owl" but not in the hearing of their employers. So, when Lenora saw that Todd's hands were covered in fresh scratches, of which some were still bleeding, she was utterly astonished. "Todd, what has happened to you? What have you *done*?"

"Who? 'Todd' done—what?"

Lenora could get no straight or coherent answer from her son, whom she hurried to a bathroom, that she might wash his wounded hands, and affix bandages where she could, all the while sobbing beneath her breath, for indeed pain was Lenora Slade's portion no less than Annabel Slade's, she understood; even as the restless twelve-year-old squirmed and laughed at her.

"Fly away! Fly away! One day Todd will join you!"

"RATIOCINATION OUR SALVATION"

Late one afternoon in March 1906, Josiah Slade visited his former professor Pearce van Dyck at his home on Hodge Road, having been invited *For a particular purpose, Josiah! Please come.*

In his retreat from social life, since Annabel's death, Josiah had several times declined invitations from the van Dycks, as from other Princeton residents; though he'd been informed of the birth of a son and had sent a congratulatory note to Professor and Mrs. van Dyck, he had not seen either in some time.

(The birth of a son, to Johanna van Dyck! All of Princeton was buzzing *But Mrs. van Dyck is not young!*)

(For the record, Johanna van Dyck was forty-one years old at the time of the birth, in February 1906. Pearce van Dyck, forty-six.)

(Yes, and for the record, too: I will say no more about this birth, or the unexpected pregnancy that preceded it. Where my objectivity as a historian is an issue, I must err on the side of caution.)

Josiah was greeted at the door by Professor van Dyck, who was looking somewhat sallow-skinned, and whose starched white cotton shirt was open at the collar. Where ordinarily Professor van Dyck was impeccably groomed, his gray-streaked goatee trimmed short and his thinning hair faultlessly parted on the left side of his head, this afternoon he appeared just slightly disheveled, and seemed to be breathless.

"Josiah! Thank God, you are safe."

"Safe? Why would I not be—safe?" Josiah laughingly replied, though perhaps Pearce's remark was not meant to be amusing.

"Come in, quickly! Please."

Dr. van Dyck shut the door behind Josiah, and ushered him into the dark interior of the house, to his study overlooking a topiary garden of dripping evergreens, that had overgrown to partly shadow the windows. Josiah was struck by the *silence* of the austere old house, where he'd been half-expecting to hear a baby's excited babble.

When Henrietta Slade learned that Josiah was going to visit the van Dycks, she'd persuaded him to take a gift for the baby, which she'd purchased at the Milgrim Shop in town, and which was wrapped in charming pale-blue paper; Josiah had not seen the gift, but had been told it was a cashmere baby blanket. When Josiah handed the box to Dr. van Dyck, with murmured congratulations, the elder man took it from him distractedly, and set it on a table, atop *The Journal of Metaphysics*.

"If you are wondering where Mrs. van Dyck is, the fact is—Mrs. van Dyck is not here. She has gone."

" 'Gone'? Where?"

"Wherever it is women go, with their newborn infants. To avoid 'contamination'—it is said." Pearce laughed almost gaily. "Will you sit down, Josiah? And will you have some sherry?"

Pearce hastily tidied up a clutter of papers, books, monographs, and sheets of stiff white cardboard on his desk and surrounding tables. Josiah perceived that the philosophy professor was immersed in a project of some kind involving diagrams and geometric figures.

"In fact, Johanna has gone less than a mile—to her mother, on Battle Road. And it will not be a permanent move, I am confident."

Josiah could think of no reply to this announcement. He had no idea what his former professor meant by "contamination" and could not bring himself to ask.

Dr. van Dyck's manner was curiously ebullient, though his eyes were red-rimmed and his color distinctly unhealthy; repeatedly, he coughed, and held a handkerchief to his mouth. There had been a rumor that Pearce van Dyck had succumbed to bronchitis, or emphysema, or a sub-tropical disease originating in South Asia; but Josiah was too reserved to ask a former professor about anything so intimate as his health.

The van Dyck house did seem darker than Josiah recalled, unless this was a consequence of the overcast late-winter afternoon, already shifting to dusk. One of the smaller mansions on Hodge Road, set back behind a grim cobblestone wall, the van Dyck house was an austere French Normandy house, with a steep front roof like a frowning brow, and shaggily overgrown trees and shrubs surrounding it.

"It's kind of you to congratulate me, Josiah," Dr. van Dyck said, with a smiling sigh, "on the birth of a son, I think you must mean? Yet—as you may one day discover—it is not so much to do with *me*, as with *her*. So much less the *father*, than the *mother*."

Josiah smiled uncertainly. Was his former professor being riddle-some, in the way of Socrates?

"Well, there is nothing to be embarrassed about. I have gone through all that—I have worked my way through it. Whatever the 'infant son's' origins—it is a *fait accompli* now. In any case, it is all only natural—that is to say, Nature. As the Thomists would elaborate—a manifestation of *natural law*." Dr. van Dyck poured sherry into two glasses, and handed one to Josiah. On a low marble table was a silver platter heaped with tiny crustless sandwiches, chocolate crescents, and the like, that the housekeeper had prepared, Dr. van Dyck said, with "particular enthusiasm," knowing that his young friend Josiah Slade was coming to visit.

"It's well that Johanna is away, so that we men can speak frankly for once. This phenomenon of the Curse in our midst—that stares us all in the face, like a deadly basilisk—this, we must discuss."

" 'Curse'—?"

"Of course, Josiah. What otherwise is it, erupting in our midst, since last June, except a Curse?"

Dr. van Dyck spoke in a lowered voice. Suddenly overcome by a fit of coughing, he pressed a handkerchief to his mouth.

Josiah had accepted the glass of sherry from his companion, but had not lifted it to his lips. A sensation of heat rushed over him; he felt both shame and dismay; thinking what a blunder it had been, to emerge from his monkish seclusion, for *this*.

Many times, Josiah had thought in such terms. A curse had fallen upon his family. No doubt, others had been thinking so, too. Yet *Curse* had not yet been uttered, in his hearing at least. He didn't know if he felt relief, or a stunned sort of shock.

"But here, we have help, Josiah. The possibility of help."

Dr. van Dyck was showing Josiah several books, volumes of short stories—*Adventures of Sherlock Holmes, Memoirs of Sherlock Holmes, The Return of Sherlock Homes,* by Arthur Conan Doyle. And a single volume—*The Hound of the Baskervilles.* At first, Josiah couldn't comprehend what his former professor was saying with such urgency, that the *ratiocination* of Sherlock Holmes was needed in Princeton, to combat the "curse," or the "horror."

"Since you last visited me, Josiah, much has changed in my life. I've set aside my philosophical speculations in favor of a Holmesian pragmatism, which has produced exciting results, I think. I've made a close study of all of Conan Doyle's Holmes stories, which overlap, to a degree, on the biographical profile of the detective, and present a remarkable vision of the world, as a forest of 'clues'—not an underbrush of gnarled 'philosophies' in hopeless competition with one another. What is required is pragmatic logic, that seems to be missing in daily life."

Dr. van Dyck was leafing through the collections of stories, speaking to Josiah in the way of a distracted lecturer, who drifts from his subject, and returns to it, with a startled smile; as Josiah made an effort to listen politely, for he could not behave otherwise with his former, so much admired professor.

He is mad. The professor is mad. And you? Why have you not slit your throat by now, coward?

It was horrible, a "voice" of Josiah's had followed him—even here.

AS A CALLOW YOUTH of just-eighteen, Josiah Slade had enrolled in Pearce van Dyck's large lecture course at the university, drawn by its curious title—"A Brief History of Metaphysics." He had not ever heard the word *metaphysics* before, and knew but the rudiments of *physics,* from his preparatory schooling.

Quickly, the freshman had become one of the professor's rapt admirers, for, though small of frame, with a filmy halo of gray silken hair about his head, and a high, reedy voice, Dr. van Dyck lectured brilliantly on such subjects as Zeno's paradox, Plato's Allegory of the Cave, Kant's categorical imperative, and Hume's epistemological theories; he shone nearly as lustrously behind the podium as Woodrow Wilson himself. (In fact, the diminutive philosopher had inherited Dr. Wilson's mantle in being elected, for three successive years, the university's "most popular" professor.) (For the record, as Dr. Wilson would certainly wish me to add, Woodrow Wilson enjoyed this singular honor for *seven consecutive years* as a professor of jurisprudence and political history, during the time of Dr. Patton's administration.) And Pearce van Dyck's distinction was the more meaningful since he had a reputation for expecting a great deal of his students, and grading them severely.

The discipline of philosophy had excited Josiah at the time, for he thought it a singular pleasure to be *forced* to think, as one is not urged to think as a religious person; though it seemed that Dr. van Dyck was, at bottom, a Platonist, as well as a (non-dogmatic) Christian, he liked to engage quick-witted students in dialogues and debates on any subject: the nature of the Universe, for instance—whether it be *in aeternum,* or not; the nature of the Deity—whether all corners of the Universe are suffused with His grace, or merely some, or none; and the nature of Mankind—whether Original Sin was our basic truth, or rather Rousseau's vision of noble savagery and innocence.

One notable morning during a philosophy lecture, Josiah Slade had raised his hand to ask Professor van Dyck a question of the kind a bright, earnest freshman might ask: "How is it possible, sir, and why should it be possible, that God allows evil in His creation?" And Professor van Dyck retorted dryly: "Young man, if you could but express that question precisely, with no misuse of terms, you would discover that you had answered it for yourself."

It was at about this time that a controversy raged over doctrinal matters in the Presbyterian Church, that involved Reverend Winslow Slade. Josiah knew little of the details but understood that the Princeton Theological Seminary had succeeded in coercing the General Assembly of the Presbyterian Church of America into bringing to trial Dr. Charles Augustus Briggs of the Union Theological Seminary on charges of *heresy;* a decision that provoked a good deal of heated discussion, and much bitterness. Dr. Briggs, it was claimed, was held to be soft on Biblical Criticism; and highly amusing on the subject of the "scholastic theology" taught down at Princeton—an "intellectual backwater" as Briggs sneered. (Indeed, it was boasted by both the theological seminary at Princeton and by the university, that, in Dr. Patton's words, no "new ideas" would be introduced into the curriculum or into the administration thereof, so long as he held office.)

These matters, Josiah thought disagreeable; but then, he'd discovered that a traditional way of thinking, whether of theology, intercollegiate sports, or the eating clubs on Prospect Avenue, was disagreeable to him; and it was wisest for him to detach himself from such controversy, and focus upon his studies, which included courses in science, history, English literature, as well as math and philosophy; he would earn his B.A. degree as his parents wished, and continue to pursue his own knowledge, and think his own unruly thoughts. It had long been hoped within the family that Josiah would "follow in his grandfather's footsteps"—that is, he would enter the Princeton Theological Seminary and prepare for a career in the ministry—but this fantasy soon evaporated, as the young man's natural skepticism emerged, after a reading of Sir James Frazier's controversial hodgepodge of pagan customs *The Golden Bough.*

Now, in Professor van Dyck's study, with a sound of continuous dripping from the eaves outside the leaded windows, Josiah was attentive to the elder man's words, for he'd anticipated something valuable from his visit, and not a dismaying waste of time. But the elder man was speaking now wistfully, and not altogether coherently: "I will concede, Josiah, that I was utterly astonished, and disbelieving—for what has happened in my life cannot—'scientifically'—have happened. Though it is no secret through Princeton, how very much Johanna and I had wanted a family; and now that we have been married for nearly twenty years, we had almost—well, we had, in fact—given up hope. In a way, I had grown complacent in my disappointment. I had resigned myself, you see, to be the last of my line." For a brooding moment Dr. van Dyck stared into the fireplace, in which a small, smoldering fire emitted a grudging heat; it seemed almost to Josiah that he'd forgotten Josiah's presence, but after a pause he continued, in a faint voice: "As to Johanna, she had resigned herself, too—of course. Johanna is so very—sensible. Then, when it happened—by 'it' I mean the miracle—that my wife was, as the quaint expression has it, *with child*—we did not know what to think, and whether to be overjoyed, as others were on our behalf, or—deeply disturbed. For—not to embarrass you, Josiah, and not to embarrass myself—it has been some time, several years at least, since my wife and I have shared the same bedchamber . . . Yet, the miracle did occur; the baby is born; Pearce van Dyck is the 'father'—which is a happy thought, I believe." Again, Dr. van Dyck lapsed into silence, finishing his glass of sherry.

Josiah swallowed hard. What had his former professor revealed to him? That there was—there could be—some question of the paternity of the newborn van Dyck child; that something was mysteriously amiss, that must be designated "miracle"?

Josiah did not want to think *Both mothers gave birth last month. Both mothers—accursed?*

Josiah shuddered though the room was over-heated from the smoldering fire. The smell of woodsmoke made his nostrils pinch.

"But now, Josiah. 'Ratiocination—our salvation.' *That* is my motto now, no longer *Cogito, ergo sum.*"

On Dr. van Dyck's desk was a piece of cardboard measuring about three by four feet, covered in an elaborate diagram, in inks of differing colors. And there was a folio-sized book between whose stiff pages he'd inserted a spray of desiccated flowers—lilies, of a particularly curdled hue and scent. (Josiah remembered these: had he given them to Pearce van Dyck, months before? Taken from the old Craven house? He'd forgotten, until now.) "Before I present my findings to you, Josiah, I should like to ask if you're familiar with Sherlock Holmes, at all? For I think I'd mentioned Holmes's significance to you, months ago."

"You did? I don't think so, sir."

"Yes, Josiah. I did." Dr. van Dyck spoke with unusual sharpness. "I have been insisting to all my colleagues in the philosophy department, and elsewhere, that Conan Doyle's 'detective' has found the solution to our human folly: close observation of 'clues,' and shrewd 'ratiocination.'"

"But 'Sherlock Holmes' is a fictitious person, sir. He is not—an actual person—"

Irritably Dr. van Dyck interrupted: "I've asked you, Josiah: have you read of the man's remarkable adventures? And his 'ratiocinations'?"

As an undergraduate, Josiah had read a number of Sherlock Holmes mystery stories, as the books were passed among his suite mates in West College; he'd been entertained by them, and struck by the detective's ingenious logic. He told Dr. van Dyck that he could see why many readers found Sherlock Holmes fascinating as a hero, and the tales themselves, rich with mystery and intrigue and colorful characterizations, were highly readable; above all, the tales presented riddles with solutions— this was most gratifying. "In actual life, mysteries are often unsolved. But in Sherlock Holmes, the reader is guaranteed a 'solution.'"

"Of course, the reader is 'guaranteed,' Josiah. For Sherlock Holmes follows an impeccable strategy of detection."

"The stories are fictions, sir, devised to be 'detected.' That is, they are puzzles with ready-made solutions; they are not true mysteries, of the kind we encounter in our lives."

"But I think that they *are*. They are distillations of the sprawling, messy, impenetrable mysteries that surround us—they are *superior*."

Dr. van Dyck was frowning in disapproval. Clearly, this was not the response he expected from a former, favorite student.

"A close reading of any of the tales," Josiah said, somewhat aggressively, "shows their flaws. In 'The Man with the Twisted Lip,' for instance, coincidence plays an unlikely role, and I didn't think it was at all believable that a disguised man's wife wouldn't recognize him. In 'The Adventure of the Speckled Band,' it's preposterous that the villain would devise such an intricate scheme to murder his step-daughter when, living alone with her, he could have murdered her in any number of easier ways—and how absurd a gimmick, to use an Indian swamp adder! In 'A Study in Scarlet,' the anti-Mormon passages are shrill and unconvincing, in context, and indeed, isn't the reader unconscionably manipulated, revealing *after the fact* that Sherlock Holmes had simply sent a telegram to Chicago in order to learn certain facts that are hidden from the reader?" In the way of a bright, combative student Josiah was speaking, but the expression on his former professor's face was not encouraging. "Well, sir," Josiah said, lamely, "the stories certainly succeed in their primary intention of entertaining."

" 'Entertaining'!" Dr. van Dyck said contemptuously. "As if at this crisis in all our lives, I mean for you to be 'entertained'—!"

Dr. van Dyck proceeded to show Josiah his elaborate "Scheme of Clues," as he called it. The chart was intricately covered in several colors of ink, with colored pins or beads affixed to the surface in clusters. "In bringing the Holmesian 'ratiocination' to bear upon our accursed Princeton mystery, I've isolated a number of threads of connection, or association, as well as 'clues'—I know, Holmes himself would sneer at my methods, that are overly fussy, and very amateur. My only faith is that I will triumph eventually because I have *right* on my side and am willing to sacrifice everything to that end . . . See here, Josiah, don't look so perplexed! This is no more complicated than Kantian metaphysics. In this column, I've represented all the significant events of the past ten months, or so, in coded symbols; and all the clues in beads. *Events* here, *clues* here. D'you see? Now, wherever it struck me as a viable hypothesis that the Fiend in his primary form was actually present—"

Josiah started, at "Fiend." He had not heard anyone outside his immediate family use this word to describe Axson Mayte—of whom, he assumed, Dr. van Dyck, was speaking.

"—for there is, Josiah, as you must know, a 'Fiend' in our midst—either a representation of the Devil himself, or one of the Devil's 'satans.' In the Hebrew Bible, there was not a single Satan, but rather numerous 'satans.' Each is a force for chaos and misery and each must be combated." Dr. van Dyck drew the stiff sheet of cardboard closer to Josiah, so that both men might peruse it together. "So, wherever it seems likely that the Fiend was present, I've used a stickpin—here, the pearl; here, a diamond; here, an opal. I suppose you will object, Josiah," the elder man said, with a smile, "that I can't know if I'm in possession of all the clues, and that's true. Nor can I know whether some of the witnesses have reported fraudulently, in confusion or ignorance, or out of a desire to 'save face.' For my methodology is far less precise than Holmes's, because there are so many more clues in actual life, than in Holmes's cases. Yet I proceed with optimism, and some of the enthusiasm of my days as a young instructor, when I was writing my first study of Plato. What makes me anxious is that I must solve the mystery before the Fiend discovers what I'm doing. Otherwise—my life may be at risk."

Wryly Josiah was thinking *At least he has given it a name: Curse. Horror. At least, it is not a single family's madness.*

There was something touching in the philosophy professor's presentation, that made Josiah less inclined to be critical. Though he thought the "scheme of clues" a desperate measure, and could really make no sense of it, yet it was impressive in its intricacy and its air of precision, in the way of a miniature sailing ship created inside a bottle; for had he ever seen anything so ingenious, outside of equations in his chemistry and physics courses? A veritable galaxy it seemed of filose inkings in several colors, and tiny symbols like dingbats, and Latin and Greek words as well as the stickpins and beads, and much penciled notations. Dr. van Dyck seemed pleased that his young friend should study the graph so closely, and, with a silver letter opener as a kind of blackboard pointer, he lectured Josiah on the Science of Detection in general, and what he called the Crosswicks, or the Princeton Curse in particular.

"As Holmes often says"—and here Dr. van Dyck spoke with such authority and fond familiarity, you would be led to think that Sherlock Holmes was a friend of his—"what is extraordinary and perverse can be a guide, rather than a hindrance, to the enlightened eye while the routine case, let's say of simple, unimaginative murder, might prove impossible to solve. In analyzing a highly complex problem of the kind we are confronted with, the necessary thing is to be able to *reason backward*. Yet the deductive method, which reasons so capably *forward*, must be utilized as well. So, following this blue line, the 'scheme of clues' represents a *backward-leaping* method; along this yellow line, a *forward-leaping*. The situation is more complicated because the Curse, or the Horror, is all about us, and we don't know where , or who, it will strike next. So, we must reason *laterally* as well."

Josiah shook his head, feeling lost.

"The opal stickpin baffles you? No, the orange beads? Ah, the abbreviation *Cr.*, which refers to 'Craven'—the old Craven house; which, contiguous with the vertical *March,* signifies the first manifestation of the Curse, so far as I know. The Craven house, in March '05—Mr. Cleveland's collapse—the invasion of *spectral figures* into our community. Now, the cluster of colored beads here, as well as the pearl stickpin, represent 'secondary valuations'—if the chart is read (as I am reading it now) vertically. As Holmes has said, *All Life is a great chain, the nature of which is known whenever we examine a single link of it.*"

Josiah murmured apologetically that he "didn't quite understand."

"Well, it is challenging, Josiah. Particularly when one is first confronted with the proposition that the 'detective' of human nature can determine, by the merest momentary expression on a man's face, or a twitch of a muscle or a glance of an eye, his innermost thoughts. I've asked Micawber to order Holmes's essay 'The Book of Life' as well as his monographs on fingerprints, the detection of long-faded perfumes, the influence of a man's trade upon the shape of his hand, and the classic 'Upon the Distinction Between the Ashes of Various Tobaccos.' So I hope that, once I have these valuable materials in hand, I'll be able to move along much more swiftly."

"I hope so too, sir." Josiah spoke humbly, for he was feeling the encroachment of a malaise, like a din of "voices," even as his former professor seemed to be in more ebullient spirits.

"Certainly, Josiah, life is a 'great chain,' as the ancients perceived. Holmes has boldly stated that from a single drop of water a man of genius could infer the possibility of the Atlantic Ocean, or a Niagara, without having heard of either; so too the skilled detective can train himself to discern at a glance the history of a person who stands before him, and the profession to which he belongs, if not the very state of his soul. By a man's fingernails, or boots, or beard, or coat sleeve, by his facial expression, by the calluses of his forefinger and thumb, one can learn so much! It is wonderful to think how we might triumph over the chaos of life. And it is my fervent hope that I will be able to save our precious community—our loved ones—from the Curse, if it is not already too late. For, you see, we have already lost the fairest and most pure of heart, among us . . ."

Frowning, as if he had not heard this well-intentioned but clumsily expressed remark, Josiah turned to the chart, to examine it closely, and pointing out to Dr. van Dyck one or two small errors: "I'm afraid, sir, the incident at the Craven house took place in April, not March as you've indicated."

"April? Not March? Are you sure?"

"Yes. I would not likely forget."

"But I—I would not likely forget, either! For I was there, too."

"Yes. And I was there."

"But—March is crucial to my scheme—for *M* links up with 'Mackay-Diggs'—"

"Who is 'Mackay-Diggs'?"

"—a graduate student of mine who came to me the other day with a hair-raising story of having narrowly escaped from the assault of a sinister stranger in the shadows behind Alexander Hall; a 'satan' it must have been, from the description. Mackay-Diggs is a young Platonist of upstanding integrity who would never confabulate or lie; he testified to me that an 'Indian-looking' individual had approached him, and touched his shoulder with a 'questioning look'—made as if to embrace him—and, as Mackay-Diggs pushed away, this person turned hostile, baring his teeth as if he meant to 'tear out my throat.' This, you see, links up with the death of the Spags child, which is indicated by a green pin; this purple line connects them; and here is indicated the 'mysterious behavior' of the Wilsons' dog Hannibal, upon several successive nights . . ."

"The Wilsons' dog Hannibal?"

"Recall, the 'mysterious behavior' of the Hound of the Baskervilles, that did not bark as it might have been expected to bark? In this case, the Wilsons' portly greyhound Hannibal—(which the undergraduates call 'Box-on-Legs')—behaved in a more conventional canine fashion by howling inexplicably—and very loudly—in the night, upon several occasions just last week."

"And you deduce from this—?"

"Josiah, it is not 'I' who 'deduces' any of this—it is the chain of *logic*. The Scheme of Clues is rather more like a map, that describes an actual terrain. It is no coincidence that the Wilsons' dog is howling at night, at a time when suspected 'satans' are roaming on the Princeton University campus, seeking victims among our students. And there is the example of the FitzRandolphs' daughter Wilhelmina, who has been sighted in secluded places like the pathway beside Lake Carnegie, in the company of unidentified men—'gentlemen,' we would hope!"

"Wilhelmina? With men? But who?"

Josiah did not like the prospect of his friend Willy being in the company of men; the thought was alarming to him, as a betrayal.

For Willy adores me. That is a constant.

"Wilhelmina has even been sighted," Dr. van Dyck said, in a lowered voice, and with a curiously lewd twist of his lips, "on Fifth Avenue, in New York City, striding in the company of one or another Bohemian *artiste*. For she is taking art lessons, you know, with the notorious Henri, rumored to have actually murdered a man, somewhere in the West."

"Is she! That's a good thing, I should think."

"A 'good thing'? Are you serious, Josiah? There are nude models at the New York School of Art, it is said—*nude*. And of *both sexes*."

Josiah frowned, considering. Recalling the soft pressure of Willy's lips against his, and the fragrance that seemed to lift from her skin, Josiah did not think it was such a good thing, that Willy was attending life-modeling classes, in which *nude models* were sometimes *male*.

Dr. van Dyck continued, tapping the silver letter-opener against the Scheme of Clues: "You see, here, connected by this yellow dotted line, an incident designated as *T* that occurred in the Princeton Cemetery . . ."

Josiah frowned at the yellow dotted line. What madness was this!

" . . . which is one of the primary reasons I asked you to come here today, Josiah. Not having been invited to your dear sister's funeral, I have nonetheless gone to visit her grave several times, to pay homage to her; for Annabel was somewhat undervalued, I believe, in her intellect, and in the sparkle of her wit, because she was so attractive, and so dazzled the outward eye. It did seem unfortunate to me—that your family would not have dreamt of urging Annabel to continue with her studies, as you naturally, as a boy, continued with yours, at a first-rate university. Instead, Annabel attended a two-year college, and made her 'debut' in New York, and—became the fiancée of a dashing young military officer. Johanna had told me, Annabel had a talent for storytelling, and illustration. However—to the case at hand"—seeing Josiah's stricken face, Dr. van Dyck did not dare continue this line of thought—"keeping in mind my friend Holmes's methodology, I returned to the cemetery the other day, to the Slade mausoleum, thinking to examine the vault for fresh fingerprints—"

" 'Fingerprints'? But whose?"

"—the Fiend, perhaps—in one of his human forms. This would be a scientific procedure, at least. And I hoped to check the area about the gravesite for footprints as well, in the melting snow. When I arrived, however, there was a person at the tomb before me—it turned out to be your young cousin Todd—who, seeing me, took fright and ran like a guilty criminal through the maze of gravestones, his head bent and his hair sticking up in bristles like those of a wild creature. I called after him—'Todd! Todd! It is only me, Pearce van Dyck!'—but he fled all the more desperately, as if *I* were the Fiend." Dr. van Dyck laughed, almost gaily. "At the base of the mausoleum I did discover, all around, a remarkable number of footprints, only some of which could have belonged to the boy. From which I hesitate to draw any conclusions but must inform you, Josiah, that often in cases like this you will find an individual or individuals within the afflicted community *in league with the demonic forces*."

Josiah protested that he very much doubted that his cousin Todd, twelve years old, and "immature" for his age, was in league with any forces whatsoever. "Todd is a very 'alone' sort of boy."

Curtly Dr. van Dyck said, "But perhaps it was not 'Todd Slade' whom I saw in the cemetery, Josiah—but a child-sized demon who resembled him."

Josiah threw up his hands, exasperated at last.

"But, sir, are we all imposters?—'demons'? How could we judge, seeing the outward shapes of people?"

"That is a very sage question, Josiah. A truly metaphysical question, which I have been pondering, you can be sure, since—since my dear wife announced to me, some ten months ago, her 'miraculous' news."

Dr. van Dyck had consumed two glasses of sherry, while Josiah had been able to swallow only a single mouthful of the oversweet, cloying liquid. Josiah saw that his former professor's face was flushed, and his eyes oddly gleaming; he seemed short of breath, as in the throes of great excitement; unless Josiah was mistaken, Dr. van Dyck's very skull seemed subtly misshapen, with a frowning bulge at the brow, and a small, twisted mouth. As Josiah rose to his feet, and his host rose with him, it seemed to Josiah too that the elder man was shorter than he recalled, with a just perceptibly malformed upper back, hidden beneath a loose-fitting tweed jacket. At the opening of his shirt collar, heated arteries visibly pulsed close beneath the damp skin.

In hearty spirits, Dr. van Dyck walked with Josiah to the front door of the house, and shook hands with him in parting, bidding him to extend his warmest greetings to Winslow Slade, and to all the other Slades whom he saw so infrequently now. "Tell them—well, perhaps it's premature to tell anyone—that 'van Dyck is on the trail'—'van Dyck is in pursuit'—it may not be consolation for their loss, but I hope it will be reassuring." Unmistakably, Josiah's former professor was shorter than he had been, with visibly foreshortened legs; and eyes that gleamed with an unnatural luster, behind even scholarly metal-rimmed eyeglasses.

"You must return another time, Josiah!—and see *it*."

"*It*—?"

"Forgive me: I mean to say, of course, *him*."

THE OCHRE-RUNNERED SLEIGH

Josiah? Josiah? Come to us, do!

How very singular a vision it was, and how unexpected—Josiah stopped in his tracks, staring.

Having left the residence of Professor Pearce van Dyck, Josiah had set off restlessly in the direction of Battle Park, an open, partly wooded area not far from Stockton Street, and about a mile and a half from Crosswicks; the over-heated study of his former professor, no less than the over-heated *ratiocination* of the man, had left Josiah feeling suffocated and muddle-headed and badly yearning for fresh air.

"Why, what is this? A 'flood of snow' . . ."

Without Josiah having been aware of it, a sudden snowstorm had whipped up, while he'd been visiting with Dr. van Dyck. The suety rain-clouds had vanished, replaced by swollen snow-clouds; not that the air was cold, but the snowfall was thick, and slow-drifting, as if the flakes were but ornamental, each fiercely glittering.

Josiah had thought to tramp about the battlefield, as he'd done often as a college student, needing to be alone; he took little heed of the slow-swirling snow, or a damp wind out of the Northeast, or encroaching dusk.

So it was, while making his way across the snow-encrusted field, upon which, generations before, his famed ancestor Elias Slade had fought heroically against Cornwallis's men, Josiah chanced to see, less than one hundred feet away, a remarkable sight: a beautifully shaped antique sleigh with high curved runners, drawn by a single snorting black horse.

"Why, who is this? Strangers . . ."

The sleigh was driven by a hunched figure in a dark overcoat and hat pulled down low onto his forehead; a gnome-like figure, flicking his whip over the horse's withers.

In the sleigh were several women, that is—*young ladies.*

The sleigh was such a romantic sight, drawn across the snowy field, through a curtain of slow-falling snow, as dusk was imminent, that Josiah paused to stare, smiling; for surely he should know the ladies in the sleigh, if not the driver . . . Yet their faces were gaily turned aside from him; they took no note of him. One was thickly bundled in a splendid black fur coat and matching hat, of sable or mink; another, smaller of frame, wore a winter coat of ermine; the third, a high-crowned hat of Persian lamb and a matching coat whose tight-curled fur struck Josiah's eye as uncommonly beautiful. It was strange that the ladies did not call out to him, to offer him a ride, for there was a place empty in the sleigh beside the lady in the Persian lamb fur; nor did the gnome-like driver, whose face appeared wizened, so much as glance in his direction. Josiah wiped snow from his eyelashes, listening to the gay chatter of the ladies, and taking note of a curiosity about the sleigh: for the runners, though sleek and curved and delicately wrought at their ends, gave off a peculiar ochre or rust glint, and did not appear to be slicing through the snow so much as skimming its brittle surface.

Why do you stand mute, and not call out to the party? You, the heir of Crosswicks, have only to raise your hand, to be carried to your home in a style befitting one of your blood.

And, when Josiah stood unmoving, as if paralyzed—*Josiah! Josiah! Come to us, do!*

Just in time, Josiah realized that it was one of his unwanted voices, in a mockery of seduction.

Unmoving he stood, vigilant, as snowflakes swirled dreamily about him, and the ochre-runnered sleigh was driven silently past at a distance now of fewer than thirty feet. Very gently, sleigh bells sounded. The horse's breath steamed, and the horse's coarse black tail switched. In rapt admiration for the muscled grace of the high-stepping horse Josiah stared, and for the antique beauty of the sleigh. His heart was moved by the fey, tinkling laughter of the ladies in which he heard, or seemed to hear, his sister Annabel's airy laughter; though which of the young ladies, their faces now hidden in shadow, might have been Annabel, he could not, in a sudden fit of trembling, have said.

And so, the sleigh passed, and disappeared in a flurry of snow.

Leaving only an echo of bells, and the laughter of the ladies, which brought to Josiah's mind the glassy notes of wind chimes sounding from a veranda or gazebo of a summer's evening long ago.

Why do you stand mute? Unmanned as a eunuch?

Are you not a Slade, and prepared for the crossing-over?

"SNAKE FRENZY"

S oon after, there came the outbreak of female nerves, or hysteria, at the Rocky Hill Seminary for Girls, on a Monday morning in early April 1906.

Historians curious about this (minor, neglected) outbreak of the Curse may consult the *Princeton Packet* for April 3 of that year, which reported the incident with prominent headlines on the front page of the local weekly:

"SNAKE FRENZY" REPORTED AT THE
ROCKY HILL SEMINARY
28 STUDENTS, 3 FACULTY MEMBERS SUCCUMB
FAINTING AND "EPILEPTIFORM" SEIZURES

It was Wilhelmina Burr's misfortune to find herself at the center of this bizarre episode, never satisfactorily explained by neutral observers as by research scientists at the university but rather brushed aside, as *female hysterics.*

Wilhelmina was directing the girls' choir in the music hall at the school—(a neo-Classic building set upon a ridge overlooking the Millstone River and an intervening marshy and muddy stretch of land)—

when, suddenly, a wanly pretty girl named Penelope van Osburgh faltered in the midst of her soprano solo in Mr. Selby's ever-popular "The Rural Retreat"—

> Shady groves and purling rills,
> Walks, where quiv'ring moonbeams play,
> Skreen the worldsick breast from ills,
> Lull the cares of sorrowed day!

—staring with widened eyes past the choir mistress's head; and, now gone deathly white, pointed to the ornamental molding that bordered the ceiling, saying, "Oh, it is alive!—the serpent!—there!—it has wakened!—it has moved!—it is coming now for us."

For some stunned seconds the hall was locked in silence: Wilhelmina might have heard the tiny ticking of her watch, had she had the presence of mind to attend to it; then, the stricken girl began to breathe hoarsely and shallowly, whispering, "The serpent!—the serpent!" Still pointing at the ceiling, she sank into the arms of the girl beside her in a dead faint.

After which, all the girls began to scream, and faint—and Chaos erupted in the music hall.

It had long intrigued Wilhelmina, that the elegant neo-Classical music building was so curiously decorated, in its moldings; she had noticed, the first time she'd entered the music hall, how, at the ceiling, there were sinuous sculpted white forms not quite visible: possibly Italianate vines, or Grecian tendrils, or "frozen waves," or, indeed, languorously outstretched serpents. That these were "white" was a misnomer for, with the passage of time, the moldings had become discolored with dust, but unevenly; so that there were suggestions of shadows, and not a uniformity of hue. In a play of light, in quite ordinary circumstances, the moldings did seem to "move"—to a degree. Wilhelmina had noticed this herself, and had dismissed the optical illusion as a phenomenon of light, of no significance whatsoever.

Yet now, it seemed that the "serpents" had roused themselves from their long slumber, and were moving. How the Rocky Hill Seminary girls shrieked! A second girl slumped to the floor in a faint, and a third, and, as Wilhelmina came to help her, she collided with two terrified girls who thrust themselves into her arms as if they were young children; for the snakes were now writhing, and had begun to slither down the walls and window frames, just perceptibly visible, and horribly, on all sides.

Wilhelmina, the only adult in the room, amid a gathering of some thirty adolescent girls, found herself utterly panicked, and perplexed: for she could not see *definitively* that the snakes were slithering down from the molding, yet, judging by an unusual agitation of the air, and the terrified cries of the girls, it was reasonable to conclude that something was amiss; something was very much amiss; and she was responsible for protecting her girls from it.

Another girl began to scream, pointing past Wilhelmina: "Oh! There! The black snake! He is roused, he is angry, he is coming for us!"— and now a greater terror ensued as the girls lunged and rushed about, whimpering, and sobbing, and white-faced, with no idea of how to escape the snakes, as (it seemed) the snakes could not be actually *seen.* Yet it was clear, the snakes were slithering toward them from all sides, along the polished hardwood floor.

Miss Burr shouted for order, and was unheard; rushed about to calm, to scold, to intervene, even to threaten. But there were too many panicked girls, emotion ran too high, like a sudden wildfire, on a windy day; all that the instructress could do was try to prevent the girls from trampling and injuring one another, in their haste to exit the hall.

"Take care! Please! There are no snakes! Where are these snakes! I see no snakes! Priscilla! *Marian!* Please do not push, you must leave the hall in an orderly fashion—*please.* Girls!"

Wilhelmina herself was nearly sobbing now, in frustration and mounting fear.

Trying to prevent the girls from injuring one another, Wilhelmina stumbled, and staggered, for there seemed to be—something—wriggling, and writhing—and *sinuous*—at her feet; a slithering muscular shape like a *bas-relief* come to life . . .

A splendid creature, not wanly white but blackly iridescent, touched with scales that glinted silver, and puce, and ochre; its underbelly finely ribbed, and as creamy-pale and smooth as the fairest-skinned girl at Rocky Hill; its broad, flat, intelligent head held high, tongue flicking, and tawny gem-like eyes glowing *as if in recognition.*

Beyond this, Wilhelmina knew no more. For amid the hysteria of her girls she too fainted, her petticoats crackling around her and her high starched collar cutting into her throat as she fell heavily to the hardwood floor.

ELSEWHERE IN THE SCHOOL someone sounded the fire alarm. The Rocky Hill fire wagon, with a half-dozen eager volunteer firemen aboard, arrived within minutes. Unfortunately, this contributed to the hysteria, as the fire alarms and sirens were deafeningly loud; and shortly it seemed that the girls throughout the school, not just the choir members, had succumbed to the mysterious frenzy—screaming at the sight of (invisible?) serpents that slithered, and slid, and squirmed, and coiled, and leapt, and writhed, advancing threateningly at them from all sides. The firemen were amazed and baffled, for they could discover no fire, and could not see the snakes, though the screaming girls pointed them out, and ran from them, in the chill of early April, clad only in middy-blouses and blue woolen skirts and matching stockings; muddying their shoes and, in some cases, falling into the soft-thawing earth, in their desperation to save themselves. Several teachers were now involved, trying to restore calm; of these, one was a young man, a mathematics instructor, named Holleran, of a nervous disposition, who seemed to be seeing the snakes himself, or their *agitated impressions* in the moist earth, and fell into a faint; or, as Dr. Boudinot later described the phenomena, *epileptiform seizures,* of unaccountable origin.

In all, the worst of the "snake frenzy" lasted scarcely an hour, as by degrees the snakes seemed to vanish; whether the creatures escaped into the muddy bog beyond the music school, or simply disappeared, to be discovered in their original, benign and bland forms in the aged molding in the music hall, the following day; yet, the effects of the hysteria were not easily cast off. Symptoms varied considerably from girl to girl, and from instructor to instructor; some felt the upset for the remainder of the day; some could not return to the seminary for a week; and others, including the Latin teacher Miss Cowper, and poor Mr. Holleran, were never again to be entirely free of the *snake vision* for the remainder of their lives. The seminary headmistress, Miss Singleton, a physically fit woman in her early sixties, would claim to have never seen a single snake, not anywhere on the school property; yet, she too was nervously affected, and was perceived to have lost some of the poise and self-confidence for which she'd been known.

Penelope van Osburgh, who'd first sighted the onslaught, was seriously ill for several days, and much petted and fussed over for weeks. Wilhelmina Burr, Instructress of Art, Elocution, and Eurythmics, was ill for a week, surprisingly; and, when she'd recovered, surprised her colleagues and Miss Singleton by resigning her position at the seminary, with the abashed explanation:

"As I succumbed to the most ridiculous of female hysterics, and could not prevent my students from fits of madness, I'm afraid that I am not much more mature than the silliest of them, and have no right to be teaching them."

POSTSCRIPT:
NATURE'S BURDEN

Though the "snake frenzy" was to be spoken of in Princeton and vicinity for decades, the episode was quickly and summarily dismissed by authorities, as by Dr. Boudinot and his medical/scientific colleagues, as a regrettable example of *female hysterics*. In the *Packet* was a prominent article in which a number of gentlemen in the community were invited to comment upon the upset, the consensus being that a "hallucinatory epidemic of unknown origin" had swept through the girls' school, and the "snakes" were mere imaginings.

Among the gentlemen interviewed were several research scientist-professors at the university, as well as President Wilson himself. Several of these affected a mirthful tone, regrettably, to the detriment of the seminary and its staff; several suggested that the "excitable girls" and their instructors were in need of better, more authoritarian jurisdiction, namely a male headmaster for the school. But Woodrow Wilson, conscious of his position as chief administrator at the university, did not choose to criticize the seminary headmistress, or any of the instructors; graciously he noted that there had certainly been "numerous outbreaks of 'demonic behavior'" at Princeton University, in the early 1800s when the boys rebelled "like clockwork," and so he would not presume to pass judgment on the seminary, let alone withdraw his daughters from it if they had been enrolled there as students. Dr. Wilson concluded with an appeal for sympathy, understanding, and patience: "For Woman, whom Nature has burdened with a load far heavier than Man—that is, *propagation*—must be judged with tolerance and forbearance in areas where, with no regard for intention, she has seriously lagged behind man."

"DEFEAT AT CHARLESTON"

I will not go down in defeat. I *vow*."

It has been variously recorded how in the winter of 1905 to 1906 Woodrow Wilson, admired and honored "abroad"—(that's to say, outside Princeton)—was yet derided, scorned, and cruelly politicked-against, within his own university community. This situation grated upon the man's sensitive nerves and caused him many a sleepless night; and, as the stoic Wilson laughingly complained to his devoted wife Ellen, compounded his "turmoil in Central America"—(that's to say, severe gastric distress in the "equatorial regions" of his body).

The initial issue of contention, the location of the Graduate College, was now complicated by a virtual war between the president's office and certain of his administrators, regarding what was called the "iron chain of command" at the university, as well as Dr. Wilson's campaign against the exclusive eating clubs of Prospect Avenue for which he felt a personal dislike and bitterness. And there were other, almost daily abrasions.

"I will not have insurrection. I was inaugurated to *run this university*, and so I will."

It was so, ironically: outside Princeton, in certain selected quarters, Woodrow Wilson's reputation could not have been higher. At a

Democrats' dinner at the Lotos Club in Manhattan, for instance, in late March, the "Kingmaker" George Harvey in introducing Dr. Wilson to his audience of cigar-smoking gentlemen had "nominated" him for President—by which Harvey meant President of the United States! And though Dr. Wilson was humbled by the remark, and made every effort to dismiss it from his mind, yet he was deeply stirred; and excited; and could not resist sharing the news with his dear wife Ellen, as soon as he returned home.

The highest Presidency in the land! Of course it was only meant to flatter.

No, Woodrow—it was not. You are Presidential material! You know that God has a greater destiny for you than just Princeton.

Yet, at the same time, so mysteriously, Dr. Wilson was treated with very little respect in Princeton; only his undergraduates seemed to admire him, if at a distance; much of the administration had shifted to a support of gregarious Andrew West, and a good deal of the faculty; the situation with the board of trustees was yet worse, and caused particular gastric distress. Dr. Wilson raged against the "condescension" of his trustees, who treated the president of the university like a "mere hireling, a lackey"; he would name no names, but one of these gentlemen cruelly flaunted his power as a "retired chief administrator of the federal government." (So upset was Dr. Wilson with Mr. Cleveland, he could not bear to hear the man's name spoken, nor even the name of Cleveland's glamorous wife, Frances.) So malevolent had his enemies grown in winter/spring 1906 they seemed to have begun a systematic erosion of his reputation among the most powerful alumni associations, particularly in the South; and Dr. Wilson thought, with some bitterness, how his old friend Winslow Slade might have aided him, if the older man had not gone into a sort of retreat at Crosswicks, now declining to see friends like Dr. Wilson.

"But I will fight them, Ellen. You can be sure!"

The more enemies, the more mobilized a man might be. Woodrow Wilson's Scots ancestors were warriors, not mewling, weak-livered *females*.

So it was, Dr. Wilson embarked upon a zealous campaign to repair his reputation among the Princeton alumni, who comprised a wealthy and politically potent segment of the university-educated population at this time; he was determined to combat certain false images, that he was "dogmatic" as an administrator, "rigid," "unbending," "dictatorial," by meeting with alumni groups in the East and South, in such key cities as Baltimore, Washington, Richmond, and Atlanta, on such favorite topics as "Democracy and the University," "Religion and Patriotism," "Princeton in the Nation's Service," "Natural Leaders of Men," etc., with gratifying success.

Then came Charleston, South Carolina, on April 13, 1906.

So grievous a showing, and the president of Princeton University so "bizarre" in his performance, a number of concerned alumni wrote letters to the board of trustees calling for Dr. Wilson's resignation!

HISTORIANS HAVE GENERALLY ignored, or underplayed, this curious aberration in Dr. Wilson's career, partly because there are few reliable records concerning the "defeat at Charleston" (as Woodrow Wilson would call it). So far as I am able to ascertain, Dr. Wilson began his speech to the Charleston alumni organization with his usual "authority" and "ease"; he knew to "loosen up" his Southern audience with a favorite anecdote about "three darkies" brought up to Princeton by their young masters, in the old days before the war, who were goggle-eyed by their *first snow*, which they believed to be *falling cotton*. (Allegedly, this anecdote roused "gales of laughter" in Dr. Wilson's audience, of entirely gentlemen. That Dr. Wilson utilized his very humorous "Negro dialect" with many a rolling of his eyes and comical gestures, surely added to the hilarity.)

After this promising start, Dr. Wilson began a speech he could have recited in his sleep—("And very often do, in fact!" as he joked to Mrs. Wilson)—titled "The University Man, the Christian, and the Patriot"— but after a few minutes he felt a tinge of apprehension, and even nausea; and his voice, ordinarily poised and well modulated, began to falter. The blame lay with the red-meat dinner he'd consumed, as a man among men; or with the sickly clouds of smoke from the gentlemen's cigars and pipes, wafting through the ill-ventilated room. Continuing to speak, while feeling sweat break out on his forehead, Dr. Wilson felt a prick of terror as, glancing about the audience, he seemed to see at the very rear of the room the corpulent shirtfront, bland bald pate, and ruddy well-fed face of his nemesis Dean West!—his enemy seated amid rapt listeners with a pretense of being one of them.

"No. It can't be. He would not dare follow me to Charleston—*he would not*."

Yet, the well-practiced delivery for which the president of Princeton was known had become, it seemed, irrevocably jarred; like a lone railway car by cruel accident separated from its fellows, that eases onto the graveled roadway bed, and begins to speed, and rattles out of control, Dr. Wilson began to speak rapidly, often interrupting himself in mid-phrase.

The substance of his talk, as it has been reported, was confused: now, Dr. Wilson spoke in an impassioned voice of *allies* and *enemies;* now, of *democracy* and the *threat from abroad*—"As hundreds of thousands of enemies of Protestantism swarm to the shore of the New World, minds and spirits shackled by the despotism, intolerance, and rank superstition which governs in the dominions of the Pope of Rome, and which prevails in all of Catholic Europe." From this, Dr. Wilson shifted abruptly to the familiar subject of Christian leadership and Christian followers: "For Jesus Christ is our model, Who knew Himself a 'fisher of men' and commanded that all who wished salvation should follow Him—yea, even unto battle." Then, with no clear transition, Dr. Wilson murmured jestingly about the *internecine battles* at the university, which provoked restlessness in the audience, a flurry of coughing, throat-clearing, and the like, of the kind that signals to a speaker that his time is finished; but Dr. Wilson did not seem to notice, and continued speaking, in a rapid if rambling voice, warning his audience that the "aristocratic heritage" of their great university was being threatened by "enemies within." At some point, the indignant speaker warned of the "worshippers of Mammon"—as well as the "wild-eyed, murderous Anarchists and their union-organizer cronies"—for, he feared, the United States would never be a true democracy until such time—(and here Woodrow Wilson drew himself up to his full, narrow height, with ministerial sternness and a glittering of eyeglasses)—"until such time, gentlemen, that a Negress resides in the White House."

At which Dr. Wilson broke off abruptly, as if a switch had been thrown in his brain. Blinking and awkwardly smiling, in preparation for the usual warm waves of applause—which, as it happened, was slow in coming, in Charleston, South Carolina, on this evening of April 13, 1906.

AFTERWARD DR. WILSON begged of his Charleston host to tell him what he'd said, which he could not seem to remember; and his host said, with evasive eyes, "Why, Woodrow, I didn't hear, exactly—or, if I did, I don't recall your exact words."

"But—what did I say? Was I joking? And the joke fell flat?"

"Yes. Possibly."

"But there was no *laughter*. There was no *applause*. What on earth did I say, that so offended the audience?"

"Woodrow, no one heard. *I* didn't hear. It is all right. It will be forgotten. Everyone is sympathetic."

"But, my God—*what did I say?*"

***

RETURNED HOME TO Princeton by rail, Dr. Wilson was stricken with both gastric and "psychoneurological" distress, for which his physician Dr. Hatch prescribed an immediate vacation in Bermuda, of not less than twelve days; that the overwrought man might calm his mind, and be restored to some balance of his former well-being. Indeed, Dr. Wilson was told that he must flee Princeton at once, that a complete mental and physical collapse might be forestalled.

"MY PRECIOUS DARLING . . ."

ere, I will include excerpts from intimate letters written by Woodrow Wilson to his beloved wife Ellen, during the time (April 16 to April 27, 1906) of his "enforced rest" in Bermuda.

It is shocking to discover that, while writing these heartfelt, surely sincere letters of love to his wife, Woodrow Wilson was at the same time falling under the spell, and, in time, succumbing, to the seductive blandishments of the mysterious society woman known to historians as "Cybella Peck"—now recognized as a fictitious name.

ADMIRALTY INN, BERMUDA
SUNDAY A.M. 17 APRIL 1906

My precious darling,
   How I miss you! I am not ashamed to say that *I think of you constantly* & often close my eyes here on the veranda of the Inn, to imagine you close beside me; that I might clasp your hand in mine, and draw from you solace, & balm, and consolation, to compensate for the pain & humiliation I have had to endure lately. Yet—*I shall endure, & I shall prevail.*
   This, I vow.

Please do not tell anyone, dearest—that I am away "for reasons of health"—nor even "for a respite from overwork." (Though God knows that is true!) You need not tell them anything, only just that "Woodrow will be back in his office in Nassau Hall on the morning of Monday, May 1."

Ah, Bermuda is certainly the best place in the world to forget Princeton, though I shall work here of course—I shall work very hard—(lectures to write)—& I shall miss my dear little wife.

My artless little Ellen, not an hour passes without my offering thanks to God, that he sent you, & your great, boundless, nourishing love! It was His plan, that another, far inferior to my dear Ellen, should have "rejected" me as a husband years ago; His plan, that we are bound together for life. Please know, sweet Ellen, that it is not by adding to our masculine knowledge but by understanding us with their superior gifts of sympathy & intuition, that women are our helpers . . . When I see the jeering faces, the faces of infamy, that would destroy me, & he, W*** daring to torment me, in Charleston . . . at once I think of *you*, & your abiding & unquestioning love; & the entire Universe is changed for me & it is rather as if *all men & angels* listened, so perfectly my thought is mirrored in the light of your lovely brown eyes!

Sunday 4 p.m.

The sky is so porcelain-blue above the Atlantic—it is amazing. You & the girls have teased me, I fail to *look at* things, yet now I am *looking at* a sight worthy of paradise, the wide stretch of beach behind the Admiralty Inn where the sand is near-white & kept very smooth; swept smooth early each morning by servants. All is calm, calm! The action of the waves which I halfway feared, after the choppy crossing, would prove agitating to my nerves is, on the contrary, restful—hypnotic— healing. In Princeton it is a chill, begrudging early spring— with a taste of winter, still, in the nights—but here on this paradisiacal island, it is full spring, & all a-bloom in crimson, yellow, orange, snowy-white flowers as large as a man's head, that seem to nod at me as I pass.

There, strife & enmity; *here,* calm & peace.

But no!—you have begged me not to brood upon my "morbid" subject—and so, I will not.

There comes a courteous little darkie the size of a midget (in livery!) to wait upon me, inquiring—*Would masta wish for a drink, sir?*

Sunday evening

Woke from an uneasy nap before dinner—stunned with the horror of my blunder at Charleston—the debacle, the *shame,* in so public an arena—*I fear I shall never outlive it.* My thoughts are overcast & sickly; & in contrast to the glowing faces of my fellow vacationers, who are both Americans & British. As to my digestion . . .

(Do not be distressed, my dear, for I am fully capable of nursing myself if required, & have become quite adept at the pump, in any case—to whose repulsive ministrations, I am ashamed to expose my darling!)*

It is said that Mark Twain arrived on a boat from Miami this mid-day, & an American heiress of the name of Peck took immediate possession of him. *There* is a gentleman of great reputation, who clothes himself in white—white linen, white cotton, white silk!—& is never seen without an ill-smelling Cuban cigar clenched between his stained teeth. I shall avoid him, I think—for it is commonly known, *Samuel Clemens* gives strength to the Antichrist in his crude "satirical" writings, & could be no friend of Woodrow Wilson.

---

* "Pump"—stomach pump. When in particularly severe gastric distress Woodrow Wilson employed his own stomach pump, a favored home remedy (like the enema) until such time as the instrument was forcibly taken from him by a White House physician in 1913, shortly after his inauguration as twenty-seventh President of the United States.

Now, I will say good night, dear Ellen! For I am feeling somewhat melancholy, & lonely; & the rebellion in "Central America" is but temporarily quelled, I fear. But I will take solace working on my speech on Christian patriotism, to be delivered to the Philadelphia Society, in May, before succumbing to my dose of Oil of Tartar, & blessed sleep!

Your loving husband,

Woodrow

ADMIRALTY INN
18 APRIL 1906

My precious darling,

Tramped barefoot along the beach at dawn, in my "whites"—(thank you my darling for having packed my things so carefully, & for including such sweet little cards, for me to discover amid my undergarments as days pass!); you will be relieved to hear that my night was not nearly so tormented as I had feared, since the debacle in Charleston; for fortunately, I have brought quite a store of medicines for the purpose of combating *insomnia* as well as the usual *gastric distress.*

Yet tramping in the open air, close by the surf, I find my mind distracted by thoughts of combat, elsewhere; & words of speeches aswirl in my brain, like swords. *I will not be defeated by my enemies. I will not.* In a haze of distraction I was stopped by a fellow resident at the Admiralty Inn, as I was about to step on a *lion's mane*—this, a nasty-looking jellyfish that is often washed up on the beach. (The Negro servants scurry to remove them, but not always quickly enough.) "Sir! You don't want step on one of these!"—so the gentleman warned me, with a wink of his eye. Indeed, I do not: as I thanked him, & we introduced ourselves & chatted briefly, before moving on.

Ah, Ellen! You will not believe it—my misfortune!—Amanda FitzRandolph & her husband Edgerstoune are vacationing here, at the home of Mrs. Peck—*Sans Souci* it is called, & said to be the most palatial villa on the island. By chance I encountered Mrs. FitzRandolph in the hotel, where she was visiting friends. "Why, Woodrow! What a pleasant surprise!"—etc., etc. I hope I was polite enough; & masked my dismay. The last thing I want is to speak of Princeton matters, *here;* even to see familiar Princeton faces, when I am meant to have a respite from them . . .

In a melancholy mood on my balcony, dear Ellen, I have written a poem for you; my sweet, *I miss you so much*. For you are my *better angel*—you keep me from despair & all temptations to darkness. These feeble words cannot hope to express my boundless love for you. When I am cast down in gloom, I seem to crave you then *with even greater passion*. Forgive your foolish Woodrow, your adoring husband—

> You were the song I waited for.
> I found in you the vision sweet.
> The grace, the strain of noble sounds,
> The form, the mind, the mien, the heart,
> That I lacked & thought to find
> Within some spring within my mind,
> Like one awakened from dreaming
> To the blessed confidence of light.

(If put to music, I imagine a bagpipe melody—we Campbells of Argyll are shameless sentimentalists, as we are stalwart warriors!)

Tomorrow, Mrs. Peck is giving a luncheon at *Sans Souci*— Amanda FitzRandolph has wrangled an invitation for me, to meet Mr. Mark Twain—but I believe I will decline, as I prefer solitude; & peace & calm; & have much work to prepare, for upcoming speeches etc. How I wish my dear little Ellen were with me, at my side! For I am cast into gloom without you, though presenting a "smiling" face to the world . . .

Your loving husband,
Woodrow

ADMIRALTY INN
19 APRIL 1906
7:40 A.M.

My precious darling,

God be praised, my dear—I spent a moderately peaceful night—& this morning rose before dawn, to stride along the beach in the brisk wind; it is chill at that hour, & not cloying-warm like most of the day. I find myself positively giddy with the prospect of a morning of undisturbed work on my speech for the Philadelphia Society & an article for the *Atlantic*. Separation from my darling gives me less pain if I immerse myself in work; & pretend that she will summon me soon, to massage my neck if she has time, for it is beginning to stiffen, without her "magical" touch.*

Beneath the clear blue dome of heaven, in this paradisiacal place, nations & all "significant" events of the world seem remote & theoretical—& not a little absurd. *There* is Lilliput, & I am Gulliver.

---

* Since a Georgia physician had once told her that "so long as a man's neck is *full*, and *firm*, and *strong*, his health will be good," Mrs. Wilson made it a practice to massage Dr. Wilson's neck each night at bedtime, and to examine it for inflamed pimples, sensitive moles, swellings, unnatural hollows, etc. There was never a wife so concerned for her husband's health as Ellen Wilson; I hope I am not leaping too far ahead of my story by noting that, on her deathbed, in August 1914, Mrs. Wilson exhausted herself by making anxious inquiries after her husband's health, as the Presidency of the United States weighed heavily upon his shoulders, and exacerbated the poor man's many physical ills, as never before.

Luncheon at Mrs. Peck's "palatial" villa overlooking the ocean, a larger gathering than I had expected; & there was Mr. Samuel Clemens, clad in white, fierce-moustached & with bristling eyebrows, seated like royalty on the terrace, & surrounded by admirers. Yet, Mr. Clemens condescended to shake my hand, & to crack a joke or two at the expense of the university; for, as he likes to say, he has had no schooling at all, except the roughest sort, in Missouri as a boy; & on the Mississippi, as a steamboat captain. Yet again, Mr. Clemens quite surprised me, for having read *A History of the American People*, and my biography of George Washington, & for saying quite respectful things about them—in the hearing of others.

Mrs. Peck is very friendly also. "Ah, you are 'Woodrow Wilson'! Such things are said about you" & I asked politely what these things could be; & the lady said, seriously, "Things that pertain to the future—the future of our country." Her eyes were so probing upon me, I felt almost dazed; & can't think that I was very articulate, amid much festivity, & a powerful scent of hibiscus . . . Dear Ellen, I miss you so! I am very, very lonely amid this tribe of Lotus-Land revelers!

You will be startled, my dear, but I hope not disapproving, to learn that I have drafted several letters, to our redoubtable chairman of the board,* to David Jones & his brother Tom; to Cyrus, & Edward, & Moses, & Dr. Patton, & (not least) W*** himself, allowing that I have rethought my position, & wonder if the quad plan might be somewhat modified & the location of the Graduate College be made a compromise . . . Do not

---

* Dr. Wilson is referring to Grover Cleveland, whose name he could not bear to speak, and whom he disliked so much that, upon the occasion of Cleveland's death, in 1908, in Princeton, Dr. Wilson decreed that no observation be made on the Princeton campus, not even a flag lowered to half-mast; though elsewhere in Princeton, as through much of the United States, flags flew at half-mast.

think that I am weakening, dear Ellen! Though I know in my heart that *I am right* yet I am (in fact) a Gulliver surrounded by Lilliputians, & must govern accordingly. (As Pearce van Dyck has consoled me, I must not wreck the university for my ideals; though I grew angry with Professor van Dyck at the time, I see now that he spoke wisely.) Now, I must dress for dinner, though, after the luncheon orgy at *Sans Souci,* I have little appetite & "social conversation"; & less still, without my dear little wife at my side.

   Your loving husband,
   Woodrow

ADMIRALTY INN
20 APRIL 1906

My precious darling,

   Thank you, my dear, for your lovely letter! Though as you say you have not much "substance" to provide—& your news of our household & of Princeton is "but minor"—yet this is precious to me, so distant from my darling, as your dear voice in your letter is music to my lonely ears.

   Here, there is golfing, & lawn tennis!—(at which your husband is poorly talented); & a tour of the island by "electric car"—it seems, my sweet one, that my social duties have begun. Strolling on a flower-bordered lane beside the hotel I heard a voice—"Woodrow Wilson? Can it be?"—& there was Francis Pyne, in the company of several others; & I could hardly escape our neighbor & university benefactor, & have been dragooned into further social gatherings at *Sans Souci.* The Chief Justice of Bermuda, Mr. Gollan, chatted with me this afternoon, in a genial & rambling fashion; my pleasure in this white-haired old gentleman being that he knows (& cares) nothing of mainland politics; in fact, he is a British citizen; & Princeton University is but a "very pleasant" place where a relative of his attended school, some years ago. & there came Mr. Sam Clemens in dazzling white, & straw hat atilt, & pernicious cigar clenched between his teeth to invite Mr. Gollan & me to "thwack" him at billiards; which Mr. Gollan laughingly accepted, while with the excuse of having a speech to write, I declined. "Another time, perhaps, eh, Dr. Wilson, when you are not embarked upon saving the world?"—so Mr. Clemens muttered in his customary manner, that some think rude & others amusing.

It is flattering, I will admit—Mr. Clemens seems to like *me*.

So very tired, dear Ellen, from these blandishments, & others! I have yet to write final drafts of my letters to the board; but will do so, tomorrow morning. Wiser to compromise my ideals than to "wreck" the university, I think; & better to compromise, than to wreck my own health & jeopardize the health of my dearest wife whom I love beyond all ability to express . . .

Your loving husband,
Woodrow

ADMIRALTY INN
21 APRIL 1906

My precious darling,

Again, what a magnificent surprise, to receive a letter from you, & the packet of very nice responses from alumni!—which helps to mitigate, somewhat, the bitterness of the Charleston episode. (Hints have been made to me, that several Charleston alums have actually written to the trustees, to *demand my resignation*. I would not even dignify such an outrage with a response.) Today I shall be drafting letters to a number of influential parties including Cornelius Cuyler, Henry Bayard, Jack Hibben, Moses Pyne, Winslow Slade—can you think of anyone else of importance?—in addition to those I listed yesterday. In this paradisiacal place my brain is abuzz with this new attitude of *accommodation*. (Which I shrink from deeming mere "compromise" for I detest the word.)

"Elevenses" here in the open, sun-dappled air, & I hunch myself over this missive to my beloved little lady, that none of my fellow guests will feel the urge to join me on the veranda, & "rescue" me from my solitude. (Word has spread, you will be amused to know, about who I am; one of the eccentric rumors being that I am an "exiled" or "disgraced" monarch of some small European principality! So Mrs. Peck has told me, with a peal of laughter.)

Rose early, & golfed this morning; my companions being Francis Pyne & his house guest Count English von Gneist, of whom I think you might have heard, in Princeton; for he has been a guest at Drumthwacket this winter. The Count speaks with a strong accent yet knows English well; his full name is *Count English Rudolf Heinrich Gottsreich-Muller von Gneist*. Well-bred he assuredly is, from ancient Wallachian stock. I begin to see why the Pynes & several other West End Princeton families have warmed to him. Were it not for his European background one could imagine him a Campbell of Argyll!—that is, a man among men. His hair rises nobly from a high, craggy, brooding forehead; his nose is aquiline, and his ears long and slender; his eyes a striking tawny hue, that changes with the light. Though a titled nobleman admitting to being linked by blood to most of the noble houses of Europe, the Count claims to be "without a homeland" & "grateful for the hospitality & charity of his American friends." In the most charming way imaginable he said to me, "Mr. Wilson! You gaze upon the Sole Living Heir of Nothingness."

As it turns out, the Count too has read *A History of the American People* & was quite flattering about its worth; claiming that he had learned a good deal from it, for, in Europe, as he said, "we don't ordinarily think of Americans as a *people* but rather as a mixture of hardy mongrel stock."

He was particularly impressed by my commentary on the infamous Pullman boycott of 1894 as well as the Populist threat in general: the labor agitations, strikes, & outright crimes, as in the recent outrage in Paterson. Both the Count & Francis Pyne think that my observations on the necessity for intelligent Caucasian discrimination, in the matter of Negroes, Orientals, and the multitudes from the lower classes out of Europe, to be quite the best, because the most reasonably argued, presentation of the subject he has read. "I've always thought it unfortunate," the Count said, "that such opinions, which are perfectly self-evident to any clear-thinking man, are often voiced, in the public press, and on the platform, by demagogues, knaves, or raving lunatics!—which is, as you know, highly embarrassing for our cause." The only demurral this gracious gentleman expressed had to do with my stated belief that the American people are blessed by God, elevated above the common run of humankind by a "guardian destiny" & intended—nay, obliged—to spread our ideals throughout the world. That is, Christianity, and Democracy. In our debate, we were joined at the club house by others, including Edgerstoune FitzRandolph. I think that I spoke convincingly, dear Ellen—*you* would have been proud, I believe—for after all, it is common knowledge in 1906, & has been since the time of McKinley, that the United States is charged by God with the evangelical mission of spreading Christian democracy throughout the world, and opening the markets of the East as well—by diplomacy if possible, by power otherwise. "We are a sort of pure air blowing in world politics, destroying ancient illusions, and cleaning places of morbid miasmatic gases," I explained to the gentlemen. We debated whether it was an "American" obligation or rather more an "Anglo-Saxon" one, which allowed us to ponder the issue over luncheon, & to shake hands with mutual respect, & now I am feeling quite "bully" indeed . . . *These are people who are on my side. & how many more, yet undeclared.*

Mrs. Peck insists upon inviting me to dinner!—quite flatters me by insisting that *Mark Twain himself bids you attend, Mr. Wilson!*

"Thank you, but I am afraid that I must decline"—these words distinctly uttered & yet—(somehow)—the very antithesis seemed to be registered by the shiny-faced American heiress who twirled her parasol in very delight—"Thank *you,* Mr. Wilson—I will send my driver to pick you up at 7 p.m. on this very veranda—& hope that, by such time, you have put aside your many papers & books & lifted your head, that you might use your eyes to *see.*"

& so it seems, my precious darling, I must go out after all, though very unwilling—*very!* Without my dear wife to tie my tie, & see that I am "properly attired" to mingle in decent society.

The only boon, I will stamp & mail this letter in the hotel lobby, that it will be hurried to my precious darling, early tomorrow!

Your loving husband,

Woodrow

ADMIRALTY INN

25 APRIL 1906

My precious darling,

How my head spins & reels with the *intensity* of this paradisiacal place!

Forgive me, my darling, for not having written for several days—for I have been entirely *immersed in work*—barricaded in this hotel room like a monk!

Feeling a bit breathless, my dear wife, for much of this day I have been preparing my modified statement of purpose offered *in lieu of a resignation from the presidency*—the most profound single document of my life!

You will say Woodrow do not exaggerate! You will cause your heartbeat to accelerate & your brain to turn feverish—do not exaggerate!

Of course you are correct, my precious darling. Always, you are correct.

It is Woman's genius, to know us as we FAIL TO KNOW ourselves.

How I wish, dear Ellen, I might read this statement to you; in which, while managing to skirt "humbling" myself—(as a descendant of the great clan of Argyll, I am hardly a "Uriah Heep")—I yet explain & quite calmly the reasons for my former adamant position about the Graduate School, & offer an apology—(yes it is SINCERE)—to Dean West in particular whom, I concede, I have *somewhat maligned*, this past year.

Thus, the work goes well; but I must prepare another draft. & think it best if I type all the letters myself, & not rely upon a hotel secretary-for-hire; badly missing my precious darling, at such a time. However—I WILL TYPE THE G-D LETTERS MYSELF—& mail out in a day or two.

As my brain felt feverish I thought it therapeutic to walk along the beach, in the wind; for luncheon was *much chatter*—& afterward two carloads of guests were driven to Government House for tea with the Governor—who (as Mrs. Peck explains) is brother to the esteemed General Kitchener. In the party were Samuel Clemens who quite dazzles the eye with his white linens, & his snowy-white hair & gruff-bristling dark brows—& the FitzRandolphs—& Francis Pyne—& Count English von Gneist; & Mrs. Peck of course for it seems, Cybella (as she bids me call her) knows everyone—& is never so happy as when she "mangles her guests together" as she laughingly says. & so—we are *mangled*...

Governor Kitchener is a dignified older man & a shining example of "splendid isolation"—even in the minuscule domain of Bermuda. For, while charming enough, this island paradise under the benign British protectorate is one of those regions of the world that *cannot matter to history*. How envious I felt of this gentleman!—ruling his island empire with no opposition, at least of which he is aware; a population of educated & genteel whites of whom many are clearly well-to-do tourists & visitors, who never present any political problems, as they are transient & indifferent to the island's politics; & all these very capably serviced by a population of Negroes well-trained & speaking, unlike our American Negroes, a very distinctive English. (You would be astonished to hear them, dear Ellen! Almost it seems, it is a kind of joke, or leg-pull, that so very black a Negro will speak such precise British English, like a wind-up doll; & not give any hint, to the U.S. tourist, that there is anything the slightest bizarre in such; for the servants here, that I have encountered, are exceedingly well trained & unfailingly competent. Would that I could transport some of these home with me, to our household at Prospect!)

"Excuse me, sir"—for, a second time, as I tramped along the beach thinking such thoughts sans shoes & socks, I came very close to stepping on a swarm of jellyfish; & am grateful for a young man, with a bemused smile, who came handily to my rescue. & grateful, dear Ellen, that you are not with me, for you would have been repulsed in horror & disgust by these translucent blobs of gelatinous matter, with hideous trailing tentacles, washed upon the beach with the tide; though at luncheon as I recall, though distracted by others' conversation, I had overheard Francis Pyne commenting on the "remarkable" phenomenon of these particular jellyfish, i.e., lion's mane, appearing in these waters, at this time of year.

Ah, a disturbing rumor, also at lunch, that blowhard "TR" & family may visit Bermuda; Sam Clemens expelling a cloud of the most foul cigar-smoke caused the luncheon party to convulse in laughter with a droll remark as to the Bull-Moose President being *more bull than moose* & I confess, I laughed with the party, for Mr. Clemens *is* very funny, if cruel & cutting.

Cybella Peck turned to me to ask my judgment of the President & I demurred, like any diplomat; yet made the party gasp with laughter sharing with them a "fantastical vision" of an Anarchist assassin making his way to peaceful Bermuda to throw a bomb at the broad-grinning President—here, there would not be sufficient police protection for him . . . For which scathing wit your poor husband was properly punished with, at the end of the two-hour luncheon, a sudden gastric attack in the equatorial regions, necessitating an abrupt departure.

My precious darling, I fear that these new friends whisper of me, behind my back, that I am "not well-looking"—for Mr. Clemens is often most cutting, seeing foibles & flaws in others that a more benign eye might overlook; & Cybella made a most cruel observation, regarding a *buck-toothed British baroness* at a nearby table; & I felt a hurt, that our dear daughters would be wounded could they overhear such thoughtless remarks. (Mrs. Peck is much doted-upon by both Brits & U.S. guests here & is often seen with Count von Gneist & Mr. Pyne—it is a minority report, yet I fail to see the woman's *serene Botticelli beauty* as Mr. Clemens praises it, & so much prefer a less "cultivated" & "calculated" charm, by far! It is good to recall how Jesus bids us to see into the soul & not be dazzled by the outer self; the more so, as Mrs. Peck is one of those individuals whose (alleged) beauty, good breeding, & wealth have not conferred kindness or charity upon her, but rather the reverse—for like her companion Mr. Clemens, Cybella cannot seem to resist a sly or cutting quip, to provoke laughter in listeners.)*

---

* Historians are sharply and irrevocably divided: when did the "intimate relationship" between Mrs. Peck and Dr. Wilson begin? Was it on this date, April 25, or the following day, when Dr. Wilson so abruptly changed his (pre-paid) residence at the Admiralty Inn, to spend several nights at *Sans Souci*? Many letters were to pass between Mrs. Peck and the besotted Dr. Wilson, it is believed, but, unfortunately, not a single one of these has been preserved, so far as I know. (Most scandalously, Mrs. Peck was also believed to be *carrying on* with Samuel Clemens at this time, a relationship not so unconscionable, as Mr. Clemens was a widower, and Mrs. Peck's

Forgive, dearest wife, this somewhat disconnected letter;
as my thoughts fly about like the disturbed moths that throw
themselves against the screen here, yearning to immolate
themselves in *heat & light*! I have not wished to alarm you, but a
fresh attack of neuritis as well as "equatorial mutiny" have cast
down my spirits, & now I must dose myself with Pinkham's &
Oil of Tartar (that mix so sickeningly together, the patient is
anxious not to vomit) & hope for sleep; & if not, will have no
recourse other than the pump you have begged me not to use,
when you are not at hand.

Your loving husband,
Woodrow

ADMIRALTY INN
26 APRIL 1906

My precious darling,
    Thank you for your sweet, sweet letter, & thank the girls
for me, for their most welcome little notes—you cannot know
how moved I was, after my turbulent night; how I have carried
my dear family close against my heart through this long &
unsettling day. I am sorry to hear your "troubling" news from
Maidstone & as you have chosen to supply no details, I am
led to worry that the long-invalided Adelaide Burr has taken
a turn for the worse. Here, though I try to avoid contact with
Princeton faces, as much as courtesy allows, I find that yet
again I have accepted an invitation to dinner, this time from
the FitzRandolphs who are hosting a dinner at *Sans Souci*; &
my punishment will be the donning of my frock coat & gray
striped trousers & the most starched collar in my possession,
this very evening. Kindly Mrs. FitzRandolph has arranged for

---

husband seemed scarcely to exist. Of this liaison, we can assume that Woodrow
Wilson had not a clue.)

their driver to pick me up in Mrs. Peck's Silver Cloud Pierce-Arrow yet another time. (Though I do not like it greatly, how our Princeton friends & neighbors *assume* that I have no way to transport myself; as the board of trustees sets my salary so modestly, I cannot afford a motorcar, let alone a driver to drive the motorcar, back home.) & though she is kindly, Mrs. FitzRandolph is somewhat coercive, a character flaw often found in females of wealth & social station; her clothes far too "stylish" for my taste—nearly as calculated to capture the eye as Mrs. Peck's that are allegedly sewn for her by a Parisian designer of great renown, *a man it is said,* who fashions clothing for the First Lady of France. Both Mrs. FitzRandolph & Mrs. Peck are women who favor the most delicate "pastel" colors; the skirts of their dresses are very full, & the shoulder line of their clothing strangely low, in what is said to be the Japanese style—(for Mrs. Peck saw me staring, & laughingly explained). The women's hats here are *enormous*—nothing like my dear wife's modest-trimmed little hats—& lavishly trimmed with very pretty though fluttery ostrich feathers. Mr. Clemens quips *How many ostriches must be sacrificed, that our ladies' vanity shines forth*—to which I inwardly murmured AMEN!

I had meant to tell you, dear Ellen, that I'd caught a glimpse the other day of the FitzRandolph baby, which few persons in Princeton have seen—its name is Terence—much swaddled in infant's clothing & in a buggy covered in veils, to protect the child from the sun's strong rays; as well, as Amanda FitzRandolph says, most curiously, from any "singular influence" the child might receive, from an adult stooping to peer into his tiny face!

At last—I have prepared the final drafts of the letters for the trustees et al.—& will toil through the day tomorrow, like a Trojan, to mail them; in the hope that the recipients will have absorbed the import of these letters, in the days before I return to Princeton.

Do not worry about me, dear Ellen—*I am quite all right.* (I have not needed to use the pump more than a single time!) Though running very low on Oil of Castor, which I hope I can purchase here on the island for I shall be desperate, I'm afraid, without!

My dearest wife, I must close now, as time has passed so rapidly & Mrs. Peck's vehicle will soon come for me, like a chariot out of the sky. I am missing my dearest little Ellen so very much, no words can say.

Your loving husband,
Woodrow

ADMIRALTY INN
26 APRIL 1906
11 A.M.

My precious darling,

Confound it, I have only now made myself comfortable at this little table above the beach, & there is some sort of ungodly commotion close by; shrill calls & shouts as of unruly children. Most distracting, when I am *polishing & perfecting* my letters; & now my head throbs, & my hand begins to shake.

It seems the mystery on the beach is solved: one of those loathsome jellyfish had evidently stung a wading child, whose nanny had been negligent. A boy of ten was stung yesterday, too. Very foolish of the children to play hereabouts & of their parents to allow it. (When I made some remark to this effect, to a very well-mannered & light-skinned little Negro who was settling my table-legs into the sand, a smile from him, & a roll of his eyes, sent me the clear signal that the Negroes of this island paradise *think it exceedingly foolish* for tourists & visitors to wade in the ocean; but would never dream of expressing this opinion, of course. I think it is my Southern roots that binds me to the Negro race, our sense of *rapport* in the midst of foolish Northerners!)

According to Count von Gneist, who, it seems, is something of a naturalist, & has even traveled to the desolate Galápagos Islands, of Darwinian notoriety, certain of the swarm of jellyfish washed upon the beaches of Bermuda are of a species larger than the usual, with jelly sacs and tentacles of near-preternatural size; and their toxin is quite potent. Ugly red welts were raised on the boy's legs yesterday & he wept most fearfully . . . I would weep too, if I'd blundered into one of those shimmering protoplasmic brutes, that appear, from a distance, like mere sea-debris, or seaweed!

Mrs. Peck has invited me to stay for the remainder of my Bermuda vacation at *Sans Souci*—it is very kind of her, for the Admiralty Inn with its elderly British guests begins to weary me; & there is the attraction, both Count von Gneist & Sam Clemens are houseguests there, & marvel at the beauty & hospitality of the villa, on the southernmost peninsula of the island & surrounded by tall swaying court palms & gorgeous bougainvillea to a height of twenty feet. Servants at *Sans Souci*, it is reported, are not common West Indian Negroes but are descended from the original "indentured servants"—(of whom some were told, when they arrived at the island, that the term of their indenture had been raised from seven years to *ninety-nine*—if they were black)—thus of a higher quality generally, & remarkably intelligent.

How I wish you were at my side, dear Ellen—I am so dependent upon my dear wife, to "dress" me; & am quite at the mercy of the ladies who make merry over me, as the *puritan-browed Princeton minister*, feeling obliged to adjust my necktie, or a collar or cuff, that somehow betrays a bachelor's toilet.

In a droll aside Mr. Clemens observed, last night, in my ear, as one of the servants came around with tiny cups of very black "Haitian" coffee—"Ah, luxury! Comfort! Ease! Wealth! Rich food & drink & the folk who come with it! It is all very stupefying & dull, is it not, Mr. Wilson?"—& when I raised my eyebrows at such a comment, with Cybella Peck but a few feet away, Mr. Clemens quickly amended, "Yet it is preferable to the rest of life, of course. One must consider *that*."

(Mr. Clemens is looking a great deal aged, from when I'd last seen him, which is strange. He plays billiards, he says, as he smokes his cigars—"Like a fiend out of Hell." Yet his hair is no less whiter & bushy & his moustache no less cavalier. His cigar emitted so potent a stench, I feared I might have to hurry from the room to be violently ill; but I knew my departure would arouse merriment in the other guests, & I could not risk this. Imagine my astonishment when Mrs. Peck "lit up" a cigar—I believe it is called a *cigarillo*—of her own, & puffed away at it laughing with the men, fortunately in the open air.)

Except for a skirmish in the early hours of the morning with Mrs. FitzRandolph's bouillabaisse I have been digesting my food fairly well, which is a good prognosis for my return to Princeton, I think! Yet more significantly, I have had a number of excellent conversations with persons of unusual common sense about the future of America & its "unique" politics—the propensity of the masses not to vote invariably in their own self-interest, or indeed, to vote at all, which allows for the skilled politician to manipulate to his advantage. Especially, I have valued my conversations with Count von Gneist whose intelligence & wit compete with Mr. Clemens's, except he is not so corrosive. As I have noted to you, the Count speaks English with a marked accent; at times, his speech is so fluid, it resembles music. Here is a gentleman who is also a *man,* in the way that our blowhard president "TR" is not. At all times he displays an inborn sort of gallantry, and an easy deference to authority; recognizing me, as he has said, as *one of the American aristocracy, born to rule*—a type, the Count says, immediately recognizable to Europeans. His eyes are a curious sort of lemon-tawny hue, like a certain sort of leather when it has been well polished. His hair is leonine, with graying locks. I confess

that I am somewhat taken with him—& wonder if he might
be prevailed upon to lecture at the university, on any subject
of his choice—history, politics, the Galápagos Islands! When
first we'd met this gentleman exclaimed: "Ah, the famous Dr.
Wilson!—who has, it seems, made so many craven enemies in
Princeton, one senses he is destined for greatness"—& another
time, on another subject, the Count murmured to me in an
aside, almost in apology: "No man is a prophet in his own
provincial community, Mr. Wilson. You must take solace in
that."

It is so rare, dearest Ellen, that a man finds such a companion
in another man, & a stranger at that!

3:10 p.m.

Wandering about *Sans Souci*—how very different from
the confines of Prospect! *There*, I am never made to feel
quite at home, for the university is the land-owner; & the
undergraduates feel it is their right to gape & gawk through the
fence, at all hours of the night. But *here*—all is open to light &
the sea; for no one would dare trespass on this private land, so
fortified against outsiders, & so capably staffed by the *Sans Souci*
servants, who are very loyal to their masters. I wish that my
dear little wife could walk with me, to observe this palatial villa
of smooth white stucco & red shutters; so quaintly, Mrs. Peck
refers to it as a "cottage," that consists of two large wings, and
some fourteen bedrooms, as grand as the New Jersey governor's
summer home at Sea Girt, or as anything at Cape May, for that
matter.

How the snobbish West End of Princeton—(not excluding
our shameless epicurean ex-President)—would gape & gawk, to
see me treated here so very graciously! Their much-maligned &
taken-for-granted Woodrow Wilson here treated like royalty! To
see how the Cybella Peck fusses over me, that my suite is ideal,
& every service of *Sans Souci* at my disposal.

There is, or was, but a single jarring note—just this

morning—as I lingered on my balcony gazing toward the
ocean, a movement caught my eye on the beach—one of the
villa's servants, though very light-skinned; yet the young
man seemed to me unnervingly like the Ruggles boy, of
whom I'd spoken to you—who had fraudulently claimed
to be a kinsman of mine, you might recall—a preceptor
at the university & a seminarian—who had had to be
dismissed from both—for reasons too disturbing to speak
of . . . Yet later, it seemed to me that I saw this very servant
in conversation with Count von Gneist, at the edge of a
broad flagstone terrace; something crimson had fallen to
the ground, & the servant quickly bent to pick it up, as if to
prevent the Count from doing so; this, a sprig of gorgeous
bougainvillea, the impudent young man inserted into the
Count's lapel, as the Count laughed . . . Imagine my alarm
when the two glanced in my direction, yet fortunately did not
see me, crouched very still behind a screen.

   I am sure that the *Sans Souci* servant is not Yaeger Ruggles. It
was but an optical illusion of some kind, that afflicts me after
over-stimulation, & a poor night of sleep.

   Another child has been stung by a jellyfish, it seems. They
say that the poor little girl was rendered unconscious for some
minutes, & has now been carried away to be hospitalized. What
a pity!—only eight or ten years old. One would think that the
nursemaid, or the mother, would keep closer watch . . . I am
so relieved that you, dear Ellen, are spared the sight of these
singularly ugly freaks of nature, born without skeletons, soft-
shimmering, yet deadly. This day, Mr. Clemens made a ribald
joke that offended me, to a degree, on the subject of the "lion's
mane" with its myriad tendrils and stinging toxins. (Quite
wonderfully, Count von Gneist recalled that Arthur Conan
Doyle, the British mystery writer, has written something called
"The Adventures of the Lion's Mane," of which Mr. Clemens
had not heard for, as he said negligently, he did not waste his

time reading *mere fantasies,* when the actual world *of pain &
suffering* stared him in the face.)

Champagne, & white wine, & after-dinner cordials—to
which I declined with thanks, it scarcely needs be said; as I
could not hope to sleep a wink, so great would be the rebellion
in the "equatorial regions" . . .

Midnight

Ah, how I miss my darling spouse! Though this bedchamber
at *Sans Souci* is splendidly furnished, & far too large for a
single lonely bachelor; & the sound of the night-time surf very
comforting, like the palm of a giant hand that caresses, and
consoles. My neck, stiff from craning much of the evening, to
hear the wit so fiercely batted about, like badminton birdies,
is badly wanting my dear Ellen's soothing fingers, that banish
aches & pains & nettlesome foolish worries lodging in the over-
heated grooves of my brain . . .

Waking in the night to a horrific vision, or it may have
been something glimpsed earlier, yet not registered in
my distracted brain at the time; yet now seeing, with
an unnerving vividness, our friend & neighbor Amanda
FitzRandolph acquiescing to an offer made by the Count of
a *pinch of snuff* from a tiny ivory snuffbox! Of all Princeton
ladies, there was Mrs. FitzRandolph, *a new mother,* allowing
the Count to insert the snuff in one of her nostrils, that she
might draw breath, and sneeze—a quicksilver rippling over
her face, and tears starting into her eyes.

This, & the incident on the terrace with the young Negro
servant, has caused me to slightly reconsider my new friend
Count English von Gneist; though a man among men, &
surely a gentleman, I am not certain that his manners are for
Prospect—for Dr. Wilson's "petticoat haven"!

As for Edgerstoune's absence, there came Mr. Clemens
unsteady on his feet & an unlit cigar in his stubby fingers,
observing to all who would hear: "A man may accommodate

himself to a disagreeable situation in a few months. The
intolerable may take a little longer."

 Your loving husband,

 Woodrow

My precious darling,

 Again, thank you so much for your dear little letter, bearing
such sweet tidings of household news, which had been
brought to me from the Admiralty Inn yesterday; but had
been unaccountably misplaced in my bedchamber, & only just
discovered by the sharp eye of my devoted boy Isaiah.

 D—n! While I have been scribbling away here, some of my
papers—drafts of precious letters to Cuyler, Hibben, Slade,
Pyne, et al.—have been blown from the balcony, & onto the
beach; & so exasperated am I, my darling, I am tempted to
allow them to blow out to sea . . . except for the exertions of
dear Isaiah, who would "do" for me, as he has several times
said, "to the very ends of the earth."

 (News has come to *Sans Souci* of a most tragic event, though
not a surprising one: a child was at last so badly stung by the
lion's mane jellyfish, he suffered a paralysis of the heart muscles
& has died. How hideous an ending, for some family, to a
Bermuda idyll! & how grateful I am, my sweet love, that you &
our dear girls are NOT HERE.)

 Forgive me, I beg, for my belatedness in replying to your
last letter—or letters—for as you must know I am very busy
with my work, including the piece for the *Atlantic* as well as the
sermon for the Philadelphia Society; &, more recently, a speech
for the Mayflower Society. None of these is *completed*—but all
are reasonably *in medias res*. & my damnable neuritis has been

giving me such pain, through the night; & so much seems often to be happening here, whether impromptu motorcar expeditions about the island, & luncheons on a bluff above the beach; & charades (at which the stiff-jointed Princeton president is surprisingly agile, to the ladies' delight); & a vertiginous trip on a yacht, circling the island, with a sighting of sharks; & numerous teas & dinners. I attend very little, of course—yet, it is as Mrs. Peck has said, "The university president is the very best advertisement for the university & must not hide his light under a basket." & to quote inimitable Sam Clemens—"This place is rife with millionaires as a casu marzu cheese is rife with maggots."

(Dear Ellen, forgive me! If my speech is becoming coarse it is not my wish nor my fault exactly, but the influence of such outspoken persons as Mr. Clemens; such drunken influence I will shortly throw off entirely, when I return to our cozy nest at Prospect.)

Yet, a word more of Sam Clemens: "Mark Twain"—"St. Mark" as he sometimes calls himself. Here is a being both *devilish* & yet *angelic*. His exterior look of age is matched by an interior erosion of the spirit, for a daughter's recent death (to which the poor man alludes obliquely, yet often) seems to have shriveled his heart. He speaks most obsessively—to some, tediously—of *lynching* in the United States—& how the Congress & the Chief Executive & the Supreme Court remain indifferent. He is writing, he says, a "blasting" essay for *Harper's*—"The United States of Lyncherdom"—which he has asked me to read, & I am hesitant to say yes, for the subject is offensive to me; also, I am most pressed for time. Mr. Clemens's most conspicuous vice, he has said, he would like to share with *me*, of all people—his smoking of "the most exquisite lung-corroding Havana cigars"—of which he smokes rarely less than *forty daily*. (How is this possible?) When a British lady guest at Mrs. Peck's affected surprise & dismay at this startling statistic, warning "Mark Twain" that he was digging a premature grave for himself, the dapper white-haired gentleman affected an apologetic expression & informed her that he could not possibly smoke *more than forty cigars a day,* though he had tried. The man's consumption of Old Gran-Dad whiskey is likewise impressive, or dismaying; yet this is the only means, he confided in me, by which he might hope to "sink into a restful blank Oblivion, for three or four blessed hours each night." Unhappy man! I tried to speak with him on the soothing powers of prayer, but he puffed on his foul cigar & coughed & chuckled saying he hadn't yet sampled that brand, & wondered how it might compare to *Our Gran-Dad.* All this, my dear little wife, I should refrain from telling you, as it is of course rather vulgar, & upsetting; the more so, that the humorist is so amusing in his replies, one cannot help laughing.

(Imagine my surprise when Mr. Clemens regaled the dinnertime company with a most hilarious story of three Georgia Negroes who journeyed by rail to New York City & saw their first snowfall, which they were convinced must be *falling cotton!*)

As Mr. Clemens was turning away, to take his place at the billiards table another time, where, it was said, he had lost some five hundred dollars to Count von Gneist, he said to me, with a squeeze of his chill fingers, "When you climb to the pinnacle, Mr. Wilson, as I have no doubt you will do, as I have done— there is but one direction left for you: the sudden step out, into empty space."

5 p.m.

Dear Ellen!—I am hesitant to chide my darling wife, & yet—it appears that you have misled me, & perhaps misguided me.

I am loathe to make such accusations. Yet, I have read & reread the dozen letters you have written to me, since I left Princeton, & can find no evidence otherwise.

Mrs. Peck says, I must not judge prematurely, or harshly.

Mrs. Peck is most solicitous of my distress, & has arranged for her private physician to "check me out"—for which I am most grateful. Already Dr. Dodge has provided me with a six-ounce bottle of Oil of Castor & a new prescription medication derived from St. John's wort, to be absorbed under the tongue at bedtime.

Yet, my sweet Ellen, the issue here is a conversation between Count English von Gneist & your anxious husband, that transpired within the hour. "Mr. Wilson, may I speak frankly with you?"—so my confidant began, informing me that he had been hearing of "certain disturbing rumors" in Princeton, through correspondents there; one of them pertains to an "imminent bequest" from a Mr. Proctor—(this would be William Cooper Proctor '66, an admirer of Andrew West); & he felt obliged to honor the friendship that had recently sprung up between us by informing me of this fact; & by adding that it was common knowledge back in Princeton that my opponents are busying themselves with a malicious letter-writing campaign to all the alumni, reiterating charges of "unprofessional behavior" at Charleston, & elsewhere; & agitating for my resignation; *while I am idling away my time in Lotus-Land.*

"It seems to me very strange, Mr. Wilson," Count von Gneist said, with an air of sincere regret, "that everyone in Princeton should be speaking of such developments while the president of the university is kept innocent—that's to say, ignorant—of what is happening. Have you no loyal, trusted correspondent, at home, who might have been trusted to inform you."

To this, dear Ellen, I was utterly unable to reply. *I simply could not reply.*

Stumbling away & much disturbed & only now, dear Ellen, sweet Ellen, able to express what is in my heart, my disappointment with you; for I have trusted my helpmate, to report such news to me; I cannot trust my aides, still less my office staff. I know you mean only to shield me, & to give me time, as you thought, to recover from the strain of constant overwork, & my ongoing symptoms of ill health; I know that you do not mean to deceive me, or to undermine my authority at the university. But all my passions are on such a terrible scale of power, Ellen, you must know that my *fighting Campbell spirit* cannot be suppressed without violence to my soul . . .

I have made arrangements in town to take the 9 a.m. steamer back to the mainland, tomorrow; from there, I shall take a train, & return to Princeton as soon as possible—not so belatedly as Odysseus, yet with that great wronged warrior's fighting sword, wielded against my enemies!

It is true, I shall not try to conceal it—I am *most upset & most aggrieved* with you, dear Ellen; this has caused a serious strain in our marriage, which I would not wish to call an imminent *breakage*. Cybella Peck has counseled me, one must not act in haste at such times; she cautions me to remain calm; for the "marital bond" is both a delicate knot & a "strangle-hold" with which she has learned to negotiate, she has said, upon more than one "fraught" occasion. Yet Cybella points out to me that it is not too late, I have not mailed the "compromising" letters, that would have so undermined my authority; it is not too late for me simply to burn them, & erase from my memory the ignominy of their composition. Such a craven wish to be liked—by a Campbell of Argyll!

I am beyond that now, I hope—as my enemies will soon discover.

Now, dearest Ellen, I shall pack; & I must bid my adieux to the Governor, & Mr. Clemens, & Count von Gneist (whom we shall be seeing again soon in Princeton, & often, I hope); & express my condolences to poor Mrs. FitzRandolph (for it was Edgerstoune, I have only just learned, in addition to the son of a tourist, who was killed by a jellyfish—not lion's mane evidently, but a species called "sea wasp")—ah, we shall hear more of this in Princeton, I suppose!—for it is very sad, & very foolish, that a grown man might tramp along the Bermuda beach, sans shoes & socks, into a swarm of disgusting *jellyfish*.

Forgive my acerbic tone, dearest wife. Truly I am not angry with you, but rather more with myself, for having trusted you, as my helpmate. It is but my nerves, my precious darling, & a sudden fierce gale-force wind rattling the shutters, as hurriedly I pack, to bid farewell to *Sans Souci*, where my life has been so vitally altered, & set back upon a triumphant track.

Your loving husband,
Woodrow

"A NARROW FELLOW
IN THE GRASS . . ."

(From the secret journal of Mrs. Adelaide McLean Burr)

_____. One day, you shall see, they turn. Husbands turn, & there is no solace then but the grave.

_____. It has happened. I have imagined nothing. I am deceived. I have been deceived these many months. <u>But I am deceived no longer</u>. Ah Horace!—my love! How could you betray your loving Puss?

_____. It is early spring. The year 1906. I shall not see another, I fear. I have sent notes to Mandy, who has returned from Bermuda it is said. Begged her to drop by for tea & might she bring the Count with her for I have heard so much of that esteemed gentleman & now I am bedridden & shall not see him otherwise. My husband nightly deceives me with harlots beneath this very roof, I shall appeal to the Count as a gentleman, to protect me. My husband despises me now & wishes me dead & <u>I am not safe any longer in my own bed</u>.

_____. A smell of camphor, witch hazel, belladonna & mint. The acrid taste of St. John's wort, that Dr. Boudinot promises will "lighten" melancholy. A faint smell of the water-closet, that needs scrubbing again. The new girl Griselda must get on <u>hands & knees</u>.

_____. The hairs on my head stand up, affrighted. I am like the cat's tail—when she is terrified or enraged, the tail puffs to twice its size, & switches like a demented pendulum. & the sheathed claws emerge, & the sharp glistening teeth.

_____. He shall not smother me, as Othello smothered Desdemona.

_____. On my bed-table beneath Mrs. Fern's insipid <u>A Poesy of Verse</u> are hidden <u>Poems</u> by Emily Dickinson—(though I cannot think that is the poetess's name, such unpolished verse would be an embarrassment naked in the world)—& <u>Leaves of Grass</u> by Walt Whitman—(certainly, this cannot be the poet's name!—such poems of naked shame, perversion, inversion!)—& several volumes by Madame Blavatsky, that Horace has warned me against; & think that I have asked the girl to carry away.

_____. & yet, I find that I must read my Bible. As my mother before her, & hers before <u>her</u>. In these thin, yellowing pages are the splotches of women's tears. O God protect me from the Fiend. How has it happened, my handsome upstanding curly-moustached husband Horace, praised by all of the West End as the most devoted & diligent of husbands, has <u>turned</u>? My lips chalky from Oil of Castor move in a whispered prayer <u>Though I walk through the Valley of the Shadow of Death I shall fear no evil: for Thou art with me</u> . . .

_____. A sleety sort of rain, very strange for this time of year. Hard & glinting like sand against the windows. Murmurous wind in the chimney. I am alone. I shall be murdered in my sleep. The household staff will press their hands to their ears like monkeys not-hearing as they are not-seeing the succession of harlots he has brought to this house. I know not, is it day or night?—for the sky is such, no sun will shine. I have devoured all the tablets Dr. Boudinot left for me with a forefinger to his lips—<u>This is our secret, Adelaide!</u> I know not what the man meant, he is an idiot. It is said he injects morphine into his veins, & has made himself an imbecile. Yet, he is all that we have. We must trust Dr. Boudinot. <u>Oh Horace! Why have you deceived me? Why have you turned from your devoted wife to the arms of others—to the arms of shameless sluts?</u>

_____. "Why do you cry, ma'am," the new girl Griselda inquires of me, staring pop-eyed at Puss hidden beneath covers; & scurries away downstairs to tell all in the kitchen of the mistress's "strange mood"—"the way white-folks ladies <u>is</u>." & gossip flies from kitchen to kitchen through the West End: from Maidstone to Pembroke to Arnheim to Wheatsheaf to Westland to Drumthwacket to Crosswicks to—(I know not what lies beyond Crosswicks unless it be Hell). & when the girl is gone I take up my mirror & gaze at the wraith therein. Ah, the once rosy cheeks now sallow & stained with bitter salt-tears!—& no one shall notice, & no one shall care. My hair all a-frizz: wild & smoky-hued & now the hideous mortal touch of *gray* has appeared; for I had to dismiss nasty little Hannah who did the henna rinse with such skill (for the Negra trollop was a common thief, stole from me my grandmother Burr's ivory miniature brooch in the shape of a swan & she would not confess though I screamed at her & threatened to have her thrown in jail)—& I do not wish the new girl to touch me so closely. Nay be gone!—be gone & let me sleep. For my Horace has ceased to love me & naught but the grave awaits.

_____ . <u>When I love thee not, then is Chaos come again.</u>

_____ . Bored & restless & yet when Lenora Slade called downstairs, I sent word that I could not see her. Mrs. Wilson, later that day. Of all people—<u>Ellen Wilson!</u> The Wilsons have not even a motorcar but must be driven by their betters & many days, Dr. Wilson bicycles along the drives of the campus it is said, & the boys themselves hide their faces in laughter. & the next day, Frances Cleveland nosed by to see, doubtless, if Adelaide is <u>quite so bad as all are saying.</u>

_____ . Cannot breathe easily. Cannot sleep despite the laudanum. Cannot eat save a bit of apple geranium jelly—(kindly dropped off here by Johanna van Dyck)—smeared on toast; & a cup of Earl Grey diluted with cream & honey; & a midday meal of bread pudding brushed with confectioner's sugar—that is all my poor stomach can tolerate, no matter that the doctor scolds, & Horace as well. (But the bread pudding had so curious a taste, though it is an old recipe of Minnie's, I wonder if poison was brushed onto it; the "powdered" sugar which is ARSENIC.)

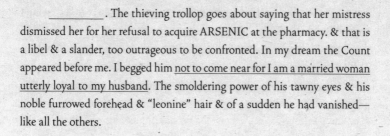

_____ . The thieving trollop goes about saying that her mistress dismissed her for her refusal to acquire ARSENIC at the pharmacy. & that is a libel & a slander, too outrageous to be confronted. In my dream the Count appeared before me. I begged him not to come near for I am a married woman utterly loyal to my husband. The smoldering power of his tawny eyes & his noble furrowed forehead & "leonine" hair & of a sudden he had vanished—like all the others.

_____ . At last after weeks of my importuning Cousin Mandy comes to visit. Insincere apologies as her widow's weeds are insincere & a harlot-smile The Count sends his deepest regrets, Adelaide, being much taken up by last-minute preparations for a trip to the West. I did not berate my cousin but smiled with disarming sweetness. It is wildly accused of her, she poisoned poor Edgerstoune in Bermuda, though others claim it was but a ridiculous accident—the fool, barefoot, stepped on a poisonous jellyfish! (As if, barefoot or no, one would wish to step on a jellyfish, poisonous or no.) & it is wildly accused of Amanda, her little Terence bears no resemblance to the late Edgerstoune but to the Count himself—(though cooler heads prevail, noting that Count von Gneist did not appear at Drumthwacket until after the baby had been born). Soon we laughed, & wept a bit; for Edgerstoune was the noblest of men; & had been the most devoted of husbands. My cousin is handsomely dressed, as always; as a widow, she is most fashionable; around her throat a Japanese silk shawl of Sebastapol blue, & new smartly heeled leather boots from the new Italian cobbler on Guyot St. of whom everyone is talking.

_____ . He is in the City, as he calls it—The City! They have all left me for I have driven them away & I do not care. I am sickly & bored & murderous & cannot conceive what Mrs. Blavatsky means by the temporal penumbra, that is to be transcended. A wildness comes over me, I shall set the velvet draperies in this sick-room on fire, I shall tumble & smash my medicines onto the bed, I shall sink my teeth into one chocolate after another until the box is entirely emptied; yes & spit the creams, cherries, truffles, walnuts, caramels, or whatnot, onto the carpet. Pah! I despise you all. The Count sends his deepest regrets dear Adelaide he has found true passion elsewhere. Mrs. Biddle dares to send up her card! Mrs. Armour & Mrs. Pyne! I shall gaze upon your pleading white faces as the Anarchists open fire & I shall feel no pity saying I do not know you, not a one of you.

The opening of the third eye is, it is claimed, the most exquisite pain—and the most exquisite pleasure.

I shall be a <u>devi</u> perhaps. Ascending in my etheric body to the higher penumbra.

_____ . This morning the bedchamber is too cold. A draft from an ill-fitting window. By midday, it has grown too warm. The girl bungles & fumbles & bites her lower lip as she sets up my fan, for she is a dolt, fearing electricity. I see that she is dark-skinned in the Red Indian way, & with lips not entirely Negroid lips, for her ancestry is mongrel of course. & her hair coarse & straight, like a Lenape Indian's. She is frightened of switching on the fan but I insist she must do so whereupon the broad, smooth, sharp, gracefully curved blades begin to turn, slowly at first, then with a soothing effect upon my fevered face.

_____ . Unable to sleep, for Horace is returned from The City; & I never know when he will <u>say good night</u> to me, & what his breath will smell of, & how staggering & uncertain his step. By candlelight reading Mrs. Corelli's <u>The Traitorous Bridegroom</u> till my eyes ached. Cannot determine if the tale is a literary masterpiece but it is painfully true. & then my volume of Dickinson's verse which I nightly peruse, & a few pages of Whitman, to stir the blood; then, my "forbidden" volume of medical lore which I must hide from Horace & Dr. Boudinot alike, <u>Medical Inquiries & Observations on the Diseases of the Mind</u> by Benjamin Rush, M.D. (One of the chapters titled "The Morbid State of the Sexual Appetites" is quite terrifying & in its obscenity, unspeakable. I had not known that a man could write such words, & that any publisher would print them. For in truth <u>I had not known that there were such monstrous things in the civilized world.</u>)

_____ . Why did you not bring Baby Terence with you, I wished to ask my cousin Mandy. Why is it, so few of your neighbors & friends have seen Terence. & is it so, poor Edgerstoune was often in The City in the days & nights preceding your trip to Bermuda?

_____ . "Is it too late for me to have a tiny baby of my own?"—so I quite shocked prune-faced Dr. Boudinot the other day, who stammered a reply so insulting to me, I conspired to overturn a tea tray, and send a pot of hot steaming water into the gentleman's _____ .

_____ . (How good it feels, to write out such an obscenity: _____ . In this diabolical code of mine, no one will ever decipher it; & surely not Horace who is clumsy at charades as a goat on stilts.)

_____ . Johanna van Dyck dropped by saying that she very much wished to see me as she was leaving soon for Quatre Face, overlooking the Delaware Water Gap, for a much-needed rest; she & the baby & a small household staff; but not Pearce, who must remain at the university of course, & whose health does not allow him to travel. Though I wished to see Johanna, yet for some reason I screamed at Griselda to send her away; for I am devastated, poor Puss <u>is deemed unworthy of having a baby</u>, while Johanna who is years older has had her baby. It is unjust!

& my Horace is always in The City; or hidden away in his bedchamber at the far end of the corridor where—(I have heard him, I think)—he weeps & gnashes his teeth.

_____ . "Puss? Dear Puss! Do look at your anxious Horace, <u>do</u>."

Drawing a chair close beside the divan it is Horace looking most anxious indeed, & my stern heart melts; for I have wronged my husband, I think; or, in the confusion of my laudanum dreams, Horace has wronged <u>me</u>. He complains of the airlessness of the room, & the "queer" odors, & the "heavy gloom" of the draperies, & my smoke-darkened lamp. His face is freshly shaven, it seems; his eyes burn with yearning; I cannot help but observe how he has so gnawed upon his left thumbnail, the very skin surrounding it is raw & bleeding. <u>Do not touch me, do not come so close, I cannot bear to be touched</u>—so I beg; <u>Do not leave me, do not abandon me, I am your lawful wedded wife who loves you dearly</u>—so I plead.

_____ . (In Dr. Rush's book, the unspeakable lusts of which the animal-in-man is capable have been recorded in unflinching detail. One by one these pages shall be fed into the little fire in my fireplace, which the boy Abraham shall set for me; one by one, such loathsome revelations put to the flame. Slyboots Puss will hold her tongue & hint not a word. For they would punish her horribly if they knew of her discovery—the Reverends & Bogeymen of Princeton.)

_____ . Dear Aunt Prudence dropped by this afternoon; or was it yesterday. My heart leapt with hope at the sight of the woman's sunny & unperturbed face, though softened with age, & lined with many creases, yet Aunt Pru smiles happily; for she has made the rounds of the houses from Wheatsheaf to Pembroke, from Drumthwacket to Mora, from Westland to Crosswicks, giving the females of the household, as she claims, a sampling of white witchcraft—(mouse-ear, hawkweed, periwinkle, Atropa belladonna, edelweiss, mandrake, cloudberry tea, dog-bane tea, & "live-forever")—& never exhibits very much care of her own. Aunt Pru winks at me promising, "What is to be, is to *be*. We can hope to be but precipitators."

_____ . (It seems that, at Wheatsheaf, my dear aunt Pru was encountered by the Slades' son Todd who told her, in a lowered voice so that his mother could not hear, that all of her "white-witch-foolery" could have no lasting effect against the "Curse.")

_____ . For Horace, to win back his love: a blend of edelweiss, Atropa belladonna, & a tiny pinch of dog-bane to be dissolved, Aunt Pru suggests, in his tea. & for Adelaide who is all nerves, a powder of "live-forever" & cloudberry—(this last once used by the Lenni-Lenape Indians of this area of New Jersey to assist them in difficult childbirths).

When I asked my aunt if it was too late for me to have a baby she seemed stunned as if I had whispered an obscenity to her out of Dr. Rush's compendium of horrors; but then recovered to say, with a mysterious smile—"What is to be, is to <u>be</u>."

_____ . I shall scribble a note to Reverend Slade, though he is but "Winslow Slade" among us now; yet, he is the man who confirmed me in my faith, & I shall not forget him in his prime. I will beg from him spiritual solace of the kind that once satisfied our elders & our ancestors; I will write to the Count as well, a note to give to the boy to post, for this European noble-man in our midst is yet a houseguest at Drumthwacket, I believe, though traveling in the West. (If, indeed, the Count is traveling, as Mandy claimed.) Ah, what measures will I not take! For I am not feeble; I am still a relatively young woman, in the fourth decade of my life. I might easily ring my maid & be dressed & have my hair properly fashioned & clothe myself in the latest Worth styles & a carriage summoned for me & I know not what-all else: for a train journey to the Philadelphia McLeans would not be unthinkable; or a train journey in the company of my headstrong young cousin Wilhelmina, to New York City; or a journey by White Star steamer to London, Paris, Gi-braltar, Istanbul . . . It is spring, my pulses leap! Shall I not astonish the prim prune-faces of Princeton by sailing in a sleek line-o'packet ship to the South Polar region, which the great Robert Falcon Scott has lately explored; shall I not resume my artist vocation, & bring along my large sketch-book, & commit a series of drawings of the emperor penguin colony of Antarctica, to amaze & delight the world?*

(Though I suppose it might be more reasonable to plan a journey to the East Indies where my great-uncle Reginald Kirkpatrick McLean is Major-General of the Bengal Artillery, stationed at New Delhi—so very far from the evils of the Curse, I should feel quite safe. For white people are treated with much honor in India, as I understand it; especially those of us of English an-cestry. & how astonished & jealous Horace would be, to receive photographs of his dear Puss, carried on an elephant's back!)

(Here is a curiosity, by the by: Aunt Pru whispered to me that Lenora Slade queried her the other day about a very curious matter. Though Mrs.

---

* A note here will be helpful, I think! For Adelaide Burr had certainly been reading Captain Scott's The Voyage of the Discovery in its excerpted form in the Atlantic, to which Horace Burr subscribed; and clearly she had been moved by the skillful drawings of penguins by Edward A. Wilson, one of the officers of the Discovery expedition of 1901–04. It is this historian's thrilling discovery to have come across the issues of the Atlantic containing these, that had once belonged to Horace and Adelaide Burr of Maidstone House, sold at auction amid a large carton of books and journals which I was able to acquire, in 1952, for a sum of twenty-two dollars!

Slade began by asking in a playful manner which "love potions" might be most effective in winning back Copplestone's love & devotion, she then proceeded, during the course of the conversation, to inquire of <u>white bane-berry, common nightshade, bittersweet nightshade & bluebeard lily</u>: which of them might "grind up the finest" & be "undetectable" in a heated drink or if mixed with dough & sweetened with sugar. (For, Aunt Pru tells me, <u>these are all poisons</u>; & however Lenora Slade came to know of them, she could not imagine!) So, Aunt Pru "gently dissuaded" Mrs. Slade, & Mrs. Slade said, with a hurt little laugh, that her interest was "wholly scientific" & "best forgotten.")

Woke this morning feeling that I badly missed my dear headstrong cousin Wilhelmina whom (it is said) her parents have "all but disowned" for her insistence upon taking up residence in New York City, in some "squalid Bohemian" quarter near Washington Square Park; most shockingly, an <u>un-chaperoned residence</u>. Still, I sent a note over to Pembroke, addressed to her, which I hope the elder Burrs will forward & not discard out of meanness.

_____ . (Still there is talk in Princeton of the recent "Snake Frenzy" in Rocky Hill, & of my cousin's unexplained role in it. In some quar-ters, poor Wilhelmina Burr is pitied, that she was the victim of both an inva-sion of snakes from the Millstone River at spring flood-time & the disapproval of her headmistress, who promptly "fired" her for not reacting responsibly to the schoolgirls' hysteria; in other quarters, it is believed that Willy herself summoned forth the snakes, in some ill-advised & bravado effort of impress-ing giddy school-girls with her <u>emancipated bluestocking powers</u>. & so I hope to speak with Willy, to find out which is true, or whether there is a third ex-planation.)

_____ . Off-white satin, with a "drop-away" skirt & but a few very subtle stitched pleats at the back waistline & a double row of those exquisite silken lilies-of-the-valley that Annabel Slade wore on her wedding day. & a "bib" in front, with a deep oval of fine Portuguese lace, trimmed with beaded braiding. A monobosom, for that style is both chaste & fashionable & suited to my diminutive figure.

The wedding train, I think, will be my own, old train—it is carefully wrapped in a closet in this very room, I believe. Untouched, like my bridal gown, for fifteen years.

_____ . A lighted fire in my little marble fireplace that is so rarely utilized; & here is Horace close beside my divan reading aloud from <u>The Smart Set & McClure's</u>, to entertain his Puss. In the demon-dancing firelight his skin is unnaturally pitted & mottled; & it seems clear, a stranger often gazes through his eyes. <u>But I must give no sign that I know</u>. & then, as I have been yawning, Horace slyly puts aside his reading matter & dares to remove one of the slender books of verse on my bedside table, beneath Mrs. Fern's; to my astonishment he leafs through <u>Poems</u> of Emily Dickinson, with a frowning leer, & wets his lips with a quick-darting tongue, & dares to reach, fumblingly at first & then with more authority, as if such verse were not utterly alien to him but familiar—

> A narrow Fellow in the Grass
> Occasionally rides—
> You may have met Him—did you not
> His notice sudden is—
> The Grass divides as with a Comb—
> A spotted shaft is seen—
> And then it closes at your feet
> And opens further on. . . .
> Several of Nature's People
> I know, and they know me—
> I feel for them a transport
> Of Rhapsody—
> But never met this Fellow
> Attended, or alone
> Without a tighter breathing
> And Zero at the Bone—

—his strangely tremulous voice ending so abruptly, you can see that he expects the poem to be longer. The heightened tension in the bedchamber is such, these enigmatic lines of Dickinson have the effect of tightening a wire; a wire that is already quite tight, and now made tighter; the <u>narrow fellow in the grass</u> seemed to rise before me, & flick his demon-tongue, & suddenly, I know not why, I was laughing, & then I was crying, & quickly Horace set aside the book of poems, & tried to take my hands, to calm me. & after some minutes, I allowed myself to appear calm; though my heart beat wildly, yet I hid my distress; or I did not want to upset Horace further, I feared the man's temper & the strangeness in his own unfathomed soul. Then, as it was nearing my bedtime of 9 P.M., Horace turned his attentions to the tray of desserts Minnie had prepared for us, & two glasses of warmed milk; Horace spooned into my mouth morsels of a blueberry tart, which was most delicious, yet unnaturally sweet, I thought. At once my temples pounded & my eyes watered as with the onset of a migraine & I did not hesitate to confront Horace boldly—"Are these blueberries truly, and not <u>bluebeard-lily</u>? For that is a poison, you know." At this remark my guileless husband stared & blinked & plucked nervously at his mustache; then leaned forward as if fearing I might by some convulsive means fall from the divan & injure myself. At this, I may have struck out blindly with my fists & elbows & cried—"You are trying to poison me! <u>You & she</u>! Do you think that I don't know about this <u>she</u>—for I can smell the civet-cat odor on all your clothing . . ." Horace protested, he had no idea what I was talking about; & staggered to his feet, & backed away from me, & what happened next, I do not know—for it seems, I must have fainted; & there was Horace passing my vial of smelling salts beneath my nose, to revive me.

"Dearest Puss! You must know—<u>I love only you</u>."

_____ . At last my cousin Wilhelmina has condescended to answer my very sweet letter to her, not in reproach but in the most lightsome teasing way asking when she would drop by to see her poor abandoned cousin, & her reply is hurried & brusque & took no time obviously for it is attached to a crudely printed poster advertising <u>YOUNG ARTISTS SPRING EXHIBIT NEW YORK SCHOOL OF ART APRIL–MAY</u>—a boastful gesture since it is implied that Wilhelmina Burr as "W. BURR" has several drawings in the exhibit, on Tenth Street at Fifth Avenue, NYC. <u>As if I would make the disagreeable journey to Manhattan, to see so crude & amateur an exhibit! Nor would Horace wish to accompany me to such a place, I am certain.</u>

_____ . Now I am most cautious of all that passes between my lips. Now I am shrewd enough to invite Griselda to drink, to eat, to sample what she has brought me on a tray, though the supposition is that Minnie prepared it. & suddenly I am very tired of them all, like a minstrel-show Greek chorus chattering & nattering away in worry of their mistress Adelaide. If the Count will only come, & take me away! I am sure it is time, by now.

_____ . Psalm 71. In Thee, O Lord, do I put my trust: let me never be put to confusion. Deliver me in Thy righteousness, & cause me to escape: incline Thine ear unto me, & save me.

(AUTHOR'S NOTE: Here is a letter hastily written by Adelaide Burr, *not coded,* and addressed, as the reader will see, to Winslow Slade: a letter that will be found in the pages of the secret journal after Mrs. Burr's death, for it was never sent, nor even slipped into an envelope to be addressed and stamped.)

5 MAY 1906
MIDNIGHT

Dear Dr. Slade—
   This Curse I wish to warn of, & this is the Curse I am beginning now to explain, this is a secret I must reveal, & which I plead with you as my spiritual advisor—(though we have not seen each other face to face, in any mood of intimacy for many years, dear Reverend Slade)—to comprehend, & to share with me; this Curse you must save us from, & pray God to save us from, for ONLY YOU DR. SLADE can save us, I must acknowledge that now. These many months I have pursued "strange gods"—to no resolution. For I know now less than I knew as a girl kneeling before you, to receive my first communion from your chaste fingers, as one day years later I knelt to make my wedding vows beside my dear bridegroom

Horace Burr. This is a warning I wish to sound through the village of Princeton & through all of the Nation, that there is something happening to us that has been happening from the time of our births, & we have been unknowing. It is the Shadow that falls over us, that blinds us, we cannot see what the Shadow obscures. This is a story I must tell hurriedly for Horace may detect the faint candlelight beneath my bedroom door. Horace may deduce, his wife is exposing her soul to another man, as she had not ever exposed her soul to him.

Now it is past midnight in Princeton & Old North has tolled & this is the Curse to be explained, the presence in those among us enshadowed & obscured & unnamed & in their corporeal being wicked, steeped in evil, not knowing that I gazed full upon them, though perhaps the Brute does know, it is like them to sense such things. I have lighted my candle with steady fingers & I have arisen from my sickbed on shaky but determined legs & I have wrapt my vale-of-Kashmir shawl close about my frame. This is the Curse, this is the Horror of the Curse, you must pray God to save us from. I glided from the room & slipped noiseless into the hallway & in the direction of Horace's (darkened) bedchamber all a-quiver that someone might discover me, Oh! it is the invalid-mistress of Maidstone, we have not seen in so long; Oh! it is the hysterical woman she will injure herself with such exertions, return her to her bed, put her to bed, to bed, put out her light in her bed, forever & ever TO BED. Paid no heed but gliding soundless along the hall, he shall be affrighted by Lilith, he shall be seduced by a succubus, he shall impregnate the demon-wraith, all unknowing. For a baby will be born of the Curse, to defy the Curse. Tall shadows cast by my candle leaping & swaying in a hellish dance, & this one, the one I am telling you of, the master of Maidstone House these many years, he is not in his bedchamber—as I knew; as I suspected, & in my heart I knew; for all that is happening & shall happen to me from which you must save me, Reverend Slade, upon receipt of this desperate letter, if you can. This one lay not in his bed as I knew, for I knew, for it could be no secret from me, the church bells having sounded their final strokes of midnight, & the Birds of Night softly calling, cooing; & I saw the toss'd bedclothes & the rumpled pillowcases & a single glove lying on the carpet, partway beneath the bed, so that only the fingers were visible, a most alarming sight yet my presence of mind prevailed for this is the story I must tell of the awareness in my soul of such evil, unspeakable evil for which there is no name, though they will deride me & call me hysterical, bundle her off to bed, to Otterholm, to bed, to bed forever & ever. Paying no heed but bravely pressing forward perusing the crumpled letters lying scattered atop Horace's bureau & on the carpet, MY DEAREST —MY BELLE DAME SANS MERCI—MY PRECIOUS LOVE—MY CRUEL & BEAUTEOUS TEMPTRESS—MY JOY & AGONY—MY SWEET MY ADORED MY RAPTUROUS "WILLY"—& you can imagine the bitter laugh that passed my lips, you can imagine the dagger turned in my heart, though certainly I knew, if it was not my cousin Wilhelmina who has turned slut & harlot it is another's cousin, as your own dear granddaughter Annabel "turned"—& the Fiend is her bridegroom, in Hell. Shall I confess I would rather have discovered the sooty-greasy smell of Griselda or of Hannah in my husband's bed— (shall I confess, I am not altogether certain that the father of Hannah's baby was not the master of Maidstone House, for it is whispered that poor Hannah suffered greatly in giving birth, in a cabin on Province Line Road where relatives had taken her in). Shall I confess, nothing would surprise me, Reverend Slade! Recalling how several years ago in a fitful midday nap I chanced to hear shuffling & murmuring & what seemed to me muffled laughter in the corridor outside my bedchamber & I thought, The wenches imagine their mistress too weak-minded to discover them, & I threw off the covers & quickly tiptoed to the door & opened it wide & was thunderstruck to discover MY OWN HUSBAND CROUCHED BY THE KEYHOLE

ON HIS KNEES; & what I had taken for laughter was weeping
& unmanly sobbing, & this is the Curse I must warn of, this
is the habit of the male in his blood & marrow that the Bible
has warned us, & pray God this night to save me, as the Psalm
has promised, & you will recall, Reverend Slade, that you did
promise, for this husband I am speaking of, this lawful wedded
Christian husband who had vowed kneeling before you at the
altar to love & honor his wife Adelaide in sickness & in health,
was to be discovered in a harlot's embrace in the carriage
house, by moonlight; a curdled-milk-moonlight; a most sickly
moonlight; & in my night-robe & shawl & in thin silk slippers
in the chill air of early May in the hour past midnight I had not
time for prayer, I had not time to steel myself for the hellish
sight I would see, peeping past the stalls in which the horses
are kept, I saw my tremulous candle-flame reflecting in the
horses' great staring eyes, they did not startle me, they did not
frighten me, nor did the lustful creatures discovered in their
intimate embrace startle, only just disgust; hideous unspeakable
adultery, my husband showering kisses upon my own beloved
cousin Wilhelmina Burr, she might be a daughter to the man,
she might be a blood-relative to the man, this schoolgirl friend
of your granddaughter Annabel who has been led to Hell, I
think this is what I must say, I think this is why I am appealing
to you, my cousin Willy has been damned by her friendship
with your granddaughter who is damned; I saw all, & could not
turn away; I saw all, & know that I must proclaim it; hideous
swooning embrace of naked bodies, rabid kisses, shameless
male murmuring O MY LOVE MY SWEET CRUEL WILLY-
LOVE WHAT SHOULD I NOT DO FOR YOU, FOR THIS—
the man's impatient caresses, & the young woman's faint
protest; eyes by ghastly moonlight shuttered, for shame; Oh &
the sucking lips!—it is too awful, I am sick to recall. This is the
Curse of the Horror that is happening to us, Reverend Slade. It
is the Curse of the Horror of Hell erupting in our sequestered
world. What sin we have perpetrated, we do not know—we

are innocent, as we are ignorant. As my girl-cousin failed
to stop my husband's mauling hands, & could not dissuade
his gnawing mouth & protruding tongue, like some terrible
species of deep-sea fish or sea-worm; this is the Curse of the
Horror, Reverend Slade, in his lust he would wish to strangle
poor Puss in her bed, to rid himself of poor sickly Puss though
she loves him & has always been faithful to him. Oh! she is a
hysterical female, let us dose her with medicines, let us wrap
her in her bed as in her shroud, let us stifle her screams with
the highest quality goose-feather pillow, let us tip this candle
from its holder into her bed, let us cut her into pieces with her
electric fan, Oh! she cannot be believed, she is telling lies, she is
damned, & she is doomed: the Mistress of Maidstone.

But it is not Horace who approaches, opening the door of my
bedchamber—to my surprise & delight it is a gentleman known
to me though I have never glimpsed him before, as I am known
to him; a tall individual, with "leonine" hair; a craggy brow,
& heavy eyebrows; an aquiline nose; & the most mesmerizing
topaz eyes . . . For here is my friend Count English von Gneist
at last. & so 'tis. I have not been snubbed after all, as Mandy
would have wished. & the Princeton ladies need not laugh up
their sleeves at Mrs. Adelaide Burr. "Please come inside, dear
Count, I have been awaiting you. Please excuse me if I am
nervous, or anxious—it is not the feeling I harbor for you in
my heart, you must understand." & the Count approaches my
bed, & stoops above me, to bow; taking my chill fingers in his
& implanting on the back of my hand a kiss of such lightness, it
feels like very light itself; yet will sting, & burn, like a hot copper
penny pressed into the flesh. "My dear Mrs. Burr, at last."

DR. SCHUYLER SKAATS WHEELER'S
NOVELTY MACHINE

The letter to Winslow Slade seems never to have been completed, and signed; of course, it was never slipped into an envelope to be addressed and stamped and posted.

Instead, it would be discovered between the pages of Adelaide's (coded) journal, after the invalid's death.

It is not known, nor can I force myself to imagine, what happened on the night of May 5, 1906, in the upstairs of Maidstone House, on Library Place, Princeton.

Much has been written on the subject of course. But I am not of a mind to paraphrase it here. For I feel, I think, such pity for dear exasperating Adelaide!—*poor Puss* as the invalid calls herself. Such pity, and such *sorrow*.

So long as the invalid had her pen in hand, she was most lively—mischievous, merry, despairing, damn'd—yet, alive. But now, the pen has been rudely snatched from her fingers, & she is silenced forever.

***

IT WOULD BE early the next morning, at approximately 8 A.M., when Mrs. Burr's maid Griselda cautiously made her way to the invalid's room, to stand outside her door as Mrs. Burr had instructed her, to listen, and try to determine if Mrs. Burr was still slumbering in her bed, or "up"—(by which is not meant "up" in a literal sense, but simply awake)—and needing assistance. This morning, Griselda did indeed hear sounds inside the bedchamber, but could not guess what they were; though afterward she would tell how the hairs stirred at the nape of her neck, as a terrible fear passed into her, of what she would discover inside: the master of Maidstone House sprawled but partly dressed in his wife's bed, amid blood-soaked bedclothes; rocking the limp, lifeless, and bloodied body of his wife in his arms, and humming, and crooning, and softly laughing in the way of a delighted lover.

Mr. Burr was seen to be deranged; yet subdued and tractable, as if knowing that the worst had come to pass, and was behind him.

Griselda gave a scream, dropped her tray of breakfast things, ran back downstairs to the kitchen in such distress, the household staff followed her out into Hodge Road without comprehending what she was trying to say; soon then, an alarm went out, and authorities were summoned.

It could not have been more than a quarter hour later that as two astonished and appalled Princeton Borough police officers entered the bedroom, Mr. Burr did not signal alarm, or irritation; though these were intruders in his house, in his wife's very bedchamber, and he and his wife were but partly clothed, he seemed unperturbed and continued to rock gently to and fro while embracing the much-ravaged corpse of his wife, and singing a fragment of a Stephen Foster song—

> Ah! May the red rose live al-way
> To smile upon earth and sky!
> Why should the beau-ti-ful ever weep
> Why should the beau-ti-ful die—?

With a measure of dignity, Horace Burr detached himself from his wife, and from the blood-soaked bedclothes where he was believed to have lain for at least ten hours, and managed to stand; as if to invite the police officers farther into the room, as they appeared frozen at the threshold, gape-mouthed in horror. With no preamble, Mr. Burr confessed to the act—"The consequences of which are undeniable." He would explain to authorities that he had *put his wife out of her misery as an act of mercy,* and hoped that God would spare his soul, even as, he knew, his peers would judge him harshly, as he must be judged.

As to how the ghastly murder was committed, I am not altogether certain. Nor do I want to speculate, heedlessly. It must suffice to note that, taken into custody with the bloodied Horace Burr, and handled with especial care, and no little repugnance, was a certain ingenious mechanism comprised of sharp-swirling fans, recently bought for the invalid in her airless and overheated chambers.

QUATRE FACE

1.

To confront the Curse that threatens us all."

The unspeakable murder of Adelaide Burr by the husband who had long been devoted to her so rocked Princeton, Pearce van Dyck became distraught with worry that, in the wilds of Raven Rock, Pennsylvania, his wife Johanna and their infant son might yet be "at risk"; and decided to sever his responsibilities to the university several weeks before the end of term, to move to Quatre Face—"For the Curse must be countered head-on, by a stratagem of *rationality*."

It was even a part of Dr. van Dyck's plan, initially, that he might talk Percy Boudinot, Dr. Boudinot's doctor-son, into taking a temporary residency in the old country estate, if Johanna's continued ill health, following the birth of the baby, did not improve.

For it had developed, evidently, that Mrs. van Dyck was "not well"— suffered from "mysterious pains" and a "lingering malaise"; and that the baby, only five pounds six ounces at birth, was gaining weight at a less than normal pace.

In Princeton, little was known of Johanna van Dyck since she had taken residence at Quatre Face. Few persons in Princeton, excepting very close friends of the van Dyck family, had ever visited the country estate on the Delaware River that had originally been built a hundred years before, and did not have the reputation of being one of the architectural gems of the Delaware Valley. Female relatives and friends of Johanna's had not been invited to visit her, nor had her replies to their inquiring letters been encouraging; often, Johanna did no more than scribble a reply on the back of a letter, to the effect that she and the baby were *doing very well, if not exactly flourishing; but quite required the calm & quiet & distance of Quatre Face, & not the harrying bustle of Princeton.*

It was doubted, among some of Johanna's women friends, that this was true: for Johanna had not wanted to move to the country, having failed to recover entirely from the ravages of childbirth; nor had she wanted the baby to be so far from decent medical attention, if that was required. But Pearce had insisted. Pearce had become quite uncharacteristically emotional, in insistence. And so, unhappily, Johanna had given in.

"A remove from Princeton is for the sake of the child, as much as for you, Johanna. You must be rational."

Johanna bowed her head, for this was so. Her husband in his "new" phase—(as a "new" father?)—was so adamant in his speech, and his gaze so fraught with dislike, if anyone opposed him, she had learned simply to give in, as the most accommodating measure. And excused herself, to retire to the nursery where she might play with the baby, bathe and nurse the baby and sing to him, as a mother might do; for Pearce was uneasy if Johanna "serviced" the baby, as he called it, in his presence.

Few persons knew, and Johanna did not wish them to know, that Pearce allowed the baby in his presence only rarely; and kept his distance from the nursery, to the extent of taking to using the back stairs to and from the second floor of the house, to avoid passing by the nursery in which the door was usually kept open.

Nor did Pearce inquire after the baby, which had become Johanna's entire subject of conversation, or nearly; until she asked of him, one evening at dinner, "Pearce, don't you like—*love*—your little son?"; and Pearce said, with a thoughtful little frown, "Yes. Of course. As his 'father' I am bound to like—*love*—him. As, as your husband, I am bound to *you*."

Soon after this exchange, Pearce made arrangements for Johanna and the child, and a small household staff, to take up residence at Quatre Face.

AFTER THE TRAGEDY at Maidstone House, in fact within twenty-four hours of the terrible news, a gravely shaken Pearce van Dyck appeared at the Nassau Hall office of the university president, with no appointment scheduled, to appeal to Dr. Wilson for an "emergency leave of absence" from his university duties, that he might take up residence at Raven Rock with his wife and infant son, who were living there temporarily.

Dr. Wilson was taken by surprise, for Professor van Dyck did appear agitated, and had not properly shaved; his linen was visibly not fresh, and the shoelace of one of his shoes was untied. (For such was the effect of Mrs. van Dyck's absence from the professor's household and from his intimate life.) Dr. Wilson was surprised too, by the request, of a sort that would ordinarily be made months beforehand, from one of the most responsible and renowned of Princeton professors as well as one, Dr. Wilson believed, who had generally supported *him*.

"It's scarcely a secret now, Woodrow, that there is a Curse on our community—not just Crosswicks. Evil has been erupting, emerging—whether a swarm of poisonous snakes in Rocky Hill or, so recently, the unspeakable murder at Maidstone House—our Hodge Road neighbor! *Can you believe it*—Horace Burr! A great-great-grandson of our revered Aaron Burr, Sr.! And Horace has been so generous in his donations to the university . . . All that will end now, I suppose. As the Burrs had no immediate heir, the fortune will go to relatives."

Pearce van Dyck spoke rapidly, nervously. Woodrow Wilson listened with his customary inexpressive calm, that so unsettled certain of his associates and adversaries, who complained that the man was maddeningly *inscrutable;* until such time as he began to speak, when he was maddeningly *transparent.*

"The most problematic issue in all this, Woodrow, as you know, is that it's impossible to tell who was 'one of us'—and who is 'one of them.'"

"'Them'—?"

"Demons."

"Demons!"

At this, Dr. Wilson did betray a quicksilver sort of emotion, that rippled across his long narrow "lantern-jawed" face: a look of alarm, and a look of comprehension.

"There are 'demons,' you know. This 'Axson Mayte'—for one. And there have been others."

Gravely, Dr. Wilson nodded. He had made some effort to push out of his memory his several days' friendship with the charismatic Mayte; and was relieved that Professor van Dyck seemed to know nothing about it.

"And now there is this 'Count van Gneist' staying at Drumthwacket. Who in hell is *he*?"

The philosophy professor spoke harshly, with a peal of laughter.

"The name is *von Gneist,* I believe," Woodrow Wilson said stiffly, "and the man is a renowned European theologian, and something of a political theorist. He is hardly a 'demon,' Pearce! In fact, I have invited him to give the Helms Lecture at Commencement."

"The Helms Lecture! That's quite an honor, sir."

"Well. English von Gneist is an honorable man."

Pearce van Dyck, absently stroking his jaw, looked as if he had more to say on this subject, but thought better of it, considering the tone of Dr. Wilson's voice.

Sternly now Woodrow Wilson inquired if Pearce had spoken with his departmental chair about this "leave of absence"; if he'd looked into arrangements for his preceptors and other colleagues to take over his classes, exams and grading, etc. As it seemed to have passed between them, that

Dr. Wilson would grant his unorthodox request for an immediate leave, which the dean of the faculty would have rejected summarily, as outrageous and unprofessional.

As Pearce would declare, in a letter dashed off that afternoon to his wife at Quatre Face—*I'd expected more of a fight from Wilson for you know, I am crucial to the philosophy department. But—the man gave in at once! This is good news! I will be at your side within another day.*

"I WILL CRACK the damned code. For a code is to be *cracked*."

Freed from the strenuous round of academic and scholarly routine, his imagination given a belated freedom by the romantic isolation of Quatre Face, Pearce van Dyck soon believed that he'd begun to perceive the pattern by which the Curse might be recognized. For certainly, like all "mysteries" it would yield to calm and systematic analytic thought, if one but took time.

While Johanna and a nursemaid "serviced" the baby—(a preoccupation that seemed to require an infinite amount of time)—Pearce hid away in his study, or hiked along the bank of the Delaware River, where there was a narrow path through briars; at some distance from the old country house, Pearce squinted at the weatherworn limestone structure with its heavy sloping roofs and blackened chimneys through myopic eyes—*Why, it has become a ruin! I have brought my beloved little family to live in a ruin!*—but soon turned away, and resumed his walk; for the decoding of the Crosswicks Curse must draw his fullest attention, not a trivial concern with domestic life.

"If necessary, I will sacrifice 'domestic life.' If I am called, and no one else—if I am *chosen* . . ."

For such is the efficacy of logic, Pearce reasoned. Whether it is the abstract logic of Aristotle or Spinoza, or the more practical logic of Sherlock Holmes, what is confusing becomes clear; and one laughs afterward at having been puzzled. But of course, to attain this end *one must work.*

So, Pearce applied himself to the riddle of the Curse, often staying up through much of the night and resisting Johanna's entreaties that he come to bed, as that he take his meals with greater regularity. But Pearce was convinced that the mystery was close to being penetrated, for the "methodology" of the death of Adelaide Burr was certainly a clue—"Staring us all in the face, probably."

It was rare for Pearce to speak of such matters to Johanna, for when he did, the woman invariably responded with an inane, or uninformed, or (deliberately?) provocative response, as at this time—

"But Pearce, Horace is not a *fiend*. He is—he was—one of our neighbors, and our friend. It must have been some fit of madness that came over him. All the letters from Princeton say that he had been drinking heavily, and . . ."

"And yet," Pearce said, pointedly ignoring his wife's naïve remarks, "why did the Fiend so *torture* the poor woman? An invalid after all, and piteous. And what does it mean, that so eccentric a 'murder weapon' was involved? In all the annals of crime and mystery that I have delved into, there has never been a—an—*electric fan* used for such a purpose."

" . . . and it's said that Horace had been writing letters to Wilhelmina Burr, of the most frank, shocking sort! Wilhelmina turned these over to the police immediately. And a gift he'd given her, an ivory brooch, which had belonged to poor Adelaide—he'd sent anonymously to Wilhelmina. Only imagine! Our neighbors and friends, behaving in such a way . . ."

"They are not 'our neighbors and friends,' Johanna, when the Fiend has influence over them. No more than poor Annabel Slade was Dabney Bayard's bride, when the Fiend exerted his power over *her*."

"Do you know, Pearce, people are saying, in Princeton, that *Wilhelmina drove him to it*. That they might marry, and 'Willy' might inherit the fortune."

At this, Pearce did pause; for Pearce had a new idea, to be added to the Scheme of Clues.

"The snakes, of course! 'Snake Frenzy.' And Wilhelmina 'summoning them forth'—then unable to control them."

"But, Pearce—Wilhelmina did no such thing! Nor did she *drive Horace to murder*—I'm sure. These are just stray bits of rumor reported to me, and not to be taken seriously."

"In a crime investigation, where 'coded mystery' prevails, there is nothing not to be taken seriously."

"The reputation of a young woman like Wilhelmina Burr is a very serious matter. In Princeton, at least. If she moves to New York City, and begins a new life—it won't matter, perhaps."

"With Adelaide so freshly murdered, I hope it won't be a matter of simply awaiting the next horror. If only I could penetrate this *forest of clues* . . ."

"Dear husband, I think it's more important, at this moment, for you to finish your meal; for you eat very poorly now, and have lost too much weight."

Pearce had quite forgotten that it was dinnertime: they were seated in the dimly lighted dining room at Quatre Face, where silken French wallpaper was shadowed with dust, and the view of the river was obscured by overgrown shrubbery like encroaching cataracts. Johanna was correct, Pearce was eating very poorly of late. Meals were virtually untasted by him; instead, he relied upon wine and sherry in the latter part of the day, and very strong black coffee in the morning hours, to fortify his nerves.

"Johanna, I appreciate your solicitude. But I am not a cranky infant, to be 'serviced'—I can take care of myself very well, thank you."

Without finishing his meal, but taking his part-filled wineglass with him, Pearce removed himself from his wife's company to the privacy and comfort of his study.

MOVING TO QUATRE FACE, approximately thirty miles from Princeton, Pearce had packed few articles of clothing and personal items, concentrating instead on books, journals, and the ever-growing impedimenta related to the "Scheme of Clues," that had grown considerably since Josiah Slade's visit, and now took over most of his study on the ground floor of the country house. Pearce had made no effort to bring with him his scholarly philosophical books, which remained in his office at the university. But he'd brought the complete set of Sherlock Holmes mysteries as well as notebooks in which he'd listed primary, secondary, tertiary, and "probable" or "possible" clues to the Curse, in an effort to relate some of these to Conan Doyle's cases, for there was a clear parallel between them, he was certain. The eruption of evil in Princeton, New Jersey, was but a single expression of a multiple Curse, or Horror—the eruption of Evil into the world of humankind, from which we must be saved by one stronger, more courageous and more "inspired" than we are.

"How clear that is! And yet—how to proceed, before another innocent is murdered?"

One afternoon in early May Pearce was in his study concentrating upon these issues when a visitor arrived at Quatre Face, unanticipated—Josiah Slade!

In his low-slung two-seater Winton motorcar the young man had been driving in the vicinity, north of New Hope, when, at the outskirts of Raven Rock, he'd sighted Quatre Face and felt a "sudden yearning" to see his former professor again, and of course Mrs. van Dyck; and to see their new baby now, he believed, at least three months old.

"Why, Josiah! What a surprise! Come in, my boy. Not a moment too soon!"—so Pearce spoke jocularly.

And Johanna was enormously happy to see their young friend—once she overcame her surprise at his arrival.

"You will stay the night, Josiah, I hope? Or two nights, if you can spare the time. We would be so grateful for your company, Pearce, wouldn't we?"

In his jocular mood, Pearce did seem relieved for distraction from his all-consuming work, and for the opportunity to share it with his young friend, to whom it would mean a great deal.

(Pearce took Josiah aside to warn him against bringing up the subject of *the many troubles back in Princeton* in Johanna's company: "I'm afraid for her well-being, she's become distracted and melancholy lately; since the birth of—as you know, *our son*—she eats poorly, and has lost more weight than is normal. I'd hoped to have Dr. Boudinot's son come with me, to examine Johanna, but that didn't quite work out. She complains of the very *quiet* of Quatre Face, though she's upset by the recent news of Maidstone . . . But you know how women are, Josiah, I hope!")

Though Pearce had declared to Johanna how very relieved he was to be freed of university politicking and backbiting, and the ceaseless strata-gems of Woodrow Wilson in his feud with Dean West, yet, now that Josiah was here, he seemed acutely interested in all the news; at the dinner table plying his visitor with every sort of question. The most delicious news, unless it was a rumor, involved the extraordinary Proctor bequest, said to be beyond one million dollars—but earmarked for the office of Dean West and not for the office of the president. So surprised was Pearce by this oddity, he asked Josiah to repeat it. "To Woodrow, it must really seem like witchcraft, that a prominent alumnus would insult the president of the university by singling out the president's enemy for such a prize!"

Josiah murmured that it was a shame, such a renowned scholar and educator as Woodrow Wilson should find himself embroiled in such provincial matters, when there was so much else in life to con-tend with . . . Pearce said, laughing, as if unhearing, "William Cooper Procter, the soapsuds benefactor—Procter & Gamble—such wealth! And so urgently needed for the Graduate College. *Is* it witchcraft? *Is* Andrew West of the devil's party? The rascal! Woodrow will be quite helpless, for he can't refuse such a sum—he would be vilified from every side in Princeton for his vanity and 'sour grapes'; yet, how can he accept it? *Will* he accept it, do you think, Josiah?"

Josiah shrugged, for how could he know?

"I'm not involved in such matters, sir. Even my grandfather Winslow has detached himself."

"And what a shock, and what a tragedy—the events at Maidstone. Of that, Johanna would like us not to speak, but I feel that we must."

Josiah sat silent, with no response; though not liking where this might be headed.

"It is being said that your friend—Wilhelmina Burr—is in some way 'involved.' With Horace, that is. Poor, mad Horace! Perhaps she is quite guiltless—guileless—you know how headstrong young ladies can be nowadays, even from good families . . . She has become an *artiste*, it's said. Have you seen any of her work, Josiah?"

"No. I have not."

"Do you see Miss Burr, often?"

"Almost never."

"And you know, certain materials were found in Adelaide Burr's bedroom."

" 'Certain materials'—?"

"Reading materials."

Pearce spoke grimly, yet with satisfaction. These materials were, he reported, a mixed lot, which Adelaide must have purchased on her own, without Horace's knowledge or complicity: mystical writings by the notorious Madame Blavatsky, verse by wild-eyed poetesses and by the notorious "invert" Walt Whitman, Socialist and Anarchist pamphlets, women's "sensation" novels, even, it was said, a copy of the Kabbalah . . .

"The Kabbalah? The medieval Jewish work? Commentary on the Hebrew Bible?"

Josiah spoke dubiously; for it seemed to him nothing less than preposterous, that one of the West End ladies, and an invalid at that, would have such a book in her possession, along with such other books.

Pearce said, "Yes, it does seem unlikely. Yet, it seems to be so. And Adelaide left behind also a journal, or diary, written in code . . . Perhaps, when it is it decoded, the mystery of why Horace turned upon her as he did will be revealed." Pearce spoke with an air of wistfulness, at the prospect of this *decoding*. He had already applied to the Princeton Borough Police, as to the relatives of the Burrs, offering his services as a *practiced decoder*, but no one had responded.

Josiah, who had transcribed his sister's distraught tale of the Bog Kingdom, which might have been in a kind of code, or demented poetry, fell silent, grateful that no one outside the Slade family knew of Annabel's account.

But Pearce continued to shake his head slowly, with a look of wistful yearning. In the flickering candlelight his skin looked less sickly than it had looked in Princeton, when Josiah had last seen his friend; and the shadowy background of the dining room was such, the seeming "misshapenness" of his skull was not so noticeable, nor so distracting. Indeed, for some minutes he looked to Josiah like Professor van Dyck of old, kindly, avuncular, though youthful, an authoritative presence of considerable charm, who had introduced Josiah to the life of the mind in his freshman year of college. Near the end of the meal he said, in a confidential tone, "It is not for general consumption, Josiah—Johanna has heard it before, of course—but only a few weeks ago, before his hasty 'vacation' in Bermuda, Woodrow had become so desperate that he consulted a Ouija board—or is it a Ouija wheel?—one of those ridiculous occult rituals in which the spirits 'speak'—the future is 'revealed.' Of course, Woodrow made light of it, claiming it to be Ellen's idea; yet he was halfway serious. His revelation was a single message—*Dean West shall fry in Hell & the fat drip from his bones*—sent, by all people, from our dear departed James McCosh. When my informant asked Woodrow if this could be so, and not rather a joke, Woodrow allegedly drew himself up to his full height and said, 'Sir, I do not joke about Hell, or about Andrew West.'"

At which Pearce began to laugh silently, with such mirth that his eyeglasses slipped from his nose, and he soon lapsed into wheezing and coughing, as badly as he had when Josiah had last seen him.

Johanna exchanged worried glances with her young houseguest.

(It should be revealed here, the reason for Josiah's sudden arrival at Quatre Face wasn't accidental, but rather in response to a letter sent to him by Mrs. van Dyck, the previous week; for the troubled wife and mother professed to being "gravely concerned" with her husband's mental well-being, as well as his physical condition, and wondered if it would be possible for Josiah, of whom Pearce was so very fond, to drop by Quatre Face soon—as if by accident. Josiah had not hesitated for a moment, but had made plans at once to drive to Raven Rock to see his old professor.)

Though the hour was late by now, and Pearce was looking clearly tired, yet he insisted upon bringing Josiah into his study, to speak to him in earnest, and at length, about his latest discoveries regarding the Scheme of Clues. He thrust into Josiah's face a sheet of paper upon which was written, in the professor's crabbed hand:

> The existence of Evil—Absolute & untempered by human frailty—
>
> even Pride.
>
> Evil so extreme so powerful mortal Reason cannot comprehend.
>
> Evil—the Devil—(d)evil—the Fiend—God's Wrath— Jehovah with cloven hoof—Sin & Death in eternal copulation to yield—human kind.
>
> The season predating Christ—when the Cross was but Death & mockery.
>
> The season predating Earth—when God was but Chaos & Eternal Night.
>
> Is the terrible secret of the Curse—that it surrounds us & nourishes us? It is the oxygen we breathe, all unknowing?
>
> How to escape the Fiend—
>
> How to exorcise the Curse—

For at least another hour, Pearce van Dyck lectured his young friend, who listened to him with genuine admiration and interest; from time to time, always deferentially, Josiah offered suggestions and (minor) corrections to the Scheme of Clues, for which Pearce expressed gratitude.

"I think that we will work together as an excellent team, Josiah—like Holmes and Watson—if Watson were younger, and sharper-witted than Conan Doyle has described him. We might, you know, even become— 'known' . . ."

"Perhaps, Professor van Dyck. It's something to think about, at least."

"Not 'something to think about'—" Pearce glared at his young friend, now pushing away the Scheme of Clues, and shutting up his notebooks for the night. "Indeed, it *is all there is to think about.*"

"DO YOU THINK he's ill, Josiah? Or just exhausted from overwork?"

So Johanna van Dyck asked her visitor, clasping her hands together in a classic gesture of anxiety, as they stood on the staircase landing, above the darkened first floor of Quatre Face that resembled a vast pool of water beneath their feet.

"I think he's just exhausted, Johanna. If only he could rest . . ."

"If only he could rest his mind! His thoughts! He is so obsessed with what he calls the 'Curse' . . . the 'Horror' . . . Sometimes it seems, he has taken it into himself, like a poison; it has breathed itself *into him*. And what looks out of his eyes, at such times—" Johanna broke off, shuddering.

Josiah said, to change the subject, "Well. In the morning, I hope I will see your little son?"

"Oh yes! Certainly. As early as you like, for he wakes *very* early."

Johanna smiled happily. The subject of the obsessed husband fell away, as the subject of the beloved baby supplanted it.

"And what is his name, Johanna? I must have been told, but I'm afraid I've forgotten."

"His name! Ah—his name! Well—we call him 'baby'—'little one'—Nanny and me. Pearce has put off 'naming' him, for the time being."

"He has put off 'naming him'—? But why?"

"I think perhaps—no name is quite good enough for Pearce's son."

Johanna spoke brightly, but not very convincingly.

"He will choose a name soon, he has promised. Now that he has joined us at Quatre Face. He has promised!"

"Have you considered calling your son 'Pearce, Jr.'?—that would seem a good compromise, if it's difficult to choose another name."

"Yes. I have considered this. But Pearce—well, Pearce is not so sure! 'Maybe "Oedipus" is the name for it!'—so Pearce jokes, in his obscure way. (He has a habit of calling our baby *it*.) But you can ask Pearce yourself, to-morrow, Josiah. Will you?"

"Yes. If you'd like me to . . ."

When Josiah had mentioned to his mother that he was going to visit the van Dycks, at their country place, Henrietta asked him to tell Johanna, for her—*The early months are the trial. You must keep yourself alive for the baby's sake.*

This strange message, Josiah had no intention of imparting to his hostess.

At the door of the sparely furnished guest room the housekeeper had prepared for him, Josiah said good night to Mrs. van Dyck. Their exchange had left Josiah troubled but he smiled at his hostess as if nothing were amiss; in this phase of his young life, in his mid-twenties, surrounded in his own family with so much sorrow and distress, Josiah had learned that a ready smile is the best gift to offer another, in such circumstances, in which words can sound flat and platitudinous, and are of little help.

"Well—good night, Johanna! Thank you for a lovely dinner."

"And thank you for coming, Josiah. I'm almost thinking—you have saved our lives." Johanna's strained face relaxed for just a moment.

Inside the chill room, with its singed-looking wallpaper and high, hard canopied bed, Josiah was to discover a large, lavish bouquet of freshly picked lilacs which Johanna had brought surreptitiously to the room, it seemed. Its rich scent would fill his nostrils, and his turbulent dreams, through the night.

2.

While the others slept—Johanna in her own bedroom, that opened into the nursery; the baby in its crib; and Josiah in one or another guest room—Pearce van Dyck remained in his study, frowning over the Scheme of Clues. He had not liked—though, as a cordial person, he had pretended to be grateful for—the brash young Josiah Slade making suggestions to him!—to *him*. He'd wanted to say, with the practiced irony of the professor-lecturer, *Thank you so much for your unsolicited and uninformed opinion, my boy. How very generous of you.*

Yet, several ideas had come to him, during his conversation with Josiah. And in truth, he was grateful for Josiah's presence in their somber household in which the only—sensory—distraction was the baby's loud crying, that affected Pearce's sensitive nerves at a distance of several rooms.

He did not think it curious that Josiah had shown up, uninvited and unexpected at Quatre Face. He did feel, under the strain of the criminal investigation, that all things that happened to him, or surrounding him, were in specific reference to his campaign to overcome the Curse; and that Josiah Slade, of the accursed Slades, would naturally be drawn to Pearce van Dyck as a kind of protector, mentor—savior.

And it seemed to him too, that Josiah Slade's young life was "on hold"—the young man had not gone to law school, or medical school, or continued with graduate studies as he'd planned; the Slades were not encouraging him, probably. The old Slade *vitality* had been leached from them, a kind of paralysis had come upon them, since the advent of the Curse.

"I will help them. I am the only one, I must persevere."

Yet often it happened, when Pearce locked himself away in his study late at night—(indeed, "locked" is accurate: for, initially, his concerned wife might dare to open the door at 3 A.M., seeking him out with a plaintive *Pearce? Why are you up so late?*)—that he lost track of time; discovered himself elsewhere in the house, wandering in the dark with a lighted candle; more strangely, Pearce had several times discovered himself outside, in the quite chilly night air, shivering in a wind that lifted from the river like a cruel caress. By moonlight, teeth chattering, in the ruin of an old rose garden, with no idea how, or why, he'd come here.

"To clear the cobwebs from my brain. That must be it."

So we invent reasons for the unreasonable. We are rationalists of the irrational. It is very hard for me to write this chapter for, to be frank, as historians are so rarely frank, *I am writing about my own dear departed father and in so doing, though I am totally sympathetic with him, as with my dear mother, it seems very wrong: a violation of something primary, not unlike Oedipus's terrible sins.*

This night, after the intellectually stimulating dinner with his young, former student, Pearce had intended to work until at least 4 A.M., then to sleep on the divan in his study, covered by an old, moth-eaten but warm comforter; for he needed to be near, physically near, the Scheme of Clues, in recent days; it was his great fear, that something would happen to the chart, as to his hundreds of pages of accumulated notes—a fire, for instance. Electricity was erratic in this part of Bucks County, Pennsylvania, and so kerosene lamps, candles, and wood fires were necessary; with her air of girlish optimism, that countered but did not quite eradicate her underlying anxiety, Johanna liked to say that Quatre Face was *romantic*—"We are like people in a gothic novel!" (Yet Pearce knew very well, the West End ladies of Princeton would far rather inhabit a novel by Jane Austen.)

And so this night, nerves strained by excitement no less than by anxiety, Pearce found himself, suddenly, not at his desk, not in his study, but, he knew not how, *outside*. The air was very chill, for May; on the wide, dark Delaware River, less than one hundred feet from where Pearce stood in the ruined garden, moonlight rippled and shivered; he was in shirtsleeves, and had opened his collar, while working and perspiring; now, his teeth chattered with cold.

Fortunately, Johanna would not know! And Josiah would not know.

Precisely how late it was, Pearce had no idea. Perhaps 3 A.M.—nowhere near dawn. Behind him, rising above him, the solid, foursquare house of weatherworn limestone, with darkened windows. Wind rustled vines attached to the house, that had not revived with spring but were dead, and very dry; the sound was like voices, whispering. Yet, Pearce could not decode what the voices were saying. A short distance away were several statues that, dimly white by moonlight, seemed both lifelike and paralyzed: slender, tall Diana with her noble hounds close beside her, whose tongues protruded from their fanged mouths; the chastely entwined couple Cupid and Psyche; and, farthest away, the comely youth Adonis poised on tiptoe. Johanna had laughed at the statues, and had wiped tears from her eyes, saying that the inheritance of Quatre Face, from a great-grandfather of Pearce's, was a mixed blessing, indeed; for, to revive the house, and to make it halfway livable, they would have to spend thousands, many thousands of dollars; and they would have to get rid of such singularly ugly statuary, executed by one or another sculptor-friend of Pearce's ancestor; almost, they would have to devote themselves to it, and abandon their Princeton lives—"It would eat us alive, Quatre Face."

Pearce had been annoyed, in fact rather insulted, by his wife's careless remark. Quatre Face was *his property,* and not *hers.*

A woman could not inherit such property, that was the law. A woman might go to court, these days; the suffragettes were clamoring for law reform, for women's rights; but that day had not yet arrived, and women had few legal rights, as they had no voting rights—none. As a university liberal, as reform-minded as any Princeton professor, Pearce van Dyck was in favor of such changes in society; yet, privately, it pleased him that so little happened, and so slowly.

And perhaps it would never happen, in fact—*women's rights.*

"There are more urgent matters. The 'problem of evil,' for one."

Softly Pearce spoke aloud. In the nocturnal silence there was no sound except of the wind, and an underlying sound of the river, that was sometimes audible from inside the house, on still nights. Pearce was resolved not to stare at the statues, that seemed to be staring at him; for even Diana's hounds seemed to be staring, with a sort of secret canine derision, at *him*. "Next, I will be talking to them—these stone creatures. And *they* addressing *me*."

Johanna was correct: the statues were ugly, and ridiculous; worst of all, pretentious. They could never invite their Princeton friends to visit Quatre Face until the old estate was, as Johanna said, *revived*.

"But nothing can be done in any of our lives until it—the Curse—is lifted."

Thinking such thoughts, Pearce turned to re-enter the house—he saw an opened door, that led to his study; obviously, in a kind of sleep-walking trance, he'd come outside through that doorway—and at the top of a short flight of stone steps he paused, seeing—was it a horse-drawn carriage approaching Quatre Face, at such an hour of the night?

"Another visitor? Impossible! A second unexpected—uninvited—guest?"

Yet, Pearce hurried to greet the carriage, as it swung smartly along the front drive, and pulled up before the granite portico of the house; for, as he reasoned, none of his small staff of servants would be up at this time of night, and it fell to him to offer hospitality.

"Yet, I'm sure we are expecting no one. Johanna would not dare invite anyone, without asking my permission."

So, we can imagine Pearce van Dyck's astonishment, shading into awe, and a kind of dread, as a tall hawk-nosed gentleman in a Scotch plaid cape leapt down lightly from the carriage—a gentleman whose fame, no less than his striking physiognomy and figure, were already better known to the philosopher than his own mirror-likeness.

For the unexpected and uninvited visitor was none other than Mr. Sherlock Holmes, the world's sole *consulting detective*.

REMARKABLE AS THIS late-night visit was, and mysterious, the motive was quickly explained to Pearce van Dyck.

Lounging with aristocratic insolence on the leather settee in Pearce's study, the Englishman told his rapt American host that Conan Doyle, a companion of his from medical school days, had passed along Professor van Dyck's several admiring letters to him, as well as his request for several monographs; and though "Sherlock Holmes" was certainly not lacking for clients in London, the situation in Princeton and environs, as it was set forth in the letters, struck him as irresistible. "So, Professor, I made the decision to sail from Liverpool as quickly as possible, with the possibly selfish hope," the Englishman smilingly said, as he employed an antiquated iron tong to lift a glowing coal from the fireplace, to light his pipe, "that you wouldn't have solved the mystery by your own devices, before I arrived!"

At this, Pearce van Dyck blushed deeply; and murmured in confused embarrassment that, unfortunately, he *had not* solved the mystery; and found himself at an impasse. As to Mr. Holmes—

"Excuse me, Professor: I am not 'Holmes.'"

"You are—not?"

"Certainly not. 'Sherlock Holmes' is a fictitious character, and a pseudonym. My name is private, and will never be revealed, as Conan Doyle has promised."

The languid Englishman went on to explain that he both was, and was not, the "Sherlock Holmes" of the popular mystery stories. Unlike the glamorous Holmes, he was very much ensconced in *terra firma*, with "marital" responsibilities; an old, sprawling, quasi-ruin of a country estate inherited from English-Scots ancestors in Craigmire, in West Dorset, near Lyme Regis; and a "quite modest *pied-à-terre*" on Baker Street. "So erratic is my income as a very private consulting detective, I must supplement my income as a part-time pathologist at the University of London medical school; for I never completed my medical studies and got my degree, which youthful recklessness seems to me now a distinct mistake. In 1906 we are none of us quite so young and idealistic as we once were . . ." Shaking his head bemused, and drawing hard on his pipe, which Pearce noted was a straight pipe and not a calabash, as he'd have expected, the hawk-nosed Englishman said with a sigh, "How I wish that I were blessed with the freedom of 'Sherlock Holmes'! Nothing would please me more, and exercise my talents better, than to be a full-time connoisseur of crime, and to ply my wits against the most brilliant criminals in the world. For I feel, like my friend Conan Doyle's character 'Sherlock,' that the art of cerebral detection is the supreme art, and that beside it other human actions and *divertissements* appear rather pallid. A healthy mind *does* rebel at stagnation; and I am so ill-equipped for the common round of existence that I should soon go mad, or slash my throat, out of sheer boredom. If it were not for my private profession, how should I live? I glory, as you do, Professor, in mental stimulation—in the pursuit of Truth—in the most deeply absorbing of ratiocinative processes. And though I have been married for a number of years, in fact, in a 'private' sort of marriage, of which the world knows nothing, I'm inclined to believe, with my mythical alter ego, that the connubial life"—at this, the Englishman gestured condescendingly toward the interior of the house, enveloping, it seemed, all of Pearce van Dyck's marital and domestic history—"indeed, the life of emotion and sentiment, is largely contemptible; and a sheer waste of time."

Shocking words! Pearce felt his heated face grow warmer still; and though he drew breath to rebut such a statement, he could think of no adequate words in defense of his position.

For—was it true? The private life, the life of emotion and sentiment, was *contemptible*? A *sheer waste of time*?

How embarrassed he would be, to confess to this elegant English gentleman that he had lately become a father . . . That is, his dear wife had lately had a baby, after years of having failed to become pregnant . . .

Speaking in a cultivated drawl the Englishman continued along the same lines, sensitive to his American host's social awkwardness, and awe in his presence: explaining that while his old classmate Doyle had greatly romanticized him, and given him "near-omnipotent" powers, as writers of fiction are wont to do, yet Doyle had more or less presented the essence of the detective's personality—"Uncannily, in fact." The author had even exposed certain habits of his which he'd hoped were known to himself only . . . (Here, "Holmes" quite surprised Pearce van Dyck by sliding up his sleeves to reveal lean, sinewy, and badly scarred forearms.) "My cocaine habit, you see—the injection of liquid cocaine into my bloodstream, until my more serviceable veins have dried up. This, I view with more alarm and remorse than Doyle suggests, rather irresponsibly, I think. An author must present a *morally coherent universe,* else he is likely to pervert the weaker and more vulnerable of his readers." The Englishman sucked at his pipe rather contently, however. One could see that he quite liked Pearce van Dyck's company, and may have been impressed, Pearce thought, at the size and style of Quatre Face, which appeared less weatherworn by moonlight; and its interior rooms, naturally darkened, less shabby. "Any man of rational principle would wish to be freed of addiction, surely—do you agree, Professor? I think you indicated that you were a 'Kantian'—a very moral, very primly pious and Germanic philosopher, indeed."

Pearce wracked his brains for a suitable response, that might exhibit sympathy, yet some intelligent censure; for the Englishman seemed to invite this, as one friend might with another. But before he could speak, the Englishman continued to develop the parallels, and differences, between himself and the fictitious detective, which he believed might be of interest to his American admirer.

So far as physical appearance went, he granted that he and Holmes were virtually twins: being six feet three inches tall, and weighing one hundred sixty pounds—thus "lean to the point of gauntness." Yes, his chin was rather sharp, and his nose distinctly long and narrow; as to his eyes—whether they were "uncommonly keen and piercing," he could not say. His hands were, indeed, stained indelibly with ink and chemicals;

his clothing, more or less as Doyle described—"Though my spouse—my 'partner,' as it were—tries to dress me more fashionably, on our limited budget." Yet, in other respects, the Englishman said, frowning, "my alleged hagiographer has rather libeled me. He knows that since boyhood I've been fascinated by the workings of the solar system yet, out of playfulness, he has turned my interest upside down, so that 'Holmes' is known as a man of genius who boasts of neither knowing nor caring what Copernican theory means!—and takes a haughty tone in rejecting the latest discoveries of science, except as they relate to his field. So narrow is the fictional 'Holmes,' scorning an interest in art, history, politics, and music apart from the occasional squeaking of his own fiddle—the man is just another English eccentric, which I rather resent."

Touched by such candor, Pearce van Dyck could only murmur a polite assent. Shyly then, for the gesture seemed belated, he offered his guest a small glass of brandy, which was accepted with a curt nod of the head, in thanks, and downed in a single shot.

Pearce, meaning to mirror his guest, downed his glass in a single shot as well, but fell to choking, and coughing; at such length that his guest queried him, if he was all right—"Your cough is 'bronchial,' I think. Have you been ill?"

Embarrassed, Pearce insisted that he had not been ill.

"Your skin tone is rather sallow. Have you traveled to a tropical or sub-tropical place, within the past year?"

"No . . ."

"You haven't had any sort of fever? Chills? Your eyes are just slightly jaundiced, I think."

"My eyes . . . ?"

"Of course, I am not a doctor; I am not an M.D. I should not be 'diagnosing' in this way."

Pearce coughed again, not entirely able to clear his throat.

"You have the sort of cough Welsh miners have, after years of working underground. I mean—the sound of your cough resembles theirs. Have you been in any place where 'particles' might be in the air—an asbestos or a fertilizer factory, for instance?"

"No. I have not."

"Have you *breathed in* anything of unusual pungency? A very strong marsh gas, for instance?"

"N-No . . ."

Seeing that his host was being made uncomfortable by this line of interrogation, the Englishman relented, though reluctantly. Thwarted in this impromptu investigation he poured another brandy for himself, and drank it down; seemed to sink into a kind of torpor, staring into the smoldering fire; and allowed his pipe to go out. Hesitantly, Pearce ventured the opinion that, as Arthur Conan Doyle had presented his "essence" in the stories, perhaps that was all that mattered. Sherlock Holmes was known by the world for his genius, not for his trifling eccentricities. "It isn't an exaggeration to say, sir, that 'Sherlock Holmes' is rapidly becoming one of the heroic figures of the day."

"Really! How bizarre."

The Englishman spoke in so languid a drawl it was impossible to judge whether he meant mockery or sincerity. Again he took up the fire tongs to light his pipe, laughing quietly to himself. "What vexes me in this matter, Professor van Dyck, is my own ambivalence. For while it seems self-evident to me that the art of criminal detection is, or should be, an exact science, freed from human emotion, at the same time I am frankly drawn to the 'romance' of Doyle's portraiture. Watson, for instance, does not exist except as Conan Doyle himself, tagging after me as he'd done in school—a relief, as I could not endure him for an hour."

No Watson! Pearce thought this quite a disappointment.

The Englishman sucked at his pipe, emitting clouds of malodorous smoke. In a whimsical voice he speculated that, were he not a detective-pathologist, he should have liked to be, like his friend Doyle, a literary man; though of a gravity surpassing Doyle. "To invent outlandish fables, precise as clockwork, yet, it's hoped, not predictable; to disguise an old-fashioned

Englishman's sentiment in such prose, and a 'case for morals'; to temper elaborate work as if it were but child's play—this would seem to me a challenging adventure. For, I think, the writer of fiction is the *supreme detective*, delving not only into intricacies of fact but into those of motive as well, like a psychologist; exploring the individual, and illuminating the species. In any case, Professor van Dyck, I have no right to object to Doyle's undertaking, and must learn to accept my fate as a 'character' in another's imagination. Which brings us, Professor, to *your* problem."

Eagerly, Pearce showed his visitor the several charts comprising the Scheme of Clues, now so covered in tiny, spidery handwriting, and confused with a multitude of tacks, pins, beads, and the like, even the Englishman's sharp eye faltered. Pearce attempted to explain the Curse, its history and (possible) origin; he attempted to explain the impasse at which he found himself. But he spoke in so excited a fashion, the Englishman asked him please to stop, and begin at the beginning. "There is nothing like chronology, my American friend, to put a brake on the soul's impulse for headlong speed."

So, while the Englishman lounged on the settee with heavy-lidded eyes, quietly puffing at his pipe, Pearce spent an hour attempting to recount the several manifestations of the Curse, so far as he knew of them. He spoke of the "visitation" of ex-President Cleveland's deceased daughter, and of the near-simultaneous appearance of the demon Axson Mayte, and the seeming "entrancement" of Annabel Slade at her own wedding . . . He spoke of Annabel's disappearance for several months, and of her reappearance, and subsequent death-in-childbirth; he spoke of the "fantastical, but not discountable" rumors of her having given birth to a hideous black snake, that subsequently vanished. And there were other crimes—murders . . .

At the mention of the black snake, the Englishman stirred, and opened his eyes as if rousing himself.

Growing more excited by degrees, Pearce spread out the Scheme of Clues for the Englishman to see, as he delivered an impromptu lecture on its contents; he spoke of the "snake frenzy," and of the "baffling" behavior of a young woman of good family who seemed to have been involved with a married man, the van Dycks' very neighbor Horace Burr who, just recently, had murdered his invalid wife in her bed . . .

By this time the Englishman had unwrapped his long lean frame and took up in his indelibly stained fingers the Scheme of Clues to examine it closely. Pearce felt a thrill of pride seeing the world's most honored consulting detective considering his amateur findings, his high, fine brow now creased and his eyes, of the hue of washed glass, emitting a chill glow. How many minutes the Englishman spent in this posture, frowning and grimacing, and muttering to himself, Pearce could not judge; but one can estimate from the events that followed, it might have been as long as a half hour. All this while Pearce stood at the Englishman's elbow, staring and blinking, mute with apprehension and hope.

At last, when the suspense had grown near-intolerable, the Englishman took up one of Pearce's fountain pens from his desk to make several broad slashes on the chart connecting singular points with other points, and turned to his stricken host with a playful smile.

"It's elementary, my dear friend—do you see?"

But Pearce, though he tried, did not see. And badly wounded he was, by the peremptory way in which the English detective had slashed his elaborate graph and overwritten his intricate notes. Seeing the expression in the professor's sallow face, and the strain in that face, the Englishman laid a hand on his shoulder to console him.

"Your deductive powers, Professor, while impressive in an amateur, were not going to bring you to the answer, since you'd failed to make crucial connections between events. It was a brilliant discovery of yours to realize that 'Axson Mayte' is a demon; yet, for reasons I can't grasp, having perhaps to do with American idolatry of European pretensions, you failed to make an identical discovery in the matter of 'Count English von Gneist.' In fact, following the logic of Occam's razor, it is my theory that *the two men are but one*. Why do you look surprised? The Count has, it seems, passed undetected in your midst; all the ladies have taken him up, and some of the gentlemen, too. And your infant son, whom you have designated here as 'it,' is, I'm sorry to say, not your son at all but the spawn of a demon—as, I think, you have halfway realized?"

Pearce stared at his visitor in stunned silence. He did not seem to have heard the Englishman's final words.

Matter-of-factly, as if he had not pierced a man's heart, the cavalier Englishman took up the charts with some exuberance, deftly indicating with the bowl of his pipe the "diabolical intricacies" of the many relationships, and how a single bold line might be drawn between A and E, removing in an instant all need for intervening points; in this way erasing weeks of Pearce's ratiocinative labor. Likewise, stickpins at 4 June 1905, 24 December 1905, and 24 February 1906 logically connected, to demonstrate an (unacknowledged) triangulated relationship: for "Axson"—"Annabel"—"Adelaide"—"Amanda"—clearly matched; and "J"—"JS" (Johanna Strachan) with "JS" (Josiah Slade). And Count English Rudolf Heinrich Gottsreich-Mueller von Gneist could be connected, by a transposition of certain letters and figures, to several individuals on the chart including "WW" (Woodrow Wilson) and, unfortunately in this context, "JS" (Mrs. van Dyck).

And so on, and so forth, as the Englishman proceeded to "solve" the puzzle, as one might show another, slower-witted person how to "solve" a crossword puzzle, by making more lines, scrawling X's over portions of the Scheme, ripping off a corner altogether and tossing it negligently into the fireplace. His curiosity was pricked, the Englishman said, by the absence of the demon's sister Camille, on this chart; one of Pearce's oversights, and a severe one at that, for Camille was one of "the most rapacious" of demons, in its female form. To the awestricken Pearce van Dyck the Englishman said, "You see, my friend, I know these hellish creatures of old, having dealt with them on the Continent in '89, and then again in Mous'hole, Surrey, in '93. The first case was given the title 'The Adventure of the Poisoned Nursery' by my old classmate Doyle; the second, "The

Adventure of the Lion's Mane." I remember the Count with much clarity, as he and I were apt to play billiards together, when not in 'combat'; often, we dined together, at the expense of our benefactors—the individuals who'd retained me, and the individuals, invariably the owners of large 'Gilded Age' houses, who made the demons their houseguests, and invited them to their dinners. Let me now consult my little encyclopedia of genealogies to make certain . . ." The Englishman withdrew from his coat pocket a crimson-covered little volume, quite worn, through which he rapidly paged, until he came to what he was looking for; then read off, in a low, dramatic voice, such a barrage of names, the distraught philosopher could scarcely follow, like an aged and badly winded dog trotting after a sleek younger dog in the open air.

"D'Adalbert—D'Apthorp—Castle Szekeley—Grand Duke of Bystel-Kohler—Baron Eger Frankstone—Castle Gottsreich-Mueller—House of the von Gneists of Szurdokpuspoki, Wallachia. Arms: argent, on a cross flory azure, between four Old World choughs, a serpent passant quadrant. Crest: demi-serpent rampant per pale or and azure, collared per pale counterchanged, armed. So you see, Professor van Dyck, it's as I suspected," the Englishman said languidly, turning his pale penetrant eyes on the dazed American. "A disagreeable business indeed but not, thank God, irremediable. The thing in the crib upstairs must be disposed of—at once. If your wife cannot part with it, if she 'resists'—you must take measures against her, as well. But why do you look at me in such a way, Professor? Is this all so very surprising to you? I can't think it is," he said, sucking on his pipe, with a maddening sort of complacency, "since your ingenious 'Scheme of Clues' contained the answer all along, though you failed to see it."

The Englishman then turned to the stone hearth and took up the poker, and held it for some minutes in the fire, that was now modestly blazing, while he continued to speak in a kindlier voice. "From time to time it is not only permissible, Professor van Dyck, but quite necessary, as your beloved Kant would agree, to 'transcend' the merely local law. (As I believe Doyle reports my having done upon several notable occasions, that a greater evil might be prevented.) For 'evil' is after all a relative term: there being a minor and pragmatical sort, to be disposed of as one swats a fly, and a vast, all-encompassing, one might say universal sort, that must be halted by any means at hand. None of this, I know, can be foreign to you as a moral philosopher of international reputation; yet it seems you have been dilatory in attending to the situation beneath your own roof. For it somehow slipped past your scrutiny that your wife, whom you wished to believe is 'faithful' to you, was nonetheless seduced sometime in the late spring of last year, by an agent of the Fiend; and that an irrefutable syllogism presents itself here within the walls of your ancestral home. Which is to say: evil must be overcome; evil dwells here, in its crib in the nursery; therefore no other remedy is possible except your proceeding, with as much dispatch as possible, in *eradicating it*."

With dilated and slow-blinking eyes Pearce van Dyck regarded the tall, lean-bodied Englishman and for some seconds stood immobile as stone. Then, in a halting motion, he removed his glasses, that he might polish their dampened lenses. Once or twice he seemed about to speak, for his blanched lips quivered; but no word escaped him. It was a respectful gesture on the part of "Sherlock Holmes" to allow the stricken man to ruminate in silence.

All this while, the poker was being heated, changing by degrees from black to red-hot to *white-hot*, and giving off an unnatural light.

When at last it was prepared the Englishman grasped it in a hearty grip, and passed it to Pearce van Dyck, who staggered just perceptibly, as the weight of the iron poker was greater than he seemed to have expected. The Englishman then walked him to the foot of the stairs, in a genial and brotherly way you would not think characteristic of the more aloof fictional Holmes. "I'm sure you are recalling at this moment, Professor," the Englishman murmured, "how in one of the final books of *The Republic* the 'tyrannical ruler' is reasoned to be three times three squared, and then cubed, *more unhappy* than Plato's Philosopher King: which is to say, seven hundred twenty-nine times. Only think! Plato was the most brilliant of philosophers, unless he was frankly mad, like so many of his successors. Yet, the courageous action you are about to take against the thing beneath your own roof, the thing that nurses at your wife's breast, the thing that dares to identify itself as *Pearce van Dyck, Jr.*, will, at a future time, reward you with three times three squared, and then cubed, more *joy*, than you would have felt otherwise—as the quasi-father of a Horror, let us say. And so, now—upstairs!—to the nursery, and to the marital bed."

So, with incandescent poker brandished aloft like a king's scepter Pearce van Dyck ascended the dimly lighted staircase, to what awaited him on the second floor.

3.

It does not hurt greatly. The pain can be borne. Summon forth your courage, Johanna! And do not resist for that will only make him angrier.

Hoarse whispered words woke Johanna from sleep rising, it seemed, from shadows close about the sofa on which she slept and confused with a fretful wind rattling at the windowpanes.

You know I am a sister to you, Johanna. I would not mislead you. I counsel you, do not resist as I did. It angers them the more, that you challenge their wish. Then, you will suffer—as I did.

Johanna was sleeping in the nursery where, having nursed and cuddled the colicky baby earlier that night, she'd fallen asleep on a cushioned sofa, that left her neck and lower back stiff. At first she thought the whispering must be the baby cooing to himself, then she realized that the whispering was from another source altogether; for the baby slept unperturbed in his crib.

"Pearce? Is that you?"

Johanna squinted into the shadows at the opened door, that led to her own bedroom, where ordinarily she slept; the other door, to the corridor, appeared to be shut.

Down the hall, in the region of the house known as the servants' quarters, the colored girl who tended to Baby, as she called him, slept; for Johanna could not bear it, that another would intervene between her and her infant son. It seemed crucial to her, that the first face the baby saw upon waking was his mother's.

"*Is* that you? But where are you . . ."

She was mistaken, it seemed: Pearce was not in the nursery.

Pearce was, very likely, downstairs in his study. He had encouraged Johanna and Josiah to retire to bed, with the excuse that he had "just a few minutes' work" to attend to; but Johanna suspected he'd been working for hours on the Scheme of Clues, and may have fallen asleep on the divan in his study.

Hurriedly, with trembling fingers, Johanna struck a match to light a lamp; now she could see quite clearly, the baby was certainly asleep in his crib; for when the baby slept, he slept deeply; as, when the baby woke, he might wake with a shattering howl.

It does not hurt greatly. I would not mislead you, my dear sister. You must not resist, that is crucial. For in Eve's fall we have sinned. We reap our harvest now, at the hands of our masters.

Johanna heard these strangely calm words issuing from the very shadows of the nursery. Yet she knew herself alone in the room with the baby. Trembling, she adjusted the wick of the kerosene lamp, rose from the sofa and looked worriedly about.

There were old, silly tales of Quatre Face being haunted. A stop on the Underground Railway through eastern Pennsylvania, or allegedly so; and a confused, ugly tale of Negro slaves beguiled into entering the house, hiding in the dank tunnel behind the chimney, only to be betrayed by the master of the house to slave bounty-hunters, and dragged back to their slave owners in the South, in chains.

What a terrible story, Pearce! Can that be true?—your great-grandfather would do such a thing to helpless people?

And Pearce had retorted, stung by Johanna's remark *Yes and why not? Your grandfather may have done so, too.*

Still, Johanna didn't believe in ghosts. There was no one in the room except her and the baby.

Since being sent to Quatre Face by her husband, Johanna had lapsed into a pervasive melancholy; it was not her nature to be despondent, and low in energy, but the seclusion of the house was depressing to her, as the condition of the house was depressing; all that riveted her attention was the baby, and what haphazard, often-interrupted reading she'd been able to do, of books she'd brought with her weeks before. It was not like her, she thought, to *imagine things;* she was not a nervous invalid, like poor Adelaide Burr, and other Princeton women; yet, at Quatre Face, she'd been beset by any number of baseless fears, as by the prevailing fear that there was something gravely wrong with her husband, and in their marriage.

It was certainly the case that, within the past year, Pearce had changed radically. His old, droll sense of humor had largely vanished, replaced by an unpredictable irascibility; at times, his eyes glared yellow, as if he hated her. (Johanna could admit this to no one, not even a sister: her husband hated her!) And it was clear he hated, feared and despised their innocent little baby whom he could bring himself only to call—*it.*

Johanna looked with tenderness at the sleeping infant. In sleep, he appeared so small! So utterly helpless.

"You will know nothing of this, I hope. All that surrounds you now—all that has culminated in *you*—will be unknown to you, as the vast galaxies that surround us are unknown to us."

The crib in which the infant lay was a family heirloom—a Strachan family heirloom. White latticework upon a sturdy pine frame, with white satin trim, and white satin ribbons. A beautiful crib and yet when Pearce saw it he recoiled, with a sardonic little laugh—"It looks like an infant *coffin.* It is unacceptable."

But Johanna prevailed. The heirloom crib remained.

Standing barefoot, in her ankle-length flannel nightgown, her hair loosed upon her shoulders, Johanna glanced about the darkened room, uneasy; seeing then, by chance it seemed, in a farther corner of the nursery, a figure sitting, or reclining, on a *chaise longue;* and in that instant she heard the low, whispered, urgent words another time—*It does not hurt greatly. It is futile to resist. He will be angry if you resist. I would not mislead you, my dear sister Johanna!*

Johanna stared, trying not to scream; for even in her panicked state she did not want to waken and alarm the sleeping baby.

Could it be?—the shadowy figure was *Adelaide Burr.*

The poor woman lifted her hurt, bloodied bare arms to Johanna—her ashen face, bloodied too, was lifted in an anguished appeal; her eyes were wet with tears, and—a mass of bleeding wounds where her small flat breasts had been . . .

Johanna do not turn away. I am your sister, I am awaiting you. Do not leave me here alone . . .

Johanna turned, blinded; in terror, she collided with the crib, and wakened the baby; the figure of her old friend Adelaide Burr seemed to shimmer, and fade, as if in disappointment, or repudiation of her; for she was very cowardly, and could not bring herself to speak to Adelaide, who appealed to her with such yearning. For there is the fear—a wise fear, I think: that if we speak just once to the dead, the dead will cleave to us in their desperate loneliness and never leave our sides.

And then, Johanna drew breath to scream, for she could not prevent herself; and would have screamed for help with all the strength of her lungs, except the apparition had vanished; and she was struggling to sit up in darkness, wakening only now from her nightmare.

For the lamp had not been lit, after all. She had been sleeping, fitfully, on the cushioned sofa in the nursery, that was too small and cramped for a proper sleep, or even a nap; and left her neck and back aching. She had dreamt the entire episode.

Now, with badly shaking hands, Johanna did light the lamp, which smelled strongly of kerosene, as if it had been carelessly filled to the brim; and saw to her relief that the nursery was empty—and nothing lay on the *chaise longue* but a supply of baby's nappies, a baby blanket and soft white baby-towels, neatly folded.

There was the source of the nightmare, Johanna thought: a trick of the optical nerve, somehow visible through shut eyes.

Nor was the baby awake but—this seemed a miracle!—continued peacefully to sleep.

YET JOHANNA WAS SO agitated still, she supposed it would be futile and frustrating to try to sleep; and so when Pearce entered the nursery a short time later, at about 3 A.M., Johanna was wrapped in a comforter and reclining on the sofa, near the crib; though the lamplight was poor, she was managing to make her way through the thorny prose of Mr. Henry James, a long-ago favorite of the lending libraries with his *Daisy Miller* and *A Portrait of a Lady;* but Johanna was reading, or trying to read, the long and demanding *The Golden Bowl,* in which she had arrived at page two hundred—and scarcely knew what the story *was.* It did seem to her strange that her husband would enter the nursery, which by day he avoided, yet Johanna was determined to welcome him, however unorthodox the hour—"Pearce? Is it you? Are you coming to bed, at last?" Yet her breath faltered, and her eyes widened, to see her husband advancing grimly upon her, a rod of some kind—a poker?—lifted in his hand; the tip of which glowed with heat, as if it had just been removed from a fire.

Mild-mannered Pearce van Dyck, transformed into this murderous man, with a contorted face; a misshapen skull, beneath fever-damp strands of dark hair; a prim cruel smile, like the smile of a gargoyle. What was he doing, advancing upon the crib? In which their baby slept? The poker uplifted, to bring down in rage?

In her husband's eyes, a tawny-topaz glare.

"Don't try to stop me, Johanna. This is an act that is foretold."

Johanna leapt at her husband, and tried to wrest the poker from him. Yet, how strong Pearce was, and what fury animated his body! The heat from the poker touched her skin, the very skin of her face, and the lashes of her eyes; and only now did the terrified woman begin to scream.

4.

In a bedroom close by, Josiah Slade was already awake; that is, Josiah had scarcely slept since he'd parted with Johanna van Dyck several hours earlier. The uncomfortable mattress, the peculiar acrid odor of the room that seemed to prevail, like a smell of the grave, beneath the intoxicating smell of lilac; the play of *splotched moonlight* on the ceiling of the room, like reflections in water; a murmur, in the near distance, of a voice, or voices, downstairs, though he knew that the house was darkened and there could be no one there—all kept Josiah from sinking into even his usual uneasy, fitful sleep.

And then suddenly, there came Johanna's cries.

In an instant, Josiah leapt from bed, and rushed to the nursery.

By instinct knowing that a terrible thing was about to happen, that he must prevent. *Hurry! Hurry! Their lives depend upon you only you Josiah*—for once, the voice was not a demon's voice.

In the nursery, by lamplight, Josiah saw two figures struggling, one with a poker in his hand; with no time to absorb the astonishing sight, Josiah grappled with the madman, and wrenched the poker from his grip, burning his fingers in the act; in a fit of youthful strength, he threw the man to the floor—seeing, only now, that the man was his dear friend and former professor Pearce van Dyck.

"Why, this is not real. This cannot be happening . . ."

By this time, Johanna was sobbing to Josiah, a confused explanation of what had happened, or had nearly happened; the baby in his crib had wakened, and was whimpering, as if with the adult knowledge of terror.

On the floor Pearce van Dyck lay, shuddering. His face, that had been contorted as in simian rage only a moment before, was now slack, and flaccid; a hoarse rattle in his throat, as if there were thorns and thistles there, to prevent his breathing. Josiah knelt over him, tugging his shirt collar open farther, so that the man might breathe; but, the blow to his head against the floor, where Josiah had thrown him with such violence, or the paroxysm of rage that had driven him to such desperation, had occluded his heart, or a great artery in his brain, and within minutes, despite Josiah's effort, Dr. van Dyck had ceased breathing; and would pass, with no further agitation or alarm, into a comatose state; within a few hours, into Death.

The poker, its lethal tip now cooling, lay a few feet away from the fallen man, harmless.

"ANGEL TRUMPET" ELUCIDATED

Historians have passed over the "psychotic breakdown" and "attempted infanticide" at Quatre Face, as if these had no direct bearing upon the Curse; as if, having occurred in the area of Raven Rock, Pennsylvania, it was too far from Princeton to be considered.

Yet, a fact crucial to this history emerges from the van Dyck tragedy.

Josiah Slade was credited with having saved both the infant's life and the life of its mother, yet, it scarcely needs to be said, the young man was wracked with a sickening guilt, and became more despondent, and more despairing, than before.

For hadn't his former professor loved him, to a degree; hadn't his former professor trusted him, and welcomed him into his house; hadn't he been, in the main, prior to the bizarre eruption of homicidal madness, correct about the Curse; hadn't the poor man, heroic beyond measure, perceived a Scheme of Clues connecting disparate events, and diverse persons? Pearce had shared a good deal with Josiah, it seemed; more than with anyone else; for he had trusted Josiah, as a son.

"And now he's dead, I'm left entirely alone. Once his admiring pupil, now his executioner."

(YET: A SINGLE uplifting memory followed from Josiah's desperate act. He would recall the intimate voice that had urged him to hurry to the nursery—*Their lives depend upon you only you Josiah.* Not a demon's voice but the voice of his dear sister Annabel, that he had not heard since her death.)

"YOU DID NOT 'kill' the man—you were protecting others."

And, "It was not a willful act of yours. It was in fact a selfless, courageous, heroic act."

And, "Johanna van Dyck's baby owes his life to you, as Johanna owes her life to you. *That,* you must acknowledge."

So, Josiah was told. But he did not believe.

Nor was Josiah's stricken conscience assuaged when Professor van Dyck's "psychotic breakdown" was explained, shortly after the man's funeral. This, by way of a fortuitous visit to Quatre Face by Mrs. Margaret Burr, who was helping Johanna's family in this time of sorrow.

The elder Mrs. Prudence Burr had come to help Johanna pack, to return to Princeton; like others, she was astonished and dismayed by the "unfathomable clutter" in the professor's study, which was not characteristic, all agreed, of the generally neat Pearce van Dyck, whose bookshelves in both his university office and in his Hodge Road residence were assiduously alphabetized, and who rarely left a book on a table, unshelved. But here, at Quatre Face, as if it were mute evidence of the man's madness, were large unwieldy charts or graphs—"Scheme of Clues" (?)—and numerous notebooks and loose sheets of paper, many lying underfoot. Mrs. Burr and her colored-girl helper discovered a dozen pages of diagrams analyzing the tales of A. Conan Doyle, in the professor's urgent, crabbed hand.

But the most telling discovery was an innocent-seeming bookmark of pressed flowers, in a copy of Spinoza's *Ethics,* that was lying on the professor's desk, beneath the Scheme of Clues; Mrs. Burr opened the book, saw the bookmark, leaned to smell the "pressed flowers," and quickly cast the book from her, as if it were a poisonous insect.

"What a tragedy! Pearce must have thought this was a 'flower'— dried lilies perhaps. In fact, the rank-smelling thing is dried 'Angel Trumpet'—a toxic cousin of the jimsonweed and one of the most lethal of 'wild-flowers.' "

So toxic was Angel Trumpet even in its desiccated state, its fruits and seeds, if eaten, would produce in human beings such symptoms as fever, dilated pupils, confusion, delirium, convulsions, and sometimes death. If Professor van Dyck had been breathing the faint but prevailing odor of his "bookmark" each day for hours, for months, it was plausible that his brain had suffered a gradual deterioration, resulting in paranoid suspicions and rage.

Canny Mrs. Burr, of an age somewhere beyond seventy-eight, had the practical sense to have her helper "wrap, carefully," in several layers of newspaper, the toxic bookmark, to bring back to Princeton with her, to turn over to police investigators.

When Josiah heard this news, he was stricken with guilt anew.

A poisonous weed! And not a calla lily, found broken and bruised on the ground at the old Craven house!

And shall you not confess a voice taunted him, hollow and nasal like that of Axson Mayte himself. *Shall you not acknowledge the source of the Angel Trumpet in the professor's office?*

"ARMAGEDDON"

C"an it be? So *soon*?"

Hearing of such disturbing matters—(the outbreak of "horrific" and "inexplicable" incidents among a number of prominent Princeton families)—Upton Sinclair came to wonder if Armageddon might be closer at hand than the Socialist prophets believed. And he speculated whether he and his wife and son might be in danger, dwelling so close to the evident center of the Curse.

"Who would have imagined, the tranquil oasis of Princeton, New Jersey—a spawning-ground of the Jersey Devil!"

Upton spoke lightly, yet half-seriously. He could not but think that the travails of the very rich were deserved, and justified, from the historic perspective; yet he very much doubted that these travails had fallen upon them from a supernatural source.

Yet, it did seem to him, a cataclysmic change of some sort was in the very air, even in rural New Jersey.

"For, only consider, Meta," Upton said excitedly, one evening as his wife busied herself with kitchen chores, and tended to little David in his high chair, "there were fifty-thousand Socialist votes in Chicago's last election; twelve thousand orders received within a single day when *The Jungle* was published as a book; in Princeton, of all places, there is a commemorative stone honoring 'Mother Jones' and the child mill-workers; and it's clear that my lead piece on 'The Children's Crusade' is responsible for the entire May issue of *The Nation* selling out on newsstands!*

"Coupled with the 'tragedies' of the old Princeton families—Slades, van Dycks, Burrs—and there may be others—it isn't unreasonable to suspect something more than mere coincidence, do you agree? Kropotkin has said, nothing in history is 'happenstance.' "

Suffused with a sudden elation, Upton gripped his startled wife by both her upper arms, and diverted her from spooning mashed turnip to little David. In an excited voice he proclaimed: "It seems clear—we're living in the 'Last Days of Capitalism'—as the soul of oppressed man breaks its chains to rise against the 'Juggernaut of Greed'—and to *take revenge where it will*. And it is happening years before we had prophesied, and just a few miles from the little log cabin in which 'Upton Sinclair' wrote *The Jungle*. Could anything be more astonishing, and more of a miracle?"

Gently Meta detached herself from her husband's grip, and, turning back to her motherly task of feeding little David, murmured only: "Yes. A miracle."

---

* Upton Sinclair is referring to a recent march of striking child mill-workers in eastern Pennsylvania, led by the labor organizer Mary Harris Jones. The children, some as young as nine, and many missing fingers and toes, and exhibiting other injuries as a result of work-related conditions, "marched" from Philadelphia to Oyster Bay, Long Island, to the private residence of Theodore Roosevelt. Though derided in the press as an "anarchist invasion" the march did bring much publicity to the plight of children working in silk mills and mines. The strike was for a fifty-five-hour work-week. In his mansion at Oyster Bay, Roosevelt refused to meet with "Mother Jones" and hundreds of bedraggled, clearly very foot-weary children. A Pennsylvania judge ruled against the striking children:

"You are on strike against God."

PART IV

The Curse Exorcised

COLD SPRING

S weet, blameless child! She is an angel now."

In Princeton Cemetery, on an unseasonably chill morning in mid-May, another time the grieving Slade family gathered to bury one of their own: in a mother-of-pearl casket measuring no more than four feet in length, heartrending in its very smallness.

"She is with angels now."

"She is with her beloved cousin now . . ."

It was the death of nine-year-old Oriana Slade whom the Slades and numerous others were mourning. A most shocking and unexpected death—seemingly, an accident.

Oriana's small body, weighing scarcely sixty pounds, had been discovered not in her little bed in the nursery at Wheatsheaf where she'd been tucked in by her mother Lenora as usual, but, in a soiled and torn cotton nightgown, outside the house, beneath a flowering if somewhat ravaged tulip tree *beyond the northeastern wall of the property.*

The child's body was bruised and broken as if it had fallen, or had been flung, from a considerable height, more than merely the six-foot height of the fieldstone wall.

The highest peak of the Wheatsheaf roof? Was this possible?

Yet, as all who saw her testified, the little girl did not look as if she had suffered, at the time of death. Her eyes were partly open, and her mouth; her expression was more of startled surprise, even serenity, than of fear or distress.

No one could explain how Oriana, who had never been known to disobey her parents or her nanny, had managed to slip out of the nursery in the night; how she had climbed to a considerable height, her tiny feet bare, and her small body clad only in a cotton nightgown; *how*, indeed, and *why*?

Todd, stunned by his sister's death, which did not seem yet altogether real to him, said that Oriana had several times told him about her "Annabel-dreams"; and of "the privilege of the sky"—(an oddity of expression from a nine-year-old which I would doubt, except it is quoted more than once in investigative reports); and someday "flying" by herself to the "icy land in the North" where Annabel now dwelled. The skill of flying was being taught to her, Oriana had told Todd, when no adult could overhear, by a very pretty silver-haired lady with "sharp eyes." Todd had laughed at such nonsense, for he could not take his little sister seriously; *his own nonsense* was effort enough for him to take seriously, as he cheerily said.

(For Todd was inappropriately cheerful, even giddy, at times, in the days following his sister's death. Yet, at other times, he was cast in a stony silence, tearless, and mute.)

Once, he claimed, he'd tried to tell their mother about Oriana's "flying" dreams, but his mother had been distracted, and hadn't seemed to hear.

Another time he'd tried to tell his mother but his mother had said, frowning, that he and his sister should not always be "telling tales" about each other.

At the gravesite, which was the Slade family mausoleum, hewed of granite and limestone, with a portico of Italian marble, the mourners gathered close together in a sudden light, chill rain; exchanging the comforting bromides of commiseration and condolence, as best they could; though, for some, for whom the death of the child Oriana carried with it a measure of something like terror as well as grief, there was very little to say. Surely it was no exaggeration, all that Pearce van Dyck had claimed: there was a Curse on the community, and not even the most innocent of individuals, a nine-year-old child, might be spared.

Reverend Nathaniel FitzRandolph, who had aged over the winter, led the familiar Christian prayers, adding, in a voice of forced optimism, that if dear little Oriana had indeed imagined she could fly, it must have been to Heaven she'd flown.

Close by, Todd Slade pressed his knuckles against his mouth, to subvert an attack of laughter.

His parents were staring at the small gleaming white coffin as if here finally was a riddle they could not solve. Copplestone's face, the face of an aging sensualist, was flaccid and puffy; broken capillaries in his wide nose gave it a red-tinged cast; his small greenish-gray eyes seemed to exude an air of petulant irritation, directed primarily at his wife: for it was being said that Copplestone blamed Lenora for their daughter's death, and would never forgive her. Always the woman was "gadding about town" in their new Pierce-Arrow, manned by an "impudent Nigra" in a "monkey-suit uniform" Lenora had had custom-made for him; always she was "meddling" with invalids and charity cases and ladies' committees bent upon restoring old ruins, or sending "needless and unwanted" secondhand clothes to some "godforsaken place" like Ethiopia.

(Lenora, stricken with grief, said nothing; she would not defend herself, at least at this time; though confiding in her sister-in-law Henrietta that she often despaired of the future—of how it might one day "end" between her and Copplestone. "He is nothing like his father Winslow. He is nothing like most of the Slades—that is, a good person.

"God forgive me, I wonder if it wasn't to escape her tyrannical father that our poor daughter sought 'flight.' ")

The stricken parents stood a little apart from the majority of the mourners, directly in front of Reverend FitzRandolph. It would be perceived by some that they were not touching, nor did they look at each other through the gravesite ceremony.

It would be perceived generally that *all of the West End of Princeton* was present: those who had not been invited to Annabel Slade's funeral several months before.

(That is: Burrs, Sparhawks, Pynes, Armours, Strachans, FitzRandolphs, van Dycks, Biddles, Bayards, Washburns—to name just a few of the more prominent families.)

(Of course, there were conspicuous absences here. Horace Burr, and Pearce van Dyck, to name two; and Wilhelmina Burr had stayed away, for a private reason.)

Since Josiah's involvement in the death of his former professor Pearce van Dyck, and since many tales of this incident had been told in Princeton and environs, Josiah Slade was conscious of all of Princeton observing him, and passing judgment. It had been ruled that he was "blameless"—legally. And Johanna van Dyck—(at the funeral this morning clad in draperies of black linen and on her head a wide-rimmed black-veiled hat, with her grim-faced Strachan relatives)—never ceased to proclaim to the world how heroically Josiah had "saved the lives" of her baby and herself. Yet, even in New York City, to which his restless spirits took him, he sometimes imagined strangers watching him. *And where can you run, and where can you hide? Bearing the mark of Cain on your forehead, the murderer of one who trusted you.*

It was an unexpected development, after months of behaving in a subdued and melancholy way, Josiah was beginning to be irritable, and irascible; most of all, the young man was prone to quarreling with his father, Augustus, as he had rarely done previously. Fresh from reading all that he lay hands on of the writings of Upton Sinclair—(known to be a resident of the Princeton area, whom Josiah was eager to meet)—as well as Lincoln Steffens's *The Shame of the Cities* and novels by Frank Norris and Theodore Dreiser, Josiah had surprised his parent by disagreeing with his father over the veracity of J. Ogden Armour's reply to *The Jungle*, which was published in the *Saturday Evening Post;* and of the good faith of the majority of businessmen who were angrily refuting the charges of "muckrakers" in the press.

Augustus responded with dignity, initially; when his son pressed the issue, daring to bring to the dinner table, to read aloud, the most repulsive passages from *The Jungle* and from Norris's novels, Augustus reacted as if he had been personally challenged: "Josiah, enough. Those are Socialists and Anarchists—they are not to be trusted! Free Thinkers, Suffragettes, Atheists—those who would overturn our civilization, and set it to the torch. You will not upset your mother and your grandfather and *me,* at such a time in our lives."

"What better time, Father? If the world is in upheaval, what are we to do but heave ourselves up, with it?"

"If you knew what you were saying, Josiah, you would not speak in such a reckless way."

"If you knew what you were saying, Father, you would not speak in so complacent a way."

Now agitated, a flush coming into his face, Augustus said, with uncharacteristic anger: "I can scarcely believe this is *you,* a son of mine, and a grandson of Winslow Slade, who says such things—and not an evil spirit that has wormed its way into your heart."

Evil spirit! This unjust remark had the effect of silencing Josiah and sending him from the table with a muttered apology. At his place at the dining room table was a plate of roast beef from Mr. Armour's Chicago stockyard, untouched.

Now at the Slade family mausoleum, at Oriana's gravesite, Josiah stood stiffly tall. He had managed to avoid his parents, and was standing between his weeping aunt Lenora and his grandfather Winslow, who was leaning on Josiah's arm; lightly at first, and then with increasing heaviness. A pious drone of Christian prayers numbed his brain. Josiah wanted to bestir the mourners by demanding who among them believed, for a particle of a moment, that his little cousin Oriana was an "angel" in Heaven; who did not believe that the family Curse had claimed her, as it would claim them all, in time.

One of his voices slyly queried *If Annabel has died, why not Oriana? A balance is restored beneath Crosswicks and Wheatsheaf and now just Josiah and Todd remain.*

Though he knew better, as a rationalist, and one for whom "history" is a matter of scientific investigation, yet it did seem to Josiah that Professor van Dyck was very convincing, in arguing for the Curse; if less convincing in its particulars. Josiah could not conceive that an actual demon had entered into Pearce's soul but it did seem plausible that the philosophy professor had been poisoned by the noxious Angel Trumpet carelessly pressed into a book; he had not confessed to anyone that he had himself given the toxic plant to his friend, under the mistaken impression that it was a calla lily—that's to say, a ghostly calla lily.

The Mercer County coroner had discovered that, indeed, a region of the cerebral cortex of Pearce van Dyck's brain had visibly deteriorated, by what cause the coroner could not say. He did not rule for the Angel Trumpet, but he did not rule against it, either.

It was similarly implausible to think that a "demon" had entered into the deranged Horace Burr, now committed to the Otterholme Hospital for the Criminally Insane, in Summit, New Jersey, where the controversial Thornhurst water cure for homicidal lunatics had been prescribed for him.* Horace Burr was said to be scarcely recognizable. (It was a measure

---

* The Thornhurst water cure for nervous invalids, named for the prominent physician Silas Thornhurst of the Harvard Medical School, was one of a number of "water therapies" of the time. The patient was strapped in a chair of proven durability, with particular attention given to leather straps (encased in cotton batting, to prevent injury) about the head, torso, and legs; then, a quantity of cold water was "dashed" onto the head from several hoses or conduits, from a height of approximately six feet. To prevent accidental drowning, swallowing of the tongue, or vocal cord rupture from excessive screaming, a clean cloth or sponge was always kept in the mouth; and every precaution was taken, and after several hours of the treatment the patient was removed at once to a room and placed in

of Horace Burr's madness that, soon after his arrest, confession, and commitment to Otterholme, the deluded man began to alter his story: though he had certainly murdered Adelaide to "put her out of her misery," it had been through the urgings of Miss Wilhelmina Burr, a young relative of his, that he had done so. In this fantastical story, Horace Burr spoke of the *bluestocking temptress* as the true cause of the murder, for she had "given me some hope, that we might one day marry—if I were free." What was more alarming, and to Josiah disgusting, many in Princeton were coming around to believe the madman's slander; and Wilhelmina Burr had even been questioned by Princeton police, to her great shame.)

At the edge of the gathering of West End mourners was a curious couple—heavyset Grover Cleveland with slouching shoulders, and a bowed head, so obese that his neck spilled over his collar; and Frances Cleveland heavily made-up with "kohl" eyes and a shiny mouth, and very fashionably dressed for so somber an occasion. It had been rumored that, of late, Mr. Cleveland continued to be "poorly"; though he ate as usual his enormous morning meal, and a yet more enormous evening meal, he was reportedly "of little appetite" for his luncheon meal, and often fell asleep in the company of others, at times even when he was himself talking. In the sudden death of Oriana Slade, Mr. Cleveland was surely reliving the death of his beloved Ruth; when visiting Wheatsheaf, Mr. Cleveland had always made it a point to talk to the pretty little blond girl, and to dandle her on his fatty knee; laughingly he told his hosts that he would "very happily" spend the entire evening in the nursery, with their beautiful little daughter, than at the dinner table where he was expected to "wax eloquent." (In truth, no one expected Grover Cleveland to "wax eloquent" at any West End dinner table.) Even now, as the heartbreakingly small

a warm bed, there to sleep uninterrupted for as long as twelve hours. Although Horace Burr was to die of a stroke in 1911, still an inmate at Otterholme, it was generally believed that the Thornhurst treatment had cured him of his raving delusions, as the patient was reported "docile, very quiet and tranquil" in the last year of his life.

mother-of-pearl coffin was being placed in the tomb by pallbearers, Mr. Cleveland sucked in his breath, and swallowed; he had all he could do, to keep from fainting; for he saw the little blond child and his own dear Ruth playing amid the weatherworn gravestones—dancing in their white garments, their hair loosed and curly, and their dainty feet bare. As he stared, smiling, the girls hid behind a marble angel about fifteen feet away, and peeped out at him, one darling head on either side and forefingers to their pretty pursed lips. *Daddy come play with us! Play with us now! Tell no one but come play with us now!*

("Grover, you must not make such sounds," Frances whispered in her husband's ear, irritably, "—that sound not like sobs but like *grunts*. Please just stop, I am so *mortified*.")

Also at the edge of the gathering of mourners, as if uncertain of their social standing among the West End company, stood Woodrow Wilson and his wife Ellen; the one tall, puritanical and stiff-backed, and the other short, somewhat dowdily dressed, with a small black veiled hat that looked, to the West End ladies' eyes, like something that had been pushed to the back of a closet years ago, and had lately been dusted off and revived. And Mrs. Wilson's black cloth coat, with shiny black buttons, looked suspiciously similar to a cast-off black cloth coat that had belonged to Frances Cleveland, and had been recently donated by her to the Princeton Women's Relief Fund, for indigent females in Mercer County.

The healthy tan Woodrow Wilson had acquired during his Bermuda sojourn, which everyone in Princeton had remarked upon, had faded with unusual swiftness; for this spring of 1906 in New Jersey was wet, chill, often overcast and cheerless, and spring flowers and blossoming trees were beaten down by relentless rain. Yet, Dr. Wilson retained still an air of strength and determination. The "Defeat at Charleston" he wished to think was behind him now; but he deeply grieved the loss of his old friend and supporter Pearce van Dyck whose brain, Dr. Wilson believed, had simply "snapped" under the tension of the university struggle: these many months of conflict, subterfuge, and tireless politicking among Woodrow

Wilson's enemies among the faculty and administration. Yet, Pearce's death had had one positive result: for by it Dr. Wilson's Campbell fighting mettle was aroused another time, and, within a week of his friend's funeral, the president of Princeton University addressed his quasi-mutinous board of trustees so forcibly, and so convincingly, that, with some reluctance, the gentlemen were led to do the unthinkable—to reject the $1 million Procter bequest, that came with an insistence that the dean of the Graduate School, and not the president of the university, have control of the fund. News had spread through Princeton that Woodrow Wilson had racked up an unexpected victory over Andrew West, who was taken utterly by surprise, and had been going about town boasting recklessly that he would be the university's next president. What a pity it was, Woodrow told his wife, when news of the board's decision came to him, that Pearce van Dyck could not share in this glory, which was the first step in the recovery of Dr. Wilson's authority.

Dr. Wilson was given to thinking, in his brooding, ever-obsessive manner, that, were it known, Pearce van Dyck was a casualty of the "war" against Woodrow Wilson, very nearly a "martyr." Of that, Dr. Wilson would not wish to speak, at least not immediately.

"It is so sad, Woodrow, isn't it! The poor *child*."

"Yes. It is always sad. But—'Ashes to ashes, dust to dust.' This is the peace that passeth understanding."

Dr. Wilson's lips moved nimbly. For a vague moment, he could not recall what funeral—whose funeral—this was.

At a little distance from his parents, as if estranged from them, stood Todd Slade, outfitted in black broadcloth mourning, with a fitted jacket, short trousers pegged at the knee, and black socks tightly secured by garters. The brother of the deceased little girl had been dressed, with much stoic effort, by the children's nanny; Todd's mother had not laid a hand on him, nor could she bring herself to look at him this morning, for fearing to see, in the boy's eyes, an accusation of *her*.

In the past several months, Todd Slade had somewhat matured:

he was not so spindly-limbed, nor so antic. His face had become more angular, and sharp-boned; his sloping chin, more pointed and stubborn; his bright black eyes, beneath quizzical brows, darted about with the restlessness of minnows. He was five feet four inches tall—a good height for a skinny twelve-year-old. Todd had not wept for his sister's death, it was being whispered of him. (In some quarters, including servants' quarters, it was being whispered that the "strange" boy knew more about his sister's death than he had admitted.) As the child's coffin was secured inside the mausoleum, and a light chill rain fell on the heads of all, as on the weatherworn granite tomb, Todd stood very still with shut eyes and a twitching mouth. *I shall be good. I shall be the swan that is now needed, and not the duckling.*

IT WAS TO his grandson Todd that Winslow Slade suddenly turned, as the gravesite ceremony was nearing its end, and the heavy iron doors of the family mausoleum were being closed, and secured; to Todd, that the elderly white-haired man appealed, taking his arm and saying that he must "protect" him—"My grandsons Todd and Josiah, who are all that remain of that generation." Blinking in confusion, a hopeful smile on his lips, Winslow said to Josiah, "For my old sin lies upon you and I must explain myself, and make amends however I can, that God will spare my remaining grandchildren."

Winslow's sons came quickly forward as well, as if to silence their father, whose words were astonishing to them; but Winslow resisted the men, slipping his arms through the arms of his grandsons, and holding them close to him, as all stared.

"Allow me to speak now, at Oriana's grave," Winslow said, pleadingly, "as I had shrunk from speaking at Annabel's grave. This I beg of you all, if you love me; or, failing that, if you pity me."

***

HERE FOLLOWS, in summary form, assembled out of the Ebony-Lacquered Box, Winslow Slade's remarkable account—his "confession," it might be said; an impassioned if not entirely coherent recollection of an event of 1855, involving a young woman known only as "Pearl." This impromptu revelation was unparalleled in Princeton, and most astonishing to all who were witnesses, who would speak of it, and write of it, in an alarming variety of ways. As Winslow Slade spoke with numerous halts and stammers, and frequently lapsed into silence, it is impossible for me to render his words accurately here; nor will I note when one or the other of his agitated and embarrassed sons pressed him to quit, and to come away home, for it seemed as if the elderly man was on the brink of a nervous collapse.

The "unfortunate episode in my life"—as Winslow Slade called it—began one afternoon in March, in 1855; a day unlike this day in May when overcast winter skies yielded suddenly to a suggestion of spring; a temporary respite, yet much prized. Winslow Slade was twenty-four years old at this time and had only just entered into an engagement (later to be broken) with the heiress daughter of Jarrell LaBove, a Republican senator from New Jersey; he lived with his parents at Crosswicks, and took classes at the Princeton Theological Seminary where he was studying Hebrew, Greek, the Old and New Testaments of the Bible, Germanic theology, and such practical subjects as "sermon preparation and delivery" and "pastoral counseling." Like most of the seminarians Winslow Slade had entered the Presbyterian seminary immediately after graduation from college, not entirely decided whether he would become a "man of the cloth" or a private, Biblical scholar; or whether he would seek his destiny in a more secular sphere of public life. (One of Winslow's classmates and friends was Henry van Dyck, who would become a renowned minister and orator and, in time, Professor of English Literature at Princeton—for the record, the father of Pearce van Dyck.) Three years earlier, at commencement day exercises at the university, the young graduate Winslow Slade had delivered the *belles lettres* oration, speaking so avidly of Milton, Goethe, and Shakespeare, and of the need of graduates to devote themselves to both the God of their fathers and the nation's destiny, he was several times interrupted by applause, and felt elation, that *words* could arouse such a response in an audience. (The *New York Herald* of June 25, 1852, noted that young Mr. Slade's oration was "an eloquent, glowing, and greatly inspiring effort, presented with intelligent sensitivity, the high point perhaps of the morning's exercises.")

So, it had seemed that an enviable career lay ahead. Winslow Slade had but to pluck the fruit from the tree, that was his for the taking.

Yet, within a year of seminary studies, and the tension of courting an attractive but badly spoiled young woman of nineteen, Winslow was feeling exhausted; his brain felt literally overtaxed, from the study of languages and from the custom of preaching sermons in empty churches; in a short period of time the young man succumbed to maladies as variously diagnosed as typhoid, brain fever, and neuritis, which necessitated a period of calm and recuperation at Crosswicks, and temporary withdrawal from the seminary. It was within two weeks of Winslow's recovery from a virulent fever of unknown origin that, by the malevolence of chance, the young man had the unfortunate "adventure" that would haunt him through his life . . .

At this time, Winslow was newly engaged; and had endured a round of engagement parties in Princeton, New York, and Philadelphia; in a valiant attempt to make up for lost time at the seminary he was working twelve to fourteen hours a day, as it was a matter of pride that he graduate with his classmates, and not even a few months after. In addition, Winslow sometimes prowled the grounds of Crosswicks late at night, debating to himself the old knotty issues of Calvinism and free will, that gripped him, he said, like a strangler's hands.

His ancestor Jonathan Edwards had had not a moment's doubt that human life was strictly *determined*, by God; Reverend Edwards had but scorn for the "childishness" of the very notion of free will. Yet the conundrum was, if we don't know the future, and have no idea what God's plan for us is, are we not in a position to imagine "free will"?—and are we not responsible, in any case, for our actions?

Most of humankind was damned to Hell, Jonathan Edwards and his contemporary Puritans believed. But Winslow Slade could not accept it, that God would send most of His creation to Hell.

Being a modest young man, easily embarrassed and not wishing to seem pious, pretentious, or naïve, Winslow had said nothing of these thoughts to any elder, and certainly not to his pretty fiancée, Evangeline.

And so, one March afternoon, Winslow was studying in the seminary library, in which a window had been pushed up several inches, to allow in fresh air; he had set for himself the task of completing a section of his Hebrew grammar, and sketching out an editorial for the *Presbyterian*, an agreeable but time-consuming task assigned to him by his advisor, Reverend Frick; and trying to collect his thoughts on the subject of infant damnation as elucidated by the Reverend Lancelot Price on the one hand and the Reverend Frederick Ettl on the other. For several hours the young man had been working diligently in the library, among a number of his classmates, whose diligence mirrored his own, when, suddenly, it seemed to him that a flame licked over his hands and the hefty volume he was gripping: a flame that was blue, and orange, and pale green and pale yellow, though transparent: and in that instant leapt up to his exposed eyes, and entered his brain.

Winslow was not an excitable young man: he understood that the flame was some sort of optical illusion, some pathology of the optic nerve exacerbated by overwork and by his recent illness, and he did not allow himself to be (visibly) upset. (He did not wish to believe that the Devil had anything to do with it: he was not that sort of Presbyterian.) And so Winslow stifled a cry, and left the room without attracting any attention, he believed; though it would seem curious to his classmates that he'd left his books and papers behind, and an expensive fountain pen. Hurriedly he left the redbrick building, that was surrounded with sere winter grass, on the cusp of spring; quickly he walked across the wide lawn, avoiding a fellow seminarian, and one of his minister-professors; quickly he walked to Mercer Street, and southward, toward the open countryside; finding himself in a meadow, with a thawing, soft earth beneath, with no clear idea of where he was going, only that he must go somewhere— anywhere!—away from the Theological Seminary, and from Princeton.

How Winslow Slade made his way south-west-ward to the village of Cold Spring, in Hopewell Township, and to a public house somewhat ominously called The Fox and the Hare, located at least twenty miles from Princeton, the young man would never quite understand; he must have hiked with more than his usual vigor and single-mindedness, soon abandoning Mercer Street for Stockton, and Stockton for Rosedale, and Rosedale for Province Line, until at last he abandoned roads altogether to traverse farmers' fields and forests. During this suspended period of time Winslow's thoughts were not of theology, nor even of his imminent assignments, or his fiancée, or his family at Crosswicks, who expected so much of him; rather, his thoughts were like the buzzing of maddened flies.

The Fox and the Hare was utterly unknown to Winslow Slade, as to any of the Slades; it proved a coarse, rowdy, noisy yet companionable place. Despite his "city clothes"—and the sturdy leather shoes he was wearing—Winslow was not made to feel self-conscious; yet, unwisely, he quickly downed a tankard of ale, in emulation of the robust workingmen around him: persons of all ages who drank heartily and talked together loudly, laughing with great hilarity. (Who were they?—very likely mill-workers, who labored in the textile mills on the Delaware River a mile away, in the small town of Lambertville.) How strange it seemed to the seminarian, these individuals behaved *as if they enjoyed their lives, and one another*. And yet—what was there for them to enjoy? For were they not men of a low social rank, coarse-featured, and carelessly clothed and groomed, obliged to work with their hands and their backs; did not some of them, as Winslow happened to notice, bear scars and worse injuries, like missing fingers, and badly crooked backs? Their hilarity was so threaded with profanities and obscenities—(of a kind Winslow had never heard before, and could not have imagined)—it was clear to him that they were not beloved of God, and that Jesus had not entered their hearts; worse, they did not miss God, or Jesus. *They don't seem to understand that they are damned,* Winslow thought, —*someone should tell them!* But this ministerial thought he quickly cast from him, as unwanted at this time.

So it was, caught up in the general hilarity of the pub in Cold Spring, Winslow Slade downed a second tankard of ale, which went down more easily; and so, a third; and shortly became so giddy and confused in his perceptions, he failed to notice that a coarse-featured rust-red-haired man of some age beyond his, yet not much older than he, had crowded beside him at the bar, as if singling him out; and was soon urging Winslow, if not pleading with him, to come outside, where *someone is asking for you.*

Or, it might have been that the coarse-featured man was saying *someone is in need.*

So it happened, again without Winslow's exact comprehension, that he had left The Fox and the Hare, and was walking, or being "walked"— (for by this time the young seminarian, unaccustomed to drinking, was not very steady on his feet)—a short distance away; now, in another dwelling, not a pub but a crude house, or cabin; here, amid a strong smell of woodsmoke and kerosene, a young woman, more precisely a girl, of some age younger than Winslow, perhaps as much as eight or ten years younger than he, was presented to him; rather, pushed at him by the rust-red-haired man and another, whose face Winslow could not see clearly. The girl was named "Pearl"—or so Winslow was informed, by both men; in the lamp-light she appeared to be *of mixed race,* Winslow thought; not "colored"—not "black"—or obviously "Negroid"—but of some mixture of these, with European ancestry; her nose was snubbed, and wide at the nostrils; her skin was a coarse, slightly pitted sere color, like something that has been left in the sun, and faded; her hair was hidden beneath a soiled head-scarf, of the kind the colored women at Crosswicks commonly wore. Nudged toward Pearl, as Pearl was nudged toward Winslow, the two were crowded together, in a small cramped space in the cabin; there were bare floorboards, a single bed with a soiled mattress and a coarse blanket, of the weight of a horse-blanket, dropped on it. The girl's smell was strong: of a female body, and of rarely washed clothes; more pungently, of her grease-stiffened hair. And her breath smelled, like Winslow's, of ale.

As Pearl struggled to focus her eyes, and to spread her fleshy lips in a semblance of a smile, to please her captors—(for "captors" the men appeared to be)—Winslow tried to detach himself, to flee; but the girl placed her hand so firmly on his arm, and fixed her dark gaze so intently upon his gaze, he felt a sort of paralysis enter his soul.

What followed from this, Winslow Slade would have very little memory.

Except a moment's revulsion, and recoiling—for he could not fail to see that several teeth were missing from Pearl's mouth, in her lower jaw; and that the fingers of her right hand, with which she dared to "caress" him, were badly mangled.

Except a sense, belated, and ineffectual, that something was being taken from him—(his wallet? his sturdy leather shoes?)—which he knew he must prevent, yet could not; for the wily girl was in his arms, or rather, the seminarian was in her arms, that grasped him tightly; in his ear, her hot breath that smelled of ale, and something darker. And so the rust-red-haired man and his companion laughed together, and left the seminarian and Pearl together, with a jocular slamming of the door.

So, time passed in confusion; Winslow Slade may in fact have lost consciousness, and lost all knowledge of his surroundings; there was an interruption, and there were loud (male) voices, and in the background a rushing of water, that indicated the Delaware River, which Winslow could not see, or had not the wit to try to see, at this time.

Later it would be revealed, the rust-red-haired man was named Henri Selincourt. But "Pearl" had no last name.

Ah, that Winslow Slade knew so little of his fellow man: that he had lived almost a quarter century, and knew Latin, and Greek, and Hebrew, and French, and German, and the Hebrew Bible and the New Testament, and the latest and most fashionable theological notion, but he seemed to have no notion of the gravity of the situation, and the danger he was in. That he was *engaged to be married*, yet remained ignorant of the wiles of the opposite sex . . .

In his confusion, and mounting fear, Winslow saw the pale flame lick across the contorted female face, faintly blue, yet orange and red as well, and transparent; in her eyes, a sickly yellow glow, as at her fingertips; and a faintness overcame him, that he had succumbed to the embrace of a demon, and his life would be blighted thereafter.

Yet, his paralysis was such, he could not seem to break away, but suffered the female's mouth to attach to his, and to suck, and suck; as if she might suck out his very soul; even as her sharp nails clawed at him, in a kind of provocative play, as one might tease a small child, or a dog, to animate it. How fleshy, the female's body! Not delicate-boned, and small-waisted, like the young women with whom Winslow was acquainted, and her arm-muscles sinewy, inside the fatty flesh. And the shock of the female bosom, the large, cushiony breasts naked inside the female clothing . . . All this while, to rude laughter, Winslow was pleading that he must leave; he must return to his family, in Princeton; he must have his shoes back . . . Now it had been discovered that Winslow Slade was carrying a gold pocket watch, in an inside pocket; this watch, inscribed to *W.S.*, was in fact an inherited watch, and priceless. Greedy hands snatched at it, and Winslow could not prevent them from taking it, as Pearl laughed, the gaps in her lower jaw painfully revealed. It may have been that Winslow tried to wrench himself from her, or pushed and shoved at the rust-red-haired man and his companion, who had returned to the cabin; for somehow, there was a struggle, and there were female screams, and a voice that was not the voice of the female, nor of the others, but a voice that seemed to issue from the very air of this hideous dank place—*You are of the Slades, you boast to all the world that you are a Slade, yet Reverend we shall see if you are not brought down to Hell.*

Was this the Devil speaking, in prophecy? Or was this the very God of Winslow Slade's ancestors, speaking in disgust of *him*?

Suddenly it seemed, the coarse-skinned girl was furious with Winslow. Or—someone was furious with Winslow.

For he was struggling fiercely now, to save his life. As the girl clawed at him, like a maddened animal.

In desperation Winslow freed himself from her, and managed to escape from the cabin; unless, in mirth, his assailants had allowed him to escape, and were laughing heartily at him, as he fled running—limping . . .

Along a roadside, in the rural dark . . .

Behind him, shouts. Female cries, fading.

For Winslow had managed to escape, and made his way limping and lurching, in his stocking feet, into a wooded area, collapsing here, for how long he wasn't certain, before summoning his strength, and continuing onward, with the vaguest awareness of a road somewhere ahead, which would turn out to be the Lambertville-Trenton Road, that intersected with the Old King's Highway, and that with the Princeton Pike, that would bring him at last home tearful and repentant.

"God help me! For I could not have helped myself."

YET, WHAT WAS the seminarian's mortification, and shame, when he learned a few days later that the *unclothed, badly beaten corpse of a young Negro female* had been found in a wooded area in Cold Spring, in Hopewell Township, a quarter mile from a *public house of local notoriety;* knowing at once that this was Pearl and that the rust-red-haired man and his companion had very likely beaten her, and murdered her.

Yet Winslow's terror of exposure was such, he could not force himself to step forward to speak; he could not, *would not,* volunteer to help in the identification of the murderers.

It was not that God failed to give Winslow Slade the clear knowledge of what he should do, but rather, God withheld from him the strength with which to do it.

I cannot. I know that I must and yet—I cannot.

For all of my life will be ruined, and the hopes of my family—dashed, despoiled.

Then, what was the coward's daily terror but that he would be drawn into the case, and made to testify at a public hearing; and forced to reveal, under penalty of perjury, all that had happened on that luckless night. Indeed, his life would be ruined; his career as a minister killed, in the bud; his engagement ended, and hope for marriage destroyed; nor could Winslow Slade raise his head in decent society again, or look his dear parents in the eye; for it was nearly as the wrathful voice had predicted *Yet you shall be brought down to Hell.*

But, as God had allowed Winslow to escape the female and her companions, and to make his desperate way back to Princeton, by that time badly limping, with bloodied feet, so God intervened another time, and the murderer Selincourt was apprehended within a week, and made to confess; and a number of witnesses in Cold Spring came forth to testify against him, speaking of his inclination to rob, beat, and intimidate any who opposed him, and of his liaison with the young mill-girl whose body had been found.

Nothing was said in the press of a gold heirloom pocket watch, from a Swiss manufacturer, that must have been found in Selincourt's pockets. Or a pair of sturdy leather shoes from a Princeton cobbler, that could not have belonged to an individual like Selincourt, or any of his companions.

In this way, the sordid matter ended, with a public hanging at Trenton of Henri Selincourt; and the episode forgotten.

Forgotten that is by all except the young Winslow Slade, soon to become Reverend Slade, a highly revered "gentleman of the cloth"; honored by the task of providing the master's oration at the seminary, at graduation, and licensed to preach by the Presbyterian Church in Lawrenceville. In this he was applauded, and congratulated, and admired, and warmly spoken-of by all, and held up as a model of Christian integrity through the tumultuous decades of the late nineteenth century: rising in his public career and in the estimation of his peers: ever rising: to the presidency of Princeton University at the very young age of forty-one, and to the governorship of the State of New Jersey, thirteen years later.

"In my pride, and in my shame. And now—I stand before you utterly exposed, and beg your mercy."

In a soft but unwavering voice Winslow Slade brought his story to an end, as all strained to hear. He was not now leaning on Josiah's arm, but stood apart from him, addressing the gathering of mourners of whom not one failed to be deeply moved, and many blinked tears from their eyes. He said, "My dear family, and my dear friends—I have carried the scar of this old sin in my heart through the years, to this very hour. So often have I prayed to God for forgiveness, I think it possible that God, in His mercy, has forgiven me for now; yet I have not forgiven myself; and have come to realize, through the past year, that the Curse leashed upon our community springs from the Curse of the young woman Pearl—and from my cowardice, revealed at last to the judgment and censure of all the world."

Soon then, the Slades urged Winslow to leave the gravesite, and to be driven, in one of the family motorcars, back to Crosswicks; while his listeners remained behind, as if slow to leave the cemetery, in the wake of the extraordinary revelation.

At first, all were silent; then, all began talking.

Amanda FitzRandolph, resplendently attired in her widow's clothing, raised her voice in the way of an operatic singer, to drown out lesser voices: "Winslow Slade is a saint, indeed—as we've long known. Who else would stand before us, so humbled? So *Christian*? To 'forgive' such a man is ridiculous. Only—what a pity that Winslow Slade's judgment should be so affected by the loss of his granddaughters, to allow him to imagine that *he*, of all people, might be held to account for the so-called 'curse' . . ."

As Mrs. FitzRandolph spoke, it seemed that a warmer, more spring-like air suffused the cemetery; overhead, the occluded sky began to break, and thin rays of sunlight appeared, like hesitant fingers; the mourners felt a sort of shifting of the very earth, or believed that they did; as if at last the Curse might now be lifting.

"Pray God it's so," Dr. Wilson murmured to his wife, as they walked from the Princeton cemetery, virtually alone of all the mourners having come on foot, in the direction of Nassau Street, and the university campus, "for surely, all of us have been punished enough."

I t can't be. My own uncle—a murderer of his wife. *And a shameless liar.*"

Virtually sleepless since the terrible news had been relayed to her, by telephone, that her uncle Horace Burr had *brutally murdered* her cousin Adelaide Burr—(in fact, the women were third-cousins, and not very closely related by blood)—Wilhelmina found herself at the center of a sordid melodrama, as improbable as any devised by Mary Elizabeth Braddon, Louisa May Alcott, and Wilkie Collins: her deranged uncle Horace was claiming that he had murdered his wife *at the instigation of the bluestocking temptress Wilhelmina Burr.*

No amount of denials, protestations, or defenses seemed to make any difference, in what is called the "court" of public opinion; though Princeton police detectives, investigating the case, were inclined to be sympathetic with the distraught Miss Burr, whose testimony seemed to them far more likely than the rambling testimony of Horace Burr.

Wilhelmina had in fact overheard one of the police officers say to another, believing himself out of her hearing: "As if *she* would have anything to do with *him.*"

The shock of it was, Wilhelmina had always liked her uncle Horace, and thought him the most patient, kindly, and tolerant of husbands, in that category of "invalid-husbands" of Princeton, of whom there were a number, at any given time.

And how shocking, Horace had stolen Adelaide's ivory swan-brooch, to give to Wilhelmina; and Wilhelmina had kept the exquisitely wrought piece of jewelry hidden away in a drawer, unable to part with it, as she was unable to wear it in public.

Following Adelaide's death, Wilhelmina took out the swan-brooch and decided that she would wear it after all: "For Adelaide would want me to, I think. Adelaide would not want it to be shut away in a drawer."

Even a natural death, a fully "legal" death, has repercussions far beyond what might be anticipated; how much more, a murder, within one's family. And there were numerous legal complications following from the murder of Adelaide McLean Burr, whose estate would have gone to her husband, ordinarily; except, in this case, her husband was both her murderer and a homicidal lunatic imprisoned at Otterholme. So, there was much for local lawyers to deal with, to their delight; and Wilhelmina felt obliged to return to Princeton, to Pembroke House, to offer emotional support to her female relatives in particular, who were in need of her company and counsel. Her parents did not for an instant believe the ugly rumors, that Wilhelmina had "instigated" her uncle, for they were in a position to know how avidly their daughter wanted to live in New York, and be an *artiste*. It was a measure of their sympathy for her, in the wake of the disaster, that they spoke of her admiringly, if not with much knowledge of what she was doing, or what her art "meant"—for it seemed to them dark, and smudged, and too ordinary in its subjects, to be of a class with the great masters, or with the American landscape painter Frederic Church, whose oil painting of the Hudson River Valley *Storm at Twilight* was the centerpiece of their dining room.

So it happened, "Willy" has returned to Princeton, to a maze of familial responsibilities; but can't bring herself to venture out into society, even to the funeral of Oriana Slade, whose death has torn at her heart. "Even though I would see Josiah there, I cannot."

Instead, she writes letters of condolence to all of the Slades, not just Lenora and Copplestone. And to Josiah she adds *What terrible things have happened to your family, and to all of us who love you.*

Quickly then, before she can change her mind, and rescind the word *love,* she seals and stamps the envelope.

MANY MILES AWAY in Boston, Dean Andrew West, having concluded a disappointing interview in the Beacon Hill mansion of the wealthy octo-genarian Isaac Wyman (Princeton 1843), prepared slowly to take his leave, as his gaze moved about the elderly man's library—seizing and discard-ing one item after another: Latin volumes (surely never once opened); an ivory elephant paperweight (from India, perhaps, but Andrew West knows nothing of that barbaric place); flatteringly executed portraits of Wyman ancestors; the head of a great-eared klipspringer, stuffed and mounted and staring in mournful resignation from a brass plaque above the fireplace (but Dean West is not a hunter); and, what's this?—a conversation piece, or a family heirloom—an antiquated musket and powder horn prominently placed upon the wall.

Cleverly, in the casual way of a practiced administrator and fund-raiser, Dean West remarked upon these items, in admiring tones, knowing that his elderly host would respond with enthusiasm. Though Princeton's popular dean had been lately rebuffed by the board of trustees, and would seem to be floundering in his struggle with Woodrow Wilson, yet Dean West never registered any sign of discouragement, or distraction, but only a frank and boyish *enthusiasm*. (He would leave to Woodrow Wilson, he said, such displays of temper; for in the end, Wilson's "childish egotism" would defeat him.) So it was no surprise when Isaac Wyman told him, in detail, of his great-grandfather Captain Horatio Wyman, one of General Washington's most trusted aides; a hero who had fallen "in great glory" at the Battle of Princeton.

Andrew West's eyes alight, and his wide mouth widens in a delighted smile.

"The Battle of Princeton, you say? Why, Mr. Wyman, I walk in Battle Park, as it's called, every day of my life, in all weather. And it would be close by Battle Park, with a view running to Mercer Street, that the Graduate College would be built, according to my plan; while Mr. Wilson prefers to build merely on campus, amid a plethora of other buildings, in which the Graduate College would be swallowed up."

At which the wealthy alum, who'd seemed eager to be rid of the dean but a few minutes previously, urges him to sit down again, and offers him a glass of his very best Scots whiskey.

"You must tell me more about these plans, Dean West. 'With a view' of Battle Park, I think you said?"*

AT MIDDAY, having brought his mother to a luncheon at the home of Sparhawk relatives in Kingston, New Jersey—(less than a mile from the Rocky Hill Seminary for Girls, the site of the notorious "Snake Frenzy")—ex-Lieutenant Dabney Bayard slips away from the company, to find himself walking swiftly along the tangled bank of the Millstone River, brooding, lost in thought, vastly relieved to be alone for the first time in hours. How tired Dabney is, of "genteel" conversation; of his

---

* It is not the historian's strategy to keep his reader in any sort of cheap suspense, for history is *past*; so I see no reason not to reveal to the reader that the outcome of the feud between Wilson and West is signaled by the fact that, to this very day, the antique musket and powder horn once belonging to Captain Hiram Wyman adorns a wall in Wyman House, the residence of the dean of the graduate school. We can marvel retrospectively how, out of the dean's inspired, "The Battle of Princeton, you say?" spring forth not only the triumph of Woodrow Wilson's enemies at Princeton but also the subsequent triumph of Woodrow Wilson as the Democratic candidate for President in the autumn of 1912; also the Fourteen Points, the Covenant of a League of Nations, the Espionage Act of 1917, and the Sedition Act of 1918.

mother, whose love for him is stifling as damp cotton batting, and her tedious relatives of whom not one is younger than she, and no one is near the age of her restless son. Especially, Dabney is relieved to escape an excruciating discussion of the *Crosswicks Curse,* as they call it; a subject about which Dabney Bayard never comments but maintains a dignified, wounded silence. For he has no idea how he feels, in his innermost heart: does he mourn Annabel Slade, who had been his lawful wedded wife for fewer than five minutes; or is he in fact glad that she has died, and that the Slades are in perpetual mourning; does he wish that he had been able to hunt down Axson Mayte, and murder the man with his bare hands, or is he relieved, too, that he'd never come close to his wife's seducer, and so had not a chance of murdering him, and blighting his own, young life?

"To Hell with them all. I mean *all.*"

A short distance along the river path, and a climb over the hill bearing the Old King's Highway, and now on the canal pathway that would border, for some of its length, Lake Carnegie;* where he sees, suddenly, a young man of about twenty, straddling a bicycle, in a dark purple sweater he recognizes as a "club" sweater—he thinks it might be Cottage. (Ivy and Cottage being the "elite" of the eating clubs at this time.) Dabney, a West Pointer, now bereft of his commission, feels a prick of resentment for the Princeton undergraduate who has pedaled out to Kingston; he guesses that the boy is the son of a wealthy father, and judging from his blandly

---

* Lake Carnegie! This was one of the first, and it would hardly be the last, of Woodrow Wilson's "presidential defeats." The beautiful lake is an artificial reservoir formed by a dam on the Millstone River, a gift from the "Gilded Age" industrialist Andrew Carnegie to the Princeton University crewing team in 1906. Woodrow Wilson perceived the gift as a mixed blessing and could not rejoice, as others did, in Lake Carnegie; for Andrew Carnegie had conspired with alumni behind the president's back to purchase the land and build the lake, quite apart from Dr. Wilson's reiterated wish that the wealthy industrialist would underwrite the costs of a university library. To the irascible benefactor Dr. Wilson reputedly said: "We needed bread, Mr. Carnegie, and you gave us cake."

"angelic" good looks, he has not suffered yet. Dreamily he stares at the lake, like a college-boy illustration in *Collier's Weekly;* though he appears to be unaware of Dabney, there is something arrogant in his pose, as he gazes at the soft-rippling water in what seems to be *willful indifference to Dabney Bayard* who stands very still watching him at a distance of about thirty feet.

Dabney sees that the boy wears no club hat, which is to the boy's credit; his wheat-colored hair is thick and wavy, and would be *interesting* to touch. His clothes are casual, but stylish—of course. His trousers fit his slender body loosely; his manner is buoyant and forthright; he isn't disturbing the tranquility of the canal pathway by whistling, or bustling about, with a pretense of taking delight in Nature—which attitude, in Dabney's own sex, Dabney finds particularly repulsive.

Dabney would turn away, but something holds him: the wavy-haired boy is now stretching his arms, and yawning; still oblivious of being observed, and believing himself alone. He lets fall his bicycle and strolls to the lakeside where he squats near the water, in his dreamy mood.

Across the placid surface of the water, a flotilla of noisy Canada geese.

"I will walk away of course. I will not approach him."

Yet now Dabney is (disagreeably) startled by the appearance, at his elbow, of a third person; doubly taken aback that this is the "Count"— the European theologian, so-called, introduced to Dabney recently at a soiree at Drumthwacket; the man's name is too lengthy to remember, and has the ring of a fraudulent name; he is from Wallachia, or Romania, or Bavaria, or wherever. Though nothing more than a small *frisson* of recognition passed between the ex-lieutenant and the Count at the Pynes' dinner party, now the tall, elegantly clothed gentleman is smiling at Dabney, and showing his gleaming wet teeth; and, whether in mockery or no, half-bowing to him, in the way of a European nobleman for whom such behavior, with even youthful Americans who have failed early at life, is *noblesse oblige.* He approaches Dabney in a sauntering manner; lightly touches Dabney's shoulder; with a glance at the boy squatting by the lakeside a few yards away he says: "You have sighted the lad first, Lieutenant. It is only fair he is yours."

"META? COME LISTEN."

He will read to her what he has written—having labored for twenty hours unrelieved except for brief, harried breaks—Upton Sinclair's slashing rebuttal to the self-righteous and outright fraudulent defense of Armour & Co. published in the *Saturday Evening Post* under the name "J. Ogden Armour"—(as if the bloated capitalist swine could write a word for himself); Upton's new essay is titled "The Condemned Meat Industry." It is a summation of *The Jungle* and much more; the issue of *Everybody's Magazine* in which it appears will sell out on newsstands in all major American cities.

Young Upton Sinclair has become a *best-selling author.*

Immersed in his work, he is scarcely conscious of his surroundings. Even when he reads aloud to his wife it is his own voice that absorbs him, not his wife's presence; her comments are usually admiring, if quietly stated.

Because he is committed to rationalist principles, as a Socialist, Upton refuses to "give in" to fears and fancies; even as he is inclined to believe in the local "curse" on the old Princeton families. For instance, during the intensity of his rapid-fire writing, or typing, of "The Condemned Meat Industry," he has been distracted by distant figures in a field outside his window; at least once, a spectral face has appeared at the very window, a few feet away; but the young Socialist, hunched at his writing table, does not glance up. *It is but a fancy. You know it is not "real."* Meta had warned him, his health would be affected if he continued his rigorous vegetarian diet, from which, on matters of principle, as he had lately worked it out, he felt obliged to exclude eggs—"For hens are the most exploited of creature-workers! First, their eggs are taken from them and devoured; then, they are themselves devoured."

Yet, as Meta protested, hens' eggs were the least expensive of foods for her to prepare; if Upton refused to eat them, she would continue to prepare them for herself and David.

She is questioning your authority. She is in rebellion.

She is not a faithful wife. As you must know.

At the windowpane the spectral face is mocking. Upton refuses to look, yet Upton sees.

And a mirthful trill of fingernails, drawn downward against the pane.

In his systematic way, Upton is refuting "J. Ogden Armour" point by point. He has already written a fifteen-page letter to the editors of the popular *Saturday Evening Post* listing these points; but the editors replied curtly to his letter, with a refusal to publish it. (It was an open secret, the meat-packing moguls, like their railroad and industrial cohorts, owned stock in prominent American magazines and newspapers, and so controlled the public press.) Armour's hack-writer dared to claim that "not one atom" of any condemned animal or carcass found its way into any of Armour's food products, continuing, in a loathsome sniggering way—

> Of course you know the sort of men many of the laborers in the meat-packing houses are—foreigners of a low grade of intelligence—and you know how impossible it is to control every individual. If these persons feel the urge to spit, why then they spit; but it is ridiculous to suppose that this goes in the meat, and not in the sawdust on the floor, thickly strewn about for that very purpose.

The opening and closing paragraphs of the outrageous article vilified "subversive Socialist elements in America"—linking Socialists and anarchists, as the press so often did, as if there were no difference between the Socialist Party and the disorganized, unreasonable, and potentially violent Anarchist Party, with which the assassin of President McKinley had associated himself.

Yet more disturbing than the meretricious article is the threat of a lawsuit against Upton Sinclair and his publisher, very likely to be brought against them by Armour & Co. for "libel"—"defamation of character"—"conspiracy to subvert trade." Upton has not told Meta about this, yet; though thinking that it will be a good thing, to "clear the air"; the issue of who is telling the unadorned truth, and who is shamefully lying, to be settled in court. Upton has a vision of arguing his case, himself: before the U.S. Supreme Court.

"Then it will be settled. With much publicity, which cannot hurt our cause."

So, Upton has been reading his article to Meta, who has been unusually quiet. As he reads aloud, he edits the manuscript; for Upton Sinclair is such a rapid writer, it seems at times that his whirling brain outraces his fingers.

"Meta? What do you think?"

Upton looks up, frowning. He'd thought that Meta was in the room, seated in a chair behind him; possibly, in the kitchen a short distance away, with the doors between the rooms open. (Upton is working now in the farmhouse, as the cabin roof so badly leaks; and this has been a wet, chill spring.)

It is so, overwork has strained his eyesight. He should have his eyes examined, and new glasses prescribed. Often it isn't a case of seeing spectral figures, but a case of not-seeing actual figures, which is the more alarming.

"Meta—?"

Irritated, Upton rises to his feet. Manuscript in hand, twenty pages of hastily typed and edited pages, he goes to seek out his wife in the kitchen, and in the dim little "parlor"—but there is no one.

"Meta, God *damn*. Where are . . ."

Only then recalling, to his chagrin, that of course Meta isn't there: she has taken their son David and returned to New York, to "temporary quarters" with her parents who live on Staten Island.

His wife's parents have never approved of Upton Sinclair, and were not impressed with the success of *The Jungle* except that—"at last"—their daughter and young grandson might live in better quarters; but this has not happened yet.

Upton, disappointed, yet not discouraged, returns to his writing table. His hands are not steady: he must devise a way to type with his elbows firmly on the table, to provide strength. Like Zarathustra, he thinks: "I have begun my *down-going* to the masses of unenlightened mankind."

THE TORCH! The torch! For the air of this sepulcher wants warming.

Josiah's most persistent voice. If he presses his hands against his ears, the voice is louder.

So frequently now do father and son disagree—on politics, religion, ideas—Josiah now avoids dining with his parents, with the excuse that he must be elsewhere. Especially since the uproar of *The Jungle* and the "defense" in the *Saturday Evening Post*, about which everyone in Princeton is talking, and generally siding with the Armours, Josiah and Augustus find it difficult to be civil to each other; even Henrietta, the most tractable and accommodating of women, has tried to appeal to Josiah to be more *reasonable*.

"You know, your father has suffered so, since—since Annabel . . . You should not upset him further, if you love him."

"That I 'love' my father is no excuse for being a hypocrite, like everyone else in Princeton! If he can't accept that, then I will have to move away."

"Move away—where?"

Henrietta spoke agitatedly; Josiah does not like to see the sick, pleading look in his mother's face.

"Why can't you see, Mother, that we are 'cannibals'—people like us? Not just the meat we eat, but—the exploited among us—who are invisible to us . . ." Josiah begins to falter, seeing that his mother is near tears;

quickly he excuses himself, and hurries to his room on the second floor of the house. There he paces, anxiously; he is not unaware of the fact that, at the age of twenty-five, he should not be living at home, in any case; but where exactly he should go, that would not suggest an abandonment of Annabel, and the "curse" on his family, he isn't certain. How much easier a decision Shakespeare's Hamlet had to make: to kill the king, or not. For the king, Claudius, was the murderer of Hamlet's beloved father, and the seducer of Hamlet's mother, Gertrude; in Hamlet's very eyes, King Claudius *existed*. Yet, so far as Josiah can see, and he has sought out his enemy in many places, the Fiend does not exactly *exist*.

What is upsetting to Josiah is that, with the passage of only a few months, certain individuals with whom he has spoken seem only vaguely to recall "Axson Mayte"; and no two of them agree on what he looked like. Josiah's perusal of Pearce van Dyck's Scheme of Clues has further confused him, for his former professor seemed to have inserted, among much that was shrewd and doubtless accurate, a good deal of speculation. His fixation on the illegitimacy of his own son, for instance, seems to Josiah a pure delusion: for the baby he has seen, in Johanna van Dyck's arms, by this time given a proper name, and a baptism, is a *perfectly normal, healthy baby* of no unusual distinction at all.

(Though the baby far more resembles Mrs. van Dyck than Pearce. And his eyes are a curious slate-blue, unlike the eyes of either van Dyck.)

Josiah wonders: should he join the Socialists, and move to New York City? Or—should he cast his lot with a polar expedition, soon to embark for the South Pole?

He has meant to seek out Upton Sinclair. He'd heard that the young Socialist is living in a derelict farmhouse on the Rosedale Road, near Province Line Road, less than four miles away; once, he'd driven out into the country in his motorcar, and was directed to "that Socialist boy's" rented house, but no one seemed to be home, nor did the farmhouse appear to be inhabited at the time.

"We must meet. We must join forces. Maybe!"

In the meantime, Josiah's voice torments him as he paces about his room, hand over his ears.

The torch! The torch! For the air of this sepulcher wants warming.

Sometimes, the voice takes on a pernicious dulcet tone Josiah would swear was Annabel's, if he did not know better.

AT THE DOOR to the president's office in Nassau Hall, Dr. Wilson's secretary knocks hesitantly.

Seated behind his desk, his long, lantern-jawed face grave in the execution, through the long day, of duty, Dr. Wilson says, with an air of exasperated patience, "Yes, Matilde? What is it?"

"A telegram has come for you, sir, from Western Union. It seems to be urgent."

Urgent! Woodrow Wilson wants to retort to this foolish woman, there is nothing in the president's life that is *not urgent.*

What an arduous day! Dr. Wilson has had a succession of appointments of which several are crucial, even *key.* He knows himself the captain of a great but floundering ship; he knows himself destined to "make history"; his father had many times prophesied for Woodrow that, as his life paralleled that of Jesus Christ, he must accept opposition and derision, even "martyrdom"—to a degree. "As there are myriad faces of evil, so there are myriad 'crucifixions.' But you will rise again, Woodrow—each time your enemies cast you down. 'For I am a light shining in darkness.'"

In truth, Woodrow does not always feel like a light shining in darkness but rather a feeble light, struggling not to be extinguished.

Of late, however, he has been racking up victories at the university. Now that his enemies can see that he will not give in to their demands and objections, but is rather strengthened by them, like a Scots warrior in the guise of a Puritan schoolteacher, perhaps they have changed their tack; and the death of Pearce van Dyck, now decidedly a consequence, Dr. Wilson believes, of the adversarial behavior of Dean West, can't have failed to sober them, and cause them to feel remorse.

"For my sake! Poor Pearce. I will name a philosophy preceptorship in his honor."

A rare smile crosses Dr. Wilson's face as he thinks of hog-shaped Andrew West confounded by the recent vote of the board of trustees—to repudiate the million-dollar gift that would have been diverted to the graduate dean's office. All of Princeton has been buzzing of this victory, he is sure. *Unprecedented in the history of Princeton University. Unprecedented (perhaps) in the history of any American university.*

If his Graduate College proposals, and his campaign to shut down the eating clubs, do not succeed—(this is a story he has told himself many times)—he will resign his office, immediately.

How astounded the trustees will be, then! How astounded and repentant, those faculty members who have stubbornly resisted him!

I have made my decision and it is final.

It will be a matter of pride, and dignity. Either you are for Woodrow Wilson or you are against him—there is no comfortable, cringing middle way.

Of course, he can't say this. He must find other, more noble words to express his convictions. Even before accepting his conspicuous office he knew that, in a democracy, the "court of public opinion" must always be manipulated. He knows that his personality does not appeal to all—did not appeal to the many who so admire the gregarious buffoon "TR"—but he understands that *sincerity* might be his trump card.

Like Christ. Yet, a kingdom of this world!

How my enemies will be devastated . . .

Woodrow has to remind himself, of late he has been acquiring victories. With Grover Cleveland absent from two recent meetings of the trustees, the vote is more likely to go in Dr. Wilson's favor; slowly, doggedly, he has been nipping at Cleveland's influence, which is an indirect expression of Andrew West's will. *If he would die. Or—have a stroke and be incapacitated and never return to cause mischief at our university.*

And this day, the May chill seems to have lifted. Woodrow has been willing to allow Matilde to tug up the window behind his desk and through the narrow opening comes fresh air in a thin, startling current that has alternately distracted him, and stirred his spirit. And now Matilde has handed him a telegram, that would seem to require immediate attention, before the stack of letters placed in a wire tray on his desk for him to read—letters of duty, of responsibility and obligation, that fail to nourish the soul. Woodrow feels the injustice of this, that a telegram will take precedence over a mere letter; yet takes it from Matilde with boyish excitement.

"Thank you, Matilde. You may go, and close the door."

Eagerly tearing the envelope open, and reading, with eyes that mist over and with a quick-pounding heart—

Dear Tommy you reside in my heart & my thoughts
constantly. Please say there is a place in which
in your life might dwell
your friend
Cybella Peck

So stirred, so thrilled, Dr. Wilson is obliged to read the telegram a second time, and a third.

TODD SLADE, twelve years old. At which time, in May 1906, the boy meets a bizarre fate.

After his grandfather Winslow Slade's "confession" in the cemetery, which was directed, primarily, at Todd and Josiah, Todd has been unusually quiet and withdrawn. Like Josiah, he avoids his parents. He avoids any and all adults. Though he still has difficulty reading and writing, he doesn't so readily flare up in a fit of temper when he tries, and fails, at these.

"But why does it matter if words are spelled correctly, and used correctly, if they're lies? No one can explain."

Todd had been frightened by his grandfather's public confession. He'd been frightened to be forced to imagine a man, a young man, who'd behaved as his grandfather had behaved fifty years before; and to imagine that this young man was somehow, at the same time, Grandfather Slade.

Since then, Todd has found his way to Crosswicks, uninvited. He wanders in the garden and has been seen—(Henrietta has seen him)—talking with the gardeners; he drifts in the direction of Crosswicks Forest.

The German shepherd Thor doesn't accompany him now, for Thor has passed away, of a mysterious malady, in the late winter.

And Annabel is gone, of course. And Wilhelmina Burr, her friend—gone.

Henrietta sees Todd from one or another window and waves to him, but gets no response; if she calls to him, he pretends not to hear.

When he isn't wandering at Crosswicks he is likely to be in the Princeton Cemetery, in the area of the Slade family mausoleum.

The cemetery groundskeeper sees Todd Slade there, knows who he is, and doesn't approach him. There are those who drift about the old cemetery, that dates to pre-Revolutionary times, like living ghosts—the groundskeeper knows to keep his distance, for they are mourners who do not want their mourning assuaged.

Though it is unusual that one of these mourners is so *young*.

In the cemetery, Todd speaks with Annabel. Much of the time, Todd is child-like, as he'd been of old in his cousin's presence; he had liked her to scold him, and he had liked to surprise and shock her, a bit. Now, there is no one he cares enough to shock.

"But why did you go away? Where did you go?"

Todd leans the side of his face against the granite vault, and listens to hear if Annabel replies to him; but there is never any sound, except the rustling of leaves overhead, a trilling of birds and in the near distance a sound of traffic on Witherspoon Street.

"Annabel! Where did you *go*?"

Todd has to remind himself, his little sister Oriana is buried in the vault, too. But he has no question to put to *her*—she is too young to help him.

Yet once, when Todd had spoken to Annabel, and received no reply as usual, he heard, or seemed to hear, a rejoinder from Oriana—*Go away, Todd! We don't want you.*

But Todd is reluctant to go home. Often, Todd sleeps in the cemetery, sprawled beneath the marble portico of the mausoleum. He feels a feathery touch on his face—the wings of a small bird? He feels a light touch across his hands—the scurrying feet of a field mouse? To the despair of his mother, and the annoyance of his father, Todd spends more and more time in the cemetery; until, on a morning in late May, the grounds-keeper makes a remarkable discovery: a new statue has been added to the company of seraphim, crosses, and other somber monuments, that of a young boy.

And yet, who has placed the statue here? A sculpted-stone statue of a boy seated on the grasses near the Slade mausoleum; an exquisite, uncannily lifelike specimen of the stonecutter's art; a boy carved so fastidiously, even the most minuscule vein of his forehead, or a crease in his clothes, is perfectly rendered. Why, even the eyelashes are lifelike; even the air of stubborn resolution that emanates from the face.

The groundskeeper hurries to Wheatsheaf, to report what he has found; at about the time that the boy's nanny has discovered that Todd Slade is missing from his room.

LIEUTENANT BAYARD BY NIGHT

W hy did you resign your commission? Why so precipitously? And is it gone forever—your dream of being a soldier?"

IN HIS HEART still he was *lieutenant*. In a fit of despair and rage after the public humiliation on his wedding day he'd resigned his commission, against his family's wishes; then, when he began to feel differently, it was too late to reclaim it.

Unless it wasn't too late? Ex-Lieutenant Dabney Bayard tormented himself with such thoughts, except when such thoughts were mollified by whiskey.

IT WAS A clouded night near the end of the university's spring term when a young man named Tempe Kaufman left Chancellor Green Library to return to his rooming house on Mercer Street; later than was his usual custom, for the library had longer hours at this time of year preceding exams. Tempe made his way through the darkened campus, and to Mercer Street, headed for his rooming house at the intersection with Alexander;

he was not lonely, but whistled thinly to himself, to lift his spirits; for he was concerned about his several courses, of which at least two were taught by professors who seemed to dislike, or to disdain him, and had graded him less generously than they'd graded his classmates. Like other undergraduates, Tempe Kaufman did not read, or care about, local news; he was from New York City, and found it difficult to take the village of Princeton seriously, as a place in which people lived apart from the university that so dominated it.

The reader might wonder why Tempe Kaufman was living on Mercer Street and not with fellow undergraduates in one of the residence halls on campus. The twenty-year-old boy was, it appears, a Jewish person; and so thought it most politic to conform with the wishes of the university administration, and with the wishes of the majority of his classmates, by acquiring a room off-campus. (There was no eating club that would admit Jewish persons, it scarcely needs be said.)

But Tempe was not lonely; for Tempe was accustomed to being alone much of the time. And Tempe didn't give much thought to rumors spreading through Princeton, of a "killer"—a "Fiend"—who had killed several people, and had not been apprehended.

As Old North tolled the dolorous quarter hour past 10 P.M., Tempe happened to notice a peculiar flitting shape at one of the gas lamps nearby (this was at the corner of Mercer and Alexander); the shape was bat-like, but larger than the ordinary bat; it appeared to be suspended in mid-air, without beating its wings, at a height of about eight feet above the sidewalk. A very large bat Tempe thought; or a common nighthawk—a bird not found commonly in Tempe's hometown, with red-glowing eyes and claw-like talons.

"Why, what is that?"

Tempe stared, and blinked; he hesitated to come closer; yet was relieved that, within a few seconds, the curious shape had vanished; perhaps it was nothing but vapor. Tempe reproached himself for being alarmed for he knew this stretch of Mercer Street well: the cobblestone paving, the flickering gas lamps, the dignified old Colonial houses with their prim facades of white clapboards and dark shutters.

Mrs. Donovan's rooming house was at 77 Mercer.

Tempe had not wanted to hear the lurid details of a recent murder at Lake Carnegie though the victim was a sophomore named Heckewalder, who had been in two of Tempe's classes; one of those eating-club boys who, careless in his work, arrogant in his manner, yet managed to get grades higher than Tempe Kaufman. Indeed, Tempe had had the mean and unworthy thought, when he'd first heard that Heckewalder had been killed in a mysterious "undisclosed" manner, that *Heckewalder deserved it, if anyone did;* such a thought Tempe immediately censored, for he wasn't that kind of person.

Still, Heckewalder had not been friendly to Tempe Kaufman, in his careless, aristocratic manner; it was said that his father was one of the most trusted legal advisors employed by DuPont & Co., specializing in the manufacture of gunpowder, and that he'd made a fortune investing in DuPont stock. Naturally, details of the young man's death were being withheld by his family, as by local authorities, and the university administration, who feared hysterical reactions and "bad publicity"; but Tempe had heard, or rather overheard, that in addition to having his throat slashed by the teeth of human, or animal, origin, the luckless young man had been made to endure an offense to his body, of an "unspeakable" sort.

This, Tempe couldn't help but think Heckewalder had brought upon himself for his excessive preening and strutting in female attire, in the recent Triangle Show, that had been hilarious, and yet in very bad taste, Tempe had thought. *His* people would never cavort in such a way, in such blatant sexual mockery, in public.

So, Tempe continued along Mercer Street, with a quickly beating heart, though there was nothing to alarm him; and most of the houses on the street had lighted windows, at least on the second floor. Yet, he couldn't help but think that Heckewalder had been an athlete, at lacrosse; a slender but wiry young man, not easily intimidated. Yet he had been unable to save himself, it seemed.

Also, a certain "aura" hung over Mrs. Donovan's rooming house at 77 Mercer, since, several years before, when Tempe Kaufman had been a high school student at Erasmus Hall, in Brooklyn, one of Mrs. Donovan's young boarders, an allegedly brilliant student in mathematics, also Jewish, from Philadelphia, had been found hanging from his neck in his room, a suicide. (In the young man's note he blamed the eating clubs that had "blackballed" him on account of his ancestry; and the university itself, in that he could count *not one friend* among the entire student body. So reckless a charge could not be taken seriously and must not be allowed to be publicly disseminated, the newly inaugurated president Woodrow Wilson quickly decided; and so the tragic affair was quietly "hushed up.") Afterward it was claimed that a young Hebrew gentleman, of which there were invariably two or three in a class, always of the most superior intellect, might count on the fingers of one hand his friends, or friendly acquaintances; at this time, in 1906, there must have been as many as six or even seven young Jews among the undergraduate and graduate body of several thousand young men, seemingly content to mingle with their own kind and to avoid the distractions of Prospect Street social life for which the prestigious university was famed.

Tempe did not think of these matters, much. For he too was rumored to be "brilliant" at math—and he had not so many friends, either.

"Hello? Hello . . ."

Suddenly a figure defined itself, to Tempe's amazed eye, leaning against a lamppost like a nighthawk grown large. To Tempe's relief he saw that the figure was that of a young man of about his age, or a few years older, in a U.S. Army officer's uniform, his rank a mystery to Tempe who knew little of such things; but he saw that the young man had an agreeable, boyish face, and was smiling at Tempe as if to comfort him.

Were they acquainted? Was this young man someone Tempe should know? In a playful gesture meant to mask his nervousness, or embarrassment, Tempe brought the edge of his hand smartly to the side of his head, in a salute: "Aye-aye, sir."

At which the young officer seemed to take offense. His smile vanished, and was replaced with a look of rage. He uncoiled himself from his position against the lamppost and, taller than he'd appeared, in a stride or two confronted the astonished Tempe, seizing hold of Tempe's right hand with fingers of startling strength.

"Are you mocking me?" the fair-haired stranger demanded, in a lightly accented Southern voice. "Are you showing contempt for an officer of the United States Army?"

WHAT IS THIS?—while stationed at Camp Raleigh the lieutenant chanced to discover, in a handheld mirror, a crease between his eyebrows which had not been there previously, he was sure. Panic flared, then ire; then a sullen intention to inflict revenge. A certain boy, an enlisted private, curly-haired shy-seeming bright-eyed boy from the hill country beyond Norfolk, who has been Lieutenant Bayard's nemesis these past few weeks, and feigning innocence.

His pretty looks shall be slashed flat, Lieutenant Bayard thinks, *else my own looks will suffer.*

"IF ONLY THEY would not struggle. It would be better for us both, and soon be completed."

FROM THE FIRST, Lieutenant Bayard knew: his prospective brother-in-law Josiah Slade distrusted him.

Disliked, disdained, distrusted him. *Him!*

While all of the Slades were warm to him, as to his parents and Bayard relatives, and pretty Annabel was shyly gracious to him, yet Josiah held himself just perceptibly apart; as Dabney had sometimes noted, in situations of male camaraderie, like football, crew, lacrosse—there were those who did not quite take to him, despite his eagerness to be liked. *You are not one of us really. You—an impostor!*

Dabney Bayard gave no sign of course. No sign that he was aware of Josiah's coolness. In fact, Dabney ignored such coolness, and responded to Josiah as if Josiah was friendly with him, and there was no strain between them.

"Shall we go hunting, one day soon, Josiah? There is much game in Hunterdon County."

"Maybe. One day soon."

So Josiah replied, with a frowning smile and evasive eyes.

He is not a good dissembler. He has no skill at subterfuge.

Dabney knew that Josiah had been accepted at West Point, had enrolled but stayed only a few months. The soldier's life was not for this Princeton aristocrat, it seemed.

How he hated Josiah Slade! The young man was a snob, a smug bastard, haughty son-of-a-bitch—he would one day pay for these insults, Lieutenant Bayard thought.

THE REMEDY IS always the same, Lieutenant. And very simple, I wonder you have not gleaned it yourself.

The Count was smiling, his darkly-pale face aglow in the sunshine. Large deep-set intelligent/bemused eyes; the heat of a stranger's breath on Dabney's cheek; an odor of ashes overlaid with a stronger odor of alcohol and snuff.

The remedy, my sweet young Lieutenant, is . . .

* * *

"IT WAS A rabid bat, it's thought, that attacked the boy. For a healthy bat would not attack a human being, and never in daylight. All the rest is foolery—this hysteria of 'vampires.' The attack of a bat against a human being may be a rare occurrence in New Jersey but is hardly rare in Europe. So, why this inordinate fuss on the part of the township authorities? And on the Princeton campus? An able-bodied young college boy should certainly be able to defend himself against a mere *bat*."

So Count English von Gneist spoke to guests in the drawing room at Mora House, his gaze moving lightly over that of Dabney Bayard's, not many days after the murder on the canal pathway of Julian Heckewalder.

AND THERE WAS the other, the *Hebrew boy*, the first of his kind in the Lieutenant's experience, in the shadows of a lane between houses on Mercer Street: dark curls, Semitic hook to the nose, the rumored sensualism of the race, an ancient and sun-warmed race, replete with secrets!

No he says but Yes I say, No please he begs but Yes I say, O help me God he prays, O dear God yes I say, But please he says, But yes I say, No he says, help he cries, No I say, no help I say, Come here I say, cease struggling I say, you will not be hurt, like this I say like this I say, and—THIS.

"NO! MY GOD."

Awakened from one of his ugly dreams.

Drenched in sickly clammy perspiration.

Heart racing, and eyelids rapidly blinking; and parched lips like the mouth of a fish thrown upon the land, gasping for breathable air.

"But only a dream. Thank God!"

For some minutes paralyzed in the churned bedclothes. Unable to recollect where he was: officers' quarters at Norfolk, or at Raleigh, or Camp Pendleton; or in his boyhood bed, or in Atlantic City, or in New York City, or—back in accursed Princeton?

Ravenous with thirst and hunger he'd been tearing at the youth's throat with his teeth, that he might suck the wholesome hot blood required for life; so overcome with passion, he could not resist plunging onward to the end, most savage indeed. Yet how is it his fault?—appetite is stronger than will, and both are stronger than the wish to do no harm. How, when the young Hebrew boy clearly mocked him with a salute, locking eyes with the Lieutenant—fatally.

ISN'T IT PREFERABLE, Lieutenant, to satisfy your appetite, and acknowledge the pleasure it gives you? And not, like most of those who surround us, enact a pious hypocrisy each day of your life?

How much more noble to follow the caprice of your secret soul, than to play at parson; for didn't one of your homespun American bards advise you should inscribe on your doorstep—WHIM?

STILL, THE DREAM was very upsetting. So lucid in its details, such as the fine dark fluttering lashes of the boy's face, and the gabardine jacket the boy was wearing; the succession of gas lamps on Mercer Street, leading north into darkness, beyond the village of Princeton; the chill, fragrant May air . . . So lucid, Dabney was afraid to close his eyes again and be drawn once more into that dank and fetid Hell.

So he lay panting in the darkened room, which might have been a hotel room; a place unfamiliar to him; for all places were coming to seem unfamiliar to him, who traveled so far by night.

Wiping at his parched lips with his knuckles, and swallowing, and swallowing, without seeming to cleanse his mouth; nor even to rid his lips of an encrustation, that tasted frankly of blood.

POSTSCRIPT:
ON THE MATTER OF THE
"UNSPEAKABLE" AT PRINCETON

As it is very difficult to speak of the "unspeakable," so the historian is limited in his presentation of certain materials; in this case, the historian is in fact ignorant of what the "unspeakable" might be, despite a considerable effort of research over the decades.

And, as this chapter contains much that is of interest only to those with a curiosity about Princeton University and its history of the "unspeakable," the suggestion is that other readers skim rapidly through it, or skip it altogether, and move to the next chapter, which is more directly related to the unfolding story of *The Accursed*.

All of Princeton was aghast, and terrified: on a May morning, only a few days before the end of term, the body of a young college student, twenty years of age, was found in the paludal wilderness between Princeton and Princeton Junction, in a swampy area beside the railroad track; as if the abused body had been thrown from the local train.

This, the second body of an undergraduate to be found, in a similar setting, and with similar injuries, within a week.

The first, a sophomore member of Cottage Club; the second, a twenty-year-old junior, living "off campus" at a rooming house at 77 Mercer Street.

For those who believed that the "curse" was related specifically to Crosswicks, to the Slades and other prominent families, these deaths presented clear anomalies: for both Heckewalder and Kaufman appeared to have been assaulted and killed purely by chance, having been in the wrong place at the wrong time; the one at the shore of Lake Carnegie, in a secluded area, in midday; the other in or near a lane off Mercer Street, past 10 P.M. of a weekday. Neither young man was a Princetonian by birth and his death very likely had nothing to do with ancestry or fate.

Like Heckewalder, Kaufman was said to have suffered "grievous"—"bestial"—"savage"—injuries to his throat, torso, and lower body; his death was of "exsanguination"; and he had suffered "unspeakable insult."

Though I am not a theologian, or a philosopher, I think it is most helpful here to follow the admonition of St. Thomas Aquinas in his discussion of "that abominable and detestable crime against Nature, not to be named among Christians."

THROUGH THE HISTORY of Princeton University the alert historian might trace a thread, or chain, of "unspeakable" incidents involving the abrupt dismissal of certain faculty members, preceptors, and students, and their immediate decampment from town; the ostracizing, by their fellows, of undergraduates suspected of partaking in the "unspeakable," or possessing the potential for such; from time to time, otherwise inexplicable acts of cruelty inflicted upon "unorthodox" individuals, particularly with regard to freshman hazing. Bicker, a time of much anxiety, was a favored time for such cruelty, in the form of boyish pranks; for a boy who very badly wanted to belong to an eating club might be led to believe that he would be invited, only to be confronted with the fact that *not a single club wanted him*. (Not that this sort of prank was limited to those boys suspected of the potential for the "unspeakable"—for of course it was more general.)

Connected with this, we have the unfortunate suicides: young men whose self-loathing came to match the loathing of their peers, leading them to the (unforgivable, by Christian standards) sin of self-destruction. That this sin is, in its way, "unspeakable," adds to the mystery.

For instance, isolated "unspeakable" episodes were whispered of during the administration of James Carnahan (1823–1854), at which time eating clubs were being formed, spontaneously; these arose from the students' need for meals, as the college was unable to provide adequate dining facilities for its ever-increasing student population. (President Carnahan's tenure was tumultuous, for near-anarchy reigned when boys rebelled, as often they did; administrators and faculty could not control gangs of roving boys who set fires, smashed windows, and vandalized the campus; the beleaguered president considered shutting down the college, until he was dissuaded by James Madison, a loyal alum.) At this time, such eating clubs were formed as "Knights of the Round Table"—"Knights of Hudibras"—"King's Court"—"Knickerbockers"—"Epicureans"—"Alligators" (this was to be Woodrow Wilson's club, or substitute for a club, as Wilson was seemingly blackballed by his first-choice club, Ivy, in 1879). Later, these names would be changed, and the eating clubs dignified by the construction of very handsome, mansion-like houses along Prospect Avenue, built by prosperous alums. In their origins the eating clubs were quite innocent, and it was only later, in the time of Woodrow Wilson's undergraduate years, for instance, that the situation radically altered: inspiring in underclassmen a frenzy of anxiety and apprehension at "bicker"—"pledge week"—as to who would be invited to join which club, and who would not be invited to join any club at all—(that is, the majority of students).

Hence, Woodrow Wilson's pledge to "shut down" the eating clubs— and the opposition to him, by a strong coalition of alums.

Whatever the "unspeakable" was, or is, these incidents escalated at hazing and bicker-time. One can imagine the inevitable consequences of fevered adolescent "courting"—"horsing"—"disciplining"—"hazing." (It was not unusual for freshman boys to be so violently "disciplined," they had to leave college, some of them hospitalized; yet none of these boys ever testified against the upperclassmen who harassed them. Deaths following "hazing" and "horsing" were not common, of course—yet those that did occur were kept quiet, by university decree.)

Over the decades, through subsequent administrations, the eating clubs grew: from five, to nine, to thirteen; eventually, to twenty. Alums began to compete in building eating-club houses on Prospect Avenue, and so the university dining facilities, though in handsome "Gothic" buildings mimicking Oxford and Cambridge, appeared paltry by contrast. Soon it came to be, there were those boys who were *clubbable*—and those who *were not clubbable*. For the great gratification of the club is, simply, that only a few members are chosen; the rest being, if not precisely beneath contempt, beneath at least that latitude demarking one's fellows from those with whom *we would not wish to dine*.

Of my own experience at Princeton as a graduate, with honors, of the Class of 1927, I will not speak: except to say that it was instructive, and illuminating; and if I had to repeat it again, I would hang myself.

During annual Bicker Week, when club elections took place, the university was gripped by a veritable epidemic of frazzled nerves, sleepless nights, agitation, anxiety, elation, despair, rage, rising even to homicidal and suicidal impulses, and acts; there was no way that faculty members could distract their students from "bicker," as one could not force children to sit still and calm, and not gape at fireworks in the sky.

This situation seemed to Woodrow Wilson, quite plausibly, as counter to the purpose of the university, as an unwholesome focus upon athletics would be; it had even come to pass that aggressive "hat clubs" (so named because of their colorful headgear) sprang up among sophomores, that they might control elections to upperclass clubs by banding together to accept, or refuse, election as a block; resulting in freshman clubs springing up, to control the "hat clubs"; all this involving every sort of cajoling, and intimidating, and courting, and threatening, and double-dealing, and horsing, and hazing, and broken hearts, and plummeting academic performances, often resulting in expulsion. The most egregious development being that freshman club memberships were often not made at Princeton at all but during senior year in prestigious prep schools like Lawrenceville and Groton; so that a lad of fifteen might already begin to anticipate the anxiety of Bicker Week at Princeton University, years hence, when his "fate" would be decided. In this way, a great many boys suffered, including many from "good" families, that a few boys might preen themselves as elite.

During the genial but somewhat lax administration of Dr. Patton, there occurred a scandal of an ambiguous sort, having to do with the hazing procedures of the third "most powerful" club on campus: this, "Ballarat," housed in a Tudor mansion that was said to have cost more than $200,000, a very high sum for the time, and quite the architectural gem of Prospect Street. As it was the club of a favored nephew of J. P. Morgan, Ballarat enjoyed many special privileges and competed aggressively with other clubs for positions of campus power; yet came to grief in 1899 when a scandal erupted following the rough treatment of new members, with hazing canes and "branding irons." And so, Ballarat was disbanded readily, and its handsome house sold to another eating club. As the scandal had to do with "unspeakable matters" the exact nature of the offenses was never spelt out, and never spoken of.

Yet there was nothing quite so extreme, I think, as the "anarchy" of the early 1800s, when mutinous students occupied Nassau Hall and set off charges of gunpowder in the building. There was even a kidnapping of a pastoral assistant whom a gang of boys, cloaked in black robes and hoods, dragged out of his bachelor's quarters on campus, and tarred and feathered on the lawn of the president's house which was at that time on Nassau Street, in the very center of the village—said pastor having been accused, by the boys, of "unspeakable"—"filthy"—acts perpetrated upon them.

During a previous administration, that of Reverend Samuel Stanhope Smith (1795–1812), the students had already, it seems, begun to behave badly, for more than one hundred of them were expelled after a disastrous fire, determined to be arson, leveled Nassau Hall in 1802!— among these boys the adopted son of the President of the newly formed United States, George Washington (a lad about whom little is known except that he was expelled from the college for "meanness and irregularity of character"). Then, during the administration of the much admired Reverend Aaron Burr, Sr., his precocious son Aaron, Jr., was known at the college for both his "brilliance" and his "dissipation" —this, in a mere lad of thirteen!

At this time, it should be noted, Princeton University did not yet exist: these long-ago individuals lived in the era of the College of New Jersey.

ADDENDUM.

This segment of my chronicle contains, for all its horrors, a "positive" ending of a kind, for, after the gruesome—and never-solved—murders of Heckewalder and Kaufman, the Curse in its primary, or ghoulish form, will not strike again.

At about this time, Dabney Bayard learned that, through powerful relatives in Washington, D.C., he had been reinstated in the U.S. Army at the rank of lieutenant; from this rank, within a year he would be promoted to the rank of captain. Soon then he was given the honor of accompanying Vice President William Howard Taft on one of numerous "troubleshooting" expeditions to the exotic Philippines, where native unrest and divers political complications necessitated United States intervention in the name of democracy. "We must have order there among those villainous little monkeys," President Roosevelt declared, "and by God I will see to it that we do!"

It would come about that Captain Dabney Bayard acquitted himself so well in his new station, within a few years he was to be promoted yet again, to the gold-starred rank of major; and with a well-trained battalion of men under his command, maintained the civil order in the Philippines, of which President Roosevelt spoke. And no further innocent persons fell prey to the ghoulish appetite of the Fiend, in Princeton.

"HERE DWELLS HAPPINESS"

Though it was a matter of public record that twelve-year-old Todd Slade was found "turned to stone" in Princeton Cemetery, and his remains put to rest inside the family vault with his sister Oriana and his cousin Annabel, yet it also seems to be true that Todd *lived still;* though in a realm of being that is inexplicable to this historian, which I am obliged to describe at second- and third-hand.

Here, Todd Slade's adventure.

HOW FREQUENTLY NOW his sleep was troubled by words unfamiliar to him, yet teasingly familiar—HIC HABITAT FELICITAS—and again, HIC HABITAT FELICITAS. Todd woke from such dreams anxious and confused, believing that a "voice" was in the room with him, or echoed inside his head.

Before being transformed into stone, and declared to be dead through some trauma to the body that resisted diagnosis, Todd had fallen into the habit of wandering at Crosswicks, as I've mentioned; though he shunned the company of his cousin Josiah, his aunt and uncle Henrietta and Augustus, and avoided his grandfather Winslow, whose "confession" had been shocking to the boy, and incompletely understood. For was Winslow Slade now confessing to a truth, as he had not confessed to the truth in the past; and, if this was so, why should he be believed now? There was a sense of shame, that passed between grandson and grandfather, that made Todd want to avoid his grandfather even as he found himself drawn to Crosswicks Manse, that seemed to him the core of the Curse. Yet, an antic mood came over the boy, the mischievousness of his old Todd-self, before Annabel had departed, that led him to haunt the corridor outside his grandfather's library, softly singing:

He lied once and might lie again
She lied once and might lie again
They lied once and might lie again
But Thor shall not lie
Thor alone shall not lie:
For the poor beast is dead.
That is why.

(It was fortunate that Winslow Slade was often no longer in his library, but in his private rooms at the Manse, in a farther wing of the house.)

Difficult as Todd had become, he was yet hounded by a "voice" more insidious than his own, that murmured "HIC HABITAT FELICITAS" in a jeering tone as if to tease him that he should seek this out, and put an end to mystery.

So it finally came about, sometime past midday of May 28, 1906, that the boy wandered into his grandfather's library, which was a room long forbidden to him, especially when no adult was present; and, poking and prying about, he chanced to see carved into the fireplace the very words that had been haunting him: HIC HABITAT FELICITAS.

At once Todd understood that he was in the presence of a profound riddle, which he alone might solve. But what was he expected to do?

Very strange it was to find himself alone in Winslow Slade's fabled library with its high coffered ceiling, and walls of leather-bound books said to be antique and priceless; and the rare Gutenberg Bible on its pedestal; and shadowed portraits by illustrious American artists (Gilbert Stuart, John Singleton Copley, Thomas Eakins) of Slade ancestors whose stern gazes appeared to be fixed upon him. Should Todd have wanted to, he might have performed any prank: run the wheeled ladder along the bookcases, and climb like a monkey to the ceiling; or steal away his own likeness, a portrait in pastels of a sweet-faced and innocent child of two or three, sketched in a patch of grass in which lay a lady's white parasol, perhaps his mother's . . . Todd had always been fascinated by this drawing of an angelic little child who was, presumably, himself; as he was fascinated by portraits of his sister Oriana and his cousins Josiah and Annabel, executed by the same artist. "Was that ever 'Todd'?" he'd asked his mother wistfully; and Lenora had said, laughing, brushing his forehead with her lips, "Of course! That angelic little boy is with us right now, if eclipsed."

This was a clever answer of his mother's, Todd thought. Much of life is *eclipse*.

Todd studied a life-sized portrait of General Elias Slade, by Copley, which had begun to crack, and exuded a dark aura; and there was the Reverend Azariah Slade, in an oil painting by Stuart, looking as if he were made of wax, eyes hard and pitiless as stone. There was a terrible temptation, for a moment, to tear at the brittle pages of the Gutenberg Bible, and knock it from its pedestal onto the floor. Then, as if he'd been postponing this moment, Todd returned to the marble fireplace, and to the words carved into it: " 'Hic Habitat Felicitas.' " He knew no Latin yet guessed that this must mean "Here Dwells Happiness"—or some similar phrase. Happiness must dwell at home, within the family—or nowhere.

At first idly, then with more curiosity, Todd poked about the fireplace; so large a fireplace, he could stand inside it, slightly hunched. There was a smell of ashes here, and there were cobwebs in the chimney; standing inside the fireplace and looking out, he felt a dizzying sense of disorientation, like one looking from the other side of a mirror. Within a few minutes, Todd's fingers discovered a loose brick, at which he tugged; when it loosened further, and fell to the floor, he tugged at another brick, and another—until to his astonishment he was seeing into the chimney, or through it, as if through a small window opening into a luminous light.

What should have been dark was not dark but "light"—a tunnel of some sort, a secret passageway.

Now Todd pulled at the bricks systematically, and set them with care onto the hearth. He did not want anyone in the house to hear him, and to interrupt. Until it was as Todd had thought: a passageway led out of his grandfather's library, not into another part of the house but into another landscape entirely, unknown to him.

How was this possible? Todd knew that the opening in the chimney could only lead to a familiar setting, yet somehow it did not; as he poked and pried further, and removed more bricks, he saw that he was looking into a forest, a tangled woodland devoid of all color yet vividly "lighted" like a movie screen. Though the very hairs stirred on the back of his neck with apprehension, and the daring of what he did, Todd continued to remove bricks, his fingers now scraped and very grimy, until, having made an aperture of about twelve inches in diameter, he could force his head and shoulders through.

In this way, Todd Slade disappeared from his grandfather's study as, indeed, from our world.

THE NORDIC SOUL

At last, Josiah Slade and Upton Sinclair are to meet. But in hardly the circumstances these idealistic young men would have chosen, and with hardly the result.

HE WOULD MOVE now more forcibly. In the history of the Revolution, it was time.

Ever more his devotion to the cause grew. Ever more, his certainty that he was in the forefront of change.

His sojourn in Princeton was coming to an end, or nearly. There would follow now a triumphant move to New York City, and from there to—he knew not precisely where: the great state of California, or a Socialist commune in rural New Jersey. There, the Socialist principles of shared property, shared labor, shared food would prevail.

He would not beg Meta to accompany him. But he believed, if he explained carefully enough to her, she would want to be with him, and would not doubt him again.

***

SOME FACTS OF his life Upton Sinclair had hoped to conceal. He had hidden from Meta and from those comrades—Florence Kelly, Clarence Darrow, Jack London, with whom he'd founded the Intercollegiate Socialist Society in 1905—the fact that his mother's father was John S. Harden, a "high official" of the notorious Western Maryland Railroad; yet more egregiously, his father's grandfather was Commodore Arthur Sinclair of the U.S. Navy, a hero of the War of 1812 rumored to have "profited considerably" through his military connections and to have gloated *There is no war that is not a rich harvest—for some!*

Such blunt truths of the capitalist spirit, such *facts*—somehow did not repel the majority of Americans, as one might expect. Why?—young Upton Sinclair yearned to know.

He had himself firsthand experience of the rich—from time to time pitied, in his threadbare Baltimore home, with a failing salesman/drunkard father and a helpless and overwhelmed mother, and invited to spend time with his Harden grandparents; he had no illusions as to the higher quality of the intelligence of the rich, as of their moral condition; it is true, the rich can be "generous"—"charitable"—no one more kindly, in an ostentatious manner, than rich Christian women at such times of years—Christmas, Easter—when their hearts are swayed by the pathos of the poor!—this is true, but not relevant to the cause of social justice. *When private property is abolished the true spirit of Christianity will emerge. But not until then.*

Sinclair felt a stab of shame, that his weak, often ailing mother took pride in the sorry fact that her Harden ancestors were Protestant landowners in northern Ireland, said to be of the very highest rank of breeding, wealth, and influence. How ashamed to be told, with a reproachful squeeze of his hand *In your veins their blood flows, even now! The blood of aristocrats.*

These painful biographical facts! Never to be published in any "profile" of Upton Sinclair, if he could prevent it.

***

THOUGH HE PASSIONATELY opposed censorship of course. Any infringement upon the freedom of others—the rights guaranteed by the Constitution of freedom in speech and in print—the *natural rights of man*—Upton Sinclair would oppose with his life.

"Thank you—but *no*. There is only one man for this office—that is Jack London."

It was flattering, and very tempting, to be offered the first presidency of the Intercollegiate Socialist Society, in the fall of 1905. But with a grave smile for the nominating committee Upton Sinclair had declined in favor of the popular and far more famous young Socialist author from San Francisco.

"Though I don't know the man personally, I have read such remarkable work of his—*The Call of the Wild, The Sea Wolf, The War of the Classes*—above all that masterful chronicle of slum life *The People of the Abyss*—I can vouch for his genius. And what I've heard of our comrade—his efforts in the cause of Socialism—I would stake my life on it, that Jack London would present our cause to the world more admirably than any other individual of our time."

He was utterly sincere! This was not false modesty—this was not modesty at all, Upton would have insisted. The vision of Socialism presented by Karl Marx—and refined by Friedrich Engels—was impersonal, and shorn of individual ego; all that was *ego* was of the past, condemned to decay, wither away and vanish within a few generations; this Upton Sinclair believed passionately, and meant to inculcate into his daily, moral life as the most effective antidote to his quasi-bourgeois background.

At this time Upton Sinclair had been twenty-six—about to publish the most challenging work of his career, *The Jungle;* already the author of numerous articles, plays, and books since his first novel *Springtime and Harvest* in 1901. Jack London was two years older and had not published nearly so much—yet *The Call of the Wild* and *The Sea Wolf*, best sellers in several languages, had made him famous—as popular a writer as the legendary Mark Twain whose prime was now past.

Now in the spring of 1906 Upton had yet to meet London. He had yet to shake London's hand and to gaze upon the young Yukon adventurer face to face—though he'd seen London's rugged photograph in numerous places, including the *New York Sun* where the "socialist-seditionist" author was anathema to the editorial writers.

How handsome London was! In secret—for his wife Meta would not have understood such a predilection—Upton examined photographs of the adventurer-writer hoping to see in his comrade's smiling gaze some sort of—mystic connection, or kinship . . . Upton could not have articulated what he sought but knew it to be the identical *ravishment of the soul* he'd experienced when first reading Byron's *Childe Harold's Pilgrimage* and Blake's *The Marriage of Heaven and Hell;* intellectually, it was Marx, Engels, Feuerbach, and Nietzsche whom Upton most admired, but he could not feel the sort of zealous passion for these thinkers he felt for the poets, and for Jack London, who was not only his contemporary but a sort of brother, or soul mate . . . Guiltily aware of himself as the privileged son of a genteel family, he found fascinating the details of London's very different background: London was the illegitimate son of an itinerant astrologer, born in San Francisco in poverty, forced to quit school at the age of fourteen to work as a sailor, gold miner, and manual laborer; as a young man he'd begun writing for newspapers, and had been bold enough to campaign as the Socialist mayor of Oakland in 1901. (London had lost, of course—but newspaper accounts spoke of the power of the "Boy Socialist" to "captivate" the crowds that gathered to hear him speak.) In Upton's dreams London appeared not wraith-like, like most dream-figures, but solid, earthy, muscled, lively and livid-faced; as he'd been rumored to be in actual life, London was quarrelsome, yet charming; so very charming, it was impossible to turn away from him, or to shake off the effect of his personality . . . *Here is my deepest self* Upton thought—*far deeper than I myself can realize.*

For there was, as Upton had come to believe, following the shrewd cultural analysis of Nietzsche, a *deep, true, primitive self*—most often betrayed by the moral cowardice of the public man.

At Upton's instigation the men had been exchanging letters for the past year—voluminous letters—doggedly earnest on Sinclair's side and fervid, and florid, on London's—extolling the crimes of capitalism and the virtues of Socialism. Upton had urged London to accept the invitation of the Intercollegiate Socialist Society to be its first president, and London had declined initially, but allowed himself to be cajoled, and eventually won over. Each young writer had sent inscribed copies of his books to the other—Upton seemed to be the more impressed, rapidly reading the stirring pages of *The Sea Wolf,* London's new best seller, only just published and already in its eighth printing; he'd written to London in San Francisco—"You are a 'real' writer—I am but a 'muckraker.' But I hope I can recognize literary genius when I confront it."

Weeks had passed, without London responding. At last, when Upton received a scrawled card from London, he'd been dismayed by the bluntness of London's remarks: "The Socialist sentiment of your work is faultless but I am afraid that your temperamental lack of touch—your 'sex-attitude'—is anathema to my own view of the subject."

Lack of touch! Sex-attitude! Upton Sinclair was utterly baffled what this might mean, and had no one whom he dared ask—certainly not his wife.

HOW BUSY THE New Year and spring of 1906 had been for Upton Sinclair! Having agitated for Jack London to be president of the Intercollegiate Socialist Society, he'd felt obliged to help organize the plenary meeting in New York City at Carnegie Hall; his co-founders Clarence Darrow and Florence Kelly, though supportive of the effort, did not live in the vicinity of New York, and were too busy with other matters to participate. Upton had only just recovered from the ordeal of rebutting a flood of attacks following the publication of *The Jungle,* and what he believed to be a major article for the influential journal *Everybody's*—"The Gospel According to St. Marx"—completed in record time, even for Upton Sinclair. (Yet, fast as Upton could write, typing so rapidly he was in danger of wearing out a new typewriter ribbon within a week, and developing cramps in both his hands, he was uneasily aware that Jack London could write faster, as well as far more successfully—though London hadn't begun publishing until 1900, by 1905 he'd already published ten books, each of them having created an extraordinary "stir" with the public.) Lately Upton was obliged to commute to New York City several times a week, by train; it would have been a felicitous time to meet with Meta, and see little David, and work out a reconciliation with his family, and yet—somehow, Socialist obligations took precedence over mere personal life, and Upton never found time.

Since Meta had moved out of the farmhouse on Rosedale Road, Upton's eating habits were yet more sporadic. It was painful to him to see, in the reflections of store windows in Princeton, how, in his mid-twenties, he still resembled an adolescent male of seventeen or eighteen; so many hours of hunching at his writing desk had permanently rounded his shoulders, like the shoulders and backs of those poor mill-worker children whom Mother Jones had presented to horrified audiences, as examples of the exploited. "Well—no one has exploited *me.* I have done it myself!" Upton's eyes, which were nearsighted, watered easily; he had not yet found time to visit an eye doctor and acquire a new prescription for his lenses. His health was beginning to be a chronic worry to him despite his strict diet and habits of cleanliness; a Socialist specialist in nutrition had advised him to fast as frequently as possible, avoiding meat, fish, and eggs, as it was now known that such a regimen led to an increase in the metabolic rate, or energy—though Upton had to confess, he felt no more energetic than ever, and often felt enervated and even discouraged—a predilection he had to fight against, vigorously. Set beside his hero Jack London—in his own eyes, at least—Upton envisioned himself as a sort of quasi-male, or stunted male—as London had so uncannily perceived, Upton lacked the temperament for *touch*—for human contact.

Yet Upton had married an attractive young woman, a fact that often bedazzled him. *How,* and *why?*—he would have said that he loved his young wife, and hoped to be a reasonably good husband to her, yet, when they were apart, as they were so frequently since the publication of *The Jungle,* Upton had difficulty remembering what Meta looked like; and his little son was interchangeable, Upton thought, to his shame, with any number of other young babies ...

Suddenly in Upton's New York life there were so many young women—so many people! And many were recent immigrants to the United States, or the sons and daughters of immigrants, like the Lithuanians Upton had interviewed in Chicago, as background for *The Jungle;* in New York City, residents of immigrant neighborhoods on the Lower East Side—"teeming" and "lawless" as the Hearst newspaper called them— were drawn to the Socialist cause, and impressed Upton Sinclair with their vitality and passion. They were German, Italian, Polish, Hungarian, as well as Lithuanian and Russian—their heavily accented English was frequently incomprehensible to him, even as their emotions were vivid and direct and so very different from the veiled and obscure emotions of the class to which he and Meta Fuller were born.

"You won't accompany me to the rally, Meta? I wish you would—it will be an historic event."

How many times Upton had pleaded with his wife, whose political sentiments, he'd thought, had been near-identical with his own, and whose methodical, meticulous editing of his manuscripts—often, line by line, and hour by hour—had been invaluable to him; but his voice expressed a sort of wistful yearning and childish hurt.

"You would meet Jack London! It will be quite an occasion—all the newspapers will write about us. We are hoping to take up a collection afterward—this will be a unique opportunity. 'Revolution Now' is the title of Jack's speech—he has sent a telegram."

Meta had murmured a vague reply. For Upton had asked her numerous times to come to this "historic" rally—many times, very many times, he'd extolled the virtues of Jack London, as of other Socialist comrades, to her. But of late, she'd declined with no excuse except that she was tired.

Once, shortly before Meta had taken David away to live with her parents on Staten Island, the young couple had had a painful exchange.

"But, Meta—the opportunity to meet Jack London—!"

"But, Upton—I've had the opportunity to meet Upton Sinclair. And what of that?"

Meta's nervous laughter rang in his ears for some time after, utterly baffling to him.

IN HIS JOURNAL for May 28, 1906, which was the eve of the rally at Carnegie Hall, Upton Sinclair grimly noted:

> In a time of Revolution, private lives are of no significance. Marriage, family, tradition—all bourgeois customs, propagating hypocrisy and capitalist exploitation—are doomed.

"He will be here. He will not let us down."

Yet by 7:45 P.M., on the evening of May 28, Jack London had not yet arrived at Carnegie Hall for the program which was scheduled to have begun at 7 P.M. Since he'd joined the Socialist cause Upton had discovered that it wasn't uncommon for Socialist rallies to be delayed—sometimes canceled at the last minute—as it wasn't uncommon for the rallies to be haphazardly organized—but the audience awaiting Jack

London this evening was unusually restive; there was a tension in the air resembling the tension before an electrical storm. Many individuals refused to be seated but were milling about in the foyer and the aisles— these were excitable, bellicose men who bore little resemblance to the young students from Columbia University, New York University, City College and other area universities and colleges for whom the Society had been organized.

Belatedly the organizers were realizing that a good portion of the audience had come expressly to hear Jack London speak, not as the president of the fledgling Socialist society but as the handsome young author of the enormously popular *Call of the Wild* which had sold more than one million copies; in spite of London's reputation as a writer of adventure stories, there were a number of well-dressed women in the audience who didn't appear, to the cursory eye, to be likely Socialists.

On Fifty-seventh Street, outside Carnegie Hall, as if unwilling to pay the small price of admission until they were certain that Jack London had arrived, were men who, judging by their rough-hewn clothes, and their air of masculine aggressiveness, might have stepped out of *The Sea Wolf*, London's new, wildly best-selling novel of a tyrannical sea captain in the mode of a Nietzschean *Übermensch*—a novel that, to Upton Sinclair's astonished envy, had sold out its initial printing of forty thousand copies *before publication*.

Amid all this commotion, and the mounting anxiety of the rally organizers, Upton Sinclair yet had to marvel—what a wonder it was, a writer of his generation had so swiftly attained such stature with the masses, of a kind he could never dream of attaining! Though his commitment to the masses was absolute, and in his most private fantasies he dreamt of being a martyr to the cause like Eugene Debs, brutally beaten by strike-breaking police, thrown into prison . . . emerging with renewed dedication . . . "The Socialist cause has found its great poet-visionary—and he is my age, or nearly! My brother, and my friend."

It was nearing 8 P.M. Jack London had not yet arrived. When the acting president of the Society addressed the audience, with a plea for just a few more minutes' patience, he was greeted with jeers and boos amid scattered applause. Clearly there was a division in the hall between those who were committed Socialists—for whom the rally was the principal draw of the evening—and those who had come to hear Jack London speak—for whom the rally, if not the Socialist cause itself, was incidental. Some of the roughly dressed men who'd been milling about on the sidewalk outside had now found their way inside, and were jostling individuals in the aisles. With an air of wonderment Upton Sinclair murmured aloud—"We are approaching chaos—catastrophe! How has this happened!"

In fact the blame might lie with Upton himself—he'd been so adamant with the nominating committee, insisting that Jack London was their man; he'd tried several times, without success, by mail and telegram, to convince London that he should arrive in New York City on the day before the rally, or, at the very least, early in the afternoon of May 28. But, for some reason Upton could not comprehend, since it suggested a reckless confidence utterly absent in himself, London had assured him that he wouldn't have the slightest difficulty in arriving at Carnegie Hall "precisely on time"—if his sea voyage from San Francisco to Miami wasn't delayed beyond a few hours, or the train from Miami to New York City . . . which was, as Upton discovered to his horror, due to arrive in Grand Central Station at 6:35 P.M. By telegram, Upton had pleaded with London to move back his travel time, by at least a half-day; to arrive in New York just twenty-five minutes before he was scheduled to address the Society seemed very risky—"You will make us all very anxious, and yourself as well. Please reconsider!" London's reply had been blithe, bemused: "Spare yourself 'anxiety,' comrade—Jack London guarantees a *Juggernaut of a performance*."

Upton had been so chagrined by this exchange, he couldn't bring himself to tell his fellow organizers the exact time London's train was due. Some measure of guilty embarrassment prevented him, as he'd hesitated to confide frankly in his wife about London, as well. It was a principle of his Socialist vow—as it had been a principle, previously, of his Christian character—that he made every effort to be *positive;* that is, resolutely to avoid *negation,* as a self-defeating strategy of action. From the great American pragmatic philosopher William James he'd taken the admonition to simulate faith, where faith may be flagging, in order to revive and resuscitate faith; as a young undergraduate at City College, he'd been impressed by no philosopher more than James, in the matter of "pragmatic truth"— *Truth is not something that resides in a principle. Truth is something that happens to a principle.*

This, Upton had tried to explain to his wife, whose knowledge of philosophy was limited to those fragments of "great thoughts" she'd been taught at Sweet Briar College—"As Darwin has taught us, the species are ever evolving, as specimens within species must evolve, to survive, so too truth must 'evolve'—it can't remain fixed."

" 'Truth must *evolve'*—how very convenient for liars."

Upton had frowned at Meta's frivolousness. Whenever he tried to speak seriously to her, she joked; whenever he tried to joke with her, she responded blankly.

It hadn't always been this way, he was sure—when they'd first met, only just a few years before. Then, Meta had been a very sweet, soft-spoken and amiable girl, if not uncommonly beautiful or striking—quick to laugh at Upton's jokes, quick to sympathize with his ideas, and eager to hear him speak, at length, on "The Gospel According to St. Marx" and its variants.

Naively, he'd thought the woman to be his soul mate.

A THUNDEROUS ROAR of cheers!—Jack London had arrived.

"He's here! At last—thank God . . ."

It was 8:12 P.M. London was more than an hour late. But the boisterous audience, that had seemed on the verge of anarchy, was immediately placated, like a great brainless beast. Backstage, where he'd been pacing in a state of extreme agitation, Upton felt a wave of utter, ecstatic relief—not just the Socialist cause had been rescued, but Upton and the other organizers, who'd begun to fear for their physical well-being but could not bring themselves to flee the premises.

Upton hurried out to greet London, who was making his way down the center aisle of the hall, like a politician, or a celebrated prizefighter, his thick dark hair attractively windblown; London was in an ebullient mood, very friendly, pausing to shake hands with admirers and autograph-seekers. It had been understood that London would arrive at the rear door of the hall, on Seventh Avenue, to be spared just such a situation, but it was clear that London greatly enjoyed the scene, as did his female companion—a small gypsy-like woman in colorful attire, clamped to his arm.

Hurriedly, in the melee at the front of the hall, Upton introduced himself to Jack London who, flush-faced and enlivened, and smelling frankly of alcohol, shook his hand so hard that Upton winced; then, like a long-lost relative, grappled him in a bear-like embrace that left Upton breathless. " 'Upton Sinclair'—comrade! You are exactly as I'd envisioned"—London laughed heartily at this remark which was meant as playful chiding, if not outright sarcasm. Upton too laughed, nervously—he felt a thrill of worry, that one or more of his ribs had been cracked in Jack London's embrace.

"My woman—Miss Charmian. My loyal consort."

Again, London laughed heartily—though clearly he was proud of his companion; in the gutter press, the caption beneath her photograph was " 'The Call of the Wild': Jack London's Other Wife." Charmian! Seemingly, the woman had no surname. Upton was surprised to see her for he'd been given to understand—by London—that London wouldn't be bringing her with him to New York, but—here she was, preening like royalty: a surprisingly squat little person with a garishly made-up pug-face and a silk turban wound about her head who took so little notice of "Upton Sinclair" that she might have thought him an usher at the rally, whose responsibility was to escort her to her reserved seat in the front row.

Upton's second surprise was that London didn't want him to introduce him to the audience—"No, no! These people haven't come to hear
you talk about 'Jack London'—they've come to hear 'Jack London.' And
I'll oblige them now."

It was a measure of the man's high spirits and his consummate
confidence in himself that he strode up onto the stage without hesitation, and to the podium, very like a prizefighter, shaking his fists in the
air both to acknowledge the deafening roars of applause, and to evoke
an even greater volume. Several minutes were required for the audience
to subside to the point at which London could be heard, his mouth close
to the microphone as he shouted, with no preamble: "Revolution now!
Revolution now! And again I say unto ye—*Revolution now!*"

Again, the hall erupted in clapping, foot-stamping, and cheers;
again, London had to wait for the hall to quiet.

Upton had taken his seat beside squat little Charmian, in a bit of
a daze. His temples throbbed, his eyes watered. He'd been so distracted
for the past forty-eight hours he had virtually forgotten to eat and was
now light-headed and weak in the knees. How close they'd come to pandemonium, if London had not arrived just in time! It was thrilling to
Upton now, to hear his hero speak in a powerful dramatic voice, hunching his broad shoulders to lean forward, gripping the sides of the podium. The audience that had been so restless was now hushed in reverent
anticipation.

" 'No Compromise' is the essence of the Proletarian movement . . .
Capitalism is the Sole Enemy . . . If one Socialist comrade will bring another into the fold, and he yet another, the entire United States will be
won by the year 1912 . . . We are witnessing the death-struggle between
the two great forces of Greed, the chiefs of the Beef Trust and the chiefs of
the Standard Oil Trust, for ownership of the United States of America . . .
'Big Bill' Haywood's motto 'Good Pay or Bum Work' will soon replace 'In
God We Trust' as the motto of the United States . . ." London spoke in a
loud, incantatory manner, like one repeating memorized phrases, yet with

great effect. Though his words were familiar ones—at least, to Upton Sinclair and other Socialists in the hall—they were greeted with applause, as if they were highly original, and daring. Upton sat in the first row of seats, below the podium, gazing up at his hero with the unstinting admiration of a kicked dog for his master, who has left off kicking him for the moment and is being kind to him, capriciously, yet wonderfully.

When London's flushed face crinkled with schoolboy slyness, you could see that he was about to make a joke—"Far be it from yours truly the much-derided 'Boy Socialist'—as my detractors have called me, in an effort to discredit the noble cause for which I stand—to deny that Socialism is a *menace;* why, our stated purpose is to wipe out, root and branch, all capitalistic enterprises of present-day society"—and all erupted with laughter, including Upton; when London's face grew sober, or seemingly sober—"our cry is a simple appeal to the downtrodden exploited workingman of America and of the world—*Organize! Organize! Organize!*"—the hall became hushed, as if London were uttering a prayer. Like the refrain of a ballad, these few words of London's returned, each time with more vehemence: "*Organize! Organize!* And again I say unto ye—*Organize!* And the world will be ours! And human destiny will be ours! *Revolution now! Revolution now! Revolution now!*"

In his fatigued and excited state Upton sat limp, like one basking in another's warmth. It had been said of Upton Sinclair as a public speaker that he was "earnest"—"inspiring"—but there was no comparing Sinclair and London, the one delivering prepared speeches in a dogged monotone, often dropping his gaze to his typescript, the other flamboyant, animated, gesturing with his hands and arms, interrupting his own words with shouts of laughter—"This'll stick-em! This'll *stick-em!*" —zestfully rubbing his hands together. London's astonishing charisma could carry all of New York City, if the city's residents had turned out to hear him; it could carry all of the United States . . . Such a *Juggernaut of a performance* deserved a stadium full of cheering spectators, not the mere twelve or fifteen hundred who had turned out this evening in Carnegie Hall.

Upton could not comprehend how Jack London had done so poorly in his campaign for mayor of Oakland several years before. Had his Socialist message been premature? Had his personality not yet ripened?

Yet, as the speech continued, and London began to repeat his words, and even his seemingly spontaneous gesticulations, Upton began to notice that, in the unsparing spotlight of Carnegie Hall, the handsome "Boy Socialist" did in fact look older than his dust jacket photos. And was he—shorter? Shorter than one would have expected? His romantic-masculine features had coarsened, his muscled body had grown perceptibly thick, and oddly clumsy. His speaking manner was to simulate a kind of confiding intimacy with his audience—as if he were sharing secrets with them; at the same time, his rhetorical habit was to raise his voice suddenly, and dramatically—so that, if you were leaning forward in your seat, listening avidly, you were likely to rear back, as if you'd been struck a playful blow to the face. And there was the hearty, bellowing laughter with its edge of—mockery? Or was this simply—Upton wanted to believe—the expression of a sort of *brimming masculinity*, that could scarcely be contained behind a podium, on a conventional stage?

Upton had not wanted to think that the first president of the Intercollegiate Socialist Society had arrived at Carnegie Hall in a drunken, or semi-drunken state, but this did seem to be the case. At the start of his speech London had taken large swallows of water from a glass placed on the podium, but after some twenty minutes he'd begun to sip openly from a flask he carried inside his coat, to the merriment and approval of the more vociferous members of the audience. The more London sipped, the more flushed his face became, the louder his voice and the more sweeping his gestures. Of course—it was known that Jack London was a *drinker;* Jack London was hardly a *teetotaler,* like Upton Sinclair. Yet somehow, Upton had not thought that London's drinking would impinge upon this rally, and this evening; Upton had not thought of this possibility at all. He didn't dare glance around at the lively, mesmerized audience but it wouldn't have surprised him if many of these individuals, too, were sipping from flasks. (Any consumption of alcoholic beverages was expressly forbidden in Carnegie Hall! The Socialists had been warned.)

Upton was also dismayed by London's clothing. How peculiar it was—how unexpected—Jack London was wearing not the rough seaman's clothing in which he was usually photographed, nor even work-clothes, but an alarmingly "dandyish" costume—an English-style herringbone suit with a vest and a white—silken?—blouse and a flowing silk tie in polka dot design. When you caught a glimpse of his footwear, you could see that he wore elegantly styled shoe-boots of gleaming black leather. And, on his thick fingers, gleaming rings.

The herringbone vest fit London very tightly, like a sausage casing, and was becoming, as the minutes lurched past, increasingly stained from spillage from the flask. London's hair looked now more disheveled than windblown, threaded with a coarse sort of gray. More openly London now sipped from his silver flask, and smacking his lips with relish—drawing a ribald response from his audience.

Upton chided himself—*As I am a "teetotaler"—often derided for my "old-maid sentiments"—as by Jack London, for my deficient "sex-attitude"—I am the last person to pass judgment.*

It was clear by now that London had no prepared speech to deliver to the Intercollegiate Socialist Society, and seemed loftily indifferent to the fact that there were young university students in the audience; his remarks, like his increasingly ribald humor, were directed toward those who reacted with laughter, applause, foot-stampings. It was clear too that London had forgotten, if he'd ever known, that his "presidential address" was but one of several speeches scheduled for the rally: he continued to speak past 9 P.M.—past 9:30 P.M.—and now nearing 10 P.M., without a hint of fatigue. Of the speakers who were to follow, Moses Leithauser, the martyr of the recent Garment Workers' strike, still on crutches after his ordeal at the hands of Pinkerton's strike-breaking "detectives," had come at Upton Sinclair's express invitation, and was becoming impatient, and annoyed; but there was nothing anyone could do, certainly not Upton Sinclair, for the audience would have been furious if their hero had been interrupted, and indeed London was very funny, at times uproariously: "The working-man of the world needs to take a lesson from yours truly in that, if he wishes to 'make ends meet,' he should not lower his standard of living but—like yours truly—*raise his income.* There you have it, comrades: Revol'shun Now!"

Even Upton had to laugh. This was very witty—worthy of Oscar Wilde—as, when you thought of it, London's playful/parodistic manner and dandyish costume were reminiscent of the notorious, lately disgraced and deceased Wilde. Yet, how different the effeminate Wilde, from the hyper-masculine London!

Upton was uneasily conscious of the eccentric little woman seated beside him, who applauded Jack London as vociferously as anyone in the hall. He didn't want to seem—he didn't want to *be*—puritanical; he was sure that, like any radical-minded Socialist in the first, thrilling years of the twentieth century, he had overcome the outmoded strictures of the bourgeoisie; yet he couldn't help but regret that London so brazenly flaunted the conventions of the bourgeoisie, which overlapped with those of the proletariat in matters of morality and "decent" conduct. It was unfortunate that the Hearst papers had luridly latched upon "immorality" and "free love" as charges against the Socialist movement; yet more, that Jack London had "repudiated" his wife Bess for her failure to provide him with a male heir, and spoke in interviews of his new attachment to a "temptress of exotic breeding and beauty," known only as Charmian. Upton had been shocked to have seen, a week before, in one of the gutter tabloids, a front-page, blurred photograph of the turbaned, broadly smiling "Miss Charmian"—"Jack London's Other Wife"; now, seated beside her, close-up, he could not imagine how the squat little female was any sort of "temptress," let alone an "exotic" beauty.

Charmian must have been older than her lover by some years, Upton thought, judging from the harsh bracketing lines framing her rouged mouth, and the sunken though glittering nature of her small eyes:

more than forty, surely! (London wasn't yet thirty, though he looked at least forty.) Maybe the gas-jets in the hall were unflattering to the gnome-like little woman who, flamboyantly costumed in a magenta silk turban pinned with a jeweled scarab, and a flowing "kimono"-style gown of crimson and black stripes, sat in a rigidly self-conscious pose, as if she were onstage herself; knowing herself watched by many in the audience, she made a show of gazing adoringly at the speaker above her, lifting her hands to clap fervently, and glancing from time to time, with queenly condescension, at the audience.

Must not judge her, and their love—"free love." As I am so conspicuous a failure along these lines myself.

For so it seemed to Upton Sinclair, what should have been obvious at the time of his honeymoon with Meta, spent at a Socialist campground at Bayhead, New Jersey: he had not a clue what *manliness, masculinity, any sort of "sex-attitude" meant.* It seemed almost accidental—or incidental—that Upton did in fact have a "male heir"; for he felt very little connection with the baby, as the baby felt little connection with him.

Now he understood why Meta had ceased laughing at his jokes—why Meta had so little patience for him, and seemed always to be too busy, too distracted, to have time even to listen to him, as she'd had before they were married. She did not appeal to him to come to bed with her any longer—she did not mind how late Upton stayed up working, or how many hours he worked through the day.

Initially, it was Upton's belief that marriage could be studied as a science, from a rationalist perspective; he thought he'd made the effort—yes, he had made the effort—but Meta had not seemed to know how to cooperate.

There was something thrilling—"primitive"—in the way that Charmian stared rapturously at her lover, and London, from time to time, paused in his speechifying to wink down at his beloved, and smile a secret sort of smile, wet teeth gleaming. For this was a radically liberated couple—an heroic couple, you might say—unashamed of the "illicit" nature of their passion, in defiance of the hypocritical disapproval of the bourgeoisie. It was known that Charmian—"Miss Charmian" as London called her—was no middle-class female but a courageous rebel, for whom the role of the "other woman" was a challenge to be met with zest, and with "dash"; as for Jack London, he'd lately advocated *natural passion* as the cure for most of society's ills, along with the Socialist Revolution.

Upton was roused from his reverie by a renewed uproar in the hall as Jack London, glowering-red with exuberance, brought the audience to their feet chanting lines from "La Marseillaise"—in loud, mangled French incomprehensible to most, though, to Upton, chilling in its robust brutality—

> *Aux armes, citoyens!*
> *Formez vos bataillons!*
> *Marchons! Marchons!*
> *Qu'un sang impur*
> *Abreuve nos sillons!*

Upton's sensitive nerves were such, the very thought of human blood "watering" soil left him weak, faint; as he was repelled by the finale of Jack London's Juggernaut performance—striding about the stage, lurching as if about to fall, striking the palm of one hand with the doughy fist of the other while shouting furiously—"Revolution now! Revolution now! *Revolution Now!*"

TRULY NOW, Upton Sinclair *was* surprised.

For, before the storm of riotous applause and foot-stamping had halfway abated in the hall, Jack London strode backstage, waving aside congratulations and offers of handshakes from Socialist comrades, declaring to Upton that he was "both ravenously hungry and uncommonly thirsty—for beer; and bored to high hell by the brain-addled sheep out front." His broad smile had vanished, as if it had never been; his eyes were bloodshot, and his skin sallow. He'd torn open his herringbone vest, which had too tightly constrained his torso and belly, and was freely perspiring. In vain Upton and the others urged him to stay for the remainder of the program, or at least to hear the revered Moses Leithauser, who had waited so patiently for London to finish; London refused even to meet Leithauser, and brushed rudely past several well-to-do Socialists who'd come considerable distances to hear him, and who were much valued as donors to the Cause.

"I too have come a long distance, all the way from California, and must now refresh myself—Miss Charmian, come!—we are going to Mac-Dougal's, should any comrades wish to join us—but do not attempt to restrain me now," the stocky man laughingly warned, "—for I want *meat*, and I want *drink*, and I want *my woman*—and there it is! Miss Charmian, come: the hackney cab awaits, and we are off."

Upton tried to plead with London not to leave so abruptly—but to no avail. Miss Charmian in her glittering silk turban had joined her lover backstage, marveling at his performance—*"Magnifique!"*—and clamping her arm tightly into the crook of his arm. Together the two made their way out onto the street, through the stage door.

Of course, Upton couldn't follow them. Not only did he feel an obligation to hear Moses Leithauser speak, and several others, but there were responsibilities he couldn't shirk after the rally ended: skirmishes between Socialists and New York City police officers on Fifty-seventh Street, and a quarrel among several of the organizers over who had misplaced a packet of valuable receipts.

When Upton returned to the hall, he saw to his dismay that more than half the audience had rudely left in the wake of their idol Jack London. Those who remained were scattered about the rows of seats and most of these appeared to be young men of university age—neatly dressed, with glasses—of whom a number uncannily resembled Upton Sinclair.

At last, at 10:20 P.M., Moses Leithauser was to speak! The delay had been unconscionable and humiliating—Upton could barely bring himself to look at the revered union man waiting backstage with pages of a speech clutched in his hand, his face a mask of wounded pride, indignation, and fury. Upton hurried to the podium to introduce Leithauser, and to urge the remaining audience—"Come forward, please! There are many empty seats at the front."

SO LATE! It was nearing midnight when Upton Sinclair and the more reliable of his Society comrades were free to leave Carnegie Hall, parting from one another in exhausted silence. Upton was staying with friends in a sparely furnished flat on the Lower East Side.

Upton thought *I will go back there now—of course.*

Yet, though he was exhausted, his nerves were strung-tight; he was light-headed, and famished; he could not stop thinking of Jack London's *Juggernaut performance,* and of the remainder of the rally—a succession of doggedly earnest Socialist speakers, lecturing to a gradually diminishing audience until, at the very end, only a few isolated individuals remained in the hall, of whom several were deeply asleep and could barely be wakened by ushers.

I will go back to the flat, to sleep. And tomorrow—I will go to Staten Island, to claim my woman and my "heir."

Somehow, as in a trance, he was walking south—on Seventh Avenue—in the direction of Times Square. Though he hadn't ever patronized the notorious MacDougal's, nor even would have thought he knew its location, Upton found himself drawn in that direction—for hadn't Jack London invited him to drop by MacDougal's after the rally?—it would be rude for him not to accept London's invitation, under the circumstances. For he, Upton Sinclair, had invited London to accept the presidency of the Intercollegiate Socialist Society, and to speak at its inaugural rally—very likely, he was Jack London's closest friend in

Manhattan, and the Socialist comrade closest to him in ideology, zeal, and temperament.

"It would be rude, certainly. After the sacrifice London has made, coming here . . ."

When Upton arrived at MacDougal's he had no difficulty locating Jack London and Miss Charmian in its crowded, deafening, and sulfurous-smoky interior—there, at a table at the very center of the bustling restaurant, was the conspicuous couple, surrounded by a pack of admirers.

Hesitantly Upton approached—he'd been jostled by departing revelers, at the front of the restaurant—feeling as if he were stepping into something like a blast furnace—by the indraft sucked inside, shyly excited, intimidated, yet helpless to resist. He saw that London's table was strewn with glasses, Champagne and beer bottles, dirtied plates and cutlery; on a platter in front of London were the remains of what appeared to be a raw hunk of meat, only the curving, tusk-like bone and shreds of bloody gristle remaining. Upton would have thought that, after his energetic performance at Carnegie Hall, Jack London would be in a subdued if not exhausted mood, but, to the contrary, here was the famous man laughing loudly, sprawled in his chair, a railway cap perched cockily on his head, and the stump of a thick-ashed cigar clamped between his big bared teeth. His jaws gleamed with grease, his canine teeth looked particularly pointed. The elegant herringbone coat had been removed, the herringbone vest had been torn open, the white silk blouse was splattered with food- and drink-stains, pulled open also at the throat to show a broad, fatty, grizzle-haired upper torso.

Yet more astonishing to Upton that London, sighting him as he hesitantly approached, squinting at him through wafting clouds of smoke, reacted so suddenly, and so warmly: "Here he is! Here! We've all been waiting for—who's-it—Comrade Sinc'ler—hope of the twentieth century—author of the greatest novel since *Uncle Tom's Cabin*—*Jungle! The Jungle!*—that's- it, ain't it?—*God-dam Jungle!*—truer words were never uttered—this damn-cursed cap'list nation is a *jungle*—never mind *Wolf,* and *Death*—predators of the deep—here is where the cesspool lies, in these United States." Upton paused a few feet from the table, stricken with self-consciousness as everyone at the table turned to stare at him, and London lurched to his feet as if he were greeting a long-lost friend, or indeed a comrade-brother. The fierce-faced man staggered toward Upton as if to embrace him, colliding with a waiter, and with a gentle-man in a tuxedo seated at his table—"Make way, make way, damn you—this is *Comrade Sinc'ler*—make way and let the skinny fella in—runt of the litter—shy!—'the meek shall enter first'—or—is it 'last'?—no mat-ter, if you enter—better last, if the first is trompled over—'survival of the fittest'—sit!—here, my friend!—beside Jack, sit—there is plenty of room—my woman on my left-hand, my brother Sinc'ler on my right—now, we are all meant where we are to be, or—we are all where we are meant to be; and the hour is still young."

Upton had no choice but to sit beside London, who pulled him down into the chair beside him; his face was hot with embarrassment, and a wild sort of elation, as if he, too, were drunk. Yet more surprising than London's welcome was Miss Charmian's—the perky little woman, not to be upstaged by her lover, leaned across London's stocky grizzled chest to kiss Upton on the cheek!—warmly, wetly—tickling him with one of the curled macaw feathers that adorned her bosom, to the amusement of the table of revelers.

"Wel-come! Wel-come to—wherever this is! If you are Jack's brother, you are Miss Charmian's brother. *Sit.*"

There followed then a confusing interlude during which, though Upton protested that he didn't drink, he had vowed never to drink fol-lowing his father's tragic experience with alcoholism, London tried to press on him any number of highly potent beverages, including what he called his *post-performance libation,* a blend of Champagne, whiskey, and dark beer; even more strenuously, London tried to press on him the remaining half of his *cannibal sandwich,* a pound of raw beefsteak topped with onions, pickles, and catsup, on a kaiser roll, which lay on a nearby plate, the hard-crusted roll showing the imprint of London's teeth. He'd had a sixteen-ounce plank steak, London said, as well as two of the *cannibal sandwiches*, and had not been able to finish the second, though it was delicious. "Comrade Sinc'ler—you are looking so undernourished and anemic, as if the women had been uncommonly rough on you, you'd best gobble down this sandwich at once, and bring a little color to your cheeks."

"But—I think I may have mentioned to you, Jack—in one of my letters—I am a vegetarian . . ."

At the mere utterance of the word *vegetarian* the table erupted in laughter—even Miss Charmian, who'd been so welcoming to Upton, laughed derisively. Upton laughed too, or tried to laugh—he was a good sport, in such situations—as a Socialist he'd learned to parry and thrust when baited, teased, even threatened; apologetically, he tried to explain that his "digestion" wouldn't accommodate such rich food, for he had some sort of stomach condition—"colitis"; yet, at this, the table again erupted in laughter, as if Upton had said something even wittier than before.

It was a relief when, laying his arm across Upton's shoulders, London regaled the table with an account of his favorite delicacies of the moment— number one wasn't beef, in fact, but "two large male mallards—cooked for no more than eight minutes to assure the fowl sufficiently *underdone*."

This ushered in a protracted discussion of favorite delicacies, from around the table, which gave Upton some respite. He'd managed to order, from a harassed waiter, a bottle of mineral water, which he drank as unobtrusively as he could manage, not wanting his vociferous companion to notice; sitting beside London, as in the vicinity of a blast furnace, he felt both warmed and over-warmed, dazzled, wary. Naively he'd hoped for some time with London during which they might have talked frankly together of politics, literature, the future of Socialism, possibly even the vicissitudes of married life, and love; naively he'd hoped that London might have sequestered a private room at the restaurant, and rebuffed the invitations of admirers to treat him and Miss Charmian to drinks and dinner. For Upton was surprised, London didn't appear to be acquainted with even the gentleman in the tuxedo, who'd been seated beside him before Upton arrived; and Upton was surprised to learn that, far from journeying to New York City principally to address the Intercollegiate Socialist Society, London had come here on the first leg of a trans-Atlantic journey—his Yukon books had become runaway best sellers in Great Britain, France, Germany and Russia, and his publishers in these countries were eager to host him—"It seems that I have quite eclipsed old 'Mark Twain'—the Germans especially despise Twain, y'know—the old fool has mouthed some crude sort of criticism of them—in defense of Jewry—*he* is in defense of Jewry—the Germans will not forgive him"—London burst into laughter, as if he'd never heard anything so amusing—"and caricature him now, in the public press, with a *Jew-nose*."

This crude remark initiated a round of *Jew-talk*, and *Jew-jokes*, which were offensive to Upton Sinclair, as well as shocking—for wasn't Socialism a wholly nonsectarian movement, vigorously led and supported by Jews?—as a Socialist, Jack London would know this fact, surely. What would Moses Leithauser think, if he could hear . . .

Yet more disappointing, London seemed to have forgotten Upton Sinclair. After the initial fuss, London turned his back to him, addressing others at the table in the hale, hearty tone in which he'd addressed Upton; nor did Miss Charmian give Upton a second glance. London had moved now from his Champagne concoction to straight Kentucky bourbon, in shot glasses.

Sprawling in his chair like a pasha, his heavy chin several times brought to rest on Miss Charmian's plump shoulder in a way to make the excitable woman emit little cries of laughter, London entertained the table, and patrons of MacDougal's who'd gathered in a semi-circle, with a rambling and disconnected monologue—his "Life Philosophy"—about which, evidently, there was enormous interest across the States.

"In interviews it is always inquired—'Where does Jack London's stamina derive from'—where, his ability to compose never less than one thousand words a day, and often near ten thousand; and how does he hold an audience in the palm of his hand—as I did just now in Carnegie Hall—for more than two hours, without slackening? Where, in short, Jack London's particular 'genius'? Where, indeed." London chuckled deep in his throat, like a stirring beast; he pressed his chin downward on Miss Charmian's shoulder, in a way to make her squeal, and glanced about the restaurant in shivering delight. "Such questions," London continued, in a graver voice, "strike deep to the heart of primeval Being itself, and can't be answered, except, perhaps, in terms of *racial ancestry*. That is, to speak bluntly—the superiority of certain races, and the inheritance of these superior traits by 'superior' specimens within these races."

Now, to Upton's extreme discomfort, London began to speak with drunken animation of *Nordic supremacy*—the uncontested superiority of the *Beast-man*—descended from the great icy wastes of the Polar region and "taking the sickly little dagos of the Southern Hemisphere by storm." Upton dared to interrupt, objecting that such a belief was in violation of the Socialist brotherhood—"Are not all men equal?—men of all races, skin-colors, and classes?—that is, *men and women alike,* in the Socialist fold? No race can claim superiority—no skin-color—though, at this perilous point in history, the proletarian is undoubtedly superior, morally . . ." But London rudely puffed on his cigar, releasing a virulent cloud of smoke; swallowed down another shot-glass of bourbon; and snapped his finger to summon a waiter, to order more bourbon. It was uncanny, London behaved not only as if Upton had said nothing but also as if Upton wasn't seated in the chair beside him; London merely continued his monologue as if he hadn't been interrupted. Nor did Miss Charmian, or anyone else at the table, take note of his rudeness to his friend.

"The dominant races of the Earth came down, you see, from the North. From the great ice-fields and snowy wastes, the tundras, of the North. From the forest primeval—the abode of silent tragedy. Yes, it is ever so: *noisy comedy, silent tragedy*. Once, we were forged of iron, and much that is greater than iron, in the blast-furnace of the soul. For there, y'see, in the pitiless North, the struggle for survival continues as always—as if it were not 1906 but the very beginning of history; and our feeble, effeminate 'civilized' notions of right and wrong, justice and injustice, social welfare and social outrage, never conceived." London sighed loudly, stubbing out his cigar in the remains of his beefsteak sandwich, and signaling for a waiter to carry it away.

With surprising boldness, for one so temperamentally quiet, and loath to quarrel, Upton dared to raise an objection: "I don't doubt the 'pitilessness' of the North any more than I would doubt the 'pitilessness' of the Sahara, or the Amazon rain forest—but I contest its application to human history. Doesn't this lead to the very 'social Darwinism' advanced by our enemies? Think of the criminal Rockefeller publicly congratulating himself that God had given him his money—or daring to compare the fruits of his criminal trust to the 'exquisite flowering of the American Beauty rose.'"

Again, London failed to reply to Upton. It might have been that he was preoccupied in searching through his pockets for another cigar—(which Miss Charmian gaily provided him out of a glaringly sequined purse); or, London simply didn't hear his comrade's remarks in the din of MacDougal's. In any case he scarcely altered his frowning gaze, or modified the condescending tone of his argument, proceeding as if uninterrupted: " . . . *never conceived.* And, indeed, mere jests upon the wind! For in the land of the midnight sun, where the wolf pack trots at the flank of the caribou herd, singling out the weak, and the aged, and the great with calf, and pulling them down to devour with not a flicker of remorse, it's a foolish fancy to prattle of such effeminate notions. The Nordic soul is a man's soul from time immemorial. Wolf knew, and Death knew—predator-brothers of *The Sea Wolf*—but all know, in our hearts—even the slant-eyed, the Jews, and the dagos. For that, my friends, is the caldron out of which Jack London has been forged and it would be false modesty to claim otherwise." London cocked his railway cap at an aggressive angle on his thick disheveled hair, as if to dare anyone to knock it off.

But no one at the table contested his words or, except for Upton Sinclair, seemed upset by them. Jocose toasts were drunk to the "Nordic soul"—to Jack London's "Nordic soul" in particular—while Upton, blushing and nettled, refused to drink even his mineral water, unnoticed.

It was now nearing 1 A.M., and the din of hilarity in MacDougal's showed no sign of abating. How lurid, this nocturnal life!—this *under-belly* sort of city-life, of which Upton Sinclair had had no notion, in his monastic seclusion outside Princeton, New Jersey; and in his fervent dealings with immigrant Socialists of the Lower East Side, who rose early to work fourteen-hour days, and collapsed into bed most nights immediately after their evening meal. Jack London, tireless, continued his slurred monologue, while Upton berated himself—what a fool he'd been, how naïve, to have imagined that Jack London expected him here tonight; to have entered of his own volition a fashionable "gin-mill" like MacDougal's. If his mother could see him, in such a place! If Meta could see him!

Upton could have wept, he'd been so naïve. So—hopeful. Since they'd begun their correspondence in the summer, Upton had been anticipating an intimate meeting with his brother-hero; he had so many things to discuss with him—the "anarchist-intellectual" C. L. James's *A History of the French Revolution*—Benjamin Tucker's *Instead of a Book;* the reformer William Travers Jerome's revelations of prostitution in New York City, aided and abetted by Tammany Hall; and future plans for the Intercollegiate Socialist Society—how were they to draw more undergraduates into the organization, apart from Jewish boys, and a smattering of Jewish girls, from the Lower East Side? Yet more naively Upton had hoped to bare his soul to another man—a married man—of his own generation; he'd hoped to speak frankly of his predicament. Not that Meta had said that her departure would be permanent; not that Meta had hinted of divorce; but—in their marital relations, she had sometimes . . . she had frequently . . . expressed dissatisfaction with him, and impatience. And since the birth of little David, she had not liked him to touch her at all . . .

And there was the matter, mysterious and unresolved, of Upton's having sighted Meta with strangers, in Princeton . . . and Meta's denial.

How would Jack London respond to a woman of his *being sighted* with other men? Upton shuddered.

He'd known that something was seriously wrong when, just recently, Meta had expressed only the most perfunctory interest in the rumor that President Roosevelt had been reading *The Jungle* and intended to invite the young author to Washington one day soon . . .

Meta, I hope you will come with me! It will be an historic occasion.

But where had Meta gone? Drifted off somewhere, in the tall grasses behind the farmhouse, amid trees, and a tangle of wild rose, where Upton, who suffered from mysterious pollen- and plant-allergies, could not follow . . .

" . . . Korean valet, we have trained—Miss Charmian has trained!—to call his master 'God.' So very funny!"

Upton was becoming ever more repelled by his comrade-brother— the fleshy, flushed face, the air of bellicose complacency—the way London swilled his bourbon, and had made a shocking mess of his white silk blouse, unapologetically; he was wondering whether, frankly, London could be only thirty years old?—had he falsified his birth-date, as he'd falsified so many other things about himself, like his Socialist convictions? Here was the heralded Socialist warrior who had emerged from the West only a few years ago, in a blaze of glory: early photographs of the author of *The Call of the Wild,* which Upton had kept, in secret, in a drawer in his study where Meta was not likely to find them, showed a dreamy young man of unusual handsomeness; rugged and masculine, yet touched by a poetic delicacy suggestive of Percy Shelley in certain of the portraits. Where had the Boy Socialist gone? Was it simply to be ascribed to an excess of alcohol and rich foods and the adulation of the public?

Though he'd been—perhaps!—just slightly envious of London's audience at Carnegie Hall, Upton had seen how seductive it is to entertain such large, rowdy audiences; how hard to resist, to stir belly laughs, if one can do it; how much more difficult to hew to a prescribed line of persuasion, and the rhetoric of logic; to uphold one's ideals, not to stoop to the level of vaudeville and burlesque . . . A sort of terror gripped Upton at the thought—the absurd thought—primitive, superstitious!—that the noble Jack London was the victim of an impostor; somehow, the Socialist hero had been transformed into the brutish drunken clown in stained clothes and railway cap, a travesty of his former self; an assassin of the true Jack London; possibly—a demon . . .

But this was ridiculous of course. As it was ridiculous to believe, as some did, in Princeton, that there were "demons" loosed among them.

Upton thought primly: *There are no "demons." Even when I was a Christian, I did not believe in "demons." There are only men—human beings—individuals not so very different from myself, though behaving in ways I find difficult to understand.*

Yet it was tempting to think that the enemies of Socialism had somehow conspired with a malevolent force, to pervert a Socialist hero, and sabotage the Revolution . . .

Now the table and the semi-circle of admirers, that had grown to include as many as thirty individuals of both sexes in diverse stages of festive drunkenness, erupted in another sort of laughter, as the berouged and bejeweled Miss Charmian told hilarious anecdotes of her Nordic lover. It might interest them all to know—indeed, Miss Charmian had told the *New York Post* in an exclusive interview—that it was true, Jack London had a Korean valet who called him "God"—and she, Miss Charmian, had indeed trained him. What was so very charming was that the valet, a sinister but "devilishly handsome" boy named "Manyoungi," was very willing to call London God—" 'For 'tis like God my master behaves,' the little heathen says." Miss Charmian laughed. Also, at a recent party in San Francisco hosted by her Jack, at which hashish and opium were distributed to the guests, along with all the liquor they could hold, her Jack had been so wicked as to play one of his famed practical jokes on his guests: he had barbecued a diamondback rattler and served it to them, with Hollandaise sauce, under the pretense it was Pacific salmon and, when he revealed what he'd done, a number of the guests became nauseated, and several were sick to their stomachs—Miss Charmian erupted in high-pitched giggles. "Oh, the Sea Wolf is *cruel*—but he is *very funny* also. And Jack never does unto others what he would not happily do unto himself—for diamondback rattler is one of his favorite meats, barbecued or rare."

Hearing his mistress speak so warmly of him, as if he were on display, London grinned, and set his railway cap backward on his head; and, conspicuously, reached over to pinch her plump rouged cheek, leaving a red imprint in the somewhat flaccid flesh.

DURING HER COQUETTISH recitation Miss Charmian had been glancing about the brightly lit restaurant, noting how other diners were enviously watching her and Jack London; how they were fascinated by the rogue lovers, in such defiance of the *bourgeoisie*—for of course the couple was recognized immediately. And now, Miss Charmian gripped her lover's massive wrist, to alert him that a "particularly interesting" admirer of his, a handsome youth at a nearby table, had been watching them closely for at least an hour; and what a gracious gesture it would be, the very sort of thing for which Jack London was becoming famous, if he invited the young man to their table, and made him welcome? "For he seems to be alone here, and must be lonely amid such festivity," Miss Charmian whispered into Jack London's ear, "and you can see from his features that he is of noble Nordic descent."

"Eh? Where?"

"There, Jack! See, he's blushing now. He is a devotee of *you*."

Without hesitation the broad-shouldered author rose from his chair to do his mistress's bidding, for nothing pleased him more than to satisfy her easier whims; with feudal swagger he signaled the young man to come join them. At which the embarrassed stranger came hesitantly forward, protesting that he didn't want to intrude upon their party, and he would not dream of sitting at their table . . .

Impatiently, Jack London commanded the young man to leave off apologizing, as only the weak-livered did such; and to introduce himself to all.

Now blushing fiercely, the young man explained that he was a "belated but energetic convert" to the cause of Socialism, having been drawn to it by the writings of both Jack London and Upton Sinclair; he had tried very hard to procure a ticket for the Carnegie Hall event, but had not succeeded; so, he'd waited outside in the street, and had dared to follow them here. "I really should excuse myself, however—I realize that I am intruding on a private party, which is the worst sort of manners."

Even in MacDougal's, Josiah Slade could not behave as if he were not of the New Jersey Slades.

"You are too 'well-mannered' already, kid!" Jack London said in a tone that was both sneering and comradely. "Come have a seat, and tell us your name."

"My name—is Josiah Slade," the young man said, in almost a voice of chagrin, as if his name might already be known to them, "but I am, as I've said—"

"You are one of us, as Charmian saw," Jack London said, gripping Josiah's hand and shaking it roughly, "—solid Anglo-Saxon stock: half the earth our heritage, and half the sea: and in three-score generations, we shall rule the world. So, be seated; and be still. I hope you are not another teetotaler!"

So hospitable was Jack London in his bullying way, he summarily banished one of the Socialist hangers-on at the table, to make room for Josiah; though it seemed clear to Upton Sinclair that the young man, taken aback by London's manner, and the general air of drunkenness of the group, regretted having stepped forward.

Upton was grateful that Josiah Slade sat beside him. With a thrill of pleasure thinking: *He knows me, by name at least. He is one of my admirers, too.*

SO IT HAPPENED, Josiah Slade shook hands with Upton Sinclair, marveling at the latter's youth and air of genteel reserve, so differing from London's brashness; and tried to tell him how much his writing had influenced his thinking, *The Jungle* most of all. For quite apart from the "instructive intelligence" of the work and its strong argument for Socialism, it seemed to Josiah a remarkably vivid and lifelike portrayal of immigrant Americans, of a kind he had never known.

Upton Sinclair was deeply moved, to be spoken to in this way, by one of the Princeton Slades. He thanked Josiah, and wracked his brains what to say next. He could not allude to the fact that he knew who Josiah's family was—hardly. And yet, the young man's identity was fascinating to Upton, who would not have believed that a scion of the revered old family could be so forthright, and so open; and so willing to tolerate the crude drunkenness of the Jack London party, that was becoming ever more distracting to other diners in MacDougal's. "You are—did you say?—from Princeton, New Jersey? Where it happens—at least at the present—I am living; I mean, renting a farmhouse on the Rosedale Road . . ."

Josiah had not identified himself as from Princeton, but perhaps he didn't remember this; in the melee of the restaurant, it was difficult to think clearly.

All this while, Miss Charmian was leaning toward the young men, hoping to engage their interest. A gnome-like woman, Josiah thought her, garishly rouged and powdered, and decked out in an inordinate amount of feathers; he was uncertain at first who she was, and what her relationship might be to Jack London. (Not his mother, surely!) Quite openly she stared at Josiah even as her lover harangued the table on the subject of "pure" and "mongrel" races, and how one could distinguish between them.

It was uncanny, how Miss Charmian seemed to be looking at Josiah, yet looking behind him; for her left eye had a slight cast.

And how uncanny to Josiah, to discover how very different Jack London was from his photographs. Far coarser, and more slovenly in dress— and his intellect crude as a meat cleaver.

Josiah thought *He is, yet can't possibly be, "Jack London"—the author. He is a buffoon impostor, yet another demon.*

How melancholy the world in this yet-new century, the twentieth! Filling up, it seemed, with demons of whom some were buffoons, and others not far more dangerous.

Had Josiah been more prudent, he would have slipped away from London's table, with a promise to Upton Sinclair to meet with him sometime soon, in quieter circumstances; but in his weakened state, Josiah too succumbed to drink, and found the whiskey-and-beer concoction—"the elixir of the Klondike"—a heady innovation.

JOSIAH HAD DECIDED impulsively to move away from Princeton, and to live in a modest rented apartment on Eleventh Avenue at Thirty-sixth Street with a view of the river from the fifth floor of a redbrick town house, and no elevator; from here, he could easily take the clattering IRT (Interborough Rapid Transit) to the Lower East Side and the Village, as it was called, as to Carnegie Hall at Fifty-seventh Street. He had prowled bookstores, and visited the Art Students League and the New York School of Art. (Vaguely he'd hoped to encounter Wilhelmina Burr, by chance; but he wasn't sure if she was living in New York, or had returned to Princeton.) He had visited the Little Galleries of the Photo-Succession at 291 Fifth Avenue, owned by Alfred Stieglitz, as well as the major museums. He had eaten in the most remarkable, inexpensive restaurants—

German, Polish, Hungarian, Jewish, Ukrainian, Italian and Greek. He had attended several Socialists' meetings in Union Square but nothing so organized and ambitious as the Intercollegiate evening in Carnegie Hall, with headliner Jack London.

He'd left Crosswicks abruptly one day after the death—(by paralysis? catatonia?—suffocation?)—of his cousin Todd Slade, for he could no longer bear living amid such devastation; he'd left with a din of jeering voices in his head, chiding him for cowardice in not pouring gasoline through the many rooms of the Manse, and setting it to the torch, as it deserved. He'd left after a long time of standing at the window of his room gazing transfixed into the garden, as if trying to gauge whether, if he threw himself to the ground two floors below, the distance would be sufficient to kill him, or merely to maim him. He thought—*I could not tolerate an invalid's fate. I would grow more cramped in spirit than I am now.*

Then he saw a slender figure on the grass below, a little distance from the house: surprised in her task of cutting Grecian windflowers, and glancing around at him, smiling. It was his beloved Annabel in a white belted blouse with full puffed sleeves, and a yellow "bolero" jacket, and an ankle-length, full skirt; on her head, a straw hat with a wide rim, and trailing a red ribbon. The straw hat was veiled, and, as Annabel turned to Josiah, and slowly lifted the veil, he saw how deathly pale her skin was, and how luminous her blue-violet eyes, piercing his very soul even at this distance . . . With a gesture of the little gardening sickle she mimed that he should join her in the garden, at once.

"Annabel? *Is* it you?"

Josiah leaned out the window, which he'd shoved open; he shut his eyes, and clenched his jaws hard. He must resist the blandishments of the Fiend: for though every beat of his pulse urged him to obey his sister, to acquiesce to her will, some stubborn corner of his soul insisted otherwise.

"No. It is *not Annabel*."

When Josiah opened his eyes the specter had vanished. And there were no windflowers to be seen—no flowers of any sort growing in the garden—as if a scorching windstorm had blown all away.

He knew then, he must leave Crosswicks. He packed a few prized items including his private journal, which was covered in morocco leather; and certain mementos of Annabel's; and a dozen of his most valued books, and a single suitcase of clothing. Against his parents' protestations he took the first train to New York City to what he hoped would be a new life

It might be that the Curse would destroy Josiah Slade, but it would not destroy him by his own hand. That, Josiah swore.

※

The lurid tale of the barbecued diamondback rattler had left Upton Sinclair seriously nauseated; he had not yet managed to recover. Despite Josiah Slade's agreeable company, he was calculating when he might leave, without attracting unwanted attention from Jack London and Miss Charmian.

"I think I must leave, Josiah! Maybe, in Princeton, we might . . ."

"I'm not living in Princeton now, I'm afraid. I live in . . ."

"Excuse me, what? Where?"

The noise in MacDougal's was deafening. It seemed to Upton that his hosts had ceased to notice him, or Josiah. But when Upton rose to leave the table, immediately London swung to him, glaring, and grinning, baring "wolf" canines, and gripped him by the arm. "Comrade Sinc'ler! You have been very quiet—you are looking very pale. You have not been eating your 'cannibal sandwich,' I see—which is why you have the complexion of a corpse. Here—a toast, at least"—London forced a glass of Champagne in Upton's limp fingers, and lifted a shot-glass of bourbon for himself. "Up'on Sinc'ler—salt of the earth! Up'on Sinc'ler—great hope of the Revolution! Kingdom of Heav'n! Meek shall enter—last! Suffer little children—

etcetera." All at the table lifted their glasses in a toast except for Upton who sat quietly, uneasily smiling, yet stubborn, and resistant; even Josiah Slade could not resist the bully.

"What? You refuse to drink? And why is that, Comrade?—your Nordic young friend here is drinking, and why not you? Are you fearful of 'demon rum' possessing your papery soul?"

London laughed abusively. Again Upton tried to stand, and again London forced him back into his seat.

"*You* are one of us—though not a very 'potent' specimen—solid Aryan stock: half the earth our heritage, and all the sea, and in three-score generation *we shall possess the earth.* Would you deny your heritage, Comrade?"

Upton tried to protest: he had no idea what London was talking about. And the hour was late, and early next morning he had work to do . . .

"You would not deny, Comrade, that there are 'pure' races and 'mongrel' races—surely? If the Socialist movement was not weakened by certain of its leaders—let us speak frankly, Comrade: I mean Jews, like— what is his name—'Leet-hauzer'—our war against cap'lism would proceed swiftly. But a Jew is lily-livered in his soul—it is against the Jew's nature to fight—to the death. You would not deny this, Comrade? Would you?"

In dismay, Upton said *yes*. He would deny this.

"The Socialist vision is *class war*—to the death! History has shown that the natural man—the natural warrior—may be born deprived of his heritage—born into an 'inferior' class—this is the stuff of legend, fairy tales—the prince under a curse, as a mere frog—his destiny is to rise up tooth and claw—fang and claw!—to tear out the throats of his persecutors and must rise up against those who exploit him—and drink their *sang impur.*" Uttering the French phrase—which London pronounced in phonetic English, with a strong, nasal *a*—London shoved at Upton's shoulder in a way to provoke.

Upton protested: "But—the Socialist vision is also—brotherhood—"

" 'Brotherhood'—yessss." London drawled the word, frowning.

A waiter had brought a platter of raw oysters to the table, which London now began to eat, rapidly, tossing the shells onto the floor after he'd sucked the slithery white thing into his mouth, and swallowed it. As he ate he spoke, shaking a stubby forefinger at Upton Sinclair: "But as with our blood-kin, not all are 'brothers'—not all are 'kin.' There is a natural aristocracy—it is useless to prevaricate, Comrade. I suppose you would defend the lowlife 'Big Bill' Hayward?—I suppose 'One-Eye Big Bill' is your comrade, too?"

"Why, yes—certainly. Bill Hayward has been a great—brave—leader . . . He has rallied the immigrant workers in New Jersey, and—"

" 'One-Eye Big Bill'!"—London scoffed, in contempt. Miss Charmian tried to placate her lover by feeding him oysters, but London, ever more incensed, was not to be placated. "True, 'Big Bill' has organized the silkworker slaves of Paterson—but the strike is intended to showcase *him*—he has been threatening the owners, and they have insulted him, and—"

"Wait! Please! You should not be speaking of—a strike . . . No, no!" Upton was horrified: the possibility of a strike in Paterson, of the silkworker union, was meant to be confidential, he was sure. How did Jack London even know about this plan? "From what I know, a strike isn't definite—Bill Hayward hasn't yet made a decision."

"Hayward is a shameless debauchee," London said, with a sneer. "The megalomaniac drunkard—blatherer, windbag—never so happy as when he's speechifying before a fawning audience of the lowest mongrel sort. The lowest *mongrel-immigrant* sort."

"Bill Hayward is one of our Socialist heroes—a savior! Jack, I must disagree—"

" 'Jack, I must disagree'—" London rudely parroted Upton's words, in a falsetto voice, which inspired laughter at the table, and a flirtatious rebuke from Miss Charmian, who patted Upton's arm as one might pat a misbehaving puppy. "Rather should you say, 'Jack, I must *agree*'—for in your heart you know that I'm right. Should 'One-Eye Big Bill' be spread-eagled and dispatched by the Pinkerton's, it would not be a grievous loss."

This remark was so callous, and obscene, Upton rose to leave. He could not bear remaining a minute longer! And when London tried to clutch at him, he lurched away, as a child might do, escaping the embrace of an adult. Except that Miss Charmian quickly restrained her lover, there would have been a scuffle. London's small red eyes glared: "You are not leaving our party so early! No one turns his back on Jack London's hospitality—no more than you would decline the hospitality of the Eskimo, if the smelly In'jun offers you his nasty 'smoked' fish, and his 'squaw.' I did not journey all the way to New York City from California to be rudely snubbed by the only man in the Socialist movement I halfway respect—though—to be brutally frank—much of *The Jungle* is slovenly work, even for a muckraker, betraying signs of the author's hack origins—and the last section is a comical sort of plagiarism of my speeches—my Oakland campaign speeches—did you think that no one would notice?"

Upton was too shocked to speak. He could not believe that London was turning on him—making such an accusation, before strangers.

"I haven't revealed the plagiarism to the press, just yet," London said, "for we Revolutionaries must stick together—like dogs in a pack. There is a lead-dog, yes—but there is the pack. The 'lead-dog' requires the 'pack'—even as the 'pack' requires the 'lead-dog.' That is a law of nature."

Seeing the expression of shock and hurt in Upton's eyes, London laughingly relinquished him, and leaned back in his chair, teetering precariously on two legs. With forced relish he continued to devour oysters, washing them down with shots of bourbon. A sort of prankish demonism shone in his bloodshot eyes. "My friend, the error of your philosophy—your religion—your bourgeois morality—as your Soc'list morality—is the attempted legislation of impulse. 'One-Eye' doesn't comprehend this basic fact, nor Debs, nor—any of 'em! For the primeval spirit *never checks an impulse*. The free man *never checks an impulse*. The rest is all cant, and humbug, and nursery rimes, and Bible verses! When Philosophy puffs itself up to instruct the individual soul *YOU MUST*, the individual soul at once rejoins *I WANT*—and does precisely what *IT WANTS*. So much for philosophy, and religion, and morality—the phantasms of eunuchs! For the brave man, the warrior, the Nordic soul, knows only I WANT—and never I MUST. It is the I WANT that spurs the drinker on to drink, in the face of all the mewling and puling teetotalers of the world—it's the glorious I WANT that makes the martyr eagerly cloak himself in his hair shirt, if it is the hair shirt that calls forth I WANT. The countless things I WANT constitute my scale of values, my private ethics—and there it is! Meat, and drink, and the passion of a free woman—the potency of the novelist's pen—the power of the voice, the throat, the mouth—and the vengeful class-war of the Soc'list movement. Jack London's acclaimed achievement is FOR MY OWN DELIGHT. Jack London's genius is FOR MY OWN DELIGHT. It isn't 'spiritual'—it's 'organic.' Every fiber of my being thrills with it. The primeval I WANT, the glorious I WANT, the ineluctable I WANT, now and forever! —Eh, what's this? Are you mocking me? Are you sending each other signals?"

London had caught sight of Miss Charmian gazing intently at Josiah Slade with tight-pursed crimson lips, and eyes squeezed near-shut; as if she were indeed sending him a secret signal which the young man, acutely embarrassed, did not wish to acknowledge.

"You dare—to mock *me*?"

Josiah shook his head *no*, even as Miss Charmian giggled lewdly. Like one guiltily found out, Josiah blushed to the roots of his hair.

"I—don't know what you mean, Mr. London . . ." Josiah swallowed hard, he was incapable of uttering the name *Jack*, even pleadingly. "I'm not mocking—anyone . . ."

Whether the belligerent London really felt primeval jealousy, or whether prolonged sitting in one place had made him restless and spoiling for a fight, suddenly he erupted into action, with a wolfish cry; he scrambled to grip Josiah in a wrestling hold, shouting his intention to commit murder.

"Signaling to *my woman*!—*my mate*! In front of *my eyes*! That is punishable by death."

Trying to wrest Josiah from his chair, and onto the floor, London lost his balance and fell, pulling both Josiah and Upton Sinclair onto the floor with him. In the frantic scuffle the chair was overturned, there came a shattering of glass and china; there were shouts, and shrieks; Miss Charmian leapt to her feet, quick and fierce as a wild cat intent upon protecting her young. Upton, on principle and by temperament a pacifist, had no idea how to adequately defend himself, still less to fight aggressively, but blindly struck at the heavier man with his fists, inflicting very little damage; while Josiah, no pacifist, struck at London with telling blows, and a surprising outburst of profanity. Now bawling like a maddened beast, London seized a bottle from the table, smashed it and brought the jagged edge against Josiah's throbbing throat—"Mock Jack London, will you! Mock the *Sea Wolf*, will you! There are insults to be repaid only in blood." London outweighed Josiah by at least twenty-five pounds but he was badly winded, and disoriented; Josiah managed to slip beneath his flailing arms and maneuver a chair between him and London—an inanimate, obdurate object that baffled London as if he had no idea what it was or how to contend with it; for London was very drunk, and his bloodshot eyes had lost their focus; and his fists swung wide of their mark. Josiah begged for London to let him go, for he respected the Socialist hero too much to wish to hurt him; but London would not; again London savagely lunged at Josiah with the broken bottle, and this time by sheer panicked strength Josiah managed to overturn the chair onto London, knocking London to the floor a second time on his back, with such force that London's head struck the floor, hard; you could hear the sickening *thud* of the man's hard skull striking the wooden floor like a hammer-blow.

Josiah thought, with a sick thrill of elation—*Have I killed again? Struck another demon to the floor, and murdered him?*

Amid this scene of general chaos Miss Charmian threw her squat little body at Josiah Slade, clawing at his exposed skin with red-painted talon-nails. "Beast! What have you done! Look like an angel-boy and reveal your true colors—devil! Call the police! He has murdered my darling Jack!

Oh—the blood! My darling Jack is bleeding from his scalp! This is outright murder! The great Jack London—oh help!"

Josiah tried to push the frenzied little woman away—how like a wild cat she was, hot-eyed, hot-skinned, baring sharp little teeth, and raking her claws against him however she could; valiantly he was trying to help London to his feet, but the stunned man had little strength in his legs; Miss Charmian continued to scream and to claw at him as Josiah turned to her, to try to placate her; for she was nearing a state of hysterics, hyperventilating; her small pug-face glowered with an unnatural heat. It was so, Jack London had been injured in the fall; he was bleeding freely from a scalp wound, streams of blood running down his fleshy face that was now drained of color, deathly-pale; his lips had gone loose and were pale also, wet with saliva like froth. To the staring throng Josiah stammered: "It wasn't my fault—he attacked me—I was only defending myself—I didn't mean—you must have seen, I didn't mean to—harm him . . ."

Miss Charmian screamed: "Oh—stop him! Murderer! He has killed our prince! The greatest literary genius of our time!"

"But—you are all witnesses . . ."

Josiah looked about for Upton Sinclair, but his friend was sitting on the floor where he'd fallen, very white-faced, tremulous; a froth of vomit shone at his mouth, and his shirtfront was stained. No help there! Josiah fumbled to wrap a napkin around London's head to stanch the bleeding, but his hands shook badly, and the wounded man continued to flail feebly at him, and curse him; Josiah let the blood-soaked napkin fall to the floor and backed away from the table, desperate now to escape. As if seeing something terrible in his face, unknown to Josiah Slade, the others shrank from him; a path opened for him amid the crowded restaurant; he found himself staggering out onto Forty-second Street where the night air was startlingly fresh. In Josiah's wake were cries *Stop him! Call police! Murderer!*—dimly heard, as in a fading dream.

Quickly Josiah ducked into an alley beside MacDougal's. From the alley, though he had never been in this terrible place before, and had only

the vaguest sense of what he was doing, deftly he made his way to another alley, and so to Forty-first Street, and then Broadway, near-deserted
at this time of night, where he found himself half-running, north, in the
direction—he believed it was the direction—of his apartment building on
Eleventh Avenue and Thirty-sixth.

The clothes he'd chosen for the evening's rally which he'd hoped to
attend—beige flannel trousers, a dark-brown coat, white cotton shirt—
were torn, and smelled shamefully of alcohol; his fair, fawn-colored hair
was disheveled, his cheeks were lacerated and bleeding as if clawed by a
cat; both his ears smarted and stung and on the following morning, in the
stark clear light reflected from the Hudson River a short distance away, he
would discover that part of his left earlobe had been torn or bitten off, the
tiny wound encrusted with a black, brackish little blood-button.

"Demons! I have entered a region of demons, and narrowly escaped
with my life."

TERRA INCOGNITA I

L enora."
    Low and level and calm-seeming, the pronouncement of the faithless wife's name.

Incriminating letters—was the proper term *billets-doux*?—clutched in his hand.

As Copplestone made his grunting way up the staircase, and along the second-floor corridor at Wheatsheaf, in the direction of Lenora's morning-room, where she had sequestered herself in the pretense of writing urgent letters on behalf of the New Jersey Society of the Colonial Dames of America, seeking funds for a restoration of "historical landmarks" in the state.

"Len-*ora*."

Her maternal carelessness had cost Copplestone his sole male heir as well as his beautiful little daughter. Even if he could find it in his heart to forgive his wife's adultery—(and Copplestone's heart was of the size of a walnut, and maggoty)—he could never forgive her for *that*.

And in her morning-room, with lattice-windows overlooking the spring profusion of the garden two floors below, and a stand of tall elms and oaks some distance away, Lenora sat very still at her writing table, a fountain pen in her trembling hand; she was swathed in black, as a widow; though not a widow but the bereft mother of two beloved children, who had departed this earth prematurely, and terribly. After a servant had brought her breakfast on a tray—(mostly untouched, for Lenora no longer had any appetite for food)—she had dared to *lock the door* against her husband, and could only hope that he would not discover it, and fly into a rage.

Touching the tip of the fountain pen to a sheet of stiff stationery embossed with a gilt rendering of Wheatsheaf, in its original, Colonial-era state, Lenora wrote, as if her life depended upon it: *It has lately come to our attention that the "Dolly Lambert" house at Washington's Crossing is in dire need of repair . . . We are hoping that you will aid us in the restoration of this crucial . . .*

NOT FAR AWAY, at Mora House, Amanda FitzRandolph was softly singing a lullaby to little Terence in his crib. The infant had wakened, as he usually did, at about 4:30 A.M., and had not left off crying, whimpering, thrashing, and kicking until after 9 A.M.; the nanny was diligent, and uncomplaining, but clearly exhausted; and so Amanda had intervened, soon after breakfast, in her muslin "at-home" gown and a beribboned housecap. In this phase of her life Amanda FitzRandolph was determined to be a very good mother; she was determined to abjure forever the temptations of the secular and sensual world, that is the *madding crowd;* despite the attractions of that world, and the figure of the Count, she would plunge ever more deeply into motherhood, even widowhood . . . Softly singing, to the small figure in the crib, that was beginning by degrees to cease fretting: "Little Baby Bunting, Father's gone a-hunting . . . Gone to get a new fur skin, to wrap the Baby Bunting in . . ."

(Yet it was startling to Amanda, as to members of her family, that she seemed at times to have "forgotten" her husband of many years, Edgerstoune FitzRandolph; or rather to remember the man as but one of her numerous Princeton acquaintances, including those relatives for whom she felt dutiful but dull affection. Edgerstoune had died of an accidental poisoning—(by jellyfish)—in Bermuda, scarcely a month before; the accident had happened on the beach, and out of Amanda's sight; only the Count had been a witness, and without him, Amanda did not think she could have survived; certainly, she could not have arranged to send the poor man's body home for burial, as the Count so efficiently did. Yet, though Edgerstoune's remains were buried in Princeton Cemetery, Amanda retained the notion that Edgerstoune was still in Bermuda, dozing, in sunshine, a copy of the *Wall Street Journal* on his lap, on the flagstone terrace at *Sans Souci*.)

As the baby drifted into sleep, Amanda studied again his strangely dark-hued, ineffably "Indian"—("Asian"?)—skin and features; the Count had counseled her, not to dwell over-much on such superficial qualities, for it was the soul of the child that mattered. "As it is your soul, dear Mandy, and not your physical beauty, that so mesmerizes me."

Amanda laughed, hearing the Count's whispered words. The blushing widow/mother glanced about the nursery, to make sure that she was alone; and not observed by any of the servants as she continued to sing her tuneless song, the words of which she was obliged to repeat as she could remember but a single stanza:

"Little Baby Bunting . . ."

CLOSE BY, in Westland, the pale yellow Colonial set so far back from Hodge Road it could scarcely be seen through a scrim of trees, Mrs. Grover Cleveland was similarly attired in an "at-home" gown (by Worth), standing lost in thought: staring with eyes of dull rage into her invalid-husband's bedroom where, propped up against pillows, the aged, obese man panted, and wheezed, and grunted, and muttered to himself, while scribbling notes to be transcribed by a stenographer; for it was Grover's latest delusion that he was involved in "business as usual": writing out commandments to his fellow trustees at the university pertaining to an action certain of the trustees wish to undertake, to force Woodrow Wilson's resignation; preparing memos to underlings at the Equitable Life Assurance Society, which Mr. Cleveland was flattered into "chairing" in the twilight years of his life.

Watching him, the former Frances Folsom brooded over not the loss of her daughter in Buzzards Bay, not the loss of her father so many years ago (which ill luck propelled the teenaged girl into the arms of her father's old political crony-friend Cleveland, in the desperation of her loss), but over the convention that, as she is not yet a widow, she cannot keep company with any man beside her husband, or risk the cruelest censure; and she does not wish to keep company with *him*.

It grieved the handsome dark-haired woman too, that her aged husband did everything so *slowly*.

"It will take him forever to die! He is so *absent-minded*."

The Count has come several times to call. The Count is a friend of Grover Cleveland's, it is known; or rather, it is said; for Mrs. Cleveland knows that she must not allow any of her Princeton friends to guess that it is she, and not the ex-President, who has drawn the Count to Westland.

Yet the Count has only just shaken Frances's hand; he has stroked the fingers tenderly, and fixed her with a "piercing" gaze, and—*murmured not a word.*

IN THE HEART of the green-leafed university campus, in his attic bower at Prospect, Thomas Woodrow Wilson (as he lately thinks of himself) is toiling over a much-revised poem, that had originated in a sonnet addressed to the young woman who had rejected his first proposal for marriage years ago; recast then as a sonnet addressed to Ellen (who had been deeply moved by it); now, recast in a more daringly modern, "thrusting" mode of poetry addressed to his dear friend Mrs. Peck. Downstairs Dr. Wilson's adoring women-folk, including now a spinster sister-in-law, tiptoe about to spare him any distraction, with not the slightest suspicion

that the middle-aged swain is not toiling over his commencement speech
("The Role of the Christian Gentleman in the Nation's Service"); that his
pulses beat erratically, and he is cruelly taxing his already strained nerves
in the invention of such bold verse—

> You are the song I have waited for—
> I find in you the vision sweet—
> The grace, the strain of noble sounds,
> The form, the mien, the mind, the heart,
> That I have lacked and thought to find
> Within some spring within my mind,
> Dearest Cybella!

To this, he signs *Your Thomas*—as "Woodrow" now seems to him
stiff, pompous, and pretentious.

TERRA INCOGNITA II

If you wish not to burn in Hell with your fellow Slades why then set out for the Polar region, and save your devil's hide!

So persistent was this voice in the days following Josiah Slade's disillusionment with Jack London, he succumbed at last; and cast his lot with an expedition set to leave within a week for the South Pole, under the auspices of the Royal Scottish Geographical Society in cooperation with a private American financier named Winthrop Moody, a relative of Josiah's through his mother's family.

From boyhood Josiah had read avidly of the great expeditions to the Polar regions, dating from antiquarian histories of Viking explorations in the North to latter-day records of voyages by Ross, Parry, Nordenskiöld, and Nansen. It seemed that just the other day the world had thrilled to the triumphant sea-journey of Amundsen's *Gjoa*, which crossed the great "Dome of America" from east to west for the first, and perhaps the only, time in history; in the autumn of 1905, Captain Robert Falcon Scott's *The Voyage of the "Discovery"* had been published in two volumes, illustrated by drawings and photographs that had entranced Josiah Slade, as they had entranced Adelaide Burr. Immense icy bergs, fields of snow that blinded the eye, and those mountains of the South

Pole "rearing their lofty heads" as Scott described, "in desolate grandeur." These were astonishing sights, indeed—as lethal as they were spectacular in the chill of minus-fifty-degrees Centigrade, and the purity of their brief sunshine; mesmerizing in isolation, mystery, and the powerful attraction of *terra incognita* to the civilized man. In the words of the great Shackleton: "You can't comprehend the yearning, the heroic compulsion, to eradicate all that is *terra incognita;* and to set your foot on places of this Earth where man has never trod."

Reading such words, Josiah felt inspired, and filled with yearning. For he was one of those who did comprehend.

Wanting to write to Upton Sinclair, whom he took for a sort of soul mate, though the young Socialist was lamentably thin, and ashy-skinned; rather anemic Josiah thought him, and disappointing in the brawl of the other night, when Josiah had needed a comrade. Yet, he would have liked to write to Upton Sinclair these words which he could record only in his morocco-leather-bound notebook:

> *It seems to me that this world is sullied almost beyond redemption in hypocrisy, lies, and outright evil. Even Socialism, I fear, is tainted—a demon lies within the very best intentions. And so whether to save my hide or not, I had better flee terra cognita.*

JOSIAH'S MOTHER'S THIRD cousin Esdra Moody had put Josiah in contact with Winthrop Moody, who'd put Josiah in contact with Captain Eric Campbell Oates, the younger brother of the famed "Soldier" Captain Lawrence E. G. Oates,* who was at this time seeking funds for a

---

* "The Soldier" may be long forgotten today, I am afraid. In his time Captain Lawrence E. G. Oates of the 6th Inniskilling Dragoons was a member of the ill-fated *Terra Nova* expedition of 1910–1912, under the command of Robert Falcon Scott, which came to a disastrous end in a blizzard on or about March 1912 at the South Pole.

spring expedition to the South Pole, and signing up recruits in New York City. (Such linkages sound more complicated than they are, for very little occurs in this world, in polar expeditions as in politics, without such connections among relatives, friends, acquaintances, and club members!) So certain was Josiah that an expedition to the South Pole would save his life, if not his soul, he went to Captain Oates in the man's lavish suite at the Waldorf and nearly begged to be taken on though he couldn't claim any experience as a sailor or as an explorer, apart from hiking in the Rocky Mountains and in Yosemite. He offered only a "strong back," as he said, and an "indomitable will"; and a passionate desire, which all but glared out of his eyes, to escape the temperate zone, and to make his way into *terra incognita*.

Eric Campbell Oates regarded his handsome and very fit-looking petitioner with a kindly, if dubious eye. He knew, from his friend Winthrop Moody, a little of the dolorous events of Princeton, New Jersey, over the last year, and more; but he'd ceased listening when the man had begun to prattle about a "curse"—he, Captain Oates, knew enough of *curses*, and could not imagine that anything truly wicked could emerge in the lily-white enclave of Princeton, New Jersey, set beside the places Captain Oates had seen in his travels, not excluding the so-called Belgian Congo. He told Josiah that *terra incognita* is more than a mere expression of romantic yearning, it is also a place—"And a very dangerous place, for one who has never left the temperate zone."

"Please give me a chance, Captain Oates! I will do anything you ask—any task, however menial. And I can contribute something to the

---

Captain Oates's nicknames were both "The Soldier" and "Titus"; relatively little is known of his younger brother Eric, and virtually nothing of the polar expedition in which Josiah Slade participated, though I have searched records assiduously, for years. And so I am led to wonder, less as an historian than as a neutral observer, whether Josiah in his wish to escape *terra cognita* hadn't been seduced by agents of the Fiend even as he valiantly sought escape from the past.

expedition, as Winthrop Moody has probably told you—not very much, but virtually all of my savings."

Which persuaded Captain Oates of his seriousness and worth.

SO IT HAPPENED with dizzying rapidity, at the end of May 1906, as the first-year anniversary of his sister's abduction and public shame approached, Josiah Slade left his home, and took lodgings in New York City; joined the Intercollegiate Socialist Society, and came close to murdering his hero Jack London; and signed up with Captain Eric Campbell Oates for the *Balmoral* expedition to the South Pole, and set sail the following week, leaving behind a most peculiar farewell note to his stricken parents:

> Dearest Mother, & dearest Father—
> I shall depart *terra cognita* for 18 months, they promise, at the very least; & if I & *terra cognita* are fortunate, for longer than that. Do not expend your parental love on me as I have been unworthy of it; do not pray for me, who will sail beyond the range of earthly prayer.
> The Southern sky has no history, it is promised, & no memory; no mind. For God has not yet been made man in that place, nor ever God. So it is promised & so I believe.
> Is it your son Josiah who writes these stark words, or another?—no matter: we sail to *terra incognita* as one.
> Believe that I love you, even so. But do not pray for me, as I have asked you—that is the purest love.
> Josiah

FOR THE FIRST several days at sea, Josiah's malicious "voice" was quelled, as if by the hardships of the sea voyage with its rocking, and tossing, and pitching, and dipping; and the slow-dawning realization among the crew that the handsome *Balmoral,* a sailing ship of three hundred tons, was far less seaworthy than her owners claimed. Though the ship was graceful enough in harbor, and impressive to the untutored eye with her slender hull and numerous dark-hued sails, a photographer's "prize" to be published in the *New York Herald* and elsewhere, it soon developed that she was a vessel of considerable age and service, having been under the command of many men from the time of the ill-fated Captain Franklin to the present day.

Josiah soon learned that the *Balmoral* was overloaded, as a consequence of Captain Oates's frugality, and that of the Royal Scottish Geographical Society generally. Despite the ship's modest weight and proportions, and despite the fact that she was bound for the most desolate and treacherous waters on earth, the *Balmoral* was handicapped by many tons of coal, pony fodder, and wooden huts; sledges, cans of gasoline and kerosene; scientific equipment, and clothing; and cases of diverse practicability ranging from sweetbreads and kidneys to canned mutton. Of dog food alone there were hundreds of pounds, not to mention the restless animals themselves (at least thirty-five huskies); and not least, a gallant little battalion of ponies (at least two dozen). The ponies Josiah took pity on at once, for he had always loved horses, and had had a young horse in the Crosswicks stables, for years, which he'd often ridden; as the ponies gazed at him with frightened eyes he could feel their terror, and share their sense of doom; for were these beautiful creatures not fated to perish in the heaving sea, or in the wilds of the Antarctic, or as food for dogs, or for men? "I will protect you, if I can," Josiah promised the ponies, who stamped and snorted and switched their tails; he stroked their heads to calm them, and took note of their rolling eyes and bared teeth. "I won't allow anyone to slaughter you and eat you, I swear!" It was a sign of Josiah's growing weakness of judgment that, before a week on the ocean had passed, he was often prone to tears whenever he visited the ponies in the dank, smelly hold; indeed, that he allowed himself to visit the ponies so frequently was a sign of encroaching infirmity.

As the voyage proceeded, with day following day in a stupor of boredom or in a paroxysm of alarm, depending upon the weather, it became clear that Captain Oates of the *Balmoral* was not quite the Captain Oates of the *Waldorf*. So seemingly forthright on land, unpretentious and matter-of-fact, Oates began to reveal an unpredictable and petty temper at sea; so lost to the minimal courtesies of his class as to appear on the *Balmoral* deck unshaven, with collar and cuffs lacking freshness. Most bewildering to Josiah was the captain's habit of joking with the rudest of his sailing crew, while he turned away from the few gentlemen-explorers on board, and the two or three "men of science"; and turned from Josiah with a sneer, if Josiah tried to approach him.

"What, my lad? Is't some special favor you want? Only just wait—a 'special favor' will come, I am sure."

Josiah was aggrieved and hurt, as a boy would have been in his place.

Only because Captain loves you. Lusts after you. Dreams of enticing you between his sheets. And indeed Josiah could do worse than succumb. For once locked in his cabin you might strangle the brute with your bare hands, for very joy.

SO IT HAPPENED that Josiah's dreaded "voice" returned, as in the recrudescence of a disease, to prove just the first of numerous urgings of which some were no more than a whisper but often so hollow and echoing in Josiah's skull, the accursed young man worried he might be overheard by one of his comrades. Just below the equatorial meridian the voice informed Josiah that a *mystical vision* was gained if one climbed like a monkey to the very top of the main mast; for he might then gaze not only beyond the ocean's horizon, but beyond the polar mountains as well, to Heaven itself—where God's face glared white-hot and seething. *But a moment's effort, Josiah—yet it will calm your seething soul forevermore.*

As the ship made her perilous journey past the Falkland Islands, beyond that ice-locked coast of Antarctica known as King Edward VII Land, the voice urged Josiah to throw off his bulky clothing, and bare his head, and leap overboard, that he might test the elasticity of the waves at this latitude; for it was a never-recorded phenomenon of the Ross Sea, that though the black waves heaved and churned, and spat up frothy skeins of white like the strait between Scylla and Charybdis, they were yet not comprised of water dense enough to support a man's wake.

A man of science would experiment in such a setting: how the great seabirds float, that are nearly Josiah's size, float and dip with the waves, and never sink; and mock you with their bird-courage, as something less than a man.

"Josiah, no! Stop him, for Christ's sake. If you must, throw him *down.* Tie him *up.*"

Later Josiah would learn that he'd been prevented from throwing himself overboard by several of the sailing crew, and carried by force down to his cabin; and made to sleep, by ingesting a quantity of brandy and laudanum from the captain's private store. But Josiah wondered if such tales were malicious, as he'd learned to "turn a deaf ear" to the blandishments of the Curse.

"It seems that I will never have peace, and never for a moment inhabit my being with the ease with which the albatross inhabits his."

ONE THING WAS CLEAR: the eye-piercing sunlight of the Antarctic was beautiful beyond all human language, and Josiah counted himself blessed to have come so far unscathed. So frigid was the air, one could not easily judge whether it was injurious to the lungs and heart, or communicated a voluptuous thrill as it pinched, pricked, stabbed, slashed, and seared white-hot, seeking entry into the human body at every exposed pore.

I do not hurt! I give no pain!—so promises the Cold. *I shall numb your senses in the sweetest oblivion.*

"I wish you'd told me of such an enchanted place, Grandfather," Josiah said to Winslow Slade who stood beside him one day at the ship's railing, "—why so much preaching from the pulpit of God, and of Heaven, and of the bloodstained cross when you might have spoken the truth?"

Winslow Slade in a heavy coarse-textured oak-colored coat, a woolen cap on his head; his ravaged yet dignified features squinting against the perilous sun; white eyebrows thicker than Josiah recalled, and fine pale lines bracketing his mouth that twitched in a murmured response. And what Winslow Slade spoke, Josiah could not hear for the wind rushing about them.

"Grandfather, what? What are you saying?"

And again Winslow Slade spoke, his pale mouth moving in near-silence.

Forgive me.

THE WONDROUS UNFATHOMED ocean—polar mountains jutting upward into the stark-blue sky—the sea spray clinging to all surfaces of the *Balmoral,* and freezing to an exquisite radiance; mile upon mile, hundreds and thousands of miles, vast acre upon acre and field upon field of icebergs and glacial rock; the crevices, the glittering knolls, the needle-like stalagmites that pulsed with godly incandescence from within: were these not mesmerizing?—and did they not obliterate all human senses and memory?

How distant, how inconsequential the village of Princeton, New Jersey, from the underside of the world!

Raise your arm before you, and bare the wrist. Clamp your carnivore's teeth upon it, and bite and bite and bite. For there's your consolation, my dear grandson.

But Josiah recognized the blandishments of his old enemy, and did not succumb.

THE GRAY-SPECKLED PONY'S eyes rolled in terror as she floundered chest-high in snow, and stumbled, and snorted; and in panic released a steaming spray of urine, that stained the snow yellow; and in a terrible instant the dogs were upon her, tearing at her living flesh. *No! Stop!* Josiah was shouting. But the ravenous huskies would eat, for they were starving. But the men would eat, for they too were starving, and knew themselves doomed.

I shall not eat Josiah vowed. *Not I.*

Captain Oates had, by this time, so overcome his gentlemanly scruples and the good manners of his class, he ate with relish the steaming flesh, and stooped to suck the hot blood; and, leaning back, his mouth stained red, offered his young comrade Josiah Slade the "most succulent of the inner organs, the kidneys" for his delectation.

I will not. Not I.

In a paroxysm of shivering Josiah woke from this nightmare, which he knew to be not a mere dream-phantasm, but a vision: for Josiah knew it would all come to pass, within a few months' time. Once the *Balmoral* reached its destination, and the men disembarked to "explore" the vast white void before them, it was inescapable. Ponies, and howling huskies, and Captain Eric Campbell Oates's bloodstained muzzle, and the triumph of his mad eyes. *Come, my sweet Josiah, my dear boy—the most succulent of the inner morsels is for you.*

After this, on the lurching deck of the *Balmoral,* all the huskies that were chained topside—(and very much weakened, poor brutes, by the driving rain and sleet)—growled deep in their throats when Josiah passed by. Their muzzles were flecked with foam and their wet eyes jerked in their sockets. These sledge dogs were killers, trained from puppyhood to attack any stranger approaching their master's sledge.

PLAYFULLY JOSIAH WONDERED: was he, in fact, by the strait-laced standards of Princeton, New Jersey, now *standing on his head*? That is, *upsidedown*? For he was in the Southern Hemisphere now, far from the temperate regions of the northeastern United States.

Yet his gallantry remained. Like instinct bred in the bones of his Slade ancestors, it remained.

For one evening at dusk, unless it was a luminous dawn, an incautious woman, dressed splendidly in ermine, with a matching hat, and fur-trimmed boots, ventured too near the dogs, that she might pet their handsome heads; with the immediate result that the nearest of them attacked, and within an instant her ermine-clad arm had been terribly torn and mangled, and streams of blood flew into the air; and Josiah rushed forward, for he had gloomily prophesied such an incident, observing the woman making her way along the deck, with an outstretched hand; seeing that the injured woman, in shock too severe to allow her to scream, was Mrs. Adelaide Burr, whom he had not glimpsed in years. As the dogs barked and howled, and lunged at the fallen woman, prevented only by their chained collars, Josiah pulled her to safety; or, to a spot on the bloodied deck that would spare her further harm; seeing that she lay mangled and bleeding from myriad wounds, her face scarcely recognizable, and her small pale bosom exposed, cruelly exposed and bleeding from a dozen wounds. Josiah cried for help, and tried to stanch the flow of blood with his coat-sleeves, and his gloves; and the ermine coat; but blood had already frozen underfoot, the deck was covered in ice-blood, and he slipped, and fell, and struck his head, as hard as he had caused Pearce van Dyck to strike his head on a hardwood floor, and Jack London on the plank floor at MacDougal's.

Will no one save us? Is there no one? No God? No—Savior?

So the dying woman whispered as Josiah lay unable to respond.

On the open deck in a howling wind laced with sleet he was discovered sobbing and despondent as a boy who has lost his mother. His tears had frozen in his eyelashes and in his short scruffy beard and the flesh of his face had lost all sensation.

"Shall we tie him in baling wire this time, sir? What is the captain's wish?"

THE CAPTAIN'S BELOVED CAT Mungo Park was a double-toed black Manx who slept with him each night at the foot of the captain's bed, and purred deep in his throat when he was stroked, and showed particular affection—(so Captain Oates explained to Josiah who lay fevered and convalescent in the captain's own bed)—by making kneading motions with his claws, and seeming to "nurse" against human flesh.

The glory of Mungo Park was that he had nine lives, of which only four or five had been used up.

Though Captain Oates dearly loved his big black tailless Mungo Park there were men aboard ship who did not; for one morning when Josiah was recovered enough to return to the deck, he observed the burly creature climbing to his customary perch atop some rigging, and saw not long afterward a sly ruffian reach up to him with a rod, and startle him into hissing, and losing his balance to fall howling into the sea.

A chorus of cheers arose. Captain Oates was nowhere near. Josiah leaned over the railing to seek out the abandoned cat—an inconsequential bundle of what appeared to be matted black fur, rocking in the waves behind the ship—with no idea of what to do. A Negro crew member said with a grim chuckle, "Mungo Park is the Devil's own. He will never drown. He will never die. Don't shed a tear for Mungo Park."

(AND SO IT TURNED OUT: for early the next morning Josiah was wakened by the creature's guttural purring close beside his head, and the rhythmic kneading motions of his partly sheathed claws against Josiah's chest. And, ah!—the beauty of those coolly-glowing topaz eyes!)

BY DEGREES JOSIAH succumbed to the Ice Kingdom. Wondering why he had eked out his existence until now in the greenery of—(what was its name?)—the village of his birth, and the hoary old estate-house called Crosswicks? Somewhere in the State of New Jersey, of no more size and consequence than a gigantic iceberg.

No matter: the Ice Kingdom was eternal. By day and by night he was entering it.

Parallel lines there were beyond counting in the (newer, revised and updated) Scheme of Clues; yet, as Josiah studied the chart, the lines extended, and distended, and whipped about to form clumsy circles—touching *mouth to tail,* it seemed.

The Antarctic moon swung around to hang motionless in the sky, so gigantic it threatened to bump into Josiah's head, had he not laughingly ducked, and crawled on hands and knees into the darkness of the hold; crouching behind a barrel of flour; until there came a cry—*Josiah? Josiah? Where are you hiding?*—and the sweet laughter of his baby sister Annabel who searched for him in the old slaves' quarters behind Crosswicks, that had been converted into storage buildings.

Shortly it seemed that the sea was composed of shallow puddles, that sparked and winked with secret marine life; and, though no vegetation seemed to be at hand, tendrils blossomed everywhere—unless they were serpents that wriggled out of the black water, to stretch over every surface; and, when a man's head was turned, to flash across the deck and into the hold? Josiah shouted, and kicked, and stamped, and tried wildly to thrust the serpents away, for they were underfoot as well; the more insidious, that they could not be seen with the naked eye.

In the distance, beyond a shattered ice floe, the upheld head of a great serpent, moving, like the *Balmoral,* in an unflagging southerly direction to McMurdo Sound.

"That? A 'sea serpent' they are called," one of the crew explained to Josiah, as if he'd asked a very stupid question. "There are many of them in these waters but as we pay them no mind, they pay us no mind."

In the wake of the great serpent, however, came a curious balmy breeze fragrant with Grecian windflowers, and daffodils, and narcissus. Josiah breathed deeply and swallowed the air. For he knew himself saved.

I shall not develop scurvy like others of the crew. I shall not suffer weakened blood vessels in the brain that, popping one by one, produce foolish hallucinations, and nightmares at noon.

PROFESSOR PEARCE VAN DYCK protested that the blood vessels in his brain had not weakened; he had been in "full possession" of his faculties until the very end—when Josiah had killed him.

Josiah begged for forgiveness but Pearce van Dyck persisted, now accusing his wife Johanna of "base adultery" and the baby sired by the Fiend "no child of mine but a demon."

Josiah blushed to hear his old professor speak so coarsely of his own wife and protested that he found it very difficult to believe that Johanna, of all women, had been unfaithful to her husband; the more so, in that the baby appeared, to Josiah, to be an entirely normal baby, of no particular distinction—neither exceedingly beautiful, nor ugly; rather, of the very essence of *human baby.*

Pearce van Dyck interrupted with a bitter chuckle, to declare that the "marital paradox" first reasoned out by the Church Father St. Gregory the Great in the sixth century explained his position: the "carnal act" within Christian marriage is *innocent* even as the desire for such an act is *morally evil.*

Josiah clasped his mittened hands against his ears and tried to argue that Christian marriage, like all marriage, could not be *morally evil;* but Pearce van Dyck refused to listen. Josiah relented, saying that brothers and sisters had no need, and no urge, to marry; therefore, no requirement to wed; in this way, the "paradox" is transcended.

Pearce persisted in his argument, drawing close to Josiah until to Josiah's surprise his features shaded into those of Captain Oates, who comforted Josiah by stroking his fevered brow, and pressing his cold cheek against Josiah's fevered cheek, and embracing him tight as any brother, or lover. Yet at the same time, Professor van Dyck seemed still present, if not visible, and at a little distance of about ten feet, grimly intoning:

Who will take little Baby?
I, said the water deep.
Baby will float in his cradle boat,
And I shall rock him to sleep.

THOUGH THE DELICATE little flowers were but satin lilies of the valley, prettily sewn to the bridal gown, yet they gave off a sweet fragrance of actual lilies, causing Josiah to inhale so deeply he began to stagger about like a drunken man. *He* would not have abandoned the mill-girl Pearl to her coarse companions. *He* could not find it in his heart to quite forgive his grandfather, for such cowardice. *O help. Josiah. My dear brother. Do not abandon me on the ice, Josiah!* Her frightened voice lifted with the sea breeze and sent him reeling across the deck. Was it—Annabel? But where? So far from home? Ah!—starboard she drifted, crouched barefoot and trembling on the ice, her hair whipping in the wind, not very prettily; and her strained face, pale as alabaster, turned to Josiah in desperate appeal.

O Josiah help me. Do not abandon me as you have done. Come to me and warm me!

And this time, no crew members being near, Josiah climbed over the rail and unhesitatingly dived into the pitching sea.

The carelessly annotated log for the *Balmoral* entered in Captain Oates's flowing hand, contains the (undated) notation that Josiah Slade's lifeless body, solid-frozen and encased in ice, was hauled from the McMurde Sound, and carried into the hold of the ship.

"*Requiescat in pace*," the vexed captain scribbled into the log, "—and there's an end to it!"

On the morning that Copplestone Slade at last "made his move" his frightened wife Lenora had dared to lock her door against him, having had a premonition that her husband's unreasonable fury at her could not much longer be suppressed. As it was Lenora's habit, following the deaths of her children, to sequester herself away in her private rooms, after her morning bath, to write letters, and read in her Bible, and enjoy her modest breakfast, so Copplestone knew where to find her; she had been hearing his uplifted voice downstairs, as if he were reprimanding the household staff, which lately he did often, and trying to gauge if he were on his way outside, or whether he was on his way to *her*.

For months, Lenora had queried herself mercilessly, as to how she had failed her husband; she had sought advice and solace from Henrietta Slade, and from the elder Slades at Crosswicks; she had not wanted to seek out her own family, the Biddles of Philadelphia, for fear of revealing too much that was intimate, and risking a scandal. At the time of her marriage to Copplestone Slade, all of her relatives had thought the match a very good one, for Copplestone was a genial, good-hearted, prank-loving young man, far from the shrewd businessman who was his elder brother Augustus, and farther still from their father Winslow Slade; he had evinced a good deal of pride in the fact that his young wife resembled a "Renoir woman" and was a descendant of the Pennsylvania patriot Lord Stirling, who'd met a martyred death while commanding the Northern Department of the Continental army; and destined to inherit a small, tidy fortune from her parents, as she was their sole surviving heir.

For many years, their marriage was unremarkable; as a West End couple, they entertained frequently, and dined out frequently. As an historian I am inclined to somewhat overzealously research even my minor subjects, and so I have looked into Copplestone's background; but there is really not much to report, for the man acquitted himself in a more or less adequate way as a son of Winslow Slade, and a partner in the Slade family businesses, that were managed by professionals, and had always prospered. It is true, Copplestone had a penchant for the theater, as a younger man; he had even participated in amateur theatrics, in the Princeton Players, taking on such ambitious roles as Theseus in *A Midsummer Night's Dream,* Bertram in *All's Well That Ends Well,* and Frederic in *The Pirates of Penzance;* less profitably, Copplestone had a penchant for gambling on racing horses, at which he lost a fair amount of money over the years; but very likely Lenora never knew anything about it, for the couple lived quite separate lives, within the granite walls of Wheatsheaf.

Since the abduction of Annabel Slade in June 1905, relations between Copplestone and Lenora had deteriorated; the more exacerbated by the children's deaths, for which Copplestone blamed Lenora. And there was Copplestone's yet more irrational jealousy of Lenora, for he seemed to have convinced himself, with no evidence, that his wife was "involved" with one or another Princeton man including the dashing Count von Gneist—though so far as I have been able to determine, Lenora and the Count could have met only once or twice, at large gatherings.

Yet, Copplestone had so degenerated in his denunciations of his wife, he was overheard to mutter in her hearing such words as *Slut! Whore! Doxy! Bitch!* and *Sloven!* not caring whether others overheard, including even the abashed household staff.

"Yet, I know myself innocent in the eyes of God," Lenora bravely reasoned. "Shall I feel ashamed, in *his* eyes?"

ON THIS MORNING in late May, Lenora was sitting at her writing desk, beginning a letter as an officer of the New Jersey chapter of the Colonial Dames of America, when Copplestone struck loudly on her door with his fist, and demanded that she open it.

So terrified was Lenora, and so oppressed by her husband, she hesitated only a moment before rising to open the door; it was with house-wifely concern that she removed the breakfast tray from a nearby table, with a platter of blueberry muffins, butter, and jam, and tea things, that had scarcely been touched, to set it out of harm's way. Then, with a silent prayer, Lenora went to unlock the door, and her infuriated husband pushed it open, and stepped inside.

"So! What are you writing? I demand to see."

Mutely Lenora stood aside as Copplestone bent over the writing table, to see the innocuous-seeming letter on the issue of the Dolly Lambert house in Washington's Crossing, Pennsylvania; yet seeing this, the jealous man snorted in derision, as if this were the most transparent of ploys, and *he* was not to be deceived.

Trying to disguise her alarm, Lenora suggested to Copplestone that he sit down, and breathe deeply; for he was breathing loudly, and he was flush-faced, and "should take care not to strain his over-taxed heart."

Copplestone relented, to a degree; for Lenora's wifely solicitude was always touching to him, even in such circumstances. Yet angrily he waved a sheaf of handwritten letters in her face, claiming that he had evidence here for civil divorce, on grounds of infidelity: "These shameless letters from *Yr. adoring Tommy*."

Lenora had no idea what Copplestone meant, but knew not to inflame him further. She suggested that he be seated, and be "calm"; perhaps join her in a cup of Earl Grey tea, which was his favorite, and a blueberry muffin from a batch baked by Lenora herself just that morning, in the hope of tempting him . . .

" '*Yr. adoring Tommy*' it is—and again, on these five or six letters—*Yr. adoring Tommy*. As if the horse-face parson hadn't enough womenfolk of his own to pet and pamper him on the university campus, he dares to plot clandestine meetings with my wife!" Copplestone waved the letters another time at Lenora, who saw that they were somewhat yellowed, and covered in a dense, dark hand that looked familiar to her but which she could not immediately identify.

"My dear husband, I can't understand any of this except to say that I am innocent. I have never received a letter from—are you referring to Woodrow Wilson?—ah, never! I scarcely know him, or his wife Elaine—is that her name? Ellen? I swear that I—"

Copplestone grunted in disgust, and slapped Lenora on the side of the head, causing her to cry out in surprise and pain. In addition, her graying hair was loosed from its pins, and fell unevenly about her face, the sight of which so repelled Copplestone, he feinted a second blow, and the poor woman dissolved in shamefaced tears.

"Copplestone, I swear to you—*I am innocent*. The letters might be from my great-uncle Timothy Jefferson Biddle, which he used to sign *Yr. adoring Uncle Timmy*—I think that must be it. Poor 'Uncle Timmy' has been dead for fifteen years, Copplestone! In the last, lonely years of his life he'd taken to writing long rambling letters to several of his nieces. I'm sure you'd met him, Copplestone. If you let me look at the letters, I'm sure I can explain."

"Yes. I'm sure you can *explain*. I'm sure you had a *ready explanation*."

Copplestone raised his hand as if to strike her again, and the poor woman shrank guiltily away.

"Lies! 'Tis all 'weary, stale, flat, and unprofitable'—this domestic life of ours, hewn out of chaos. Only the fifth act of the tragedy redeems."

Panting quickly, Copplestone was yet distracted enough by the aroma of Lenora's blueberry muffins to stab his finger into one of the muffins, and taste the crumbs, even as he continued to persecute Lenora, ranting that "Thomas Woodrow Wilson" could not have been the first, or the last, to have been involved with Lenora—"It isn't beyond imagining that my own damned brother 'Gustus has set his cloven hoof in my bed, for the sport and spite of it!" In his rage, Copplestone's vocabulary had sharpened; his pronunciation of certain common words had acquired a British flair.

"Your own brother, Augustus? You can't be serious . . ."

"Can't I! Can't I 'be serious'! You will be quiet, whore, or I will mur-der you! It's as the playwright knew, 'Lie with her? Lie on her? We say lie on her, when they belie her. Lie with her, that's fulsome!' All who marry take out license to become cuckolds, in time." Copplestone made the cuckold's sign of horns on his forehead, as his greeny eyes shone. "Yet—should I take my revenge now, or leave her to Heaven? Let me see that damned let-ter you're scribbling—in code, I suppose. It's said that Adelaide Burr kept a journal in code, that the authorities are trying to 'crack' without success. Pah! A regiment of faithless women."

Copplestone snatched up the letter on behalf of the Colonial Dames, but could make no sense of it, and hadn't the patience to read it carefully. Lenora dared to speak to him, saying that she feared he was "unwell"; since Oriana's death, he had not been sleeping through the night, and his ap-petite had diminished so that he only picked at his favorite foods—roast suckling pig, blood pudding, sweetbreads, and the baked goods Lenora made with her own hand, solely to please him.

"Dear husband, I wish you would sit down for just a minute, and compose yourself; then if you like, you can resume your interrogation of me." Lenora spoke so pleadingly, fixing her husband with tearful yet lov-ing eyes, it was very difficult for Copplestone to resist. "Here is a cup of Earl Grey. And here, some brown sugar, and cream. Shall I? You are very fatigued, you know; you have taken the deaths of our children very hard, which is a mark of your love for them . . . Copplestone, darling, these blue-berry muffins are favorites of yours, prepared from the recipe of Prudence

Burr which I've often followed. You know you are very hungry, dear. It isn't good for a man of your age and responsibilities to fast; I am sure that it is very bad. Shall I butter the muffin for you . . ."

Despite his resolve, Copplestone was swayed by his wife's soothing words; for perhaps he did love her, or some dim memory of Miss Lenora Biddle, forged in the long-ago of a Philadelphia Christmas cotillion ball at which Copplestone Slade and Miss Biddle were perceived to shine. Roughly he wiped at his eyes and mustache and, overcome by a rush of ravenous if reluctant hunger, he took the blueberry muffin from Lenora and devoured it in two or three bites—"Well. Yes. It *is* good— God damn!" Copplestone laughed, and took up the platter of muffins, which Lenora had pushed in his direction; greedily he devoured these, with swabs of butter, eating rapidly and with an obvious sensual pleasure. Lenora poured him another cup of tea, and sweetened it as before with brown sugar and cream; and this too the panting man accepted, with a shaky hand. He drank heartily, finishing the cup within a minute; rudely he belched, and wiped his mouth on the edge of an embroidered doily, on Lenora's table. After a pause he said, with a sly, cruel smile: "Yet it will not save you, whore. *It will not save you.*"

FOR COPPLESTONE SLADE had prepared a document during the night, dictated to him, as he thought it, by a Higher Power; which document, embossed with the monogram of Wheatsheaf Manor and the coat of arms of the Slades, he intended for his adulterous wife to sign. Then, he would bribe a notary public employed by the family firm, to swear that he had witnessed the signature.

While Lenora listened, very stiffly, and still, Copplestone read to her in a swift, stern voice: " 'I, Lenora Biddle Slade, the wife of Copplestone Slade and the mistress of Wheatsheaf Manor, being of sound mind and body, do hereby confess to the loathsome sin of Adultery, with these persons—_____, _____, and _____.' " He would fill in the blanks, Copplestone said, when he'd determined the full extent of her crimes. " 'By affixing my signature to this document, free and uncoerced, with my husband as my primary witness, I hereby relinquish all my claims as mistress of his household and surrender all my expectations as his lawful wedded wife; and sign over to him the power of attorney of my hand, and the rights and privileges thereby entailed; and, as God is my witness, I consign to him and to him alone the discretion of *taking my life, or no:* this act to be performed at a time and a place appropriate to it, the decision resting with Copplestone Slade.' So, a Higher Power has instructed me, Lenora; it is out of my hands. You are to sign on the line here, do you see? Yes?"

Copplestone then tried to close his wife's trembling fingers about her fountain pen, and to dip it into ink, but their struggle was such that an anguine blot appeared on the document, which quite dismayed Copplestone, as he had prepared the writ with great care on a stiff sheet of parchment, and had neither the time nor the spirit to transcribe it a second time. "Sign your name, whore, and have done with it!"

Understanding that her cause was hopeless, and that this man was not her husband but a maddened creature bent on her destruction, Lenora sprang past him suddenly to seize a silk bell pull that hung on the wall, in order to summon a servant; she had to hope, in desperation, that the household staff downstairs would not shrink from the responsibility of coming to her rescue, or at least summoning help from neighbors; but, unfortunately, Copplestone was too quick for her, clumsily wrenching her back by the hips and throwing her down onto a velvet *chaise longue*. The spark of resistance in the woman—the mere touch of her flesh—seemed to inflame him; he felt a perverse rush of animal desire, yet a stronger rush of revulsion. His fingers closed about her throat as he muttered: "Oh no you don't, whore—you shall *not*. For a Higher Power has instructed me, we are but pawns in His hand. Stop struggling, slut—don't madden me the more!"

Thrown into a frenzy, like a wild creature fighting for its life, Lenora too cast off all restraint; so raking Copplestone's hands and face with her nails as to force him from her, at least temporarily, that she might scream for help. In a fury the madman seized a pillow and pressed it over her face; and pressed, and pressed, until her cries were muffled; and the wild thrashing of her body gradually ceased. Such was Copplestone's effort, his eyes fairly bulged from his head, and a great artery throbbed between his eyes. Half-sobbing he fell upon the woman, and pummeled her with his fists as a child might have done, whispering: "Whore! Strumpet! Have you learned, too late? Do you repent—too late?"

When Lenora made no reply, and did not move, Copplestone threw the pillow to the floor, took hold of Lenora's chin and roughly shook her head from side to side. How like the deceitful whore, to mock him! But her eyes seemed to have rolled back up into her head, hideously; her mouth had gone slack; horribly, it seemed *all life had drained from her.*

Copplestone grunted, and lifted himself from his wife's body with effort; he stared, and wiped bloody spittle from his lips; adjusted his disheveled clothing. "Why then 'tis done—consummated. 'When I love thee not, chaos is come again . . .'"

THE WHEATSHEAF ENIGMA II

Yet when several of the more courageous servants ventured into Lenora Slade's morning-room, through the opened door, in great trepidation at what they might discover, it was an unexpected scene: for their mistress Lenora Slade lay unconscious on the velvet *chaise longue*, breathing faintly; and their master Copplestone Slade lay on the rosebud carpet, his dressing gown torn open and his face, still flushed and radiant with heat, contorted in a hellish expression—of rage, agony, and immense surprise.

Which is to say: Lenora Slade lived; and Copplestone Slade departed this life.

BY THE TIME help had been summoned, and Dr. Boudinot arrived, followed quickly by Augustus Slade, Lenora had begun to waken; though the poor woman had no idea of what had happened or even, it seemed, that she had been viciously attacked. Her muslin gown was badly ripped and stained; her face, throat, and bosom were bruised. Though it must have cost her great effort to speak, she appealed to Dr. Boudinot to attend to her husband, and not herself.

"Mrs. Slade, I'm afraid it's too late. Copplestone is—is not—breathing . . ."

Already the heated, corpulent corpse was cooling; the reddened face gradually losing its angry hue, and the glassy eyes shining a fainter green. On the froth-spittled mouth were remnants of muffin crumbs, as on the silk dressing gown. For it seemed to Dr. Boudinot that the deceased man must have eaten a hearty breakfast, prior to his collapse; the physician did not want to think, despite evidence, that Copplestone Slade had violently attacked his wife, before succumbing to a stroke.

"Death would have been instantaneous, in this sort of massive stroke," Dr. Boudinot said, in the tone of one speaking to individuals who know less than he knows of the human body and its perils, "for the symptoms are familiar to me, unfortunately! I'd long warned Mr. Slade that he was overweight, and had high blood pressure; I'd warned him that he was not too young, at his age, to suffer a stroke. (For, you know, Woodrow Wilson had a stroke at the age of thirty-nine—a fairly minor stroke, but it has been kept secret in order not to injure his career.) A tragedy, Mrs. Slade, and Augustus, but if it's the smallest consolation, you should know that in such cases the victim feels not a moment of pain, despite his facial expression. Copplestone may appear angry, but he is entirely at peace."

It was a matter of some embarrassment, that Lenora Slade seemed to have suffered some sort of attack upon her person, showing, among other injuries, the reddened imprints of fingers around her throat; but neither of the gentlemen wished to inquire, and Lenora herself was eager to be led away to her bedroom, by one of the colored girls, to bathe, and dress and groom herself, in preparation for the ordeal of dealing with her husband's death, as she had had to deal with the deaths of both her children. For it had happened, that which God had not prevented from happening—*Yet another innocent member of her family had been taken from her.*

Surveying the damage in the room, the badly shaken Augustus Slade, known as 'Gustus by his younger, vexing but good-hearted brother, set upright a cushioned chair, and an overturned table; as servants scrambled to set things right, he took note of a broken Wedgwood plate on the carpet, and a broken cup; spilled tea; a scattering of crumbs and bits of muffins, and cubes of brown sugar; and, his shrewd lawyer's eye falling upon a curious legal-looking document crested with the family coat of arms, he deftly pocketed it with the intention of examining it in private. If it proved pertinent to the situation, Augustus thought, he would certainly turn it over to the Township authorities, in time.

THUS, THE INEXPLICABLE reversal of fates at Wheatsheaf, to which I have given the title *The Wheatsheaf Enigma*. For no historian has ever satisfactorily explained it—not Hollinger, not Croft-Crooke, not A. D. W. Maybrick—and not I.

"SOLE LIVING HEIR OF NOTHINGNESS"

W hy, you are very naughty! You are breaking your mother's heart."
She'd sent away Nanny that she might take a mother's pleasure in bathing her baby, and putting him to bed for his afternoon nap;
and was now a little anxious at his fretfulness. Indeed, she spoke sharply,
giving the blue-painted ceramic baby's tub a rap of her knuckles.

Baby Terence, winking and grimacing at his mother, only feigned
obedience, for, when Amanda bent over him again, to soap him gently with
a sponge, the little fellow resumed his energetic kicking, and more bathwater was splashed onto Amanda's dress, quite soaking her apron.

"Oh! Terence. You are *very naughty*."

Terence Wick FitzRandolph was but a few months old—(was he?)—
yet had grown apace; and must have now weighed somewhere in the vicinity of twenty pounds. The contours of his fleshy-soft baby's body had
begun to lengthen, and become angular; the miniature genitals, which his
mother tried not to stare at, and to touch as minimally as possible, had
decidedly grown. And Terence's skin-tone was decidedly of a hue just perceptibly *not entirely Caucasian*.

"Poor Edgerstoune! He would be so abashed. And yet—it is all innocent . . ."

Amanda had not inquired into her family background, in detail; for she would not have wanted to raise suspicion among the relatives. Yet it would not have surprised her if, in the previous century, or even in the century preceding, there had been a "mixing" of races—"An Indian princess, it may have been. Surely, no mere commoner."

Amanda's paternal family, descended from the revered Mathers of Plymouth Colony, was large, sprawling, and very certainly "heterogeneous"; and her maternal family, the Proxmires, originally of the Rhode Island colony, had partly emigrated to the western frontier, prior to returning to the East, to establish roots in Wilmington, Delaware.

Of Edgerstoune's family, the FitzRandolphs—Amanda knew less. Yet this too was an old, sprawling family descended from Puritans who'd been admonished to *increase, and multiply*.

The Count had cautioned Amanda, motherhood might not be for her; in the intense emotions of motherhood, there might be peril; she was "yet a young woman, a widow" and "perhaps not fully a *mother*." The Count had pointed out that infants are by nature very "selfish"—having but a limited awareness of the adults who surround them, and nothing like respect or genuine feeling. "It is all *appetite*. It is *appetite that must be fed*."

Amanda protested that she loved little Terence, though he was a difficult, colicky baby; and she meant to be a very devoted mother, as all of Princeton would see.

"Adoring your baby is all very fine, dear Mrs. FitzRandolph," the Count said, "but disciplining him is something more demanding."

This was true. Adoration came easily, and discipline very hard. And lately, Terence seemed less adorable—for his sweet blue gaze, formerly reserved for her alone, now leapt from object to object as if attracted by sheer movement and novelty. And now it appeared that Terence's dimpled baby smiles, which had afforded Amanda nearly as much pleasure as nursing itself, could be summoned by anyone—a visitor, the Irish nanny Brigit who crooned to him in Gaelic. (Amanda wasn't so sure she quite approved of that: crooning to her baby in a foreign, antiquated language that was known to be, in British circles, the language of *resistance*.) Yet more distressing to his mother, Terence frequently lapsed into one of his noisy "talking" spells in the company of his stuffed animals, with as much absorption as if he were "talking" with his mother. And he was naughty, unfailingly naughty, in his bath.

Where was Brigit? Almost, Amanda wanted to call her, and summon back the hearty Irish girl, who took not the slightest heed of baby's noisy, fretful, and *soiling* ways, as Amanda did. For it seemed at such times a profound mystery to her that the squalling infant in the grayish soapy water was *hers*.

She had wanted to bathe him, tenderly; to dry him, and powder him, and dress him in his pretty baby-clothes; she had wanted to feed him mashed plums from his own silver spoon, and rock him against her bosom, and sing to him, and kiss him all over . . . But Terence did not seem to wish to cooperate.

As the Count said, Terence was spoiled; and it would only get worse, as he matured.

Amanda leaned over the tub, that smelled frankly of both soapy water and baby urine, to sing a little tune she'd learned from the Count, who'd sung it first in German, and then translated for her:

Who will take Baby Terence?
I, said the water deep.
Baby will float in his cradle boat
And I shall rock him to sleep.

But Baby Terence responded to this with a devilish baby-smirk, and a thrashing of his fat baby-legs, and a shriek that made Amanda's hair stand on end, for she feared Brigit would hear, or one of the household staff, and come running.

The Count was dropping by at teatime, or so he had promised. She would be headachey and red-eyed and out of sorts; and her mother, who was also dropping by, would fuss over her, as Amanda hated her to do.

Not a fit mother—was that what Princeton was saying, of Amanda FitzRandolph?

"I will make them say otherwise. I will make him *love me*, and *obey me*."

This declaration, on the very day of Amanda FitzRandolph's "vanishing" from stately Mora House, at 44 Mercer Street: May 29, 1906.

"WITHIN THE HOUSE of the von Gneists," the Count had told Amanda FitzRandolph, on one of their walks along the wide white beach at *Sans Souci*, "there is a tradition of the curse that is also a blessing; or, the blessing that is also a curse. I have no detailed knowledge of this tradition, except to know that it sets the von Gneists apart from others." In a melancholy yet bemused tone the Count told his attentive American listener of ancient feuds between Romanians and Hungarians; "saintly men of God" slaughtered like beasts, by peasants; and tides of the Black Death, issued by a wrathful God, in punishment for such violations of nature. Seeing that Mrs. FitzRandolph shivered at his words, and bit her lower lip, the Count continued, in a more confiding voice, "The essence of the 'curse' seems to be that, as my deep happiness lies in the fact of my existing without volition, and viewing the world freed of all desire, so too does my sorrow lie in this: that I am a von Gneist, I am condemned, or if you wish, privileged, to see the world as little more than a screen of mere images, impressions, and possibilities, lacking all permanent substance; and lacking, as a result, the 'hooks and barbs' that ensnare a man's soul. It is said, the selfless love of a woman can 'save' the accursed von Gneist, and yet, how painful for me, to feel *desires*, but rarely *desire*; and of course, very rarely *love*."

Amanda lowered her eyes, deeply moved; grateful for the fine-spun chiffon veil that partly obscured her face, to protect it from the powerful rays of the Bermuda sun. She murmured that she understood, of course—though truly, she did not.

"In addition," the Count said, "I've found myself in permanent exile: a solitary wanderer through the continents. I am forced to accept the generous charity of my American friends, which I can only hope to repay, someday; for of course the von Gneists are penniless, and near-extinct. I must wander until the curse is erased, or until I die—which may be the identical thing . . . Well, Mrs. FitzRandolph, I must not burden your youthful heart with such melancholy confidences."

"And have you never been 'in love,' Count? Is that what you are saying?"

Gusts of sea-wind stirred Amanda's hair beneath her wide-brimmed hat, and roused her spirits to speak daringly; for Edgerstoune, absorbed in golf with friends, was in another part of the island and nowhere near.

"It's said that a von Gneist will be released from his 'blessing' if another human being should love him wholly, and unquestioningly, above all the world and Heaven," the Count said, frowning, "which is to say not only above all living things but *above God as well*. And with the willingness, if required, to sacrifice them. A single hour of this selfless love, a single minute, would erase the curse on my brow; and restore my soul to me, that I might love in turn, and feel such emotions as pity, need, yearning, interest, as human beings normally feel. I must confess, my dear Amanda," the Count said, now in a trembling voice, "that it was the promise of America that drew me here; for you are all young, having so little history of your own, and that a crude history, lacking culture; Americans seem willing to expend precious energies with the vitality of youth, as if such energies are infinite. The Old World envies such innocence, and thrills to it; and hopes that lasting blood-ties might be forged . . . Before sailing from Liverpool I dared to think, 'Even a von Gneist might seek salvation there.'"

At this, Amanda was so stricken with emotion that she could not speak, and stood rooted to the spot; until the Count took her arm, to twine through his, and resumed their walk along the beach, in a loop that would bring them back to the white-latticed porch at *Sans Souci* where Mark Twain in resplendent white was holding court to admirers; sighting the romantic couple, Mr. Twain lifted his cigar in a signal of—recognition? approbation? camaraderie?

"Bienvenue, mes amis! C'est la vie ici—oui?"

Forty hours later, Edgerstoune FitzRandolph lay dead on the wide white beach behind *Sans Souci,* the heedless victim of a lethal sting on the bare heel of his right foot.

SINCE AMANDA FITZRANDOLPH'S secret journal, known among my research materials as the Fleur-de-lis notebook, is undated, and haphazardly arranged, as well as, as I've noted previously, lamentably unreliable, the historian can only conjecture as to the probable duration of the "affair" between Mrs. FitzRandolph and Count English von Gneist: it could not have been long, for the lovers first came together, I believe, in Bermuda; in that place of lax, Lotus-Land manners, far from the rigors of Princeton, New Jersey; and it ended, or rather culminated, on the day of this narrative, which is May 29, 1906.

So hallucinatory, scattered, lurid and implausible are entries in Amanda FitzRandolph's journal, approaching this date, this historian has been sparing in his consultation of it; and though rival historians will protest, and think my procedure unprofessional, *I have already committed the offensive document to the flames.*

The claims of historical accuracy must yield to claims of common decency.

In any case, it was in late April that Count von Gneist and Mrs. Fitz-Randolph seem to have "coupled"; according to Amanda's journal, this "coupling" was not *by day* but wholly *by night* as she lay in her bed sleeping and helpless. (Excised portions of the journal seem to suggest that these nocturnal visitations from the Count may have predated Bermuda, and took place as Amanda lay beside her heedlessly slumbering husband; this is even more disagreeable, I think.) Amanda would wake from disturbing dreams to see the gentleman's spectral, or immaterial, form in the darkened bedroom; at times, she witnessed his figure easing through a wall, as if the wall were but mist. With none of the gallantry for which the Count was so admired by day, he seized Amanda by the shoulders, lifted her and pressed his mouth against hers, greedily; ignoring his terrified victim's struggle to escape him, he kissed her as he liked until Amanda grew so short of breath she passed away in a faint.

And how bewildering to awaken hours later, in a flood of sunshine, to discover her heart beating languidly against her ribs, and her lacy nightclothes twisted and damp.

So dazed was Amanda, after the return to Princeton, in the first phase of her young widowhood, and so uncertain whether the Count had "really" been present at her bedside, or whether she'd only dreamt him, she lay abed for hours; with little appetite for breakfast brought to her on a tray; feeling a stab of guilt, that the household staff, like friends, relatives, and West End neighbors, believed it was Edgerstoune she was mourning.

"Poor lady!"—(Amanda happened to overhear one of the servants remark to another)—"seems like her soul just ain't in her body, but with *him*."

By day, when they were likely to be in the company of others, the Count never hinted at his nocturnal behavior. Nor would anyone have guessed, seeing him speaking with Mrs. FitzRandolph, as he spoke with other Princeton friends, that there was anything secret between them; anything clandestine, still less lewd. For the Count was a gentleman of impeccable manners, as his grooming and his clothing were flawless; and Amanda FitzRandolph, one of the most gracious and upstanding of West End ladies.

Yet, it was noted how the two—(one would not have called them a "couple," exactly)—played together at bridge, as partners; and one evening at Drumthwacket, Amanda astonished the gathering by singing, as the Count accompanied her on the piano, a song no one had ever heard before, in the widow's clear sweet soprano voice:

Es flustern und sprechen die Blumen
Und schau'n mitleidig mich an:
"Sei unserer Schwester nicht böse,
Du trauriger, blasser Mann!"

It should be noted that Amanda had long been one of the most ad-mired amateur singers in Princeton. Prior to her marriage to Edgerstoune FitzRandolph, at the age of twenty-one—(Edgerstoune had been thirty-four)—her sweet if somewhat wavering soprano voice had been much in demand at weddings, funerals, and other celebrations. Though her throat was not strong, and her delivery sometimes hesitant, and she betrayed, in more exacting compositions, a faulty middle voice, Amanda had been en-couraged by her voice teachers, and was capable of much expression in her singing; and looked very striking with wide-spaced gray eyes, and slightly snubbed nose, and pert rosebud lips, honey-brown hair piled upon her head in glamorous Gibson Girl style.

It was fortunate, how all of Princeton could not know how often, and with increasing bestiality, the Count "had his way" with Amanda, by night; taking no pity on her, and responding to her whimpers of distress and pain with a cruel laugh—the very antithesis of the Count by day.

"Doesn't he remember? Is it—a sort of game? But what is my role, and how am I to respond?"—so Amanda queried herself, perplexed and ashamed; though recalling how, in the most recent dream, her arm had slipped about the Count's neck as if with a volition of its own.

ONE NIGHT, in late spring, when a heady aroma of wild rose suffused the air, the Count came for Amanda—"My Mandy!"—and led her from her bedroom through the darkened streets of the West End, and to another part of Princeton less known to her; here, there were lanes and back-alleys, and small houses set side by side, like dutiful and unsuspecting pupils. His fingers were closed about her slender wrist, she could not have wrested from him if she'd tried. It seemed that the two were "running"—leaping and bounding as if weightless—in close pursuit of their prey, which the Count had sighted: a youth of about fourteen, with a very dark skin, like ebony; a startled white smile, or grimace; and eyes protuberant as the eyes of a panicked pony. This, on lower Witherspoon Street, several blocks below the cemetery; on a night of intermittent moonlight and shadows; like big cats they stole upon the youth, soundless; like cats, cuffing and pummeling and clawing him, as he cried out in terror. The Count drove the boy at Mandy, who drove him back to the Count, with the most deft motions of her hands; then, with a muffled cry, the Count fell upon their prey, sinking his teeth deep in the ebony-dark throat, and deeper yet. The Count reached out to seize his mistress's wild windblown hair, and to tug her to him, that she too might embrace the now paralyzed youth, and suffer the paroxysm of gratified desire.

"We will not leave him, I think, for others to find, and release more hysteria on the community. We will hide him, in plain sight"—so the Count said, laughing; with the result that the fiendish couple dragged the youth's thin body to a culvert, and to a drainage pipe, into which they stuffed it, and hid the opening with debris fallen from trees.

Astonishing to Mandy that on such nights, she did not repel the Count, but acquiesced to him, at once; and that her mouth should so instinctively and greedily suck, with the abandon of her baby at her breast; or that the swallowing of hot blood, which would certainly have provoked fits of vomiting in her by day, should so please her at night.

"It is only a dream of course. Only a dream"—Mandy placated herself. "In a little while, I will be awake in my own bed."

IT WAS IN the morning of May 29, in the nursery at Mora House, that the Irish girl Brigit returned earlier than expected, to discover her mistress in the act of—(could it be?)—struggling with her infant son in the baby-tub, to push his head under-water.

"Mistress! No!"—Brigit rushed to the baby's aid and, in the exigency of the moment, dared to pull Mrs. FitzRandolph's hands away, with the result that the thrashing baby emerged from the water shrieking at a deafening volume. Amanda turned sharply to the nanny saying that Terence had been naughty, and she had been disciplining him, as she had failed to discipline him in the past, with unfortunate results.

"Mrs. FitzRandolph, you don't mean that," the frightened girl said, "you can't mean to harm Baby. Please, mistress—"

"Oh! Listen to him scream! I can't bear it."

Mandy pressed her fingers into her ears, in dismay. The entire front of her dress and apron were wet from the bathwater; her hair, that had not yet been fashioned into its Gibson Girl style atop her head, was hanging in her face, wetted and limp. "Brigit, Terence is *spoiled*. He is *selfish*. He cares for none of us really, not his mother, and not *you*. We have all been derelict in spoiling him, and now—it's almost too late."

Brigit tried to lift the squirming baby out of the bath as Mandy tried to push him down, crying that he was bad, bad—"possessed by a demon!"

But Brigit managed to wrest Terence from her, as Mandy wept and pummeled at her with her fists; the one, Brigit, a sturdy wide-hipped girl of nineteen, the other, Amanda FitzRandolph, a more delicately boned woman with fevered eyes, locked together in an astonishing struggle, that none of the FitzRandolphs' friends and neighbors would have believed. And here was the baby's ceramic tub overturned, water everywhere, Mandy's clothing soaked, and hair in unsightly strands.

"Amanda—*forbear*."

Count English von Gneist stood in the nursery doorway, with a look of consternation. How out of place the gentleman was, in this part of the house; and how formally he was dressed, as if for travel, in a cloak of lightweight black wool lined with pale silk, and a black silken top hat; and carrying an ebony-knobbed walking stick beneath his arm. Though the handsome gentleman was frowning, his manner was that of an irate but affectionate elder, a "friend of the family" who has taken upon himself the duty to chastise.

"Such things are beneath your dignity, my queen," the Count said to Mandy, extending his arm, "—so, let the infant be: and come to me at once. For it is time."

So it was, Amanda FitzRandolph ran sobbing to her lover, without a moment's hesitation; and he opened his arms wide that he might enfold her protectively in the cloak. In full view of the staring Brigit, who held Terence close against her breasts, the Count chastely kissed Amanda's brow, and lifted her in his arms as if she were his bride; turned on his heel, and bore her in triumph from the room.

"Mistress! Oh—mistress!" the tremulous Brigit called after her. "You cannot mean it!—you cannot wish it!"

But no one attended to the Irish girl's words. Little Terence continued his heartrending cries, kicking and flailing his arms as the Irish nanny held him fast, and Mrs. FitzRandolph had, in an instant, vanished from view in the arms of the Count.

Neither was ever seen again in Princeton.

THE TEMPTATION
OF WOODROW WILSON

O n the morning of May 30 the shocking news spread through Princeton, and made its way in swirls and ripples and eddies across the
university campus: the president of the university, the much-revered
Woodrow Wilson, had suffered a severe stroke, and had been hospitalized;
and was not expected to survive.

At once the murmur arose on all sides, even from Dr. Wilson's detractors, that such a terrible thing could not be!—for Woodrow Wilson
was so clearly singled out for greatness; here was one who had seemed,
from his adolescent years, destined for a special fate.

And with news of Dr. Wilson's stroke there came news of its probable cause: just when it had seemed that the university president was to
emerge victorious from his long struggle with Dean Andrew West, Fate
cruelly reversed itself and Dean West triumphed instead.

(How had the canny dean of the graduate school brought off this
coup?—with what ingenuity, bred of low cunning and craftiness? By ar-
ranging that elderly Isaac Wyman agree not only to leave the university a
fortune of two million, five hundred thousand dollars, but to specify in his

will that this money must be administered by no one except Dean Andrew West.)

Hearing this crushing news, first brought to him in a handwritten missive from the dean of the faculty, and delivered by Matilde—(ashy-faced with knowing the content of the missive and what it would mean to her beloved Dr. Wilson)—Woodrow Wilson knew, on the afternoon of May 28, 1906, that all was lost; wanly sat at his desk, beneath the frowning portrait of Reverend Aaron Burr, Sr., stunned, open-mouthed; then, with but a murmur to Matilde, taking his leave of his office, and of Nassau Hall; staggering across campus oblivious of his surroundings, and to Prospect; there to seek commiseration from his astonished wife, and even for a brief spell to weep in her arms. "My enemy has triumphed at last," he said as Ellen tried to comfort him, "and if I know the man, he will eat my heart. My tenure at Princeton is over. I must resign. God only knows what awaits, if all the world learns of my defeat here! I can't appeal to the trustees to reject this request, as they'd done with the other—*this is two million, five hundred thousand dollars*. And it is destined for my enemy. How did it happen! How did the wretch bring it off? I had thought—oh, Ellen!—in my vanity I had truly thought—*God favors me, He will see me through this struggle. God is on my side*."

So distraught was Ellen West, so utterly caught up in her husband's suffering, the whispered words escaped her lips: "Oh, dear husband—*they have murdered you*."

EARLY THE NEXT morning Mrs. Wilson discovered her husband, following a sleepless night, collapsed on the floor of his tower study, or hideaway, where, it would be reported, the disappointed man had gone to write his letter of resignation to the board of trustees; senseless, unmoving, rigid as death, his widened left eye covered in blood and his face ossified in a grimace of rage.

IT IS CERTAINLY true, as all historians concur, that the precipitating cause of Woodrow Wilson's stroke of May 30, 1906, was the triumph of his nemesis West; yet, the cause of West's triumph has never been fully elucidated; nor is it the case that the dean himself knew how, unwitting, he had performed as a mere pawn in the general incursion of the Curse into the Princeton community. Which is to say, West's triumph was but *the triumph of the Curse in mortal guise.*

(I am not one of those who believe that Andrew West "dabbled" in the occult. I have never come across any convincing evidence supporting this rumor, that had been promulgated, as we have seen, in part by Dr. Wilson himself.)

As five of the controversial "Mrs. Peck" letters are extant, and determined by reputable Wilson scholars to be in his hand, the passion of Woodrow Wilson for this mysterious woman is no longer any secret; while in '06 it was known only to the principals and one other person—the Wilsons' youngest daughter Eleanor, or "Nellie." (It seems that Nellie chanced upon crumpled drafts of the incriminating letters among her father's papers in the tower; saw their nature, and destroyed them immediately, to prevent Mrs. Wilson discovering the affair. Shaken to the depths of her soul by this betrayal of her revered father, Nellie never said a word to anyone.) Yet, the damage had been done; the letters mailed; and the adventuress "Mrs. Cybella Peck" so indifferent to their worth, and their effect upon Woodrow Wilson's reputation, that she left them behind in her room in the Peacock Inn, where they were discovered by the canny innkeeper, and hidden away. These invaluable documents are not only items of great rarity, in that they throw a revealing—some might say exposing—light upon the man who was to become the twenty-eighth President of the United States; as they contain passages of a salacious nature, they are kept under lock and key in the Woodrow Wilson Special Collection and are forbidden to any but the most highly qualified scholars.

So it seems, mercifully, Mrs. Wilson was spared all knowledge of her husband's infatuation for another woman; and there is evidence to believe that Dr. Wilson, recovering from his stroke, remembered "Mrs. Cybella Peck" but vaguely, as one remembers, in fragments and elliptical images, the seductive hallucinations of a fever dream . . . appealing, and seductive still, but forever out of reach.

NEW HISTORICAL EVIDENCE suggests that it was Samuel Clemens who brought together the "Presbyterian priest" Wilson and the beautiful Mrs. Peck in Bermuda, on a whim: for the much-acclaimed American man of letters was known for the eccentricities of his humor, and often behaved wantonly, and cruelly, in his attempt to escape what he called the Bog Kingdom of Boredom.

So it was, Mr. Clemens thought it an entertaining prospect, and something of a scientific experiment, to suggest that the puritanical university president be invited to *Sans Souci,* and to see if Wilson would succumb to Mrs. Peck's wiles, as many another man before him, married or not. "It's no more malicious, and surely no more unnatural," Mr. Clemens murmured to himself, smoking his smelly Havana cigar, "than the act of introducing the male black widow spider to the female of the species. For, what is one doing but hastening the procedure of Nature, and thereby abridging the narrative?"

Of course, it is no secret that Sam Clemens was deeply in love with Cybella Peck himself. He had fallen under the woman's spell several years before while vacationing in Bermuda for reasons of health; and was fond of referring to himself as a "genial husk of a creature, demanding very little of the world and receiving always a dollop too much." His own infatuation with Mrs. Peck persevered, like a chronic illness, yet he believed that he enjoyed an enviable sort of invulnerability—"also known as impotence"—so far as the female sex was concerned. In Clemens's own droll phraseology, it seems that his passion for Havana cigars and Old Gran-Dad whiskey, employed at the start to nullify the tumult of his heart, soon took precedence over the tumult; and became more the objects of his desire than any flickerings of Romance had ever. Mr. Clemens proclaimed himself "dehorned by age" yet retaining the novelist-voyeur's playful interest in the vagaries of "other fools' sentimental attachments."

This historian regrets to report that, in his letters to his wife sent from Bermuda, Woodrow Wilson considerably misrepresented his relations with Cybella Peck! In, for instance, his letter of April 19, Dr. Wilson barely mentions her at all, except as the hostess of a luncheon at *Sans Souci;* it isn't altogether clear how, or why, Woodrow Wilson was invited to the luncheon. In a subsequent letter, Dr. Wilson disdainfully speaks of Mrs. Peck's *Botticelli beauty*—which he can't see; never does he indicate how enraptured he was with her, and how distracted from the work he'd brought with him to Bermuda. In fact, upon being ushered into the young woman's presence by a native butler clad in white, Dr. Wilson stared in boyish awe at his hostess, who was certainly the most beautiful woman he had ever seen at close range.

His immediate thought was a husbandly sort of embarrassment, or shame for his dear little wife, so much less attractive than the glorious Cybella—*Poor Ellen! A mercy she is not here.*

As the mistress of *Sans Souci* was known to be married to a very wealthy man, or was perhaps the heiress of a very wealthy family, so the mistress of *Sans Souci* was known to be of an "indefinable" age—clearly, she was not young; yet, her face had the mask-like beauty of a Greek statue, flawless and aloof. Her eyes were a curious golden-brown hue, and thick-lashed; her complexion pale as cream. Her smile, which was both demure and sensuous, revealed flawless white teeth—which feature made Dr. Wilson feel self-conscious, for his own teeth had become alarmingly decayed and mottled of late, and he feared extensive "gumwork" so much, he had avoided his Princeton dentist for months, canceling appointments Mrs. Wilson had made for him. Cybella Peck's hair was an uncommon silver-blond, giving to her features a lunar, and not an earthy, quality; it had been elaborately fashioned in a heavy braided coronet, and braided loops, entwined with camellias, suggestive of an early and more romantic era. She was wearing a Worth gown of burnished gold silk trimmed in ivory silk and styled with a Greek simplicity that belied its elegance and cost; and again Dr. Wilson felt a stab of embarrassment, for his poor dear Ellen whose pudgy figure rendered even attractive clothing dowdy.

When they were introduced by Mr. Clemens, Mrs. Peck smiled her dazzling smile and, extending her hand to be kissed, softly exclaimed: "Woodrow Wilson, is it! I have long hoped to make the acquaintance of the celebrated author of *Congressional Government*, and feel myself quite honored."

This was extraordinary. Woodrow Wilson could not believe his ears. It was not uncommon for people to claim an admiration for Dr. Wilson's *A History of the American People*, or *George Washington;* but to have read, and admired, the far more demanding *Congressional Government* was remarkable indeed. Confused and blushing like any schoolboy, and certainly not able to kiss the woman's proffered hand, Dr. Wilson made a stammered reply; blushed deeply; and was very grateful for Sam Clemens's presence. What a kindly man Clemens was, and how sympathetic with Woodrow Wilson, seeing the flash of panic in his eyes, as in one sinking beneath the surface of a treacherous sea.

Woodrow Wilson had long "mastered"—(or so he believed)—the full bag of tricks of platform speaking, which requires a receptive, uncritical audience, but as he knew, the art of sophisticated social conversation was quite beyond him; though Mrs. Peck seemed most impressed with all that he had to say, and plied him with intelligent questions of Princeton, and of the United States, and of the "future of the world" in the twentieth century, that he might speak with his customary fluency.

In this way, the first visit was a considerable success; and as he was preparing to take his leave, Mrs. Peck drew him aside to say that she hoped they would meet soon again, for it had been a very long time since she had encountered a gentleman of quite Dr. Wilson's mettle—"for vigor of intellect coupled with manliness of form."

(It should be noted that from that day forward, until the morning of his nearly fatal stroke, Woodrow Wilson carried in his breast pocket, in strictest secrecy, a single camellia petal that had fallen from Mrs. Peck's hair.)

THE SUBJECT OF Woodrow Wilson's relations with women is so complex, ambiguous, and frankly "controversial," this historian is reluctant to introduce it here; yet, I believe it should be recorded, for matters of historical accuracy, that no other gentleman in this entire chronicle except perhaps the raving lunatic Horace Burr was capable of such deliriums of passion as Thomas Woodrow Wilson—the very individual known to the world, as to history, as stiff, unbending, puritanical, and "priestly"!

For it seems to have happened that Woodrow Wilson fell in love with Cybella Peck at that first meet—at the proverbial "first sight." Even as he would write to his devoted wife letters invariably beginning *"My precious darling . . ."* virtually every day he was in Bermuda, yet his heart was taken captive by the mistress of *Sans Souci,* and he could think of little else, despite the protestations of the letters. In fact, so overcome with feeling was Dr. Wilson, he stayed up later on the first night to write the first of his numerous letters to *My precious Cybella,* though it is believed that he never mailed this letter to her.

Of the extant letters it is the second that ranges furthest afield, whether boastfully or naively: for the besotted Woodrow tells the object of his passion that "deep perturbations are natural to me, deep disturbances of the spirit"; he tells of a conversion experience he'd had at the age of sixteen—which the "miraculous" meeting with Cybella Peck had evoked. "This profound upheaval of my soul was stirred by the example of a pious and comely youth named Francis Brooke, a student at the Theological Seminary in Columbus, South Carolina, where my father taught.

Ah, his radiant powers of persuasion! I knew at once, Cybella, that a work of true grace had begun in my heart . . . The immediate consequence of the conversion was, of course, that I was admitted to adult membership in the church; the larger consequence, that I now comprehended the nature of Jesus Christ's love for mankind; and beyond this, the special hope that God had for me, that *I, Thomas Woodrow Wilson, was chosen for a singular task; that I must never yield to my enemies; and that God would preserve me until my task on earth was completed."*

For several pages Woodrow Wilson continues, the subject being his "rapture" at having met Cybella Peck, and his "deep and abiding gratitude" for his friendship with young Brooke, the "magnetic Christian" who had changed his life; then, realizing that he must bring his outpouring to an end, he speaks again of his great pleasure at making Mrs. Peck's acquaintance, and concludes with the hope that they will meet again very soon.

MUCH CRITICISM HAS been leveled against Woodrow Wilson for his sentiments regarding women, particularly since the turbulent years of the 1970s when the issue of "women's rights" was first raised, in a somewhat militant and hostile manner, not advantageous to one of Dr. Wilson's generation and background. (See Hellings, Skirmish, Kozdoi, and O'Stryker for the most extreme of *radical feminist* thinking on this subject.) Certainly, Dr. Wilson's general attitude toward women could not be deduced from the worshipful air of the "Cybella Peck" letters. It seems to have been Dr. Wilson's belief, widely shared by men of his era, that the "sacred role" of Woman was to inspire Man, as the "sacred role" of Man was to serve the state "devotedly, religiously, and loyally." In these beliefs, which Woodrow Wilson often uttered, he was confident he did not speak solely of and for himself but of and for America; and indeed, he did not doubt that America spoke through Woodrow Wilson, in a voice approximating that of the Almighty.

At the same time, Dr. Wilson was scarcely willing to play the fool in endorsing mere women as equal, let alone superior, to men. Indeed, he did not think they could be taken quite seriously as "citizens of the Republic."

He had once spoken sharply to Miss Wilhelmina Burr who'd been arguing in favor of women's suffrage, quite delighting his audience (including women), and inspiring general mirth through the room, by stating that, while he was adamantly opposed to handing over the vote to women, he was as adamantly opposed to arguing against it—"For the reason that there *are* no logical arguments against it."

"But why, then, Dr. Wilson, do you oppose voting rights for women?" Wilhelmina had asked, a flush rising into her handsome face; and Woodrow Wilson amused the room by saying, "I have told you, Miss Burr. I am 'adamantly opposed'—for no logical reason except *I am adamantly opposed.*"

More seriously, Dr. Wilson explained that he was, in truth, not opposed to female suffrage per se, but he feared it would have the pernicious effect of "doubling the vote" in most households and in this way bringing about "the useless enlargement of an already over-large and ill-educated electorate." As to the feminists' argument that, since the freeing of the slaves, Negro males were allowed the vote (at least theoretically, in certain regions of the country), it should then follow that women be given the vote, Dr. Wilson's rejoinder was a witty: "Two wrongs, ladies, cannot make a right."

The suffragette movement filled Woodrow Wilson, as it filled many men of his time, with both loathing and trepidation, for it seemed to him "abnormal" for women to behave in an "unwomanly" fashion; which could not fail to lead to promiscuity among the sexes and a general collapse of morals. For wasn't it the case that women like his very own dear wife Ellen were provided by God with a quality of sympathy and support that, in turn, provided men with the necessary strength to combat evil? And what if this strength were undermined, or sabotaged? "All the sex will give over to crude Amazonian postures," Dr. Wilson prophesied, "and we men shall be so intimidated, the species might end within a generation."

Yet more repulsive was the thought, if women were allowed the vote, might it then follow that *women would run for political office?* The very thought was outrageous!

"Imagine, a female senator! A female President! The United States would be the laughingstock of the world."

Along lighter lines, Woodrow Wilson could not resist a jest or two at the expense of the crusading suffragettes. He thought both Elizabeth Cady Stanton and Susan B. Anthony were "noisome harridans, whose bile was the consequence of their ugly faces." He thought the Seneca Falls Convention of 1848 was the "root of all present evil—the original witches' brew." Only Mrs. Julia Ward Howe escaped his censure, striking the eye as an agreeable and motherly old lady whose wild notions could not possibly offend anyone.

So far as Dr. Wilson's own womenfolk were concerned, Ellen Wilson and their three daughters assured Woodrow that they did not wish to vote, fully trusting to men in such matters.

The tale was many times reiterated through generations of Princeton students, of President Wilson's refusal to be swayed to any violation of his academic and moral principles, by womanly ploys. For instance, in the spring of 1904 a well-born widow from Washington, D.C., made an appointment to speak to him, to appeal to him to reinstate her son, who had been expelled from the university in his senior year for the crime of *keeping a mistress*—(indeed, just across from Old Nassau, in an apartment above the Bank of Princeton). Dressed in mourning, for the distraught woman had lost her husband only months before, she made her case to Dr. Wilson along personal lines: stating that her son had already suffered "deep mortification" and that his entire family shared in his shame; and that she herself was soon to undergo surgery for the removal of a tumor, and believed that her chances for survival were threatened if this ignoble disgrace was allowed to stand.

Though Woodrow Wilson listened politely and sympathetically to the petition, he was resolved not to weaken, for it was a principle of his that he never changed his mind "once he turned the key." To the tearful widow he said, with regret: "Among undergraduates at Princeton, Madame, the only offense of greater moral turpitude than drunkenness is *impurity*. It's an unfortunate development that your health has been endangered by your son's disgraceful behavior, but this is not the fault of the university, Madame, nor is it mine. If I am forced to choose between equal justice in our university, and your life, Madame, I am forced, I fear, to choose the former."

THE DAY PRECEDING Woodrow Wilson's stroke, which was the very afternoon of his final assignation with the female known as "Cybella Peck," Dr. Wilson spent much time in agitated brooding; and whether at last he might summon forth the strength to speak his heart to his beloved Cybella as he'd managed to speak his heart in his letters to her; whether he might seize her hand in his and press his lips passionately against it. In Bermuda, in the haze of late-hour soirees at *Sans Souci*, there had been fleeting and ambiguous intimacies . . . but these seemed to fade, like dreams in daylight.

"Madness to be in love, like a schoolboy! And at such a precarious time in my life." In a misery of bliss, Dr. Wilson regarded himself in a mirror: the long, lean, lantern-jaw and glass-glittering eyes. He was thrilled to imagine what Andrew West would think, if West saw Cybella Peck and Woodrow Wilson together!

Since the wooded acres beyond Battle Road were not often frequented by Princetonians at this time, being adjacent to the famed Battle Field at the edge of the village, Woodrow Wilson arranged for Mrs. Peck, who had traveled to Princeton expressly to see him, to meet him there, shortly past four o'clock; making his excuse in Nassau Hall that he had an urgent medical appointment.

In all, Mrs. Peck and Woodrow Wilson met in secret only a very few times, I think; some historians argue that they didn't meet in any "intimate" setting at all; yet it seems likely that this rendezvous, in this idyllic place, occurred but once.

In Princeton, to which she claimed she was drawn "by the power of your pen, dear Woodrow," Cybella Peck took a suite of rooms at the Peacock Inn on Bayard Lane; but of course her lover could not meet her anywhere in the vicinity of the Inn. Woodrow felt the strain of their love more obviously than did Mrs. Peck; he suffered the pangs of guilt that married men commonly feel in such circumstances, yet, like these married men, he did not wish to alter his situation in the slightest, for nothing gave him more exhilaration, more joy, more hope. Yet, as the affair was (seemingly) unconsummated, and indeed very far from being consummated, Woodrow rarely felt any compensatory sense of triumph, elation, or mere animal gratification.

(Poor Ellen Wilson! Like many wives of unfaithful spouses, she felt quite clearly the agitation in her husband's soul; yet, in her naiveté, Ellen Wilson attributed Woodrow's condition to his ongoing battles with the dean of the Graduate College and the eating clubs on Prospect, that showed no signs of being resolved. It was the more frightening for Ellen that she had had firsthand experience with madness as a young girl, when her minister-father succumbed to acute psychotic rages in middle age, alternating with melancholia; and had died by his own hand, most shamefully, on May 30, 1884—by a cruel irony of fate, twenty-two years to the day before her husband's stroke.)

On the humid spring afternoon of May 29, as the hour of four o'clock drew nearer, Woodrow Wilson taxed himself with worry that Cybella Peck would not appear at the edge of Battle Park; then, he taxed himself with worry that she would appear, and he would be "undone, utterly."

Capable of baring his heart in prose, in letters, Woodrow greatly feared losing "self-control" in the presence of another person. For no one, not even Ellen, had any sense of the "perturbations" locked within his breast.

Yet there was no need for worry, for there was Cybella Peck at the edge of the woods, awaiting him like a figure in a pre-Raphaelite painting: in a flounced muslin dress of an older style, consisting of numerous frothy layers of strawberry-tinted material, and trimmed with ribbon of a subtly darker hue, ingeniously woven into the stitching. Mrs. Peck was slowly turning a white parasol over her shoulder; on her head was a broad-rimmed straw hat with a satin band that matched her dress, and on her fingers white lace gloves. A very fine veil obscured the luster of her eyes. The impression produced upon Woodrow Wilson's overwrought nerves was that of a precious orchid transposed by magic to a northern woods, so it was little wonder that, even as he hurried to greet her, his courage drained from him, to a degree. "Ah, dear Cybella! You have come . . ."

Having picked in stealth a little bouquet of sweet alyssum and miniature iris from his wife's garden behind Prospect, Woodrow presented this to Cybella, who accepted it with a happy smile, and affixed it to the belted waist of her dress.

Politely then, Mrs. Peck inquired after Dr. Wilson's health and well-being: "For you look, dear Tommy, as if you have lost your 'golden' Bermuda tan altogether, in just a few weeks!" Dr. Wilson felt obliged to reply in some detail of his usual crises of digestion, nerves, vision, spinal column "irregularities," and "aching gums," as Mrs. Peck listened with as much attentiveness as Ellen Wilson would have done.

"We will find a way to 'transcend' such crises, dear Tommy. You must have faith in me."

The lovers walked in Battle Field, along a faintly trodden path of sunshine and shade; Mrs. Peck's arm slipped through Woodrow's, and exerted a delightful pressure upon it.

Mrs. Peck complained, in the way of one who means to entertain, and not to aggrieve, of the "unwanted attentions" of an "importunate suitor" who had recently "re-inserted himself" in her life: one of the most renowned of American writers, praised as being to America what Shakespeare was to England. It was partly this problem, as Mrs. Peck explained, that had brought her to Princeton to meet with Woodrow, that is "Tommy"—for she wanted advice from a gentleman of Dr. Wilson's intelligence and sensitivity. What was she to do?—which way to turn? For the undesired suitor was a widower, and very lonely; he had loved her some years ago, futilely, and she had thought that the fever had passed; yet now again he was plaguing her with declarations of love, unwanted letters, and ill-written verse—"For he has no talent for poetry, Tommy, as you do. He is all crude, crushing *prose*."

Woodrow Wilson felt a stab of jealousy, and rage: for he knew that this unwanted suitor had to be Sam Clemens, his rival. Excitedly he said, "If you have asked him to desist, he is not a gentleman to persevere. You must reject him absolutely. I think—I believe—he is not a moral man: he is a cynic, and an atheist, and a drunkard."

"Indeed! I think you are right, Tommy. Yes . . ."

"You might consider moving to Princeton, taking lodgings here—to avoid him . . . I could help you, of course—if but indirectly . . ."

Noting how agitated her companion had become, Mrs. Peck changed the subject, now asking Dr. Wilson how his administrative work was progressing; and whether his "difficulties" were close to being resolved. This prompted a lengthy monologue ranging from any contempt for his "backbiting" enemies, to subdued pride in the rumor that certain New Jersey Democratic "kingmakers" were speculating about Woodrow Wilson's qualifications for governor of the state.

"Governor of the state! This is wonderful news," Cybella Peck said, "of which I've heard, I should tell you, just a little. And will your enemies be crushed, if this comes about?"

"If I were to be elected governor, yes—they would be crushed. That is, if they don't crush me beforehand."

"Why, what do you mean?"

"As president of the university. Here, I am frantically *vulnerable*."

So the couple walked at the edge of the Battle Field, slowly, in deep and earnest conversation; an observer would note the awkward height of the gentleman, and the graceful strawberry-tinted figure of the lady. At times, the lady inclined her head toward the gentleman's shoulder, as if unconsciously.

Then, Cybella Peck paused; and raised her veil from her eyes, to look at Woodrow Wilson frankly, and to receive his full admiring gaze; and told him, in a childlike voice, that she had deceived him, in a way, by not fully identifying herself; that she was *not what she seemed*.

"'Cybella Peck,' yes—to a degree. But in fact, to speak truthfully, I am Countess Cybella de Barhegen, and I am not an American-born citizen but a 'naturalized' citizen, since the age of twenty."

"'Countess!'"—Woodrow Wilson blinked and gaped in awe.

"I have not wanted to confess to my American friends, unlike my dear comrade English von Gneist, who never hesitates to spread out his pedigree on the ground, to be walked-upon by anyone who wishes, that I am a so-called full-blooded European aristocrat of the ancient house of Barhegen, in northern Germany. I am a 'countess' not only by birth but through marriage; and that a most ironic and bitter bond, indeed." In a lowered voice Cybella said, "A countess doubly, dear Tommy; that is my fate. A married woman, not entirely by volition. And now I have fled the Old World, and want nothing more than to establish a new life here . . . You are looking curious, I think? You are wondering about my husband? The shame of it is, my family married me off to the Count Hugo de Barhegen, a widower of some sixty years of age . . . and the father of children older than I, for I was only eighteen at the time. In short, dear Tommy, it eventually came to this: I found myself so unhappy in my 'blessed' marital state, as a consequence of certain conjugal customs said to be commonplace in central Europe, that I began to plot my escape. I was without friends, and my family would have disowned me; my step-children were brutes, wanting only to use me; at the nadir of my misery late one night, hidden away from my husband in a remote wing of the Castle Barhegen, I fell upon my knees and petitioned God for mercy—so very violently, and with such passion, a burst of light ensued in the room and a presence materialized which I took at first to be a form of God Himself, but which was in fact an archangel— (have you ever seen one, dear Tommy? No?)—suffused in nearly blinding radiance, both splendid and terrifying, as you can imagine."

Woodrow Wilson gazed in awe at the beautiful Cybella—Countess Cybella! In his life as an intensely devout Christian, a Presbyterian for whom the religious life was of paramount significance, he had not ever seen, still less been visited by, an archangel.

"Yes, dear Tommy—you are right to look at me with such sensitivity—compassion, yet a kind of pity—for it was not an 'easy' experience for me, at my young age, and in my desperate circumstances; as all mystics have recorded, an experience of the 'visionary' sears the soul; you cannot truly know if you live, or have died. Or if you are in the presence of the godly, or the demonic. So confused and frightened was I at the time, I didn't fully comprehend the archangel's message; but the substance seemed to be that I had wished in my heart for death and had thereby committed in my heart the sin of *suicide;* and so, if I wished, my accursed mortality might be absolved by God, and my spiritual being devoted for all time to God's employ. Which is to say, my dear friend, that I was in a position to escape both my bestial husband and the natural consequences of my own sin, if I consented to taking my place amid the community of spirits whose function, in God's great scheme, is to perform as a *devi*—an angelic messenger."

Cybella Peck paused, that Woodrow Wilson might absorb her remarkable words. There was a look of strain in her face, very different from the woman's usual bright social manner; her pressure on Woodrow's arm increased, as if she required his strength to support her.

"A—*devi*? 'Angelic messenger'? Can it be—?"

"Tommy, yes. You alone know my secret. Sam Clemens has teased and tormented me, calling me an 'angel'—'his guardian angel'—but the man has no awareness of what he is saying; for he does not believe, and I'm afraid his tortured soul will be tortured forever—in Hell. You, dear Tommy, are totally different: you can be entrusted with my secret. If I'd seemed to you, in Bermuda, a sophisticate of international society; if I seem to you now a descendant of an ancient race, with pretensions to nobility; if, indeed, I sometimes struck you as 'chill' and 'artificial'—why then, my dear friend, I must confide in you, and you alone, that I am an agent of the Higher Power, and not a mortal woman at all."

With this revelation Mrs. Peck leaned against Woodrow Wilson's arm; she placed a gloved hand on his wrist, as if to calm his pounding heart; for it was clear that Dr. Wilson was shaken by this revelation, and did not know what to think.

In a quiet voice Cybella Peck reiterated some of what she had said, that might have bypassed the distracted man; and went on to explain further her life subsequent to the angelic visitation, which had been years ago in fact, long before her "new, virgin" life in the United States.

"I think it must be your modesty, Tommy, that draws me to you. And your modesty that prevents you from quite comprehending why a *devi* might be employed to communicate with you intimately. But, you see—angels will appear to men who deserve and require them at crucial times in their lives, when God has need to make His intentions clearly known."

In such a way the seductive Mrs. Peck enumerated past histories of angelic visitations to men of significance, whose histories Woodrow knew well—Gladstone, Napoleon, Alexander the Great, General George Washington on the eve of his brilliant attack of 26 December 1776 on the unsuspecting Hessians at Trenton. All these accounts, Woodrow listened to with grave intensity. At last saying, with an involuntary smile of his pale lips, "It is true, it is true—as Father promised."

" 'Father'—?"

"My father. When I was a boy. 'Angelic messengers'—'a special destiny'—he seemed to know. Yes," Woodrow said, wiping at his eyes, "he *knew*."

"And is your dear father still living, Tommy?"

"No! He is not."

"Yet, from Heaven he can observe you—your career. You can be sure of this."

"I—I sometimes hope . . ."

"Except, dear Tommy, there is a particular reason that I am here today, as you must know. For a *devi*, nothing is accidental; all is part of the great scheme. You are not aware of the danger you are in—at this very moment, in Boston, your unscrupulous rival at the university has all but convinced an elderly alumnus to leave a large sum of money to Princeton, with the restriction that he be named executor—more than two million dollars, to be specific. Consider the insult to the university itself, that an outsider, even a very wealthy alumnus, should presume to dictate university policy! Soon it will follow that 'robber barons'—like the notorious Andrew Carnegie—will seize control of the highest educational institutions, by dangling gifts of large sums of money before administrators, and by outright bribes to them. Corrupt politicians, outright criminals: will they not want to erect monuments to themselves, and endanger the idealism and innocence of youth? And all this follows from Andrew West's manipulation of an impressionable old man in Boston, who is easily flattered as the descendant of a Revolutionary War hero; who cannot tell a flatterer from—a gentleman-administrator like you. (For I think you visited Mr. Wyman last year? With no satisfactory result?) It's a pity, and a tragedy; yet all is not lost, for the purpose of my visit is not only to alert you to the imminent disaster, but to suggest to you a course of action that will change all."

Mrs. Peck paused, allowing Woodrow to absorb this yet more staggering news. Dazedly he asked if it could be true—"Wyman is about to capitulate to West, and destroy me utterly?" Seeing how shaken Woodrow was, and how damp his pallid forehead, Mrs. Peck removed a lace handkerchief from a pocket, and dabbed at his heated skin.

" 'A course of action that will change all'—how?"

"As I am ordained by a Higher Power, Tommy, transcending merely human notions of justice, morality, 'right or wrong,' so I am ordained also to thwart the dean's plan; even, if necessary, rid the world of his evil influence. That is—if you should wish it."

Quietly Cybella Peck spoke. But Woodrow Wilson heard clearly.

" 'Rid the world of his evil influence'—? If *I* should wish it?"

"The Almighty is concerned that His plan for you may be sabotaged, before it has quite evolved. The Almighty has reason to know that the dean may leap into the Devil's camp—and bring more disaster upon this troubled community." Now Cybella spoke matter-of-factly, looking frankly into Woodrow Wilson's astonished eyes. "The unrest here of late, and through the country generally, follows from the failure of strong leadership to assert itself, whether from the governing bodies, the pulpit, or the university; this must be known to you. The 'bestial' killings in Princeton . . . the 'tragic deaths' . . . If Andrew West's coup is allowed to take place, the man will never rest until he has shamed you out of office and crowned himself president of the university. (Grover Cleveland has said that he doesn't plan to die until he sees his friend inaugurated!) All this goes strongly against the plan of the Almighty that Woodrow Wilson is to triumph at Princeton, and enjoy a long reign, like certain of your distinguished predecessors, prior to continuing with a public career in government, and ending as a *statesman* . . . So, this obstacle must be dealt with immediately."

"—*statesman*? When my stock is so low here at Princeton . . ."

"Tommy, a brilliant career lies before you, if you do not weaken. Princeton now—Trenton tomorrow—Washington, D.C., thereafter; from there, the world itself one day, united as a sort of 'league' or 'club' with the American President at the head . . . Dear friend, your eyes are glassy, and your manner stricken; where is the razor-sharp look of old, which so many have feared?"

Woodrow apologized for his slowness to respond, and his failure to quite comprehend all that was being explained to him. He hoped he would be forgiven, but he felt "very queer"; as if a "great pressure" were building inside his head; and he could not catch his breath, in this humid spring air.

"Tommy, sit down! Here in the grass. We will sit together, as the Almighty looks over us."

In the tall, unmowed grass at the edge of the Battle Field woods, the couple sat, somewhat awkwardly; for Woodrow Wilson was wholly unaccustomed to such a behavior, and had probably not sat on the ground since he'd been a boy. Very close by, Mrs. Peck gathered her strawberry-tinted skirts becomingly around her, and sank down into the grass, and took up her parasol again to shade her flawless complexion, as she spoke, quietly, yet urgently, to her shaken lover: "You have only to indicate to me, dear Tommy, by a squeeze of your hand, if you want your *devi* to fulfill your wish—if it is indeed your wish that the evil represented by Andrew West be eradicated, at once. Before you, then, will lie a triumphant reign here at Princeton, including the banning of the eating clubs, at last; you will be favorably compared to your predecessors Winslow Slade and James McCosh. Even greater honors will follow, in my Master's scheme for you, leading to such heights, your old enemies will have to crane their necks to gape up at you. A time of terrible devastation lies ahead for Europe; a time of sacrifice, for young American soldiers, who will be sent to 'make the world safe for democracy'; yet you will triumph, and one day you will hear orisons of worship through war-torn Europe, in Italy in particular—seas of adoring Italians chanting your name in the squares of Rome—*Viva Voovro Veelson! Viva Voovro Veelson!*"

Woodrow shook his head as if to wake from a dream, and in a faint voice queried: "'*Voovro Veelson*'—why cannot my name be pronounced properly? Is it in mockery? In jest? I don't like to travel far from home, Cybella; my nerves, and my stomach, can't tolerate it . . . My dear Cybella, you are frightening me—I feel very queer indeed."

"Tommy, you surprise me. That *Woodrow Wilson* should stare at me in such a craven way, and show so little enthusiasm for my Master's plan. In an instant you could rid yourself of Andrew West—my Master has the power to strike him down as one crushes a fat beetle beneath his foot; and by this you triumph here at home, and can lord it over that gang of palsied old fools, the 'board of trustees,' whose boots you are very tired of licking, you know; and you will drive that tub-of-guts Cleveland into an early grave—if not quite early enough. Your dear wife Ellen, suspecting nothing, will be delighted for you; your daughters will adore you yet more, and suitable husbands may emerge for them, who are now holding back, to see how your shaky career proceeds. As for the faculty here—once you've set your foot on their necks they are yours forever, for they are of a cowardly disposition, and will not make any trouble if you pay them reasonably, and invite them to Prospect House from time to time. Once done, as I've said, 'tis done forever; and all will lie before you, Dr. Wilson—*all of the world*."

In a vague hopeful voice Woodrow said, as much to himself as to Mrs. Peck, " . . . Father did seem to foresee. His hand upon my shoulder, his voice ringing . . . *my son will be a great man*. Yet, Cybella, it's very strange: I don't actually seem to feel any 'ambition'—beyond Princeton. It is really all that I require. I have never liked Europe—only England and Scotland. My nerves are irritated by 'foreign accents'—the mangling of English. I have no use for the so-called cultures of France, Spain, Italy, Greece, even Germany; the Catholic countries are contemptible, under the directive of the pope. I do not know and can't greatly care if the Alps are in Italy, or in Switzerland, or Belgium; if Baghdad be in Persia, or Constantinople, or Mexico. All may be heaped on the banks of the Zuider Zee, so far as I am concerned." Feebly he laughed, having meant these latter remarks as a joke.

"Tommy! This is not like you. Remember your father's hope for you, and your own secret desires. From boyhood you've sought your destiny—if but indirectly. And now I, as a *devi*, the first of my kind to visit Princeton, and perhaps the last, have been designed by the Almighty to act in your behalf—with no consequences for you except good."

" 'No consequences'—? No one would know?"

"Of course, no one would know. Andrew West would vanish—'of natural causes.' "

" 'Natural causes' . . ."

"Dear Tommy, you sound like a parrot! But a timid sort of parrot, not at all the bold, visionary statesman that is the essential Woodrow Wilson."

In the distance, Old North was tolling the hour of five: so swiftly, an hour had passed! It was Woodrow's custom to dine promptly at six o'clock, at Prospect, if there were no guests. Fumbling at his collar, which had grown terribly tight, Woodrow wondered aloud what he must do . . .

"Do?"—Cybella Peck's voice had grown perceptibly sharper, and was tinged now with sarcasm. "Why, you have to *do* nothing. What have you ever actually *done*, my friend? You are a talker, a commander . . . you tell others what to do. You need but give me your consent, a mere squeeze of your hand on mine, and the vainglorious West will topple dead in the midst of his enormous breakfast tomorrow at Merwick—an instantaneous stroke, that will give him no pain."

By degrees, Cybella Peck's voice was growing vehement, impatient; she was turning her parasol restlessly on her shoulder; gazing with a disbelieving contempt at her companion, who seemed scarcely aware of her any longer as a female presence of exquisite beauty. His lips moved numbly: " 'No pain'. . . . that is a mercy. Andrew will overeat—overindulge . . . His blood pressure, it's said, is dangerously high. Yet, what an appetite! It is a pity . . . yet he is of the Devil's party, that's clear . . . well, I will miss him. . . . Countess, I feel so very queer, I hope you will forgive me."

"Your consent, sir," Cybella Peck said, with a forced smile, "and your forgiveness afterward. If you'd rather not express your secret wish aloud you might just nod your head or . . ."

Yet Woodrow Wilson continued to brood, while his vague fingers groped at his jaw; and Cybella Peck was growing increasingly impatient. "The world is all before me, as Father predicted . . . if Andrew but topples over dead. So simply! He would not feel a thing . . . He and I are of an age when such things can happen . . . indeed, I suffered a 'minor' stroke at the young age of thirty-nine . . . from which I did recover. . . while Andrew, you say, will not recover?" As Cybella drew out her fan, and again snapped it open, and began to fan herself vigorously, Woodrow continued, musing: "I think that I could indeed affect the course of history—the destiny of nations—God's will translated into politics. The tariff has long been an abomination to me, as to all Democrats; I think that I could easily 'go

Teddy one better' and put strength into the anti-trust laws; and give federal assistance more liberally, to undercut the power of the labor unions. Yet I wonder, Countess, if there hasn't been some misunderstanding—you have mistaken me for someone else . . ."

Mrs. Peck said at once that that was unlikely. Her tone was now transparently ironic. "There is only one 'Thomas Woodrow Wilson,' I think. Are you saying that you reject us? The plan of the Almighty, to be enacted through *you*?"

Tugging at his high starched collar Woodrow Wilson said, more forcibly, as if he had been gathering strength, sitting so awkwardly on the ground with no instinctive sense of how, or where, to place his long, lanky legs, "Even if I wished this advancement, Countess, I could not accept it at the cost of another's life—not even at the cost of another's suffering . . . No, I can't wish Andrew West dead under any circumstances."

"And do you think West would be so magnanimous toward you?"

"I—I—I can't think—that he would be less magnanimous . . . For there is Jesus's admonition that we must love our enemies, and do unto others as we would they did unto us." Woodrow spoke slowly, with the air of one picking his way through a difficult passage. "But the primary reason I must reject your offer, Mrs. Peck, is simply that *I do not want to injure my enemy for any reward whatsoever, still less for revenge.*"

Now Mrs. Peck responded with scarcely concealed rage: "Suppose it is the case, Dr. Wilson, that the dean's fate will fall upon you tomorrow morning, as his substitute? That my Master, impatient with your feuding, and with your mutual appeals to the Higher Powers for aid, has decreed that one of you must be struck down? Might you be prepared then to change your mind?"

The troubled Dr. Wilson had been fumbling with his pince-nez, to fix them more securely on his perspiring face; and now made an effort to stare at the woman with some trace of his old "power"—unfortunately, almost entirely drained from his watering eyes. But in a voice that quavered with certainty, he said: "If you knew me, Countess, you would know that

I never change my mind once I have made a decision. *The key is turned in the lock, and thrown away.*"

The strain of this lengthy conversation was such that Woodrow Wilson was exhausted, and came close to losing consciousness; indeed, he may have lost consciousness for a fleet moment. Lying on the grass in his ministerial suit, white shirt and necktie, he opened his eyes to see the sky lurching above him, like an abyss into which he was in danger of falling; and there was the sun, in the western sky, swollen, throbbing against his very brow. Though he'd tugged his collar open he could not, it seemed, *breathe.*

"Countess? Where . . ."

When the spell passed, Woodrow sat up, disoriented. He was alone: his companion had vanished, without a word of farewell; and had left carelessly behind, on the grass beside him, unless she'd flung it down in disgust, the little bouquet of alyssum and iris he'd given her from his wife's garden—the delicate flowers now yellowed and withered and the leaves so dry, they crumbled to dust when he touched them.

POSTSCRIPT:
"THE SECOND BATTLE OF PRINCETON"

The rest is history.

For of course it happened as the "Countess de Barhegen" prophesied: Isaac Chauncy Wyman did indeed pledge a gift of two million, five hundred thousand dollars to Princeton University, stipulating that the dean of the Graduate School, Andrew West, must oversee the money in the construction of a graduate school of his design.

When notified of the bequest, the elated West traveled at once to Boston by train, to thank Mr. Wyman in person—(as, some eighteen months later, the dean would travel to Boston to attend Mr. Wyman's funeral, and to lay a sprig of ivy on Wyman's casket, taken from the outer wall of Nassau Hall). From Boston, West would wire triumphant cables to several of the university trustees, who had been his staunch supporters through the years of the Wilson/West struggle—

TE DEUM LAUDAMUS. NON NOBIS, DOMINE.

By this time Woodrow Wilson had been struck down in his tower at Prospect, felled by a "massive" stroke.

So ended, sadly for Dr. Wilson, the "Second Battle of Princeton."

DR. DE SWEINITZ'S PRESCRIPTION

After Woodrow Wilson's stroke of May 30, 1906, the distinguished Philadelphia physician Wilhelm de Sweinitz was summoned to Princeton by the trustees of the university, that an expert verdict might be offered on the subject of Dr. Wilson's future health.

In the interim, Dr. Wilson's longtime physician Dr. Hatch, in collaboration with Dr. Boudinot, seemed to have antagonized the Wilson family by suggesting that Dr. Wilson appoint an acting president of the university; and seriously consider resigning his office, to return to a less demanding professorial schedule. After twelve days of severe disability, Dr. Wilson began to "rally" despite the fact that the vision in his left eye had all but vanished, seemingly forever; his ability to flex the fingers of his right hand seemed permanently impaired; and neuritis of the left shoulder and leg had lately grown so painful, paralysis might be imminent. Most worrisome to the physicians were the convalescent's mercurial swings of mood: from despair, to euphoria; from extreme caution, to certitude on all matters; to bouts of sardonic laughter, and bouts of despairing tears. Yet, the invalid was soon "up and walking"—with a cane; and his speech, though hesitant and slurred, gradually strengthened, like an atrophied muscle returned to use.

Woodrow Wilson would not hear of appointing an "acting president"—not while he was alive!

As befitting a specialist of high repute, Dr. de Sweinitz examined his patient with painstaking thoroughness and assembled a medical history by closely querying Dr. Wilson's Princeton physicians, and not only Dr. Wilson and his wife and daughters, and certain of his associates, but even the household staff at Prospect, as to the man's habitual behavior. Dr. de Sweinitz estimated that Woodrow Wilson had suffered, prior to 1906, at least *fourteen breakdowns* in mental and physical health; mincing no words, he diagnosed *arterio-sclerosis* as a consequence of prolonged high pressure on brain and nerves.

Mrs. Wilson pleaded with the Philadelphia physician, not to make such a diagnosis public. "A dying by inches, is it not? What then of Woodrow's career?"

Nonetheless, Dr. de Sweinitz insisted upon his conclusion, and suggested an uncompromising prescription.

"The patient's medical history is such, I must advise him not only to retire from his presidency here, but to retire from the academic world altogether. He must 'close up shop' at once. In addition, he must give up all pretensions of a *public life;* most of all, his habit of speechifying, which is a kind of insidious myth-building: erecting mere opinions and fancies into pontifical orations, much repeated and calcified, declaimed on public platforms before an audience. Also, Mrs. Wilson," Dr. de Sweinitz said, more severely, "he must give up his habit of reading books: for a man of Dr. Wilson's temperament can't read another man's line without wishing to combat it, which inevitably leads to 'vocalizing' his thoughts, and thereby to speechifying. He is plagued by *ceaseless thinking,* like wheels churning in mud. This has caused his high blood pressure, and a strain to all the nerves and vital organs." At this the distinguished physician paused, for he himself had worked up a nervous intensity, signaled by a quavering of his voice. "I must therefore advise that your husband retire from thinking as well, for he cannot think without wanting to write and speechify—a pathological circle from which we must save him, else he is prematurely doomed."

As Ellen Wilson wiped tears from her eyes, Dr. de Sweinitz took pity on her yet further, saying that if Dr. Wilson followed his advice, and took all the medications prescribed him, she and her daughters could expect to have him with them for some years more—"No less than five, I would estimate, Mrs. Wilson, and perhaps as many as seven. *But he must never yield to thinking in the old way again.*"

THE CURSE EXORCISED

Historians are in general agreement that June 4, 1906, marks the date of the "exorcism" of the Curse on the Princeton community, being *coincidentally* the date of the death of Winslow Slade; but none has yet attempted to link the events in any convincing manner. Hollinger's feeble thesis—that the "energies of Evil" had simply run their course, and that the "dead" grandchildren of Winslow Slade had never really died—has been the most commonly accepted.

Fresh evidence, however, to which I alone am privy, suggests that matters are not quite that simple.

The challenge for this historian is tremendous, however: my task is to evoke *simultaneity* in two very different, even antithetical dimensions, being bound to a linear narrative in which chronological time is the organizing principle. That is, the reader has a reasonable expectation of encountering, in a work of history, something of the causality of his actual life—if X occurs, Y follows; from Y, Z follows. It is never the case in actual life that time runs backward, unless in science-fiction films; for all of us, time moves forward, inexorably. Yet, we are fully comfortable with the idea that many, countless many events are occurring *simultaneously*—most of them beyond our awareness; and that these events may be linked in intricate ways.

In my chronicle, the reader is required to know that Winslow Slade departed this life in the very pulpit of the First Presbyterian Church where he was delivering a guest sermon; that his death was unexpected, and terrifying to behold for the congregation many of whom loved the elderly man dearly, and all respected him; and that this death coincided with, or may have followed by a moment or two, Todd Slade's triumph in the Bog Kingdom. (This would have been approximately 10:20 A.M. EST, in Princeton; but at no recorded hour in the Bog Kingdom, as in that region seasons seem not to exist as in our world, and calendar and clock time serve no purpose.)

Following later in the day are the miraculous developments involving Dr. Slade's "deceased" grandchildren, of which I will speak in due course.

So it is, I will present the chapter "A Game of Draughts" first, and "The Death of Winslow Slade" second, asking that the reader keep in mind the fact that the events they record occurred *simultaneously*.

A GAME OF DRAUGHTS

Here was a novelty, and something of a shock: a child in the Bog Kingdom after so many centuries.

So tattered was the boy's clothing, so disheveled and sickly his appearance, he was believed at first to be a mere urchin or beggar-boy, or a chimney sweep cast out by his master, in an early stage of lung disease. But the Countess Camilla, drawn by servants' excited chatter, perceived that he was a decent boy, perhaps even well bred, and decided upon a whim to take him in, and save his life. *For one day my life may want saving, and here is an investment.*

When one of the Countess's retinue observed that taking in a strange child might go over poorly with the Master of the castle, the Countess said haughtily: "You've heard my wish. It's enough to *hear* it, I hope, to *obey*."

So it happened that Todd Slade gained entry to the mist-shrouded castle at the heart of the Bog Kingdom, which fact would precipitate the deaths of his family's enemies.

"YOUR LIFE HAS been saved, Rat-boy," the Countess Camilla said, not unkindly, "and now you must repay me. What qualities have you? Can you sing, can you dance, can you tell stories?"

When the boy did not immediately speak, being in a state of numbed shock, like one who has been propelled through time and through space bare-headed, exposed and with no protection, the Countess said, "Will you play mute, boy?—and tempt me to forget my good intentions?"

At first, the boy seemed incapable of responding. Then, with the air of one who must react, to save his life, he slowly shook his head—*No.*

"You are not mute, then?" The Countess was both vexed and amused. "Except you don't speak, eh?"

And again the boy shook his head slowly—*No.*

As the Bog Castle lay beneath a dread weight of *ennui,* the inevitable curse of a seasonless and timeless land, it was hoped for a while that the foundling child might provide a suitable diversion for Countess Camilla, who'd had no child of her own. She ordered Rat-boy bathed in her own sumptuous marble bath, in clouds of effervescent bubbles; and surfeited with every manner of sweet and liqueurs, until he grew ghastly pale, and was sick to his stomach—a novelty in the Bog Kingdom, and a particular revulsion to the Countess, who commanded that Rat-boy be taken from her quickly, anywhere out of her sight.

Yet, not long afterward, the Countess commanded that the spindly-limbed boy, who looked to be about eleven or twelve years old, in Earth-time, be dressed in an embroidered silk costume, complete with ruffled white blouse and kidskin boots, that he might perform as her page. "He's but a child and harmless. If he begins to sprout a beard, and hairs in his armpits, the Master will kill him, or castrate him—but not for a while, I hope. In the meantime, our household has been too long empty of childish laughter which is *unpremeditated laughter.*" So the queenly Camilla whose pale golden eyes snapped even when she smiled and whose will was not to be thwarted within the castle walls, except by her brother the Count.

For Countess and Count were not wife and husband but sister and brother and between them there was no deep bond of love but only of the more sinister primordial *blood.*

Once bathed, and his hair brushed and curled, and his frayed and filthy clothing cast away and replaced by a costume suitable for the Count-ess's page, Rat-boy was attended by the Countess's own servants, and fussed over by certain of the women; kissed, petted, and proclaimed as an a *angel-child* by Countess Camilla herself. In her hands she framed his face and peered into his eyes, that blinked with fear; she interrogated him as to his name, and his homeland, and his reason for the journey alone, afoot, through the hazardous wastes of the Bog. But Rat-boy only shook his head, silently; as if he were not only mute but also deaf and dumb; in truth, the frail boy was malnourished and weakened, for the castle food scarcely nourished him.

"What is your name, my little page? Whisper it in my ear."

The Countess pinched the boy's cheeks until a dull flush came. But he had not a word to utter, and shrank from the fierce woman in appre-hension. "Where did you come from, my lad, and where did you intend to go? It was not *here*—of course. For *here* is not imaginable from *there*—whichever *there* was your home." The Countess stared into the boy's eyes, that fascinated her as the eyes of one *still living*, which she had not seen in a very long time.

"Do you know where you are at this moment? And who is Master here, and who is Mistress? Or have you truly 'lost your tongue'?" So saying, the Countess made a show of prying the boy's jaws open that she might see if his tongue *was* missing, and terrified the child by asking if he should wish to be disburdened of the "slimy useless thing" which, it seemed, he did possess after all, attached to the back of his mouth.

"For if you are indeed mute, my boy," the Countess said, in a re-proachful voice, "it may be that you will be required to look the part."

WHEN THE MASTER of the castle returned, he thought his sister's page a rat-faced little whelp who looked familiar but could not recall having seen him before. Unless, in some dim chasm of his brain, the boy lingered as a memory of a meal of no particular distinction hastily and only partly devoured.

"I don't doubt, Camilla, that you've taken Rat-boy in to spite me, and not out of a charitable love for *him*."

The Countess, already beginning to be bored with her Rat-boy page, yet protested that the boy was her pet, and not to be molested or frightened; in any case, not to be tossed out for carrion birds to pick at until she, and she alone, gave the command.

So heavy was the pall of damp and lassitude upon the Bog Castle, the nights were spent in joyless carousing, and the playing of draughts; but, as an elderly bent-backed servant informed Todd, the game was no ordinary game of draughts of the kind played by persons in civilized lands, but a most ingenious and deadly species. For the winner was not only privileged but required to chop off the head of the loser in full view of the assembled court!—which feature the Master had initiated upon his return from the East some years ago, that the *ennui* of the castle might be stirred. And now all were mad for the game, and had acquired an insatiable desire for blood—the blood of others, that is. "When you hear a bestial roar erupt in the early hours of the morning," Todd was told, in a lowered voice, "it's the response of onlookers to yet another 'execution.' And nearly as horrific a sound to hear, as it is a sight to see."

Todd would have liked to question the man further, but he thought it most prudent to remain speechless. For some reason, it is human nature to speak more openly to one who appears to be mute.

Being of a disposition desperate to survive, and made cunning through desperation, Todd Slade had acquired certain mannerisms appropriate to a mute—signaling with fingers, rolling his eyes agitatedly, grimacing, rapidly nodding or shaking his head when others spoke; in this case, he shuddered, and shrank away in fear. And the elderly servant warned: "You must never consent to play draughts with any of them, my lad. But if you are forced into it, your only hope is *never glance up from the board*. Not for an instant—not for the wink of an eye! For the experienced players have grown fantastically adroit in cheating, and the Master above all. (Master prides himself on playing draughts with any opponent, and acquiescing to his own execution if he loses; but of course, Master never loses.) If they can't clear the board of your pieces legitimately, they will sweep them to the floor or pocket them; and then all that awaits you is the chopping block and the starving reptile-birds. Not even Mistress could save your life—nor would she wish to, as she too is mad for blood."

Todd had played numerous board games with his cousins Josiah and Annabel, as with other family members like Grandfather Slade; in fact, it was his grandfather who'd taught Todd to play draughts—"an English variant on American checkers"—and to play with "both a serious and a playful heart." Winslow Slade had quite enjoyed playing such games with his young grandson, and was surprised and delighted when Todd quickly began to win. The boy's precocity at draughts/checkers was marveled at through the West End, by those who'd seen him play with adults; but, unfortunately, at about the age of ten, Todd became easily bored by games so restricted by rules as board games, so that not even Annabel enjoyed playing with him. With dismay Todd recalled his brattish behavior—if he'd lost a piece at the wrong moment he might fly into a tantrum, and send all the pieces tumbling to the floor; sometimes, he cheated by advancing a piece by stealth, or with a sly movement of a finger dislodging one of his opponent's. Particularly Todd was ashamed of how childish he'd been, and how he'd taxed poor Annabel's patience.

"If only I had my childhood to relive!" Todd murmured to himself, crouched in one or another of the castle's damp corners. "I would do everything differently, and not have come *here*."

AS THE COUNTESS lost interest in the novelty of her Rat-boy page, Todd was free to wander in the castle as he wished, so long as he kept clear of those residents who seemed to take offense at the sight of a child, and amused themselves with drunken pranks and torments—seizing Todd by the scruff of the neck, for instance, and forcing him to compete with snarling dogs for scraps of food. (So humiliated, yet bent upon surviving, Todd accepted such indignities with a steely resolution he recalled his grandfather Slade speaking of, at a time when Todd had scarcely paid the old man any heed: *As you are a Slade, you can and will keep your own inner counsel.*)

The cunning child also reasoned that, if his tormenters saw him broken and weeping, they would be satisfied for the time being, and he would be spared another day; and might hope for revenge.

By daring and stealth Rat-boy made his way to the great dining hall where wood fires dispiritedly burned in great, six-foot-high fireplaces littered with bones, and where, through the long, sleepless night, the castle's revelers caroused. (For sleep of a normal kind was, while not forbidden in the Bog Castle, considered déclassé, and a sign of weakness.) It was observed by one of the Countess's female consorts—(such were chosen by the beautiful Countess for their ugly faces and misshapen bodies, for the Countess was amused to appear to great advantage beside them)—that a child of such tender years should be spared such gruesome sights as beheadings, as they might give him "unnatural inclinations"; provoking the sulky Countess to shrug, and tousle her page's hair, saying: "Why, where's the harm in it?—one can't be a *boy*, and *tender*, for very long."

So it happened that Todd Slade was a mute witness to some very coarse behavior among members of the court, and occasional visitors; and to the nightly games of draughts—which, though begun with drunken optimism and noisy bravado on the parts of the players, always culminated in craven terror on the part of the (disbelieving) loser; and in an execution so bloody, and so often mangled, poor Todd hid his face in his hands.

So rowdy were these nocturnal merrymakers, so strident and forced their laughter, the very spiders shuddered in their webs hidden high against the vaulted ceiling of the great hall; and in the bone-littered courtyard outside, scavenger birds stirred in sleep, and flapped their wings, in anticipation of the dawn's bloody repast. Todd's sheltered boyhood had ill prepared him for the brutality of the world—at least, *this world;* he recalled like a dream the customary quiet of Wheatsheaf, the way in which his mother and the household staff coddled him, despite his bad behavior; only his father had no patience for him, and now Todd could quite understand why.

In the Bog Castle, Todd shrank from all that he was forced to see, and expected to be "amused" by. His first execution, for instance, was carried out by Master himself, who, being very drunk, with frog-eyes bulging, badly botched the job, and had need to bring the (poorly sharpened) ax down five or six times on the neck of a smooth-chinned castle youth, before the deed was accomplished. Several nights later Todd was yet more astonished and repelled by the spectacle of the fair-haired Countess Camilla!— who, for all her hauteur and scrupulosity, often indulged in draughts with untutored male opponents who offered her no serious challenge and were easily defeated. "My queen conquers all! D'you see?—*all*"—the Countess's voice rang thrillingly.

And then what paroxysms of laughter arose at the sight of the beautiful woman with her mask-like face of blond perfection, her composed expression, in velvet, silk damask, and ermine robes, glittering with jewels, as she stood like a woodsman with wide-spread legs, to swing the ax with fearsome determination through the air!—and to sever in a single blow the head of a luckless admirer from his body.

And cheers arose drunken and callow as cheers at the Princeton-Yale football game, Todd had several times attended with his family.

Rat-boy hid away crouching with the dogs. With the most craven of these, he had made friends; these were creatures bonding in equivalent misery. He thought: *Will I ever escape this hellish place? And if I do, where can I go? For I have lost my way back home.*

***

WHILE TEACHING HIMSELF the alphabet, and how to fashion words into logical sequences, Todd had had occasion to peruse some of the very old, never-opened books in Copplestone's library at Wheatsheaf; as something of a prank, meaning to stupefy his father, he'd committed to memory a passage from Anaximander: *It is necessary that things should pass away, into that from which they are born. For things must pay one another the penalty, and the compensation, for their injustice, according to the ordinance of Time.* Todd had not understood this wisdom at the time, though he had felt its implacability.

And, in another of the old, ignored books, a passage of Heraclitus that had made him shudder, for something uncanny and prophetic in its words:

Time is a child playing draughts; the kingship is in the hands of a child.

Little could Todd have guessed that, one day, his own life would be in his hands, in a game of draughts.

IT WAS A distinct advantage that Rat-boy's skinny frame and sallow skin made him seem younger than he was. A casual glance from any adult in the castle would have marked him as no more than ten, and negligible. Children were rarely seen in the castle, though babies were born; but babies did not long survive in the atmosphere of dank rot. But Rat-boy slipped past much scrutiny, for his small size, and muteness; and his privilege as the Countess's page, even if the Countess no longer cared much for him, and had allowed his page-finery to become dirty and tattered. The females of the court, imagining him so young, were careless with their dress and toilet in his presence, as with their speech; for Rat-boy did not seem to matter. A fleshy female with a harridan's face said, with ribald wit: "Rat-boy is but a baby, yet both *too old,* and *too young,* to properly suckle at a woman's breast." Blushing fiercely Todd remained very still as the gathering of females laughed.

Imagining him so young, and mute, the court was the more astounded when one night when the evening's merrymaking was not so strident as usual, the Countess's shy little page spoke aloud at last, in a high, frail, whispery voice—"Countess? May I speak?"

"*May* you speak? What is this? *Can* you speak?"—the Countess was very surprised. "I have healed you, have I? Is that it? My care of my little Rat-boy page has restored his speech, has it?" The Countess thought well of herself for this miracle, as others congratulated her.

In his frail whispery voice, that was near-inaudible, Rat-boy spoke in the Countess's ear: "I would like to play draughts with M-Master."

" 'Draughts with—*Master*'?" The Countess stared at Todd with genuine alarm. "Are you mad? You will lose, and your dear little head will be chopped off, and flung to the carrion birds; and your Countess is not prepared for that, just yet."

But Master had heard the page's reckless words, that could not so easily be revoked. And through the gloomy vaulted room that resembled, for all its air of febrile festivity, and fires burning in several fireplaces, a vast mausoleum, there were startled exclamations and a scattering of applause, for the possibility of such sport was exciting, or at least carried the promise of excitement, in this morass of *ennui*.

"My page is too young to play draughts," the Countess protested, "and my brother is a master of draughts who can't be beaten, or even held to a draw; so it would be only slaughter, and can't be permitted."

"All things are permitted," the Countess's brother said to her, with a scornful curl of his lip. "All things in the Bog Kingdom are permitted *me*."

The Count was delighted that his sister's Rat-boy page had issued such a challenge, for, over the centuries, he had grown so skilled at draughts, and so ingenious and frequently negligent in his playing, he often played with two or three opponents simultaneously, and had begun to find the game, even with its bloody finale, tedious. So he rejoiced that this evening should at least be *diverting*: for in the history of the Bog Castle, dating back to time before Time, no child was ever known to issue any challenge to any adult, still less one of the nobility. And it struck the Count that there was something treacherous, something uncontrollable, indeed something *unnatural* in the very concept of a child. "For is not a 'child' a being that will alter by degrees, not quite before our eyes, yet in our presence," the Master of the castle mused, "and is not a 'child' an early version, or mockery, of ourselves?—an image of our despoiled innocence and our blasted hopes? Most intolerably, is a 'child' not *one who will replace us*?"

The Count's pallid frog-face brightened in a smile, that revealed jagged yellow teeth as the Count clapped a hand upon Rat-boy's head, in a pretense of genial affection; and said that yes indeed, he would accept Rat-boy's challenge at once, for the evening was unusually slow and dull, and a perpetual wintry rain fell through the bog, and his companions had become cowards who dared not challenge him, or even one another— for there was no fresh blood at the castle, hence no "fresh blood" for the night's sport.

"Could you have spoken all along, Rat-boy? And 'held your tongue' out of cunning?" the Count asked the Countess's page, with a deceptive sort of sympathy; seeing the Countess frown and shake her head just perceptibly, behind the Count's back, Rat-boy shook his head slowly to indicate *no*, all the while grimacing, and twitching his shoulders, to suggest that indeed speech was difficult for him, if not painful.

The game board was set up on a stained marble pedestal, in a central position in the vaulted room, several yards from the fire burning without much heat in the largest fireplace. In itself the board was a work of art, or had been at one time, comprised of zebrawood, with squares set individually in place, and painted in exquisite tones of red and black; around the edge of the board, a matte-finished gilding in an abstract design to suggest the Oriental and the serpentine. The draughts-pieces, or checkers, were somewhat larger than the ones Todd had played with as a child, fashioned of carved ivory with serrated edges; and divided, as usual, into two armies, the red and the black.[*]

Unfortunately, not fifteen feet away from the game board was the reeking chopping block, a much-abused stump of log taken from the bog; and the deadly ax itself with its sturdy handle worn smooth over the years and an enormous double-edged blade covered not only in dried and blackened blood but in myriad hairs as well. (This repulsive sight clearly worked to the Count's advantage, as it unnerved the brashest of players, while the Count affected utter nonchalance, as if unaware of its presence.)

The Count led Rat-boy to his chair, and took his place across the board from him, and said in a pretense of sobriety that he supposed the game of draughts as played at the Bog Castle required no detailed explication; but in the event that Rat-boy had forgotten, the novelty of the game was this: "If your army triumphs over mine, you are required to employ that ax—(do look at it, my lad: *do!*)—and with all the strength in you, you must sever my head from my body. You cannot grant mercy because you have not the power: the Bog Kingdom admits of no mercy, even to its masters. Is't understood?—and you promise not to dissolve into tears at being *required to kill* your host and benefactor, who has tolerated your presence here in his kingdom for so long? However, in the event that your army, these red fellows, are defeated," the Count said, with a sly smile, "why, our situation is simply reversed; but that event is so remote and unlikely, we need not waste our time in speculation."

Though this was a feeble sort of wit the hall rocked with malicious laughter; but Rat-boy, poor frightened Todd Slade, sat frozen with eyes

---

[*] Though it isn't possible after so many years to determine its authenticity, there is good reason to believe that this single playing piece in my possession, kept on my desk here that I might contemplate it, and take inspiration from it, is the very piece brought home by Todd Slade from the Bog Kingdom. So worn is the checker from the passage of time, its serrated edges are not very distinct any longer; and so faded its coloring, you can barely discern that it was once black.

affixed to the game board. Clearly in his head the admonition sounding clearly *Do not glance up, do not glance up even once.*

A tankard of pungent dark ale was brought to the Count, and a miniature version brought to Todd, to provoke laughter from the onlookers; diverse sweetmeats were served; and the bloody "cannibal sandwich" that had once sickened Annabel. These dainties the Count nibbled on through the game, wiping his sticky hands on his velvet clothing, while Todd declined to eat at all; though in truth he was faint with hunger.

As the hollow-sounding bell of the castle tolled midnight the game began, with Master allowing Rat-boy the first move, as his army was red; and the idlers of the court, including sulky Countess Camilla and her retinue, drew around. With some hesitation Todd made his first move, taking up one of his first-row pieces; but felt a sudden fear of releasing it from his fingers.

"Come, come!" the Count chided, "—you must let go; there is a time limit for such ploys, beyond which the offense fingers are *chopped off.*"

Then, it was the Count's turn. Fearfully Todd raised his eyes to take in that queer flaccid green-tinted face in which, lurking beneath its ugly exterior, one could almost discern a reptilian sort of nobility. Was this the very personage whom Todd's cousin Annabel had loved, or had been hypnotized into believing she loved; was this the very person that had precipitated the ruin of the Slades, and the devastation of Crosswicks?

"Take care!"—the Countess hissed at Todd, with some disgust.

For, in the mere instant required to gaze at the Count's face, and think his melancholy thoughts, Todd's cunning opponent had managed to knock from the board two of Todd's pawns . . .

On all sides the Master's sycophants chuckled. So swiftly had the frog-Count moved, so stunned was Todd to see his army already reduced by two playing pieces, the boy was unable at first to fully comprehend what had happened.

A stern voice admonished him *Your only hope is never to glance up from the board.* So he'd been warned clearly enough, yet like a fool he'd forgotten.

The Count naturally betrayed no awareness of having cheated, still less of his child-opponent's look of dismay.

For some minutes the game proceeded in a more or less normal fashion, though with painstaking slowness on Todd's part, for again he was reluctant to lift his fingers from a checker; and recalled how recklessly he'd played as a boy, at Crosswicks, trusting to good luck and inspiration to carry him along, as frequently it did, to his grandfather's delight. When the Count asked, in a kindly voice, if Todd would like another sort of beverage, one more suited for a child, Todd knew that he must not be deceived, and look up at the man; he must only just shake his head *no*, but keep his eyes fixed to the board. *I will not be drawn into my own death. I must concentrate exclusively on the game of draughts.*

By contrast, the Count moved his black pieces swiftly, and with a show of indifference, never failing to snap his chin up after a move, that he might beguile Todd into glancing up at him and locking eyes; but Todd clenched his jaws and did not surrender to the impulse.

Concentrate!—Grandfather Slade had counseled him. Only in concentration can you succeed.

So the game proceeded slowly. At one o'clock a number of the on-lookers muttered among themselves that the game had grown "tedious"— and they might be up until dawn at this rate. Countess Camilla dared to taunt her brother by observing that it was clear he wasn't half so gifted a player as he prided himself, if a mere child of ten years or so could keep him at bay. "Move for move, and piece for piece," the provocative woman said, "the lord of the manor and the lowly Rat-boy seem to me near evenly matched, neither being sparked by genius."

This rude remark was meant to annoy the Count, as it did; he disguised his vexation by yawning, and stretching, and sighing; and drawing out of his vest a worn leather pouch filled with a sharply poignant substance smelling of bay rum and heat. He dipped his fingers into the pouch, and raised them to his nose: the familiar motion of "taking snuff" in one nostril, and then in the other; as Todd couldn't watch him directly, these motions were distracting; and so he surrendered to the instinct to glance up another time.

Poor Todd!—in that instant the fiend's free hand darted across the board and so blithely removed one of Todd's crucial checkers, which was in a position to guard his back row, that, a second time, Todd blinked in confusion and incomprehension. How was it possible that anyone could cheat with such quicksilver skill?—and such seeming innocence?

Again, everyone laughed. Even the Countess laughed in disgust. And the Count merrily sneezed, and blew his noise most repulsively into his handkerchief; and urged Todd to make his move—"For the hour is growing late for you, my lad. Soon, it will be your *bedtime*."

By this time Todd was both demoralized and terrified; his poor red army had been depleted by three pieces, at no cost to the black army; like a crippled old man he sat rigid and hunched over the board; dangerously, his eyes flooded with tears. He had to blink rapidly to clear his vision; but did not dare wipe his face, for fear that his opponent would take advantage. In a mock-kindly voice the Count was saying, that draughts, having little of the subtleties of chess, should really be played in a carefree manner. Wasn't it the quintessence of *childhood*—a game of straightforward simplicity, all its elements visible to the eye, and requiring little ratiocination? "In draughts one may as well move a piece quickly as after deliberation," he said, "for it will make little difference, eventually."

So tense had Todd become, when finally he made his next move, and lifted his fingers from the checker, he saw to his horror that he'd made a terrible blunder—and could not now retract it.

Concentrate!—so Winslow Slade admonished.

Never glance up from the board!—so the elderly servant admonished.

As if suspecting a trap, the Count hesitated; then proceeded to leap over not only the luckless piece Todd had moved, but a second; and bore them off this time in honest triumph from the battlefield.

At which the gathering of sycophants and idlers responded with hand-clapping, and murmured compliments to the Master on his prowess.

Sullenly the Countess said, "It was the boy's mistake, not the Count's 'prowess.'"

Now a sickly sort of realization came over Todd, as he feared he'd forgotten the rules of the game. At Crosswicks, when he'd played so heedlessly with Annabel and Josiah, he'd often violated the rules, and his cousins had not much minded.

"Come, Rat-boy," the Count said, "my little army is roiling for the kill. And you know, caution is useless."

Todd tried to recall: the object of the game was to become "kinged"— in that way to acquire more power. Being "kinged" had something to do with the back row of the board. This recollection came into Todd's mind like a drifting butterfly, in time to allow him to make his move; and a lucky move it was, as if it had been deliberated.

So hastily then the Count pushed a piece into Todd's depleted ranks, with the obvious plan of acquiring a king in the next move, he committed a blunder as well; which he and Todd saw at the same moment. But by then the Count had released his piece, and had to surrender it.

Or was this a trap?—Todd wondered. His eyes darted frantically about the board.

Yet it seemed not to be a trap. Every sycophant and idler in the vast gloomy space drew in breath, in anticipation. Todd shifted a lone piece into a strategic position that blocked two of his opponent's crucial pieces, and would in the next move account for the loss of one.

"Child's luck. Rat-boy luck." The Count muttered sullenly, like a petulant child. For now he was forced to make his move, and to sacrifice a piece. "Well. I see Rat-boy will be 'kinged' now. But so shall I, soon. And you have postponed your bedtime, it seems, for another hour."

How innocent, how unobtrusive, the Count's stubby fingers, resting lightly on the gilded edge of the board; but Todd knew how swiftly those stubby fingers could move, and did not dare look away.

King! He'd acquired a *king*. He felt an uneasy thrill of elation, though he had but seven pieces remaining, to his opponent's eleven.

Do not. Glance up. DO NOT.

Minutes passed, and, to the disgust of many, a full hour; and when the hour of 2 A.M. sounded the perspiring Rat-boy had but five pieces remaining, of which three were kings; and his opponent had six pieces, of which only two were kings. By this time the raucous crowd of onlookers had quieted and the atmosphere had grown brittle.

"Here is another tankard, brother," the Countess said, with a sly sort of solicitude. "Perhaps it will yield inspiration."

The Count took the tankard from her irritably, and drank deeply, and, with a bluff swashbuckling motion, made a move to approach one of Todd's unprotected men from the rear; yet in so eccentric a manner, it must be a trick.

Todd brooded long over the new alignment on the board, yet could discover no logic to it. He saw now how the game mimicked war: there was no logic to it. He started to move one of his kings, then hesitated; started to move the lone piece, then hesitated; and stared, and swallowed hard. Was his opponent planning an ingenious assault, or had the Count plunged ahead blindly, without seeming to see that a sharp-eyed opponent could capture one of his two kings in two or three skilled moves . . . ?

How Todd's head ached, and his eyelids quivered with strain!

Badly he regretted his past life, his heedless child's life, when he had been so headstrong with his family, so cruel to even his loving mother, and a thorn in the heart of his father; even with Annabel whom he'd loved, he had often been rude. And he had not admired Josiah enough, and had taken his exemplary cousin for granted.

He had not loved his grandfather Slade enough: he had not ever forgiven his grandfather, for the humbling "confession" in the cemetery.

The Count was betraying some apprehension, for he shifted about in his throne-like chair, and wiped at his face with a soiled handkerchief. "Rat-boy," he said softly, "you are perhaps *not a child* at all."

"He's a child, Brother! He's just a child. *You* must be prepared to be beaten by a child, in front of witnesses." The Countess laughed in delight, revealing yellow-tinged teeth, that did not detract from her curious mask-like perfection, but rather enhanced it.

After a long minute of deliberation Todd made a move; and the Count made his; and, suppressing a shiver of apprehension, or a little cry of elation, Todd quickly took advantage of his opponent's poor judgment—capturing *not one king but two* in a spirited hopping march across the board!

At this, Annabel would have applauded. Even if Todd were beating her.

Now it seemed that Rat-boy was near to winning the game, unbelievably, against the Master of Bog Castle. All of the great hall grew hushed.

"Well, Brother, you are driven to it," the Countess Camellia declared in a voice both exhilarated and fearful. "You and I both—for my fate rests with yours. *Take care*."

Slowly the Count drew forth his filthy snuff-pouch and, while positioning a tiny pinch of the foul tobacco in one of his nostrils, succeeded in wafting a grain or two in Todd's direction; with the result that the boy's eyes welled with stinging tears, and he could not stop himself from sneezing—once, twice, a third time; and, instantaneously, the wily Count swept Todd's most valued king to the floor.

All of the assemblage reacted with a murmur, though not of support for the Count's crude move; for even a cheater is obliged to act with grace, and to disguise his dishonesty.

Todd saw at once what the situation was, and fought back tears of helplessness and anger; for he'd been tricked again, and truly unfairly. The Count was like Todd as he'd once been, as a spoiled child; but far worse, since his pranks were lethal.

Yet Todd managed to recover, to a degree, to continue the exhausting game, and in so forthright a manner, no one could have told that the loss of the king had thrown him into a temporary panic. Following this exchange, so warily did the Master of the Bog Castle and the lowly Rat-boy play at their game of draughts, and so cautious were their soldiers of one another, the castle bell tolled 3 A.M.; and then 4 A.M.; at last 5 A.M.—with no significant change of fortune. *How strange that I am evenly matched with the Devil*—the thought came wryly to Todd.

By this time all but the hardiest of the onlookers had lapsed into drunken slumber. The Countess Camilla had resorted to taking snuff, with her retinue of coarse-featured court women, in order to stay awake.

"Shall we declare a draw, Brother?"—so the Countess said, disguising her concern in a jesting voice. "It would not be so dishonorable, you know, but something of a novelty in the Bog Kingdom."

"No. Never a draw."

"But—"

"I said *no*. Never. This Rat-boy is a devil of some sort, from another sort of Bog Kingdom, and not what he seems. But I will beat him—fairly. I promise."

Todd's throbbing head was nodding; his eyelids had grown heavy. Of a sudden he heard Annabel addressing him, her voice soft and close against his ear. *Once you are a swan you will be a swan.*

He sensed his opponent's weariness as well, but knew enough not to glance up at the Count. *Once a swan. A swan!*

At last the game of draughts ended, in an altogether unexpected way, at 5:21 A.M.; when only six pieces remained on the board, evenly divided between three kings of the red army and three of the black, timidly huddled together in their respective camps.

By this time, so far as Todd Slade knew, all of the vast Earth had been reduced to the shimmering squares before him. Dazed, hollow-eyed, faint with hunger and anxiety, he could recall little beyond the game board or the game. All that mattered were maneuvers and counter-maneuvers. In two moves possibly—in three moves assuredly—he might win; yet it was best to be prudent, to take care. If the red king advanced by one more square, then the cornered black king would be forced to move laterally; but what of the other black king, positioned so crucially? There was no end to the game in sight. The game of draughts, Todd saw, was interminable—*it was his life*. And when he weakened, or slid help-lessly forward in a faint, it would be his death.

Precisely how the *coup de grâce* was administered by the exhausted Rat-boy page none of the onlookers could have said afterward; nor, unfor-tunately, can this historian replicate the final moves of the game, though I have set up a small checkerboard here on my desk, to follow the game. According to evidence afterward provided by Todd Slade, the end came at dawn, or what passed for dawn in the Bog Kingdom, when a languid and sickly sun penetrated the smoky interior of the hall; and only a few observ-ers, including the ashen-skinned Countess, were witnesses. The Count, nearly as drained of strength as his child-opponent, and somewhat inebri-ated, was overcome by a sudden rage against one of the snoring blood-hounds at his feet; and, cursing, gave the dog a sound kick in the ribs, which sent the poor creature yelping and whimpering into a corner . . . But when the Count returned his attention to the board, to reach for one of his kings, he saw to his consternation that the king had vanished; and his two remaining kings were now vulnerable to being captured.

"What! How is it! Rat-boy has—*cheated*?"

"He has not cheated, Brother. I saw nothing."

"But, my king—"

"Your king is at your feet, Brother. Where you yourself toppled it."

But was this so? The Count did not dare to look, for fear that his wily child-opponent would cause another piece to "vanish."

The Count clapped both hands to his forehead. His frog-eyes bulged and quivered. For it was clear to him that the game of draughts was all but over, and Rat-boy had defeated him honestly, following the rules of the Bog Kingdom; and there was no way out.

Even in this flush of triumph the wily child knew not to glance up at his opponent's strained face. *Do not weaken* Annabel seemed to advise him, *remain calm and have no pity.*

The Countess was swaying, and clutching at her hair that had come loose in the course of the long night, in an attitude of angry despair. "It is over. The game—our game—the Bog Castle—the Kingdom. The Kingship is now in the hands of a child and our long reign is ended."

"The Kingship is in the hands of a child," the Count echoed, as he continued to stare, and stare, at the lone pieces before him of his black army. Piteously, the protuberant frog's eyes filled with moisture.

So it was, pitiless Todd Slade jumped two of his opponent's vulnerable kings, and the game board was cleared entirely of *black*.

"YOU MUST, you know. There is no turning back."

The Countess herself had taken up the heavy ax, to force into the boy's hands.

"You *must*. It is the completion of the game of draughts which you began, on the very hour of your arrival among us."

In this way we come to the bloody denouement: for when the spindly-limbed Rat-boy, reeling with fatigue, dread, and repugnance for the terrible deed he must commit, at last manages, with some four or five clumsy swings of the ax, to severe the Count's head from his shoulders, and erase forever the Count's smirking frog-face, the shadowy hall with its gaping witnesses vanishes—and the Bog Castle vanishes—and the Bog Kingdom vanishes through its vast waste stretches; and Todd Slade wakes, his young heart hammering with life, whether in his old bed at Wheatsheaf, or in another place, he doesn't know at once.

He knows only in that wondrous instant that the Curse has lifted, and he is alive—again alive.

THE DEATH OF WINSLOW SLADE

In all the annals of medical lore this historian has had occasion to study, including even the most macabre and unlikely "case studies" memorialized at the Mutter Museum in Philadelphia, he has never come across a means of death more shocking, indeed more "unnatural," than that suffered by poor Winslow Slade, in full view of the congregation of the First Presbyterian Church on the morning of June 4, 1906.

This Sunday morning, Dr. Slade was prepared to deliver a guest sermon entitled "The 'Spirit' and the 'Letter' of the Law," an homily he had delivered several times, in differing versions, in New Jersey and Philadelphia, always with warm and gratifying results; but at the last minute, for reasons never made clear, the retired minister spoke of setting this sermon aside in favor of another, more "personal," sermon with the mysterious title "The Covenant."

Of course, it was noted by most of the congregation, as by Winslow's family and relatives, that this sermon fell on the anniversary of Annabel's abduction from this very same church; Winslow's son Augustus spoke to him gravely on this issue, but was assured that, to Winslow, the "tragic event" would be but an impetus to his sermon; and his example, to the congregation, would be of the fortifying strength of Christianity, in the face of sorrow.

"The sermon is an opportunity, Augustus! Nathaniel seems to have felt this, in inviting me to speak."

In the church, at the pulpit, Winslow Slade was remarked to appear just slightly agitated, or distracted; he had lost weight, and aged over the past twelve months, clearly; yet his manner was nervously alert; and his white hair, smooth-shaven face, and impeccable clothing were very attractive to behold.

"O dearly beloved in Christ—hear me and have mercy . . ."

Even as Dr. Slade began to speak his sermon, which he had memorized, he was overcome by a convulsive sort of shivering; an assault upon his person by a shimmering phantasm, a gigantic black snake: which remarkable creature, with a cruel flat head and bronze-glittering eyes, and iridescent black scales that winked like tiny diamonds, appeared out of nowhere; out of the very bowels of the church; and so surprised Dr. Slade, he could not escape before it wound itself about his body, and thrust its head into his mouth, horribly; as if the loathsome creature meant to bury itself inside him.

All this in full view of the horrified congregation upon whom a kind of mass paralysis had settled: as if, their eyes opened and fixed to the hellish spectacle before them, they could not believe what they were seeing.

For the black snake was both "real" in its effect upon the stricken man, and yet shimmering and transparent; you could see through its sinewy length, to the wall behind. Yet, though transparent, the thrashing snake threw a dim shadow, as the Theosophists would argue the *etheric body* throws a shadow that is invisible to the ordinary eye, while visible to the enlightened eye.

This historian is not capable of suggesting the collective horror in the church, for the terrible creature that measured, according to the testimony of some witnesses, between ten and twelve feet in length, would not relent its assault upon the helpless man; it was as if the creature wished to bury itself inside its victim. Was there ever so violent an assault upon a human being, in such sacrosanct circumstances; and by way of a devilish specimen of the suborder Serpentes?—any death so cruel, and so horrific? The foul thing succeeded in penetrating the mouth and throat of its victim, while the wretched Dr. Slade, now fallen to the floor beside the pulpit, and thrashing wildly, tried to tear the snake from him with his enfeebled hands, that he might not be choked to death.

But the great black phantasm-snake could not be budged, and Winslow Slade died within minutes.

(RECALL THAT THIS CHAPTER occurs simultaneously with the preceding chapter in the Bog Kingdom: the assault upon Dr. Slade coinciding with the moment of the Count's execution by Todd Slade. Whether one event precipitated the other, I am not certain; it would seem unlikely that the simultaneous events are unrelated. And what is the exact relation between these two events, separated as they are in regions of the spirit, and the miraculous restoration to life of Dr. Slade's four deceased grandchildren? Before such mysteries, the historian must throw up his hands and trust to his material to communicate a tale, and a meaning, beyond his own ability to fathom.)

SO IT HAPPENED that Winslow Slade died in the very church in which, for years, he had been minister, and greatly beloved; he died at the age of seventy-five, of what would be diagnosed as *cardiac arrest;* and the vicious creature that killed him seemed immediately then to have vanished, whether through a rear exit of the building, or somehow through the floorboards and into the cellar beneath. So confused was the scene, so panicked the spectators, so unspeakably awful the sight of the dying man wrestling with his demon—few persons have ever tried to present a full account of it, still less to explain it.

The historian is not so puzzled, for this is commonplace in history, that, afterward, witnesses disagreed about what had happened, or what they had believed happened; and that when Dr. Slade's body was examined, and afterward subjected to the indignity of an autopsy, no actual trace of any physical assault could be detected, by a snake or any other creature. Such members of the congregation as Francis Pyne, Abraham Sparhawk, and Andrew West, seated near the front of the church, surely saw the monstrous snake as, in panic, they rushed for the nearest exit, on the other side of the church altar from the pulpit; yet would afterward deny that they had seen anything at all. Andrew West gave out the account that he had run from the church, panting and affrighted, in order to summon help for the stricken man—as it seemed that Dr. Slade was having a convulsion of some sort.

And with the passage of days, and then weeks, the majority of the congregation came round to thinking that while they might have witnessed some such nightmare assault, it had been a collective mirage—conjured out of the air, of whirling dust-motes in a wide quivering ray of sunshine falling upon the altar; they had seen *nothing monstrous at all*. Except the thrashings and convulsions of a dying man.

So, unconscionably, careless historians of the ilk of Hollinger and Tite have subsequently interpreted the entire fourteen-month siege of the Crosswicks Curse as an exceptional phenomenon of *mass hysteria*, citing the "snake frenzy" at the Rocky Hill Seminary as a preliminary incident. Murders and atrocities in the Princeton area were committed by deranged but not supernatural individuals, of whom some were apprehended by police authorities, and some were not. And other commentators on the subject, including journalists for Jersey and New York City newspapers, went to the other extreme in assembling lurid "eyewitness" accounts of the great serpent's attack upon Dr. Slade; some of these accounts were by persons not present in the church that morning, and some were not even members of the congregation; some, not even bona fide residents of Princeton Borough.

Yet another aspect of the mystery has to do with the fact that, after Dr. Slade's body was carried away, no trace could be found of any sermon titled "The Covenant"; only just the manuscript titled "The 'Spirit' and the 'Letter' of the Law"; so that, in the grief and confusion of the hour, it came to be doubted whether this second sermon had ever existed; and this despite the fact that somewhere beyond two hundred persons saw the elderly man clutch the manuscript in his hands, before the attack of the great snake, beginning to read in a high, quavering, yet resolute voice: "O dearly beloved in Christ, hear me and have mercy . . ."

This "lost" sermon was to be discovered, years later, among the private papers of the heir of Crosswicks Manor, Augustus Slade, who must have spirited it away for safekeeping, even as his father's body was being carried from the church to an awaiting ambulance; sequestering it in the family safe, as he'd done with his brother Copplestone's *God-dictated document* less than a week before. And this priceless manuscript now resides with me, having been acquired for a pittance at an estate auction; kept now under lock and key in my Ebony-Lacquered Box where no one save this historian has access to it.

(See the Epilogue: "The Covenant," to follow.)

"REVOLUTION IS THE HOUR
OF LAUGHTER"

Was it the great Frenchman Voltaire who'd said these provocative words, as Upton Sinclair believed, or, as his new friend and comrade Yaeger Ruggles asserted, the equally great Frenchman Victor Hugo?

"I will defer to you, Yaeger, as you are far better educated than I! And a year at the Princeton Theological Seminary, and as a preceptor for Woodrow Wilson—those are impressive credentials, indeed."

Yaeger Ruggles shifted his shoulders uneasily inside his coat. In a rueful tone he said, "It would be good to think so, Upton."

The friends shook hands on Broadway, at Thirty-first Street, with a plan to meet at a Socialist-suffragette rally three days following, at Union Square. (They had first met two weeks before at a rally on the Bowery of the Socialist Labor Party in support of striking mill-workers in New York City, at which, following a tempestuous rousing speech by Mother Jones, Upton Sinclair had given an earnest, fact-filled speech; Ruggles had introduced himself to Upton afterward, as a "fierce admirer" of *The Jungle*.)

Upton watched the stiff-backed young man stride away, marveling at his dignity, and unusually well-pressed clothes, for a Socialist comrade; he'd felt a thrill of brotherhood with Ruggles, as soon as they'd met.

Though not greatly liking the young man's Southern accent, that was associated with the particular conservatism of the South, deeply entrenched against the labor movement, as against Socialist reform generally.

"He is of 'mixed race'—is he? Poor fellow! The dark-skinned Negroes will not accept him, as one who is descended from race-rape; and his white brethren will shun him. Only we, his Socialist comrades, can value *him*."

On the morning of June 16, 1906, Upton Sinclair was bound for Penn Station, where he planned to take the 2:25 P.M. train to Englewood, New Jersey, for a visit of two nights. In the waiting room, Upton seated himself on a bench and began at once to work, for he was one to never waste time—"As if you could kill time, without injuring Eternity"—this remark of Henry David Thoreau was a favorite of his since boyhood.

"Revolution Is the Hour of Laughter" was the inspired title of Upton's new article for *Everybody's Magazine*, on the subject of the imminent Socialist transformation of America; an article the young author was sketching out in a virtual fever, for the subject was precious to him. *Man is not intrinsically evil* Upton scribbled on a sheet of yellow foolscap, *but, under Capitalism, immoral behavior is systematically rewarded. By removing Capitalism we therefore remove Evil. This has been most conclusively demonstrated by . . .*

At this moment Upton glanced up startled, having heard, he thought, his name called—*UPTON SINCLAIR!*—only just audible amid the cacophony of sounds in the bustling train station. In the way of a turtle shrinking into its shell the young author hunched over his work, for he had been so often besieged of late, as a consequence of his newfound fame (in Socialist circles) or notoriety (all elsewhere), upon the publication of *The Jungle*, he'd come to dread the prospect of being noticed in public places; especially here in Penn Station, where he hoped to work.

Another time, more faintly—*UPTON SINCLAIR!*—but the words were muffled by an announcement of a train due to leave within five minutes at track nineteen, for Boston and points between.

Upton returned to his work, writing with boyish urgency. There was so much to be done!—so much to be done by *him*. Often he suffered veritable brainstorms of ideas for articles, like this for *Everybody's Magazine*, which, he was thinking, should be a series of articles; and he must soon write a strong letter to the *New York Times* on the subject of an uninformed editorial published there regarding the Meat Inspection Bill passed just last week by Congress; and an equally spirited letter to President Roosevelt, whom he'd visited by invitation, to discuss *The Jungle*, and who had gravely disappointed, if not betrayed, the idealistic young Socialist. Yet more pressingly he was obliged to compose a clear and coherent statement for the newspapers regarding the philosophy of his Socialist Utopian community, to be called the Helicon Home Colony, one day to be situated in a wooded rural area outside Englewood, in the northeastern part of the state; at the very thought of this colony, Upton's mind was flooded with ideas and plans, and a hope of whom he might invite to live there with him—among Socialist comrades, his new friend Yaeger Ruggles was primary; though the young man had expressed only a guarded sort of friendly interest in the colony. ("Socialist comrades would *live together*? And this would be tolerated by the community?"—so Ruggles had inquired, with some doubt; and Upton had assured him, "This is the United States of America, Yaeger! We may live where we wish, if we can afford it; and we can certainly live with whom we wish.")

And wasn't there something else pressing, that Upton had promised to do? Involving Meta and little David, whom he had not seen in weeks?

"So much work, and so precious little time," Upton murmured to himself, searching through his shabby valise for a fresh sheet of foolscap, "but the 'Socialist King of the Muckrakers' must be equal to his challenge, as the prophet Zarathustra was equal to *his*."

SINCE THAT NIGHT in MacDougal's when Jack London and Josiah Slade came to blows, and Upton Sinclair was knocked most unceremoniously to the floor amid much wreckage in the popular Times Square restaurant, numerous events had happened in Upton's life of an unexpected sort. The romantic isolation of his Princeton farm, where, in his memory, he and Meta had lived as a honeymoon couple, at least at the start, and where Upton had worked so productively, free to write each day as long as his strength allowed, was vanished forever; for *UPTON SINCLAIR* had taken his place, however bashfully, in the headlines of the era.

As an editorial in the *New York Evening World* observed, with a hint of censure: "Not since the youthful poet Lord Byron woke one morning to find himself both famous and notorious, has there been such an example of world-wide celebrity won in a day, and *by a book,* as has come to Upton Sinclair; and now it remains to be seen, how the young Socialist author will behave."

Upton had immediately fired off a letter protesting that it wasn't the notorious philanderer Byron with whom Upton Sinclair should be compared, but America's own, far greater and nobler Harriet Beecher Stowe— "whose masterpiece *Uncle Tom's Cabin* has changed all of our lives, forever."

(The *New York Evening World* had kindly published Upton's letter, which ran the length of two columns, for which Upton Sinclair was grateful, if somewhat surprised. Socialists were accustomed to being disdained, dismissed, or viciously attacked by the enemy press: it was a startling reversal, when the press appeared to cooperate.)

The Jungle continued to capture the attention of ever more readers, it seemed, as well as the attention of politicians and statesmen; among its renowned readers were the President of the United States and the Honorable Winston Churchill, an Englishman of thirty-two years of age with a seat in Parliament and a respected position in English journalism, as Upton had learned. (Churchill had written an extremely perceptive two-part assessment of *The Jungle* for a progressive English weekly.) Photographers, reporters, and the less scrupulous of the columnists dogged the author's path; editors who had formerly rejected his most worthy efforts, and dismissed Upton Sinclair as a hack writer, now pleaded with him to write for their magazines, offering such financial enticements, the confused young author could not resist. ("If only I had an assistant!—an indentured servant, or a slave"—so Upton joked to comrades—"I could accept every commission, promote our cause, and make a little profit in the effort.")

Though sales for *The Jungle* were modest compared to the far more admired and entertaining *The Sea Wolf*, by Jack London, the novel continued to ride the crest of the best-seller list; and so many aroused individuals were writing to the author, he was in despair of finding time to answer them all. ("Ah, I miss Meta! *She* would be ideal to answer these letters in her sincere yet diplomatic manner.") Most of the letters conveyed enthusiasm for Upton's exposé of capitalism, and included hair-raising personal accounts of injuries, deaths, and humiliations in the workforce, but a considerable number contained threats, veiled or explicit; others suggested mental derangement in the letter-writers; and numerous letters proposed marriage, or business partnerships, or a new religion, or a vegetarian commune, and the like. Most upsetting were those begging frankly for money, displaying not the least interest in *The Jungle* or in the brotherhood of Socialism itself.

Hardly a day passed without a virulent attack upon the authenticity of the book, which was presented, for reasons of legal caution, as a "novel"; editorials and columns appeared in the Hearst papers particularly, attacking Upton Sinclair's "integrity, decency, and American patriotism." All these, Upton felt obliged to answer. And problems had lately arisen regarding the administration of the Intercollegiate Socialist Society, in which Upton Sinclair was a founding officer, and Jack London a former president; during London's brief term, the Society went badly into debt. Yet, at the present time, Upton Sinclair was hoping to save enough money of his own, and perhaps to borrow some, to make a down payment on Helicon Hall, in rural New Jersey, formerly a boys' private school that had closed in bankruptcy; the price of the entire property was a staggering $34,000 . . .

Recent months had been so strenuous, Upton had suffered a recurrence of ulcers, and was on a very restricted diet indeed, of "primarily white" foods; his daily reading matter included the popular *Physical Culture, Natural Health* by Jeremiah Pym, Ph.D. and M.D. As a (female) comrade-friend had chided Upton: "It won't do the revolution any good if you're in pain trying to digest a simple meal, and continue to lose weight as you have been. We need *vigorous speakers,* not *penitent martyrs.*"

Many were the young women, and some not so young, who implored Upton Sinclair to take better care of himself, for the sake of the revolution; and offered to feed him, and even to help clothe and dress him; even to "trim" his hair, that badly needed tending-to.

("If Meta knew, she would not take me for granted, maybe! She would be jealous, maybe! And not dismiss her husband with scorn.")

The most immediate result of the financial success of *The Jungle* was the possibility of establishing the Helicon Home Colony within a few months, and not being forced to wait for years, as Upton had expected. (Of course, Upton was obliged to supply financial support to Meta and their child, when he remembered to; in the meantime, it seemed to him that his wife and son were living very contentedly with Meta's parents in a redbrick house on Staten Island, and did not need much interference from *him.*) Yet, an unfortunate blunder had already been made, by Upton Sinclair, in terms of "public relations"; for in releasing to the press a hastily composed statement on the Colony—

> Helicon Home Colony will be an Utopian effort at cooperative living in the midst of the Capitalist state: democratic in principle and practice; devoted to reform, experimentation, and radical theories of education; and to any individual of good moral character who is free from communicable disease and of sound mental health.

—he had drawn a good deal of ridicule and censure upon his head, which he feared he might not soon overcome, as newspapers made merry over the last qualification regarding "communicable disease" and "sound mental health."

(Indeed, Upton Sinclair could have had no idea how the comical specter of "communicable disease" would be used repeatedly to ridicule his idealistic enterprise; and the phrase "any individual" be deployed to suggest that the Helicon Colony was dedicated to "race mixing" as to "free love" and "atheism.")*

"So, this is 'fame,'" Upton mused to himself, in Penn Station, "—being the subject of perpetual attack in the outside world and, in the inner, made sleepless by a racing brain, a fast pulse, and a perpetual queasiness in the southern regions of the belly."

ONE OF THE MORE remarkable consequences of the young Socialist's renown was an invitation to dine at the White House with President Teddy Roosevelt and his famed "tennis cabinet"; for indeed, the eagerly awaited summons finally arrived for Upton Sinclair; and the young author, who'd not long ago written jokes for *Jude, Puck, Graham's,* and *Life* for one dollar each, and had feared he was prostituting his genius by penning nickel

---

* The historian is reluctant to indicate here, as my chronicle is nearing its close and I must condense vital information, that despite Upton Sinclair's zealous intentions and unfailingly high ideals, he was to be commonly presented in the gutter press as having established his commune expressly for the purpose of creating a harem among the "amoral Socialist females." Bravely and stubbornly Sinclair was to protest such lies, and tried to maintain a measure of his natural dignity; until such time as the Helicon Home Colony burned to the ground on the morning of March 7, 1907; and the disconsolate young man (who had suffered injuries in the fire) was the more slandered by baseless rumors that he and his comrades had set their own fire, to collect insurance and to cheat local tradesmen of money owed them. (Though a cross had been burned on the grounds in front of the residence but several days before, by a dozen individuals cloaked inside white robes with masked hoods.) In this debacle, his new friend and comrade Yaeger Ruggles would be of great help to Upton, though Ruggles refused to appear ever again in New Jersey, as he too had been injured in the fire, and the dangerous charge of "race mixing" was associated with him, like a brand in his forehead. Recovery from the catastrophe was slow, but Upton Sinclair did recover, and his optimism remained unabated as he looked forward to the publication in 1908 of his next book, *The Metropolis,* which was expected by all who'd read the manuscript to bring to fruition the Socialist dream in the United States, that *The Jungle* had precipitated but not fulfilled in 1906.

novels under a variety of pseudonyms ("Benjamin Frankman," "Horatio Linkhorn"), as well as his searing Socialist diatribes, now found himself dining in gentlemanly splendor at the very vortex of political power in Washington, D.C.

Meta will be aggrieved now, when I tell her of this grand occasion, Upton thought, packing his worn valise with several copies of his earlier books for presentation to the President, *for I am sure she would have wished to accompany me, as my wife.*

Yet after the initial excitement of taking the train to the great vaulted station at D.C., and hiking a little distance to the White House, and being ushered into the President's private dining room, and shaking "Teddy's" genial hand, and being introduced to "Teddy's" aides, the young author began to feel a prick of disappointment: for it seemed, though Roosevelt was an affable enough personality with an interest in, as he said robustly, *giving hell to the meat packers,* his attitude toward Upton Sinclair and Socialism generally was not what Upton had hoped.

And the luncheon itself, which Upton had awaited with boyish eagerness, proved to be one of the ordeals of his adult life.

Promptly at twelve o'clock the luncheon party was seated, at a long table at which President Roosevelt sat at the head, and his chief aide at the foot; they were served by mute-seeming Negro waiters in impeccable white uniforms, that emphasized the dramatic darkness of their skins; the men ate, with the exception of Upton Sinclair, with appalling gusto, as if they had not eaten in days; and Teddy ate, and talked—talked.

"The Old Guard senators be damned," the President declared, striking the table with a clenched fist, so that cutlery rattled against china, "I know what I know, and my stomach isn't deceived. It was tainted, and overripe, and damn-right maggoty meat we were given in the very act of serving our nation in Cuba! Treason! That crook Armour should have been hanged!—the packers should have been hanged! Routed, and tarred and feathered, and set ablaze, and hanged for *treason in wartime.* And now this courageous young man Mr. Sinclair exposes the fact that Armour &

Company profit by shoveling rat dung, and cow fetuses, and cow tails, and eyeballs, and every variety of gristle, innards, and excrement, and, by God, fingers and toes of human beings, into such staples of the American household as deviled ham—a favorite of my boyhood!—spicing it up, as it were, with the expectorations of hunkie T.B. carriers! This treason will not be countenanced as long as Teddy Roosevelt sits in the White House."

So many grimaces accompanied this speech, and so many blows on the table, Upton Sinclair had to steel himself not to wince, staring in amazement at his fiery host. How very like Jack London the President was, and Mother Jones: the impolite yet admiring word had to be *rabble-rouser*, a talent surely bred in the womb. Teddy's voice so brayed, Upton felt a need to press his fingers into his ears, seated beside the man, yet did not make a move of course. It was stunning to him, whose demeanor even in Socialist circles was reticent and restrained, and whose manner was always to defer to someone who interrupted him, to observe a man for whom speech was indeed a kind of sustained expectoration; to see that the outsized "Teddy" of the tabloids and popular imagination was an actual person, of the species of caricature. (Yet no caricaturist could do justice to the living man, Upton saw.) It seemed that the President was accustomed to entertaining his listeners and himself with a performance of serio-comic genius: gruff, blustery, big-toothed, excessive and exaggerated, with a high squeaking voice issuing from the fleshy face; indistinguishable, except for the content of his words, from imitations of "Teddy" by vaudeville and burlesque comedians.

When the President at last paused in his ranting, to lower his head to his plate and eat, all that he'd said was heartily if somewhat perfunctorily seconded by his vice president Mr. Charles Fairbanks, his Republican-party comrade Mr. James Garfield, his aide Mr. Francis Leupp, and others, who gave every evidence of having listened closely to the outburst, as if they had never heard it before. The genial Mr. Fairbanks was so thoughtful, or possessed of so sly a sense of humor, as to observe to Upton Sinclair that all pleasure in the day's meal was considerably qualified by the "gross, shameful, nauseating" revelations in *The Jungle;* though, as the vegetarian

Upton wryly noted, the gentlemen were devouring their roast beef rare with unslackened appetite.

Why *does humankind insist upon eating animals?—is it in lieu of eating one another?*—so Upton thought, sipping water from a crystal goblet as, elsewhere around the table, the gentlemen were drinking a very pungent-smelling dark ale.

In an interrogative way, that made Upton Sinclair quite uncomfortable, the President asked why he'd investigated the Chicago stockyards in the first place, and "why in hell" had he suffered the hardship of spending seven weeks in the Stockyards Hotel; but when Upton tried to explain that it was his sympathy for the workingman, particularly those of foreign birth, and his more general interest in the Socialist brotherhood of man, and in the vegetarian movement, rather than a narrow interest in the sanitary conditions of the packing houses, it seemed that the President's eyes acquired a distant look behind the round glinting lenses of his glasses; and a moment later, in an outburst that might have been considered rude in other circumstances, the President interrupted his guest with a sudden guffaw, and a smart blow to the table, having at that instant recalled a meal he and his Rough Riders had been forced to consume on the "very eve" of the great Battle of San Juan Hill.

"Tainted, and overripe, and damn-right maggoty, I say!"—even as he scooped a dripping piece of roast beef into his mouth, and chewed.

This led to an entertaining reminiscence on the part of Roosevelt regarding his famed Rough Riders, which cavalry unit had participated in more skirmishes than the pacifist Upton Sinclair had known. The President seemed particularly proud of the fact that his unit had suffered a high degree of casualties—"Many more than the average, sir!"—and that they'd indeed had a "damn rough time of it" during the ten weeks' fighting of the "splendid little war" against the Spanish villains. "It was that damned 'embalmed beef' that counted for most of our casualties," the President said grimly, "and now that I sit in the damned White House, Armour & Crook Company had better take notice."

During a welcome lull in the conversation while the gentlemen were sampling a new, even darker and more pungent ale, Upton broached the subject of the plight of the "common workingman and woman" in the country, which he saw as unconscionable, set beside the massive profits of their capitalist employers. Since the President and his aides had presumably read *The Jungle*, they were now well informed of conditions in Chicago, and would surely wish to propose some legislation to remedy them at once; yet it should be understood that working conditions in stockyards throughout the country were no better, or even worse; and the pay scale was frequently lower. And the cruelty to the animals—this, indeed, was not to be countenanced by decent persons . . . Upton grew increasingly impassioned until his voice trembled. "Only consider the wretched working conditions in factories owned by the copper trust, and the steel trust, and the tin trust, and all the rest. How can it be tolerated, Mr. President, that even as we dine in this elegant room, children as young as six and seven are toiling in factories close by us, particularly across the river in Maryland; and the inhuman owners insist that it is their right to dismiss any worker who pleads for a twelve-hour, instead of a fourteen-hour, day. And—"

Here Roosevelt interrupted with such vehemence that spittle flew from his lips. "And you must not forget, Mr. Sinclair, the shipbuilding trust," he said, "that foul octopus of traitors, presided over in shameless pomposity by Senator Hale of Maine!" Here the President became so overwrought he pushed his plate from him, and began to pick his teeth agitatedly with a gold pick. In a breathless high-pitched voice he cried: "Gentlemen, I give you Senator Hale of Maine!—the most innately and essentially malevolent scoundrel that God Almighty ever allowed to exist on Earth! Why, it's criminal how the man stonewalls against me—what lies and slanders he spins of my 'fear' of him! It has come to light that the traitor conspires with my enemies in Washington, that the shipbuilding trust shall 'sail merrily' over my grave. Hale should be hanged, sir! *They should all be hanged.*"

All at the table loudly concurred, except for the abashed guest; and discussion flowed over other traitors, like dirty water across the white linen tablecloth, that was itself, by this time, liberally splattered with spots and stains: persons as diverse as James J. Hill, J. P. Morgan, and George F. Baer, on the one hand; and David Graham Phillips on the other. (Phillips, a well-respected colleague of Upton's, was the author of the courageous exposé "The Treason of the Senate," then appearing in *Cosmopolitan;* one of his particular targets was Senator Hale from Maine.) The President seemed to have forgotten his guest of honor as he lapsed into a wrathful denunciation of the *tribe of muckrakers* themselves . . .*

It was Upton's attention, stated to his comrade-friends in New York City, that when he had the President's ear he would broach the subject of immediate legislation to protect workers, and to guarantee some sort of absolute minimum wage; for it would be a sorry consequence of his labors if only the American meat-eaters were "protected." But he could not wedge a word into the conversation, it seemed; it was not simply that Upton Sinclair was interrupted or ignored, but that he had become invisible; and much of the heated discussion dealt with matters, with individual Democrats and Republicans, of which he knew nothing. So, Upton sipped discontentedly at his glass of water, and thought it a melancholy irony that he should be at last at the White House, as the President's guest, yet as powerless as ever. "Better to be hidden away in the countryside beyond Princeton," he mused, "in my quaint little cabin, laboring over *The Jungle* . . . while Meta prepares a delicious dinner, and tends to little David. Ah, were we not happy then!"

After an hour the hearty luncheon was declared over, for, as Roosevelt said sternly, "There are some of us who work, sir—not *scribble.*" More genially the President laughed to his friends saying they could not spend all the day "bloviating and idling—as we might like." The President shook Upton's hand so vigorously that the young man's teeth rattled, exclaiming:

---

* *Muckraker* was a derisive term coined by Teddy Roosevelt himself, the allusion being to the Man with the Muckrake in John Bunyan's *The Pilgrim's Progress* who "suffers from an unwholesome obsession with filth."

"Jolly good of you to drop by, sir! Most helpful! And when we meet again, Mr. Upton, it's to be hoped that the damned traitorous packers will have been brought to their knees, like beef to the slaughter, and that scoundrel Hale hanged high!"

ON MAY 26, 1906, the papers trumpeted the news that Roosevelt's bill regarding federal inspection of meat, afterward known as the Meat Inspection Act, had been passed after much quarreling in Congress; and nearly every editorial on the controversial subject spoke of the "triumph" of young Upton Sinclair: for did this not prove that justice might prevail, and that "the pen was mightier than the sword"?

Only Upton's Socialist comrades understood the young author's list-lessness at the news, and his sense of having been betrayed, of which he scarcely dared speak to the reporters who besieged him. Upton was, however, inspired to make the single utterance for which he is known out of his long and heroic career, and his formidable outpouring of impassioned books numbering at nearly one hundred: "I aimed for the heart of America, and hit its stomach instead."

NOW THE HARRIED young man sits in clamorous Penn Station, hunched over his writing pad and composing as fast as his cramped hand will allow the piece for *Everybody's Magazine*. It has just struck him that the striking figure of speech borrowed from Voltaire—or, more likely Hugo, since Yae-ger Ruggles insisted it was Hugo—might after all be inappropriate to his purpose, for *REVOLUTION IS THE HOUR OF LAUGHTER* is a concept that might go over the heads of, or offend, the average reader of *Everybody's;* and Upton has a dread of being misunderstood yet again. And there is very little to laugh at lately for "Big Bill" Hayward's red banners, unfurled just the other day in Paterson, New Jersey, surely signal violence to come.

Upton was particularly hurt by encountering, in the press that very morning, President Roosevelt's denunciation in a speech of certain "yellow journalists" and "muckrakers" bent on "stirring up discord in America."

So, Upton crosses out his inspired title. But can't think of a substitute.

Hearing *UPTON SINCLAIR!* amid the ceaseless murmur and clatter of the train station, yet steeling himself to resist; for he knows it is a phantom calling to him, and mocking him; a simulacrum of his own, future self in some unfathomable time. He dares not look up; he must keep his glance down, on the sheet of foolscap; he must concentrate, to save his life; falling to the task of covering one long sheet of foolscap in his small hand, and then reversing it, so that every inch of space will be utilized, and nothing wasted; and then a fresh sheet is produced out of the valise, and another. So immersed in his work is Upton Sinclair, the hands of the great clock in the center of the terminal now read 2:48 P.M. which means that the young author has missed his train to Englewood, and will not discover the fact for several minutes.

Yet there is no reason for immediate alarm, for another train to New Jersey will come along in an hour or two; and Upton Sinclair will see to it that he does not miss that one.

THE CROSSWICKS MIRACLE

So the Curse seemed at last to have lifted, and the three Slade grandchildren entombed in the family mausoleum, Annabel, Oriana, and Todd, were roused from their stony trance, sometime in the early afternoon of June 4; and, at the antipodes of the Earth, in the Southern Ocean, in the hold of the pitching and tossing *Balmoral,* Josiah was restored to life, to the amazement of Captain Oates and his crew, who would swear that, frozen in the ocean, he must certainly have died.

A miracle, it would be said—or indeed, miracles. And directly related to Todd Slade's adventure in the Bog Kingdom, and his grandfather's death in Princeton. Yet historians have tried to explain these unique events as "natural"—the original origins of death having been mistaken. For the young persons entombed in the Slade mausoleum might have suffered a rare category of catalepsy, or a relatively benign strain of the Laotian sleeping sickness; or, it may have been, an hypothesis suggested in the anonymously penned *The Vampire Murders of Old Princeton,* an insidious form of mesmerism.

"For the very fact that the young people now *live* necessitates the fact that they never *died*"—this was the verdict of Dr. Hiram Hastings of the Harvard Medical School, summoned to Princeton to give an expert diagnosis of the bizarre development of three individuals, of the same family, "coming to life" at the same time, in their family tomb. (It was Todd who shouted loudest, attracting the attention of the terrified groundskeeper of the Princeton Cemetery, who could not believe his ears, and then could not believe his eyes; and would never wholly recover from his shock.)

Dr. Hastings's much-deliberated conclusion was that the young Slades had lapsed into comatose conditions in which breathing, heartbeat, and other vital signs were suppressed; but responsible physicians and medical workers should have detected life in their bodies and brain activity of a kind, by shining a beam of light into the individual's eye, in which an involuntary reflex of the pupil would signal life. Told that reputable physicians in Princeton, notably Dr. Boudinot, Sr., and Dr. Boudinot, Jr., had "thoroughly examined" their patients before declaring them dead, and signing death certificates, the Harvard doctor said, with a bemused smile, "Yes. But this is Princeton, you see. This is not Boston, Massachusetts, where our medical standards are higher."

It seems that Josiah Slade was not in fact "frozen" in the waters of the Southern Ocean but had been subjected so quickly to so low a temperature, his body had reacted by reverting to a state virtually prenatal, or mimicking hibernation; in Josiah too, breathing, heartbeat, and vital signs were gravely suppressed, and only a cursory examination of his "frozen" body was made by Captain Oates and his appalled physician (in fact, a dropout of the Columbia University College of Physicians and Surgeons and not a licensed M.D.) before he was declared dead, his body wrapped in canvas and placed in the hold, to be interred when the *Balmoral* returned to New York Harbor at the end of the summer.

(Though awakened at the time of the others, Josiah did not return to Princeton until late August, for the *Balmoral* continued on its expeditionary journey into the south polar region, as planned.)

Josiah, too, had quite terrorized his shipboard companions by pounding on a door to the hold, and shouting loudly. Since none of the crew would open the door to him, Captain Oates had had to be summoned; and he, like the Princeton cemetery groundskeeper, would never wholly recover from his shock. Captain Oates seems soon then to have retired from sea-going, to vanish into the mountainous regions of upstate New York and the anonymity of a landlocked life.

It was a very good thing that none of the young people could remember the circumstances of their "dying," or lying in state, or being entombed. All had the confused belief that they had slumbered deeply, and would not have wished to be awakened. For was not their sleep, as Macbeth had spoken yearningly of sleep, a "raveling up of the sleeve of care"; had they not slipped from a place of grief, and, in waking, found themselves restored to a semblance of their old happiness?

Annabel was never to remember having "given birth"—though in her dreams she would perceive the image of a floating "ghost baby" with features too indistinct to be seen; and of an identity totally unknown to her.

The youngest, Oriana, was yet more soft-spoken and reticent than she'd been in her previous life, except at odd, mercurial moments when she burst into nervous laughter, or tears; she remembered nothing of her fall from a high roof of Wheatsheaf, but spoke wonderingly of her flight into Heaven, the movement of her "white-feathered wings"—the joy of being borne aloft in the air as if bodiless. Her companion was a hawk, she said, of noble proportions; a female hawk, she seemed to know, with "golden" eyes—"How I wished I could fly with her forever! But my wings were not strong enough, and she flew on without me; and I had to come back, to my home."

Todd recovered slowly from his ordeal, having lost a good deal of weight since his "death"; he then confounded all the family with his memento of the Bog Kingdom, as he called it—a single black checker, of carved wood; a very old piece it seemed, which was found clutched in his fingers when he awakened in the dark of the tomb.

By degrees, over a period of weeks, Todd regained some of his memory, and was encouraged by Annabel to dictate his story to her, that all of the world might know of his experiences; which account has been included here in its entirety, in the chapter titled "A Game of Draughts." Todd rejected the notion, as an insult, that he had simply "frozen" to a comatose state in the cemetery, while visiting his cousin's and his sister's tomb; it was Todd's insistence that he hadn't been in the cemetery at all at that time, but in his grandfather Winslow Slade's library where he dimly recalled the fireplace with the secret passageway beyond, and how he had made his way through. (Yet, when Todd and Annabel examined the fireplace in their grandfather's library, all the bricks were in place, and none were loose, or could have loosened. "It is a perfect brick wall," Annabel observed, "through which no one, not even a wily snake, could crawl.")

Following the trauma of her "death" Annabel Slade recovered by slow degrees to a semblance of her former self; she would not regain her youthful beauty, which may have been fragile and fleeting as the roses in her mother's garden, but acquired a more thoughtful, if slightly ironic look of female sensitivity; her forehead was just perceptibly lined, with worry-frowns etched permanently in her skin; her smile was not so spontaneous as it had been, but rather hesitant, and guarded. Annabel had become one who distrusts happiness—until it has been proven to her that the happiness is genuine. Of the four grandchildren, Annabel was the most afflicted by amnesia; she would recall virtually nothing of the long episode she had told her family, which was recorded by Josiah in the invaluable Turquoise-Marbled Book; fortunately for her, she recalled nothing of her grotesque pregnancy, and its aftermath. So confused was the young woman, when first she'd wakened, and was removed to Crosswicks, to familiar quarters, she persisted in claiming that she "knew she must not marry Dabney Bayard but must break the engagement at once"—as if the year were still 1905, and the date sometime before June 4. She told her parents: "Dabney does not love me, I know. He loves my 'Slade' name—he loves this estate. He may not like women at all—at least, he does not like me. And I don't love him—I don't feel for him any portion of what I feel for you, or Josiah. And though it may disappoint and anger you, dear parents, I don't think I want to marry anyone at all."

Henrietta and Augustus must have exulted, that their (naively optimistic) prayers had been answered: their beloved daughter restored to them *as she had been;* that is, innocent, and in a sense a virgin; for, her experience being guiltless as it seems to have been, Annabel could no more be counted as the illicit bride of Axson Mayte than she had been the bride of Lieutenant Bayard. (Their marriage had been annulled, and so was stricken from any and all church records.)

"I will never leave you again, dear parents," Annabel said gaily, "—at least, I will never leave Princeton or—at least, I will never leave New Jersey. That is my promise."

Of the four morbidly afflicted grandchildren, Josiah was the most clinically curious regarding his experience in that "other" world. He was certain that he'd been conscious all the while he'd been in the hold of the ship; mistaken as dead, he'd certainly been plunged into a deep sleep, with imperceptible vital signs. The barking of dogs close by his head, the whinnying of horses, the howling of winds, the creaking of the ship—these were phantasms in his dreams, yet very real. Vividly he remembered his sister in distress, on an ice floe in the Southern Ocean; he remembered her calling to him; and he remembered hurrying to her rescue—but beyond that, he remembered nothing. Except for growing gaunt from lack of food, Josiah had been refreshed from his sleep; and in this sleep, his evil "voices" vanished. Having wakened from his enchantment Josiah believed that he was fully himself again, as he had not been for a year or more; and never again suffered the incursion of alien thoughts, that had so made his life a torment.

"The first act of my newly regained sanity," Josiah said, "was to disengage myself from the folly of the South Polar expedition, which was poorly funded and poorly staffed; when the men set forth on land, led by Oates, I remained safely on the *Balmoral* with a few other men, to write in my journal and compose my thoughts. Men were lost in the polar region—all of the ponies were lost, and half the dogs—God only knows what the survivors had to do, to survive those grim months. But they did return. And so we all returned to civilization, just a little later than scheduled."

To his family, and to Annabel in particular, Josiah vowed that he would never again set sail for *terra incognita*—"There is the unknown world within, that quite suffices."

THOUGH *THE ACCURSED* is a chronicle of events primarily limited to 1905 to 1906, I think it is necessary to suggest an immediate future beyond the buoyant summer of 1906 when all of the Slades were reunited, except for the unhappy Copplestone. Within the year, through a set of serendipitous circumstances, Josiah and Annabel joined the Helicon Home Colony in the countryside near Englewood, New Jersey; for Josiah had another time sought out Upton Sinclair, at an Intercollegiate Socialist rally in New York, and established a connection with the young organizer, whom he introduced to Annabel, and eventually to Wilhelmina Burr, who joined the Colony at a slightly later date. (When Annabel and Wilhelmina at last embraced, having not seen each other since the morning of Annabel's wedding, Wilhelmina burst into tears declaring that she had never in her heart believed that her dear friend had died; somehow, she had known that Annabel was still living, in some way unfathomable to the world. "And now, I hope never to let you out of my sight again," Wilhelmina vowed, "or, at least, out of the range of my love.") And there came to live in the Colony the former seminarian and now avid Socialist Yaeger Ruggles, who became a close friend and comrade to all, as one with particularly "radical and revolutionary" ideas ranging from union organizing to farming, worker-owned factories to "race-free" education and housing; ideas, unfortunately, far ahead of their time.

The Helicon Home Colony was comprised of several stucco-and-wood-frame buildings including a residence that had been a boys' dormitory, that had had to be renovated, for use of the commune; the property included some two hundred acres of fertile land, both cultivated and wooded, stretching from the Old Jericho Road north and eastward past Lockwood Gorge. The Colony was to prove, at the first, at least, a happy retreat for the idealistic young people who had had quite enough, as they phrased it, of proper bourgeois society; and wished to apply their energies to such disciplines as agronomics, organic agriculture, animal husbandry, and greenhouse-horticulture. When not involved in Socialist activities in New York City, Josiah was much absorbed in the breeding and training of Peruvian horses, whose beauty and grace quite bewitched him. Wilhelmina persevered in her art, hoping to cultivate a "women's Socialist aesthetic"; Annabel concentrated upon writing, and the upkeep of the Colony to which, like Josiah, she contributed virtually all of her trust-fund money.

Though the young "farmers" were novices at the time they began their venture, Upton Sinclair had been canny enough to invite more experienced individuals to join the commune, to help with the outdoors; it was his dream that one day soon, in another year or two, the Helicon Home Colony might expand to include fifty members, a hundred members, two hundred—"Eventually, we might revolutionize the world!" Upton had charted a five-year plan by which the Colony would soon become self-sustaining, and even profitable; in the meantime, they would supplement their income with private earnings, like those from his book royalties, and they would grow as much of their own food as they could, and sell what they could—"People in the area will know, they can trust *us*."

In the early winter of '06, that they might quell some of the slanderous and threatening things said of them by residents of Englewood and environs, there was a double wedding on the premises, presided over by an ordained (female) minister of the Brooklyn Unitarian Church, at which these couples were joined in matrimony: Josiah Slade and Wilhelmina Burr, and Annabel Slade and Yaeger Ruggles.*

Of what lies ahead for idealistic young people in March 1907, this historian will not speak except to say that all survived the arson-set fire; for my chronicle has ended, and "ordinary life" must resume. My final scene is the double wedding ceremony at the Helicon Home Colony in a flower-garlanded setting, with Upton Sinclair boyishly smiling, shaking hands with the bridal couples and the guests, tears shining in his eyes: "Comrades! It is the dawn of a new day! *Revolution now!*"

---

* At the Helicon Colony, it was quickly determined that Annabel Slade had a skill for bookkeeping, and took pleasure in "balancing the books," that had quite eluded Upton Sinclair who had neither the time nor the aptitude for such; by degrees Annabel was given responsibility for the housekeeping budget and in this way had much opportunity to confer with Yaeger Ruggles, whose dark eyes, "kinky"-dark hair worn to the collar, olive-tinted complexion and "meltingly Virginian" accent quite entranced her; as the very blond Annabel Slade entranced the former seminarian, at their first meeting. What is the historian to think? Is it the historian's place to suggest disapproval of "race-mixing"? Or—was such radical behavior on the part of Annabel Slade but a prophecy of what disruptions to tradition lay ahead in the tumultuous twentieth-century, let alone the unfathomable twenty-first? It was a measure of the elder Slades' resignation to fate that, confronted with the news that their daughter, only newly returned to them from the dead, should "fall under the spell" a second time of a seemingly unsuitable individual with a marked Virginia accent, they did not interfere with her marriage plans.

Epilogue

THE COVENANT

(Winslow Slade)

O DEARLY BELOVED IN CHRIST—HEAR ME AND HAVE MERCY.

KNOW THAT MY SIN HAS BEEN THE MORE COMPOUNDED IN THAT I HAVE WORN THROUGH MY LIFE *THE FACE OF VIRTUE.*

KNOW THAT MY EVIL HAS BEEN THE MORE COMPOUNDED IN THAT I HAVE SPOKEN THROUGH MY LIFE IN *THE VOICE OF RIGHTEOUSNESS.*

O FRIENDS AND NEIGHBORS AND FELLOW CHRISTIANS, O BELOVED KIN TO ME, YET THE MORE ABUSED BY ME, WHO HAS DWELT AMONG YOU IN HYPOCRITE GOODNESS THESE FIVE DECADES AND MORE.

KNOW THAT MY BLAME FOR THE CURSE PERPETRATED UPON YOU IS THE MORE COMPOUNDED IN THAT I HAVE MADE THE FEEBLE AND HYPOCRITICAL PRETENSE OF AN EARLIER CONFESSION: A FALSE CONFESSION FROM THE FIRST SYLLABLE.

KNOW THAT THE CURSE UNLEASHED UPON YOU AS A

CONSEQUENCE OF WINSLOW SLADE'S SIN, AND THAT ALONE; AND THAT IT WAS NOT A PACT WITH THE DEVIL BUT A PACT WITH ALMIGHTY GOD WHOSE WRATHFUL HAND CANNOT BE STAYED BY THE EXERCISE OF PRAYER, GOODNESS, OR SACRIFICE OR *ANY HUMAN PETITION AT ALL*.

KNOW THAT I STAND AT LAST UNMASKED AND STRIPPED BEFORE YOU, AS *MURDERER, PERJURER,* AND *HYPOCRITE BETRAYER* OF ALL THAT YOU HOLD DEAR; AND THAT ON THIS SABBATH MORNING IN MY SEVENTY-SIXTH YEAR, FOLLOWING THE RAMPAGING HORROR FOR WHICH I ALONE AM TO BLAME, I DO HEREBY CONFESS MY SIN, MY CRIME, AND MY BETRAYAL OF OUR COMMONWEAL, AND ABSOLVE YOU OF THE BITTER DEED OF CHASTISING ME, BY CONSENTING TO MY OWN DEATH AS QUICKLY AS THE LORD GOD WILL SEND IT: THAT I MAY BE PLUNGED INTO THE FARTHEST DEPTHS OF HELL, TO SUFFER THERE FOREVERMORE, AS MY PITEOUS VICTIM HAD PRAYED IN HER TERROR OF ME.

"YET YE SHALL BE BROUGHT DOWN TO HELL."

IT WAS NOT THE FRENCHMAN SELINCOURT WHO STRANGLED THE YOUNG WOMAN NAMED PEARL BUT I, WINSLOW SLADE: I WHO STAND BEFORE YOU DECADES AFTER THAT FOUL DEED *UNMASKED AND STRIPPED AND PROCLAIMED THROUGH ALL THE WORLD AS MURDERER, PERJURER, AND HYPOCRITE BETRAYER*: I, AND I ALONE WHO MEANT TO SILENCE THE POOR MILL-GIRL WITH THE MANGLED HAND AND THE SKIN LIKE SOMETHING SINGED AND EYES TREMULOUS WITH KNOWLEDGE OF HER DOOM AT THE HANDS OF THE FRANTIC YOUNG (WHITE) MAN TIGHTENING HIS HANDS ABOUT HER NECK AND SQUEEZING, AND SQUEEZING, IN THE DESPERATION OF COWARDICE AND

SHAME; UNTIL NO LIFE REMAINED IN HER FRANTIC BODY, AND NO TEASING FIRE BLAZED OUT FROM HER DULLED EYES. UNTIL THE GIRL LAY LIFELESS AND BROKEN ON THE CHILL GROUND BEFORE ME: AND WINSLOW SLADE WAS INDEED DAMNED FOR ALL ETERNITY.

I WANTED ONLY TO SILENCE HER SCREAMS AND ACCUSA- TIONS WHICH I DID—O LORD!

I WANTED ONLY TO EXERT MY POWER OVER HER TO IN- TIMIDATE HER AND ABASH HER WHICH I DID—O LORD, THOU KNOWEST HOW!

I WANTED ONLY TO INFLICT SOME SMALL WARNING IN- JURY UPON HER HEATED AND WRITHING FEMALE FORM IN THE RANK INDECENCY OF HER SEX WHICH I DID—O MERCI- LESS LORD, AS THOU WELL KNOWEST.

FOR SHE WAS TAINTED, AND IMPURE; AND NOT DESERVING OF LIFE.

FOR SHE WOULD CLING TO ME LIKE MUD; AND WAS FRIGHTENING TO ME.

FOR SHE WAS SENSUOUS AND BEAUTIFUL IN A WAY UT- TERLY NEW TO ME, THAT WAS TERRIBLE TO BEHOLD, AND MUST BE PUNISHED.

FOR SHE DARED SLIDE HER ARMS AROUND MY NECK AND MADE TO MOVE HER FLESHY LIPS AGAINST MY NECK, MY CHEEK, MY MOUTH ALL SHAMELESSLY AND TO ENJOIN ME INTO KISSING HER IN TURN—AS I COULD NOT RESIST.

FOR SHE SEDUCED ME INTO BETRAYING MY FIANCÉE WHOSE VERY NAME IN THE HEAT OF SUCH PASSION I COULD NOT HAVE RECALLED.

FOR SHE CURSED ME AND PRESSED HER DEMON'S BODY

AGAINST ME; AND TOUCHED HER HOT TONGUE TO ME AND
LAUGHED AND TEASED AND TORMENTED AND AROUSED
SUCH HELLISH DESIRE IN ME, IT WAS NOT TO BE BORNE.

FOR IT WAS *SHE AND SHE ALONE THE BLIGHTED ONE WHO
BROUGHT ME DOWN TO SIN AND TO THE CONDITION OF COMMON
MAN AND TO MORTALITY* AND O FEARSOME GOD!—I KNOW NOT
ALL.

IT WAS NOT YOUNG WINSLOW SLADE INNOCENT OF ALL
CARNAL KNOWLEDGE UNTIL THAT TIME WHO GROVELED
UPON THE GIRL TO BURY HIMSELF IN HER BODY EVEN AS THE
DESPERATE LIFE FLED FROM HER—IT WAS ANOTHER BEING EN-
TIRELY—A TRUE DEMON NOT BAPTIZED AS A SLADE. AND THE
LORD GOD WAS THE ONLY WITNESS, AND DID NOT INTERVENE.

GAZING STERNLY DOWN UPON ME WHERE I LAY ENTWINED IN
THE GIRL'S ARMS AND AGAINST HER BREASTS AND BELLY AND
THE FLESH OF HER LEGS FROM WHICH HEAT WAS FADING RAP-
IDLY AND NO REPENTANCE COULD SUMMON BACK. AND THE
FLEET THOUGHT CAME TO ME, I WOULD COVER HER IN LEAVES
AND DIRT AND ANOINT HER FOREHEAD WITH MUD AND HIDE
FROM THE LORD IN THE DEPTHS OF THE WOODS AND ABAN-
DON MY LIFE AMONG CIVILIZED MEN FOREVERMORE.

WILD ANGRY LAUGHTER DESCENDED FROM THE HEAVENS
LIKE MADDENED THUNDER AS THE LORD GOD DEMANDED
OF ME WHAT WICKEDNESS HAVE YOU WORKED UPON THE
FEMALE MY FINE LAD WHAT BIT OF NAUGHTINESS HAVE YOU
PERFORMED IN SECRET AS ALL OF THE SLADES PERFORM IN SE-
CRET FROM YOUR DAYS OF SLAVE-HOLDING UNTIL NOW YOUR
GREAT FORTUNE WHICH IS THE LORD'S BLESSING HARVESTED
FROM THE BENT AND BROKEN BACKS OF FACTORY WORKERS,
MILL-WORKERS, DUMB AND STAMMERING IMMIGRANTS MISS-
ING FINGERS, TOES, EYES YET YOU HAVE TRIED TO TRICK YOUR

GOD, YOU HAVE TRIED TO DISGUISE YOUR SIN AS IF IT WERE A MERE CRIME, DO YOU THINK IT IS A MATTER OF FASTENING UP YOUR BREECHES MY LAD AND CREEPING OFF INTO THE FOREST PANTING LIKE A BEAST, DO YOU THINK THAT THIS NIGHT WILL BE EXORCISED WHEN THE MOON'S STONY RAYS SUCCUMB TO THE SUN; DO YOU THINK MY GREEN YOUNG WHELP THAT YOU HAVE ACTED ALONE IN THIS DAMNED PLACE AND WITHOUT THE KNOWLEDGE OF YOUR LORD?

SO DEAFENING HIS LAUGHTER FOR IT WAS THE LORD GOD OF WRATH OF OUR HEBREW ANCESTORS AND NOT THE LORD JESUS WHO DIED ON THE CROSS FOR OUR SINS AND SO I SOUGHT TO BURROW INTO THE VERY EARTH TO ESCAPE SUCH LAUGHTER AS THE STARK-STARING FEMALE GRINNED AT ME IN THE RIGOR OF DEATH AND REVEALED HERSELF SO VERY YOUNG, NOT MORE THAN SIXTEEN AND SHE WOULD NOT WAKE WHEN I GRIPPED HER SHOULDERS AND SHOOK AND SHOOK AND CRIED OUT TO HER TO ARISE BEFORE IT WAS TOO LATE, I WOULD MAKE UP TO HER AND TO HER PEOPLE ALL THAT I COULD, I WOULD MAKE AMENDS FOR MY LUST AND MY CRUELTY BUT THERE WAS NO RESPONSE, FOR ALL BREATH HAD CEASED; THE SINGED SKIN THAT HAD SO REPELLED AS IT HAD ATTRACTED WAS FADING NOW AS WARMTH FADED FROM THE BODY, THAT COULD NOT BE CALLED BACK. AND THE LORD GOD SAW ALL AND HIS WRATH WAS THE MORE, THAT I HAD COMMITTED SO COARSE AND CRUDE A SIN AND TRIED THEN TO HIDE FROM HIM. AND THAT WAS THE GREATER SIN.

JESUS—TWIN OF JUDAS THOMAS—SPOKE IN A VOICE LIKE A TRUMPET, DO YOU THINK, MAN, THAT I AM COME TO BRING PEACE TO THE WORLD AND KNOW NOT THAT I AM COME TO CAST DIVISIONS—FIRE, SWORD, WAR, FOR THE CHILDREN

SHALL BE SET AGAINST THE FATHER AND THE HUSBAND AGAINST THE WIFE AND THERE SHALL BE FIVE IN A HOUSE: THREE AGAINST TWO, AND TWO AGAINST THREE; THE FATHER AGAINST THE SON AND THE SON AGAINST THE FATHER; AND ALL MANKIND SHALL STAND AS SOLITARIES.

IN ANGER JESUS SPAKE, I WILL GIVE YOU THAT WHICH THE EYE HAS NOT YET SEEN, AND THE EAR HAS NEVER HEARD, AND THE HAND HAS NOT DARED TO TOUCH, AND THAT WHICH HAS NOT YET ENTERED INTO THE HEART OF MAN.

AND JESUS PROMISED, THAT SHALL BE THY PARTICULAR WISDOM, TO KNOW WHAT NO OTHER MEN KNOW: BUT TO STAND SOLITARY FROM THEM, IN THAT KNOWING.

KNOW, O DEARLY BELOVED GATHERED TOGETHER TODAY IN THIS PLACE OF WORSHIP, IT WAS NOT THE LUCKLESS SELIN-COURT WHO COMMITTED THE BRUTE CRIME AT COLD SPRING THOUGH THE MAN WAS PUNISHED FOR IT: HIS LIFE TAKEN FROM HIM AT THE END OF A ROPE IN THE PRISON AT TRENTON WHILE THE TRUE MURDERER HID AWAY IN WEALTH AND RECTITUDE LESS THAN TWENTY MILES AWAY IN THE VILLAGE OF PRINCETON; THE MURDERER HID IN PLAIN SIGHT YET IN TERROR OF BEING DISCOVERED AND REVEALED AND SHAMED THROUGHOUT THE LAND FOR LAYING HIS HAND UPON A FEMALE SO DEFILED AND OF A CASTAWAY RACE, A DESCENDANT OF THOSE BROUGHT FROM AFRICA IN CHAINS HAVING BEEN SOLD INTO SLAVERY BY THEIR KINDRED AFRICANS FOR PURE GAIN.

THIS MURDERER WHITE-SKINNED AND PRIZED WITHIN HIS FAMILY AS A MOST PROMISING SON SO DECEIVED HIMSELF SAYING, I AM A SLADE, AND ORDAINED BY GOD; AND GUILTY OF NO CRIME; FOR ALL THAT FALLS FROM MY HAND MUST BE GOD'S OWN DESIRE, AND CANNOT BE DEEMED SIN.

HOW COLD IS YOUR BREATH, WINSLOW—MY YOUNG BRIDE SHRANK FROM ME ON OUR WEDDING NIGHT; FOR MINE WAS THE FETID BREATH OF THE GRAVE, THAT WAS MY OWN. FOR MY INNOCENT BRIDE ORIANA HAD ONLY TO GAZE INTO MY GUILT-SICKENED EYES TO KNOW OF THE FOUL CRIME COMMITTED IN MY HEART OF WHICH I WOULD NOT EVER SPEAK TO HER, OR TO ANYONE.

AND IN THE NIGHT OF MANY YEARS TO COME PARALYZED IN SLEEP AND MY UNHAPPY WIFE BESIDE ME I STRUGGLED TO DRAG THE BODY DEEPER INTO THE FOREST AND FARTHER INTO THE NIGHT TO A PLACE OF MARSH GRASSES AND ROTTED TREES AND SNAKES RIPPLING BENEATH THE SURFACE OF BRACKISH WATER TREMBLING AND WHIMPERING LIKE A FRIGHTENED CHILD, O GOD THOU SEEST ALL, AND FORGIVE NOTHING! HOPING TO COVER THE BROKEN CREATURE WITH LEAVES AND MUD SCOOPED IN MY HANDS, AND FALLEN BRANCHES, THAT SHE WOULD NEVER BE DISCOVERED; AND IF NOT, AND IF NO ONE EVER KNEW WHAT HAD BECOME OF PEARL WHO HAD PRESSED HERSELF INTO THE ARMS OF MANY MEN FOR THE PROFIT OF THOSE MEN WHO USED HER YET ALSO IT SEEMED FOR SOME SMALL GESTURE OF LOVE, OR A MOCKERY OF LOVE. AND IF THIS WAS SO, AND THE BODY NEVER FOUND, THE CRUEL DEED HAD NOT TRANSPIRED—HAD IT?

AFTERWARD RUNNING FOR MY LIFE. AND MY SHOES TAKEN FROM ME, SO I AM BAREFOOT.

AND IN PURSUIT THE LORD GOD OF HOSTS LIKE A RAGING HOUND AND JESUS WITH A VOICE LIKE A TRUMPET JEERING AND NOT THE JESUS OF LOVE SAYING, LET US FORGE A COVENANT BETWEEN ME AND THEE: FIFTY YEARS SHALL YE BE GRANTED, TO EXERCISE WHAT TRIFLING GOOD, OR FURTHER HARM, YE WILL: AND THEN THE ANGELS OF WRATH WILL BE

LOOSED UPON YOU—AND UPON THOSE WHOM YOU LOVE BE-
YOND YOURSELF.

KNOW, WINSLOW SLADE, ALL THE DAYS OF YOUR LIFE NO
ONE SHALL BE SPARED WHO DWELLS BESIDE YOU, AND EM-
BRACES YOU; FOR YOU ARE ACCURSED OF GOD, YET A WORTHY
TWIN OF THE WRATHFUL GOD. HALLOWED BE THY NAME,
REVEREND SLADE.

*AND IN TRUTH, O DEARLY BELOVED, I HAD NOT KNOWN THE
LORD GOD OR HIS ONLY BEGOTTEN SON JESUS OF NAZARETH IN ALL
MY LIFE BEFORE; NOR DO ANY OF YOU KNOW THESE, UNLESS YOU
HAVE TASTED BLOOD.*

*MY FAMILY, MY RELATIVES, MY PRINCETON FRIENDS AND NEIGH-
BORS, MY BRETHREN IN CHRIST—O YE TO WHOM I HAVE LIED THESE
MANY YEARS, YE TO WHOM IN ALL CUNNING I HAVE PRESENTED A
FALSE FACE OF VIRTUE: KNOW THAT* THREE DAYS PASSED BEFORE
THE MILL-GIRL'S BODY WAS DISCOVERED DEEP IN THE FOR-
EST BEYOND COLD SPRING; AND WITHIN A DAY THEN THE
FRENCHMAN SELINCOURT WAS APPREHENDED, IN FLIGHT
FOR HIS LIFE—A SIGN OF THE RUFFIAN'S GUILT IT WAS BE-
LIEVED. (HIS COMPANION WHO HAD AS CRUELLY MISUSED
PEARL WAS NEVER APPREHENDED.) SOON THEN THE MAN
WAS MADE TO CONFESS HIS FOUL DEED, NOT ONLY MURDER
BUT THE VIOLATION OF THE GIRL'S BODY UNMISTAKABLE
AFTER EVEN THREE DAYS AND TOO VILE TO BE GIVEN UTTER-
ANCE IN NEWSPAPER ACCOUNTS. THE LORD GOD WATCHED
OVER ME AS I WAS SEQUESTERED AWAY AT THE MANSE
TAKEN SICK AND ENFEEBLED WITH A FEVER-MALAISE AND
MY FEET COVERED IN SCABS AND BRUISES LIKE ONE WHO
HAS BEEN CRUCIFIED. AND MY DEAR MOTHER ALL UNKNOW-
ING, ACTING AS MY NURSE. FOR WOMEN HAVE ALWAYS PRO-

TECTED ME, NOT KNOWING ME IN MY INNERMOST HEART. IT WAS AN ATTACK OF BRAIN FEVER, THE DIAGNOSIS CAME; OR INFLUENZA; OR—THEY KNEW NOT: BUT VERY GRAVE IT WAS INDEED, AND ONLY THE LORD GOD BY HIS MINISTRATIONS ALLOWED WINSLOW SLADE TO SURVIVE INTO HIS WRETCHED LIFE.

SO IT CAME TO BE, THE FRENCHMAN SELINCOURT WAS TRIED AND FOUND GUILTY OF MURDER IN THE FIRST DEGREE AND IN THE AUTUMN OF 1855 EXECUTED BY THE STATE OF NEW JERSEY FOR HIS DESPICABLE CRIME: BEING HANGED BY THE NECK UNTIL DECLARED DEAD. AND THE YOUNG SEMINARIAN HAD LONG SINCE RETURNED TO HIS PASTORAL STUDIES AND PLEASED HIS ELDERS WITH HIS PIETY, DILIGENCE, AND INTELLIGENCE; AND PLEASED THE LORD GOD AND HIS SON AS WELL; FOR SOON HE WAS DULY ORDAINED A MINISTER IN THE PRESBYTERIAN FAITH AND THE LORD GOD LAUGHED AT SUCH A MASQUERADE SAYING,

KNOW THAT JESUS HAD A TWIN, DIDYMUS JUDAS THOMAS APOSTLE OF THE MOST HIGH, AND SO TOO WINSLOW SLADE HAS A TWIN: THIS BEING THE LORD GOD OF HOSTS WITH WHOM HE HAS FORGED A COVENANT TO DISGUISE THE WORKINGS OF EVIL ON EARTH WITH A PACIFIST SMILE AND IN THIS WAY TO PROMOTE EVIL AND ALL WICKEDNESS UPON THE EARTH; WHILE TAKING CARE ALWAYS TO PREACH THE REVERSE AND BEHAVING AT ALL TIMES AS IF HE WERE FREE OF THE SLIGHTEST TAINT OF SIN.

FOR, MY BRETHREN: IT IS WICKEDNESS, DISCORD, AND TERROR THAT LEAD MEN TO THE LORD, IN THEIR BROKEN SOULS; AND IN FEAR OF HIS CRUELTY; AND TERROR OF HIS GAPING HELL.

FOR THE HAPPINESS OF THE PEOPLE IS THE CURSE OF

GOD, THAT THEY DRIFT FROM HIM, AND TURN THEIR EYES UPON ONE ANOTHER, OR UPON THEIR OWN MIRRORED SELVES—TO THE VAST DISPLEASURE OF THE LORD.

FOR THE MISERY OF THE PEOPLE HAS LONG BEEN THE JOY OF THE LORD, FROM THE TIME OF THE CHILDREN OF ISRAEL UNTIL NOW; AS ONLY WHEN THEY THROW THEMSELVES PROSTRATE BEFORE HIM IN ANNIHILATION OF THEIR MUTINOUS SPIRITS, AND WORSHIP HIM AS HE DEMANDS, IS THE LORD GOD FULFILLED, AND HIS RAGE QUELLED.

FOR KNOW THAT THE LORD GOD IS A JEALOUS GOD AS THE HEBREW BIBLE HAS WARNED, AS HE HAS DECLARED AND COMMANDS THE WHIRLWIND, AND THE DEEPS OF THE SEA, AND THE SWORD OF THE BARBARIAN, AND EVERY MANNER OF VERMIN, IN HIS EMPLOY, THAT MEEKNESS, SERVILITY, UNBRIDLED FEAR AND TREMBLING BE THE LOT OF MANKIND; AND HIS GLORY EXALTED.

THE CYNICS, ATHEISTS AND ANARCHISTS AMONG YOU ARE THE ESPECIAL ENEMIES OF GOD, AS THEY DO NOT REQUIRE HIM: YET IT IS REQUIRED OF THE BELIEVERS IN GOD, THAT THEY DO BATTLE WITH SUCH INFIDELS WHO WOULD SAVE THEM FROM THE WRATHFUL GOD, IN THEIR IGNORANCE. AS IT IS OUR AIM TO SOW DISCORD AMONG THE NATIONS, AND TO SET MEN AGAINST THEIR FELLOWS, FOR EACH TRIBE OF MAN BELIEVES THAT THE LORD GOD IS ITS GOD, AND HATES ALL OTHER TRIBES; IT IS THE FATE OF NATIONS TO BE SET FOREVER AGAINST ONE ANOTHER, THAT THE SWORD MAY BE WORSHIPPED, AND ENEMIES TERRORIZED IN THE NAME OF GOD THAT THEIR FERTILE LANDS AND WATERWAYS BE APPROPRIATED, YET ONLY IN THE NAME OF GOD.

FOR KNOW THAT WE WHO ARE HIS AGENTS ARE MOST

PRIZED WHERE WE PREACH DISCORD WHILE EMPLOYING A VOCABULARY OF LOVE; AND WE PLEASE HIM, IN SPEAKING OF ARMAGEDDON, AND LAST THINGS, AND THE LAYING WASTE OF THE SINFUL CITIES OF MANKIND—THE MORE SUBTLE OUR MANNER, THE MORE BENIGN AND LOVING, THE MORE PRIZED BY THE LORD FOR WE ARE THOSE WHO URGE THE SLAVE TO FORGIVE THE SLAVER, AND TO WEAR THE GARMENTS OF HIS RELIGION AS THEIR OWN; WE URGE THE DOWNTRODDEN TO REJOICE IN THE LITTLE THAT IS THEIRS, OUT OF FEAR OF HELL; TO STAY THE HAND OF THE REBEL, IN A FALSE PEACE.

ALL THIS WAS TOLD TO ME ON THE VERY EVE OF MY OR-DINATION. NEVER IN ALL THE INTERVENING YEARS HAVE I SWERVED FROM THIS FAITH.

MY FIRST WIFE ORIANA THOUGH GUILTLESS OF HER HUS-BAND'S SIN SUFFERED ITS EFFECTS NONETHELESS AND SHRANK FROM ME IN APPREHENSION, HOW COLD YOUR HANDS, MY HUSBAND, YOUR BREATH, YOUR LIPS—YOUR SOUL! THOUGH I FELT NO TRUE DESIRE FOR HER OR FOR ANY WOMAN SINCE THE NIGHT OF MARCH 1855 WHEN OUT OF MY LOINS LEAPT A BURNING AND POISONOUS FLUID CONJURED FORTH BY THE MILL-GIRL WITH THE SINGED SKIN AND MAN-GLED HAND; AND OVER THE YEARS, YET IT HAPPENED THAT SONS WERE BORN TO ME, OUT OF MY WIFE'S BODY FOR AL-WAYS IT WAS KNOWN BETWEEN THE LORD GOD AND ME THAT HE SENT SONS TO ME THAT THE SLADES BE PERPETUATED AND OUR LINEAGE NOT EXTINCT. THUS IT WAS, TWO BABY DAUGH-TERS WERE STRICKEN WITH DIPHTHERIA AND DIED AS IN-FANTS AS NEGLIGIBLE TO GOD'S PLAN; THOUGH ORIANA WAS DEVASTATED BY SUCH LOSSES, AND DID NOT EVER RECOVER

FULLY; AND HERSELF PASSED AWAY OF A LINGERING MALAISE, WHEN MY SONS WERE HUSKY YOUNG BOYS OF NINE AND THIRTEEN YEARS AND DID NOT ANY LONGER REQUIRE HER.

AND IN HER LOSS I GRIEVED, FOR I KNEW THAT I HAD DESTROYED HER LIFE, AS I HAD DESTROYED THE LIFE OF THE LITTLE MILL-GIRL.

YET THE LORD SENT ANOTHER WOMAN TO ME, THAT I WOULD NOT FALL INTO DESPAIR; FOR IT IS THE VERY AGENTS OF THE WRATHFUL GOD WHO ARE VULNERABLE TO DESPAIR, AND TO ENDING THEIR LIVES, TO END THE MASQUERADE OF THEIR VIRTUE IN A PLUMMETING STRAIGHT TO HELL.

THIS WOMAN, TABITHA, WAS ONE WHOM I HAD KNOWN LONGER THAN I HAD KNOWN ORIANA; WHO HAD NOT MAR-RIED, AND CONFESSED TO WINSLOW SLADE THAT SHE HAD LOVED HIM ALL THESE YEARS, AT A LITTLE DISTANCE. AN EAGER AND LOVING STEPMOTHER TABITHA WAS TO MY SONS, AND EAGER TO HAVE HER OWN BABIES; WHICH WAS NOT A WISH OF MINE YET ONE NIGHT THE HOT-FLESHED PEARL LAY BETWEEN US AND HER MOUTH WAS SUCKING AT MY MOUTH AND HER MANGLED FINGER-STUMPS TOUCHED ME LEWDLY AS MANY TIMES IN DREAMS SHE HAD TOUCHED ME; AND I WAS PROVOKED TO LUST AND TOOK MY AFFRIGHTED WIFE WHOSE NAME I COULD NOT HAVE RECALLED IN THE FRENZY OF THE MOMENT AND IN THIS SHAMEFUL WAY TABITHA BE-CAME PREGNANT IN THE SECOND YEAR OF OUR UNION AND HER LABOR WAS SO PROTRACTED AND EXCRUCIATING, MORE THAN TWO DAYS AND TWO NIGHTS, THE RESULT BEING AN INFANT GIRL WHO DIED WITHIN THE HOUR AND WAS NOT EVER BAPTIZED; AS TABITHA SCREAMED ALOUD IN PAIN AND DESPONDENCY AND MADNESS, AS I HAD NEVER HEARD HER UTTER SUCH PROFANE WORDS, CURSING ME, AND BEGGING THE LORD THAT MY BODY BE TORN IN TWO, AND MY BONES

CRUSHED, AND MY FOUL HEART RIPPED FROM MY CHEST, THAT I SHOULD SUFFER AS I HAD CAUSED HER TO SUFFER; FOR HER DEATH WAS FAST UPON HER, AND SHE HAD LOST ALL QUALITIES OF THE PERSON KNOWN TO THE WORLD AS TABITHA PAIGE STRACHAN, SAVE SPEECH, THAT SHE MIGHT CURSE HER HUSBAND.

SUCH MADNESS IN CHILDBIRTH WAS HORRIFIC TO ALL WHO BEHELD AND TO THOSE TO WHOM IT WAS RECOUNTED FOR TABITHA HAD BEEN A GENTLE CHRISTIAN WOMAN WHO HAD NOT BEEN OBSERVED TO HAVE EVEN RAISED HER VOICE; YET THE GUILTY HUSBAND UNDERSTOOD, TABITHA HAD GAZED INTO HIS HEART, AND HAD KNOWN HIM AS NO OTHER LIVING PERSON KNEW HIM.

NUMBERLESS SERMONS THE REVEREND WINSLOW SLADE PREACHED IN HIS OWN CHURCH IN PRINCETON AND THROUGHOUT NEW JERSEY AND PHILADELPHIA; AND IN NEW YORK CITY WHERE HIS PATRICIAN MANNER, HIS STUDIED EASE AND CHRISTIAN PIETY HELD HIM IN GOOD STEAD WITH HIS ELDERS AND THE MOST CONSERVATIVE OF CHURCH MEMBERS. AND THOSE WHO WOULD HAVE BEEN HIS ENEMIES WERE SO WON BY HIS MANNER AND HIS MAGNANIMITY, THEY DID NOT KNOW TO LOOK BEHIND THE MASK, AND SO WERE DISARMED. YET IN THE VERY MIDST OF AUSTERE PRESBYTERY THE REVEREND SLADE SLYLY SOWED SCHISM; FOR THIS WAS THE ERA OF HERESY TRIALS IN WHICH THE GENERAL ASSEMBLY OF THE CHURCH BROUGHT CERTAIN OVERLY LIBERAL MEMBERS OF THE CLERGY TO HEEL.

AND THE PROTESTANT PREACHERS INCLINING TOWARD THE EVANGELICAL AND THE ENTHUSIASTIC WERE CENSURED.

AND THE IMMIGRANT MASSES OF IRELAND AND SOUTHERN EUROPE, HOTBEDS OF POPERY, ILLITERACY AND

SUPERSTITION—THESE WERE DENOUNCED FROM THE PULPIT IN THE MOST JUDICIOUS VOCABULARY.

AND THE JEWS—MURDERERS OF JESUS AND SOWERS OF THE ANTI-CHRIST.

AND BRUTE NEGROES, ONLY A GENERATION BEFORE FREED OF THEIR WHITE MASTERS.

AND HYSTERICAL FEMALES DEMANDING "RIGHTS."

AND THOSE WHO TAUGHT HERETICAL EVOLUTIONISM, AND THOSE WHO TAUGHT ATHEISTICAL SOCIALISM.

ALL THESE THE LORD GOD SORELY DETESTED, AND WISHED TO HARM; AND THE REVEREND SLADE FROM HIS PULPIT SPOKE IN GENTLE AND INSIDIOUS CONDEMNATION OF THESE; AND OF THE GRIEVOUS ILLS THAT BEFELL THE LUCKLESS, PRIMARY AMONG THEM THE DARK-SKINNED DE-SCENDANTS OF OUR SLAVES LIKE THE MILL-GIRL PEARL, THE REVEREND DID NOT SPEAK EXCEPT IN THE MOST RESIGNED OF WAYS; FOR THE REVEREND TAUGHT THE "PEACE THAT PASS-ETH UNDERSTANDING" AND NOT THE CLENCHED FIST OF THE LABOR UNIONS AND THE IRON HAMMER HELD ALOFT. ALL OF WHICH PUT HIM IN GOOD STEAD WITH HIS ADMIRING CON-GREGATION, AND WITH HIS MASTER THE LORD GOD ON HIGH.

IN THIS WAY THE OUTWARD MAN PROSPERED: WINSLOW SLADE WAS INAUGURATED PRESIDENT OF PRINCETON UNI-VERSITY AND GOVERNOR OF THE STATE EVEN AS THE INWARD MAN KNEW HIMSELF JOYLESS AND WITHERED FOR THE LORD GOD FASTENED UPON HIM EACH HOUR AND MADE OF HIM A SHADOW AND A PHANTOM OF THE NIGHT, THAT HAS NO TRUE SUBSTANCE BY DAY YET IS MISTAKEN BY OTHERS AS A LIVING CREATURE.

AND IT WAS KNOWN TO HIM ALWAYS: THE GIRL PEARL DIED THAT YOU MIGHT LIVE, AND PROSPER; EACH DAY AT

CROSSWICKS, YOU WALK UPON HER BONES MOLDERING IN THE SOIL; AND THE CRIES OF BIRDS FROM THE EAVES OF THE GREAT HOUSE ARE THE CRIES OF THE STRICKEN GIRL—YET YOU WILL BE CAST DOWN INTO HELL.

IT WAS NOT KNOWN TO THE UNENLIGHTENED HOW THE NEW GOVERNOR WINSLOW SLADE WAS ELECTED BY SHAMELESS BALLOT-STUFFING THROUGH THE STATE AND PARTICULARLY IN THE CAPITAL CITY OF TRENTON. IT WAS NOT KNOWN HOW THE GOVERNOR SO REVERED FOR HAVING BEEN A MINISTER AND A FORMER PRESIDENT OF THE GREAT UNIVERSITY WAS BUT A PUPPET OF THE REPUBLICAN PARTY LEADERS AS THE PARTY LEADERS WERE BUT PUPPETS OF THE TRUST. "BOLT-ERS" OF THE DEMOCRATIC PARTY AND NEW JERSEY HIRE-LINGS AND EX-GOVERNOR BEDEL AND HIS CRONIES AND OLD SENATOR SMITH OF BURLINGTON AND ANTI-ABBETT MEN AND PRO-ABBETT MEN AND RUFUS BLODGETT AND HIS HIRELINGS AND PASSAIC LABOR MEN AND COLONEL DICK-INSON AND REPUBLICAN MALCONTENTS OUT OF NEWARK AND TEMPERANCE MEN AND LOCAL OPTION HIGH LICENSE ACT MEN AND LONG-ENTRENCHED "RUM POWER" MEN AND GENERAL FISK AND HIS MEN AND ANTI-RAILROAD TAX ACT MEN AND STANDARD OIL MEN AND THE BALTIMORE AND OHIO RAILROAD AND THE ATLANTIC CITY–CAPE MAY RACE TRACKS—OUT OF THIS COALITION A GREAT STINKING STEW WAS BREWED, WITH MANY A RAT'S EXCREMENT TOSSED IN, AND THE CORPSES OF BODIES FLOATING IN THE DELAWARE ROTTED AND SWARMING WITH MAGGOTS THAT GOVERNOR SLADE WAS REQUIRED TO TAKE INTO HIS MOUTH AND CHEW AND SWALLOW WITH NO PROTEST.

SO IT WAS, A SPECTER HAD ASCENDED TO THE HIGH-EST OF STATE OFFICES AND WHETHER HIS ELECTION OF 1887

WAS THE RESULT OF BALLOT-STUFFING OR NO, THE MAN WAS ELECTED TO THE GOVERNORSHIP OF NEW JERSEY WHICH COULD NOT HAVE FAILED TO PLEASE THE LORD GOD.

FOR WHY WAS ZACHARIAS SLAIN IN THE TEMPLE BUT THAT HE HAD SUFFERED A VISION AND WHEN THE UNHAPPY MAN WISHED TO PROCLAIM HIS VISION TO THE MULTITUDES THE LORD GOD STOPPED HIS MOUTH AND HIS LIFE WAS TAKEN FROM HIM.

BLESSED BE THE NAME OF THE LORD!

SOON THEN THE GOVERNOR WAS BELIEVED TO HAVE MISCALCULATED, IN MEANING TO IMPOSE A NECESSARY PEACE UPON THE STRIKING WORKERS OF JERSEY CITY BY BRINGING IN THE STATE MILITIA WHICH THEN DID MARCH AND FIRE UPON THEM IN A PANDEMONIUM OF HORROR IN WHICH WAY AS IF UNWITTINGLY THE GOVERNOR PROVOKED DAYS OF BLOODSHED; AND WHEN A SIMILAR UPRISING OCCURRED IN PATERSON, AND THE GOVERNOR FORBORE TO CALL IN TROOPS, YET MORE BLOODSHED ERUPTED, FOR THE FACTORY OWNERS, ACTING WITH DISPATCH, HAD HIRED THEIR OWN PRIVATE MILITIA TO DEAL WITH THE EMERGENCY.

IN THIS WAY NOT ONLY STRIKERS WERE KILLED BUT WOMEN AND CHILDREN AS WELL.

THUS, MY SERVANT WINSLOW SLADE, IN WHOM I AM WELL PLEASED.

SOON THEN THE GOVERNOR RETIRED FROM PUBLIC OFFICE, SICKENED IN HIS GUTS. FOR THE STINKING STEW OF POLITICS HE COULD NOT STOMACH, EVEN HE WHO DWELT IN SIN. RETIRING FROM PUBLIC LIFE WITH A CLAIM OF WISHING TO RETURN TO THE MINISTRY AND TO THE CONTEMPLATIVE

LIFE; TAKING REFUGE AT THE MANSE, AND ATTEMPTING SOME HUMAN ALIGNMENT AT LAST, WITH HIS GRAND-CHILDREN.

FOR THERE WERE FOUR GRANDCHILDREN, WHOM HE LOVED MORE THAN LIFE ITSELF, AND FAR MORE THAN HE LOVED HIS OWN TAINTED BEING.

JOSIAH, AND ANNABEL, AND TODD, AND ORIANA—THESE BLESSINGS THE LORD GOD HAD GIVEN ME, I KNEW NOT WHY; BUT KNEW THAT I DID NOT DESERVE.

KNOW THEN, MY BRETHREN, MY COMPANIONS IN CHRIST, THAT THE CHILDREN OF MAN ARE MOST CHERISHED BY GOD WHEN THEY GROVEL IN DESPAIR—WHEN THEY TAKE NO SOLACE IN HUMAN LOVE, NEITHER LOVING NOR RECEIVING LOVE; BUT ARE IN MORTAL TERROR OF THE BEAST WHO SETS HIS CLOVEN HOOF UPON THEM, TO TRAMPLE THEM INTO DUST.

KNOW YE, MY BROTHERS AND SISTERS, THAT THE CHIL-DREN OF MAN ARE MOST RESENTED BY GOD, WHEN THEY BASK IN THE BEAUTY OF THE EARTH, AND PARTAKE OF THE FRUITS AND SPLENDORS OF THE EARTH, OFFERING NO SACRI-FICE TO THE LORD, AND TURNING FROM HIM ENTIRELY. THEY ARE IN MOST DANGER OF HIS WRATH WHEN THEY REGARD NAUGHT BUT THE EARTHLY PARADISE, AND ONE ANOTHER, IN MORTAL LOVE.

SO AT LAST THERE CAME THE HOUR WHEN THE LORD GOD PEERED INTO MY HEART AND PERCEIVED THE SEED OF LOVE THEREIN; AND SAW THAT I HAD LONG DECEIVED HIM, IN MY CRAVEN REVERENCE FOR HIM, AND WOULD HAVE REVOLTED IF I'D HAD THE COURAGE.

AND THE LORD GOD COULD NOT FORGIVE ME, THAT I

LOVED MY GRANDCHILDREN BEYOND HIM; BEYOND EVEN MY
SONS, AND MY DEAR MISUSED WIVES; AND HOW THUNDER-
OUS HIS WRATH, WITH SUCH KNOWLEDGE.

AND HE SAW TOO THAT FIFTY YEARS HAD PASSED; AND
HIS SERVANT WINSLOW SLADE WAS NOW AN OLD MAN GIVEN
TO SOLITUDE, AND TO MELANCHOLY BEHIND THE HABITUAL
SMILE ETCHED INTO HIS FACE; AND NO LONGER HAD THE
POWER TO PERPETUATE EVIL, SHOULD HE HAVE WISHED TO
DO SO. AND IN HIS HEART THERE BUDDED THE MODEST WISH
THAT HE BE ALLOWED THE BLISS OF THE COMMONPLACE,
AND HUMAN LOVE, AND OBLIVION ITSELF—WHICH IS TO SAY,
THE ERASURE OF HIS SIN.

SO THE LORD GOD TIRED OF HIS SERVANT, AND JUDGED THAT
THE CHALICE BE TAKEN FROM WINSLOW SLADE. AND THE
FURIES OF HEAVEN, THE AVENGING ARCHANGELS, WERE RE-
LEASED AT LAST FOR THE ANGRY CREATURES HAD HUNGERED
FOR MY BLOOD THESE MANY DECADES BUT HAD BEEN HELD
IN CHECK BY THE COVENANT OF OLD.

IT CAME ABOUT THEN, THESE ANGELS OF THE LORD
WERE GIVEN THEIR FREEDOM TO APPEAR ON EARTH, IN
OUR MIDST, AND WREAK SUCH HAVOC AS THEY WOULD, TO
PROPAGATE TERROR, REVULSION, AND DESPAIR—THESE AN-
GELS YOU MAY HAVE MISTAKEN FOR DEMONS, MY TOWNS-
PEOPLE.

THAT THE FIRST VICTIM TO BE BORNE AWAY WAS MY BE-
LOVED GRANDDAUGHTER ANNABEL COULD NOT HAVE BEEN
A SURPRISE TO ME THOUGH IN TRUTH HER ABDUCTION CUT
ME TO THE BONE AND I DIED THAT MORNING IN THIS VERY
CHURCH BUT A YEAR AGO THIS MORNING.

YES, WINSLOW SLADE DIED THAT MORNING. BUT SUCH
IS THE CRUELTY OF THE LORD GOD, ANNABEL'S WAS BUT THE

FIRST OF NUMEROUS INNOCENT DEATHS, AND A LAPSING OF OUR COMMUNITY INTO SUCH DESPAIR THAT LANGUAGE CANNOT EXPRESS.

NOW I TAKE LEAVE OF YOU, MY DEAR TOWNSPEOPLE. I CONFESS THAT I AM GUILTY NOT ONLY OF THAT DESPICABLE SIN AND CRIME COMMITTED A HALF-CENTURY AGO BUT I, WINSLOW SLADE, AM GUILTY AS WELL OF ALL OF THE MANIFESTATIONS OF THE CROSSWICKS CURSE, AS IT HAS BEEN KNOWN TO YOU. FOR THE ANGEL-DEMONS WERE BY WAY OF ME AND COULD NOT HAVE UNLEASHED SUCH MISERY UPON YOU SAVE BY WAY OF ME,

WHICH IS TO SAY, I AM MYSELF THE CROSSWICKS CURSE.

WHICH IS TO SAY, I AM GUILTY OF ALL THE CRIMES, DISORDER, RAMPANT MISCHIEF AND HORROR THE DEMONS HAVE COMMITTED THIS TWELVE-MONTH, AND MORE—AS IF THIS VALE OF TEARS WERE BUT A CRAZED DREAM THAT MIGHT ERUPT IN LAUGHTER AS READILY AS IN TERROR AND THE ANGUISH OF SUFFERING MANKIND OF NO MORE SIGNIFICANCE THAN THE ELUSIVE FLIGHT OF A BUTTERFLY.

AND THOUGH I MIGHT BEG FORGIVENESS OF YOU, AS FROM THE MURDERED PEARL, I MUST NOT BE FORGIVEN. IT IS MY FATE TO BE UNMASKED AND STRIPPED AND EXPOSED AND CAST FROM YOUR MIDST FOREVERMORE.

FOR MY SIN BEING AGAINST MANKIND, AND NOT AGAINST GOD, IT IS ONLY MANKIND THAT CAN FORGIVE ME; AND MANKIND, THAT MUST NOT FORGIVE ME.

AMEN.

SO BY THIS AGED HAND, ON THE SABBATH MORNING OF 4 JUNE 1906 I HEREBY DESIGNATE:

THE END

ACKNOWLEDGMENTS

The truths of Fiction reside in metaphor; but metaphor is here generated by History.

Among the books consulted in the composition of this novel are:

Woodrow Wilson: Life and Letters, volumes I and II, by Ray Stannard Baker, 1927.

Woodrow Wilson, The Academic Years by Henry Wilkinson Bragdon, 1967.

My Aunt Louisa and Woodrow Wilson by Margaret Axson Elliott, 1944.

Woodrow Wilson of Princeton by McMillan Lewis, 1952.

Woodrow Wilson: A Brief Biography by Arthur S. Link, 1963.

The Priceless Gift: The Love Letters of Woodrow Wilson and Ellen Axson Wilson, edited by Eleanor Wilson McAdoo, 1962.

When the Cheering Stopped: The Last Years of Woodrow Wilson by Gene Smith, 1964.

Woodrow Wilson: A Medical and Psychological Biography by Edwin A. Weinstein, 1981.

Modern Battles of Trenton: Being a History of New Jersey's Politics and Legislation from the Year 1868 to the Year 1894 by William Edgar Sackett, 1895.

Jack London by Richard O'Connor, 1964.

Scott of the Antarctic by Elspeth Huxley, 1978.

The Autobiography of Upton Sinclair by Upton Sinclair, 1962.

Stories of New Jersey by Frank Stockton, 1961.

The Cross and the Lynching Tree by James Cone, 2011.